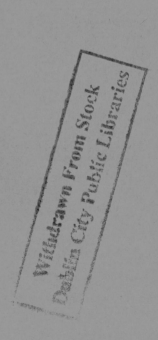

HOLLOW EMPIRE

www.penguin.co.uk

ALSO BY SAM HAWKE

City of Lies

HOLLOW EMPIRE

A POISON WAR NOVEL

SAM HAWKE

BANTAM PRESS

TRANSWORLD PUBLISHERS
Penguin Random House, One Embassy Gardens,
8 Viaduct Gardens, London SW11 7BW
www.penguin.co.uk

Transworld is part of the Penguin Random House group of companies
whose addresses can be found at global.penguinrandomhouse.com

Penguin
Random House
UK

First published in Great Britain in 2020 by Bantam Press
an imprint of Transworld Publishers

First published in the United States of America by St Martin's Press LLC

A CIP catalogue record for this book
is available from the British Library.

ISBNs
9781787631038 (hb)
9781787631052 (tpb)

Printed and bound in Great Britain by Clays Ltd, Elcograf S.p.A.

Penguin Random House is committed to a sustainable
future for our business, our readers and our planet. This book
is made from Forest Stewardship Council® certified paper.

MIX
Paper from
responsible sources
FSC® C018179

To loved ones lost, in the hope that they still hear the stories you never got to share.

HOLLOW EMPIRE

INCIDENT: Suspected poisoning of Credola Valleya Reed

POISON: Lockwort

INCIDENT NOTES: Gradual temperament change and weight loss noted by colleagues as symptoms of old age. Retirement and replacement by great-nephew suggested in Council, proofer sought excuse to examine torso and confirmed distinctive broken capillaries and encouraged C. Valleya to seek medical attention. Suspect regular dose of lockwort (powdered in beverage?) by nephew. Internal Reed matter, no further action.

(from proofing notes of Credola Jaya Oromani)

1

Jovan

You never get used to poisoning a child.

Dija Oromani arrived in Silasta four months after the siege ended, in that strange period teetering between chaos and routine, when my sister's health had recovered enough for her to return home but not to work, and the last of the billeted citizens had returned to the lower city. At eleven years old, the youngest daughter of my second cousin, Dija radiated quiet earnestness, with thick glasses over bright clever eyes that reminded me of my uncle, and a cloud of hair like Kalina's. How easily she had slipped into our household. The Oromani family needed an heir to eventually inherit my Council seat, one young enough to learn the machinations of government and strong enough to withstand the other requirements of my position.

Six months after she arrived, I poisoned her for the first time.

I knew it was too early in her training. In better conditions we would have studied for several years, building a base of knowledge before taking that critical step. But at eleven, almost twelve, she had been five years behind the ideal starting age for proofing. We couldn't afford to wait years. It was with an anxious heart and shaking hands that I added bloodroot to the ground oku meat in our evening meal, and a long night of doubts and guilt as I sat beside her bed, holding her vomit pail and cooling her sweaty forehead with a wet cloth, murmuring weak comforts. She had recovered, and apologized—apologized!—for failing to detect it. Almost two years had passed since that first night, but I remembered the twisting discomfort in my own stomach. Harming a child was wrong; it was against every deep biological instinct. And yet.

And yet I had poisoned her then, and again, and again. In minuscule quantities, over the two years she had been my apprentice, to build her immunity to some of the most common, but non-lethal, poisons she was likely to encounter. In larger doses, to demonstrate the cues, only learned through experience, that could one day save her life and her charge's. Occasionally, to surprise or test her. The last I hated the most, but it formed the most critical part of our training.

I had failed Tain once. In his thin face and dulled complexion, his drastically reduced appetite, his swiftness to tire, the reminders of that failure faced me every day. I was determined never to so fail again. But one day, through poison or some other means, I would be gone, and Dija would be the last quiet shield between the Chancellor and those who meant him harm. It was my responsibility to ensure her readiness. Perhaps one day there would be no need to fear a silent attack on Sjona's ruling family from within or without. Until then, though it tugged at my heart and slow-soured my relationship with Hadrea, I would lace Dija's morning tea and prepare small, dangerous tablets, and nurse her back to health, and remember that our country, for all its flaws, was worth this. Worth my life. Worth hers.

It had to be.

The darkened theater was too hot, and the glare from the single focused lamp on the stage left bright smears behind my eyelids when I squeezed my eyes shut.

"Eyes open or you'll miss it." A whisper in my left ear.

I kept them closed. "I have a headache."

Can a grin be audible? I could have sworn I heard one. "Another one? You should see a physic about that, Jov. You might be allergic to something."

I opened my eyes a crack to scowl at my friend. Even in the darkness of the audience seating the brightness of his teeth revealed the width of his smile. "I *am* allergic to something," I muttered. "I'm allergic to this sh—"

"Shh!" I shifted my glare to my other side. Kalina was two seats down, and though it was too dim to read her expression, her tone was severe. "They've worked hard and you're being *very* rude."

"It's all right for you," I grumbled back. Down on the stage, the lights had expanded to reveal the actor playing my sister, crying far more attractively than any human had a right to at a simulation of Chancellor Caslav's funeral.

Stagehands cunningly hidden from view fanned the actor so her dress caught dramatically in the "breeze," and the roguish young man cast as Tain—all right, I could admit he was a reasonable likeness—laid a comforting arm around her shoulders. A heavy chord sounded from the small orchestra and the light narrowed in on an ascetic figure who had been lurking behind the glamorous pair. I tried not to bristle. The Jovan character, while ostensibly one of the protagonists of the play, skulked and glared, creeping around the stage, tailing after the luminous pair of Kalina and Tain like some kind of tame but badly socialized animal.

"He's quite handsome, Uncle," Dija whispered from beside me. Her gaze looked innocent behind her thick glasses. I couldn't tell if she was teasing me, or offering serious consolation. Someone on my other side suppressed a small snort or chuckle.

"Maybe you should try wearing those pants, Jov," Tain suggested. "They're all the rage now, and they'd really show off your thighs."

"Shh," I hissed back. "They've worked very hard and you're being *rude*, Chancellor."

He buried a laugh with a hasty cough.

I'd read the script in advance, but the text had not quite conveyed the *tone* of the play, and I understood now why the Theater-Guilder had been so insistent I see the early showing, before the rest of the city was talking about it. It was going to draw attention to me again, and from the looks of it, reignite speculation about my relationship with Tain. The stage Jovan seemed more poisoner than proofer, whispering worries about traitors and urging Tain to take action against them, and presented more as spy and adviser than friend. After all, my part in the public story could be distilled merely to the most dramatic and violent events. Tain had discovered and owned up to the city's dark past and secured peace between the rebels and the city citizens; Kalina had uncovered the plot by the Warrior-Guilder, Aven, almost dying to warn us all of her treachery, and Hadrea of course had taken on the powerful water spirit, Os-Woorin, and saved the city from destruction. But me? I had covered up Tain's poisoning, killed the traitor Marco, and blown off the Council chamber roof to free the trapped Council from the fire. My part was not so easily smoothed into celebrated heroism.

Just when my brief fame—or notoriety—after the siege was starting to fade away, too. I tried not to sigh. This was far from the first production of the siege of Silasta; apparently the residents of this city didn't mind reliving their own trauma in dramatized form, as there'd been a string of the bloody things. But this one had three times the budget of its most recent competitor, and as the highlight show of the karodee, guaranteed high audience numbers. The international guests currently swelling our population seemed fascinated by our brief civil war and the apparent reemergence of an ancient magic. I hadn't even been a character in several of the earlier productions but now I could look forward to being the source of scrutiny and fascination once more.

As if she'd heard my thoughts, Varina swiveled round in front of me, an apologetic wince and spread hands conveying her helplessness. The Performers' Guild contributed to funding the play, but did not control its script or its dramatic choices. The producers could have cast me as the villain and there'd have been no recourse. At least this way I was forewarned.

I shrugged at Varina. *Be a good sport about it,* Kalina had beseeched me, and lo, here I was, being as sporting as sporting could be.

I squirmed in my seat as the rebel army came onstage, complete with actors under cunningly flexible coverings to portray animal mounts, dancing together to threatening music from the orchestra. Someone in the audience sucked in their breath loudly when the peace negotiator was shot down in alarmingly realistic fashion and collapsed in a spotlight in the center of the stage, halfway between the army and the cleverly designed wall set. I was uncomfortably aware real people had died in this conflict. Chancellor Caslav and my uncle Etan had been the first victims, but no less important had been the hundreds on both sides, caught in an engineered conflict that had claimed their lives. This wasn't some ancient tale about people who lived long ago. That peace negotiator had worked at the Administrative Guild, just like my sister. Her family probably lived here. How would they feel, seeing this actor lying so still, punctured with crimson for the entertainment of the audience? It was a real thing that happened, not a story.

And yet. *Stories are important,* Tain had told me when we'd been given the script and the warning. *Stories are how we talk about who we are, and who we want to be.* We were trying to build something out of the twisted mess of old wounds that were the foundation of this country, and we needed a narrative to carry people on both sides along with it. And I had to admit, if grudgingly, that while it wasn't fun to experience us all portrayed like fictional characters, the "story" being told was, overall, a fair one.

The production had split the narrative between the city and the countryfolk. Tain, the earnest young leader, passionate but humble; Kalina, his brilliant, overlooked strategist; and me . . . well. Me as the suspicious, mistrustful harbinger of doom, lurking and scowling. They contrasted our crisis with a Darfri family who personified the effects of the slow, poisonous oppression our families had inflicted on the estates, and the depths to which working people had been driven to seek justice.

The political commentary was sharp enough that no one could call the play propaganda. They hadn't crafted it to pander to the Council; the audience would be left in no doubt as to how the rich and powerful had set the pieces in motion that would be used so effectively against us all. But they hadn't cast us all as villains, either. Still, I burned with remembered shame watching the three of us onstage, floundering as we tried to understand the rebellion, blocked at every turn by faceless, pompous actors playing our fellow Councilors. Literally faceless. Rather than identify individual Councilors, the company had elected to portray most of the old Council as a dozen or so actors dressed alike, faces hidden by blank dark masks, dancing together as a single monolith.

"Listen, at least you got a face," Tain whispered, as if he'd read my mind, and even I had to grin. Most of the surviving members of that original Council were in this theater, watching, and some of them would be extremely annoyed to find themselves relegated to "dancer-third-from-the-left." On the other hand, some of them ought to be grateful they'd been absorbed into the monolith rather than had their individual actions scrutinized. I caught Dija watching me and smoothed my face. Resolving to be a better example for my young apprentice, I settled back on the bench, rested my chin in my hands, and tried to watch the play as if I were just an ordinary spectator.

I could acknowledge—in the spirit of good sportsmanship—that while the music was a little obvious and wouldn't win the composers acclaim, the actors were decent, the dancers good, and the production and props top notch. The tumblers who rolled backward down the ladders during the first attempt at the walls (crafted of stackable light blocks, and assembled with supernatural swiftness in the scene changes) fell so convincingly I was sure they'd be injured, and when one of the Darfri family characters was killed on the walls by the hand of the enormous man playing Marco, the acting Warrior-Guilder, sniffs and stifled sobs could be heard throughout the dark chamber. Sometimes a conversation was eerily accurate (albeit with rather more pirouettes than I remembered) and other times I found myself confused about the sequence of events, even though I'd lived through them. The fake headache had become all too real.

During the fight in the dark tunnels under the city, when miners had dug their way under the walls, the whole theater went pitch black, the only light a weak, bobbing lantern as Tain raced around unseen obstacles across the stage. The harsh clang of metal on metal burst suddenly from behind us, in the back corners of the theater; Dija squeaked with fright and I jumped at the shock of both the noise and the sudden presence of her small, warm hand, clutching at mine. I squeezed it uncertainly. The noise was disorienting and alarming, but the fear and confusion the sounds in the dark evoked did pull me back to that horrible night.

And yet, there was something more bothering me than just the scene on the stage. I looked around surreptitiously, trying to make out the dark shapes at the edges of the seating. Actors and stagehands had made their way past us—or come through some concealed entrance—without me noticing. A familiar prickle of fear crawled down the back of my neck and lodged in my chest at the thought that we had been quietly surrounded, albeit benignly.

If I kept my eyes away from the chaotic lantern on the stage, my vision adjusted and I could make out the distinctive markings on the uniforms of the men and women stationed at both back doors. Tain's personal guard, nicknamed the blackstripes, were now a permanent feature of his public life. After everything that had happened, it was nonsensical and potentially destabilizing to continue the polite social fiction that Tain wasn't being protected. But though they were dedicated and alert, I was never able to relax when Tain was in a crowd, and over time my concern had started to be seen by others as paranoia.

In the immediate aftermath of the siege everyone had listened, and the Council had been all too eager to have Aven and the mercenaries we had captured questioned, to fund audits of the payments that had supported the rebellion, but as the search dragged on and answers never surfaced, interest in finding out who had backed and incited Aven fizzled out. The longer we went without another strike from our unknown enemy, the more people convinced themselves the threat had passed, or worse, that it had gone no deeper than a corrupt Warrior-Guilder looking to create her own empire. Attention and funding turned to tolerance, to mollification, disinterest, and eventually faint embarrassment. Even staunch allies had taken to suggesting I was making connections where there were none, imagining assassins in the shadows.

But I had heard what Aven had said, and I had seen the numbers and the records and spoken to everyone we knew to be involved. Our country still had an enemy out there, no matter how convenient the Council found it to forget. Karodee, a triumphant celebration of the recovery of our country and its return to stability with Tain at the helm, provided a perfect storm of opportunities for an enemy to reach him to disrupt that.

I set my attention back on the play. At some point Hadrea had appeared, played by a luminous young woman with none of Hadrea's actual prickly charm. Here she was a poor, passionate Darfri woman who had bravely snuck into the city to try to avert a war, her character something of an amalgam of her and Salvea, with all Hadrea's bravery and determination merged with her mother's smooth edges and conciliatory manner. I wondered whether Hadrea would be amused or annoyed at her portrayal. She could still surprise me by laughing when I expected her temper to flare, or the reverse. I glanced automatically down the aisle before remembering she had refused to come, and the twisty ache in my chest stole any semblance of good humor I'd had left.

The onstage rebels broke through the wall and the Silastians retreated across the lake to the upper city, the audience oohing and ahhing over the clever portrayal of Darfri magic, with wispy silks on hidden sticks simulating the wind that had diverted our arrows and hidden the rebels' movements. But I found myself searching the dark corners of the theater again. I felt unsettled, like the uneasy feeling on waking knowing some dreaded task or event awaited before being awake enough to remember what it was. I didn't like it.

The feeling persisted through Tain's onstage poisoning, Kalina's brave escape from the city under the water gate, and even several of Jovan's most significant scenes: finding a cure for the poison, confronting the traitor and poisoner, Marco. I barely followed any of it.

"Is something the matter, Uncle?" Dija whispered at last.

"It's nothing. I just need a little air," I whispered, and ducking awkwardly I edged to the aisle, grateful we had come in late and were seated near the end of the bench. I leaned against the heavy drapes, my eyes averted from the bright stage, hands squeezing alternately into fists as I counted silently in my head. Shadowy figures moved at the edges of the theater; someone in an alcove near the front was operating a remote pulley system to work the fake catapults on the stage, several musicians were playing instruments at key moments to enhance the atmosphere, and the occasional audience member slipped in or out of their seats, moving slowly in the dark.

When a creepy, echoing windy sound erupted right next to me, I started, one hand flying into my paluma to reach for the concealed pouches there, before I realized there was a young man on a perch above, concealed by the curtain, playing a long, tubular instrument that created the eerie sound of wind. Rather than releasing the tension it only looped it tighter inside me.

And then I saw him. Perhaps he moved, or was caught in a bit of reflected light from the stage, or maybe my restless gaze simply happened on the right place at the right time, but I looked up, and in the shadows of the ceiling, balanced on a support beam in the center back of the room, there he was. A man—or a figure, anyway, but already my brain was filling in the rough shape, barely lit in reflected stage light—crouched above the audience, utterly still. Not moving ropes or directing lights, he might have been part of the structure itself if I hadn't seen the gleam of brown skin, an unmistakable curl of hair against a cheek. Already the ceiling had fallen into darkness again and there was nothing to see but indistinct blackness.

A cool, hard sensation filled my chest. There was no pleasure in being right. It was *him*, the man I'd glimpsed following the Chancellor over the past few months, a man with unremarkable features and the studied air of normalcy only a fellow practitioner could identify. Every time I'd seen him he had disappeared before I could point him out to the blackstripes, and I suspected even they thought I was imagining things. But this time he was here, ready to act, and so was I. Staying tight against the curtains, I moved slowly up the aisle, my eyes fixed on the mass of black, trying to find him again. My heart pounded. Of course it *could* be someone from the production staff. But almost all the people I cared about most in the world were sitting below, clumped together and vulnerable, and I wouldn't risk their safety for the sake of my pride.

I glanced behind at the blackstripes. The two on the nearest door weren't looking in my direction; one had her back half-turned, eyes roaming the audience, while the other seemed to be watching the play, his posture bored and languid. I started toward them, but had only taken a few steps when someone opened the door at the other side of the theater and the dim light leaking in illuminated the ceiling for a moment. My head snapped up and I saw him again, crouching like a statue on a wall, something drawn to his face—a thin stick of some kind—and instinct took over.

"Assassin!" I yelled.

In the temporary quiet, my cry rang out, explosive. The door slapped shut and patrons leapt to their feet, the crowd erupting into chaos in the darkness. Someone screamed. Panicked voices swept the room. On the stage, the performance stopped and someone swung one of the big focused-beam lamps in our direction, so the writhing black mess of bodies disappeared in an explosion of white across my eyes. When it cleared I could no longer make out the figure on the beams above. And from behind, someone strong seized my arms and hauled me backward.

I struggled to turn, to pull free, but no sooner had I yanked one arm loose than a thick forearm was around my neck. Terror filled me. How many were there? I'd been so focused on the person above I hadn't stopped to think they might have accomplices. My vision was streaked with spots and stripes, obscuring my view of the crowd now struggling to escape their rows, so I could not make out Tain, or Dija, or Lini, or anyone. People were streaming past me, pushing for the exits, too many for the blackstripes to contain. Someone shoved into us and the grip around my neck tightened. Dizziness closed in around my head.

Then, "Uncle Jovan! Let him go!"

"Let him go, by the fortunes! That's Credo Jovan."

The pressure around my neck released abruptly, and I half-stepped, half-slid away. It was one of Tain's blackstripes, the man by the door, who'd had me. Dija pushed her way over, her glasses askew and her eyes frightened, but apparently unhurt. I patted her shoulder weakly as I scanned the room. The high lamps on the walls were stuttering and starting, and though I searched out the interlocking beams on the ceiling, there was no sign anyone had ever been there. Tain appeared a moment later, his hand on my shoulder to steady me as I sagged with relief to see him safe.

"Are you all right? What happened?"

I shook my head and massaged my throat, scanning the crowd, looking for the man whose ordinary face I would surely recognize. Half the theater had already emptied, and those who had stayed were standing, staring, their alarm fading. Most of the half-lit figures were people I knew, and none looked suspicious, merely confused. Hot frustration doused me. "There was someone there. On the beams in the ceiling."

"What did you see, Credo?" the blackstripe asked politely. Tain's brows were drawn in concern, and Kalina joined us, breathing heavily.

"Someone was crouched on the beam, there, above the Chancellor," I said, gesturing to the ceiling. "I saw them put something to their mouth. I thought—" My voice faded. It would be too specific to say they'd had some kind of projectile, perhaps a poison dart like the Marutian one that had killed Chancellor Ardana eighty years ago. Kalina was frowning, following my gaze; she knew what I had suspected of the man who had been watching Tain. I cleared my throat and tried again. "I only saw them for a moment when the light from the door came in."

"And you got out of your seat?"

"No. I was already in the aisle, I—" Again, I dropped off, not wanting to admit it had only been a feeling that something was wrong. Already the expressions of the people listening were changing, growing skeptical. I cleared my throat. "I was going to go out for some air. I saw movement and noticed the person on the ceiling."

"It was very dark," the other blackstripe offered, her voice not *quite* disbelieving. She stared up at the obviously empty beams. "You might have been mistaken?"

"I suppose," I said, unable to keep the stiffness from my reply.

The first blackstripe's expression remained neutral, without judgment. "Sorry for grabbing you, Credo. I heard the cry and you were in the aisle, rushing in, like. Thought you were the threat."

"That's understandable," I said. As the alarm died down, more and more of the remaining people were peering curiously at our little huddle. The show manager, in obvious distress about the ruin of her opening night, was in close conversation with Varina, who kept trying to make eye contact with me. "It was so dark in here, it's perfect conditions for an assassin."

Tain squeezed my shoulder. "Are you sure you're all right? You don't look—"

"I'm fine," I snapped. "I'm not seeing things, if that's what you're—"

"Jov," he interrupted gently. "I just meant, is your neck all right? My man half-choked you there. I didn't doubt you saw something." He glanced around. "Not sure we can do much about it now, though."

If there had been anyone trying to get to him, they were gone now, and even my certainty was slipping. What if it had been a member of the theater staff, up there for some innocent purpose and holding a pen or a straw or a stick of janjan in their mouth, who had simply panicked when I'd cried out?

Most patrons seemed to be regarding the incident as a false alarm, their initial panic fading to be replaced by whispers and condescending looks in my direction. My face grew hot.

"If the Chancellor's guard check our audience carefully, may we continue the performance?" the show manager asked. Tain hesitated and looked at me, and other heads swiveled in my direction. I had to shrug. An assassin who had waited for us in a dark theater would be unlikely to try again once we were on alert. I couldn't think of a reason why the play could not go on, other than the obvious reason that I did not want to keep watching it.

"You don't have to stay," Kalina said quietly as people began filing back to the benches, and the actors, with nervous looks and some muttering, took their positions again. Kalina's onstage counterpart, having undertaken a brave and desperate journey to bring word to our army, had uncovered the Warrior-Guilder's betrayal and was about to be chased down. I had ruined one of the most dramatic moments in the story. "I can keep an eye on things here, and the blackstripes will be patrolling."

It was tempting. If it had felt strange and wrong watching actors "die" in the earlier battle scenes, it would be nothing to the unpleasantness of watching a reenactment of my sister's near-death at Aven's hands. But if I left now it would only make the whole thing look more like a stunt. And I'd be even worse stewing outside, wondering if I'd missed something in there. At least this way I could keep eyes on Tain, Dija, and Kalina. I took my seat again.

This time, the lanterns stayed lit at the edges of the room, and the black-stripes patrolled, alert. One part worried, one part embarrassed, I sat through the remainder of the play in a familiar internal storm of self-recrimination, counting squeezes of my hands to keep the anxious dread at bay, hardly following the events unfolding onstage. So focused was I on staying calm and not jumping at every movement in my peripheral vision, I barely took in the impressive choreography of the battle at the lake, the cunning use of color and light to suggest water. I watched Tain's grand plea for peace, and numbly noted the cleverness of the production when, just as the battle seemed to be over, the real Os-Woorin emerged, a fluid and strange shape created by acrobats balancing on each other's shoulders underneath a semi-diaphanous fabric shroud. It shouldn't have worked but it did; something in the combination of grace and unnaturalness of the thing genuinely recalled the weird and awesome sight of an ancient spirit. I missed Hadrea all over again when her onstage counterpart fought the spirit and felt a bone-deep relief when at last it was over.

I stood with everyone else, politely applauding, counting the moments until I could flee. Varina, in the row below us, turned around. "I know the cast were keen to meet you three," she said over the applause and the general hubbub. "But if you slip out before the manager gets up here, I'll make your apologies." Technically she was addressing the three of us, but her gaze was on me.

"I'm feeling a bit unwell, Uncle Jovan," Dija said, in a clear, carrying voice. "Would you mind if we went straight home?"

Kalina gave my apprentice a very soft look. Affection and gratitude swamped me, tinged with guilt that she'd already had to learn how to handle me.

"I'll tell them you had to take her home," Tain said easily, understanding me immediately and regarding us without judgment. "I hope you feel better soon, Dee," he added gravely, and she bobbed her head in thanks.

"I could walk her home if you like, Credo?" Tain's page, Erel, a few years older than Dija, had appeared at the end of our row with the kind of beaming smile and helpful attitude that had propelled him from messenger to Tain's personal page. I tried not to glare at him.

"That's fine, thanks, Erel. I've got a lot to do at home anyway."

"It's no trouble at all, Credo."

I started to answer, but Tain interrupted with a tap on my shoulder and a whisper. "Looks like Bradomir didn't appreciate being faceless, eh?" He gestured below and to the right, where Credo Bradomir, in contrast to everyone else, had not stood to applaud.

I shrugged. "I guess they already had enough villains for the narrative." Bradomir had resigned his Council seat under considerable pressure in the aftermath of the siege and revelations about the extent of his role in the abuses at his estates. Though his family still held considerable wealth and power, their honor and social standing—Bradomir's particularly—had diminished as a result. "I'm surprised he even came."

"Gotta keep up appearances," Tain muttered. "Speaking of those, you'd better head out before we get caught."

Dija took my hand and started to lead me out just as the show manager called out, "Honored Chancellor!" and I hurriedly followed. Kalina, whose energy levels had not increased with her public profile, joined us without a word. But we'd only taken a few steps when a woman's voice, raised in alarm, cut through the chatter of the crowd.

"Uncle!"

I glanced back. Credola Karista, Bradomir's niece and replacement on the Council, was shaking his shoulder, urgent. "Uncle!"

Only then did I register his slumped posture, the tilt of his head. Warmth drained out of my body as if we'd just stepped out into a cold wind. Bradomir wasn't standing, not because he was an angry old man, refusing to show appreciation for a show he had not enjoyed. He wasn't standing because he couldn't.

"Call a physic!" the elderly woman on his other side cried. Varina turned from her conversation with the theater manager, the bright beads in her hair swinging as she spun about and stared up. I sometimes forgot she was a Leka— our relationship had somewhat surprisingly evolved into mutual respect, even friendship—but in that moment her resemblance to Bradomir was vivid.

"I think it's his heart," Karista moaned. She took Bradomir's cheeks in her hands and stared into his face. "Uncle. Uncle."

I half-turned away, not wanting to gawk, as a physic in the audience pushed his way through the crowd. If Bradomir's heart had given way, I could say I was neither surprised, given his overindulgent lifestyle and general ill health, nor saddened. But I did not want to intrude on the legitimacy of his family's grief, either. Before I could make my polite escape, though, Karista's eyes locked on mine as if she'd sought me specifically out of the crowd, and their hostility took me aback. She didn't like me, had never liked me—as peers at school, my particular oddities and compulsions had been a cause of much mockery from her—but this was a look of unabashed hatred and fury.

Uncomfortable, I tried to convey sympathy in my expression. Whatever my feelings about her uncle or her personally, I knew the devastation of the unexpected loss of a mentor. Two years on, I still felt Etan's absence every day as I floundered around my attempts to be a good teacher for Dija, and despite Bradomir's public withdrawal, rumor had it that Karista still leaned heavily on her uncle's advice in managing Leka interests.

Her glare only intensified, and unpleasant understanding struck me as I turned away. Her look was an accusation. Just like the Ash family after Credola Nara died, as if my ill will had contributed to her heart failure. Irritation replaced my initial sympathetic urge. Disliking Bradomir or Nara couldn't cause their deaths or they'd have died a long time earlier, and not just because of me.

But the thought did occur to me, as I slipped from the theater with my sister and ward, that the assassin I had been so sure I had seen targeting Tain could just as easily have reached Bradomir, seated only a row in front of the Chancellor.

Other families' poisonings weren't my business, I told myself firmly. My job was to protect the Chancellor, not to usurp the significant protections the other Councilors employed. If Bradomir had made an enemy, that was not unexpected and absolutely *not* my problem.

"And how is this your problem, precisely?"

Thendra sounded more irritable than usual, and barely slowed her pace, forcing me to trot after her. The physic's skin gleamed with sweat and her arms were laden with supplies; belatedly I hurried forward to awkwardly share the pile. The hospital was crowded with physics, assistants, and patients, with people moving in every direction and a constant hum of noise and activity. I followed along down the corridor and into a treatment room with four separate patients on pallets, where Thendra handed off her pile to a harried-looking assistant and gestured for me to do the same, before pivoting from the room again.

"It's busy today," I said, avoiding her question by stating the obvious.

"The city is overrun, Credo," she replied without so much as glancing at me. I didn't need telling. Every guesthouse in the city (and plenty of opportunistic un-Guilded private residences and businesses) had long since filled, and even the rougher options in the fledgling settlement outside the walls were bursting. "More disease, more accidents, more foolishness, more conflicts." The last was snapped with obvious disapproval. With the population of the city multiplied past capacity, including people whose homelands had a higher tolerance for violence than Sjona, the karodee influx had led to additional disputes and injuries, both accidental and deliberate. "We will need a second hospital if this is to be sustained."

"Karodee will be over in a few days, at least."

"This is not a karodee problem," she replied, terse. "It is a population issue, Credo. It did not start with the festival."

It was true. Over time the city *had* changed. Immigration led to a denser population, more competition for resources, more pressure on the Guilds and consequently more un-Guilded work at lower standards. We had greater crime and constant pressure on the determination council adjudicating petty and serious disputes. It would be easy to miss the peaceful, sophisticated city of my memory if only that enforced civilization had not been bought and paid for by the suffering of others.

"These gangs, these drugs . . ." Thendra was continuing, her expression grim. "I am seeing things I have never seen in all my years' practice here."

I sighed, fists clenching. "I know." There was always crime in a big city, but its apparently successful organization was a new phenomenon. Chen, the Captain of the Order Guards, seemed to be locked in a perpetual battle with the most powerful gang. It was likely linked to the increased use of recreational drugs, but drugs were one more entry on the list of problems my fellow Councilors had no appetite to pursue. Encouraging the government to act on an issue was challenging when a good proportion of them, I suspected, had come to enjoy that particular vice. "I've raised it, Chen's raised it. They'll give you more funding."

"I do not like what I am seeing. When it is one of their family members in here on my table, hmm? Or their homes broken into?"

"Sooner or later it will be," I muttered. "Listen, Thendra, about Bradomir . . ."

"Well, I asked you, did I not?" She glanced back at me. "I do not mean to be rude, Credo, but is there some special reason I should interfere with a matter that has nothing to do with me—or with you, no?"

I cleared my throat and met her gaze; she held it for a moment and then let out her breath in a rush. Her lips thinned and she shook her head, but her bristly impatience softened. "Very well."

"Thank you." Relieved and grateful, I fell into silence as she led me downstairs into the basement, where the hospital kept bodies until formal burial. Thendra and I had never had an honest conversation about what my job entailed but she knew, or at least suspected, and she had done me plenty of favors in the past.

Bradomir's body was clean and wrapped, smaller in death than it had appeared in life. I felt hollow looking down on his blank, slumped face. I did not pity him, exactly, but death never felt trivial. I was glad Dija wasn't with me.

"Did you examine him?"

She shot me a look brimming with irritation. "Do not be foolish, Credo. The Families do not submit to such things. Credola Karista would have me thrown from the Guild for even speaking to you about this."

I examined his face, crouched to better see his neck, letting the silence drag on, until words were tugged inevitably from her like I'd been winding a well rope. "His heart failed, it seems."

"Mm." I glanced at her, and her gaze slipped off to the side. "Sometimes these things happen." She pointedly didn't look at me as I checked the skin around his neck, checking for signs of a puncture. After a moment, she cleared her throat.

"The wrappings need some adjustment. Would you mind assisting, Credo, since you are here?"

"Of course." Together we rolled the body to its side, and Thendra fussed with the wrapping around one arm, determinedly avoiding my gaze as she revealed a shoulder muscle. I frowned at the tiny pin mark, faintly discoloring Bradomir's skin but so small—a mere blemish to the casual glance. My heart sank; for once, I would have preferred to have been wrong. "But it would have had to come through the clothing," I muttered. I remembered Karista holding her uncle's shoulders, trying to shake him to consciousness. Could she have unknowingly dislodged a tiny dart? One meant for Tain, but whose trajectory had been disrupted by my shout? A pinprick on his arm could easily have been overlooked in that sudden press of bodies and the stampede to get out of the theater. He had been well enough when everyone had resumed their seats, but dead half an hour later.

There were a few poisons that could kill if injected and against which a proofer was no use, the most dangerous of which was a rare and expensive poison called rucho, the death feather, extracted from the feathers of a bird found only on islands off the far west coast of the continent. Not the kind of substance easily obtainable by a disgruntled family member or business partner, but one only found in the kits of assassins.

I helped Thendra restore the body to its former position, still deep in thought. Karista had looked as if she had believed me responsible—and perhaps I was, indirectly, if the target had been Tain—but, despite that, she was not willing to ask the physics to look for signs of murder. Perhaps proclaiming it a murder might draw attention to the reasons why someone would wish the former Councilor ill, and bring further dishonor to her already humiliated family. Reputation and honor were still a currency of this city, for all our shuffling of power in the last few years.

Thendra was watching me, her lips still thin. "Thank you," I said quietly.

She nodded. Then, after a long and thoughtful pause, "Be careful, Credo. This country has had its share of instability, yes? I would prefer not to see you down here again."

INCIDENT: Attempted poisoning of Chancellor Caslav Iliri

POISON: Zarnika

INCIDENT NOTES: Bottle of fortified kavcha delivered to Manor in purported celebration of birth of Chancellor's niece, proofed and tested by self, found to contain non-fatal dose of zarnika. Given proximity to vote on junction boundary, suspect attempt to incapacitate Chancellor by Ash family. No further action at present.

(from proofing notes of Credo Etan Oromani)

2

Kalina

There's a fine line between diplomacy and dishonesty. As I stepped away from my broken cup (sending a silent apology for the disrespect to good porcelain) and made a show of being surprised by the man who had looked around at the crash, I thought the line was rather easier to cross than I'd once assumed.

"Credola Kalina!" Ectar sprang to his feet at the sight of me, almost dropping his own cup.

"Lord Ectar." My best rueful smile and a murmured apology to the boy who had appeared out of nowhere to clean up my mess. "I'm afraid you've caught me at my clumsiest."

The Talafan nobleman, grandson to the Emperor and survivor of the siege of Silasta, hurried over. He was immaculately dressed and coiffed, his pale yellow hair bound with a jeweled clip and his floor-length nihep cut to emphasize his slim—thin, by my people's standards—physique. The Talafan silk and metallic embroidery gave him an otherworldly sheen in the sunlight from the window. Sincere delight manifested in his fluttering hands and the pitch of his voice, rather than in any overt change in the expression on his elaborately made-up face.

He took my hand and touched the back of it to his cheek, a gesture marking respectful and polite affection in the Empire. "Clumsy? You are never clumsy. I taught you to shoot a bow, do you remember?" He held on to the hand a fraction longer than would be proper in his homeland, I suspected. "I didn't see you there before. Please, come and join us!" He stepped aside and indicated the cushioned alcove in which another Talafan man sat cross-legged,

sipping from a sweet-smelling cup of kavcha. Its scent mingled with the perfume from a heated pot of oil in the center of the low table. He regarded me
with a combination of curiosity and distrust.

"Oh, I must not intrude," I demurred in Talafan, nodding politely to the
other man. "I was about to leave in any case—there is a ribbon dancing performance at the arena I have been looking forward to. It was a pleasure to see
you again, Lord Ectar."

"But no!" Ectar's hands fluttered. "Please! We too are attending the ribbon dancing. Won't you come with us?" He added, in slightly stilted Sjon, "I
have been hoping to see you."

Since the Talafan delegation had arrived for karodee, Ectar had sent several messages, asking me to various private engagements. Indeed, he had
written to me often in the time since the siege, expressing his pleasure over
my recovery and his hope to return to the city one day. He was a learned and
pleasant correspondent, but his letters had taken on a concerning tone in recent months. I had begged health issues or other commitments to deter him
so far. I did not want to see Ectar in private, and build on his obvious hopes.
Nor did I need to probe the motives of someone who had risked his life to
help us two years ago. It was the other members of the Talafan party I needed
information from, and Ectar was my best ticket to gain entry to them.

"What a lovely coincidence," I lied. Even surrounded by Talafan guards-
men Ectar was comically easy to survey, because like all Talafan noblemen
he had been conditioned to pay no attention to servants. It had been a simple
matter to learn of his plans today. "If you are already going, then I would be
very pleased to accompany you."

"Wonderful! Your fine Council has arranged a magnificent area for viewing the events in the arena—there is plenty of room. Credola, have you met
the Foreign Minister, Master Kokush?"

"I have not." I offered my hand, Talafan style, to the Minister. He was a
shrewd-looking fellow with a thick mustache and small eyeglasses, and he
clasped my hand firmly enough, his face still as he looked me over.

"Credola Kalina," the Minister repeated slowly, as if searching his memory. "Credola Kalina. Ah! The Hero of Silasta, isn't it?"

"Not an official title, I'm afraid," I said, chuckling as if he'd made a fine
joke. He knew exactly who I was, and he'd been stonewalling the Administrative Guild's requests for a meeting with me ever since he'd arrived in the
city. What I needed to find out was why. For now I smiled, going along with

the pretense that he was struggling to place me. "It is an honor to meet you, Minister. I met your predecessor some years ago and I was sorry to hear what happened."

"Very unfortunate," the Minister said, his face neutral.

"He was a fearsome negotiator, but fair. I enjoyed dealing with him." An exaggeration; I had still been in recovery when the former Minister had come to Silasta to negotiate reparations and compensations for the disruption and broken trade contracts surrounding the rebellion. When my health was better, though, I'd been able to participate, and the Minister had been a clever and determined man, ruthless in his pursuit of good terms for his country, but a reasonable one. We'd scrutinized him for any sign that Talafar had been involved in the plot that had torn our country apart, and found no grounds for suspicion.

Things were different now.

The former Minister had drowned in a boating accident, and Kokush had replaced him. Coincidence, perhaps, but one of many such coincidences that had gradually changed the makeup of Talafar's Imperial government. Sjona and Talafar had a secure treaty and had been firm allies during the Emperor's long rule, but our spies' reports, the impressions of our former Ambassador Astor, and my own private correspondence with Ectar all confirmed the past two years had seen a gradual shift of power from the elderly Emperor to his eldest son and heir. Crown Prince Hiukipi's intentions toward the Empire's southern neighbor were uncertain; we had no spies close to the Prince, and since Astor's expulsion from the capital we'd even lost intelligence from more official sources.

The Crown Prince was here in Silasta but seemed determined to avoid any diplomatic engagement. Whether we were dealing with a wealthy noble who just wanted to indulge in everything Silasta and karodee had to offer, or one deliberately snubbing our officials for more sinister reasons, we didn't know. In the last eighteen months Talafar had undertaken two conquests—"liberation and annexation" was the politer term—of small neighboring territories on Imperial borders, reportedly under Hiukipi's direction. Clearly he was more aggressively minded than his father. The critical information I needed was whether his sights and ambitions had drifted south. Someone with resources had funded a rebellion to weaken us, and if it was the Prince then I would find out.

"Well. Nothing to negotiate for now," Ectar said, placing a hand on my

shoulder blades, almost possessively. "There is a litter waiting. If you've finished your drink, Kokush?"

The Minister paused before setting down his cup, and did not hasten to his
feet, but nor did he dawdle to the point of rudeness. I pretended to brush my
clothes for the last of the fragments of broken porcelain as an excuse to observe
this subtle tussle between nobility and bureaucrat.

"Are you enjoying the karodee?" I directed the question to both men
as we boarded the waiting litter outside the teahouse. While Ectar gave
enthusiastic affirmation, Kokush gazed through the fluttering fabric at the
passing traffic and took his time answering. He looked at me in an assessing
manner.

"It is a very grand affair," he said at last. "Quite the celebration." His manner was faintly hostile, but I couldn't quite pinpoint why. Many conservative
Talafan would disapprove of aspects of the karodee celebrations, most notably
the adult ones confined to nighttime. Or perhaps I personally was the source
of his distaste. Some in the Administrative Guild had resisted my application
for Ambassador on the basis that women did not hold government positions
in Talafar and a female diplomat could find some Empire officials hostile
due to gender prejudices. Yet it seemed unlikely the Empire would appoint a
Foreign Minister who was offended by foreign customs and social standards.

"Have you seen ribbon dancing before, Minister?" I prompted. "It's quite
beautiful."

"Never," he replied gravely, without looking at me.

"Dancing is a social event in Izruitn," Ectar clarified. "It will feel strange to
only watch!" Then, as if he thought he might have offended, he added, "But I
am looking forward to it, of course."

A brief tug of affection—he really was trying very hard—preceded a
stronger one of guilt for how I was using him. But a degree of dishonesty to
all but those closest to me was a necessity of my role. Etan had explained that
all those years ago, and I'd agreed willingly enough. "There will be dancing
during the masquerade, so I hope you still brought your dancing shoes, Lord
Ectar."

"Do you dance, Credola?" he asked hopefully.

"I'm afraid I don't have the stamina."

Ectar's hands stilled, stricken. "Of course! I'm sorry." Not the first time he
had forgotten, or even disbelieved, my limitations.

Kokush looked at my stomach, suddenly attentive, confirming my guess that he had always known precisely who I was. The ugly knot of hard tissue and the web of pale surgical scars beneath my clothing served as permanent reminders of my encounter with Aven, but aside from the occasional random twinge the injury rarely bothered me. What she'd done to me had left different marks. But for most people it was more comfortable to attribute my slow recovery and any ongoing health issues, however unrelated, to the dramatic story that had defined the last few years of my life.

I would use that; I would turn it and everything else into a tool at my disposal to protect what was important to me.

"I'm quite recovered from my injuries," I assured him, and turned the conversation to a discussion of Ectar's trading ventures. While Ectar happily expounded on the new demand for leather clothing in the mountainous Doran kingdom, the Minister visibly relaxed. I was glad of the hours of practice learning body language cues with my Talafan language tutor, because Kokush, unlike Ectar, never wavered in his facial control, and clues to his mood and emotions were in the rise and fall of his breathing, the movement of his hands, the occasional shift in his seat. The more we talked business and trade, the more comfortable he seemed. By the time we arrived at the arena, Kokush's guarded manner had eased and he had joined the conversation.

The Stone-Guilder, Eliska, and her team had spent months transforming our old sporting grounds into this imposing, impressive structure capable of seating thousands at capacity. A smiling attendant led us to seats reserved for our international guests. Keeping pace with the men as we ascended took much of my energy—fortunes, I hated stairs—but I was determined to stay with Kokush now he was opening up. My lungs burned beneath my ribs and my legs were warm with a dull ache that preceded exhaustion. I would pay for this little excursion.

The guest area, with its unparalleled view of the whole arena, had its own roof to protect it from weather, and resembled a cozy room with its fine cushions, rugs, and lamps. A far cry from the plain benches ringing the lower levels where I had watched several earlier events, but I preferred the anonymity and unpolished excitement of the public section. This afternoon the area was empty but for a few guests from the western nations in one corner, engaged in an intense conversation. I recognized several Marutian Dukes with their decorated beards and flat hats, and the imposing, veiled High Priestess from Perest-Avana. One of the latter's accompanying officials, a tall woman with a sculptured face accentuated by very short hair, smiled at us warmly, but none of the others looked up from the conversation. A Talafan servant led us to a cushioned bench in the corner of the partitioned section.

"You were telling me about your family's business, Minister," I reminded Kokush. "Where did you grow up?"

"My family is from the northwest, originally," Kokush said, lowering himself beside me. Ectar, who had turned away to hand his hat to the attendant, looked put out as he swung back and found himself on the far side of the Minister.

Behind us, several other groups entered the area; I pretended to adjust my position on the seat to scan them. It was not the Crown Prince, as I had hoped, but a group of Talafan noblewomen. At their center was a beautiful woman with an intelligent face, long curls the color of sunlit honey, and a kind of gentle grace in her movements I couldn't have imitated with months of practice. That must be the celebrated Princess Zhafi, the Crown Prince's younger sister, by decades, and by all reports their father the Emperor's most favored daughter.

She was surrounded by a handful of other noblewomen and trailed by several maidservants. A glowering and primly dressed man directed them to seats as far from the other guests as possible, his gestures and tone as they took their seats reminiscent of a bad-tempered schoolteacher. In their gleaming multicolored silk pants and elaborate headdresses, the ladies looked more like a flock of exotic birds than unruly children, and their smooth, doll-like painted faces and perfect composure made his forceful treatment incongruous. Ectar bowed his head to the ladies but did not speak, and Kokush gave no sign he'd even noticed their entry. "The province of Lokapir."

I blinked, returning my attention to the Minister. Though some of the women had looked over at us with curiosity, it was apparent none of the men thought it worth introducing us. It took me a moment to recall what the Minister was talking about, but I recognized the name, for more than one reason. "The home of the famous Lokapir parumb? The most marvelous dried parumb found their way here last year and I have been trying to get more ever since. My mother wants to use them in tea."

"It will be a while, I'm afraid," Kokush said, the barest suggestion of a frown in his voice if not his expression. "It is grown near the border and most of the season's harvest and many of next year's plants were destroyed in the annexation of Lios. There was a fire." His eyes darted to the pack of women on the opposite side of the seating area, then returned.

My shocked groan was an easy lie. Of course I had heard about the fire; the price of the dried fruit had blown out immediately, to my mother's ire. However, the parumb were not the victims of the annexation with whom I was concerned. "How dreadful. But of course we did hear about Lios, even all the way down here. Is it true the Crown Prince himself rode in to take the fortress?"

Against my innocently curious words, the Minister's guarded air returned like a cloak had been thrown around him. "General Zoho led the liberation force, but His Highness the Prince followed soon after to greet our new citizens and establish the Imperial Governor."

The liberation force. Is that what you'd call it if he sent his army down here? I wanted to ask, *And how did those new citizens feel about their "liberation"?* but instead I smiled sweetly. "How fortunate for your new citizens."

Ectar made a sound that might have been laughter or might have been agreement.

"I have not yet had the pleasure of speaking to His Highness, of course." I looked under my eyelashes at Ectar, willing him to walk the path I had laid out for him. "Will he be here today?" But instead, it was his turn to look disquieted.

"No, no. My uncle the Prince is . . . a very busy and powerful man. He is not familiar with your city or your customs, Credola Kalina. He does not speak Sjon, and does not like to rely too much on translators." He reached over and patted my forearm. "Do not trouble yourself—I daresay I can keep you entertained! Besides, there will be plenty of time for formality if you come to Izruitn."

Kokush swiveled to Ectar, his shoulders tense. "What do you mean by that, my lord?"

"I forget rumors don't always worm their way down every hole," Ectar said airily, and the Minister's nostrils flared. "Credola Kalina is to be the nominated Ambassador for Sjona." His pleasure in conveying information the Minister lacked was obvious.

"My appointment has not been finalized," I said, truthfully. The Administrative Guild had not even formally proposed the appointment, let alone had it accepted by the Talafan government, though the Guild deliberations had been far from secret. My fame and my family name gave me a high profile, but counting against me were not only the gender issues in the Empire but also my relative inexperience, and my well-known health issues. The old Kalina would never have put herself forward against arguably worthier candidates, but the old Kalina had not known the capabilities of our country's enemies, and what we could lose if they struck again. Someone Tain could rely on absolutely needed to be digging into the Empire's position, and on whom could he ever rely more than me? "Perhaps it is fortunate we have run into each other, Minister Kokush. It will be easier for you to assess my suitability face-to-face, rather than as a mere figure in a story, do you not think?"

His hands closed together purposefully. There was a long pause, then he nodded. "Indeed, Credola Kalina. Very fortunate. Your Talafan is very good, I must say."

"Thank you. I have worked hard to improve." When I had been too ill to leave my bed, Jov had hired me a Talafan tutor. Focusing on improving those skills had kept me sane in my confinement, and kept my mind occupied on something other than the fears that waited for me whenever my thoughts drifted.

"Ah look! The first dancers have arrived!"

We all leaned forward to see dancers filing out onto the freestanding performance stage below, bare-legged, palumas pale against their dark skin, bright crisscrossed cording up their torsos and down their arms. "Where are the ribbons?" Ectar asked.

I smiled. "Just watch."

The music sounded faint and wispy from here. But ribbon dancing was about making music visual, and quickly Kokush and Ectar became transfixed as the dancers spun, at first gently and then more forcefully, and began to release their costumes with the rhythmic contortions that unwound what had appeared to be ordinary cording into long, bright ribbons. Ectar exclaimed in delight as the dancers all unwound the last of the binding around their hips and flung the rippling ends of ribbon into the center of the stage. They hurled themselves around the space with athleticism and elegance, and soon the entire stage was filled with a constant swirl of color and motion. So entrancing was the performance that when a servant appeared at our side to offer sweet and savory crusted nuts, it took her three attempts to get the men's attention.

"Such control!" Kokush murmured, absently accepting a little cone of nuts without taking his eyes from the stage. "The ribbons are longer than the dancers. How do they not become entangled?"

"With rather a lot of practice," I said. "And probably a lot of swearing in the process."

He surprised me by laughing. Across the room, the dour ladies' escort stopped eating to give a sharp look in our direction.

Onstage, attendants threw out a change of ribbons, all blues and greens, and the dancers moved in alternating patterns, the ribbons flowing like beautiful waves. "It is like water," Ectar said, and I nodded.

"This is an homage to our traditional sea dance."

Kokush glanced at me quizzically. "But Sjona has no ocean, Credola Kalina."

"There is a very fine painting of the ocean in the guesthouse, too," Ectar pointed out. "I assumed a foreign artist."

I smiled again. "It's a very old dance, Minister. And the painting in the Leaning Lady is a very old painting, by one of our most beloved artists. Ribbon dancing, and memories of the ocean, were carried to Sjona by early refugees, I believe."

I was about to ask about the ocean—Izruitn was, after all, partly an island city—but Ectar pointed at the grounds. "Ah, now the competition begins?"

The group routine had ended and most of the dancers were leaving the stage. "Yes. There will be pairs, first, then single dancers."

The pairs did not disappoint. Two extremely acrobatic men threw each other across the stage so lightly they seemed on wing, an adorable young pair of siblings performed some innovative moves with stiff ribbons held between them like ropes, and there were several romantic numbers with much binding and unbinding. One tragic routine between two women had such intense chemistry in their movements apart and together, conveying a desperate, passionate desire to unwrap each other down to their very core, that I felt sure they must have real romantic history. Ectar and Kokush shifted uncomfortably during this routine; in the Empire much of their social culture was bound up with their religion, and they might never have seen women dancing in such a manner before.

The Marutians and Perest-Avani seemed silently captivated, and the group of Talafan noblewomen giggled and gasped their way through the performances. Several times when I glanced over, one of the ladies looked back in apparent curiosity. More disconcertingly, I caught the escort staring at me, eyes gleaming with unexplained hostility.

The solo dances were last, performed with a ribbon in each hand, dancers attempting to keep themselves and the whipping, flying fabric in constant flowing motion across the stage. The best was a powerful woman with bloodred ribbons, and the story told in her dance was brutally resonant. The deep silence of the arena as she danced, and for several full breaths after it ended, was a testament to her performance.

The applause after the stunned silence was the loudest yet, including within the room; Ectar and Kokush both stood, clapping hard, and so did the women, and the roaring and pounding of hands and feet in the seating below and around our area made the whole place shake faintly. Amidst all that tumult, a harsh coughing sounded a few times before I noticed and turned to see who was struggling with such an unpleasant raspy hack.

It was the Talafan ladies' chaperone, and one look was enough. He was not coughing. The sound had all but gone: he was red-faced and gasping for breath. "Help!" I shouted, and sprang to my feet. "That man is choking!"

I had cried out in Sjon; by the time I realized, I was already at the chaperone's side. Someone screamed. His flushed skin was turning bluish pale around the lips. One hand clawed at his throat, pulling at the skin and the high neck of his nihep, leaving deep gouges; the other flailed uselessly. Guards at either corner of the room raced in as if propelled but then stumbled to an awkward, almost comical, halt, evidently unsure what to do. One of the ladies emitted little high-pitched scream-squeaks, like a terrified animal, and another was crying noisily in panicked gulps. Ectar and Kokush had both risen from their seats but were staring transfixed, unmoving.

"He is *choking*," I shouted again, this time in the right language, and when no one responded with anything but open-mouthed stares, I threw up my hands, stepped behind the man, and hit him hard between the shoulder blades with a flat hand.

He spasmed, staggering forward, but nothing dislodged and he continued to grope and gasp. One of the guards had made as if to grab me when I'd struck the chaperone but now dropped back, looking anxiously at his colleague. Everyone was staring. "Lean forward," I told the chaperone firmly. I hit him again, then a third time, and on the fourth slap a projectile finally broke free and bounced down between the benches.

The man's legs sagged as if the nut obstructing his airway had also been holding him upright. Now, at last, the guards and servants rushed in to assist. Breathing heavily, I stepped out of their way. But the chaperone shoved them back furiously and staggered to a bench to sit alone.

"I am well, I am *well*," he snapped as a servant tried to offer him water.

"He will be fine. He just needs some space to breathe," I suggested to the servant, and she gave me an odd look, as if surprised to be addressed directly—or perhaps simply surprised to be addressed politely. I glanced around at the room full of shocked faces. The westerners were whispering to one another, and most of the Talafan women had sunk to their own benches, obviously distressed. Ectar and Kokush looked pale and embarrassed. I struggled to believe they had never seen a person choking before—even if they'd had no contact with children, adults eating at parties were equally talented at attracting this particular disaster.

The chaperone glared at me. "I am fine. It was this . . . this ridiculous food." He kicked at the spilled nuts scattered around beneath his feet. Apparently, he had more than one thing in common with a toddler. A servant, kneeling, swept up the mess with her hands. I crouched to help her.

"My lady, please, no, no, I will do this!" She looked thoroughly alarmed, her hands shaking as she half-shooed me away, somehow combining insistence with deference. As I started to stand I noticed under the bench what looked like a discarded toy poppet, about as big as my forearm. Thinking it must be a toy dropped by some child, I was about to retrieve it when Ectar's paralysis finally lifted, and he swooped in to help me to my feet with a trembling grip.

"Thank our holy God for the Credola Kalina," he announced to the room, brandishing me like a trophy.

"She saved his life," one of the ladies said in a carrying whisper. One of the Marutian Dukes raised his cup in my direction with a faint smile, and the High Priestess whispered in her attendant's ear, but her veiled face was turned toward me. The pretty woman who had smiled at me earlier beamed again, and I felt my cheeks warm under all the sudden regard.

The man did not look thankful. Once he had recovered his breath and his composure, he stood, nodded stiffly in my general direction without making eye contact, and returned to his post with the women as if nothing had happened.

"Come, sit," Ectar said, and, somewhat nonplussed, I returned to the bench. We had missed several routines and the incident had left me disconcerted, but everyone else seemed to find the man's strange behavior unremarkable. I glanced at him a few times but he kept his back to us.

"Do not be troubled," Ectar said in a lowered voice, speaking in Sjon. His accent had improved. "His manners are . . . wanting. I am sorry he does you dishonor. He was lucky you are here."

I replied in an equally quiet voice, though taking care to keep my tone light. "And who is my brusque friend?"

Kokush's mouth made a thin line and he surprised me by joining the conversation in Sjon. "Brother Lu is the Emperor's own spiritual adviser, Credola, sent to accompany the Princesses and the ladies, to provide guidance and counsel."

Ectar turned a look on Lu that was, for a Talafan, unsubtle in its dislike. "The Church was concerned about Princess Zhafi. She is unmarried, you know, and my grandfather is protective of her. Her ladies are very sheltered and their dignity and purity are very important to the Church. Brother Lu is charged with ensuring they are not, ah, tainted by the . . ." He trailed off, perhaps struggling to find the right words in our language, or perhaps simply unable to come up with a polite euphemism.

"The terrible temptations of our city?" I filled in, struggling between amusement and pity. I knew something of the powerful Talafan religion and its views on things Sjons would regard as basic freedoms of a civilized society. If mere exposure to Silasta was a danger to adult women, how could a single man's presence—however disapproving—offset its apparent wickedness? But how sad for those poor women.

Ectar patted my arm again, still leaning across Kokush, apparently oblivious to the other man's irritation. "Do not concern yourself, Credola. There are many rules for the ladies of the Young Empress's court, it is very . . . uh . . . complicated. I apologize again for the rudeness, and pray you do not take it to heart." An anxious note had crept into his voice and I smiled, reassuring him.

"I won't," I said, then switched back to Talafan, and a normal volume, forcing my attention and theirs back to the dancing. "Look, this is Siris. He won the crown at the Games last year."

The remainder of the event passed without incident. "Quite remarkable," Ectar said, shaking his head as the crowning ceremony concluded. "Extraordinary."

"It is one of my favorite events," I said.

Ectar was looking over at the ladies' group as they all got to their feet, chattering quietly again. His face wore the slightest smile and to my surprise, one of the ladies raised a hand to wave at him. She was a tiny thing in a pale green suit, with a soft, gathered mass of long, pale yellow hair, and her delicate painted mouth curved in an answering tiny smile. "My dear Lady Reuta," he said, beckoning her forward. "Did you enjoy the dancing?"

"Very much," she said, bowing her head. She walked in dainty, soft steps, her suit barely moving, giving the impression of her gliding over to us. Coupled with her pretty, doll-like face, it gave her an otherworldly appearance. "It was beautiful. Did you like it, my lord?" Her words were directed at him but her gaze was on me.

He nodded enthusiastically. "Remarkable!" he repeated. "My dear, won't you come and meet my correspondent, Credola Kalina?" The woman missed—or ignored—the low noise of protest from the chaperone, who had been herding the ladies toward the door. Ectar brought the young woman's hand to his cheek affectionately, then held it out to me. "Credola Kalina, this is the Lady of Agarata, Lady Reuta. My youngest sister."

The resemblance was there, now he said it, in the shape of her nose and her small, pointed chin. "It is a pleasure," I said, offering my hand.

"It is my pleasure. You were so brave just now with Brother Lu, Credola Kalina," she said, but before we could shake hands, the chaperone had stepped in, stony-faced and rigid-spined.

"Excuse me, my lord, but the ladies are required to return to their accommodations. My lady, if you will please?" His manner made it clear it was not a request. Brother Lu steered Reuta back toward the others, taking obvious care to avoid the Perest-Avani Priestess and her attendants as they left the area. Ectar opened his mouth as if he might protest, but then shrugged and turned back to us, his eyes bright with some impending suggestion.

"I must beg forgiveness and take my leave as well," I said, before he could issue any further invitations. "Thank you for the company, Lord Ectar, Minister Kokush. It was an honor to be invited here. I promised to collect my niece, and I fear I may already be late." Jov was collecting Dee, but I needed to rest, soon, and to strategize. And now I wanted to do more reading about the Church in Talafar. Brother Lu's barely concealed hostility, even in the face of me literally having saved his life, was intriguing, and the Church's feelings on violence and conquest would be very interesting to know.

"Thank *you*, Credola," the Minister said. I noted with satisfaction the thaw in his manner. Perhaps he would not avoid our next meeting. "Brother Lu is lucky we ran into you this morning, or this might have turned into quite the tragedy."

"Are you sure you must go?" Ectar asked plaintively. For all his sophistication and occasional charm, he was still a wealthy and powerful man, accustomed to getting what he wanted.

"Very sure. But thank you."

Ectar, disappointed at my insistence, touched the back of my hand to his face. "We are all lucky, as the Minister says. We shall meet again soon, Credola."

We started toward the exit, following the disappearing party of noble-women, before I remembered the poppet I'd seen under the bench. "One moment, Lord Ectar," I apologized, and ducked down to where I'd seen the doll. I tugged it out. "Are there any children with the ladies? I think someone dropped a toy." Though even as I said it, I realized it was unlikely to be the toy of a noble child. It was an ugly little thing, clumsily made, with one deformed leg and grubby string wound round to form the neck. Its dress was a black scrap of fabric. Holding it now, I found I didn't like it at all; it reminded me of the big dummies we had used as fake sentries in the siege, or of the targets we had practiced archery on. More reminiscent of weapons and war than a play.

Ectar shrugged. "I don't think so," he said carelessly, though I doubted he'd have paid enough attention to the dozens of servants in their party to be able to tell. Some poor toddler was likely already missing their favorite toy, hideous or not.

An elderly servant was carrying a pile of the ladies' shawls, hats, and other belongings toward the exit. "Excuse me," I said. She did not look up, but bowed deeply in my direction.

"My lady?" Her voice was soft and quavering, as if she feared reprimand. "At your service?" It made me uncomfortable seeing the Talafan staff's degree of deference compared to the workers in our employ: our housekeeper, Sjease, who had taken over our household in the space of less than a month and now shamelessly bossed us all around at leisure; my guard Lara with her cheeky good humor and long-winded stories about her son; or Tain's earnest young page, Erel. I'd seen some bad treatment of staff in this city, but even the most self-important wealthy Silastians would find the level of worshipful service apparently expected of Talafan servants disconcerting.

I held out the poppet. "Is there a child traveling with your party? I think someone dropped this."

She looked up with a little jerk, and took the doll so swiftly it was almost sleight of hand. "Of course, of course, thank you, my lady, thank you," she murmured, and backed away, the poppet already lost in the piles in her arms. I felt strangely relieved at having handed it over. I wiped my hand on the side of my hip as if I could remove the touch of it. I noticed one of the Marutian

Dukes, still sitting at the back of the area, was watching me with his head cocked to one side, one hand stroking his beard. Not for the first time, I felt unsettled at having been watched by a stranger.

"Come, you'll be late for your niece!" Ectar said, and I wondered if I'd irritated him, but as we proceeded down the steps of the arena he chuckled indulgently instead. It reminded me that he still thought of me as a strange and exotic marvel, not quite of the same species as himself. Though my limbs trembled with weariness, I sped up so his hand fell away from my back. I was not a spectacle for anyone's entertainment, and I'd had enough of acting that part for the day.

I was descending a few lengths behind Brother Lu, at the tail end of the ladies' procession, when he fell.

The priest was stepping confidently, if stiffly, his arms folded behind his back, when his leg simply . . . crumpled, like soggy paper, just as he transferred his weight. No one had pushed or even touched him. Nor did he miss his step or slip for an obvious reason, and the steps were clear of debris. But he went down hard, and fast, and with nothing more than a yelp.

"My God!" Ectar, perhaps embarrassed by his inaction with the choking, sprang forward immediately this time. "Are you all right, Brother?"

This time, the man couldn't foist off the assistance; his leg had gone between two steps and he howled in pain. Ectar, sweat breaking out on his wide-eyed face, pulled back the man's nihep, and one of the women screamed. The ugly break was horrifically apparent in the protrusion of white bone through a jagged, bloody gash in his shin. Vomit rose in my throat and I clapped a hand over my mouth.

"Get a physic," I cried, and heard the shake in my own voice.

Then I let myself be caught up in the crowd of concerned onlookers and away from the Talafan party. I didn't understand what had just happened but for whatever reason, the ugly poppet sprang back into my mind, its throat tight with string and one leg missing or deformed. The mental image was a sinister and unpleasant thing. I wanted very much to be away from this odd party of hostile priests and corralled women and opaque officials. There was something wrong in this Talafan camp.

Incident: Mass poisoning at Silverstream village town hall

Poison: Scatterburr

Incident notes: Scatterburr plants burned as kindling during town meeting; combination of cold weather and virulent Maiso, poor ventilation and blockage in chimney led to concentration of toxic fumes. Four dead, six treated in hospital. No signs of deliberate sabotage, suggest resources toward education on estates about toxic nature of certain plants.

(from proofing notes of Credo Etan Oromani)

3

Jovan

Closeted in the alcove in my bedroom with a pot of tea, I hovered my pen under Bradomir's name on my list of confirmed incidents. Long gone were the days when I could spread my work over the table. With extra relatives from the estates staying in the city for karodee, I had retreated from the chaos of the main apartments to spend most of my time in here. I sat among piles of notes on Aven, the mercenaries, the funding trail, every incident that could be connected to the rebellion and every suspicion we held about other countries and potential enemies. And now, an assassination attempt.

Without recovering the dart, and in the absence of a proper examination at the hospital, I could not prove Bradomir's death was murder, nor even intimate such to the Council. I had made my case to the Warrior-Guilder and the captains of the Order Guards and the blackstripes, respectively, but had made little ground. While no one had said outright that they disbelieved my account, the meetings had felt more like polite indulgence than serious discussions. Tain was already well protected, they had told me. Yes, they would search any premises before he attended in the future, even the rafters of a theater. But a single incident witnessed by no one but me was not proof of a broader plot, and their doubts were palpable.

Fresh from Thendra's confirmation at the hospital, I'd been barely managing my compulsions that day and had been unable to keep some of my more obvious tics from surfacing during the meeting. Physical signs of anxiety always made others perceive me as less trustworthy, even hysterical. Even among people who trusted my devotion to Tain and to Sjona, that had an impact. The bloody play (despite, or perhaps because of, its dramatic pre-opening) was proving wildly popular, fanning public speculation about me, and even though these men and women had known me for years, its influence crept into our interactions. I wasn't a joke to them, not quite yet, but the Chancellor's eccentric friend had become a person to be managed, rather than listened to.

A tap on the doorframe interrupted my train of thought.

"Credo Jovan?" Al-Sjease, our household manager and my secretary, peered around the corner. Tall and slender, with a smooth, androgynous face and wooly braids bursting from a stripe down the middle of their head, Sjease wore an expression somewhere between exasperation and tolerance, one I'd grown to know all too well over the course of the last two years. "You aren't dressed. The rowing final—I did leave you a reminder. Did you forget the time?"

I sighed and gulped down the last of my tea. "Yes. Sorry. I did see the note, but I got sidetracked." I rubbed my forehead.

Seeing my expression, Sjease's own softened. "Are you feeling all right, Credo? You seem . . . distracted."

"Just a headache," I said, waving a hand dismissively, and Sjease accepted the lie without comment. I hadn't wanted a housekeeper—or indeed a servant of any kind—and had worried that it would risk exposing our family's secrets. But Kalina and I couldn't be home with Dija every evening, so I'd had to accept it. Over time, my initial concerns about bringing a stranger into our home had faded. If Sjease was curious about my strange behavior and obsessions then they hid it well enough to fool me.

"I laid out your clothes earlier, but if you need assistance?" They scooped away my cup and pot and their eyes twinkled as I grumbled a negative. Within the first week on the job Sjease had pronounced my clothes chest "utterly devoid of personality" and their quest to clothe me more fashionably had worn me down over time. I knew better than to argue by now. So while Sjease swept out of the room with my tea things I grudgingly changed from my plain clothes into the more colorful outfit on my bed.

Long gone were the days when a gleam of metallic thread in the cording of a plain paluma could pass for formal wear. Now blending in among my peers meant lace and beading and exotic dyes in my clothes, and new cuts and fabrics and fastenings every few months, it seemed. This garment, with its loose sleeves and structured torso, barely resembled a paluma anymore. It was so snug the cording was more decorative than functional, though it still had enough room around my middle to accommodate the belt of pockets Kalina had sewed to fit a useful array of my tools of trade.

"Not bad," Sjease said when I emerged a short time later. Deft fingers adjusted the scalloped edging around my neck with practiced ease, and added a pendant necklace I'd pretended not to see on the bed.

"Very handsome," Kalina agreed as she looked me over with a suppressed smile. "Is everyone ready, then?"

We collected our assortment of accompanying relatives—Dija and her mother and grandmother, her two brothers, and two excited third cousins—and the collection of personal guards we were required to ferry around to every official function. I even managed polite small talk with the group on the way down to the lake. The streets were loud and merry, overwhelming my senses with color and noise and competing smells both fair and foul. Massive karodee flags by the lake crackled and flapped in a colorful dance in the heavy spring winds. Glazed pots bursting with riotous flowers and swinging merry ribbons decorated every shop front and doorframe, heralding the arrival of spring and the recovery of our city. Silasta thrived once more, and its residents celebrated that. Well, most of its residents.

"Isn't it exciting, Uncle Jovan?" one of Dija's brothers asked, face split into a grin as he swiveled his head around this way and that, eyes shining. His first visit to the capital must have seemed a thrilling change of pace from life in Telasa, the smaller northern border city. He didn't seem to need an answer; something else took his attention and he grabbed at his older brother's arm to point it out, sparing me having to fake an appropriate level of excitement.

Once we were on the crowded lower streets approaching the lake, I found an anonymity I'd sorely missed in the constant giddy press of excited bodies, the food carts and street games, and the laughter, whoops of encouragement, and ever-changing wagers. A performer collecting a crowd for their balancing act called out for our attention, a man asked me to "Buy us a drink, mate, go on?," and a girl with a slick smile tugged at the cording on my clothes with a murmured, "Fancy a game of spots?," but otherwise our group went largely unnoticed.

Large colorful marquees decorated the grassy east bank of the lake, and the competitors' boats waited at the start point. Etrika, Dija's grandmother and Etan's first cousin once removed, took off her hat and fanned her face with it. "Find me a spot to sit down, would you, loves?" she said to the boys. "An old lady needs a rest after all that walking."

I sent her a sharp look. Etrika was barely seventy, a hale and formidable woman. She had been happily walking around the city for weeks, refusing a litter, and during the rushuk ball match last week she'd leapt out of her seat, swearing so enthusiastically I'd worried she'd been about to start a fight with the referee. "There'll be plenty of room in the Council marquee for family—" I began, but she met my look with innocent wide eyes and cut me off.

"Oh, no, no. I couldn't be expected to stand around with all those Councilors and important people. Not at my age, Jovan. My constitution, you know." She fanned herself once or twice more, for good measure.

"Yeah, mine too," I muttered, and she winked.

I would have skipped the event if I could, but Tain and Merenda, his cousin and heir, would both be there. His blackstripes would be on high alert, access to the marquee would be carefully restricted, and no one with a weapon would be anywhere near the Chancellor. And Tain's ongoing health issues meant everyone had grown accustomed to him rarely eating in public, so my actual proofing duties were limited. But given our mysterious enemy was armed with quiet and lethal substances like rucho darts, I wouldn't take any chances.

A servant ushered Dija, Lini, and me inside the grandest of the marquees. He was dressed the same as the others, but with muscular arms straining the seams of the tunic and the posture of a swordsman, not a butler, I'd have known him as a blackstripe even if I didn't recognize his face. "The staff first, then Merenda," I murmured to Dija. My apprentice nodded and slipped away from us into the milling crowd, a convincing look of wonder on her round face, as if she were a small child being given a treat.

Probably half the Council was here already, as well as many of our international guests. An explosion of gold and glimmering jewels visible through a gap identified the Crown Prince of Talafar, Prince Hiukipi, flanked by Imperial soldiers with hard, attentive faces and stiff uniforms bearing the Emperor's symbol: a crenelated crown. Kalina made a small noise of satisfaction. She'd been trying to get a meeting with the Prince since his arrival, and the strange accident that had befallen the priest had only increased her interest. "Go work some charm," I encouraged her. "See what you can find out."

Kalina headed determinedly in that direction and I accepted a cup of warm and sweet-smelling kavcha from a servant and sipped, my gaze roaming as I mentally cataloged the spices. I marked out the blackstripes in the crowd and watched Dija speaking earnestly to a servant bearing a heavy tray.

I'd taught her to first count the number of servants in the room, to note their faces and their manner, and report back to me what each was carrying. Then she was to stick close to Merenda and observe anything out of the ordinary. Everyone was used to seeing her publicly attached to the Heir, and I knew they whispered that warm, gentle Merenda was a better influence than Dija's odd uncle.

"Isn't the tent interesting?" Dija asked breathlessly, returning to my side. She had tucked a yellow flower into the side of her glasses and her fingers fluttered; she looked for all the world like a girl at her first party, over-whelmed with the glamour. She recited the food available in the same ex-cited tone. "There's fried fishballs and honey figs, and those little nut pastries with corin that Auntie Kalina likes, and bread with orange paste, and sugar crisps . . . can I eat anything I like, Uncle Jovan?" Several passing Councilors exchanged indulgent smiles with me. Where Etan and I had both cultivated an air of dull ordinariness, my apprentice's cover was something different.

"Let's try some of everything," I agreed, and let her lead me around until we had sampled everything being offered to guests. I kept an eye on Tain, who was with Kalina in conversation with the Talafan, and Dija relayed a detailed story about what had happened in the previous rowing heat one of our cousins had been in, providing her observations about the food and as-sessment of the ingredients in between commentary about the various teams.

"Oh, look, they're getting ready to start!" she said, taking a delicate nibble of a fishball on a stick. Then, as if as an aside, "The Honored Heir wouldn't like these, you know, she told me the other day how she gets a headache from too much pepper. I should tell her."

"It wouldn't do to have a headache during the race," I agreed, keeping my tone neutral, but giving an approving smile at her subtle signal about the masking flavor that made the fishballs a risk. "Go on, then."

When I checked on Tain again he had left the Talafan and was chatting with one of the Doranite Chieftains. His face brightened and he beckoned me over. I wove through the fray, keeping my senses attuned for anything out of the ordinary. There were so many people here. The tense, suffocating feeling of dread I'd felt in the theater returned, and the urge to start pacing twitched in my feet.

"The elusive Credo Jovan at last." A Doranite servant translated in heav-ily accented Sjon the booming greeting of one of the Chieftains as I ap-proached. I had met and briefly conversed with the King of Doran on his arrival several weeks before, but had exchanged only bare greetings with the half dozen Chieftains accompanying him. The Chieftain who had hailed me was a good head taller than I, with spiked hair and decorative colored-glass fragments glued across one of her cheekbones. She wore a glossy brown fur across her shoulders in defiance of the warm spring weather. "We heard much about you across the border." The servant paused, gave a sidelong, uncomfortable glance at the grinning Chieftain, and shifted weight between his feet before translating the last, his head lowered. "The . . . uh, the Chancellor's little attack pet, yes?"

Tain stiffened. "Credo Jovan is my most trusted adviser and dear friend," he said, drawing me to his side with a hard hand on my shoulder. "And one of our most esteemed members of the Council. You have heard his name because he was instrumental both in defending our city and securing ongoing peace. None of us would be enjoying these festivities if not for him."

Rather than being cowed, the Chieftain laughed, clapped her own enormous hand on my other shoulder, and said something in a jovial tone. "Oh yes, a very useful pet!" the servant clarified reluctantly, his creamy brown face flushing. "We attended your most excellent play last night, you know. We do not have such things at home. We are too busy training to beat you at rowing!"

I had already followed the line of the Chieftain's gaze down to the lake before the servant finished translating. Enormous-shouldered Doranites were swinging their arms in powerful circles, warming up beside the water. The course was marked out as a set of arches and bobbing buoys, bright little jewels on the shining surface. The nearby Sjon team, and the pale-skinned Talafan, looked like children by comparison.

"The race is about to start," Tain said to the Chieftain, his tone still stiff. "Please, why don't you have a seat."

Apparently unoffended by being brushed off, the Chieftain grinned and nodded. "I would not miss this! It will be over quickly. Like the climbing! Why do you have so many climbing sports when your country is so flat? You cannot compete with true mountaineers." She shook her head and slapped her thigh as if it were a great joke.

Tain steered me away. "Sorry," he sighed, once we were out of earshot. "I know we need to keep things smooth with the other countries, but honor-down, they make it hard sometimes. The Talafan Prince was bloody rude to

Lini, and I've no idea what passes for manners in Doran, but I think it's lost in translation."

I shrugged. "What was it the Ambassador told us the other week? 'Good manners in Doran is waiting until the other person takes off their best cloak before trying to take their head off'?" I gave Tain a wan smile. "Anyway, I prefer it when they're open about it. I'll take insults over assassins any day."

Down at the river, the horn sounded the beginning of the race. Tain gave me a reassuring smile over the cheers of the crowd. "We've got through it all so far. I know the thing with Bradomir was—"

"You know I was right about Bradomir," I said quietly, hovering to the back of the crowd as most of the group moved toward the open side of the marquee to watch the boats fly forward. I added sarcastically, "Since it wasn't *me* who poisoned him, despite what certain others seem to think."

He looked at me sharply, then changed it to a pleasant smile as another Councilor moved nearer to us. Down on the Bright Lake, the athletes cut across the surface of the water with smooth precision, calling out with their powerful strokes. The red Talafar boat had taken an early lead. We watched for a moment before Tain murmured, "We can't be sure about anything. Bradomir had plenty of enemies. Fortunes know I won't miss him."

I shook my head, and fought to keep my irritation down. "It was the same man, Tain, the same one who's been watching you. He'll try again, I'm certain. I've talked with your Captain but think—"

"Honored Chancellor, Credo Jovan, how pleasant." Sjistevo Ash had slithered up without me realizing. There was no black left in his hair or beard but he wore more perfumed oil than a man half his age. "I've barely seen you this karodee. I suppose we don't need to be worried about assassins in the rafters today?" His smirk left his cold eyes unchanged.

"Let's hope not," I replied levelly. Honor-down, I was tired of this nonsense. "We've got a team to support down there." Said boat was in a distant third; the Doranites' inexorable rhythm had taken them past the Talafan boat and into what looked like an insurmountable lead, cutting the gleaming water of the Bright Lake like a gliding bird across still skies.

"I heard your Tashen pulled out of the wrestling," Tain said innocently. "That was a shame. But I suppose it's for the best—he wouldn't have come off that well against some of our international competitors, would he?"

"He was *injured*," Sjistevo retorted, nostrils flaring. "After some Darfri woman took offense at something he said, he *supposedly* slipped on the edge of the canal and broke his elbow. On a perfectly flat bit of ground, mind you." He glanced around, eyes fixing on several of the Darfri Councilors. He didn't trouble to lower his voice. "Doesn't pay to offend the Darfri now, does it?" Sjistevo glared at me before striding away, and Tain sighed wearily. All of the Families had been required to pay reparations to the Darfri and other citizens of the estates they had mistreated, in addition to funding schooling and Guild sponsorships, but they had done so with various degrees of resentment. For all that the city had purportedly embraced its religious history—having that religion come dramatically to life by exploding the lake in our faces made it rather difficult to refute, after all—there remained factions ready and willing to blame Darfri magic for everything that went wrong in their lives.

"They can't seem to make up their minds, can they?" I took a sip of my kavcha and took my attention from the race to check on Dija. She was midmouthful, lines of concentration on her small brow. "Am I a paranoid recluse, seeing conspiracies that aren't there, or am I some secret assassin behind everything they don't like?"

A grin. "I've always said you have many skills."

"Ha. Shame understanding Darfri magic isn't one of them." I hadn't meant it to come out so sour, but Tain understood, as he always did. He put a comforting hand on my shoulder.

"It's a new world for all of us, but especially Hadrea," he murmured, while the rest of the crowd oohed in appreciation at a particularly close passage through the final arch. "It's been a lot for her to digest."

The Compact reached with the Darfri elders after the siege had guaranteed funding for fresken training of potential Speakers, including Hadrea, who had reached adulthood without being taught how to develop and use that potential. It was what Hadrea had wanted her whole life, but frustration with her teacher and the pace of her learning was apparent in her bristling defensiveness or sullen silences if the subject came up. "She's having a hard time," I agreed neutrally. I had no desire to talk about it, so I looked around instead. "Where's Kalina? You said the Prince insulted her?" Hiukipi was watching the race with one of the western nobles but my sister wasn't with him.

Sudden applause erupted as the Doranite team sailed through the finish point. To my disquiet, as I turned to say something to Tain, the Darfri Speaker An-Ostada stood there instead as if we had summoned her.

She was a large and impressive woman, a charismatic presence who commanded attention and respect without effort. She wore traditional Darfristyled clothing, with layered skirts and a brightly embroidered scarf covering her speckled gray-and-black hair. Heavy decorative earrings pulled her lobes low and swung down near her shoulders, and her eyes, dark and bright in her wrinkled face, passed over me coolly.

"Credo Jovan," she said.

"An-Ostada. That was . . . uh, a good race, don't you think?"

She shrugged one shoulder, as if to admonish me for my petty enjoyment of such trifles. "I need a word with you."

I blinked. "With me?"

"Was I unclear?" An-Ostada had reached an age and level of power and influence that overwhelmed any instinct for politeness. As I hesitated, she clicked her tongue, visibly irritated. "Outside, please. I do not wish to be overheard."

I glanced around the marquee. Dija was still at Merenda's side, listening to the older woman explain something about the race. Merenda had been something of an athlete, and had competed at the Games herself a few years back. An attractive Perest-Avani diplomat had waylaid Tain, but two blackstripes were within arm's reach, alert. Still no sign of Kalina.

An-Ostada clicked her tongue again. "All right," I said awkwardly, and followed her outside the tent. Cries and cheers of the crowd, including large thickets of exultant Doranites, clattered around us. We'd never spoken privately before. In Council and in conversations with Tain and the Darfri Councilors, An-Ostada was reluctant to discuss any matters relating to the spirits or fresken and vocally opposed what she regarded as government interference in religious matters. My apprehension turned hopeful; perhaps this attempt at a private conversation meant she was finally ready to have a more candid discussion.

"What can I do for you, An-Ostada? Is there more news from the estates?" For much of the year An-Ostada and her students had been traveling to the various regions of Sjona, learning to connect to the spirits of the land and educating the local populations about how to live harmoniously with these otherworldly beings. In the last few months, though, they had found regions where local spirits had vanished without explanation, and to the bafflement of locals. An-Ostada appeared to consider it an exclusively Darfri matter, but it seemed either a troubling sign our attempts at restoring balance and correcting our errors were failing, or something more sinister. "The Chancellor is taking it seriously, I hope you know, and so am I."

She fixed me with her stare, long enough to make me squirm uncomfortably like a child in trouble. "It is about An-Hadrea," she said at last. "I have some concerns. Perhaps if you spoke to her about her attitude?"

A laugh almost escaped me. I wanted to say, *Have you* met *Hadrea?* "Hadrea is her own woman," I said warily. "I would not presume to interfere in Darfri business."

An-Ostada shook her head, sending her earrings rattling. "I had concerns about temperament in the beginning. There is an openness and a humility necessary in our practice that is the antithesis of stubbornness and ambition. This is why we begin teaching children when they are very young."

An ominous flutter in my chest. Hadrea might resent her teacher but she had always wanted to be a Speaker, had always known she was meant to be one. She'd saved the whole bloody city when An-Ostada and the rest of the elders had been powerless to stop Os-Woorin tearing it apart. Honor-down, she was a near-mythic figure in this city; she couldn't be denied her heritage, no matter how frustrating a student she might be. "You promised to teach her. That was part of the Compact. You haven't forgotten what she did for everyone?"

Her reply was drowned by a horn blast. Not too far from where we stood, the karodee committee were preparing to present the winners' ribbon to the Doranite rowers, who were standing, strong arms raised and clasped, enormous grins on their faces. I was momentarily distracted looking over at the announcers. "I'm sorry, I didn't catch—" But then I broke off. Because I had seen, suddenly and with perfect clarity, a familiar face. A man walking in the opposite direction to the main press of bodies moving toward the winners, back toward the Council marquee. Ordinary, studied ordinariness, but no one is *that* ordinary.

And he'd seen me, too.

In a flash, he had changed direction and gone. I spared one quick look for my own guard, for a blackstripe, for Tain or Kalina or anyone of use, but there was nobody within immediate range and he was disappearing even now. *Not this time,* I decided, and with an apologetic shrug at An-Ostada, I sprang after him.

My obsessive tendencies were sometimes useful. I'd pictured his face, his hair, the shape of him, so many times, gone over and over my brief glimpses, that I could follow his head and shoulders as he pushed through the crowd. His haircut wasn't *quite* fashionable. He carried his right shoulder fractionally higher than his left. The press of people worked against both of us and it wasn't until he had almost reached the pedestrian bridge—what had once been Bell's Bridge, now the rebuilt and renamed Compact Bridge—that he could lengthen his stride and make any distance on me. *This is stupid, he's an assassin, what are you going to do if you catch him?* But we had no chance of finding this nondescript man in a city bursting with visitors. If I didn't track him now, the next time could be too late. My hands found the pouches Kalina had sewed inside my clothing. I wasn't without my own defenses.

He turned, then; a casual turn, just a man shielding his face from the sun, but his gaze swept over the crowd from which he'd emerged. I stepped swiftly behind a taller woman, whose headscarf had loosened in the breeze, shielding me, and held my breath. When I chanced a glance around my shelter he had moved on, striding toward the Compact Bridge steps in a less hurried fashion. Hopefully he assumed he'd lost me. I continued, taking extra care to keep several people between us.

The docks were quieter than usual, with little trade taking place in these last few hectic days of karodee, and no boat traffic permitted because of the water events. Still, there were enough people moving about between boats, warehouses, and the harbormaster's offices that I had to concentrate hard to keep my eyes on my quarry.

He passed into the industrial district beyond the docks known as the Fives, striding unconcernedly, looking every inch an ordinary merchant. I kept my distance and stayed behind carts and pedestrians as much as possible. The clang of industry drowned out the distant rise and fall of the crowd at the rushuk ball game in the arena, the cries of hawking of un-Guilded street wares, the blessings called out from upper-story windows. I smelled oil, metal, and fire in the air. No ribbons or flags adorned the functional buildings in this area.

Once, the man stepped swiftly into an alley, and from behind the cabbage-laden cart I was using as shelter I saw his profile as he backed in, his movements easy and deliberate. A certain calm, set look about his plain face chilled me. He hadn't assumed I'd lost him, then. The various powders and phials in my pouches suddenly felt less than adequate. I silently cursed myself for having left without my own houseguard, or a blackstripe—someone, anyone, who could have helped, or at the very least witnessed that it was a real person, not a phantom. Coming alone had been foolish; going into that alley after him would be even more so.

Before I could decide to abort the entire effort, though, the man emerged, a stick of janjan in his mouth, and strolled on with no obvious caution. Still, I waited for the next cart to rumble up the street before I followed behind it, my breath short. The assassin turned to the left, then to the left again, moving into quieter streets. Soon I had no wagon traffic to shelter me, only small carts and pedestrians. It was growing harder to find ways to stay out of sight but I dared not expose myself.

Finally I saw him duck between two buildings into an alley shabby with graffiti and refuse, and when I drew level with it from the other side of the street I was just in time to see his dark head disappear into a doorway. Excitement pounded in my chest, and trepidation. After all this time, weeks spent worrying about this man, of wondering in weaker moments whether I really was cracking up, seeing dangers that weren't there, now I had a location. We were deep in the Fives, on a street I couldn't name, but I marked the graffiti on the bricks near the alley: a picture of a kitsa, a few Darfri symbols, a crown. I could find this again. I could leave, find an Order Guard on patrol at the docks, send for Chen. Or go straight to the blackstripes captain and leave it in their hands.

But what if it's too late? I crossed the street and sidled down the alley, trying to determine which door he'd entered. There were several, but no windows; most of these buildings were shared-wall workshops and storage facilities. I risked going closer. *What if he's only meeting someone here, or changing clothes, or what if he's here to assassinate someone else?* Leaving was a risk as well, a risk he would not be here when I came back with reinforcements, a risk there would be nothing in this dingy-looking place to identify or implicate him. But if I could get inside, confirm whether this was a place he was likely to return to . . .

"'S the right place," a voice sounded from the shadows, making me jump. My fingers had gripped a powder packet but released it as the speaker revealed themself: a child of no obvious gender with a face of baked-on grime and shrewd toughness. They'd been so still beside a heap of broken and discarded buckets, some oozing a mystery black oily substance, that they'd blended in with the surroundings.

"What's that?" I asked carefully. "What did you say just now?"

The child stretched their arms out with threaded fingers and made a show of yawning. "Was just saying, it's the right place. You look like you're wondering if you're at the right door, is all."

Scrambling for time, I slipped a hand inside my paluma to find my purse. Family chits were no good at most of the temporary karodee stalls and attractions, so even Credolen had taken to carrying coin. I flicked one down to the child, deciding the voice indicated a girl, and gave her a rueful smile. "Am I that obvious?"

She inspected the coin then tucked it away with lightning fingers. "You got the look is all. Too rich and clean to be down here except for *that*."

Grateful my tattoos were hidden by my sleeves, I admitted, "First time," and she grinned, her teeth yellow. I couldn't resist adding, "Have you got somewhere warm to stay tonight, kid? It's still cold at night."

She curled her lip. "You reckon I don't know exactly how cold it is, mate?"

Feeling stupid, and embarrassed, I dropped my smile. "I just meant, go to any of the Guildhalls, they'll organize you a hot meal if you haven't got anyone looking out for you."

"I got people," she snapped back, her jaw hard and hands balled into fists, angry as an animal whose tail had been pulled. "I'm no kid. Don't assume nothing about me, mate."

"Sorry, I didn't mean—" But she had already grabbed her small bag of belongings and disappeared through a gap in a rickety fence. Regretfully, I turned back to the silent face of the building she'd indicated. If random strangers regularly entered the building, it likely wasn't the assassin's private lair; it might only be a thoroughfare, or a drop-off location. If I left now for help, the chances of finding him again would fall.

I stepped across to the door and listened. Nothing: no voices, no movement. I tried the handle gently. It was bolted, but the door was a poorly fitted one with a reasonable crack, so a squirt of Malek's acid made short work of the bolt. I opened the door a handswidth, holding my breath, but there was no light and no shout of alarm from inside.

Just as I was slipping into the darkness, a movement in the alley caught my eye. I could have sworn a small figure had ducked behind the debris to my right. Unsettling, perhaps, but not enough to deter me. Tain's safety was at stake.

It was unlit inside, but enough light crept in through cracks in the external door and the one on the far side to see the rough outlines of looming equipment and crates. A chair by the door, still warm to my touch, indicated someone had been keeping guard there until recently. I padded across the room to the other door. I just needed information, nothing more. A sense of what this place was, something to give me enough to find the assassin again.

Voices filtered through, faint but audible. At least two or three. I crouched low, risked pushing the door an agonizingly gentle crack, and listened.

It took some time to follow the conversation, but it became clear it was a business discussion of some kind. There were two men, one with a very deep, rumbling voice, and a woman who interjected occasionally; by the way the others immediately silenced at her words I surmised she was in charge. They were talking about selling something in various districts of the city. Something un-Guilded at least, illegal probably, but nothing about the Chancellor or assassinations. I sat back on my heels, suddenly uncertain I even had the right place.

". . . if he gives you some trouble," the woman interjected slowly, her voice husky, strained, like a singer who'd performed too long, "then we'll give *him* some trouble."

"He'll come 'round," the higher-voiced man said. "Everyone knows by now Void's where the money is."

I realized, at last, what I was overhearing, and swore silently. This was nothing to do with an assassination. Void was the drug so prevalent in Silasta these days, and these must be drug dealers, probably part of the gang that had been giving Chen such trouble. The kid in the alley must have sent me in here thinking I was looking to buy. *You got the look,* she'd said. I felt like the worst kind of fool. It had been stupidly risky to follow him in the first place, but equally stupid to have lost him wasting my time eavesdropping on petty criminals.

Leaning forward again, I pushed the door a little more. I couldn't rule out the possibility that the assassin was working with a gang; crime was crime, after all, even if I doubted the man with his months of patient observation and his exotic poison darts was in this grimy room talking about selling drugs on street corners. Still, I would get a glimpse of the trio inside and confirm the assassin wasn't one of them before I cut my losses.

The angle was wrong; they were sitting on the left-hand side of the room, below the yellowish light of the lantern. The angle had been to my advantage in concealing me but it worked against me now. I crouched there a moment, still and frustrated, then felt down the front of my clothes with a sudden burst of amusement. The necklace Sjease had forced on me, with its plump glass jewel, was nestled there, and it had a flat, reflective facet. *I really need to raise Sjease's salary.* I slipped it carefully through the crack, angling it until I could see, like a tiny mirror, the wonky reflections of the three people sitting on cushions in the room.

It was a poor image but it told me all I needed to know in an instant. None of the three resembled my assassin—the woman sat with her back to me, with matted black hair spilling all the way down to the ground; one man was hulking, enormous, with darkest brown skin and a bald or shaved head; and the other was thin and small with a lot of facial hair. I pulled the pendant back and thrust it into my pocket, frustration a furnace inside me.

The light alerted me before the sound. The crack from the external door had painted a musty pale line of light a length or so from me, and for a moment it went dark; I was already turning when a tiny creak sounded. Someone was standing at the doorway, watching; someone small. I stood swiftly but my unthinking movement jolted the door I'd been hiding behind, and the voices in the next room broke off suddenly.

Fear momentarily froze me in place. By the time I sprang toward the external door—perhaps the street kid had lured me into danger deliberately, but I'd take my chances with her over three adult criminals—the internal door burst open, and before I could get a hand into my pouches something struck me across the side of the head.

Lights and pain exploded in my skull, blinding me, deafening me, and I hit the ground hard, too dazed to break my fall. The second blow was a sharp kick to the back of my ribs, and I barely had the breath to grunt with this renewed pain. I tried to get to my knees but only succeeded in a pitiful roll, not enough to avoid another kick. I just had time to register the sound of a childish gasp, and raised my chin to focus on the gap in the door.

The terrified face there was not the street kid I'd inadvertently insulted. It was Dija.

INCIDENT: Poisoning of Shelle Cha

POISON: Gravalana (false goaberry)

INCIDENT NOTES: Shelle (well-regarded portrait painter) reported blistering rash on hands, unable to paint for approx. 1 mth—causing cancelation of commissions including portrait of C. Devin. Likely culprit diluted goaberry serum mixed in hand-washing water in studio (painting assistant suffered similar reaction on hands). ~~Suspect: rival artist Josip Nojak who took commission in Shelle's stead.~~ *Update:* Noting subsequent public scandal involving Josip emerging immediately after reveal of portrait, likely part of broader scheme to embarrass C. Devin by linking her to Josip. Suspect rival family, no further action at this time (continue to monitor).

(from proofing notes of Credo Osi Oromani)

4

Kalina

I left Jov to inspect the marquee and keep an eye on Dee, and made a line toward Prince Hiukipi. Nearby, as I'd hoped, was Minister Kokush, deep in conversation with several of the western visitors. He touched his clothing often, fidgeting with sleeves and dangling adornments, as if he feared he was overdressed. The Prince was speaking to the Perest-Avani High Priestess, but his gaze strayed hungrily to the woman beside her, whom I recognized as the same one who had smiled at me during the ribbon dancing. I guessed she must be the Priestess's translator from the way the latter's veiled head drew often down toward her as she spoke.

I smoothed my paluma, willing my nerves away. I had listened in on Council meetings, hidden in unlikely spaces, and had once pretended to be an ignorant innocent in the face of the most dangerous woman I'd ever met. All I had planned for today was to ask questions and make observations. Strange dolls and mysterious injuries aside, there was nothing to be frightened of in that.

"You all right, Lini?" Tain appeared at my side and took my arm in his. His page, Erel, trailed behind, scribbling some notes in his ever-present notebook, a little frown line between his eyes.

"Just thinking." About Hiukipi, and what kind of man he might be. About Brother Lu and his apparent misfortune. Jov had showed me a poison that made bones brittle, and another that could have subtly swollen Lu's throat to make him more susceptible to choking. Whether an accident or an attack, there was no need for me to dwell so on the poppet under the bench that had carried such an ominous air. I shook my head. "I'm fine." I glanced at his page and smiled. "Erel, he's not making you work through this, is he? You can just watch the race."

Erel's eyes went wide. "Oh, the Chancellor isn't making me," he began, and Tain laughed.

"She's right. I can remember who's who on my own today. Go have some fun with your friends." As Erel hesitated, Tain made a shooing motion and the lad tucked the notebook away and ducked away, grinning, into the crowded marquee.

My smile slipped off as I turned back to my friend, scrutinizing his thin face. Honor-down, I couldn't help the little pang of sadness at the physical change in him since the siege. "Are *you* all right? Since when did you need help remembering names?"

But his dark eyes still crinkled up with his smile, warm as it had ever been. "The kid just likes feeling useful." He tilted his head at the Talafan group. "Not sure the Prince is all that well disposed toward us, but you'll make sure I don't make an idiot of myself, eh?" I was so used to the false cheer in his tone that it almost fooled me. Almost, but not quite. I'd been faking health far longer than him, after all. Karodee on this scale had taken most of the year to plan, and no one had been under more pressure than Tain.

I squeezed his arm. "Stop you making an idiot of yourself? That's what I'm best at," I said, and he laughed.

As we drew closer to the group, the Marutian who had been speaking stopped abruptly. All of the men looked at Tain; only Kokush looked at me, and inclined his head. "Chancellor Tain!" the Marutian boomed. A broad smile split his heavy black beard but his eyes did not change. "A pleasure to see you again."

"Duke Lago," Tain replied, returning the man's short bow, then introduced me to the others in turn: Kokush of course I knew, but I had not met his Costkati counterpart, who was good-looking, fat, and impeccably dressed, nor the Tocatican Prince, Hanichii, who was handsome too but unappealingly aware of it, holding his head like a man who had practiced the most flattering angle in a looking glass for hours. "I hope you are all enjoying the entertainment," Tain said. "The race should start soon."

"Yes, yes. This is what we were doing just now. We were having a small wager," Lago lied baldly. Whatever they'd been talking about, it hadn't been sports. Clearly we weren't the only ones using the karodee for diplomacy, though I wondered what all the western representatives, famously unable to maintain peace for more than a few years at a time, were doing together looking so chummy. Trying to show Kokush that they could work cooperatively to offer an alternative trade route? I looked the men over thoughtfully. Together, they had a lot to gain from Sjon instability. As if she'd heard my thought, the Perest-Avani translator glanced over at me and caught my eye, and flashed another dazzling smile.

"And who is your money on, your Grace?" Tain asked, smiling pleasantly.

"The Talafan team was the fastest in the heats," Lago said, tipping his head toward Kokush. "But my people know waterways. Your little pond here is very tranquil, of course, but Marutians learn to handle boats on the mighty rivers of the west."

"Such a beautiful patchwork of waterways," I agreed. "Well suited for sports. Our river is far better suited for trade and transport, of course."

Lago's eyes narrowed, but it was Prince Hanichii who answered. Our languages shared many similarities and I could *almost* understand him, but not well enough to gauge tone or intent. "You would be surprised at the speed we can move cargo on river." Hanichii's translator conveyed the Prince's words, and though he had ostensibly answered me, his eyes were on Kokush. "There is swift passage for heavy goods from Ja Baii in the north through to Branasque on the Doran border. Weight is no obstacle. Why, the Minister could ride on his mighty koule all the way onboard if he so chose."

"It must have been inconvenient, having to travel by carriage to Sjona instead of koule," Lago said to Kokush. His beard made it difficult to say for sure, but I thought from the sudden sparkle in his eyes that he was genuinely smiling for the first time. "Because of the unfortunate bogs and swamps?" The preferred mode of transport in the Empire, koule were massive horned animals as big as a house, and far too heavy for the northern barges.

"Yes, the marshes are a wonderful defense," I mused before Kokush could respond. "Did you know that until our engineers worked out how to channel the marshes, no one could safely cross them? The tides are so treacherous that you could go out in a boat one afternoon and never make it home again. Imagine those overconfident fishermen, thinking they could easily handle the situation, not knowing they would drown out there. Very sad."

"Sjona's engineers are world renowned," Kokush agreed, and I read amusement in his hands, which had stilled their fidgeting.

Hanichii smiled broader still. "Your engineers are among the finest in the world," he said. "With such discord and crime in your country, many have fled west and found new lives in our cities." The smile never slipped as the translator, impassive, relayed his words. Tain shot me a glance, but I was already responding.

"Competition is fierce in this city," I said. "It's no surprise some lower-tier Guild members may feel they have greater opportunities for renown in a less challenging environment." I leaned closer to the Prince. "Give them a chance, Your Highness. After all, what is the saying from your poet, Hanir?" I smiled. "Even the sourest *happi* is sweeter than a *faya*?"

There was definite laughter in Kokush's tone. "Lucky for me, today will test our nations' arms, not our wits," he said. "My money, Honored Chancellor, is safe in Imperial hands."

Tain, seemingly grateful for the interruption to our little game, gave Kokush a jovial grin. "I don't think I'd take that bet, Minister. Your countrymen were very impressive in the heats."

"In fact I heard that the Crown Prince himself is a sailor of some renown?" I added, and Kokush, bless him, took my hint.

"Indeed. I must introduce you to His Highness," he said, though with a tension that hadn't been there a moment before. He turned to the group beside us and bowed. "Your Highness, may I interrupt?"

The Prince's large frame was bedecked with jewels, his pale, thick neck was circled with gold, and his face, broad-jawed and handsome with elaborately painted whorls of color around his eyes and cheeks, wore a faintly bored expression. "What is it, Kokush?" He shifted his gaze to Tain. "Ah! Chancellor. A fine day for a race." He strode over to shake Tain's hand, the older man dwarfing the younger in breadth. Though well into his sixties, the Prince had the build of an athlete or a laborer rather than a wealthy nobleman. His arms from wrist to massive shoulder were thick with muscle. Astor had spoken of his skills as a sailor and a hunter and his deep enthusiasm for competition.

The Prince's translator, an elderly man with a tea-colored complexion and ink on his fingers, repeated the words in Sjon as Tain accepted Hiukipi's hand.

"A pleasure to see you again, Your Highness," Tain said in passable Talafan. Prince Hiukipi released his hand and turned to me with a heavy, assessing gaze that trailed my entire body, and would have been extremely rude in any ordinary Silastian gathering. A tightening of Tain's jaw told me he had not missed it, but I silently urged him to hold his temper. "Your Highness,"

Tain said loudly. "May I introduce our proposed Ambassador, Credola Kalina Oro—"

"Oromani, yes," Hiukipi drawled, in a tone that matched his eyes. "I've heard of her. Your . . . I don't know what you would call it in your language." He gestured a slow hand to indicate my whole frame and his lips curled in an unpleasant smile. "Mistress? You do not have wives here, I understand. My wife is with her women." He gestured carelessly out onto the grass, where a separate silken marquee had been set up nearby. "In Talafar we do not bring our women where they do not belong."

Kokush cleared his throat and interrupted the interpreter before he could finish translating, the Minister's hands fluttering wildly in embarrassment as he avoided looking at me. "Honored Chancellor," he said in rapid Sjon. "There must have been a miscommunication. His Highness does not understand, or I did not adequately explain, the Credola Kalina's role in your Guild business. I thought—" In the background, the interpreter was murmuring a translation to Hiukipi, who looked amused. "—I thought I had made clear the proposed position." He bowed his head to the Prince and switched to Talafan. "Credola Kalina is from the Sjon *government*, Your Highness," he said, his tone beseeching. "She is not anyone's wife or mistress."

Tain looked at me, confused by the various exchanges and the stunted translation, and I shook my head fractionally. If this was how it was going to be, I would handle it; we didn't need his sense of honor and manners getting in the way. Besides, I suspected this display was more for my benefit than Tain's. I squared my shoulders. "An honor to meet you, Your Highness," I said, in Talafan, as if he had greeted me politely. I offered my hand.

Hiukipi didn't look surprised to hear me speak Talafan, and certainly not embarrassed, which made it clear the rudeness had been meant to land directly on me. His hesitation in taking my hand was obvious enough that I detected a flicker of anger or frustration from Kokush. But the Prince shook firmly enough. His palm was hot and unpleasant. I gave my best impression of a demure smile. "Are you enjoying the karodee, Your Highness? Ambassador Astor mentioned your prowess as a sailor."

"All men should sail," he asserted. "There is nothing like it. I learned as a boy, from the finest sailor in the world. Rowing a flat lake is not the same as battling the waves of the ocean. These you call athletes, they would not so lightly cope with the Copper Sea."

"Perhaps you should have entered the Games, Your Highness. You could have shown those we call athletes how it is done."

Even under thick cosmetics the color in his face deepened and his gaze intensified, but it wasn't clear if he had taken it as flattery or insult. "Perhaps I will show you some things, Kalina, Hero of Silasta," he said, in a low voice that, despite the lack of translation, made Tain bristle at my side.

"I'm afraid I see some of our southern guests looking for us, Your Highness," he said, taking my arm again and making eye contact with a group of Doranite Chieftains. "Please enjoy the race, and the hospitality." I only had time to bow my head to the Talafan before Tain had steered me firmly away.

I pulled my arm loose, cross. "I can't learn anything from people if you leave the second they start showing us who they are, Tain."

"I think we learned plenty," he said. "What did he say to you at the end there?"

"It doesn't matter," I sighed. "Look, the Chieftains are expecting you now. I'll catch up with you later." I spotted Jov patrolling a short distance away but before I could head in his direction, someone touched my shoulder.

"Credola Kalina?" A Talafan servant bowed low. "Her Highness has extended an invitation to her marquee, if you would be so good?"

Taken aback, I glanced at Tain, but he was already having his back thoroughly clapped by several enormous Doranites. Jov, several treads away, was talking to Dee and seemed to be proofing something from a passing servant. What did a Talafan Princess want with me? "Of course," I said. "I would be honored."

Feeling a little like a schoolchild being led impatiently by a long-suffering teacher, I followed the servant's quick steps out of the front of the big central marquee and into the small violet silk one to its right. Two young Imperial soldiers guarded its entrance, which was shielded by a fluttery gauze fabric like the sides of a closed litter, and through which there carried muffled voices and tinkling high music. It stopped abruptly as the servant parted the curtain and gestured me through.

It was a pleasant space, easily as luxurious as the Council marquee, shady and furnished with beautifully patterned cushions. In a dizzying array of beauty, four ladies were arranged on the cushions like a necklace of finest jewels, all gleaming sumptuous fabrics and beaded headdresses in bright colors. While their pale skin ranged from pink to light golden brown, and their long hair various warm yellow and woody shades, their still faces were styled so similarly with heavy cosmetics that they looked like sisters. One stood by an upright string instrument, the evident source of the music, and another sewed an elaborate shawl or scarf with several different kinds of needles. Princess Zhafi, the Crown Prince's younger sister, sat in the middle, a book open on her lap.

"The Credola Kalina Oromani," the servant introduced me, then immediately withdrew.

"Good day," I said, trying to sound as if this had been a planned visit. I was at a sudden social loss, painfully aware of the gaps in my knowledge.

Princess Zhafi got to her feet gracefully. She was lavishly dressed in a split-leg dress like the wings of a bright bird wrapped around her, the full embroidered sleeves wound with strings of beads. The silk fabric barely rustled as she moved.

"Your Highness." I inclined my head.

"Credola Kalina, welcome." She shook my hand—her palm was cool and firm—and gestured. "Please, come and sit. Thank you for joining us."

"Thank you for the invitation." For it was immediately clear which of the Princesses must have extended it. Zhafi was even lovelier up close than in my fleeting observation the other day. Her face was pretty and her honey curls as shiny as her clothing, but it was her manner that distinguished her, the way she held herself, a certain thoughtfulness in her blue gaze. I'd had the impression of intelligence when I'd seen her before and sensed it again, but there was also warmth there, and a dimple in her cheek that was faintly mischievous. I sat, trying not to convey my confusion.

"It is a pleasure to meet you all," I said. An elderly servant appeared silently at my elbow and poured me a small cup of something cold and herbaceous; I copied the other ladies and stirred it with the fragrant stick of garmony. She inclined her wispy gray head at my thanks and melted away. I was reminded of the servant who had taken the poppet from me in the arena, but it was impossible to be sure, with their downcast eyes and identical clothing. The Talafan disregard for the faces and individuality of their servants was exploitable, and I was always wary of people who could move in and out of spaces practically invisibly. I'd used that skill to my advantage too many times to disregard it in others.

Princess Zhafi fluttered one long, pale hand at the other ladies. "Please, may I also introduce Her Highness, Princess Josta, the Lady Mosecca, and I believe you have met the Lady Reuta."

I greeted them all in turn. Princess Josta, the Crown Prince's wife, had eyes like a startled animal in her thin face, and she dropped her gaze immediately from mine. Lady Mosecca had a calm face beneath dramatic, dark brows, and I could not remember how she was related to the Emperor; a cousin, perhaps? Talafan family trees were so much more complicated than ours, with all of their interlinking separate families and their focus on paternal lineage. "I was sorry not to meet you all properly at the dancing," I said.

"Oh, you were busy with the men," Zhafi said with a careless shrug. "We understand how they are." She shook her head. "We loved your ribbon dancing, but it did go rather terribly at the end, didn't it? Poor dear Brother Lu. What an extraordinarily bad day he had."

In a Silastian woman I'd have taken it as sarcasm—surely Lu could not have been popular, given his manner—but this was my first real conversation with Talafan noblewomen and I was at a disadvantage with language and custom. I tried to keep my tone neutral when I asked after the man's health.

"Your healers are quite extraordinary," Reuta said. "They think he will make a full recovery. He is being treated in your . . ." She stopped, clearly short of a word. There was no equivalent to *hospital* in Talafan, which had no centralized medical care, only healer priests who worked individually. "Your medical facility. I am sure he is praising God you were there, or he might not have been so fortunate."

Mosecca was watching me over the rim of her cup. "That was remarkable, Credola Kalina," she said. Her voice was throaty and deep. "Very brave. You are a woman of many talents, clearly."

In the distance, the horns sounded for the start of the race, but the women appeared utterly disinterested. Zhafi gestured to my cup. "Do try it! It is not quite like your tea, but it is good. We make it with a root vegetable that I do not think you can grow this far south."

I took a sip. Jov would probably be able to identify the root vegetable; to me it tasted like warm bark, but I smiled politely. Jov would probably also be furious with me for taking drinks from foreign strangers, especially when I was trying to investigate our country's enemies.

"But we should not speak to you of tea, should we?" Zhafi said, her cheek dimpling. "Oromani tea is famous even in our part of the world. Even my father the Emperor has taken a liking to it."

"A talented family," Mosecca added, but the look she gave me was cautious, as if she were regarding an unpredictable animal that might prove dangerous.

"My mother deserves most of the credit," I replied carefully. "She would be delighted to hear her tea is being enjoyed so far from home." Ha! My mother knew perfectly well the Emperor's sudden interest in our product had led to substantial export profits in the north, but she did not care; she measured success only against her own exacting standards. Other people's opinions mattered nothing to her.

"Oh, yes, certain parties are *very* fascinated with all things southern." Mosecca glanced at the other women and picked up her sewing again. The needles clacked away rapidly in her hands as she spoke. "Sjona will always be a source of fascination for young people in the Empire. Our most exotic neighbor." A palpable ripple of tension passed around the room; the women all suddenly seemed intensely interested in their hands or hair or their crafts. Zhafi turned a page in her book, but her fingers trembled. My awkward discomfort sharpened into something else. There might be something important to be learned from the ladies.

"I am just as fascinated by Talafar," I said, leaning forward. I widened my eyes, made my voice higher and softer. "Such a vast empire, with so much to see. I imagine a person could travel all over and never see it all. And it is ever-expanding, so I hear."

That definitely landed, with both the Princesses. Josta's fingers faltered on her instrument, and Zhafi looked up from her book to meet my gaze. Her face was smooth, the dimple absent. I continued, pretending to struggle to recall. "Is it . . . Lios? The newest province? The Foreign Minister told me—"

"Yes." Zhafi's voice sounded a little hoarse. "Yes, it is called Lios."

"Your grandfather is the General, is he not? General Zoho?" Zhafi's mother was the First Empress—not the Emperor's first wife chronologically, but in social standing and importance—the daughter of the celebrated General Zoho, who'd led the conquest force.

She nodded. Her gaze locked on mine, she looked trapped. Outside, cheers and roars sounded from the lake.

"Enough about us, Credola Kalina," Mosecca said firmly. She set down her sewing and folded her hands in her lap. "We are eager to hear more of you. We have heard tales of your adventures, even in Izruitn, you know. Your daring escape up the river. They call you the Hero of Silasta, do they not?"

Now it was my turn to deflect. "Everyone likes a story," I said, shrugging, with a gesture toward Zhafi's novel. The Princess seemed to have recovered her poise. She tilted her head to one side.

"They say only you were clever enough to see the true face of your treacherous Commander behind her noble mask. Is that your great skill, Kalina of Silasta? To see through a mask?"

I paused, taking my time as she looked over my face with obvious interest. Eventually, I raised an eyebrow. "Well, I promise it isn't swimming," I said, and was rewarded with an actual laugh, albeit an extremely delicate one. The dimple on Zhafi's cheek deepened.

"Of course, it is Reuta's brother who has been telling us such tales, you must have guessed." She bestowed on me another small smile. "Dear Lord Ectar. He had promised to introduce us today but he didn't feel well this morning, so I admit I took matters into my own hands."

"He is the baby of the family, and none of my other brothers have much time for him," Reuta said, and this time affection warmed her voice. "Or my father. But we are close in age, and Ectar has always been kind to me. He is determined to make a name for himself. He makes bold trades and has amassed quite a fortune. We tease him that he wished to bring home an exotic foreign wife, to further stand out from the rest of them." She shot me an appraising look under her lashes.

I suppressed a sigh and took a moment to formulate a careful answer. "I have found Lord Ectar a kind and generous friend. And he was a remarkable ally during the siege, risking his own safety countless times. We are forever grateful. But I hope he—and all of you—can make better memories here this time. Celebrations are far preferable to wars, I think."

I scanned their reactions to that bait, especially Josta, but this time it returned not so much as a flicker of a response from any of them.

"It is certainly a celebration," Zhafi said, sounding wistful. She pivoted to gaze out of the marquee. The excited movement of the crowd and the glint of the Bright Lake were a fuzzy backdrop, and a bearded young Imperial soldier patrolled back and forth, at constant alert. I felt a sudden burst of pity. The joy of karodee wasn't in watching an occasional elite sport or performance from a lofty, distant stand or behind a veil, but in the hectic fun of the streets. A solid week of ribbons and flags and bells, and hot fried meat and spicy seeds and apples and papna stuffed with honey nuts on every corner, and games and contests of luck and skill on every scale, to be participated in or wagered on.

Of joyful greetings called to strangers, of songs by those with voices ill-suited to the stage, but eminently appropriate for a merry crowd. Karodee—Silasta—couldn't be understood from a cloister. Our city's heart was in the sculpture garden, the amphitheaters, the teahouses, the library, in the Darfri shrines and the gallery of arts. I couldn't help but feel sorry for these women, traveling weeks to come here only to be trapped inside buildings with the very people they saw every day.

"We heard such stories about what it would be. There is a dance tonight, is there not? A masquerade?"

"Yes, people dress up for the spring parade through the streets this afternoon. And then at sunset, the Darfri elders will perform a ritual at the lake, giving thanks and offerings to the great lake spirit, Os-Woorin. After, there will be more music and dancing well into the evening." I stopped there. The evening part of the masquerade was *not* an event Talafan noblewomen would find appropriate. The revelry by the lake was intense, and flamboyant, and usually ended with . . . well, with a lot of good-natured outdoor sex with strangers in masks, but I had no idea how to politely explain that to women with wildly different social expectations. I hurried to distract them. "And other activities all around the city. There will be poetry recitals, and games, and the northwestern sculpture garden always has a beautiful candle walk."

There had been a palpable change in the atmosphere. "Os-Woorin, you said?" Mosecca pronounced it haltingly, but her eyes gleamed with fascination. "This is the spirit who they say rose from the lake at the end of your civil war?"

"Ectar will not speak of it," Reuta said, her voice a little breathy. "And Brother Lu said it is blasphemous to ask in any case. Some stories say a statue came alive? It does not sound believable. Did you see this happen?"

I hesitated. "I did not see it, no. I was injured at the time. But it is certainly true the spirit rose from the lake—and a statue, but they weren't the same thing. . . ." Flustered, I stopped, but they only looked more fascinated.

"And tonight, at this ritual? Will the spirit rise again then?"

Princess Josta sounded more frightened than excited, and Zhafi leaned over to pat her hand. "Don't be silly, dear one." But she was watching me closely. Evidently *this* was the topic of greatest interest to them, perhaps the reason I had been invited; they'd hoped to get confirmation of Ectar's stories from a Silastian.

"I doubt we will see Os-Woorin tonight. It took three armies to rouse the spirit last time." They all looked a little disappointed, and Mosecca took a breath to say something else, but, reluctant to continue the story, I added, "But I think you will enjoy the costumes and masks of the parade this afternoon. It's traditional to give flowers and other favors to acknowledge those you like the best."

"What fun! Will you be in it?"

I shook my head. "I find walking long distances, and dancing, difficult, I'm afraid." Like Kokush the other day, Mosecca and Zhafi both glanced at my stomach. Before they could ask further questions, I said, "Our housekeeper, Sjease, will be in the parade, though. Look out for the most magnificent sun mask, we've been working on it for weeks." Sjease had been delighted to find another member of the household with sewing experience, because they had an eye for fashion but neither the purse to buy what they wanted, nor the skill to make things themself. I enjoyed helping with their designs, and it gave me easy cover for working certain additions into my brother's and my wardrobe, as well. We had made the mask together, and while it was nothing to rival a proper mask-maker's or even a Guilded hatter or seamster's, we were proud of the result.

"In some of the western tribes, they worship the sun as a god," Mosecca said mildly. "The new Perest-Avani Ambassador in the Imperial City does the most graceful dance to honor the sun in the mornings. I have seen him outside Government House. It is quite a sight."

I worked hard to keep surprise from my face, but my mind raced. "Is there a new Ambassador, then?"

"Oh, you know how diplomacy works," Zhafi said. "Governments change, and people grow tired of the same faces, over and over."

Mosecca studied her painted nails. "Some at the Palace had grown weary of Astor's face, I'm afraid. But perhaps the next will be more pleasing."

I sipped my drink again. Mosecca's smooth face and gentle eyes were as still as a painting, and I couldn't tell if this was a peace offering or a warning. "Our great countries have been friends and allies for so long," I said. "I can't imagine we couldn't find a face we agree on with enough time to talk about it."

"'For there are no wounds nor wars that cannot be helped or healed or hindered with the power of words.'" Zhafi's voice was soft, and I glanced at her in surprised recognition.

"Is that Kosahi? From the, er, 'The Ocean of Sounds'?"

"It is my favorite of her poems," Zhafi said, leaning toward me, enthusiasm obvious. "Have you read the short novel published before she died?"

"No, she is famous here for her poems and philosophy. I did not know she wrote a novel."

"There is a copy in the library in Izruitn," Zhafi began, but stopped when a voice on a speaking trumpet sounded from the lake.

"They're announcing the winners," I explained when the ladies looked puzzled.

"Oh!" Zhafi sighed. "We have made you miss the whole thing. I *am* sorry." The servant who had brought me here parted the curtain, coughed, apologized for the interruption, then moved across to Princess Zhafi to murmur something in her ear. *Zhafi*, I noted, *not Josta, even though it's Josta who's poised to become an Empress.* It was clear where the power lay here. Zhafi looked over at me with an unreadable expression, and with the slightest movement of her hand, the other ladies fell silent.

"Credola Kalina, I understand my brother the Prince would like me to join him to watch the presentation. Perhaps we could walk back together?"

"Of course, Your Highness." I looked around at the other ladies as I stood. "Thank you for the company. It was a pleasure."

We stepped out into the afternoon sunshine but Zhafi held back with deliberately slow steps, so the servant quickly outpaced us. She didn't speak, but lingered, staring out at the lake, trailing her hand along the fabric cover of her book. There was a smudge of black ink along the outside line of her left hand, which she rubbed at absently with the other. The signs of a person with something to say. I let the silence build, and eventually she stopped her contemplation and swung around to face me, a spring released.

"You are close with the Chancellor, are you not?"

"We have been friends since childhood," I said carefully, knowing the assumptions strangers often made about our relationship.

"What sort of man is he?"

I hesitated. She'd caught me off guard, but there was no benefit in lying. "He is a good man, Your Highness. Generous and fair. He has done a remarkable job bringing together this new Council and rebuilding our city." While we were being honest: "What sort of man is your brother the Prince?"

She blinked, perhaps caught off guard, too. "I . . . I do not know that I can say, Credola Kalina," she admitted. Her tone was melancholy. She gazed back at the marquee, her eyes tracking the young guard walking back and forth as if watching the swing of a pendulum. "I would say he is a man who is accustomed to his wants being met. We are far apart in age, and in influence, and he has no time for ladies of the court, not even . . ." She broke off, visibly correcting herself, like a drunk walking too close to the edge of a cliff. "My father the Emperor has granted me many freedoms, but lives of Princes and Princesses do not often intersect, and my brother has strong views about how noblewomen should live and what they should be allowed to do."

Ah. So we were not the only ones concerned about the transfer of power. "I am sure your brother appreciates the work you do, Your Highness," I said. "I understand you are lauded in Izruitn for your charitable efforts, and that you personally fund and maintain orphanages, workhouses, and farms." Astor had said they called her the City Princess, and that she was deeply beloved in circles high and low for such works.

A spark animated her face for a moment. "The Imperial City is much larger than Silasta," she said. "And there are many who need help. Many war orphans, especially. They need safe places to stay, and schooling, and productive work to do. Praise God His Majesty my father allows me to do what I can to fund orphanages and workhouses to help. For now." The spark faded, and her gaze returned to the marquee again.

And just like that, I put together the little clues that had been dancing around before me this whole time. "The new province of Lios," I said softly. The pattern matched what our spies had reported. The Empire conquered, and occupied, but installed one surviving member of the previous ruling hierarchy to be married into or adopted by some minor member of the Talafan Royal Family. DeRamata, the Violet Islands, and now Lios. Princess Zhafi had been allowed to remain in the capital and in her father's household for a decade past the age when all of her sisters had been sent away, but it seemed the Emperor's protection of his favorite daughter might finally be waning with his ill health. Was Zhafi to be the latest balm the Empire offered its new conquests to warm to their new overlords? Swallowed and subsumed, eaten up by the beast that was the Empire. "Is that where you are headed next, Your Highness?"

Zhafi had stiffened at my words, but then she sighed, her body slumping as if the pressure of holding it inside her had been released, and gave me such a frank look with her expressive blue eyes that I forgot, for a moment, that we were strangers to each other, not dear friends confiding. A taste of her powerful charisma; apparently I was far from immune. She looked away, lovely face grieved, and the urge to wrap an arm around her shoulders the way I might Hadrea or Dija was strong.

She was silent a long time. "I begged to be allowed to come here," she said eventually, so softly that I had to stand close beside her, almost touching, to hear. "Once I am in the north, there will be no more such opportunities. I have read so much, heard so many stories. But in some ways it is worse, now I am here. The *kandu kesibor* is very great."

I didn't know the phrase. "Kandu . . . ?"

"It is, er. A feeling." Her hands fluttered as she searched for the words. "It is like, to glimpse the pool, but not be allowed to bathe."

That I understood all too well. The ink stains on her hands, the insight in her questions, the appreciation of poetry and philosophy and, if I wasn't mistaken about the wording glimpsed on the book in her hands, the ability to read at least one other language; this was a learned and intelligent woman glimpsing a society in which she might have more fully thrived. I didn't know what to say that wouldn't sound patronizing.

Zhafi took a breath and then turned to face me, face composed again. "I am being maudlin. I *am* sorry, Credola Kalina. What must you think of me—my father and brother have given me so much, and here I stand, ungrateful." She gave her head a little shake and tucked the book away in the folds of her clothes. The warmth in her eyes and the dimple in her cheek made her look younger. "I would have liked to watch your parade tonight, and give flowers and favors to all the suns who pass us by. Perhaps the Prince will allow it, even without Brother Lu to escort us." She touched my hand. "Now, come! Your Chancellor and my brother will be wondering where we are."

As if he had been waiting for this, the servant reappeared from the main marquee and ran over. "Your Highness!" he said plaintively.

"We are coming," she said, head downcast.

The crowd had already begun moving out of the marquee and down to the stage by the water, though I doubted we'd even hear the ceremony over the cheerful roaring of the Doranites. Zhafi and I joined Hiukipi and Kokush, who were talking with Prince Hanichii and Duke Lago. Lago caught my eye and smirked as he leaned down to say something to Kokush that I couldn't hear. A few paces ahead, several Councilors were speaking to the Perest-Avani delegation, and Karista shot me a cool look.

I spotted Tain, but not my brother. Erel was with the Chancellor, looking a bit bewildered, and gave a relieved smile in my direction, tapping Tain on the shoulder. Tain strode over at once, and took my hand. "I lost track of you. Is everything all right?" he asked urgently, in a low tone, and I smiled widely and squeezed his hand back, hoping he would be reassured by that private code if not my words. The Foreign Minister, at least, could understand our language.

"Of course, Honored Chancellor. I have been well entertained by the Princess."

Tain favored Zhafi with one of his more charming smiles and offered a hand. "Thank you for returning my friend, Your Highness," he said.

"Where's Jov?" I murmured, and Tain frowned.

"He went off somewhere with Dee, I think," he said. "I haven't seen either of them for a while. He's supposed to come with me to the winners' lunch after the ceremony."

"You have been with the women, Credola?" Hiukipi broke off his conversation with Hanichii and casually dropped his half-eaten fishball into a servant's hands as he turned around to face us. "What a dull time! All they do is sit and gossip."

The translator, a red flush creeping up his neck and onto his cheeks, stammered as he translated the Prince's words, and Zhafi stiffened, but did not comment. Her confident rule over the women's court might never have been, for all her meekness now. Tain, however, looked like he'd reached the end of his tether with the Prince.

"Forgive us," he said firmly, taking my arm and creating a larger space between us and the Prince. "Credola Kalina and I have another engagement right after the ceremony and I have a few more people to say goodbye to. It has been most interesting to talk with you, Your Highness. Thank you, Minister Kokush," he added.

"Thank you, Honored Chancellor," Kokush said, in Sjon, then bowed to me and added, "I hope we will have a chance to talk properly soon, Credola, about your forthcoming appointment."

But Hiukipi, for whatever reason, seemed to have taken renewed interest in me. "I shall come to this luncheon, yes?" he announced.

Kokush shifted weight between his feet and interrupted the translator before he could get more than a few words out. "Your Highness, you and the Princess Josta were to attend—"

"Rearrange as you need to," Hiukipi said, with the blithe unconcern of a person others carved their lives around, and who had never been inconvenienced.

A man accustomed to having his wants met, Zhafi had said. Perhaps it would be good for the Prince to have to work a bit harder for something. "The Prince is going to accompany you," I translated to Tain, whose pained look, bless him, signaled that he understood what I was about to do. I turned back to Hiukipi. "What a wonderful idea, Your Highness. And that frees your lovely lady wife to enjoy the masquerade parade with the other ladies this afternoon. Princess Zhafi, were you not just saying how much you wished to attend?"

The Princess ducked her head, but the hint of a dimple appeared before she did. "Yes, Credola Kalina, that would be most lovely—but we have no masks, I fear."

"I feel quite confident your excellent staff can make arrangements," I said smoothly, smiling at the servant. "That is no trouble, is it, sir? And I will speak personally to the owner of the Leaning Lady to lend you a staff member to assist with language, if you need it, because Trade will only get you so far if you need to explain the last-minute rush. Most of the shops will be sold out, but I know some people who could probably help."

Hiukipi said nothing, his eyes glittering as he watched me and his plump lips pressed together in a firm line. Helpless, the servant nodded. "Yes, my lady, I suppose we can—"

"I have heard about this masquerade," Hiukipi said. "I am not sure it is a godly event."

"We would only watch the parade, of course," Zhafi said, head bowed. "I understand that without Brother Lu, His Majesty our father would be concerned for our safety."

There was a long pause. Then, "Send the servant out for masks," he said, waving a lazy hand. "You can watch from the guesthouse garden. I wish to attend the celebration. I hear it is an opportunity to get to know many of the locals, eh?"

When the translator converted it to Sjon, he omitted the leer, but Tain nevertheless looked vaguely revolted and I stepped on his foot before he smoothed his expression. "The parties can be quite raucous, Your Highness," he said carefully. "It is a very emotional celebration for many people. Perhaps instead you might prefer the candle walk through the sculpture garden or—"

"Do *you* dance in this celebration, Credola?"

The translator dutifully translated, but once again Tain seemed to have read enough in the tone and body language to understand. His expression had cooled, and I spoke before he could. "I fear not," I said. "I have a health condition." I was conscious of Hiukipi's pale eyes traveling over my body. "But thank you for your concern. In fact, you are right, Your Highness. I shall stay with Princess Zhafi. I can help acquire costumes and then we can watch the parade together. As you say, we ladies do love to sit and gossip."

By the time the translator had finished relaying my words, Tain released his breath very slowly, and shot me a look under his lashes, the merest twitch of his lips betraying his combination of irritation and amusement. Hiukipi's face had gone pink under his makeup. "I will look for you later, then," he said. He whirled on the manager. "Well? Move, man!"

Zhafi had her head bowed, her posture docile, but the moment her brother's attention had moved away from her, she shot me—so subtly I might have imagined it—the tiniest wink.

INCIDENT: Poisoning of Kai Doorevat

POISON: Salgar (red death)

INCIDENT NOTES: Victim experienced throat and abdominal pain and bloody stools for several days, missed vital speeches for Guild elections at which she had been lead contender for Stone-Guilder. Recently attended production of *Casabi's Lament* by visiting dancing troupe—recalls lead dancer kissing her at conclusion of performance. Suspect salgar mixed with lip paint transferred to victim. Order Guards took troupe into custody in Telasa, arrested lead dancer, rumored to be notorious assassin known as "Red Piper." Suspect escaped from Telasan jail, unable to confirm. Further investigation warranted?

(from proofing notes of Credola Jaya Oromani)

5

Jovan

For a few blessed moments upon waking, the only sign that something was wrong was my unusually dry mouth. So dry and sticky I could barely swallow, in fact. And then the pain kicked in.

"I would not recommend trying to sit up just now," a wry voice suggested. I blinked gummy eyes open, trying to focus on the figure in front of me, but my eyes were as dry as my mouth.

"Can I have some water, Thendra?" My croaky voice was, apparently, a few moments quicker on the uptake than my brain, because only after I said the physic's name did the crash of emotions follow. Thendra. I was in the hospital. I was alive, thank the fortunes, and . . .

"Thendra?" A papery chuckle. "Oh, sweetie. Where do you think you are?"

My senses were slowly coming back, fitting together again into a terrifying whole. The ground, gritty and hard under one of my shoulders. Deep, sullen pain in my abdomen and chest. My wrists behind my back, something rough binding them. My head pounded. The woman crouched in front of me seemed to be made of abstract geometric shapes and patterns, black and white. I licked my dry lips and blinked harder until she resolved into a proper human shape—or at least, something close to one. It still looked more skull than face, striped black and white, and long, tattery black hair flowed around her like ragged shadows. A nightmare face, a creature from my blackest childhood dreams.

"Wraith," I whispered. The evocative and creepy mythological villain in old folktales we'd all read as children, the Wraith was supposedly a spirit who had been trapped and tortured by humans thousands of years ago and sought eternal revenge. Yet there she was, right before me, straight out of a story.

She sat back on her heels and laughed.

"I haven't given you *that* much yet, precious." Her rough hand gripped my chin and held it fast even as I tried to yank away. She forced something small and hard between my lips. "Let's have some more, then. Here, come on and swallow, now." When I clamped my teeth together and pulled my head out of her hands, another set of hands, bigger and heavier, seized my shoulders and forced me flat, cracking my skull hard on the ground. They tipped my chin back, and suddenly water, warm and stale, filled my mouth, my nose, my throat, while the Wraith woman pressed down on my forehead. I thrashed around fruitlessly, sharp pain bursting in my torso as I struggled, but eventually had to swallow. The hands released me and I turned weakly onto my side, choking and coughing. I squinted up at the man. He was huge and his face, too, was unreal, a flat black circle with a long, vertical slit for a mouth, and no eyes I could make out.

A whisperer. My confused, frightened brain made the link. The whisperers in folktales were the Wraith's minions, spirit-world creatures that crept into homes at night and whispered dark and murderous thoughts into sleeping ears. They also happened to be the most hated monster of my childhood, the one peculiarly resonant with my personal fears. All too easily I could be that boy again, lying in bed, besieged by one dreadful whisper of a thought that then burrowed into my mind and took root. Whisperers were the part of myself I hated, given form.

I'm dreaming, I told myself, as my vision swam and the shadows seemed to lengthen, to loom. *This is a nightmare.* As if in response to the thought, the pressure and pain eased. My head became light, so light I couldn't tell anymore if it was touching the ground or floating. The spikes of fear grew in intensity. Already my brain was throwing up hateful thoughts of my youth. *What if you spend all this time on poisons because you actually want to hurt people? What if you poisoned Tain by accident? On purpose? Why would you even think that, if you didn't want to do it? Your mother knew you were like this, that's why she left, she couldn't stand to be around you.*

I pressed my head to the ground, suddenly afraid it would detach and float away. The room seemed to be moving. The whisperer leaned in and I tried to back away. *She knew something wasn't right about you.* I could see my mother, in my head, her face young, but lined with exhaustion. *Fortunes, can't you make him stop, Etan? I can't handle this.* Her anger. *What is wrong with him?*

"Stay with me now," the Wraith said, sounding amused. "Don't you go anywhere just yet. How interesting you've come to visit us, Credo Jovan, at such a crucial time. My superiors have such *plans* for you."

That was my name. The Wraith knew my name. That seemed both strange and funny, but when I tried to laugh nothing came out but an odd croak. That was funny, too, so I rasped on the floor. Was I on a ship? We definitely seemed to be moving.

"How much did you give him?" The man didn't sound amused. He didn't sound anything. His voice was a deep, oddly expressionless rumble.

"Relax. It won't kill him."

"What we gonna do now?" A third voice. Reedy. Like a complaining child. *Child.* Something snagged in my train of thought. A child. There was a child. *Dija.*

It was as though someone had slapped me. My mother's voice receded. I had someone else to fail now, someone for whom I was responsible, who depended on me. And I'd led her into danger, I knew that, even if the details were elusive in my strange, fizzy head. *How much did you give him,* he'd asked. They'd forced me to swallow something—some narcotic—and that was why I couldn't think straight, why my nightmares walked before me. And oh, fortunes, where was Dija? I squeezed my eyes shut at the remembered image of her scared face through the crack in a door, the door of the building I'd gone into . . . I'd . . .

This time someone really *did* slap me. "Don't go off on a dream, now, Credo." The Wraith was close enough for me to smell the sweet-sour tang of janjan on her breath. *Not* the Wraith. Just a woman in a karodee mask. I scrambled to make sense of it all. Whatever they'd given me, it was making it hard to hold thoughts together in my head, hard to trust my senses. But I could trust one thing: Dija could still be somewhere nearby, and that meant she was in danger. I clung to that motivation.

She was wearing a mask. Just makeup and a mask. I didn't need to be afraid of her, she wasn't a villain from a story come to get supernatural revenge. She was, however, holding me prisoner and force-feeding me drugs, so perhaps fear wasn't entirely inappropriate. "What do you want?" I managed to say.

"What do I want?" The black-and-white horror of her face split into a skeletal grin. "Sweetie, I just want to give you a good time."

They were moving me. For a while I'd lost my sense of self and certainly of time, breaking in and out of dreaming hallucinations, a mix of physical and psychological sensations that left me dazed. Now I was being walked between two people, propped up with my arms over their shoulders. A hot wave of pain fizzed up one of my legs with every step we took, and something weighed my head down, obscuring my vision. A bag over my head? It was very loud, all of a sudden. We were outside. The sensations and realizations came slow as treacle, as once again my addled brain tried to pull itself out of the mire and back to the real world.

Outside. Surely Dija would have gone for help. Or had she stayed, too frightened to leave me there? What would I have done in the same position? Would Tain or Kalina have noticed my absence from the ceremony? I tried to swallow—honor-down, my mouth was so dry again—but there was something in the way. A gag. They'd gagged me, and put something over my head; a bag, perhaps, and now we were walking down what sounded like a busy street full of merry laughter, singing, and the smell and sizzle of sweet and savory foods being cooked on the street. *Karodee*. The bastards were walking me through the bloody masquerade.

I tried to yell out, but managed only a muffled squawk. With so much background babble it was doubtful anyone could have heard me anyway.

A prick of fresh new pain distracted me. Something sharp against my ribs. "None of that now, Credo," the woman's voice sounded in my ear. "You've just had a bit too much to drink, eh? Let's not make it anything more serious."

Fuck that. I dropped all of my weight, going boneless, and they both immediately staggered under the sudden jolt, enough for me to twist hard and pull my arms free. I plunged forward, hobbling blind, trying to get as much distance as I could, screaming into my gag for help. My left leg slowed me, made me clumsy. Voices chattered all around me; someone would help, someone would—

Smack. A tiny, disorienting moment where I was flying, and then something flat, hard, and immense smashed into my face and body, like someone had thrown a building at me. Dazed, I could do nothing as I felt hands at my shoulders, at my waist, concerned voices.

"This one likes karodee a bit too much," I heard someone say, and tried to answer, to shout again, but then the world was swinging confusingly again and I realized I'd been flat on my face, on the ground, and now I was back between my two captors, my wrists gripped so hard as they slung them over their shoulders it felt like they might snap in two. "First time on Void, you know the rich ones can't handle it," the Wraith said, and a few people laughed. "I'll get him home, don't you worry. Come on, Credo, you've had enough."

And the crowd was parting for her, I could feel them moving away, the good-natured jovial relaxation of it all, and I wanted to scream, but couldn't. The knife in my ribs bit through my clothes, into my flesh. "I can get a corpse up the hill if I need to, Credo," she hissed, not amused now. "Or dump it in the lake if it's too heavy. But if it's all the same to you, I'd rather you got through the night alive, eh?"

Get through the night alive. I wished I could feel comforted. Another wave of pain washed over me as I stumbled on the bad leg, this time accompanied by a rolling nausea. A vivid and gruesome image of Credo Tamago, who'd choked on his own vomit after eating a toxic baked eel when I was fifteen, sprang to mind. Gagged and apparently masked, vomit would be a real risk right now.

The agonizing, disorientating walk seemed to take hours. I could tell when we crossed Compact Bridge because they half-dragged me up some stairs and the wind picked up, the bells hanging below ringing in an insultingly cheerful manner. In one of my more aware periods I registered us walking uphill, but though I'd paced the streets of the upper city countless times, it didn't help me work out where we were. My feet scraped on the ground as often as they stepped, and the mask and blindfold were thick enough that the only clue to my whereabouts was the faint increase and decrease in light as we walked. *Lamps.* So at least a few hours had passed since I'd been captured. I held on to this new bit of information, as if holding one thing in my head would help me piece the rest together. I counted the gaps between the brightest spots to try to estimate how far apart the lamps were. I focused on that and soon realized it was irregular. A spike of excitement. There was one section of the city where streetlamps had been added and there had been a mistake in the planning so they were not at regular intervals; it was near Potbelly Square and the old markets. That gave me something to work with. Thinking of escape gave me something to concentrate on, and made the painful, jolting walk more bearable.

Then, all of a sudden, we stopped. The pressure on my wrists suddenly lessened and I was lowered off my captors' shoulders against something hard and rough. They let me slump and slide down until I was sitting, back against a wall, injured leg out in front of me, panting with pain and fear. Then an increase in brightness and the welcome lick of fresh air on my cheeks as first the mask came off, then the blindfold. The soggy, unpleasant gag stayed put. I blinked into dusk light, half-dazed.

"No yelling, now," the Wraith warned. She crouched in front of me. Her mask and makeup still looked creepy, but not quite so nightmarish. I held on to that. This was just a woman, and what was addling my brain was just a drug. I could get through this. Think through it. If my pouches were still there— was that their comforting weight, pressing against my stomach?—then I had a purge. Maybe I could get some of this stuff out of my system. "I'm going to take this off, but things'll go better for you if you don't disturb any nice folks around here. Understand? Nod if you understand."

I nodded. The motion sent pain ricocheting down my neck and spine, and my vision blurred. She leaned in and loosened the knot at the back of my head. I spat the gag out.

"That's better." She smiled, wide and gruesome. "Now, open up, you're going to need something more to properly enjoy this particular party. No, no, don't struggle." Something different was forced against my face, a wet cloth carrying the distinctive smell of the sedative Art's tonic. I tried turning away but it was no good. Already the pain was fading, my limbs growing heavy, my vision closing further. "Good boy. You relax there."

Dimly, I heard the rap of knuckles on a door. The sound of a door swinging open. I turned my head, heavy as an overripe melon, to see a woman in a sleeping robe, with tousled hair and a small lamp in one hand, blinking out at us. She took the Wraith in with a startled jolt. "Madam," she said, ducking her head. The glimpse I had of her face looked cowed. Maybe even frightened.

"Got a special guest for you," the Wraith purred. "Gonna leave you my boy here to look after him, but I'll be back."

The woman peered around the door at me, and raised an eyebrow. "All right, darling," she said. "Come on down, then."

I couldn't hold my head up, let alone stand, but the big man hauled me to my feet. She ushered us inside, closed the door behind us, then took off her robe and hung it by the door. Under the robe she was wearing a very filmy sort of dress. She smelled cloyingly sweet and her eyes looked glazed. My own felt heavy. I closed them just for a second, but when I opened them, everything had changed.

I was on a pile of cushions. The atmosphere was cloying, stifling, pungent, a room resembling a large underground gaming room. People drank at low tables lit by colored-glass lamps and oil braziers burned all over the room. Several instruments provided background music and two men were singing in intoxicated harmony. But it was all twisted slightly, like the way in which a subtle wrongness in a familiar place can bend a dream into a nightmare. The people weren't quite people, they were animals and monsters and mythological creatures—masquerade masks, I told myself, just masks, but it was so hard to hold on to a coherent thought. Instead of playing riddles or muse or betting on dice, people were gathered around a fight between two small animals tearing bloody chunks from each other with low growls and snarls. Another group was half-undressed and having what looked like fairly frenetic sex in another corner. It was hot, so hot, and a dull, smoky haze hung over the place.

I couldn't remember what I was doing here, only that something was wrong. A battle raged inside my body, which was both desperately shouting alarms but also sliding into a kind of deep, hot-bath state. I worried my heart might be failing, the way it lurched between acceleration and deceleration. Once I thought I saw a familiar face, round and serious, peering round a doorway. *Dee?* But I blinked and it was gone, just another hallucination.

Smoke from the brazier made my head fuzzier with the scent of snakeleaf oil, a relaxant, and something floral. There was someone beside me on the cushions, his hot skin pressed against mine; a handsome man with a generous white smile in his smooth dark face. He brought a honeyed pastry to my lips and I obediently took a bite. It tasted terribly sweet. There was something wrong, though, I remembered suddenly, and stopped eating, and tried to push away from him, but my body was sluggish and noncompliant.

"Have another drink," the man suggested, and there was a cup in my hand I had no memory of accepting, and my mouth was sticky with the taste of kori and sugar syrup. "Some more!"

Though I didn't like the drink, it seemed polite to sip again. The room had darkened, the music notes twanging closer, vibrating around the space. It was too hot. And people were too close. I tried to stand, but my leg hurt, and my chest and head. The smiling man was right beside me, helping me up, and a pretty ebony-skinned woman was on my other side, her hair rippling over my arm and chest, offering me another drink, or would I like to dance?

"I need some air," I tried to say, but my tongue was too big for my mouth. I staggered away from the pair of them and moved through the crowd, looking for a door. Lots of people were smiling at me, and I didn't know any of them. My heart was pounding but I also felt on the verge of falling asleep. *Why can't I remember?* My body wouldn't cooperate as I tried to find an exit. Other people were laughing and relaxed, dancing lazily around me, but this hypersensitivity, all this accidental touching, triggered every anxious response in my body. I felt even stranger, dizzier, and it was more than just whatever the intoxicant was in the air, there was something else, a peculiar, draining feeling.

Something drew my attention to an alcove at the far side of the room, from which emerged low laughter and astonished gasps, like the audience at a show, and the slow beating of a skin drum. I shrugged off my companions and stepped toward it, feet stumbling as if some unseen force propelled me. It was a dark corner of the room, the space lit only by candles, and a small group was gathered around a woman sitting in front of a painted clay urn and gesturing and talking quietly to the group of onlookers. She was naked and her skin was covered in swirling patterns too thick and glossy to be tattoos. At her feet sat a small boy playing a drum. I staggered, dizziness intensifying, my ears ringing so I couldn't hear what she was saying. The sight of it, combined with what I felt, made me desperately afraid.

A hand seized my arm. I turned and there he was, the big masked whisperer, looming before me, expressionless and passive, implacable. He took hold of one of my arms and moved me back to the pile of cushions as if I weighed no more than a kitsa. I stumbled down, understanding flooding back, and with it the panicked recrimination for forgetting. *How long have I been here? What do they want from me?* And more frightening still: Why had no one come? *What happened to Dija?*

My head hurt and my vision wavered. Whatever they'd dosed me with had been strong. The pain from my various injuries pulsed away in the distance, but muted. But I had enough presence of mind to slowly work a hand toward my stomach. It was hard to say how closely the whisperer was watching me since his eyes were obscured by the strange flat mask. He didn't react. I let my head slump backward as if lacking the strength to hold it up, and crawled my hand in through the concealed gap in my clothing.

My fingers found familiar shapes and relief coursed through me. They hadn't found the pouches. Perhaps they'd assumed if I'd had a weapon it would have been in my hand. I was still afraid, still confused, but I wasn't without weapons or defense, not entirely. The order of contents had been jumbled at some point so I couldn't be sure exactly what was what, but my slow, groping fingers closed around a paper packet and a small cloth bag. A weapon and a defense. Agonizingly slowly, I worked one of the little compressed chew cubes out of the bag. Vomiting might get some of the drug out of my system, but if the whisperer saw me being sick he'd just dose me again. Would they let me go to relieve myself? Honor-down, I still didn't grasp what they wanted. They'd beaten me, but left me with no serious injuries. They'd drugged me, but so far only to keep me at a party half–passed out. What was it all *for*?

I flopped my head forward. "Need to . . ." I slurred, my tongue fat. I coughed and when the whisperer stood, I said, "Need to piss."

The mask tilted to one side, as if he were considering. Then his rumbly, low voice came through. "No one's stopping you."

Hardly daring to believe my luck, I struggled to sit up again, but the big man pushed me back down. "Didn't say you could go anywhere," he said flatly. "Shit yourself if you want to."

My fingers closed around the first packet. Whatever their plan was, I didn't want to stay here and find out. The guy was a lot bigger than me but after a face full of powdered stingbark he'd not be in a position to chase me down, clumsy or not.

"Getting bored?"

My brief spike of energy and determination washed away. The Wraith was back. No one else seemed alarmed by the specter stalking through the room—just another karodee costume. "Don't worry. I found you a friend," she said. "I *told* you you'd have a good time tonight."

She tugged a man along from behind her. He had a sweet face, pale, with a brown beard and big, liquid eyes, and he grinned stupidly at me and said something I couldn't understand. *Talafan*, I thought, *he's from the Empire*, and though my head hurt too much to understand why, a heightened sense of danger and anxiety threatened to choke me.

The Wraith looked over at the whisperer man. "The boss suggested it," she said, with none of the silky tone she'd used on me. "He'll do nicely."

The Talafan man's movements as he looked around the room looked wrong, twitchy and awkward. The Wraith smiled indulgently. "Why don't the two of you get to know each other? It's too crowded in here. Let's go somewhere a bit more private."

The whisperer twisted my left arm up behind my back and drove me forward. The pain in my shoulder sent more waves of black over my vision, more strange lightness. I stumbled up the stairs, my bad leg throbbing with pain from the ankle up. There were no Order Guards coming to rescue me. Maybe I had never seen Dija back at that building, just imagined her like I'd imagined her here a short while ago. Maybe no one knew I was here. All these people, they could all see me, but no one was reacting. *What is wrong with everyone?* I wanted to scream.

They got us up two flights of stairs and then, smothering my attempts to struggle, into a small room, a regular sleeping chamber. The flickering lights and distant sounds of karodee filtered in through a narrow open window. The Talafan man, oblivious to the danger, flopped dramatically on the bed, spread-eagled. "I want more!" he moaned in Trade, very obviously utterly out of his mind on whatever they'd given him. Given us.

"Of course you can have some more," the Wraith crooned. "It makes you feel so good, doesn't it?"

"Good," he agreed, his smile beatific.

"Don't take that," I warned him, as the Wraith slunk closer. If he heard me he gave no sign. She scooped a pale amber powder from a packet onto one finger, which the man eagerly took into his mouth, licking and sucking like a baby animal at the teat. My stomach turned.

"He was so bereft when I got hold of him, you know," she told me conversationally. She stroked between his legs while he continued to suck on her fingers. "He'd been rejected, you know, and his whole karodee spoiled. I'm doing him a favor, really. Or should I say, *you're* doing him a favor." She increased the rapid movement of her hand and glanced back over at me. "Do you want to help? No? I hear you weren't so stuck-up an hour ago, darling."

The man's grip on my wrist never slackened, but I dragged together every skerrick of my self-possession. I might only get one chance at this. The purge and the poison were still clutched in my closed palm, twisted behind my back. With this leg and my disorientation I'd never get out the way we'd come. How far was the drop to the street, if I could make it to the window? I tried to remember the number of stairs we'd come up.

If my captors noticed my frantic assessment, they didn't react. The Wraith was still pleasuring the now almost completely incapacitated Talafan man. "You two silly boys," she said, smiling at me with her skeleton smile. "You shouldn't have had so much. Didn't anyone warn you not to combine highs? Things got out of hand, didn't they? Oh dear. You'll live through the night, Credo, I told you, but I can't promise you'll have a good day tomorrow."

It had to be now. I maneuvered my free right hand behind me to the base of my spine, closed my eyes, calling in any good fortune I'd ever earned, and opened my left fist.

The soft contents dropped and I felt them brush my open, stretching fingers, but my reflexes were too slow. My palm closed on nothing. But no time to swear or hesitate; I took a sudden staggering step forward, clearing a space between us, then pivoted sharply back in toward my captor, driving my free elbow into his face. He grunted and I wrapped my arm under his and up behind his shoulder, forcing him forward in a bow, straight into my waiting knee. He released my wrist at last and I dove straight for the powder I'd dropped. My hand closed around something just as pain exploded in my jaw and my head cracked into the wall.

The Wraith's foot came down on my chest, all her playfulness gone. Dazed, head ringing, pain radiating from my jaw, I squeezed my fingers around my last weapon, but knew by the terrible solid feel of it that I'd grabbed the wrong thing. I had a purge, only a purge. I'd lost my only chance. "Enough," the Wraith said coldly. "Do it now."

It took a moment to realize she wasn't talking to me, but to her comrade, and he had the Talafan man's neck in his massive hands. *Shit, shit, no,* I thought, but I was out of energy, out of coordination, out of tricks. "No," I croaked, but the Wraith only watched me impassively as the weak gurgles and thrashing on the bed slowed and eventually stopped.

INCIDENT: Poisoning of Lord Niceames, son of the 2nd Duke of Maru

POISON: Graybore

INCIDENT NOTES: Lord Niceames visited Silasta on a recreational trip and took to life in the city, thereafter refusing to return to his duties in homeland. Presented to the hospital with a bloody cough and hair loss after apparent weeks of increasing illness. Physics diagnosed graybore poisoning but Niceames died shortly thereafter. Traces of graybore later found in the man's favorite perfume bottle. Political background suggests manservant may have been instructed by the Duke to carry out the gradual poisoning. Servant left Sjona soon after the man's death and determination council elected not to pursue further.

(from proofing notes of Credola Thoraiya Oromani)

6

Kalina

It transpired that bribery was more than enough to overcome the initial protests of the costumer who had made my masquerade outfit. Several hours after the boating, and considerably poorer, I had ensured the Talafan noblewomen had dresses and masks from his private stocks. While I might have been rash in antagonizing the Prince, it hadn't been a fruitless gesture; the ladies had insisted on bringing me back with them to the Leaning Lady, the guesthouse that had been commandeered for the Royal Family's visit. Perhaps I could learn something more about the Prince from his household. Or about Brother Lu.

We had returned to Zhafi's private room at the guesthouse after our shopping, and the ladies' servants fussed around assisting the women into their dresses. Reuta had a coral-and-red firebird mask with a beautiful spray of feathers and a slightly sinister beak, and Mosecca a brown kitsa. The Princess, who was having her nails carefully filed by a yellow-haired servant kneeling by the bed, held her mask up to her face. It was green with mottled gold scaling across the cheeks and brow, and thin glass panels in the eye sockets. "What did you say this was called, Kalina?"

I masked my instinctive shiver. "It's called a riverring," I said. "I do not know the word in Talafan, I am sorry. It is a creature from children's stories. Riverring are twin water spirits who live in the depths of rivers and lure in unwary children."

Reuta made a theatrical little shudder. "How horrid!"

"They are more mischievous than bad," I clarified. "I suppose they are a cautionary tale, meant to keep children safe in the shallows. But they mean to play with the children, not harm them. You'll probably see a few pairs of them in the parade; it is a popular costume."

Zhafi, looking interested, pulled the mask over her head and her smoothly bound hair. It was a full mask, mostly fabric, that covered her down to her neck, and Reuta gasped in horror at the sight—"Those eyes, they're so awful!" I forced a smile, but in truth I agreed; the glassy eyepieces *were* creepy, and it was impossible to separate my feelings about silly old children's stories from my very real memories of cold water closing over my face, my blood darkening the wispy river reeds around me. It had been more than two years ago, but the fear of water, the nightmares, seemed determined to stay with me, a ghostly partner in everything I did.

Zhafi took the mask off and placed it on the bed.

"Do you think Princess Josta will join us?" I asked. The older woman had not accompanied us to the costumer's but Zhafi, optimistic, had bought the matching twin set of her riverring costume in case the Princess changed her mind.

Zhafi sighed. "Dear Josta. She says she is feeling unwell." The slightest movement of her eyebrow suggested skepticism of this claim. "She worries so about what her lord husband will think, you see. The Prince can be very . . . forthright in his opinions."

I'll bet. "That is a shame," I said. Guiltily, I hoped my little stunt with the Prince had not created problems for Josta. "Are you traveling with your husband, too, Lady Mosecca?"

She shook her head. "I am a widow, Credola. His Imperial Majesty permits me to live at the Palace to reside as one of the Young Empress's ladies, praise God."

"Praise God, praise His Majesty the Emperor," Zhafi agreed.

It had taken me a moment to recognize the word: *widow* meant her husband had died. "I am sorry," I said awkwardly.

But if Mosecca was distraught, she hid it. "I am blessed with fine children and kind friends," she said, inclining her head.

The servant who had been filing Zhafi's nails, a fair-haired woman, finished her work. "Your hands are ready, Your Highness," she murmured.

"Thank you, Esma," Zhafi said, surprising me by calling the young woman by name, warmth in her tone. "Could you make sure Her Highness has her costume, just in case?" Esma left the room, laden with mounds of green fabric.

"We are all right now, thank you," Zhafi said to the rest of the servants. "You can all leave us."

The sight of servants filing out reminded me of something else I'd hoped to learn here. Feigning only mild interest, as if the question had just occurred to me, I asked, "Did any young children come with you to the city?"

"My son is in the Imperial force and my daughters are all married," Mosecca replied, a faint smile at the edge of her lips.

"With one of the servants, I thought perhaps?"

"I don't think so," Reuta said, playing idly with the feathers on her mask as she adjusted it in the small looking glass. "Why?"

"There was a—" I stopped. I still felt strongly that there was something strange about the servant and the toy, but for all I knew anyone here could be involved. I shrugged. "There was a sound just now, I thought it was a child crying. I must have been mistaken."

"How peculiar," Reuta said, frowning and looking around. "I didn't hear anything."

None of them looked the slightest bit suspicious of my question, at least. "I'm probably hearing things." I smiled. "In fact I ought to be going back home to get dressed myself." I brandished my own mask, a silver cloud lizard.

Zhafi reached across and touched my hand. "Thank you for helping us with our costumes, Kalina. And for your suggestion to my brother. I think you must know it is only due to you that we have such a treat."

"Ectar told us you were kind," Reuta said. "I hope . . ." She stopped, smothered what sounded suspiciously like a giggle. Mosecca gave her a severe look and she cleared her throat. "I hope we can be friends, too."

"I would like that very much," I said, and was surprised to realize I meant it. Friendship and diplomacy were uneasy bedfellows, went the saying, but perhaps, I thought, they could find a balance.

I found Etrika, Ana, and Dija's two older brothers in the apartments, the boys itching with urgency to leave and join the fun and delighted by my costume. Salvea had dropped off her young son Davi, who had taken a liking to the boys and was alternating between following them around worshipfully, and sprinting excitedly underfoot. But no Jovan or Dee; they still hadn't re-turned home from wherever they'd gone during the rowing.

Knowing my brother, it was unlikely he'd simply decided to take Dee to some karodee event as a treat. More likely he'd thought of some additional lesson or test for her. "He'll look after her, don't worry," I reassured Etrika lightly, but it worried *me*, a little. Fun and relaxation were important ways to build bonds, and Jov never indulged in enough of it with his young charge. Even without the added scrutiny of her immediate family staying with us, I knew he felt inadequate to the task of raising her. He had expected many more years with Etan to perfect his own craft before taking on his own Tashi. I just wasn't sure if it was a lack of self-confidence holding him back from properly bonding with Dija, or an unconscious protection against the pain he'd experienced when Etan died.

The pain *we'd* experienced. Etan had been my Tashi too, my teacher too, I had to remind myself, because even with all I'd shared with my uncle, he had always belonged to Jovan, with me the outsider at the window, handprints on the glass the marks of my desire to belong. I shook my head. Here I was being maudlin, and every bit as self-indulgent as I would tease my brother for being.

Perhaps I'd been unfair, anyway. Perhaps Jovan had not been inspired by the rowing final to go and quiz Dee on the possible uses of the venom from the toads found in the marshlands, but was instead taking her on a trip to the market to buy her a spiced meat skewer, or letting her play sticks and shoes with children on the street. It didn't matter. He'd have to be back soon to get dressed and go up to the Manor. He'd want to be by Tain's side during the masquerade, in case of trouble.

But time stretched on without them turning up, and soon the boys were muttering anxiously and Ana, never particularly talkative or expressive, paced back and forth in a manner reminiscent of my absent brother. She had an impressive line of scowls and heavy footfalls, and theatrically expressive eyebrows. "We'll have to go without them," she eventually announced, face pinched with disapproval. "If Jovan will keep her out so late, he can take her with him."

"We might see them there," I suggested, masking my own disappoint-ment; I itched to share with Jov what I'd learned about the westerners, and Lios. I might not have gotten any closer to solving the Brother Lu mystery, but at least I'd confirmed the Prince was an ass. I didn't point out how dif-ficult it would be to find anyone in the masquerade crowd, even knowing each other's masks. Unless he could find us, poor Dee might end up being forced to accompany the Chancellor around, too. Hardly the most exciting masquerade for a child her age. Then again, my niece wasn't precisely a normal child.

The parade was already underway by the time we left our apartments, so we made our way down to join the crowds by the shores of the Bright Lake to watch the long procession of costumed people of all shapes and sizes and ages joining in the fun.

"You didn't want to be in the parade, darling?" Etrika asked Davi, who was balanced on her cheerfully tolerant eldest grandson's shoulders, watching with excitement. Davi looked down and shook his head as if she'd asked something foolish.

"How would I see everything, if I was *in* the parade?"

I smiled as he pointed out his favorite costumes, and the older boys played spotting games: *Find five kitsas. Spot a geniope with a red hat. Two identical Sunch the Golden Pens.* We saw animals, mythological creatures, fearsome warriors, and famous Chancellors. Davi screamed with delight when he spotted a beaming Sjease, whose entire face was painted gold within the massive, multi-pronged sun mask. Groups of gleeful children danced together in their masks and face paint, giggling and spinning. Darfri spectators called out blessings, and people thrust flowers and gifts into the paraders' hands, and others in higher windows threw handfuls of dyed seed husks that fell over the parade like tiny, brightly colored raindrops.

My usual enjoyment was dampened, though. I found myself watching the crowds more than the parade, searching for Jov and Dee. I forgot to hand out flowers or favors and eventually the boys commandeered my supply and doled them out on my behalf. "Aren't you having fun, Kalina?" Davi asked, looking disappointed when he saw me staring off into the distance instead of watching a group of children in pink performing acrobatics around a fountain.

"Of course I am," I said, catching his hand and turning my full attention to the somersaulting children. "Lizards just like to soak in the sun, that's all."

We all had kavcha and various sticky sweet treats, and played several games of chance run by men and women with toothy smiles who cheerfully took our money as they apologized for our bad "luck," and one of the older boys made gooey eyes at a very pretty young baker boy making cheese-and-date rolls shaped like karodee bells. Ana steered us firmly away from there and the brothers began grumbling with disappointment about being treated like "little kids." I distracted them by buying Davi a ribbon flag, and after everyone had been poked with the stick end as he waved it with great enthusiasm and poor coordination, they were all too busy fantasizing about snapping it in half to worry about the disagreement.

As the sun began to set, the crowd started to settle around the giant Darfri shrine by the water on the southeast side of the lake, finding positions to watch the offering performance by the Speakers. Soon Davi was yawning and dragging his feet, and drooping his head against our waists. "Best we take you home, little chappie," Etrika suggested, and though the older boys protested, a sharp word from their mother silenced them. Ana watched her eldest son with firebird eyes, and reminded him he was not old enough to stay for the nighttime part of the festival.

I bade them all goodnight as the first of the Darfri drums sounded, but avoided the main crowds settling for the ceremony, preferring to stay on the fringes. I felt unsettled, and tired, and some part of me would have preferred to return home with the family, but I wanted to at least try to catch Jov and Tain. Once I saw someone in a speckled drake costume up on Compact Bridge that I thought was Tain, but it must have been someone wearing the same costume, because no Jov in his graspad outfit stood beside him. There were likely other friends and occasional lovers mixed in among this crowd but nobody with whom I hoped to celebrate into the night this year.

The kavcha switched to the fortified version, and bottles of wine and kori and sticks of janjan and karodee cakes—a traditional Darfri sweet rolled in egg and powdered sugar—were exchanged. A plump woman with a horned half mask and an elegant neck offered me a cup of strong-smelling kori and a suggestive broad smile, and several men sitting nearby tried to cajole me into their circle, but I waved them all off. I tried to conjure the celebratory feeling of the previous karodee, one nowhere near as big as this, but full of frenetic energy, when I had been so grateful to be alive, and half-drunk on my strange visibility, when it seemed half the city had hoped to share a drink or a kiss with me. But that abandon was elusive. The merrier the crowd became, the more disengaged I grew.

The Darfri Speakers chanted in unison, the deep booming drumbeat forming a primal rhythm. I couldn't see more than a blur of the dancing, but the crowd embraced it, swinging and nodding along. For some Darfri in the crowd, this would be the first time their own religious ceremony had been given such social prominence; I saw that joyful satisfaction, and even tears, in many among the crowd. It was beautiful, but it also made me feel more alone.

When the sun dropped below the line of the walls, and the lamps and fires were lit, the formal part of the ritual concluded. Young families and older people, and those not interested in the nighttime dancing and festivities, drifted away, to return home or to head off to the more sedate entertainments throughout the city, clearing space that was quickly filled by more musicians, performers, and costumed people laughing and dancing. I wondered where Tain and Jov were; buried somewhere in the crowd, no doubt, enjoying rare anonymity. Tain's cheap, feathery costume was a secret, with only a small handful of us having seen it. Perhaps he would enjoy a chance to celebrate and unwind tonight. He needed it.

Before the siege Tain had socialized regularly, visited his favorite bath-house, and enjoyed the company of a range of lovers—once, though it felt now like a long time ago, I had even wanted to be one of them. Now he only attended official functions, and rumor had it he no longer used the cur-tained sections of any bathhouse in the city, nor invited anyone to his private chambers. I worried for him. He seemed lonely. Maybe tonight he'd indulge himself in a bit of relaxation.

The crowd certainly seemed in the masquerade night spirit. There was plenty of dancing and talking but people were also setting up on blankets, cushions, and even little tents near small fires now, and I smelled sweet and spicy scents in the air from intoxicating oil burners, and heard laughter and flirtations and tipsy singing from all sides. I still felt no inclination to join any groups, but took some amusement from watching the odd sight of vari-ous animals and mythological and historical figures gathered together. Al-ready, creative anatomical combinations were happening in darkened spaces. I let myself be spun around in a dance or two and had a bite of a karodee cake offered from a smiling woman in a half-face geniope mask, but it tin-gled oddly on my tongue and tasted as if something had been mixed into the sugar; thinking of Jov's worries about the prevalence of new narcotics around the city, I quickly abandoned it. Perhaps that was the source of the overly intense atmosphere and the euphoric expressions on many faces. As it grew dark, I had to accept I would not find Jov or Tain, and might as well go home. I was weary and my face felt very hot. I reached up to take my mask off, then stopped.

Hiukipi was right before me. His mask was a simple half-face style, but jeweled like a crown; it only took me a second to identify him, surrounded as he was by a small group of Talafan guards and servants without costume. The

Prince strode through the crowd with the expectation others would move out of his path; broad, strong shoulders squared, radiating confidence, and his wealth and privilege obvious from his manner even more than from his expensive clothing. I pushed my mask back in place; hot or not, I was suddenly grateful to be a lizard.

His expression was greedy as he stared at the women he passed. He was free with his hands, touching without seeking leave and pressing too close and too tight in dances. I watched him grow visibly frustrated at rejection after rejection, but he seemed to lack even the most basic of charm or manners—or at least was not choosing to waste them on masked strangers. It could not be more obvious he had expected to be treated to a buffet of available partners, but he had never been required to seek free consent from a woman before, and lacked the skills even in this extremely conducive environment. Plenty of foreigners, men especially, struggled to adapt to Silastian sensibilities, and did not realize how gaining a poor reputation could see one thoroughly shut out of social engagements. Masquerade night always revealed a number of them.

Even as I started away, Hiukipi had begun again to dance with another woman, this one visibly drunk and the long line of her throat exposed as she threw her head back to laugh as they spun. The Prince was a good dancer, and picked the woman up easily by the waist to lift her to and fro in rhythm with the music. But on the third spin he shifted his hands lower, grasping her backside, and thrust her hard up against him. One hand pinning her there, he started to pull apart the ties of her dress.

The woman jerked backward, shoving the hand away, and wiggled out of his grip, her affront obvious even through her mask, and stormed away. I saw her signaling other dancers and pointing Hiukipi out, and people melted back away from him, passively excluding him from their circles.

He noticed it, too, and a dull flush of red marred his neck and lower face. His building temper and frustrated entitlement was a physical thing, straining like steam in a lidded pot. "They are rutting on the ground like animals, but they say no to me?" I heard him spit at one of his guards or servants.

Reasonably satisfied no Silastian woman would wake up with this unpleasant specimen on the grass beside her, I pushed my way out of the dancing, my only remaining emotion a deep desire for sleep.

I was moving away from the lake when, in the flickering light of dusk, fires, and lamps, a green dress and a scaled mask passed in front of me. A riverring, styled so similarly to Princess Zhafi's and worn by a woman the right height and frame that for a panicked moment I feared the ladies had left the guesthouse. After all, they had been extremely interested in the idea of the Darfri ceremony. Perhaps no one had explained the nature of the evening celebrations.

Uneasy, I tried to get a closer look. The crush of people had thickened and many of them were wearing costumes, so feathers and hats and scarves kept catching on my limbs or poking me in the face. It was only a function of moving against the flow of the crowd but I grew flustered all the same. A burly costumed man shouldered me aside accidentally with a grunt of an apology, and my resultant stumble knocked me into a woman, causing her to spill her picnic basket. As papna fruit and honey pastries scattered and were crushed beneath the feet of other revelers, she rounded on me with a shriek of outrage. I apologized, scrambling to help her pick up her things, and when I looked up I'd almost lost the riverring woman.

It can't be, I told myself, but my chest was tight with my lack of certainty. She wore a long dress, mask, and gloves, so I couldn't see her skin or hair, but she had the same graceful poise, the same gliding walk. When she spun happily in time to the music her elegance made her stand out from the other merrymakers. And Hiukipi was nearby. My breath caught in my throat. I had taken a risk as it was, baiting the Prince, but I'd had no desire to begin a diplomatic incident. The woman was not engaging with the crowd, only drifting along with it, head swiveling to watch, like a person at their first karodee masquerade. I was almost on the brink of calling out, but then I breathed out in heavy relief as a man walking near the woman touched her shoulder and she turned and flung her arms around him. *Thank the fortunes.* Clearly the man was not a stranger. They continued walking together, and the man slipped a hand very familiarly around her waist as he bit into a karodee cake with the other hand. *Definitely not a Talafan Princess,* I thought, and smiled at my own foolishness.

I followed the couple; not deliberately, but because they were heading away from the celebrations in the same direction as me. An otter, a Chancellor Telasa, and a pair of already half-undressed firebirds called out to me as I walked, but I shook my head and they faded away back to their own groups. On the nearest street, the couple stopped to prop against a wall near a lamppost, just outside the bright circle of its light, giggling and kissing with their masks half-on. The man in particular seemed frenetic in his passion, clumsily pushing up the woman's skirt with one hand as he tugged up his own tunic with the other. I averted my head to give them privacy as I passed, but not before the woman's bared leg caught in the light, and the pale exposed skin sent an icy chill of certainty down my body. *Honor-down.*

They hadn't noticed me, and I stood stationary, stricken, my mind temporarily buzzing and frozen. *Shit, oh shit, oh* shit. The man pushed her mask up and tossed his own to the ground, revealing a profile vaguely familiar, light skinned with a neat beard dusted with powdered sugar. My brain clicked with recognition. The Talafan soldier, the young one who had been patrolling outside the marquee, back and forth.

That was enough to drag my thoughts back to coherence. Of course it was that guard. She'd not been staring idly as she spoke honestly to me of things denied her, she'd been staring specifically at *him*. And then she'd tricked me and, I assumed, at least some of her household as well, with a servant her own size and coloring in an identical outfit. Esma, the maid who had taken Josta's costume from the room. Even now, perhaps, Esma sat outside in the garden with the other ladies, mask on, enough to fool the household manager. I shook my head, impressed despite myself at her cleverness.

It wasn't my business if a woman about to be sent off to live with some potentially hostile stranger in a conquered territory wanted to take some joy and passion where she could. I'd felt sorry for Zhafi before and I felt no less sorry for her now, cunning tricks aside. She wasn't hurting anybody, and to be denied basic physical pleasures, and autonomy over her own body, was a cruel fate for anyone. My instinct was to let them be. On the other hand, they were being far from discreet; this street might not be filled with revelers but there were still dozens of people passing in various states of inebriation and high spirits, heading to and from the celebrations. What if someone else recognized them as I had, and word got back to the Talafan delegation somehow; the Crown Prince and the Foreign Minister had both witnessed me creating this opportunity for the Princess. Would they assume I was a willing conspirator? What would happen to Zhafi, if her reputation was publicly damaged and her value to the Empire suddenly diminished?

I couldn't do nothing, I decided, and risk someone less sympathetic finding her. The Prince himself might soon grow tired of being denied willing partners and return to the guesthouse; I couldn't leave them here to be potentially exposed. But honor-down, this had to be handled carefully. They were well underway, and I could hardly just wander up and tap her on the shoulder. I sank back around the nearest building corner, amidst a small garden of flower bushes and decorative stones, and thought. Something to distract them, get their attention, so I could subtly warn her to go home. I could feign drunkenness and bump into them, or make a loud noise . . . *Ah*. I'd played a lot of bannerskids with Jov and Tain as children and was a decent shot with a small ball. I scooped up a fair-sized pebble from the little ornamental garden and took aim.

The lamp broke with a satisfyingly loud smash, causing passersby to yelp in surprise and, critically, the couple to jump apart at the sound. "We must have annoyed one of the spirits," someone on the street suggested, and a few people laughed. I used the confusion, as the other people in the street diverted to avoid the broken glass and the apparent mischievous lamp-exploding spirit, to sidle quickly up to Zhafi and her guard companion, both of whom were looking at the lamppost in alarm.

"Go home," I whispered in her ear, and she jerked to face me. Her companion had taken a few steps away and was looking down the street anxiously as he readjusted his clothing. The commotion seemed to have reminded him exactly how dangerous his behavior could be. I didn't like to imagine his fate if they were caught. "The Prince is walking the streets," I hissed. "You could be seen."

"I . . ." She stopped, her hand flying up to her mask and tugging it in place. "Kalina? I don't—oh, God forgive me. I just—"

"Don't explain, just get out of here." I glanced at her partner. "And don't eat any more of the powdered-sugar cakes."

Trembling, she dropped her hand, then nodded. "You . . . you won't . . . ?"

"Of course not. But go, now."

Her man turned around just as I stepped away, and as I strode up the street I heard her say, "I am so sorry, Tuhash. This was a mistake." I let myself breathe again. If the fortunes favored her, and me, she would get back into the guesthouse before anyone noticed anything amiss. And hopefully she would not be so foolish again.

If I had felt tired before, I was positively drained now. I needed solitude and my bed, and a night free from nightmares for once. My diplomatic career seemed to be getting off to too exciting a beginning for my liking. Though, I thought, trudging weakly up toward our street, it was no small thing for a Princess to be in one's debt.

The others were abed already, but when I checked Dija's room I found it empty, and Jov's the same. Ana and Etrika, sharing space in the long disused part of the apartments we had hastily cleaned out for their visit, were awake by the sound of their breathing, but neither spoke when I checked in on them, and I felt the silent judgment of their daughter and granddaughter's late night hanging awkwardly in the air between us. Perhaps Jov had relented and decided to take Dee somewhere fun—to the sculpture walk, perhaps, or an age-appropriate play. I had to maintain my own irritation with his irresponsibility—he did, after all, forget sometimes how young she was—because if I didn't concentrate on the annoyance it started to turn to worry.

I sat on my bed, exhausted, knowing sleep would not come until I'd heard them safely home.

It was in a half-dozing state I found myself, and when a rap came on my window I jolted as if I'd been shocked awake. Someone was there, outside, despite the fact that our apartments were guarded. My mind leapt to assassins and dangers before I shook those foolish fears clear. Assassins did not knock. I climbed wearily out of bed and went to the window.

"Hadrea?" Moonlight illuminated my friend's face. I pushed the window open, my tired fog lifting with alarm. Hadrea was bare-chested, her body painted elaborately in Darfri symbols, and charms hung heavily around her neck. She might have been interrupted during the ritual itself, such was the air about her; sweat drenched her hairline, and she had a strange, buzzing energy about her, as if she were flush with power, slightly unstable, like one of Etan's old chemical experiments bubbling away in a glass beaker in our little laboratory. More alarmingly still, Dija emerged from the shadows at her side, visibly twisted with anxiety as my brother at his worst. "Dee. What on earth are you doing out there? Why didn't you come to the door?"

I rubbed my eyes and looked at her properly, taking in her shabby appearance swiftly. She had never changed into her costume; those were the same clothes she'd been in this morning. And they were covered in—"Is that blood?" My chest felt tight.

She wiped a hand on her cheek with an impatient swat. "It's all right, Auntie, it's not—I mean, it's not all right, but it's not my blood."

My heart started up a *tat-tat* rhythm and my face burned with a sudden rush of heat. *Jov.* "What happened?"

"You must come," Hadrea said tersely. "Dee found me because it was easier than scouring a crowd full of masks. She did not want to alert the Guards."

"Hadrea, what *happened*?"

"It is Jovan," she replied, short and tight. "He is in trouble."

Hadrea lent me her strong arms to lever me out the window. Panic fluttered hard inside me, like a live thing trying to escape my rib cage. I smelled a whiff of woody smoke on the air. "Where is he?"

"He is in a house in the old market district."

"And he's in trouble how?"

Hadrea held up one hand to quiet me and pressed the other against my chest, holding me back. "Wait," she whispered. She crept forward toward the edge of the garden and disappeared briefly from view in the line of plants beside the wall. Moments later she was back, beckoning us, and offered a boost to get up onto the wall.

"Where are our guards?" Friend of the family or not, she should not have been able to get around to our sleeping quarters, and we should not be able to cross this wall without challenge.

"Shh. It was not their fault." Hadrea picked Dee up easily and placed her on the wall beside me. "I confused them."

She hoisted herself up and over, graceful as an acrobat, and I watched, uneasy, unsure what she meant. There was something odd about her manner, something almost furtive, like a child sneaking honey pastries in the middle of the night. She stretched out her arms and Dee slid easily down into them. I got down with considerably less grace. We crept out across the road and used the shortcut through the gardens between the Leka and Ash apartments. "All right, will one of you tell me what's going on? Why are we slipping our own guards, and what's happened to Jov? Is he hurt?" I sniffed the air. "Is there a fire?"

"He is hurt, but it is not life-threatening," Hadrea said. She hesitated, glancing back over her shoulder at Dija, so I dropped to look at the child directly.

"Dee. What did you see? What is going on? You two never came back after the race—where did Jov take you?"

"He didn't," she said miserably, scuffing one foot on the ground. "I followed him. He left the event when we were supposed to be there together, we were supposed to be watching the Chancellor and the Heir, and then he just suddenly left. So I followed." Her voice was very small. "I wanted to see if I could track him without him noticing."

And we hadn't worried too much about her absence, thinking she was with Jovan and therefore safe. What stupidity. My brother was perfectly capable of getting himself into plenty of trouble, and of course Dija would have made a game out of trying to get one up over her inaccessible teacher, to try to crack his facade. She was only thirteen years old, and while proofing was a deadly serious and significant role, aspects of the training involved games and tests of skill. I couldn't blame her, and I was too worried about Jov right now to waste time dwelling on blaming him, either. "All right. So what happened to him and why is it so secretive?" My voice shook.

Hadrea glanced back at me, her face grave. "We must be secretive because he is being set up to be dishonored. If we call the Guards he is going to be found in a compromising position. Kalina, we need to move now. We do not have much time."

My chest felt tight with the effort of staying calm, but I obeyed, following her as she strode downhill and south. "Compromising how?"

Hadrea looked at Dee again, but the girl had her head down as she scurried along beside me, legs moving double the steps as compared to my friend's confident strides. Hadrea sighed. "They have drugged him and left him with a dead body. Unless we get him out of there before the Order Guards find them, it is going to look like a karodee night gone bad."

I shook my head, as if that would settle the information into a coherent pattern. "Wait, what? Who's drugged him?" *Jov*, of all people, being drugged? How would anyone trick a proofer into taking a drug? "Fine, we'll go, but Dee, tell me from the beginning."

With her head down and voice low, Dija gave me as much detail as she could about what had happened. It had started as a game, an exercise, but she'd quickly figured out he was following someone himself, and then everything had gone horribly wrong. I guessed who he must have been following; the only reason Jov would abandon Tain is if it related to the person he considered the greatest direct threat to the Chancellor—the mysterious assassin figure he kept seeing everywhere. My chest felt tight. By the time Dee had realized what was happening, she was isolated, far from anyone else who could help. She'd been too afraid to intervene and once they had moved him, she'd been unable to seek help or risk losing them.

"I thought they were going to kill him," Dee muttered. "So many times. I didn't know what to do. I didn't have anything with me and I was just too scared. I didn't—" She stopped, composed herself, adjusted her glasses. "I was too scared. He was on the floor and they were kicking and kicking, and I just did nothing but watch. And then when they realized who he was, one of them left to get instructions, and I didn't want to follow him, but I couldn't think of any way to help. And then in the house, I got in and I could even see him from the back stairs, but I couldn't think of a way to get close enough to do anything."

"That is all you could and should have done," Hadrea interjected. She held us back in a shadowy side street as a group of people passed up the street, singing, their arms slung over one another's shoulders. "If you had intervened directly at any point, what do you think would have happened, little one? We would be finding *you* somewhere terrible in the morning. And Jovan would be no better off." The people moved out of earshot and she urged us on. I patted Dee's shoulder reassuringly. The thought of her creeping into a strange house and spying on the people who were torturing my brother made me feel sick. What *would* they have done if they'd caught her? We took two more turns down increasingly narrow streets into the old market district, where what had originally been the city's main commercial area had been converted into a meld of higher-end shops, offices, and residences. "Is this it?" Hadrea asked in a low voice, indicating the building across the lane.

There was no indication of a party. The building was dark and the windows gave no hint of life. But Dee was completely confident as she pointed to the first-story window. "He was in there," she said, equally softly. There was no one on the street—we hadn't seen anyone for a while—but that window, at least, was open, and sound carried.

"You are sure?" Hadrea asked her. She looked grim. "If it is the wrong room, this could get ugly, little one."

"I'm sure. It was the only one open, that's how I got in." Dee pointed to the gnarled crangelter espaliered against the north wall of the adjacent building in its small garden. "I climbed up there."

Despite the urgency, I stared at the gap between the buildings. It was three treads at least, maybe more. Dee was a clever and dedicated child, but an athlete she was not. "You didn't jump?"

She peered up at me through her glasses gravely. "Of course not, Auntie. Look." I peered into the black space where she indicated and made out a post wedged between the bricks of the two. "I borrowed it from their garden. I'll put it back after we get him out," she added, as if I'd chastised her for stealing. Rather, I was both deeply impressed and horrified to think of her risking her weight to that stake. Hadrea clapped her on the shoulder and gave a faint grin.

"That was well done. Perhaps you should have been in the Games."

Despite everything, Dee turned toward that praise like a flower to the sun, and a little stab of referred guilt pierced me. We must be starving her of compliments. She was such a hard little worker Jovan rarely faulted her for anything as an apprentice, but the distance I'd been worrying about earlier might also have made him a teacher she was growing desperate to please. What if she had gotten hurt trying to impress him and prove herself tonight?

"Can you manage it?" Hadrea asked me, and I shuddered. I was already so worn out, and I didn't trust my coordination when my energy was this low. But Dee had not been able to rouse or move Jov, and strong as she was, Hadrea would need help getting an unconscious body out a window. I nodded, and she accepted it briskly, moving into the garden. That was her way; she never questioned or asked twice. Me saying I could do a thing was all the evidence she needed to be confident it was handled. It was one of my favorite things about her, in fact. I smiled at myself in the dark as I recognized the same response in myself that Dee had just shown. Hadrea was my friend—a difficult person to be close to at times, but we *had* grown close all the same— but even after years of knowing each other I still retained the desire to impress her. She had turned the tide of a war, she had fought and subdued something very like a god. Who could not be a little bit like the flower to the sun around a person like that?

"He's so heavy," Dee said, to nobody in particular.

I touched her shoulder gently, knowing what had prompted the comment. "You did everything you could," I said fiercely. "I couldn't move an unconscious man and I'm more than twice your age. I need you to stop wondering if you should have done things differently. You got us here and we're going to get him out, all right?"

She didn't answer. "All right?" I repeated, and stared down at her until she gave a tentative nod.

"All right," she said. She hastily wiped under her glasses with the edge of her scarf and I pretended not to notice.

Hadrea was already halfway up the crangelter, which seemed to comfortably bear her weight. "You're on watch," I said to Dee. "Keep out of sight but you let us know if it's not clear for us to get out. No one can see us."

She nodded, and melted back into the garden. The street had been quiet but if there was a private party in this building, doubtless people would continue to come and go throughout the evening. It wasn't even midnight yet. I breathed out, trying to let my body relax, but it was a lost cause; hauling myself up the thick, rough bark of the tree was an exercise in sheer nerves, especially knowing the horror that might greet me at the other end if we made it safely. *One shitty thing at a time,* I told myself.

The tree wasn't that bad. My hands shook but I never felt in real danger of falling because the windy trunk was solid against the brick. It was the gap between the buildings that made my heart race and my throat go dry and thick with fear. Dee had wedged the stake firmly and Hadrea crossed easily with only one light step on it, with no sign of movement of the makeshift bridge. But it still involved taking a step into a dark chasm. I wished, as I stood there, sweating, panting, shaking with exhaustion, that I was as small as Dee and could crawl across it, but at my size there was no way to safely balance, not to mention it would involve too much time relying on the stake to hold.

Hadrea had made the window ledge and was looking back at me, mouthing *come on*. After a moment's hesitation, I blew out my breath again, blinked hard, then took the step.

For just a sliver of a moment I thought I'd mistimed it or stepped at the wrong angle; my left foot slipped on the stake as I tried to transfer to my right and for that tiny moment I thought I was going to fall. Then I was thumping ungracefully against the wall, my cheek hitting brick, and Hadrea's strong arm slapped around my back, keeping me safely pressed against the wall until my bearings returned.

"Thanks," I whispered. We both shrank to a careful crouch; the sill wasn't really wide enough to accommodate adult visitors, but there were plenty of handholds here at least. The open shutters provided us with cover but also made it hard to see into the room. "Can you hear anything?"

"Someone groaning," she breathed back. My heart did a strange palpitation, simultaneously relieved Jov was alive and worried about what state he would be in. "Nothing else. I think we go in."

I squeezed her hand in reply, and we edged our way past the shutter.

The room was quiet and unlit, though the full moon provided some cold and thin illumination. We hovered there a moment, looking for signs of movement, but no one stirred. Hadrea slipped in and dropped noiselessly to the floor, and I followed, legs shaking with relief to be back on solid ground.

There were two figures on the bed, but Hadrea crossed straight to the door and looked for a latch. She had a short, decorated stick prop from the Darfri ceremony that she unhooked from her skirt and held aloft now as a weapon. It looked comfortable in her grip. She gave me a jerk of the head and I crossed quickly, but reluctantly, to the bed. Part of me didn't want to look, because once I looked we had moved into the next step, the step where Jov was definitely hurt and I had to find out how badly.

The next shitty thing, then.

Dija had said he'd been put in a compromising position, and she'd not exaggerated. The strong smell of vomit and bile overwhelmed me. Jov was facing me, lying next to a pool of what must have been his own vomit, his eyes open only a slit and his breath coming out in a weak pant. "Jov," I whispered, touching his cheek with a hand as gently as I could. "Jov, can you hear me?"

He stopped panting. There was an agonizing moment when I thought he had stopped breathing altogether, and my heart plummeted in my chest, but then he took a breath so deep and slow it reminded me of water coming up from a well. His brown eyes opened wider, meeting my gaze. They looked glazed and unfocused, but they were definitely responding to my voice. I found his slack, warm hands and put them in my own, pressing our palms together and entwining our fingers. My eyes pricked with tears. "Jov," I said again. "It's me. Wake up."

Something changed in his vacant expression. His eyes narrowed and his eyebrows came together. "Lini?" Like he was struggling to remember a long-lost cousin.

"Yes, Jov. Come on. You have to—"

Something seemed to swell in my chest and throat, cutting off my breathing.

A man lay right beside Jovan, pressed up against his back, his pale chest bare, ribs and hip bones protruding. There was a fraction of a moment in which I froze, afraid we would wake him, but then the fear intensified in the worst possible way. We wouldn't wake him, because he was dead. Demonstrably, indisputably dead. And worse: I knew him.

It took a moment to understand why, to place the bearded face, but then it clicked. This poor soul was Tuhash, the guard I'd had to break apart from the Talafan Princess. What in all the fortunes had happened between then and now? How had he found his way to this party, not even speaking Sjon, in such a short space of time? What had happened here?

I stared at him, paralyzed with horror, unable to move, unable to think, to process it. He was dead, and partially nude, lying facing Jov, the smell of alcohol and sex and smokes and perfumes mingling with the stench of the vomit, wrapping the corpse, clutching at me. I couldn't breathe. Bright fabric stood out against the pale skin of his neck and chest, wound round his neck like some strange fashion, its riotous colors an obscene contrast to his blank face. I recognized the fabric as the cording from my brother's paluma. The man's eyes were wide open, too wide, almost bulging. A shocking pink sliver of tongue protruded from between his lips and the faint dusting of sugar still lightened his beard below his mouth. It was grotesque. I couldn't look away, could barely blink.

Jovan finally saw where I was looking, and a kind of visible tension bound up his shoulders so his neck got smaller and smaller; he looked so *sad*, so alone, so guilty, that I was sure he had been conscious enough to understand what was happening to him, even if he'd been unable to do anything about it. "He's not much more than a kid," he grunted through gritted teeth. "I tried to fight. Couldn't stop them." His hands slapped weakly at his clothes and I knew he was looking for his concealed pouches. "I tried to dose the big one but I didn't make it. I got the purge, but dropped the powder."

I looked at the vomit with sudden relieved understanding. "You threw up some of the drugs." Likely the only reason he was awake and able to sit up. "Come on, we have to get you out of here." I tried to help my brother maneuver around the smelly sick puddle but his coordination was impaired.

"Hadrea?" Jov blinked across the room, where she stood by the door, on guard. She gave him a weary smile but kept her attention on the door and the hallway.

"Jov, we have to move *fast*. He's Talafan." I nodded to the body, trying not to convey the full extent of my horror at this. "He's an Imperial soldier. I . . ." I cleared my throat. "I saw him earlier. He's got connections. We can't be found with his body."

"I hear something," Hadrea hissed suddenly. "Move." I redoubled my efforts but Jov was heavy and clumsy and struggled to bear his own weight. We needed to be gone before anyone discovered us; it was going to be hard to get him safely out that window but a hell of a lot easier than being chased down by criminals or Order Guards.

We got to the window but Jov was so unbalanced as he tried to mount the sill he was certain to fall off the other side, and even at my most healthy and energized I wouldn't be confident of being able to hold him up. Now? I had no chance. "Hadrea, you're going to have to take him," I whispered, and she took in the situation with a single glance, then nodded. She strode over and handed me the baton before slipping under Jov's arm, propping him up with her shoulders.

"I have you," she said to him quietly.

I tracked back across the room, baton slipping in my sweaty hand. Hadrea had eased the door open a narrow crack but there was no lighting in the hall and I couldn't see if anyone was approaching. It was silent. Maybe Hadrea had imagined it. I glanced back over my shoulder. I could see the shape of their figures silhouetted on the sill. Back to the doorway; still nothing. I relaxed, just a fraction. We might still make this without anyone knowing.

Then, a distinct noise. A thud, like someone bumping heavily against a wall. Footsteps. Heart pounding, sweat wetting the back of my neck, baton trembling, I watched. Nothing, yet. I chanced a quick glance at the window. I could no longer see Hadrea and Jov. Did I risk following them now, or stay to give them more time? I could try to pull furniture in front of this door, stop anyone coming in, but then it would be obvious where we'd gone. Or did I wait it out, hope whoever it was wasn't coming in for us?

Jov needed to be away. I couldn't risk us being found escaping out a window—that would make everything worse. So I stayed, weak and terrified, at the door, hoping.

He appeared, a hulking shadow, up the second set of steps and into the hallway. The sheer size of him, a blacker shape barely distinguishable in the dimness, made my heart race even faster. It was hard to release the stale air in my lungs or to listen properly over the roar in my head. The figure moved with a strange gait, plodding, going from side to side in the hallway like he was sweeping up after a particularly messy child. Was he looking for something? Listening at doors? The frustrating lack of light, and my narrow viewing slit, made it impossible to tell. Then, another thud as he appeared to collide with the wall. The figure stopped.

Drunk. Just a bloody drunk, lurching around, barely able to keep his balance. The fear leaked out of me, leaving me dizzy with relief. But I still didn't want him trying this door; there was no way to lock it and my body weight wouldn't stop him pushing it open. I took a steadying breath, counting as I held it, the way I would during one of my lung episodes.

Then I stepped out of the doorway swiftly and closed it behind me.

The man took a comically long time to react. I was already halfway toward him by the time he had focused on me, and I saw with some relief that up close and with my eyes adjusted to the dim light, I did not recognize him. He was a fat, handsome man, perhaps in his thirties or forties, not a Credo, but wealthy, by the look of his clothes, even rumpled as they were. He blinked at me, started to say something, and burped.

"Excuse me, *excuse* me," he said, catching his balance by throwing out a hand to prop on the wall. "Sorry about that. Where's the—" He burped again, but this time turned his head away, covering his mouth with incongruous delicacy. "Where's the washchamber? I swear they said go upstairs, but these—" He thumped the nearest door with one big hand to demonstrate. "—these are all locked."

I gave my best attempt at a giggle. "I came up for the same reason! But I tried every door down this hall and not one is a washchamber. I reckon—" And here I paused, held up a finger, giggled again. His drunken gaze focused on the finger like a beacon. "I reckon we came up too many stairs. Let's go back down." Very gently I indicated the direction from which he'd come, and he obediently turned his head and began to shuffle back down the hall.

Then he spun around, faster than I expected.

"Or we could just piss in the hall!" he suggested. "Their own fault for making it so bloody hard." Ignoring my gentle protests, he grabbed fistfuls of his long tunic and adopted a broad stance facing the wall. Honor-down, I'd not have been surprised if he pissed pure alcohol, but I was in no mood to find out exactly how much urine he could produce, not when Hadrea and Jov were waiting for me, probably starting to get worried.

"You know what'd be funnier," I said quickly. "What'd really show them? Why don't we go piss on the stairs back to the basement. Then when they come upstairs they'll see firsthand what happens when you don't give clear directions."

He blinked, staring at me, both hands still in the process of lifting his clothing. Then his face split into a huge grin and he dropped the tunic to slap me on the shoulder instead. "I like the way you think," he boomed. Laughing, he preceded me down the hall and began lumbering down the stairs, still chuckling. I felt a moment of vague remorse when he adopted his pose again at the landing; this kind of behavior at a party was likely to stifle his social invitations for a good period, but then again, given the crowd he was partying with, I'd likely done him a favor.

While he was busy letting out what sounded like an unhealthily forceful waterfall of piss down the stairs, I slipped back up silently, then fled down the corridor and back to the room I'd abandoned. I raced to the window and peered down. Dee's anxious face was visible in the foliage next door, and I saw the relief in her as she pointed me out to my brother, slumped next to her. Hadrea, whose nimble form was halfway back up the tree, gave me an anxious look, and I waved her back down. I was halfway out onto the sill before I remembered.

The cording.

I'd nearly forgotten. I sprinted over to the bed, my stomach turning over and over like washing sluiced in a pail, threatening to overwhelm me. I didn't want to touch him, but there was no way of unwinding the cord from his neck without it. *I'm sorry,* I thought, trying to avoid his dead, empty gaze. *Shit, shit, I'm so sorry, Tuhash.* The waxy feeling of his skin beneath my fingers as I unwound it was repulsive. *You deserved better than this from our country.* It was taking too long. *Move faster!* Fortunes, his face. I'd separated him from the Princess and a few hours later he was dead, a victim of a plot against a family he knew nothing about. I pushed the guilt back down, concentrated on the cord, and then it was free at last. The indignity of leaving him here, vulnerable and half-dressed, seemed a final cruelty. I was able to tug the sheet free and throw it over him, covering up to his shoulders. It wasn't much, but it was all I could do for him now.

INCIDENT: Poisoning of Sjemma "Meg" Iliri, Heir to Chancellor Jay Iliri

POISON: Bluehood

INCIDENT NOTES: On tour of Moncasta, the Heir's recurring long-term illness suddenly increased in severity. Two days later the Heir was urgently returned by boat to Silasta after displaying additional motor weakness, vomiting, and diarrhea. Physics in Silasta concluded that the local physic in Moncasta, possibly due to pressure of unexpectedly treating the Heir, accidentally administered treatment of bluehood instead of sunfinger tincture to ease symptoms, thus causing the additional damage. Heir made full recovery and incident was deemed accidental.

(from proofing notes of Credola Robynn Oromani)

7

Jovan

This time when I woke up and saw a figure by my bed, I did not assume it was a physic. Instead, I feigned sleep, and stole a hand to my waist to retrieve a weapon sooner rather than later. But there was nothing there. My chest was bare and my clothes, pouches and all, gone. That blow struck hard, but weapons or not, this time I wouldn't wait around to have more control ceded from me. I rolled hard to the opposite side of the bed and almost sent myself crashing out. Firm hands caught and steadied me.

"It's all right, Jov. You're safe." My sister's voice, it was definitely my sister's voice. My vision blurred and wobbled and then cleared.

"Lini," I said, and my eyes felt suddenly wet. "It's really you."

"It's really me." A smile in her voice even though her expression was serious. She took my hand and smoothed my hair back from my forehead. We were in my bedchamber, and the lamp was lit; it was not yet dawn. Also there, watchful and solemn, was the physic Thendra; I blinked a few times to make sure it was really her, this time. Hadrea hovered on the other side of the bed. She looked terrible, her hair matted and face smeared with the remnants of face paint. She was wearing a plain dress I recognized as Kalina's, and I caught a faint hint of woodsmoke as she shifted.

"Are you hurt?" I asked. Confused, messy memories of the last day tumbled back. "And Dija, where's Dija? Is she all right?"

Hadrea had a strange expression on her face as she perched awkwardly by the side of the pallet, but her voice was gentle. "I am not hurt. I was just inadequately dressed." She shot Thendra a look, then added, "And yes, Dee is fine. She is asleep now. She was frightened and worried half to death but none of them ever saw her. She has more stealth in her than you do, Jovan."

I managed a smile at the longstanding joke. "Wouldn't be hard."

"No." The silence following turned brittle; Hadrea and Kalina exchanged a look, but neither spoke.

Thendra handed me a cup of water, which I gratefully drank and only half-spilled. "You are asking about everyone else, Credo. It is for you that I have been dragged from my patients in the middle of the night."

Experimentally, I tried moving various body parts. My arms and hands felt fine, but moving my left ankle made me wince, and I could not take a deep breath without several sharp pains in my chest. I'd damaged ribs before, and had not particularly wanted to repeat the sensation. Thendra watched me wince and pulled away the bed coverings to examine my ankle. "It is swollen," she said. "But I do not think there is a broken bone. Now you are awake, I would recommend submerging your foot in a bucket of water, to keep it cool. The ribs—" She gestured to the bruising already visible on my skin. "—there is not so much I can do for you. There is a bruising poultice by the bed." She frowned. "I was also informed you had substances in your system, yes?"

"Yes." I felt embarrassed, as though I had done it on purpose; Thendra wore a rather schoolteachery judgment on her face that made me squirm. "I don't know what drugs they gave me, exactly. Something initially that knocked me out and left me a bit woozy—praconis leaf or Art's tonic, probably—then something that must have been a recreational drug they're using. It was in a compressed powder pill, and it was . . . disorienting. Mood altering. I couldn't think straight."

She looked at me with narrow eyes. "I will need you to be more specific."

"I saw things. Remembered things. I don't know if it was so much hallucinations as it was . . . just, everything around me suddenly seeming more sinister or threatening." Feeling foolish, I described the strange sensations, the spikes of fear and the blurring of reality and imagination, how the masks and costumes worn by my tormenters had transformed them into mythological monsters. It had been almost akin to the kind of runaway panic I could find myself in during an episode, when being aware of the irrationality of the root cause did not help me rein the emotions in. "I don't know why anyone would take that on purpose."

Thendra gave the weary sigh and shrug of a physic who had seen far too many inexplicable decisions by the citizens of this city to try to puzzle out motives.

"Then they gave me something else, it definitely had Art's tonic in it, but something else, too. I lost a good . . . hour? Several hours?" I looked hopelessly at Kalina and Hadrea, watching quietly on the other side of the bed. "Dija would know the timing better than me. I woke up much later with no memory of what happened in the interim. I . . . made myself sick when I got a chance, so I got some of it out of my system."

She must have followed us all the way to the house and through the terrible party. She must—oh, fortunes, she must have seen how they had left me, with the Talafan man. A child should not have had to see such a thing. I squeezed my eyes shut, wishing so hard that I could take it all back. I had been a fool, I had been careless. Following the assassin might have been a necessary move at the time, but once he entered that house I should never have gone in. I'd not only put myself at risk, and a fat lot of good I would be protecting Tain if I was dead on the floor of some abandoned warehouse, but I had risked Dija's safety, too. Proofing was not a job without risks, but they were supposed to be measurable, manageable risks. My little bit of foolishness had expanded on them into unacceptable territory, and from the undercurrent flowing dangerously between the women in the room, the topic would be discussed in the very near future.

"Thendra," Kalina said suddenly, in a tone rarely heard from her: openly authoritative. "Like I was trying to tell you earlier, what happened to Jov tonight is part of an attempt to discredit him. Over the next day or so he's very likely going to be accused of having voluntarily gone to these events and then . . ." She paused, swallowed, then continued. ". . . then hurting someone. Another man."

"They killed him," I said, hating how stark those words sounded out loud. I'd seen so many deaths, now. Deaths of people who didn't deserve it. Deaths of people I had loved. But never had someone died so pointlessly, so blamelessly, for the sole purpose of harming me. "I couldn't stop them." I couldn't look at Thendra. As a healer, what would she think of me?

"His body is going to come in, likely in the morning," my sister continued. "He was drugged and then strangled."

"I see." The physic had gone very still. "And where is this poor fellow now?"

"We couldn't get him out safely. He's still at a residence in the upper city, but I assume whoever set this in motion will have arranged for him to be found."

She propped one hand on her hip, and regarded the three of us grimly. "And what is it you wish me to do?"

Kalina hesitated, then said, "Nothing inappropriate. If asked, say you treated Jov for a turned ankle and bruising after he reported he was waylaid and attacked by thieves. That's true." She paused, visibly considering her next words. She had a particular look about her, a feverish air, that worried me; she was clearly thinking up a plan on the fly, but it was obvious she'd not slept, and it was taking its toll. "Just—if you could, if you were asked, not volunteer anything else you know. He didn't hurt that man," she added hastily, as Thendra raised a silent eyebrow, "and if they can't prove he was there, all they can do is make baseless accusations."

"The evidence is there on Credo Jovan's body, yes?" Thendra pointed out, her eyebrow still favoring us with her skepticism. "He *was* beaten. Why can you not tell the truth about the full extent of the attack?"

I shook my head, already seeing Kalina's strategy. Little bitter cuts opened up inside me. I could tell everyone what happened, and offer supporting evidence, and even a witness. But faced with the choice between my outlandish story, and the more dramatic and almost-plausible idea that a Credo had overindulged or experimented with some street drugs and ended up in some kind of terrible romantic encounter gone wrong, some, at least, would favor the latter. Having my own heir as a witness would hardly provide unbiased proof. No doubt there were witnesses who would attest they saw me at the party. Things were still a bit foggy but I remembered the sly comment the Wraith had made—*you weren't so stuck-up an hour ago*—and the man with the smile, pressed up against me, the woman with the rippling hair, catching the lamplight so enticingly, on the other side. Cup in my hand, the taste of food and drink on my tongue. I had not been unconscious that entire time, only unable to recall it.

"Reputation is everything on the Council," Hadrea said, before I could say anything, and there was a familiar and unwelcome twist to her lips as she watched me. "His will be damaged by the accusation, and any part in it he admits will lend credence to it."

"You don't have to lie for me," I said to the physic, determinedly avoiding looking at Hadrea, trying to ignore the stab of hurt at her words. "I wouldn't try to make you. It's just . . . you know me. You know I have enemies, both within the city and without. This was meant to ruin me."

"It'll be bad enough anyway," Kalina said, shaking her head. "The dead man was one of the Talafan Imperial soldiers."

Only when she said that aloud did I remember her saying it to me, in that hazy fog of the rescue. My heart plummeted all over again. This hadn't *just* been a setup for me. It had also created a diplomatic incident. How would the Imperial delegation react when one of their own men was pulled out of that house?

Thendra looked at us all in turn. "And your young niece, she saw someone else murder this man?"

"No, thank the fortunes," Kalina said. "She was hiding. She didn't have to see . . . that."

But I thought I understood why Thendra had asked it; not out of concern for Dija's composure, having witnessed a murder, but because she was determining whether there was a true witness.

She clucked her tongue and began to pack up her things. "I have heard many disturbing things about what people are capable of under the influence of these evil narcotics," she said. "But I do not wish to believe you would strangle a man even in those circumstances, Credo Jovan."

"Don't wish to, or don't?" Kalina pressed her. She had subtly repositioned herself to be between Thendra and the door; the physic's eyes darted momentarily to the exit and then, resigned, back to my sister. She didn't say anything, and by the fortunes, that hurt, too. We weren't close personal friends, so I had no right to her unconditional loyalty, but even so. She had known me for years, known my absolute loyalty to the Chancellor and the country. She must know I was no killer.

"The man who strangled him," I said quietly, staring down at my own hands. "He had enormous hands. Far bigger than mine. Is there a way to tell, on the body . . . would that make a difference?"

She looked back at me over her shoulder, one hand fussing with the case of potions and bandages she carried. "I will look closely at any body that comes in," she said.

"Thank you," Kalina said, letting her pass.

When Thendra had safely left the apartments, Hadrea settled herself down cross-legged at the end of my bed. "She will not cover for you," she observed. "If she is not satisfied you could not have killed that man."

Kalina's lips were very tight. "Thendra's known our family her whole career. She's never let on, but I think she knows what we do. We've always trusted her, that's why she was the only one I'd have let come here tonight. But I wonder, now." She bit her lip, looking thoughtful. "I wonder whether that stupid rumor . . ."

"More poisoner than proofer." The play that kept on giving.

"I guess we can't blame her. There is a certain element of . . . violence, about our family." She gazed into the middle distance, assessing, wearing a strange expression I didn't recognize. What was she thinking about? "You should get some more rest, Jov. We need you to be coherent tomorrow if someone comes knocking."

Someone came knocking just after dawn. I was already awake, remembering fragments of the evening in all their humiliating glory, but unwilling to get out of bed and face it all. I heard Sjease's smooth tones, the sounds of other voices. Guards? Despite everything, a coil of fear was building in my stomach. I should have found Tain last night, at least left him a message. Would he find out after the fact that his best friend, his closest adviser, the person supposed to protect him, had been dragged out of bed and arrested?

But it was Sjease who came first to my door. "You have guests," they said quietly, not bothering to pretend they thought I was asleep.

"You sound far too chipper for someone on the morning after the masquerade," I muttered, trying for a smile. *They wouldn't haul me anywhere. I wasn't there, no one can prove I was there.* "Didn't I say you weren't to work today?"

Sjease crossed to my bedside. They were dressed in a bright robe and their skin and eyes looked clear. The only sign of the late night our house manager must have had was the faintest trace of gold paint still speckling their cheekbones and chin. If anything, that seemed like an arrestable offense. They handed me a warmed cup, which I sniffed carefully. Ginger, and the color suggested milkwort. "That should soothe your stomach."

I realized they must think I had overindulged at karodee, but I felt grateful all the same. I was partway through a sip when they added, quietly, "The Captain of the Order Guards is here to see you. I've left her outside, for now. Your sister is sleeping and looks unwell, so I didn't want to wake her. Credo . . . I saw the physic come in late in the night." My gaze was drawn up, almost involuntarily, to meet theirs. Sjease's eyes were arresting, a layered dark brown that always appeared to be seeing right into me. Their gaze now was sympathetic, but very knowing, and left me feeling uncomfortably scrutinized, not knowing quite what to say.

"Yes," I said slowly, trying to think and finding my head frustratingly thick. I wanted Kalina here, always quick with a convincing story.

But Sjease spoke before I could make up some explanation. "Do you remember what I told you when you hired me?"

My lips twitched into an involuntary smile. Etan, Lini, and I had always managed on our own, even when we had to deal with my mother's occasional visits leaving the household scattered like the aftermath of the Maiso. But after the siege, after Dija moved in, we needed a third adult to be in the apartments, as Kalina and I were often required to attend the same nighttime functions. And I had needed a secretary to stop me failing at managing the laborious burdens of being a Councilor during a period of dramatic change for the country. I remembered very well interviewing Sjease for the first time—Al-Sjease, as we called them then, the formal Darfri address for a person who was neither male nor female. They had worked in Telasa in the north, and on some of both our family's and Tain's lands farther west, and had been the first candidate to make Dija laugh. And I remembered what they'd said that had sealed the decision. I'd told them our family's needs were perhaps a bit peculiar; unlike many other Credol Families our apartments housed just me, Kalina, and Dija, with occasional disruptive visits from our mother, Lailana.

"We like to cook, so we'd keep doing most of the food preparation ourselves," I'd said. "We're very tidy—"

"Credola Lailana isn't," Dija had said. "She needs tidying after."

"—and so we would just really be looking for someone who can help us with ordinary household cleaning and administrative tasks, responding to routine invitations and such, managing our schedule. It would be a live-in position, because one of the things I'd need would be someone to be home to supervise Dija when my sister and I have to go out at night."

"I don't really need any supervising," Dee had interjected.

"Does that sound like the sort of job you'd be interested in?"

"Yes, Credo. You can see from my background I've done work as a clerk, too, and I cared for children at several of my placings." I remembered being skewered on the end of their rather thorough gaze. "If you don't mind me saying, I heard a bit about your family from servants who've worked for the Chancellor, and I think we might be a good fit. I gather you like your space and your privacy and I'm very quiet and *spectacularly* un-nosy about things that aren't my business." Al-Sjease paused, then added, "I should say though, I'm an excellent cook, you're missing out if you ban me from the kitchen."

The memory made me smile. Sjease was a perceptive and insightful person, but they had not exaggerated; if they were curious about the strange activities our family indulged in, they hid it so thoroughly it was impossible to tell from the outside.

"I said I knew a bit about your family," Sjease said. "And I had a sense, even then, what kind of people I was joining in with, so to speak." They looked me over. "Overindulging in something isn't what I'd call in character for you, Credo."

I sipped the milkwort beverage gratefully and returned Sjease's gaze with bleary eyes. Suddenly, perhaps recklessly, I realized I did trust them. For all our careful rules we'd established, and however well they'd played along with them, over the course of the last few years they'd become a member of the household in their own right, and I wouldn't lie and pretend we were dealing with a bit of karodee foolishness. "No. You're right. That wasn't me overindulging."

"Is everything all right?"

I took a breath. The man, kicking feebly, his pleasurable oblivion turning to panic and fear before the end. "No. Not really." The steam from the cup made a misty, warm coating on my face. Honor-down, my head hurt, but at least I could think. I had to stay calm, had to get through whatever interrogation I was about to suffer, and get this new information to Tain as quickly as possible. I took a calming breath, trying to silence the clamor of increasingly awful scenarios vying for attention in my head. "Sjease. Do you trust me?"

Sjease cocked their head to one side. With their habitual carefully organized locks spilling from the central topknot, wound with a variety of beads and ribbons, and the remnants of gold paint giving their angular face a gleaming edge, there was something almost alien about the look. "I've lived with you and yours for two years now, Credo. I'd say if I was still here and I didn't, the problem'd be with me."

Some of the tension in my fists released. "There was some trouble last night. I followed someone and ended up in the middle of something I shouldn't have. Kalina and Hadrea got me out, but I don't know if we did enough. People are going to ask questions."

A pause as they considered this. "Well, then. You know sticking my nose in isn't my style, so I'll just ask you this: Is there something I can help with? What can I get you that's going to help you manage this?"

I couldn't stop Dija and Kalina from being involved, but at least I could insulate the others, stop them having to lie for me if at all possible. "I don't want anyone involved who doesn't have to be, I don't think. Can you keep Etrika and Ana and the boys from coming out to talk to the Guards?"

They must have noticed who I left out; a tiny flinch, barely registered, passed over their features. Sjease was very protective of our youngest family member; they'd grown close, and perhaps the fiction of incuriosity about our affairs did not extend to indifference to dangers to which Dija might be subject. "I can. Anything else?"

I grimaced. "A new head?"

"All out of those at the market last I was there, but I do have some very refreshing finger-limes, fancy one of those?"

"Sjease, could you just be fractionally less cheerful?" I muttered, rubbing my pounding forehead.

"Yes, sir, somber it is." They gave me an appropriately serious look. "How much time do you need for the Order Guards?"

"I'll be out before you make the tea. Just—delay them a little, all right?"

They left the room and I struggled to dress myself without aggravating my injuries. The cold bucket last night hadn't been pleasant but it seemed to have improved the ankle a little—I could walk on it, at least—but moving my arms enough to pull on a tunic and paluma set off a range of fresh pains in my chest and ribs. I heard Sjease's voice at the external door, and Chen's crisp tones in reply, then the door shut again.

I creaked myself out of my room; Sjease stood looking between me and the door in turn, an unreadable expression on their face. Dija was emerging from her room, wrapped in a robe and her small face determined. There was no sign of Kalina, but perhaps she would sleep through this—last night would have cost her dearly in energy.

"Are you all right? Are you ill?" I hastened over but Dija only nodded impatiently. She had a sick pan in one hand and she smelled like she'd just thrown up. She set it down beside her and grabbed one of my hands.

"Sjease, was that the door? Would you mind getting it? I'm feeling unwell and Uncle Jov is too sore to get up." Her voice was firm, and she looked at me with eyes entirely too knowing. "Trust me, please, Uncle," she added quietly. Her gaze flashed to the kitchen, to the entrance to our hidden workroom.

Sjease looked at me, unsure, and though my heart felt like it was in my throat, I closed my mouth and nodded.

Chen and two other Order Guards had come. The Captain led the way, moving a little stiffly on her artificial leg. "Morning, Credo Jovan," she said, nodding pleasantly enough, but instead of her usual welcoming grin, her face was closed and grim. The two men behind her likewise gave nothing away, following wordlessly. "Young Credola," she added to Dija, the overly jovial way she delivered it obviously designed to mask that she'd forgotten my apprentice's name. Dija gave her a wan smile.

"Hello, Captain," she said, in an entirely different voice than the one she'd used on Sjease a moment ago. She sounded young and her voice slightly croaky as if speaking hurt her. I resolutely did not look at the kitchen. What had she done?

"Good morning, Captain," I said calmly, as she approached. "Won't you sit down? Is that leg all right?"

Chen sighed and took the seat Sjease offered her and the cup of tea apparently summoned from nowhere; another of Sjease's invaluable skills. Her back was stiff, her gaze uncertain; she seemed reluctant to begin. She rubbed the lower part of her thigh, where her false leg began. "Been a long night, as you can imagine, Credo. I'm not as good on my feet as I used to be. Wears you down after a while."

"Yes, I'm sure it does." Chen had lost the lower part of one leg in the final battle during the siege. Likely she didn't patrol much, now she sat at the top of the ranks at the Order Guards, but karodee was stretching her resources as it was, let alone the additional frivolities they'd have had to cover last night. "I don't want to extend what must have already been a very long night for all of you." I set my cup down. "You must have important news to bring it in person."

"Not news, as such." She cleared her throat awkwardly. "Perhaps the young one ought to . . . ?"

I started to agree, but Dija frowned. "To leave? But Captain, you'll need me to help explain what happened, won't you? Uncle Jov got hit in the head so he didn't see everything."

"Hit in the—what?" Chen was staring, perplexed, at Dija, which was fortunate or she might have seen my expression. I tried to catch Dija's attention to shut down the story, reaching for her under the table, but she was already speaking again.

"You're here about the muggers, aren't you? I thought Auntie Kalina or the physic might call on you." She glanced at me, looking anxious. "Uncle Jov didn't want to bother you but just because they got scared off before stealing anything doesn't mean we shouldn't report it, right, Captain? Maybe you'll catch them? There were two men and a woman, but they were wearing masks."

Chen finally looked at me, her face a comedy of confusion, but I kept my face as smooth as I could, and she turned back to Dija. "I'm sorry, Credola . . ."

"Dija."

"Credola Dija, but I'm not—"

"You're not going to catch them? Don't worry, I'm not a baby, I know it's hard to catch criminals. These ones were in costumes so I really couldn't see that much. But I could tell you how tall they were, and what their masks looked like. Maybe someone else saw them."

Chen looked helplessly at me. "I think," she said at last, "you'd better start from the start. If you're able to, Credola Dija. Are you well? Do you need a cup of water?"

Dija had one, gulping it down and then seeming to regret it, squeezing her mouth and eyes shut and holding her stomach. "Sorry, Uncle, I know I promised to get some rest, but since the Captain's here—" She broke off and gulped, her eyes closing. Smooth as if they'd rehearsed it, Sjease grabbed the pan and brought it swiftly to her in time for her to be noisily sick. The two Guards took abrupt steps backward and Chen's face was a rictus of attempted politeness as her hands pressed down on the table, as if she were physically restraining the impulse to push away. Dija accepted a cloth from Sjease and wiped her face, looking shaky. "Please forgive me, Captain."

Chen nodded, but seemed unsure what to say. I knew how she felt; I had no idea where Dija was going with this story, but she'd asked me to trust her and it was too late to stop her now.

"Uncle Jov thought at first I'd just had too many sweets," Dija said, glancing over at me. "But we think now it was probably some bad meat, or I wouldn't have been up all night sick."

"Up all night sick, you say?" Chen glanced back at her companions and her fingers stilled on her cup of tea.

"After we got home." She wiped her face again, as though this was taxing her, then straightened up. "Uncle Jov was supposed to take me home after the Darfri ceremony but I . . ." She looked down at her hands, as if embarrassed, starting to mumble rather than speak clearly. "I didn't want to go home. This is my first karodee in the city, I missed out last year, and I begged him to let me stay out, not to the party at the lake, I know I'm too young for that, but there are other things on, plays and music and stuff."

Not wanting to come across as a mere spectator in this apparent alibi for my evening, I thought it safe to say, "She wore me down."

"You're a bit of a soft touch, are you, Credo?" Chen gave me a half grin. "Should have known it." She was starting to look visibly relieved. "So you went . . . where?"

"Some of the kids were playing rushuk ball in the arena, so we got honey sticks and watched for a bit, then when it got dark we went and did the candle walk at the sculpture garden. It was lovely, have you seen it? They light up all the statues and things and they look so different with the shadows and light, like they're all alive." She smiled at Chen, so utterly convincing in her dreamy recollection of a trip we had not taken that I was almost as alarmed as impressed. Then the smile dropped, her face crumpling. "It was after that it happened. I think most people were down at the party, it was quiet, and I didn't want to go home yet, so I kept suggesting other things I wanted to see, and I was quarreling a bit. . . ." She stopped, sniffed, wiped her eyes behind her glasses as if trying to force tears away. "We didn't hear them, they just came out of nowhere."

"Who?"

She blinked. "The people who attacked Uncle Jov, of course. They tried to rob him. Isn't . . . isn't that why you're here, Captain? I thought someone must have called you. He wouldn't go to the hospital, he said it would be too busy, but I know it was because he wanted to get me straight home."

"I should never have had you out so late," I said quietly. "I put you in danger. You could have been . . ." My turn to trail off. Unlike my apprentice, I wasn't lying.

"We found Hadrea and she helped get him home, and then Auntie Kalina got one of the physics from the hospital to come and make sure he was all right."

"I'm all right," I added, when Chen cast a concerned gaze over me, perhaps noticing my stiff posture for the first time. "Bit of a blow to the head, a lot of bruised ribs. One of them stomped on my ankle, but Thendra didn't think it was broken and it's moving all right today." I ran a hand through my hair, thinking fast. Honor-down, but Dija's story had been good. She'd managed to provide an alibi, explain my injuries, and give a timeline that did not require Thendra to lie about her treatment.

"They kicked him a lot. I couldn't do anything," Dija said in a small voice, and this time I knew she too was speaking with full honesty. It must have been traumatic, watching through that crack in the door and not knowing if I would make it out alive. That only made me feel guiltier. And here I was, involving her in deception against the Order Guards. And not just anyone, but Chen, who I'd personally suggested and recommended for Captain of the Order Guards based on her work in the Oromani quarter during the siege. She was a friend, or at least something like a friend, and lying to her wasn't something I was enjoying.

"I wasn't going to bother reporting it, to be honest," I said to her now. "You've got enough on during karodee and with everything else. We've got no way of identifying who attacked us. They were wearing masks, like Dija said."

Chen nodded vaguely, but she was looking back at her companions again, openly relieved. "So you two were together during the evening, got attacked, and then went home. With An-Hadrea and Credola Kalina, did you say?" When we both nodded, she went on, "And then . . . you stayed here for the rest of the night?"

"Well, the physic came," I said. "Thendra, from the hospital, you know. She patched me up and treated the ankle, but didn't think it was worth going to the hospital."

"And then I started throwing up," Dija interjected ruefully, "and ruined the *rest* of his sleep."

"You'll have to excuse us," I murmured. "I imagine we look a bit disheveled. Neither of us had much sleep."

Chen set her cup down, positively cheerful. "Well. I'm very sorry to hear you were hurt, Credo Jovan. About that other matter—you might not be able to help me, though."

I tried a casual shrug, as if it were neither here nor there, and smiled politely. "Sorry, what was the other matter?"

"There was an incident last night—we got a report you were there."

Sjease gave a small chuckle. "Forgive me, Captain, but unless the incident involved the inside of a sick pan, my employer is unlikely to be much help."

Sjease too! Why was everyone in my household such a terrifyingly smooth liar? I turned to my apprentice. "You go back to bed, Dija. You really shouldn't have got up, I could have explained to the Captain. Being up is taxing you. Sjease, could you assist, make sure she has water?"

I waited until they were out of the room before looking frankly at Chen. "What incident? What's up?"

She looked troubled again, but her expression was no longer the closed, stiff face of a person facing a dreaded task. "Bit of an unpleasant death, actually. A strangling. Woman claimed she'd seen you, uh, socializing with the chap who died, and that you left together. Seemed pretty confident it was you." She stared uncomfortably at her empty cup. I refilled it wordlessly, not bothering to hide my wince of pain at the movement, and she nodded a thanks. "Didn't put much stock in it, myself, but people know we're acquainted, I didn't want to be seen to . . . you know. Ignore information."

I met her eyes as I set down the teapot again. "Well, I promise you I haven't strangled anyone, Chen."

"I never thought you—" She broke off, gave me a shamefaced grin, and took a noisy sip of tea, then sighed. "Anyway. Someone's been wasting our time, lads. Sorry, Credo."

"Not a problem." I pushed myself to my feet, not having to feign difficulty. "But I'd quite like to know more about this party I was supposed to be at. Funny, I don't remember any invitations."

Chen grinned again. "Me neither. Some secretive thing, for the very rich, I got the impression." Her face turned grim. "There's no one in the house now, but it was in the upper city, an expensive place. I've heard a bit about these sorts of parties before, and let's just say I'm not overly surprised someone's ended up dead."

From what I'd seen, I privately agreed. "And the woman who said she saw me. Who was she? Was she just mistaken, or is someone trying to cause trouble?"

"She wouldn't leave her name. Said there were a lot of powerful people at that party and she was afraid of the Credol Families and repercussions." Chen shot me another embarrassed look. "I'll look into it some more."

"Please do," I said sincerely. I dropped my voice. "I'm not the most popular member of the Council, Chen. If someone's falsely accusing me of murder on the same night I'm attacked by some supposedly random thugs, I can't help but wonder if there's a connection."

She slapped my shoulder. "I'll find out."

As she was about to leave, halfway through the threshold, she stopped, turned back to me, and said thoughtfully, "You said masks. Just out of curiosity. What masks were they wearing?"

"Oh." I tried to look lighthearted, as though I hadn't found them alarming. "The woman had a wraith mask and the men were whisperers, you know, with the blank faces and the slits, like in a play. They were probably looking to blend in with the masquerade crowd. Why? Does that mean something to you?"

She hesitated. Then, almost reluctantly, she nodded. "I've heard the Hands wear masks sometimes, is all."

"The Hands?"

"The Prince's Hands." She said it with a snort. "One of the gangs, fancies 'ruling' the lower city, I guess that's why they call themselves that. Anyway, it's hard to get anyone to talk about the leaders but we've had one or two reports that they wear masks like that. This is the first time I've heard of them messing with the Credolen, though."

"They're the ones selling the narcotics, right?" I said slowly. "That new drug, what's it called?" They'd been talking about distributing it when I'd first overheard them. And I remembered something else, fuzzy at the edges: the woman's voice, laughing at me in the crowd. *First time on Void.*

Chen blew out her lips. "Void. Yes. I keep telling the Council, if you don't mind me saying, Credo, I keep telling them we need to be on top of the drugs because it's where the money's coming from, but they seem to think it's a bit of harmless fun. When we've had businesses vandalized and owners attacked, too scared to say who's responsible. I reckon the Hands've got a hold over a good portion of the lower city now, but I don't have the resources to . . ." She trailed off, shook her head again. The men behind her exchanged a glance suggesting they'd heard the spiel a number of times. "You know this, Credo. I don't likely forget you're an ally on that Council and I know you've been supporting me there."

"And I'll keep at it. Karodee's been a big distraction. Hopefully after that we'll be able to convince them it needs attention." Already my brain was racing. What connection did an increasingly powerful street gang have to the potential assassination of the Chancellor? Chance couldn't have led the assassin to that particular house at that particular time; he'd taken me there on purpose, and they'd known who I was and put me in that position. What did the

Hands have to do with me, or Tain? It was a big step up from intimidating businesses and selling drugs to assassinating Councilors. Unless the Hands hired out assassins to third parties . . .

"Mm." She didn't sound hopeful. She rubbed her leg, then straightened and shook out her shoulders. "Anyway, sorry to trouble you so early. Should have known it was a mistake, or someone looking to cause trouble. Between this and the fire, it's been a hell of a night."

"The fire?"

She sighed heavily. "Oh, one of the Ash boats sank last night, there was a fire and it looks deliberate. No one was aboard and no one was injured, but I've had half the bloody Ash family down in the Guardhouse, shouting about sabotage. The way they're talking, that boat was the most expensive bit of real estate in the city." She shook her head. "Not the worst thing that's ever happened during karodee, but a bloody hassle for us, gotta get the harbor-master involved, and the Ashes are going to want someone to blame. Like I said, it's been a hell of a night."

Nothing, I reflected to myself after Chen and the others had left with more apologies, *I said was untrue, strictly.* Which was more than I could say for the other members of my household. I stalked into Dija's room and perched on the edge of her bed.

"You poisoned yourself?" I asked grimly.

She was propped up, looking genuinely ill, but her jaw was set and her sweet round face was as stubborn as I'd ever seen it. "I heard Auntie Kalina and Hadrea talking last night about what could happen. You were in trouble."

"I—" Of all the things I had involved her in, this seemed somehow the worst. Mistake compounding on mistake. I dropped my head into my hands. "Honor-down, Dija. Yes, I was in trouble. But I don't want *you* to be in any. Not for my sake."

"How am I supposed to protect the Chancellor without you?" she asked. She reminded me suddenly and intensely both of my uncle and my sister, with their gentle exteriors and their solid cores, and I felt very tired and very old, and an utter failure at everything that mattered. I was alive only because an enemy had apparently decided to target my reputation instead of my life, and I was doing shit-all to protect the people for whom I was responsible. Dija was trying so hard, seeking my approval, and this was all wrong, I was using this intelligent, good-natured little soul for things she should never have had to be involved in.

We are who we are. I'd thought it before, and what a cold bloody thing that was.

When I checked in on Kalina she was sleeping deeply but, as was often the case with illness-induced exhaustion, it did not look like a restful slumber. Deep lines divided her eyes and her mouth looked pinched. I smoothed unruly curls off her face and hovered there, watching and worrying. It didn't count if she didn't catch me doing it.

"Credo?"

Sjease was behind me at the door. I turned wearily and followed them out. "It's Jovan, please. I think once you've given false witness for someone you're past the point of titles."

A pause. Sjease's eyes were sharp and serious. What they'd heard Chen describe had unsettled them. But instead of questioning me further, they simply said, "Your other family members will wake soon. What do you want them to be told?"

"They don't need to know about Chen coming unless they ask," I said quickly. "I'll have to apologize for keeping Dija out so late."

"To go to the sculpture walk, and eat honey sticks," Sjease repeated neutrally.

"I—yes."

"She's very persuasive. I don't blame you."

"They'll be upset about what happened. The attack." An understatement. Ana in particular had a way of looking at me with her eyes lowered slightly, as if my chin had offended her, which conveyed her disapproval of her daughter's new lifestyle. And how could I blame her? There had always been risks, sending Dija here to be my heir. But I was sure those risks had sounded a lot more abstract when they had made the decision.

"I'm sure." Another long pause. "Look. Cre—Jovan. I've worked for people before who demanded loyalty and didn't deserve it. I think you're the other type, but I want you to tell me now if I'm wrong."

"You're not wrong, Sjease," Dija called out fiercely. "He's a good person." Her loyalty hurt like fire in my chest. What had I ever done to earn it?

"I'm not going to pretend the explanation we gave was true," I said to Sjease flatly. "Or that it's not my fault, in a roundabout way at least, that a man is dead. I have to live with that. Our family has enemies, and sometimes it can be dangerous being around us. But I didn't strangle anyone."

They gave me a weak smile. "Never doubted that for a moment."

"I can't promise more trouble won't follow this," I said. "What we told them now should get us through today, especially if Thendra backs it up. But if the only witness able to say I wasn't at that party is my own heir, a thirteen-year-old girl, they're not going to give up that easily. Who's to say I came back here with Dija? My sister, my lover, my employee? Hardly impartial witnesses." I shook my head. "This could get ugly, Sjease. I wish neither of you were mixed up in it." I found myself irrationally angry, not with Sjease, but with myself. Once again, control was slipping from my grip, and I was afraid, so very afraid, I was going to let everyone down yet again.

INCIDENT: Poisoning of Credola Kathrin Ash

POISON: Bitterseed

INCIDENT NOTES: Well-known costumer and seamster, victim had complained to family members of shortness of breath, repeated headaches, and dizziness. Eventually suffered seizure and died. Rumors suggested involvement of one of a number of rivals in Craft Guild. This proofer undertook private investigation and found evidence that insides of C. Kathrin's gloves and at least one collared dress contained traces of bitterseed. Anonymous information left with Order Guards. Suggest continued observation of C. Rowenna Reed (seamstress and hatter) and Il-Obro esIana (costumer) as likely suspects.

(from proofing notes of Credola Ettenna Oromani)

8

Kalina

The day following masquerade was always a subdued one. It functioned as a recovery day, particularly for athletes and performers who still had events on before the close, and there were few official functions. No doubt the story of what had happened to the Talafan guard was being shared, but today it would be a trickle rather than a flood. Tomorrow might be a different story.

Ana and Etrika accepted the explanation for our delay and the "mugging," Ana thin-lipped as Jov apologized for her daughter's proximity to danger. Dija, whose illness had cleared up with the judicious consumption of a counteragent but who was confined to bed for the day to maintain the image, emphasized how he had prioritized getting her home safe before even having his injuries seen to. Clearly, though, this mess had cost Jov any little ground he might have gained with her mother over the course of the stay.

The boys, on the other hand, seemed to think the entire thing sounded exciting and were only annoyed their little sister had been out later than they'd been allowed. Etrika, too, had been unconcerned. "There are thieves in Telasa, too, darling," she'd pointed out mildly. "An unfortunate tax on city life, isn't it?"

"Yes, I suppose." Ana had returned to her book, signaling an end to the conversation, but her eyes hadn't moved on the page. I did understand, and sympathize; our story was preferable to the truth, but it still made Jov seem a naive, undisciplined guardian.

By the time Tain arrived, as discreetly as possible, Sjease was playing muse with Dija in her chambers, and Ana and the boys had gone to visit some of the other families who had come from Telasa for karodee. At the sight of the

Chancellor, Etrika too excused herself to meet up with a friend. I made the tea while Jov relayed the whole sorry story in all the detail he could remember, halting and visibly ashamed.

Tain had a plate of harpea dip and black bread on his lap, and while the bread was occasionally venturing into the paste and around the plate as he listened, it rarely made it anywhere near his mouth.

"You have to eat," I reminded him. Usually I left the nagging to Jov, but he was distracted and, honor-down, Tain looked thin. Obligingly, he ate a piece of now slightly sodden bread, chewing without enthusiasm.

"I've fucked up," Jov finished baldly. "I've gotten someone killed and we're in a lot more trouble than we thought."

Tain raked his hands through his hair. "But you're sure you're all right?"

"Sore. Sorry for myself." Jovan shrugged. "Battered and bruised but no permanent damage."

"And you, Lini?" Tain's sharp gaze took in my hands, shaking as I poured the tea, and he took the pot from me wordlessly. I appreciated it. Frustratingly I'd been unable to summon the energy to get much farther than from my bed to the main apartment, and the effort of maintaining a conversation, let alone an important one, was wearing on me. A lifetime of this cursed illness had taught me that when my energy was depleted, no level of willpower could increase it, and trying only made things worse. "Leaving me out of your adventures again," he chided me, and I laughed.

"You do get in the way, you know."

"Always." For a second his smile made him look his old self. Then it dropped away and his face once again looked drained, wrung out like a juiced fruit.

"Are *you* all right?" I asked. "Nothing happened to you last night?"

"No, no, I'm fine." He waved a hand impatiently. "Other than worrying myself sick about why you didn't turn up, Jov. The one bloody night of the year it's impossible to find anyone."

"Sorry."

That elicited a faint grin. "Yeah, that's right, idiot," he said fondly. "Time your elaborate beatings and kidnappings so as not to upset me, next time."

Jov squeezed his shoulder and sighed. "So Chen didn't bring any of this direct to you? I've been in here just waiting for someone else to come knocking."

"She sent the Guards' report of the night, but I haven't gone through it yet. I assume it's in that."

"They mustn't have identified the body yet," I said thoughtfully. "I mean it's obvious he's Talafan, but if they knew he was with the Imperial party then Chen wouldn't just be reporting it as an ordinary crime. It'll be a whole diplomatic incident."

"He wasn't wearing a uniform," my brother mumbled. "When they brought him in. He was dressed like a Silastian." He narrowed his eyes at Tain. "Finish your meal."

Tain sighed and tore off another small piece of bread.

"He wouldn't have wanted to look like an Imperial soldier," I said quietly. "I didn't get a chance to say last night, but there's a complication. The reason I knew who he was is that I caught him with the Princess at the masquerade."

"With the Princess? Zhafi, you mean, the yellow-haired one?"

"Yes, and I mean *with* the Princess."

Tain blinked. "Fuck."

"Unfortunately, yes. Exactly." I scratched my hand through my hair, feeling it stand up higher. "People were giving out dosed karodee cakes, and he was eating one when I saw him. He might have been an easy target, not knowing anyone or the language but being high and heartbroken." I swallowed. "I can take some blame for it, too. If I hadn't meddled, the women wouldn't have been allowed to get dressed up and watch the masquerade, which is how Zhafi got away from the guesthouse without raising an alarm."

We looked at each other glumly. Bad enough anyone had died, but it felt like the fortunes were actively conspiring against us here. "Maybe they knew who he was?" Jov said at last. "Honor-down, what are the chances of them pulling someone off the street who was sleeping with the Emperor's daughter? Of all the people to have gotten caught up in this mess!"

I hesitated. "Presumably the Princess is going to worry when he doesn't show back up at the guesthouse, but she's not exactly going to run to her brother. She's not supposed to have a lover."

"She's not married, is she?" Tain looked curious. "Astor went on about her a fair bit when he found out she was coming. I thought he rather fancied her, actually."

That was an understatement of our former Ambassador's extensive and effusive praise for the Princess. He was a pompous type, the kind who loved ceremony and the sound of his own voice, and he seemed determined both to resent me for taking the position and to impress upon me the full extent of his knowledge and expertise. "No, she's not married. I suspect the Emperor, or Hiukipi, whoever's running things, has plans to marry her off to their puppet

ruler in the new province. She intimated as much to me yesterday. This might
have been one last-ditch play for freedom."

"You liked her." Tain regarded me with his head cocked to one side,
thoughtful. "I saw that yesterday. She must have made an impression."

"I did like her." I stared at my hands. "Honor-down, I felt sorry for her,
too. And now . . . she's going to find out he's dead and not even be allowed to
be seen to grieve."

We all fell into silence. I stood up and returned the pot to the kitchen
along with the rest of Tain's abandoned food. When I came back, Jov was
fidgeting, moving his empty cup from one hand to the other and back again.
"I've been thinking," he said quietly. "This morning. About what happened,
and about our assassin. What if I've been looking at this wrong? What if the
assassin wasn't at those events to kill you, Tain? What if *I'm* the target?"

I blinked. "Well, then I'd say he's not a very good assassin, Jov."

"Not to kill me." The cup was still moving back and forth, back and forth.
"He could have killed me yesterday if he'd wanted. Instead he led me to these
Prince's Hands, and *they* could have killed me, but instead they staged this
elaborate mess. Why? I'd never even heard their name until today."

"They're criminals. They could have been paid to discredit you, I suppose?" Tain frowned. "There's plenty of people who'd like your family to be
a bit less well respected and powerful."

"What about the theater?" I said. "Your assassin was up in the rafters with
poison darts, he wasn't there to start rumors."

"I thought he was aiming at Tain, and I assumed killing Bradomir was an
accident, but what if it wasn't?" He set the cup down with visible effort. "Karista
looked like she blamed me at the time. Even though the Lekas called it heart
failure, I wouldn't be surprised if she's been telling people otherwise in private."

"So this was meant to stir up trouble between your family and the Lekas?"

I took a seat again; my legs were weak and I was suddenly unsure of my
footing. "Bradomir hated us, but *especially* you. And everyone knew it. When
he was forced to resign his Council seat to Sjistevo, remember that speech he
gave?" Bradomir had stood outside the Manor gates, fueled by the rage of a
once-powerful man forced from what he considered his rightful place, and
delivered a scathing indictment of the "shadowy figures" who he claimed had
spread lies about his family and holdings for their own benefit. I doubted our
family had a more publicly known enemy.

Jov labored to his feet and hobbled into his own chambers without speaking. Tain and I glanced at each other, but when it became clear he wouldn't be returning, we followed. My brother was at his desk, pen in hand, papers full of his neat handwriting and diagrams spread before him. He tapped his pen under a line of text and looked up, his eyes burning with excitement. "This here. This was the first time I remember seeing him at an event. It was the opening of the arena, remember? Then this is every other time, and everyone I can remember being there. I kept wondering how he knew we were going to be at all of these places because at least two"—here he tapped another two entries—"were times we weren't at or on our way to a scheduled event. I'd been trying to work out *why* he'd chosen those times and places, or if he was just watching you all the time and I only occasionally noticed."

"So now, let's look in a different way," I murmured. "Imagine Tain wasn't the target. Did anything else happen, anything affecting *you*, at any of these events?"

We studied the list. It was a confusing, apparently patternless set of data, a combination of public events and ordinary political business. No murders. But Tain pointed to one entry.

"What about this one?"

"The Paractus retirement party?" Jov said. "Nothing happened there. I proofed the meal, it was fine."

The Paractuses were a wealthy merchant family, well connected, but I hadn't been at the party. I raised an eyebrow and he elaborated. "Ruzo Paractus was retiring as head of the family business. He made a party of it, said some rude things about his competitors, then at the end of the night shocked everyone by naming his nephew instead of his niece as the new head. Should have been in the Performers' Guild, really. But no one died."

"Ruzo's niece made a total idiot of herself, remember? Got drunk, insulted her mother, claimed they stole the design for that water-resistant fabric from the Stones . . ."

Jov nodded, smiling faintly. "Yeah, but that wasn't suspicious, was it? She was drunk because she was pissed off her Tashi picked her brother to take over the business. She drank too much and ran her mouth off."

"And you were pleased," Tain said.

"Yeah," Jov agreed, "and so were you, because Kasha Paractus is a giant asshole."

But I was remembering the other reason the Paractus family name was familiar. They'd been in dispute with our family over irrigation contracts.

"Kasha was threatening to take us to the determination council," I said. "And then it all went away because Rikto didn't care and just canceled the contract and paid the fees."

"If Kasha had been declared heir, like everyone expected, she wouldn't have let that contract go," Tain said. "But I'm not sure what an assassin could have done to cause it."

"Kasha didn't come in drunk," Jov acknowledged a little gruffly. "She said something to me on the way in, I remember, and she was her usual self—rude and smug. It was only after she lost control and embarrassed Ruzo that he announced Rikto instead. What if someone was dosing her drinks?"

Working the list, we were able to find three more incidents that had affected the health or reputation of someone that had ultimately been to our family's benefit, and one that had been to Tain's. "It's almost like this guy is trying to . . . *help* our families," Tain said in frustration. "Until last night at least."

I noticed one last entry that jogged a memory. "This one," I said slowly.

Jov squinted. It had been an exhibition by a promising young painter using a new technique. "We went because the artist was at school with us."

"I remember her work," Tain commented. "But we didn't stay long; Jov saw the man in the crowd and made us go out the back early. And you weren't there, Lini, were you?"

"No," I murmured, "but I remember it because her Tashi used to work in the diplomatic office in the Guild, and his heart failed right after the show. It was very sad, but he was elderly. I only remember because I had a meeting scheduled with him the next day."

"What was the meeting about?" Jov asked.

"Nothing important. He was retired, but he mentioned some business contacts in Izruitn he wanted to introduce me to, or tell me about, or something. I think he was just trying to help me out if I took the Ambassador position." I shrugged. "I can't imagine what could have been important enough to our family that the assassin would kill him to stop that meeting."

"If the goal is discrediting you, they could do it a lot easier than this," Tain said, gesturing at the complicated lists and diagrams across the table. "If it took us this much effort to even notice it's happening, it's hardly a cunning strategy, is it?"

But the subtlety worried me. It felt less like the flailing of an incompetent villain and more like the scaffolding of a careful plan we could not yet fathom. This play against Jovan had been an impulsive thing. *It* was the outlier, a rare direct attack.

"What we need," Jovan said suddenly, as if I'd shared the thought out loud, "are the missing pieces of the puzzle. A full picture of everything they've been doing so we can find the connections."

Tain scratched his cheek. "What if we asked at the hospital, to see whether anyone came in injured or were brought in dead on or around these dates? Then we could check whether any of the victims were at these events. We might find extra connections that way, maybe figure out what's coming next."

"Actually, that's a smart idea," Jov said.

"You don't have to sound so surprised," Tain muttered, grinning.

"In the meantime, you should stay out of sight, Jov," I said. "You're injured, you can legitimately stay home to recover."

But Jov was shaking his head. "There're still one or two public events Tain has to be at. I *have* to be anywhere he is. No one else knows what the assassin looks like. Maybe his plan doesn't involve killing you, Tain, but I'm not having you out there as a target on that chance."

"And what about *you*?" I pointed out, a bit sharper than intended. "You're lucky you're not tied up in an investigation right now. Do I need to remind you how close we came?"

My brother looked at me and I immediately regretted saying it. Every death he'd caused hurt him, but this one . . . this one had been particularly bad. I'd dreamed about Tuhash's terrible dead face, his protruding tongue, his eyes, the feel of his skin under my fumbling fingers at his neck. I shivered, and put one hand over Jov's; he squeezed it back in understanding.

Tain put a tentative hand on Jov's shoulder across the table. "Nothing's going to happen, all right? The body was found in a house. It won't be hard to figure out who hosted the party, and they'll find the connection with the Hands. Chen's people will find the real killers and this will all sound as ridiculous as it is." He gave Jovan's shoulder a little affectionate shake. "But listen, Lini's right, I think you should lie low for a few days. I promise I'll be careful when I go out, I'll have the blackstripes on high alert and make sure they don't let any strangers within spitting distance of me. We'll travel by different routes, leave late or early, keep it unpredictable. We just have to ride out a few more days, then karodee will be done, we can package up and send home all our important guests and get to the bottom of this."

I nodded with false cheer. We had a glimpse of a plan but no idea who was behind it, and Chen had been chasing the Hands for the better part of a year and still knew barely anything about them. I couldn't be confident she'd have any better luck tracing the real killer. And how would Talafar react when they found out one of their own soldiers had been murdered here under our noses, especially if rumors about Jov reached their camp?

"I'd better get moving," Tain said, rising. "I was only meant to be checking on you. I'm supposed to be meeting Eliska later about—" He stopped, scratched his head, and sighed. "Honor-down, I don't remember. Sewers in the village, or something. I'd better go. You two, rest up and stay out of trouble, all right?"

But before he could move, there was another knock at the door, and all three of us jumped. Sjease emerged swiftly from Dija's room, looking annoyingly fresh. "It's your day off, remember?" I reminded them as they swept past.

"What is it now?" Jov asked, his tone tight with dread. On the floor, his toes clenched convulsively.

When the door opened, though, some of the building tension dropped away as I recognized the slightly warbly tones of Tain's page, Erel. Not an Order Guard, not Chen, not some furious member of the Administrative Guild come to see who had so damaged the relations between our countries.

"Through here, lad," Sjease said. Every time I saw Erel he seemed to have grown, but he still had all his youthful enthusiasm and even the tuft of hair that always stuck up like a little crest.

"What is it, Erel?" Tain was frowning, and Erel's expression was anxious, his hands threaded tight together as he bobbed on the spot. "Out with it, kid."

"There's Councilors looking for you at the Manor, Honored Chancellor," the boy said. "You didn't tell Argo where you were going and you've nothing scheduled on right now, so the messengers didn't know where to find you. I made a guess." His eyes darted to my brother and then back to Tain. "I think there's trouble, Chancellor. They're riling each other up. You might need to go calm them all down."

Despite his humble upbringing—an orphan found abandoned in a remote village by a Guilded scribe, who had earned extra coin carrying messages and cleaning the Guild and making himself useful—or perhaps because of it, Erel had a good nose for reading a situation. He was an excellent messenger, fast and accurate, but it was a waste of what Tain had sensed was a quick mind and willingness to learn. He'd been elevated from Tain's personal messenger to his page more than a year ago, and by the time he was an adult I imagined he might well be one of the Chancellor's trusted advisers.

"Riling each other up about what, do you know?"

I held my breath. Surely word couldn't have gotten out so soon. It had only been a few hours since Chen had come round, and with a Talafan victim there would be no reason to inform any of the Families of the incident. Unless, of course, one of the Families was the source of the conspiracy in the first place.

"There was a fire at the shipyard," Erel said. "One of Credo Sjistevo's ships burned down last night."

Tain raised an eyebrow. "Not the worst accident we've had during a masquerade night. I'm sure Sjistevo's annoyed, but that's not enough to get half the Council out of bed before midday, today of all days."

Erel was demonstrating an admirable fascination for his own feet. He briefly looked up at Jovan, then dropped his gaze back to the floor. "No, Honored Chancellor, it's not just the ship, though Credo Sjistevo's right angry about that, claiming all sorts of things were on it. It's . . . it's what they're saying happened to it." He looked at Jovan again, bouncing off quickly as if burnt.

Tain scrubbed his fingers through his hair and sighed. "Erel, spit it out, whatever it is."

The lad swallowed. "They're saying, well, Credo Sjistevo's saying, and he's saying he's got witnesses, that it was a group of Darfri mages. You know. Speakers or what have you. Burned it down with magic."

"What?" Jov blurted out. "That's ridiculous."

Tain, though, just made an exasperated noise. "Why am I not surprised? He'd blame the Darfri for stubbing his toe if he thought he'd get away with it." He glanced over at me, and added, "You don't see him in Council, but he and Karista complain about the bloody reparations every chance they get. They're always stirring things up. Sjistevo was going on about his great-nephew's broken elbow yesterday, claiming some Darfri woman cursed him, and Karista accused a local family out on her estates of infecting three fields of her crops with kaki beetles. I've thought they were going to come to blows with Il-Yoro at least three times in the last month or so." He sighed again, and got to his feet. "I'd better handle it before it all gets worse. They'll all have sore heads and be in tempers for being dragged out of bed, no doubt."

"You'd better come too if you don't mind me saying, Credo Jovan," Erel said, bobbing his head. "It's like to turn into a full Council meeting at any rate, and . . ." He stopped, licked his lips nervously, then added all in a rush, the words bolting out in a jumble like scared animals, ". . . and I heard An-Hadrea's name mentioned."

"What?" Jov said again, stupidly. "What do you mean, her name was mentioned?" This, I realized, was why the lad had been afraid to look at him. "You don't mean—"

"Credo Sjistevo's saying witnesses saw her with the Darfri group who started the fire," he mumbled. "He hasn't got anyone with him, mind, so it could just be gossip, but, well, it's gossip, and it's spreading. Just thought you ought to know."

This, at least, was enough to rouse Tain to anger. "Hadrea saved every one of their stinking necks. Using her in one of these damnable political stunts is pretty low." He scowled. "Bastards can bloody well try to say that to our faces. Can you walk all right, Jov?"

Erel looked at Jovan curiously as I helped my brother to his feet. "You can borrow my stick," I said, quick to take the excuse to turn away. A strange and unpleasant tightness had taken up residency in my chest. Because I was remembering, now, when Hadrea had come to my room in the night, and helped me out the window. I'd smelled smoke on her. I'd not thought much of it at the time. *There were campfires all around the lake,* I told myself, *and if she'd been sitting beside one she'd naturally have picked up the scent.* I fetched my stick from beside the door, where it had been gathering dust. After my initial recovery I had still had occasional sudden pains around the wound—the knife had caused some nerve or muscular damage—and had used this sturdy-based stick in case of unsteadiness. *What about the guards? She shouldn't have been able to get past our houseguards.* And now I'd started, I was remembering her odd, furtive manner, and comparing it with the anger always bubbling under the surface, these days.

I handed the stick to Jov and he gratefully took pressure off his left foot with a sigh. It was well bandaged so he couldn't move the ankle but it obviously still hurt to walk.

"Are you all right, Credo?" Erel asked, wide-eyed, as Jov grunted his way to the door with Tain.

"Absolutely bloody brilliant," he grumbled back.

INCIDENT: Harrow village poisonings (assorted)

POISON: Laceleaf

INCIDENT NOTES: A series of heart failures in elderly residents of Harrow caused by apparent accidental poisoning by use of laceleaf in cooking instead of sicero. May have gone unnoticed but for visiting relative noticing the prevalence of laceleaf in communal garden. I suspect a single source of information about the potential for substitution of which a number of disgruntled relatives took advantage. Note poison supplier was likely traveling herbalist using (assumed) name of "Alix," offering "natural remedies" for a range of conditions. Disappeared before I arrived in Harrow. Advise keeping contacts on lookout for "Alix" in villages across country.

(from proofing notes of Credo Etan Oromani)

9

Jovan

Erel hadn't exaggerated. Half the Council was at the Manor by the time we made it back up the hill in Tain's anonymous, unmarked litter and in through the private side entrance. Argo informed us, with some stiff exasperation, that he had ferried them all to the Council chamber. "They were shouting in my entrance hall in a most improper fashion," he wheezed, clearly agitated. He adjusted his glasses and passed a pile of papers to Tain. "Further messages for you, Honored Chancellor."

"Erel, can you get a servant to find Merenda? I'm going to try to head this off before we're hosting a whole bloody Council meeting, but if we aren't out in ten minutes you'll need to arrange to send someone to fetch the rest of the Councilors who aren't here, too. If we leave anyone out we'll only have to repeat it when they wake up and find out they've missed the drama." He ran his eyes over several messages in turn. "Great, these look . . . these are all great news. Excellent." He took a steadying sort of breath and gestured for me to precede him into the Council chamber.

No one looked up as we slipped in. They weren't yelling, but the room vibrated with tension. Credo Sjistevo stood, one quivering finger pointed directly at Salvea, who sat with a stiff spine and tight lips.

"—undermined. Now they have been caught at the scene, and still I am hearing protests. No family has been forced to provide greater recompense than mine. No family has been subjected to more criticism, more dishonorable treatment."

"No family brought as much dishonor to themselves as yours," Salvea said. Her voice was low and shaking. Her hands were folded together so tightly the fingers were discolored. Unlike Sjistevo, who looked disheveled from what must have been an extremely long night, Salvea was clear-eyed, impeccable, her dark hair confined smoothly under a bright scarf. "Not one. You are doing the bare minimum this Council forces you to do and still you drag your heels every step."

"The bare minimum?" Sjistevo retorted. "I ask you! New Compact, shrines round half the city, you've *crippled* my family's quarries and rivers with those 'replenishment' regulations . . ." He thumped a dramatic fist on the table. "We're being punished for things that happened before we were even born!"

Il-Yoro, a powerfully built man with a round chest and a wall-shaking voice, made a contemptuous gesture. "*We* are still being punished for the decisions your families have made for generations," he roared. "You want to wave your hand and make it all go away! It does not work like that, my boy. This Council is supposed to be making things right, not covering them over with cheap plaster. A few seats in here, one lousy Guild for workers, and you think the job is done?"

"Do you see? Do you see this attitude? It's never enough! Two years of emptying our coffers paying compensation, funding education—"

"The money in your coffers wasn't yours," Tain said. His voice was very cold, and everyone in the room turned to look at us immediately, falling into silence. "Your family stole it. Just like mine did, like every Credol Family did. It is only through the generosity of others that we are still sitting in this Council, that we still have coffers to empty."

"Honored Chancellor, the Credol Families built this country—" he began.

Il-Yoro, on the other side of the table, thumped a fist on its surface. "The Credol Families represent people who helped shape Silasta centuries ago, yes, but every week it seems you are standing up in this chamber claiming you personally are not responsible for the behavior of your aunt, or her mother, or her brother. You cannot have it both ways, Credo Sjistevo. If your family owns its wealth, it owns its sins."

Sjistevo was breathing hard now. He seemed unable to come up with a sufficient retort so instead he pivoted back to Tain and made his voice softer, obsequious. "Honored Chancellor. These are no doubt important issues to be considered as we move forward to the fair future we all desire for our country. But they are not the issue at hand. I came to you this morning with an important complaint, and I find myself hijacked."

"I heard about your family's boat," Tain said, sitting down calmly. "And it's very unfortunate, but it's not the first time a boat has burnt, or things have gotten a bit out of hand during the masquerade. The Guards are already aware of the issue, and you've been in touch with the harbormaster, I understand, because I have a complaint from her on my desk that she was woken at dawn by your servants." He waved one of the papers in his hand, and set the rest down on the table. The other Councilors also sat, with varying degrees of hesitation. However fractured this room could be, it warmed me to see how fully and competently Tain had settled into this role as leader. He had their respect, even if it was sometimes grudging. But that pleasant thought only brought on the inevitable worry tailing it, as always. His ability to bring together this group of people with widely varying, sometimes directly conflicting, interests, his capacity to compromise and to encourage others to compromise, made him a good Chancellor, but it also made him an ideal target for anyone seeking to divide us. I glanced over at Merenda, who had slipped in quietly during the argument. She was shifting uncomfortably in her seat, her brow furrowed. Doubtless she would increase in confidence and grow into the Heir's role in time, but if power passed to her too soon, it might all fall apart under the strain.

"The loss of your goods is no doubt very distressing," Tain said, "but was this a matter worthy of dragging everyone into an emergency Council? We have a meeting scheduled for next week, when karodee is over. Could this not have waited?"

Sjistevo's lips had gone very tight, barely moving when he spoke. "I brought this directly to you, rather than referring it to the determination council, because of the *sensitivity* of the issue." His eyes flashed to Salvea, and my heart sank. "Your daughter is well known around the city, you know. One of Silasta's 'heroes,' they say. Well then she should be more careful, because she was easily recognized with this group of rogue Darfri, and she is out there wreaking havoc on our city and undermining all your assurances."

"I know my daughter, thank you," Salvea said, and for the first time she raised her voice.

Tain sounded calm, but his anger was plain. "Credo, it is very fortunate you didn't bring this complaint to the determination council. You're accusing the daughter of a Councilor, not to mention a person to whom everyone here owes their lives, of petty property destruction? Frankly, I'm shocked you would countenance such a claim."

Credola Karista cleared her throat. "I agree it is shocking, Honored Chancellor, but this is no petty damage. Valuable cargo, an expensive purpose-built ship . . . it is one thing to dismiss claims of people falling into canals, of the *numerous* instances of damage of crops, of mysterious injuries and ailments that seem to plague anyone who so much as dares criticize a Darfri person—"

"No one has dismissed anything," Budua, the Scribe-Guilder, pointed out dryly. "Indeed it seems every second complaint going to the determination council relates to something of this nature. It's just that as you know perfectly well, Credola Karista, no one as yet has been able to satisfy a determination council there is any complaint at all to answer."

Karista continued as if Budua had not spoken. "—but this? This is indisputable, flagrant sabotage."

"No one is disputing the sabotage," Tain said, with cold patience, "only the saboteurs."

"I mean to say! The Darfri group was seen at the wharfs right before the fire started!" Sjistevo spread his hands expansively. "Multiple witnesses say they approached, intoxicated, loud, aggressive, half-undressed, covered in Darfri symbols. We all know what they look like now, you accept? They were singing—chanting—and the boat went up all in a burst. An-Hadrea was identified there shortly after."

"Your witness claims they saw Hadrea setting a fire?" Tain said. "Or just that she was there, afterward?"

He blustered a little. "No one saw the fire being lit, but they wouldn't, would they? If it was by magic. Witnesses heard chanting and drumming. Just like during the war! Ordinary folk aren't likely to forget what it sounds like, I promise you. Her daughter was there with other Darfri and it was their magic that burned our boat." He pointed at Salvea again. "We've sat here for two years listening to them insist their magic can't be used to help the city or make our lives easier, honor-down, we shouldn't expect that, oh no. But it's funny how magic is suddenly available when it's grudge settling."

"This is a very disturbing accusation," Karista cut in smoothly. She was like a miniature Bradomir, elegant as a reptile and as cold-blooded. "Not just because of An-Hadrea's . . . er . . . potential role in this but in terms of how Darfri magic is regulated more broadly. We have all seen it used as a destructive force, to the detriment of the city. We all voted on how this was to be taught. One central teacher, carefully selected students. There were agreements, assurances. If there are unregulated . . . what are they called? Speakers? Running around the city, that affects *all* of us."

Silence greeted her words, and a noticeable change in the atmosphere. Other Councilors murmured to one another, and uncomfortable memories of being on the wrong side of Darfri magic clawed at me. And something else flashed to mind: the woman and the drum, last night, her body painted with symbols, and the feeling I'd had. But I pushed it aside and met Salvea's gaze. My heart skipped a beat at the trust in her expression. "Credo Jovan!" Her voice shook. I'd never seen her angry before. "Perhaps you can assist with this nonsense about Hadrea. It is absurd!"

For the first time, everyone looked at me. I saw immediately that regardless of what Chen had said or we had hoped, rumors had reached some ears. Lazar flinched, looking away, and Javesto gave me an appraising look, his brows furrowed. A sinking, sick feeling churned my stomach. They were friendly colleagues at least, and I'd have thought they wouldn't believe me capable of strangling someone, under the influence of narcotics or not.

Sjistevo dismissed me with a glance and glared at Salvea with a false bark of a laugh. "*You* may play a reasonable voice in this room, Councilor An-Salvea, but your daughter is not so politic! She hates my family, she's open about it! She hates every Credol Family, anyone who isn't Darfri, and now she and her friends are getting their revenge by—"

"It *is* absurd," I said. "I'm sure there were a lot of Darfri celebrations last night, as we would hope and expect, given what we were honoring. I've no doubt witnesses saw Darfri groups, and likely they were singing and dancing, same as most of you probably were. But if we're looking at crime and destruction I think we should be looking elsewhere." So much for playing down my little mishap. "I came afoul of criminals myself last night, from the 'Prince's Hands,' the same gang Captain Chen's been warning us about, and we've been failing to resource her to deal with." I pushed back awkwardly from the table and gestured at my bandaged ankle, my borrowed walking stick. Sjistevo and Karista peered curiously at me, forgetting to look affronted for a moment in their apparent surprise. If they'd known about it in advance, they were fine actors. But Javesto chewed thoughtfully at his lip, and Lazar was once again avoiding eye contact.

"Are you all right, Credo Jovan?" Budua asked, frowning over her glasses.

"Yes," I said. "A simple mugging, maybe, though I'll be interested to see whether there are other reports of robberies or whether I was singled out." I looked around significantly, and saw a few faces twitch in response, whether out of alarm at the prospect of Credolen being targeted, or something else. "Fortunately for me, my young niece went for help and managed to find Hadrea. And then Hadrea stayed with me and organized a doctor, which would have rather put a cramp in any recreational fire starting, don't you agree?" I smiled pleasantly. "I assume no one here is accusing me of setting fire to anyone's boat."

Sjistevo looked at me, then at Tain, then back. "Of course not," he conceded. "But—"

"I suspect both of our problems would be better handled by the Order Guards than by half a hungover Council," I continued, which elicited some chuckles and approving nods. The tension in the room was leaking out. "I'm sure most of you here would probably prefer to be spending this morning in bed with a quiet pot of tea."

Budua got to her feet. "I daresay," she agreed. "Anything you need from us, Chancellor?"

Tain shook his head. "I agree with Credo Jovan that more attention needs to be focused on these organized criminals, so I propose we discuss that as a matter of priority at our next scheduled meeting." He gestured wearily to the pile of messages he'd left on the table. "This is just from last night alone. Reports of thefts and property destruction over the city—the Ash boat was far from the only thing damaged. The hospital is reporting dozens of people with alcohol- and drug-related issues this morning, not to mention a man's apparently been murdered at a party."

I felt eyes on me, and kept my face bland as if I'd not heard anything about it. Not just Lazar, but also the Warrior-Guilder and one of the estate representatives were looking at me now. I counted breaths, trying to stay focused. Blood rushed to my cheeks. I had spoken out against the use of recreational drugs on multiple occasions. Did they think me such a hypocrite?

"I'll bring Captain Chen in for a full report next week. We've avoided dealing with this drug issue too long." Tain turned wearily to Sjistevo. "Credo, the Guards and the harbormaster can work out what happened to your boat. As long as your family filed the proper papers I'm sure there'll be no difficulty reconciling your lost goods."

People stood and began to move toward the door. Sjistevo stared at me, unblinking, muscles of his jaw working silently. He looked both furious and flummoxed. Karista, by his side, glared at me with dislike and calculation. But they both stood eventually and made to leave.

"Wait." Salvea, gentlest and calmest person I knew, was now visibly shaking with rage. "No, I do not think we should move on quite so quickly. Credo Sjistevo owes my family an apology for the disgusting accusation."

"I had good evidence, Councilor," he said stiffly. "I accept Credo Jovan's testimony as to your daughter's whereabouts, but how was I to know that in advance?"

"Not just to us," Salvea said, as if he hadn't spoken. "You owe an apology to every Darfri person in this room, and the ones not here. You have insulted us all with your childish claims. Our focus has always—*always*—been to restore the tah that has been diminished by the Credol Families, yours more than any other. An-Ostada is a woman of impeccable honor and integrity and she is training her students—our children, whose heritage would have forever been denied them if your family had its way—to restore that balance. These are honorable young people learning to right the wrongs of the past, and you accuse them of such low behavior. It is unacceptable."

"I had good evidence," he repeated, his face very tight.

"I understand the fire was quite sudden and alarming, Salvea," Moest, the Warrior-Guilder, said gently. "Witnesses heard chanting and drumming. Likely it was just singing, or even just some passing Darfri locals, like Credo Jovan said, but you must understand how it could call to mind the most frightening parts of the siege for some people."

"I must understand?" Her voice went up several notes. "Why is it always us who must understand, who must be tolerant and polite, to not make you uncomfortable? Darfri songs are our heritage—not just mine, yours too! Our culture is not some alien and dangerous practice to be greeted with suspicion and blame!"

"Salvea," Tain said. She whipped her head to face him and something passed between them; was that a plea in his eyes, or an admonishment? Whatever it was, it sapped her energy; she closed her mouth and dropped her gaze. There was a long silence. Then he cleared his throat. "I agree, you are owed an apology. And I offer mine, not just for this incident but for all the ones preceding it. Some have been wont to blame Darfri for every problem that materializes. We have to do better." He gave Sjistevo a hard look. "Don't you agree, Credo?"

Sjistevo did not resemble his late aunt Nara in looks, but for a moment I could see her looking out with familiar calculating bitterness from his narrowed eyes. But the Ash family had been dishonored by the revelations about estate behavior and his influence on the Council accordingly lowered. He didn't strike me as particularly intelligent but nor was he a fool. "I apologize, Councilor," he said, inclining his head dramatically. "I apologize to all Darfri. My distress at the malicious damage left my emotions high. It must have been an unfortunate coincidence."

Or another way of discrediting me, and those close to me. Of course the Ashes and the Lekas, even the Reeds to some extent, had an inherent interest in turning Council sentiment against the Darfri. Their bitterness about being forced to make right some of the wrongs we had caused was equal only to their resentment that the Darfri spirits could not be trotted out to do our bidding when convenient. They could have started the rumor themselves. But I couldn't help but wonder if our enemies had taken advantage of yet another opportunity to sow discord. Our city was balanced in a strange state, with most of its residents—me included—indisputably convinced of the existence of supernatural forces, but lacking the foundational religious beliefs that put those forces in a context we could make sense of. It was such an obvious pressure point for the Council, consisting as it did of an uneasy mix of the old Families, the Guilders, and the regional representatives. To have Darfri residents openly using magic against fellow citizens would make a lie of the restrictions on the use of fresken An-Ostada had insisted on, and re-emphasize the differences we had worked so hard to blur.

On the way out of the room Lazar made accidental eye contact with me and then brushed past so fast he almost knocked me over, unbalanced as I was with the walking stick. Someone caught me by the elbow and steadied me; I turned to thank them and found Credo Javesto at my side. He had puffy lumps under his eyes, and a certain delicacy in his movements suggested he'd enjoyed the festivities rather well the previous night.

"Be careful there now," he said. I readjusted the stick and nodded a bit stiffly. I tried to sound natural but my thanks sounded wrong, high and tight. He glanced over his shoulder, then, satisfied no one else was paying attention, dropped his voice. "My nephew's in the Order Guards, Jovan. He told me they interviewed you this morning."

I opened my mouth to respond but he held up a hand, shaking his head conciliatorily. "He said Chen's blaming it on a bad witness. But some of the

Guards who talked to her first found her rather convincing, describing you there. Listen, friend, I've had a party or two myself that's gotten out of hand. Happens to the best of us. I've not—"

"Like I told Chen," I replied, trying to keep my response pleasant, my tone light. Javesto wasn't a bad sort, but he certainly had a reputation for enjoying a party and I didn't need him sympathetically trying to relate. "I was never at any party last night. I took my niece out and then I was mugged."

"I've no doubt this was all a mistake," Javesto reassured me, but the way he smoothed his beard down his round chin and glanced away as he said it put a lie to that statement. "I just thought it best you knew that unless—until!— the investigation turns up the real killer, it's possible there will be . . . talk. My nephew told me as he knows I hold you in the highest regard. But the witness spoke to more than one Guard, and, well, you know how things are. With the play, and with Bradomir, and—"

"You might remember *I* was the only one who thought Bradomir was as- sassinated," I said, irritated to be proved right in my theory. "The Lekas said he had a heart condition and everyone acted like I was a lunatic for saying there was an assassin. What's that got to do with anything?"

"It's just . . . it's one more thing, Jovan," Javesto said, almost a whisper. He cleared his throat. "Some people have started to take notice. Things have gone well for the Oromanis since the siege, you know as well as I do, and it just seems your political rivals don't last for long, anymore. People are start- ing to say the fortunes may favor you a little too much." Seeing my face, he shook his head again, raising both hands. "I warn you out of friendship! I stood by you at the battle of the bridge, did I not? Raised a sword in this pudgy ill-suited arm to defend you and what you said was right? And I owe you my life for getting us safely out of the fire, don't think I'd ever forget. I'm just warning you people are talking. Keep your head down for a bit, eh? Don't make things worse."

Before I could respond, Tain turned and called out to me, and when I glanced back it was to see Javesto's retreating back, hurrying from the room.

I wanted to tell Tain we'd been right about how my reputation was being at- tacked, but Erel was waiting for us right outside with an armful of daily reports, along with the Manor undersecretary, and two more officials from the karodee planning committee whose names I'd forgotten; I nodded along and racked my brain to remember them as they rattled off things that needed attending to. There were last preparations for the closing ceremony in three days' time,

and additional dramas that had sprung up overnight, including an outbreak
of a contagious pox among some of the karodee committee members and
key staff—"Of all the timing!" one of them exclaimed—as well as property
damage and robberies in the industrial district affecting the engineer Baina's
stores, and potentially putting her much-anticipated closing ceremony display at risk.

"That's dangerous stuff to steal," Tain muttered as he ran a finger down a
list. "Chemicals and such. Baina thinks the thieves might dump them once
they realize they're not useful to sell, and they're all pretty toxic. We'll have to
put out alerts in case anything ends up near the canals or the lake."

"The sky fire display won't be affected, will it?" one of the committee members asked, twisting her scarf ends between her fingers anxiously.
"That's the crowning glory of the evening! Without that the whole thing will
be spoilt. What will we all do in the dark?"

I quickly lost track of the conversation. The possibility we might have to
close the karodee without all of the intended entertainments wasn't exactly
my top worry right now. Our enemies had made a move against me yesterday,
but not a fatal one; what we needed to know was what was coming next. We
were missing something, I was sure.

And I had the strongest sense we were about to run out of time to work
it out.

It was hours before I finally saw Hadrea to warn her about what had happened at the impromptu Council meeting this morning. She turned up at
the apartments, her brother Davi racing in beside her. "It is windy today,"
she said, shaking her coat off and striding in. She'd obviously had a better
rest than either of us; she looked energetic, vital even, her skin clear and eyes
bright, and her wind-tangled hair clean and shining. I felt, like I often did
when seeing her unexpectedly, as if someone had just winded me. "How are
you both feeling?"

"The ankle's sore and it hurts to breathe," I said. "And I feel like I'm going
to have a headache for a week. But otherwise, great."

Davi, who even now retained the wary, wild-animal air about him when
around me, edged around the back of the room. "Hi, Davi," Kalina said, and
he shot her a bright smile in return. "Dee's in her room, if you want to go say
hi. She's been sick but she's all right now."

He didn't need telling twice, skidding out of sight, a fistful of cards in his hand.

"Some of the schoolchildren taught him how to play fire-fire," Hadrea said, smiling indulgently at her disappearing brother. "No, no, do not get up. You both need rest." She settled down with us instead, scrubbing her hair out of her face and winding an affectionate arm around my waist. Her hair smelled like rain as she leaned on my shoulder. "Has our northern friend been identified yet?"

We filled her in on what we'd learned over the course of the day, including what Chen had reported to Tain about the house the body had been found in—now deserted, but according to the neighbors, owned by a rich merchant family who had let their home out for the duration of karodee. They would not be the only ones in the city risking the Guild's wrath to supply un-Guilded accommodation at an inflated price. No one seemed to know anything about the current occupants, except that there had been lots of visitors observed in the evenings.

Hadrea listened well enough, but I had the sense she was distracted. Her eyes strayed often to the window and several times she asked me to repeat something. Kalina, too, looked odd, staring at Hadrea during those moments as if deep in unsettling thought.

"I suppose it would be safer," Hadrea said, when we had finished explaining Tain's request that we stay out of sight. She winked. "Anyway, it is tiring being worried about you all the time."

"Well, I know you like to keep busy," I retorted, and the answering sparkle in her eye reminded me, momentarily, of happier times. "Speaking of being worried about you," I said, annoyed my voice sounded falsely casual, too bright. "Something else came up at Council."

The positive energy that had radiated from her on arrival faltered, faded. "Yes, my mother informed me," she said neutrally.

"I said you were helping me, and they accepted that."

"Yes." Hadrea shifted, straightening her posture and creating a gap between us. "Thank you. I do not need more of those puffed-up songbirds poking their beaks into my business."

There was a long pause. Hadrea had crossed her legs and was studying her hands as intently and with as much curiosity as if they'd just sprouted tentacles. Kalina pushed back away from the table fractionally. We both knew Hadrea had a temper and this particular subject was a sensitive one. "They're going to try to keep poking," I said. "It's not in their interests to let it go. I just wish I knew whether this was the Ashes or other Credolen inventing the problem or whether someone else started the rumor to increase division. If the city thinks there's a bunch of rogue Darfri running around performing magic outside An-Ostada's control, it'll do a lot of damage. We could end up right back where we started, even if for different reasons."

I swallowed, eyeing her warily. I hated prodding her on sensitive subjects, especially when she was already on edge. But on top of what was happening in Council, we couldn't risk ignoring it, either. "Also, I saw something—at least, I thought I saw something—at the party." Kalina looked up, brow furrowed in a confused frown, and I realized, despite my best intentions to tell her everything, I had left this out of my story. "There was a . . . woman at the party. Maybe a Darfri woman." I described the scene as best I could from my fragmented memory. The chants, the drum, the symbols, even, though with some hesitation, the sensation I'd briefly felt, the draining current of energy being drawn using fresken.

Hadrea bristled. "A sham. They are using our culture as a show for rich, spoiled city folk who do not understand it," she said, her tone low and furious. She had dropped my hand.

"I did feel something," I said, reluctant in the face of her rising temper. "It felt like how I remembered the fresken at the lake."

Kalina sucked in her breath, looking alarmed, but Hadrea waved a dismissive hand. "You were on Void, and the fortunes know what else, Jovan. You can hardly trust your feelings. No, no Darfri would use their connection to the spirits for the entertainment of drunken fools. It was just a show, a parody for the rich." She scowled. "I should have expected this. If they are not allowed to attack us directly they will just seize the parts of us they want and use them for their own. You people only know how to take—"

"You people?" It was my turn to be prickly. "Aren't we past that, Hadrea?"

She shifted, scowling further still. "You want to be past that because it is convenient for you to be. We are years into the new Compact and you are tired of the effort? You want to be able to say, well, I stood up against your enemies once, is that not enough?"

"That's not what I'm saying," I said, flustered. The conversation was spiraling out of my control, and I wrestled to get it back. "I'm on your side here."

Hadrea didn't answer. I realized my left hand was crushing the fingers of my right and couldn't make the grip relax. My knuckles felt like they were going to break. Our relationship had arisen out of a time of great tension and stress and I had never really expected we would be a long-term romantic pairing like Marjeta and Budua, or Eliska and Dara; such things were unusual beasts in Silasta. Still, I thought our friendship would endure even if her attraction to me faded over time. Instead, the physical side of our relationship had continued—more intensely than ever in the last few months—but she kept things from me, and I realized, staring at her tense profile, that I was no longer sure she trusted me.

"Hadrea," I said, beseeching. Honor-down, though, I wanted to make it right.

Kalina, wordless, leaned over and took both my hands in hers. I caught my breath and relaxed, slowly, under her even pressure. But we had gone so far, and I had one more highly uncomfortable thing to bring up. "All right, you're right, it must have just been a sham. But there's one more thing I meant to ask you. An-Ostada said something to me yesterday." Hadrea's eyebrows drew down at the mention of her teacher's name. "Did something happen in your classes recently, or while you were out touring the villages? She seemed a bit . . . worked up."

Hadrea read the implied understatement, because she made a scornful noise and suppressed what looked like the beginnings of a rude hand gesture. "She is always worked up about something. She wishes to teach us like we are toddlers, learning to walk and talk, and she does not trust or respect her students. Already she has lost several, and—" She stopped, pressing her lips together.

"She's lost students?" Kalina asked reluctantly into the silence. "How many? Does the Council know?"

It didn't—*I* didn't. Anger was churning in me, but I couldn't tell whether it was directed at An-Ostada or Hadrea, or both.

"She would not have wanted to tell you people had left. Then she would have to admit to her failings as a teacher. She is too proud." Instead of snapping at me, Hadrea reached over suddenly and pushed hair from my forehead, her touch gentle and her gaze honest and direct. "It is difficult for everyone, I think. Always, she talks of old ways, even in the face of new challenges, for that is what she learned. But we are not children and we have all seen our people powerless and abused with the old ways not there to protect us. If she only teaches us the old ways, if we are not prepared, there will be no new defenses to come to our rescue next time." She gestured to the piles of papers, the empty teacups, the evidence of our long afternoon of researching and thinking, and sighed. "Sometimes it feels like we are the only handful of people in this city who remember your Warrior-Guilder was not this country's only enemy. We must be ready to protect ourselves again."

"I agree," I said, relieved. "Last time that enemy didn't restrict themselves to working within the boundaries of the city, so why would we expect them to do it again? We need to understand what's going on in those villages, with the missing spirits. Maybe there's a connection."

Hadrea frowned. "Yes. I told you that I did not believe this was mere neglect; the people there were no more careless or disrespectful than anywhere else. There is no good reason for the spirits to be gone in those places. It feels like something is happening out there, something we do not understand yet."

We all looked at one another, but no one voiced the worry we felt. Our enemy had used tensions among our own people to raise a rebellion two years ago, and though good changes had come out of the Compact, we'd be fools to pretend there weren't still exploitable cracks in our society. I knew our enemy would come for us again; this time, we had to hope, they would not be able to use us against one another.

"We only have to get through a few more days and some of the pressure will be off," Kalina said with bracing optimism. "We can all lie low together till karodee is over, at least."

"As long as we get through karodee," I muttered.

It took almost a full day for Tuhash's absence to be noticed by the Talafan delegation; evidently he had not been scheduled to work on masquerade evening and another soldier had covered for him for the morning shift, assuming he had overindulged. It was not until late in the day that Tuhash's failure to return to the guesthouse had been noticed. The Talafan alerted the diplomatic office, who had passed it on to the Order Guards, and only then did anyone on the Silastian side—other than us—link the unidentified dead man in the hospital and the missing Imperial guest.

To compound the disaster, it transpired Tuhash had not only been a soldier, but also a minor noble. Unlike in Sjona, where at least until recently the Warrior Guild was made up almost entirely of people with less fortunate backgrounds since the wealthiest and most powerful families did not encourage their children to pursue a martial career, according to Kalina the

Imperial soldiers of Talafar were prestigious, full of young noble boys trying to distinguish themselves and retired army officials who had earned a well-respected post closer to home. Tuhash came from a noble family and, worse still, his mother—a direct, albeit distant, relative of the Emperor—was here in Sjona as part of the Princesses' entourage. Kalina had even met her. Tain had gone around in the evening to offer formal condolences in person, and had reported back that the Foreign Minister had revealed little of how the family might be taking the news. "He didn't even ask questions," Tain had told us, somewhat bewildered. "Maybe it was the language barrier, but I was expecting him to really press me for details on what happened and what we were doing about investigating, and I had all these careful answers prepared, but he just looked like he'd rather be anywhere else."

I suspected the Talafan were assessing their response and waiting to see what we would do. It was certainly too much to expect that they would simply allow us to conduct the investigation without their involvement. One more thing to plague and worry me.

Sjease went early to the market and the rest of the family, even Kalina, left soon after to attend the puppetry at the open theater, leaving the house blessedly silent, and my thoughts unpleasantly loud. No further revelations had emerged from my review of papers and half-formed theories. I would have liked to take a break myself, to walk the city and think clearly out in the open to the tune of familiar steps, but that was neither practical nor wise in my current state.

So instead I continued to trace lines and circle potential connections and wonder, and speculate. Bits and pieces of the night's events were coming back to me, fragmented and confusing, but there were clues to be found there when combined with what Dee had witnessed. The assassin might have lured me purposefully to where the Hands were doing business, but he hadn't told them to expect me, and they hadn't known who I was at first. Dee confirmed they'd stopped their assault once they noticed my tattoos and realized who I was. According to her, one of them had gone to seek orders from someone else, someone above the Wraith, perhaps someone with an interest in me personally. Someone who had not only directed the Hands to place me at that party but had also supplied the victim. *The boss suggested it*, the Wraith had said when she produced the Talafan man. Could the assassin and the Hands both be working for the same employer?

And what had been happening with the woman in the alcove? I had dreamed of it last night, in terrifying flashes reliving the feelings, the fear. I had been drugged, disoriented, confused; likely I'd mistaken the sensation in that state, but it had *felt* like magic, like being swept up in something not of my understanding. Hadrea had dismissed that idea easily enough, and of course she was likely right, because what Darfri woman would use their sacred arts for the entertainment of others? But in my dreams logic and reason made no difference. It was all too real in my head.

I started at the sound of the door, imagining the Order Guards returning, perhaps, or some other bad news, but it was only Sjease returning from the market, laden with purchases. I raised a weary hand in greeting, relieved.

"How's the ankle feeling, Credo?"

"About the same." I watched them walk past, avoiding my gaze. "What is it?"

Sjease set the basket of market goods down and regarded me seriously. "There's talk already," they said bluntly, and I didn't need to ask about what. My heart sank. "I heard the cook's assistant from the Brooks and two maids from the Reeds talking while I was getting these." They brandished two hanging bindies before laying them down beside the basket.

"Talk?" I asked, pulse quickening, blood rushing to my face. Javesto had warned me word might leak out through the Order Guards, and I lived on the same street as the Brooks and the Reeds; anyone could have seen Chen and her Guards visiting in the early hours of the morning. Or someone else could easily have seen me at the party. I suspected, from the gaps in my memory and the Wraith's mocking comments, that I had not been simply sitting in a stupor the whole time but had interacted with at least some other guests. Again, I remembered with a chill the press of a man's body on one side of me, the touch of a woman's unbound hair on the other. *You weren't so stuck-up an hour ago, darling.* Everyone may have been intoxicated, but it was a lot to hope that no one had recognized me. I swallowed. I was in more trouble than I'd realized. Chen might believe one "witness" was lying or mistaken, but she'd have a much harder time buying my alibi in the face of multiple accusations, if it came to that.

"They stopped talking when they saw me," Sjease said. Businesslike, they unpacked the eggs and refilled jars of spices from the basket, then began rinsing the harpeas with the jug of water, still avoiding looking directly at me. "But I overheard a fair bit before they noticed."

"And?" I cleared my throat. "Sjease. What were they saying?"

"Largely what the Captain reported this morning," Sjease said reluctantly. "That you were high on something at a private party, went to a bedroom with a man who ended up dead." They cleared their throat, giving the harpeas rather more attention than they needed. "Then they were sharing rumors about your . . . uh . . . preferences, I suppose. Not the kind of nonsense that'd bear repeating in the normal circumstances, but I thought you might want to know in this particular case."

There had always been some talk about my lack of regular participation in the Silastian social scene, including my avoidance of romantic relationships with my peers; a product of both the secrecy of my role and the inconvenient workings of my brain. It hadn't bothered me for a long time. But it had, of course, left me vulnerable to rumors speculating more sinister reasons for my privacy. I supposed a penchant for violence in intimate settings fit the narrative of me as a skulking assassin for the Chancellor far better than the truth. "Did you hear where it came from? The rumor, I mean."

"Not straight out, but if I had to guess, it seemed like one of the maids had heard it from someone from her own household who was at the party." They unpacked the last item from the basket—a pungent cloth-wrapped cheese. My stomach, which had been unable to tolerate any food all day, grumbled, and my mouth started to water. "For the sousuk tonight, not for you," Sjease warned, shifting the cheese out of my reach. I grinned. Sousuk, a baked egg-and-herb dish, was one of my childhood favorites, and though they wouldn't say so I knew Sjease was making it to try to bring some cheer to the household. I appreciated the gesture even though it was a futile one.

"That'll be round all the Families by nightfall, then," I muttered.

"Not all servants are gossips."

I raised an eyebrow.

Sjease sighed. "It'll be round all the Families by nightfall if it isn't already." They hung the basket on its hook on the wall. "But I don't know if it'll go further. The way they were talking about the party I had the impression it was the kind the Families wouldn't admit to attending, at least not officially."

True, there was a difference between talk and formal reports. Whenever I'd brought up Void in Council, the Families had maintained a pretense that none of their households contained users. Maybe they'd be reluctant to make an official complaint. Something about my housekeeper's tone made me ask, "Do you know anything about these parties, Sjease?"

They shrugged. "They're not the kind of parties servants get invited to, and not the type Guilded servants work, but you hear things." They set out the bowl to make the sousuk mix and began cracking eggs while I chopped the carrots. "This is all off-books stuff. Not in official businesses. People's houses, certain parks, places the Order Guards don't go near. Everything's by invitation, you pay to get in." They twitched, clearly uncomfortable. "People say Silasta's changing. After the siege, the city opened up, you changed the game table. Lots of wealthy people here suddenly find things very different to what they're used to."

There was an openness about the way Sjease spoke to me now that drew attention to its previous absence. A trusted and respected member of the household they were, but they had never volunteered a critique of society before; we'd never had a conversation like this in two years of living and working together. I kept my eyes on my carrots and listened. There were different cities within my city I knew little about, even those inhabited by my closest peers. Perhaps especially those.

After a pause, Sjease continued hesitantly, as if unsure of the reception this would receive. "See, the problem with Silasta is you had a whole lot of people used to living an exclusive life, elevated above the rest, then suddenly they're being told they have to share it without complaint. Seems to me there are a lot of younger daughters and excess sons around the upper city and they've spent their lives being told about honor and contribution to their family, but now they're not sure what their family means in the scheme of things. And now there are people in their ears, telling them it doesn't have to be that way. They don't have to slide into mediocrity the way they fear. They still have money, and they can still have things other people don't have."

"And they want . . . what?" Nothing about that party had been appealing to me. It had been the worst aspects of every social situation compressed into one hideous room.

"It doesn't matter what it is," Sjease told me seriously. "That's not the point, Jovan. The point is it is a secret and you have to be rich to get into it. They can't call someone an earther in their favorite teahouse anymore without social repercussions, so they find a way to make new rules."

"And there are people ready and willing to step up and give them what they want," I said slowly. "The gangs. That's how they're getting the upper city. Selling the same drugs to the rich as to the poor but in a different package."

It fit. The woman running the party had known the Wraith and her henchman, and acted like a subordinate. If the Hands were running parties like this, within walking distance of the Manor and the homes of the city's richest and most powerful, supplying drugs to the elite, there *must* be a way of finding out who their leader was. Someone among my peers had the connections. The Hands had targeted me for a reason, and it couldn't be a coincidence that the assassin had led me right into their clutches.

"Thank you," I said, and Sjease took my finished carrots without comment. I went back to my table and started writing, on a separate new list, names of people I knew who might be the type to be involved in that sort of scene. Not actual Councilors—there was still a certain level of propriety—but more remote family members, children of wealthy merchant and artisan families, especially ones who weren't in Guilds and had more leisure time than sense. It could, I thought, be quite a long list.

"Credo?"

"Mm?" I glanced up from my work. Sjease stood there, one hand clutching a bunch of fresh-picked herbs for the meal, the other balled into a fist by their side.

"Can you come to the garden?" There was a very strange look on their usually composed face, something unsettled; perhaps not afraid, but at least worried. Enough that I put aside the paper I was scribbling on and rose immediately, wincing on my sore leg.

"What's the matter?"

"Just . . . come out."

I followed them into the small garden at the back and side of our apartment, where I grew a variety of herbs and edible plants, and where our uncle was buried. It was a peaceful walled space, protected from the wind, and the path between the greenery was well trodden with the tracks of years of my pacing passage. There was no one out there, no sign of a disturbance. "What's the matter?" I asked again, but Sjease was already leading me to a leafy corner and pushing aside a heavy branch laden with flowers still drooping from morning condensation.

My question died in my throat. Something was hanging there, slung over the wall on a string, mostly concealed by leaves. Sjease, careful not to touch it, pulled back the foliage and stepped aside to give me a proper view. "I only saw it because I was bending over the parsley."

We both leaned in. It was a lumpy brown thing, stained in ways I found repulsive without fully understanding why; rather like a small, misshapen sack. What looked like wet, clumped feathers protruded from the top, as if someone had killed a bird and stuffed it in a bag without dressing it. Yet there was also something disturbingly deliberate about it, a precision in the binding, and, looking closer, tiny stitching down the side of the seam that resembled writing, though not in any language I recognized. I took the knife Sjease had been using to cut herbs and carefully sawed through the string from which it was hanging. We both stared at in silence as I straightened, dangling it from its string, and shared a look of uncomfortable revulsion.

It was not a dead bird, as I had first thought, though I was far from convinced the brownish stains on the fabric were not blood. I cut it open on the kitchen bench while Sjease watched, silent but visibly distressed, hovering just beside me. My slice exposed a strange interior. A sticky, pungent clump of dark, matted feathers, stones, and dirt. At the center lay something round and brown like a seed, about the size of an eye, and around it a little cross frame of wood wound through with yarn in an interlocking pattern. I recoiled from the thing. I still could not have said why it had affected us so but there was something almost malevolent radiating from it, inexplicable but undeniable. If I had been alone perhaps I might have convinced myself it was an overreaction, but Sjease's tight face and shallow breathing echoed my own.

"What *is* it?" Sjease asked at last, voice hesitant and shaken.

"I honestly have no clue," I said, regarding the thing with suspicion, a coil of dread in my stomach.

"And where did it come from? That wasn't there yesterday, I'm sure of it. Who left it there?"

I imagined the scene as if I'd witnessed it; a shadowy figure throwing it up and over the wall, then slipping away into the night. But *why?* What were we looking at? "I have no clue about that, either," I said quietly, "but I think it's safe to assume they aren't wishing us well."

INCIDENT: Poisoning of Credola Devin Leka

POISON: Zarnika

INCIDENT NOTES: Series of incidents targeting C. Devin's reputation observed over a period (see further notes at page d77); Leka family standing affected. C. Devin ceased appearing in public, rumors of a facial condition emerged. Investigation through household servants suggested extreme facial swelling and vomiting. Suspect zarnika poisoning through hair tonic but family refused further investigation (internal?? consider C. Keiran, noting unfortunate feud beginning when C. Devin made reference to C. Keiran's 'skin flaps' in public).

(from proofing notes of Credo Osi Oromani)

10

Kalina

Lord Ectar did not answer my first note, nor my second. By the end of the second day keeping a low profile in our apartments, Jov's injuries were healing but his mood had darkened; first there had been word of the rumors spreading through the servants, then the strange and disturbing parcel thrown over our wall, and then upon turning up in exasperation to try to see them in person, I was told everyone in the Talafan entourage was feeling "poorly" and could take no visitors. This despite the fact that I had arrived as several other visitors were leaving, including the Perest-Avani High Priestess and her disconcertingly attractive translator, who smiled at me with surprising warmth as we crossed paths.

"Please pass on my regards and my sympathies to the delegation," I had told the household manager, covering my frustration with a bow. I had no way of knowing whether the refusal was being extended to all Sjon or if it was targeted at me or my family. The women were isolated in that household, so how would they have learned gossip about the circumstances of a death, without contacts here in the city? Yet as I left the gardens and glanced back, the pale shape of a face at the window gazed back at me, unmoving. I raised a tentative hand in a wave, and it snapped back out of sight so fast it might never have been there. It left me unsettled. Tuhash had been Zhafi's lover and Lady Mosecca's son. If they believed the rumors, they likely hated my brother, and perhaps me by extension. Quite apart from the effect this might have on my future position as Ambassador, it made my insides heavy with regret.

Afterward, in the interests of maintaining appearances, Hadrea and I had taken Davi and Dee along with the rest of the family to make kites and fly them from the city walls. I tried to ignore the whispering, the sidelong looks, the carefully phrased questions, but it grew harder the more I smiled through them, ignoring their subtle digs and forays. It wasn't quite at scandal level, not yet, but momentum was building. Nor did it help that Hadrea was by my side, defiant and unfazed, provocative in her complete disregard for their opinions. I watched her now, striding confidently along the wall with Davi, showing him how to catch the wind and keep it. As with most physical activities she seemed almost supernaturally good at it, her snapping bright colors gliding and soaring with precision. If she even noticed people staring she gave no sign, but there was an awkwardness between us, an unseen block of questions I wanted to ask her but could not.

"Is it not bad manners to stare in any culture?" Hadrea said to me suddenly, and I blinked in surprise, and felt blood rush to my cheeks. I opened my mouth to apologize before she nodded once to her left and I snapped it shut again, realizing she was not talking about me at all. Through the merry crowd filling the walkway atop the walls, watching the kites and flying them, I saw her, too: a pale-faced figure, hair bound in a sensible scarf, her gaze locked on our group, twisting the end of her kite string in both hands. She was too distant to make out the detail of her face but as I peered at her it felt as if our eyes met. Unease spread through me like a growing stain, then a group of chattering young people crossed her path and she was lost to the crowd.

"She was Talafan?" Hadrea was looking at me curiously, her head cocked to one side and a concerned question in her eyes. I had been staring at the space where the woman had been, my mouth slightly open, my hands clenched in nervous fists. I shook myself and forced a shrug and a smile.

"I guess so." There was no reason to feel uneasy, but I realized even as I tried to shake it off that I did. Probably inevitable after spending two days obsessively poring over theories of conspiracies and assassins. My smile widened. "You are famous, to be fair."

Hadrea tossed her head with a snort. "She was not looking at me. Who do they call the Hero of Silasta, eh?" And she laughed when I ducked my head, embarrassed.

Silly or not, I kept an eye out for our observer, but with no luck: she had disappeared.

"Whoops, we're getting tangled." A much smaller kite was dancing dangerously close to the one Dee was controlling—and I ignored the tingling sensation down my spine, knowing it was only my imagination reacting to having been watched. Our assassin was not a northern woman, and no matter how intense her glare it was not a threat on our lives. It did make me wonder, though, how fast rumors of the manner of Tuhash's demise had spread. Could she be someone from the Talafan party who had known him? I thought again of the face at the window at the Leaning Lady and then for some reason of the old woman in the viewing box who had taken the doll from me. I shivered at the memory of the latter.

"Auntie!" Dee called out, half-laughing. "Help!"

The smaller kite, pale white against the blue sky, was butting up against our larger, brighter one. I put a hand on Dee's and gestured with my other in the opposite direction. "Here, let's move this way." We started to move away, but they were tangled and it had no effect. I started to pull our kite in, but Dee gasped, her eyes wide, and I whirled around even as I heard a heavy, menacing beat of air behind me. I had an impression of white and motion and a high-pitched shrieking cry, and then fiery sharp pain erupted as something seized my shoulder and slashed at my forehead. I flung my arms up to protect my face from the attack, and beside me Dee screamed and screamed. The heavy pounding of powerful wings, a stabbing, slashing beak, claws like a metal trap around my upper arm . . . blinded by my own bleeding forearms, I staggered sideways into the side of the parapet and crushed the great bird between my shoulder and the stone. Its claws released my arm and it slid off me, stunned at the blow. I sucked in a mouthful of grateful, desperate air but even as I tried to regain my balance the creature had flung itself aloft, wings beating hard enough to raise a cloud of dust from the walkway, and then with another terrifying swoop, latched onto Ana.

She howled with pain as it dug its claws directly into her short curly hair. She ran, panicking, down the walkway, stumbling and screaming all the while, the frightened crowd parting around her in alarm. I dragged blood out of my own eye and followed after her, but the kite cord was caught in my legs somehow and I almost tripped.

"Mama!" one of the boys yelled, trying to beat at the bird but succeeding only in collecting some slashes on his forearms as it turned its beak on him. Still it maintained its horrible clawing grip on Ana and her screams only intensified. Then Hadrea was there, what looked like a walking stick in her hands, striding past me.

"Stay still!" she barked, in such a forceful tone that Ana, hysterical as she was, stopped spinning and screaming for a moment. Without hesitation Hadrea swung the stick in a swift arc above Ana's head, striking the bird across its chest and wing and sending it tumbling off Ana and onto the walkway. There was a moment of silence as the crowd stared. Hadrea, letting out her breath, passed the stick from one hand to the other and then returned it to an elderly man standing nearby. "Thank you," she said calmly.

I tugged and scrambled to untangle myself from the kite cord then, free at last, crossed the last of the distance. "Are you all right?" I asked Ana. Large gouges shone red and gleaming from her scalp and she had gone a strange color. "Boys!" Her sons scrambled up and caught their mother on their shoulders as she slumped back, drained and beginning to cry. Etrika pressed her scarf to the worst of the cuts on Ana's head and someone from the crowd offered theirs to her son for his arm.

"Are *you* all right?" Hadrea, with a wary glance at the stunned bird on the ground, put a gentle hand on my shoulder and brushed hair out of the cuts on my face. "These are not too bad," she said, then frowned at the other shoulder. "These are worse. We will need to get you both to the hospital." I risked a glance down at my own arm and felt my stomach roil unpleasantly. There were deep wounds in the flesh of my upper arm and shoulder where the bird had clung to me. As if seeing them close somehow activated the pain, they stung and burned with fresh intensity. I peered down at the bird cautiously, noting the size of the claws.

It was a rorutus, a powerful hunter bird that preyed on small mammals out in the plains and rarely came near the city. I'd never seen one up close before, though Arjai Reed had a stuffed one he'd showed me once. It was magnificent, even dazed and with its beak and claws scarlet with our blood. I started to crouch beside it but the rorutus shook its great head as if startled then flapped its wings frantically as it tried to right itself. The whole crowd, myself included, sprang backward, and a child started crying somewhere in the circle we had inadvertently formed around the struggling bird.

My chest tightened with pity for the thing even as I recoiled. Hadrea closed her hands into fists, but her face looked grim and sad and I knew she felt it, too. But then the rorutus got both its feet on the ground, shook its head again, beak glinting menacingly, and flapped its wings again, and suddenly it was airborne once more. I flinched back, heart pounding, and I wasn't the only one; several people nearby screamed, and everyone pushed away still farther. But whatever interest or instinct had been driving the bird toward me and Ana, it was gone now, and so was my feathered enemy; swooping, sailing, sometimes lurching lopsidedly and being buffeted by the wind, it took off into the blue sky without so much as a squawk.

The crowd returned to life as if a spell had been broken. The wall walk filled with people crowding around me, asking questions, checking my wounds, staring. A bit of nervous laughter even rippled through the gathering; feeling on the edge of hysteria myself, I understood the urge. It had all happened so quickly and so unexpectedly. But Hadrea scowled around at them, unamused. "Clear the way so we can go to the hospital," she said loudly, and she looked so fierce people scrambled to obey.

Ana was still crying but had calmed enough to be led to the nearest stairs by one of the boys while the other raced ahead to call a litter. Dee, silent and wide-eyed but ever practical, recovered our kite while Hadrea bound her scarf around my arm to stop the bleeding. Still shaken, but recognizing the drama had ended, most people drifted back to their kites or their conversations. I saw a flash of white out of the corner of my eye and whirled, but it was only the white kite that had bumped into ours; it had lost the high wind and was slowly descending to the marshes outside the city, its string apparently abandoned. The owner must have lost hold during my tangled drag or in the confusion. Even so, I squinted at my feathered attacker and kept watch as it disappeared into the distance, some part of me afraid to turn my back on it in case it returned.

"I have never seen a bird do that before," Hadrea said at my side, soft enough that only I could hear.

"Neither have I," I said, trying to keep my tone even and not reveal the extent to which it had unsettled me. It had just been a random thing. A wild bird. Unfortunate, but hardly sinister. But Hadrea was looking at me with a funny expression, and with an unpleasant jolt I recognized it. Fear. I wasn't sure I had ever seen her afraid before, and it made my own anxious stomach worse. "Do you . . . do you think this is the kind of thing that can be . . . done?" I felt stupid saying it aloud. But I had seen a man choke and then break his leg in strange and suspicious circumstances only a few days prior, and there was just something about this incident that felt similarly improbable.

Hadrea didn't answer, but she still looked worried.

"Auntie, we should go," Dee interjected, appearing beside me.

I nodded to her, but risked a further question, almost whispered, to Hadrea. "Is it something that could be done with fresken?"

Her head snapped around and her eyes were sharp, her jaw tight. "No." Then she shook her head, her face softening. "No," she continued in a more conciliatory tone. "That is not how fresken works."

There was a short, tight silence. "Hadrea," I said tentatively. "About the other night . . ."

But she had turned away again. "Come on." She steered me gently by my uninjured arm. "Dee is right. You will need those cleaned. Birds can be dirty creatures and their wounds can turn bad."

"There are some diseases that spread by bird contact," Dee began, "and there's this horrible one that makes you bleed from the—" She caught herself and her enthusiastic expression slipped away. "Sorry, Auntie."

"Oh, good, I was worried it was just going to be a scratch or two," I said. I tried to smile to show her I was joking, but the pain was building and I was starting to feel dizzy. "You know how I like the attention."

Cleaning the wounds hurt more than having them inflicted, and by the time the physic had finished stitching up the worst of the cuts I was deeply grateful for having been unconscious and having no memory of any of my surgery after the river. The pain-numbing agent worked well enough but the sound and sensation of the skin being stitched together, especially on my scalp, was nightmarish.

"You'll need to stay here for at least a few hours," the physic told me briskly as he tied off the last of the thread. "Yes, yes, I know you're extremely busy," he added, raising a hand to cut off my protest, "and I'm aware it is in the middle of karodee. Nevertheless, my responsibility is to make sure you are properly recovered, and that there are no complications. With your medical history, you have to be careful, Credola. And there are a number of diseases linked to birds, some of which can be very serious."

"Yes, I hear I could end up bleeding out of some unpleasant place," I muttered, rolling over on the pallet and taking a deep, frustrated breath.

"What was that, Credola?" The physic had already started to move to the next patient.

"Never mind." A few hours, I could hold off a few hours. "How's my cousin?"

"Ana Oromani? With the scalp wounds?" He scratched his cheek. "She's doing well. There was a lot of blood, but no damage to her skull. She'll be fine."

"Good." With the mood Ana had been in lately, I couldn't imagine a random bird attack would have improved it in any case, but at least she hadn't suffered any permanent harm.

Still, when I asked Dee how her mother was an hour later when she came by to see me, she twisted one foot awkwardly on the ground and stared at it as she answered. "She's all right. She's . . . a bit upset. It was very scary," she added, as if I'd criticized her mother for weakness. Then the set of her jaw changed fractionally, and her tone took on a studied evenness. "She doesn't much like it here. Grandma told her there are birds in Telasa too and she got really cross."

My mouth twitched but I smoothed it out. "It *was* scary. I'm so glad she's all right though."

"I'm sorry I said the thing about the bleeding eyes disease," Dee said, peering at me earnestly through smudged glasses.

"Oh, eyes, was it?" I muttered dryly.

"I just thought of it. Sometimes I say things without thinking. I'm sorry, Auntie."

I reached out with my unbandaged arm and ruffled her hair. "It's fine. Look, can you do me a favor? Can you go home with Etrika and check on Jov?" Hadrea, once satisfied I was being properly cared for, had gone to our apartments to report what had happened, and I knew how worried he'd be. I'd been lucky: a lot of scratches on my forearms and some on my face and head, plus the gouges in my arm from the claws, but nothing that wouldn't heal, eyeball bleeding aside. But it was another blow against our family, even if one without malicious source.

Once Dee left I passed the time having silent arguments with myself in my head. *Had* it just been a random incident? Hadrea had said definitively that Darfri magic could not control an animal. It sounded absurd even in my head. But also . . . there were other magics in the world, other things we didn't fully understand. Uniform religion was intrinsically tied to the Talafan Empire and its expansion over the centuries: the Emperor was the anointed leader and their Star God tolerated no competition. Yet no land as vast as Talafar and all the territories it had swallowed could be a monolith of culture or spirituality. Talafan folklore was infested with witches and their strange magics; my brother had brought me a book of their children's stories before the siege, and it had been full of tales of witchmothers and flying princesses escaping towers and cruel princes and feeding hearts to hungry mountains. And animals that befriended lonely children and did the bidding of witches. Witches were part of Talafan folklore, and perhaps they, like the Darfri in my homeland, persisted in the face of indifference or opposition from the dominant culture. Once I might have assumed them to be no more than tales, children's stories, but we had been criminally, stupidly wrong about Darfri beliefs and magic and I wouldn't make that mistake again.

On the other hand, there were very real and very legitimate forces working against us that were *not* supernatural, and untangling that conspiracy needed our full attention. I couldn't let myself become distracted.

"Credola!" A familiar voice startled me out of my contemplation. "Half the city is talking about it. I saw the Perest-Avani diplomat, what is her name? Abae-something? And she said you were attacked on the walls by a monstrous winged beast!" Ectar swooped in and crouched beside me, eyes wide with dismay. "The poor thing was very distressed. Are you all right? How badly are you hurt?" His eyes traveled anxiously over my bandaged upper arm and shoulder, and the various cuts on my face.

"I'm fine," I reassured him. "Just scratched up a bit. It was just a bird." His expression, if anything, grew even more alarmed, so I smiled and patted his hand. "It was kind of you to come, anyway."

His hands gripped the edge of the pallet. Shook, then steadied. "Of course," he said.

"I heard they found your missing soldier," I said softly. "And I wanted to say I was so sorry it happened here in my city. I had hoped you would see Silasta without violence this time."

"Ah." He fidgeted, did not meet my gaze. "An unpleasant business, yes."

"The whole household must be so upset," I continued, risking a sidelong look; his head was tilted firmly down, staring at his hands, the bed, anywhere but me. "Poor Lady Mosecca. I met her, you know, a few days ago, and wanted to pass on my condolences."

"The lady is distraught, of course," he said. He pulled at the collar of his nihep as if it were too tight around his neck. "She is . . . It is a very difficult time. She had lost her husband not so long ago and Tuhash was her only son."

"I wanted to reassure you I personally know the Captain of our Order

Guards, and our determination council is very good. They'll investigate and find the person who did this."

Ectar looked at me quite sharply. "There must not be any investigation, Credola." At my perplexed frown he stopped and softened his tone. "I mean no offense, but you must understand. The circumstances in which he was found . . . it is very embarrassing. My grandfather His Majesty would not have such a thing made public. An investigation would be most ill-advised."

I blinked at him, genuinely surprised. "But—Ectar. He was killed. Do you not want to find out who, and see them punished?"

"He should not have been where he was," Ectar said, almost a whisper now. His face had flushed red, the shade clearly visible even through his cosmetics. "He had no business in some local house, doing the Great Lord only knows what. My grandfather's own spiritual adviser is here, you know this, even if he is confined currently due to injury. If Brother Lu hears any of this, it will go back to the Church. It must not. Lady Mosecca is a member of the royal household, Credola. She is a member of the Young Empress's court! The shame!"

I had known this was a risk, though I hadn't been sure how much the Talafan would infer from the circumstances in which Tuhash had been found. A rented house, hastily abandoned, evidence of a party gone too far, and the body in a compromising position. The Talafan Church was a powerful and strict master and its believers were not permitted certain freedoms. But still, the callousness was startling.

"Please. Convey to the right people that it would be most humiliating if the Royal Family were linked in any way to this scandal. I am confident my uncle the Prince has accepted the personal apologies given by your most honored Chancellor and your Administrative Guild. Please, let it go no further."

I hesitated. If he had heard this much, he would no doubt have heard the entirety of the rumor. "Ectar," I said quietly. "There are rumors, false rumors, but rumors you may hear—"

"They will not reach any further." There was a strange set to his jaw, and the speed of his reply told me whatever his sources of information, the rumor had at least reached him. I felt doubly grateful he had come to see me. "Your family is a valued trading partner, and a friend to the Empire. And, I would hope you know, to me." He cleared his throat, the flush on his neck deepening further still. "I would dismiss such things as nonsense, and would tell any as much, even someone in my own family."

I was oddly touched by his loyalty. "Thank you."

There was a long and awkward silence, in which he darted small, furtive glances at me, but did not speak. To break the moment, I asked, "Have you done much business with our western friends lately? I noticed the nations seem to be on better terms than usual, and Duke Lago and Prince Hanichii were extolling the virtues of their new waterway system to Minister Kokush earlier."

Ectar nodded, seeming grateful for the subject change. "Where opportunities present themselves, I am always interested. You are right to say that Tocatica and Maru, and Perest-Avana and Costkat, too, are working more cooperatively. Never have I seen so many westerners together in Izruitn than over the last few years. Why, the Tocatican delegation at Government House has tripled, I think." He chuckled. "But you need not fear I will forget my southern friends, Credola, if that is what you are worried about! There are many opportunities for all. You will see when you come to the Empire, do not worry. Minister Kokush was quite impressed with you, you know, and I have dozens of friends and colleagues who are awaiting your acquaintance with much anticipation. Many of us have been doing business in Sjona for years. I know there can be some cultural differences"—and here the sudden flush up the skin of his neck told me he'd heard of my encounter with Hiukipi—"but businessmen understand how things are here."

Cultural differences were one thing but rudeness was rudeness, and I hadn't mistaken Hiukipi's behavior for the former. But I smiled, to let him know I had taken no insult. "I wouldn't be much of a diplomat if I expected every culture to have the same standards and rules, Lord Ectar."

"Your interest in our culture and traditions is a pleasure to me, I admit it."

"It is a fascinating country," I said. And then, seized by impulse and curiosity, I added, "Some of the texts in our library are so dry. I would love to know more about some of your culture from you directly."

"Oh, yes?" He was gazing at me with an indulgent smile now, composure fully restored. "I would be delighted!"

"What can you tell me about witches?"

"What?" The word came out so aggressively he stumbled to add, "I mean, I am sorry, Kalina. What did you say? I did not quite understand the word."

"I am interested in Talafan folklore," I said innocently. "I started reading some of your myths and legends while I was recovering from my injuries. It is a lovely way to improve my language skills and learn something about the ancient cultures of your beautiful land. The word is *witch*, is it not? I have a book of your children's stories and several stories feature witches. It is not a concept we have in Sjona, and I am curious."

Ectar smoothed his impeccable nihep, looking over his shoulder as if fearing to be overheard. "Please." He sounded almost frightened. "That word is . . ."

I stared at him, curious about the reaction. "It is an . . . insulting word? A forbidden one? But I read it in a children's book."

"Witchcraft has been forbidden for decades, but in recent years the Church has decreed all talk of witchcraft a sin," he whispered, and his hand trembled on his sleeve as he brushed away imaginary lint. "You should not mention a child's tale like that to anyone, especially in the presence of Brother Lu. Or anywhere when you come to the capital. It could get you in trouble. Such stories are no longer permitted."

I blinked. "I did not know. My apologies, Ectar. I had read some stories and wondered whether it was something like our Darfri magic, if you would call it that."

A shadow and a shudder passed over him, and I knew he was recalling what he had seen in the siege.

"I won't bring it up again," I promised, and turned the subject to his business dealings; always a safe topic. While he gratefully seized the opportunity to tell me about some reclusive Sjon gemstone merchant he had been trying to do business with, inside my thoughts raced. Far from reassuring me, the conversation had convinced me there was much more to these legends than stories for children, and we should ignore that at our peril.

INCIDENT: Hallucinogenic honey from Chakra township

POISON: Atrapis

INCIDENT NOTES: Several guests at Beaton family party in Silasta, including prominent legal scholar Jacin Dimi, writer Shan Borti, and chief librarian Aidenna Khehir, appeared to suffer significant dramatic hallucinations and died from a fall from the roof. Witnesses attested the women were convinced they had grown wings (it appears they became tangled in a tablecloth). Several elderly guests hospitalized. Source of intoxication eventually traced to honey pastries consumed at party. Entire batch contaminated with atrapis; investigation in source at Chakra revealed wild atrapis in bee feeding zone. Honey seized and Leka family fined for negligence of beekeepers under care of steward. (Unofficial trade in unrecovered honey continues at a premium within the cities.)

(from proofing notes of Credo Bobi Oromani)

11

Jovan

I had been in effective exile for days now, and we were out of fresh ideas. Rather than being short of information, we now had too much of it.

I didn't know what to make of the business with the bird. Kalina and Ana had been injured, and too many unsettling and unpleasant things had occurred to dismiss the possibility of supernatural forces at work, whether native to our country or not. Once alerted to the possibility of such things, I found myself seeing them everywhere. An oven that flared too high and fast, catching my sleeve alight. A passing worker who had slipped on a stone on the street outside our apartments and almost crushed my foot with his fallen load of bricks. Little accidents and incidents ordinarily no more than bad fortune felt like miniature staged attacks on our family. Poisons, deceptions and lies, even assassins, these things we were at least trained to deal with, but against the supernatural I had no armor.

And all the while, our enemies circled, drawing closer. I could smell it, yet here I was stuck in my apartments, doing nothing for Tain other than preparing his food, forced to leave him in the hands of the blackstripes who would not recognize the assassin if they saw him. And no matter how hard Kalina and I studied what we knew, tried to identify things we might have missed, speculated about what was planned next, we were no closer to an answer. My leg and rib injuries hobbled me, preventing me from moving around with ease, and so my compulsive habits felt concentrated somehow, more intense, for the lack of being able to use my whole body in them. Sitting at the table together for hours, it was natural to fidget as we read and drew lines connecting linked theories and talked out possible motivations for the thousandth time, but the distractions interrupted my patterns and wound up the tension inside me. Kalina didn't comment, she never did, but it was clear my relentless tapping, flicking, and tensing was affecting her, too.

"If this is part of a single plan—"

"It's too convoluted. I can't even work out what we're thinking here," Kalina said, gesturing to the piles of paper, the scrawls and the lines and the jumbled mess of our thoughts, and I couldn't argue. *We look mad. Paranoid and mad. If anyone came in here now they'd not listen to a thing we said, and I couldn't blame them.* "We *think* the man you keep seeing is connected to the Hands, because he led you right to them, but from what Dee says, they were surprised to find you there, so he didn't warn them. And we know they're connected to these new drugs, and they've either got a grudge against you or are working for someone who does. But I don't know how this connects to the rebellion, or to anything to do with the Darfri. Can this really be all part of some giant scheme? Are we just overcomplicating everything?"

Frustration, exhaustion, a mild sense of panic, it all seemed to rise in a wave. The fact was, there were too many moving parts, and it was impossible to know which were connected. Darfri agitators in the city could be a false problem manufactured by Credolen with a grudge against the Darfri or at least self-interest in diminishing the growing power of the lower classes. Or it could be a legitimate expression of dissatisfaction by people still angry about how slowly progress had been made and the continued existence of the Credol seats on the Council. We knew there were spirits dying, even if we didn't know why. Maybe some Darfri really had gotten drunk and set fire to a boat, or pushed someone into a canal, though I doubted any magic was actually involved in either of those incidents. Or—perhaps more likely—it could be the enemy who had helped incite us to a civil war only a few years ago was once again creating wedges between our people, trying to turn us on each other.

"It could be the same group that's already working against me. Everyone knows I'm a 'Darfri sympathizer,' to use the charming phrase I heard out of one of Karista's younger sisters recently, and lots of people know about my relationship with Hadrea. Naming her as a perpetrator not only hurts Darfri relations in the Council, it hurts me personally, too." I ran my fingers through my hair. "It all has to be coming to something, doesn't it? They can't be separate, unrelated problems, not when everything is just converging like this, all around the karodee."

Even to myself it sounded more hopeful than convinced. Perhaps I only wanted it to be a single problem, because that left open the possibility that if we just *thought* hard enough, we could solve it.

The list from the hospital had finally arrived today. Thendra had included a short note on top, in her own hand. *I conclude are looking for a man with very large hands, based on the marks on the neck.* Something had unwound in my chest in relief, knowing that was her way of telling us she accepted our explanation and would keep our confidence. My reputation had suffered, but servants gossiping in markets and peers whispering behind their hands was a very different matter from getting hauled before a determination council, accused of murder.

Here is your list of deaths, no doubt for the purposes of research. I have not completed the more complex task of identifying all presentations to the hospital, as you can imagine, but for now, I have enclosed presentations in the last week as they were on hand. Some poor clerk at the hospital had obviously been tasked with compiling the list; over the past three months there had been forty-eight deaths recorded. "Is that a lot?" Kalina had wondered aloud. "For natural or unnatural causes?"

I had shaken my head absently. "Not really. Etan told me once it was usually something like two hundred a year, in a city this size, with our medical care. It'd be a higher rate outside Silasta because we have the best physics here. Probably way higher in the Empire, especially among the lower classes. But violent deaths are rare . . . well, less rare since the siege, but still not exactly common."

The list contained bare details, just a name and a cause of death. I had circled any reasonably proximate to the dates I'd seen the assassin. I read the list more generally now, hoping something would jump out at me as significant.

"Only a few murders, that's some—that's gruesome," Kalina said, pausing at an entry for a man found in a canal with his throat slit. "Honor-down, there's two of them."

"Chen told me about those when they happened. She thought those were gang retaliations," I said, without looking up. "She says the gang—these Prince's Hands—collect money from businesses in the lower city and send thugs to beat up anyone who doesn't pay. Then all the business owners are too scared to talk to Chen's people. And they're even harsher on their own members." It was sickening to think of such a thing happening here, of all places. Our non-violent city had no place for such brutality. Despite the siege and the battle and all the mistakes we'd made, I still wanted to believe we were better than the kind of city where people were found in canals with their throats slit.

"I don't know half these names," I muttered, frustrated. "How are we supposed to know if a death is significant if we don't know who it was? Do any of these sound familiar to you?"

Kalina scanned my list of deaths near the relevant dates. "Traviso Oskata. He's an Order Guard, isn't he? Pretty senior, too."

"Yeah," I said, looking more closely at that entry. "Ex-soldier. He was here during the siege. Always smoked too much janjan and had that cough." According to the list he'd died of apparent lung disease, which accorded with my memory of a thin, reedy man who coughed often. "Can't imagine why he'd have been a target. Though . . ." I checked back on his list of events. "He died, what, two days after the arena opening, that's the first event on my list. He might have been working security for it, definitely." I chewed my lip, but I was feeling slightly more encouraged. "What else is there?"

A few members of Guilds, a couple of Credolen and merchants; plenty of deaths that appeared to be accidental, but could easily enough have been caused by someone who knew what they were doing around poisons. *Like us.* The list of presentations for accidents and illnesses was longer than the death list despite only covering a week. In addition to a range of accidents and alcohol- or narcotic-related admissions from masquerade night, evidently there had been a good dozen people admitted for apparent burning pox the following day. "I know some of these names," Kalina said, pointing to the section on pox sufferers. "This woman, An-Kake, is on the karodee committee, I was talking to her about ticketing for the closing ceremony."

I glanced up. "Yes, someone else from the committee was complaining about that the other day," I said, thinking back to the little group of frantic committee members I'd dodged after that particularly tense Council meeting. "They were worried about how they were going to manage the ceremony with half their members out if they didn't get better soon."

Kalina squinted at a little note beside the first of the pox cases, in Thendra's handwriting. "'Unsure of diagnosis at this time,'" she read out. "She's not sure it's pox?"

"Huh." I stopped what I was doing. I suddenly felt very aware of my breathing, yet I felt strangely calm.

"What is it?"

"It's just . . . burning pox is pretty distinctive. I only know one thing that presents like it but isn't," I said slowly. "If you got them handling false goaberries they'd get a rash with hives that look pretty similar to the pox. And it's burning, incredibly painful. They'll be in the hospital for weeks if they handled the juice." The beginnings of an understanding were creeping up on me. I took a breath, got my own composure steady. I needed not to chase the thought too hard and lose it. "The one thing we can be certain of is what happened to me. Whether it was impromptu or the assassin deliberately lured me to the Hands, either way, *why* did they do what they did?"

Kalina leaned back, thoughtful. She started to tuck her hands behind her head but flinched and stopped; her arm was still bound and the nasty gouges from the bird must have still hurt. "If the plan had worked, if you'd been caught with Tuhash's body like they hoped, what would have happened?"

"I'd have been under investigation by the determination council, for starters."

"And if a formal investigation was indicated, you wouldn't be free to wander around in public, acting like everything was normal. If their plan had worked, you might not be in jail but you certainly wouldn't be attending public events. Even if you weren't formally accused, the Talafan contingent will be at the closing ceremony, and it makes sense you wouldn't stand right there in their faces. Maybe that's why, out of every drunk they could have pulled out of the masquerade, they chose a Talafan one."

"All right, but that's where I am anyway, isn't it?" I tried to keep the bitterness out of my voice. "If they wanted me out of the way, it worked. I've been stuck here for days because we thought that was the right thing to do."

"But why out of the way and *not dead*? Dead is easier. If you're causing them trouble, why bother discrediting you when they could just kill you? Because if you were dead," she answered herself slowly, "imagine what would have happened. Would your best friend in all the world, your brother practically, be heading out to the closing ceremony tomorrow?"

I blinked. If I were dead, Tain would be in deepest mourning. "No. Of course he wouldn't."

"Then what if *that's* what they wanted. For *you* to miss the closing ceremony, but not Tain."

I poked the list with one finger. "Honor-down. Lini, I think you're right. There are going to be people missing from the ceremony planning staff. Maybe at least one Order Guard who was meant to be on security." I flexed my hands in turn, the count almost forgotten as my gaze skidded over the papers before us, rapid and anxious, but almost exhilarated; it felt like we were on the edge of understanding. "They're planning something, and it's *got* to be at the closing ceremony. Could they be inciting a riot? Another miniature rebellion? We didn't notice the signs last time, but they knew how to turn people against each other, all right. They were bloody experts at it." There would be thousands of people packed into the arena. Had things really gotten so bad again between the classes without us noticing? Even with all of the steps we'd taken? "How in all the fortunes could we guard against something like that happening?"

"It would distract everyone," Kalina said. "Create chaos. Having some key staff out of the picture will make it harder to control the event."

"Or," I muttered, thinking, "it's the opposite. We're worrying about riots and things that could go wrong on a big scale, but think about this: the closing ceremony is the only event Tain can't, or won't, skip. And he'll be visible, they'll know where he's going to be, but the opposite won't be true; half the bloody city is going to be packed into the arena, anyone could hide. If the assassin, or whatever he is, and the Hands are working together, the fortunes only know how many people they've got at their disposal."

"You're saying this time it really *could* be an assassination," Kalina said grimly. "Because this time you're not supposed to be there, so it's not a setup for you. What if they're really going to try to kill Tain this time." She took a hard breath. "He'll be in the viewing box, with all of the representatives from the other countries. They'll have armed guards, all of them, they got special dispensation from the Council, remember? If one of them, or more than one of them, is behind this . . ."

I stood abruptly, took a step, having forgotten my sore ankle, swore, and caught myself on the windowsill. "We'll tell him he can't go."

"We can try," she said doubtfully.

"We'll bring this to the blackstripes and the Order Guards. If they agree there's a threat, they won't let him go, or they'll cancel the whole thing."

She shook her head. "And how would that look? He can't tell our supposed allies he suspects one of us might have financed our own civil war and might still be working against them. Besides, it's his big event, Jov. He's worked himself to the bone for this. I think he thinks—" She stopped, a strange, worried shadow passing over her face. "I think he thinks the country's legacy, and the new Council and everything he's worked for, will be kind of cemented, if this karodee is a success."

"Well, he should be less concerned with his legacy and more concerned with living long enough to *have* one," I retorted. "One thing at a time."

She gave me a funny look, her brow furrowed, her eyes searching, as if I'd misunderstood her, but after a moment she shook her head and laid a hand on my arm. "Assume no one is going to agree to cancel the ceremony unless we bring absolutely watertight evidence about what's going to happen. Let's concentrate on getting Tain not to go. If we sound paranoid they'll dismiss us, so we need to simplify this, find the most convincing bits of information to take to them to show them there's a real threat."

"They have to listen," I said, but I could already see their faces. The polite incredulity. The *tolerance*. The dismissal. "Lini, I just know there's something wrong, and I don't ignore that feeling anymore, not ever, not ever again."

I realized I was sweating, breathing heavily. My sister's hand shifted from my arm to my forehead, testing temperature. "Your skin feels hot," she said, frowning. "Maybe we ought to have Thendra look at you again. You don't seem well and we don't really know what those drugs could have done to you."

"I'm fine. It's probably the strain of being cooped up here." It came out sharper than I'd meant it to, and I regretted it when hurt slid across her features. She knew better than anyone what it was like to be cooped up involuntarily, and complaining about my brief stint made me something of an entitled baby. "Sorry."

"It's all right. Look, I don't think we should ignore the instinct, either. We just need to work through it first though. There's no point bursting into the Manor demanding we cancel a ceremony people have spent literally months planning without being able to offer a firm threat. They won't listen to you."

The anger dropped from me and I slumped, deflated. "I know." They hadn't listened about the assassin and they weren't listening about the dead spirits on the estates, or the spread of Void, or anything else that upset their illusion that the mistakes of the past were over and the country was safe. They wanted to believe Aven had somehow funded all her machinations herself, had forgotten or ignored her admission in front of witnesses that she was an agent of another party. But here in front of us, fractured as it was, was evidence another move was being made against us. "We'll prepare something, and we'll *make* them listen."

INCIDENT: Poisoning of Warrior-Guilder Ana Stefevo

POISON: Poison rookgrass

INCIDENT NOTES: Warrior-Guilder Ana collapsed and suffered a series of convulsions at site of battle with White Taskjer tribe (Doran). Several senior officers suffered similar but less severe effects, traced to consumption of roasted bindie; contents of stomach revealed distinctive yellowed flesh suggesting bindie consumed poison rookgrass. Tactical disadvantage of incapacitation of key officers suggests Doranite infiltration of camp. Warrior Guild to conduct own internal investigation in search of spies.

(from proofing notes of Credola Tasuri Oromani)

12

Kalina

"They didn't listen."

Even if he hadn't said it, I'd have known it from the visible combination of anger and exhaustion written on my brother's face as he slumped into the apartment. My heart sank. *Maybe I should have gone*, I thought guiltily. *Even if I'm not a Councilor, maybe it would have been taken more seriously coming from someone else.*

"Who came to the meeting?" I asked, clearing some space between Dija and me at the table. Dija glanced nervously at Jovan as he sat, but had the presence of mind to quietly pour him a tea, which he took gratefully.

"Captain and Second of the blackstripes at the start," he said, voice hollow. He took a long sip. "And Moest showed up near the end, and then a few of the karodee committee. Tain was the only one not looking at me like I was the simple child in the room who needed to be accommodated. They made a show of listening, but they just don't believe it." He hesitated, looking at Dija, then glanced around the room. We were alone, Sjease having agreed to take today as their day off, and the rest of the family having gone out with some of their Telasan friends this morning.

"It's just us here," I reassured him, but his gaze lingered on his apprentice, uncertain. I knew he was feeling guilty about what she had seen and done on his behalf. Had Etan felt this way, I wondered suddenly, when he had trained us? Had there been a point where the games and tests had become so serious he had worried it was wrong to involve children? Most of those early skills had felt more like games than traumas: stay unseen in this room for an hour; find out the name of a popular singer's favorite pet; steal a letter from a pile for delivery, causing a slight and a fractured relationship between two families, and ultimately prevent a particular business deal. I had never felt any reluctance on his part, and on mine I had wanted so desperately to be useful, to earn the right to honor on my own behalf, even if only a private renown between my Tashi and myself. But it would have been different with Jov. Proofing was more dangerous than my quiet arts, and the training required punishing the body again and again. It could not have been easy for Etan to do that to his beloved nephew, not even with the best and most honorable of motives. He had given his life and his devotion to Chancellor Caslav and his family, but he had loved us.

Jov caught my eye and I sensed his reluctance to speak in front of Dija. He might have to poison her, because there was no other way to teach the ways of our family's art, but she didn't need to be embroiled in politics at this stage, nor did she need to grapple with the mystery of Aven's financier and their apparent grudge against our country. She could be young, a little longer.

But stubbornness was an Oromani trait if anything was, and Dija squared her little jaw and asked, her voice small but firm, "Is there going to be another attack on the Chancellor?"

He looked surprised, then cross, then worried, all in the space of a few breaths. Then he sighed. "Yes," he said at last. "Yes, we think so, Dija. There's been a range of poisonings, we think, of people who are involved in the closing ceremony, maybe to make it easier for them to get someone in position for whatever they're planning. And we think the reason I was attacked and then set up was to make sure I didn't come."

She swirled the tea in her cup around in a manner reminiscent of how Etan used to do it. "And they didn't listen? The Chancellor doesn't believe you?"

"Of course he believes me," Jov replied sourly. "And he told them so. But he thinks they can keep him safe anyway, or at least he's willing to pretend he thinks that. The committee head looked like she was going to faint when I suggested we cancel the ceremony and just formally end the karodee at some smaller, private event."

I bit back the curses springing to my tongue. I hadn't really thought they'd be willing to cancel the event, but hearing it dismissed out loud was still painful.

"They kept saying they'll look into things, take all our concerns seriously, and they'll take precautions, but . . . I don't know, Lini. Either they never really believed Aven wasn't working alone or two years of peace have made them complacent. They'll be on the lookout for an assassin but I couldn't really make them understand we could be dealing with an entire criminal gang."

I frowned. "Did they say anything about the dead man?"

"Directly? No. But they'd absolutely heard about it already. Even little Erel was giving me some funny looks. One of them made a bit of a snide comment and Tain took it head-on, said he thought rumors to that effect were part of a pattern of discrediting me. No idea if the Captain believed him or not." He shook his head. "So much for the honor of the Oromanis, eh? Famous the country wide for uncovering a conspiracy, but fortunes forbid anyone should listen to us when we're warning them about another one. You'd think," he said, acquiring a knife and stabbing into a piece of cold meat with unnecessary vigor, "all that bloody fame would at least earn us the right to be taken seriously when we're trying to save lives."

But there, of course, was the paradox. The careful actions over time, the poisonings, the unnatural good luck in our political and business life had done their work in sowing suspicions about my brother's true nature; the irony was by identifying the deaths and injuries as suspicious, they already had evidence of a thoughtful, careful planner. Yet presenting these actions as part of a conspiracy rather than a random series of events was scoffed at, called paranoid.

"What changes are they making, then? Presumably Tain reassured them you were to be listened to on this. Right? Is he staying away, at least?"

He scoffed. "No, you were right. He wouldn't hear of it. You said it yourself, he's too invested in this going well."

"Do you think . . ." I stopped. I'd tried to bring this up yesterday, but even then I'd not been able to properly articulate what had bothered me. There were just things Tain had said, impressions he'd given off, that unsettled me in an indefinable way. "He worries me sometimes. He's so focused on the karodee, and he said something to me about Merenda, about her being accepted as Heir . . ."

Jov looked up sharply from his food. "What about Merenda? She seems competent enough, and Tain likes her."

"He said something about not wanting her to have to deal with what he dealt with. Being thrown into a disaster and having to be a Chancellor in a crisis instead of one in peace."

He looked at me, a deep line between his eyes. "What's he worrying about that for, of all things? We can't control now what the country will look like in forty or fifty years. We have to focus on our problems *now*. He's got enough to be going along with." He drained the last of his tea. "Chances are Merenda won't ever have to rule anyway. Her daughters are going to join her here next year, and it'll likely be one of them who eventually joins the Council."

He'd missed my point. I opened my mouth to explain that what worried me was Tain seeming to see only far ahead enough to contemplate a position of stability, as if that were the end of the line. As if that were the end of *his* line. But instead I pressed my lips together again. There was no point sharing that particular anxiety with someone who already carried too many. "If he's going, what are they doing to protect him then?"

"They'll change the route they take tonight. And Tain will show up for the obstacle course final but not move up to the box until after that's finished, so he'll approach from an unexpected area." He sighed. "It's not enough. He's still going to end up in that viewing box and there's only so many ways of getting there, and none at all I can guarantee won't be blocked."

"What can we do?" Dija asked. I was proud of her composure even as I worried about it. Jovan must have felt the same way because he looked at her more warily than appreciatively.

"You don't need to do anything," he said. "I'm going to have to break it to your mother and grandmother that all of you should stay home tonight. I've got no idea what will happen, but if we can't have the bloody thing canceled then at least you can stay safe here. But in the meantime, you're going to go to the craft markets this afternoon with your aunt, same as we promised." He stabbed another piece of meat and scowled at it. "And I am going to search my papers another time to see if I can find anything we've missed that will serve as incontrovertible proof."

Dija set down her cup, and a little tea sloshed out of it, the only sign of her displeasure. "I don't want to go to the craft markets while the Chancellor is in danger," she said. "I would rather help you. That's what I'm here for, isn't it?" Her tone was polite, but there was a little of her frustration in that last sentence.

"This one's bigger than you, little one," I said gently. I, in any case, still wanted to go to the market, had banked on going to the market, because it was where I had asked Zhafi to meet me. "Jovan has told the Chancellor's guard what we know. There's nothing we can add unless we have more information."

She nodded, but carried the tension in her shoulders all throughout the remainder of the meal. By the time we were ready to leave for the market, later, Jov was already buried in papers again, a frown of concentration on his face. I squeezed his shoulder. "Have you considered just poisoning all of them so they're too sick to come?"

"Haven't ruled it out," he said with a scowl.

Bright canopied stalls lined the edges of the market, not selling their normal array of everyday goods this afternoon but instead offering various karodee crafts. Dee and I wore ribbon crowns and strolled together through the crowd, trailed at a discreet distance by our houseguard Lara, and I feigned smiles and casual conversation with other festivalgoers, exchanging ribbons and pretending the peaceful enjoyment that should have characterized the last day of karodee. Dee bounced along beside me, eyes wide and watchful and a faint smile at the corners of her mouth. She seemed to have recovered well from her ordeal, or at least she played the part well enough. A day in bed had done me good, too; we had still come down to the lower city by litter, but so far neither my legs nor my lungs had protested the gentle activity.

We made paper boats that were supposed to carry the year's bad luck away, and sailed them together in the canal, dodged giggling children holding hands and solving clues to the great citywide treasure hunt, and fed the last of our seed cones to persistent gulls hopping hopefully among the thicket of legs. All the while I watched the gently moving crowds, looking for telltale pale skin, or broad-brimmed hats among the ribbon crowns. There were plenty of northerners in the crowd, along with tall Doranites and various westerners, some bedecked in local fashion and exchanging ribbons, some merely watching our rituals, but I recognized no one from the official Talafan delegation.

Perhaps Zhafi had not received my note, or not found it hidden in the book I had sent her. Perhaps the low rumblings of scandal around my family had reached her after all, or perhaps she blamed me for Tuhash's fate. Or perhaps she simply had no desire to go out in public so soon after receiving terrible news. But I had to *try*, at least, to see her. Perhaps the other women knew her secret and were comforting her. Certainly at least some of them must have known she had slipped out at masquerade, but did they know the extent of it? The possibility that she was alone in her grief, unable to disclose to anyone what she was feeling, had haunted me for days. I already pitied her lonely lifestyle and her lack of self-determination; I couldn't bear the thought that she might have to hide herself when she most needed support.

I had not sought a reply; it would be difficult, perhaps impossible, for her to send a messenger with a private message in ordinary circumstances, let alone if sentiment in the Prince's household had turned against us. There was no doubt the rumors about Jovan had now spread widely, judging by the speculative, sidelong looks and whispers that followed my passage. Some people gave me overly warm greetings, their gazes intense and searching, their grips too earnest. Others avoided me altogether.

"Is your brother here today?" one of the Reed cousins asked me, only moments after handing over a bright red ribbon in exchange for one of my greens. She threaded it into her crown with an innocent smile. "I've heard he's a bit more sociable than he used to be."

I didn't like her sly giggle and took my time fastening her ribbon to my crown. "No, I'm afraid he's been injured. He was attacked a few nights ago. Attempted robbery. Didn't you hear?"

She gave a theatrical gasp, clapping her hands to her mouth. I touched her arm and gave a sympathetic smile. "You know, people say the Reeds are always the last to know anything, but I don't think it matters. It's just gossip, isn't it? Anyway, a bounteous and fortunate season to you." I finished with the ribbon and turned down to Dija. "Let's get something to eat, Dee, what do you think?"

We diverted to a long table nearby where people were making pastries, leaving the Reed woman behind, her mouth working in silent fury.

"That was a bit mean," Dija said, looking up at me solemnly as we took our place at the bench.

"It was," I agreed. I wouldn't apologize for it. "There's nothing the Reeds fear more than being left behind the news." It was Lazar's great paranoia to be always trailing a trend or a word of gossip, and he'd infected his whole family with it.

A line of half a dozen cooks with powerful arms and sweating, cheerful faces pounded the flour behind the bench, and someone passed us a section of the sticky finished product. Dija surprised me by turning an extremely cheeky grin on me. "I've never seen you be mean. Properly mean. Not just teasing."

"Oh, sweetie," I murmured, rolling my ball of pastry with a little more vigor than was strictly called for. "If they come after our family, they'll be seeing more of that."

We rolled the little rice pastries and stuffed each one full of sharp orange and creamy barbanut paste, Dee with an oddly satisfied look on her face.

"Credola." A soft voice to my left as someone joined the group.

"Your Highness." I started to turn toward her but Zhafi made a small sound of protest or warning. Under the guise of adjusting my crown I looked around. Zhafi's blond servant, Esma, stood on her other side, but I saw no other Talafan ladies about. However, a clot of hard-faced Imperial soldiers were behind her and, at their core, Brother Lu in a wheeled chair borrowed from our hospital. He swatted insects and glared around as if looking for an excuse to end the excursion. Fortunately, market day was the most innocent and harmless part of karodee. I glanced at Zhafi without being too obvious about it. She wore a broad-brimmed hat that hung down, shading her cheeks, a ribbon crown fashioned around its band. "A bounteous and fortunate season to you," I said in Sjon.

"A bounteous and fortunate season to you," Dee piped up politely from my other side. We both untied a ribbon from our crowns and Zhafi, fumbling slightly, did the same. I chanced a quick look back at her grim entourage. Several of them looked bored, the others wary, but no one seemed to object to the Princess exchanging spring greetings or ribbons. It was not clear whether any of them had recognized me.

"A . . . bounteous and fortunate season to you, too," Zhafi replied softly, and I had to mask my surprise. Either she had practiced the greeting extensively by rote, or she actually spoke some of our language, because her Sjon was easily understandable. "What are you making?" she asked in Talafan, and there was something brittle in her tone.

"Sweet buns." I handed her a piece of fresh dough, and passed my completed cakes over to the cook steaming buns over a big pot at the end of the table. "Here, you roll it like this."

She pushed it tentatively against the table. "Like this?"

"You'll need to put a bit more wrist into it," I said. I glanced around the table casually. No one I recognized. I dropped my tone further all the same. "Are you all right?"

Her hands paused, bright-painted nails digging into the white dough. "I didn't know what else to do," she whispered, and my chest ached with the childlike helplessness in her words.

"I am so sorry."

She seemed to have gotten the knack of rolling the ball, and accepted the bowl of paste from me, silently copying the thumb action to make a hole for the filling. When she spoke it sounded like she was fighting back tears. "We thought about running away, you know. On this trip. My brother is selling me off just when I had dared hope I might be free."

I had to strain and concentrate to understand her. She spoke so fast and so low, the words draining from her like I'd lanced a boil. "I was foolish. I thought myself so worldly because my father let me fund orphanages and workhouses and travel the Empire. But I was never really independent, I just thought I was. As soon as a better use was found for me than generating goodwill in the capital, it can all be taken away." A hand darted up, quick as a kitsa catching an insect, to wipe her cheek. "But Tuhash loved me. He was not like any of the other men of the court, who treated me like blown glass. He knew me and he wanted me, for *me*."

That struck such a chord in my heart that I dared reach out and briefly touch her hand. Fortunes, I knew what it was like to covet the sensation of being properly seen. The touch seemed to puncture her; the hat slumped and her spine loosened, and she let out a tiny hurt sound like a small animal in pain, quickly suppressed.

I knew grief. Even though it had been more than two years, Jov and I still liked to sit late in the night sometimes and talk about Etan; remembering and sharing stories about the kind of man he had been, or relaying those stories to Dee. It helped. "What was he like?" I asked.

"He was . . . exciting." Her voice strengthened. "A little wicked, perhaps. He had such wild dreams, and when he spoke of us together taking on the world, it felt real. He was so handsome, and charming, and he had a way of making me feel like I was the only woman in the world, like he would not be able to breathe if I was not kissing him. He could have told me to throw myself in the ocean and I'd have done it." Her head was tilted firmly down, apparently concentrating on her task, but there was the hint of pride and pleasure in her words now. I felt sure she had not said this aloud before.

Beside me, Dee was a little too still, clearly unable to stop listening even if she did not understand the language we were speaking. Gently, under the bench, I touched her foot with mine, and she gave a tiny start and began stuffing her rice buns again. The first batch was cooked now, and the smiling cook slid the board back to our end of the bench, laden with the fragrant sticky steamed cakes. "Here, try this," I said in Sjon, and offered Zhafi one of the fresh cakes. "It's a karodee special."

I took a bite of a bun myself, enjoying the contrast of flavors and textures; smooth, silky outside, creamy and crunchy inside. "Zhafi," I said slowly, because I could not bear to leave unacknowledged the part I'd played in this mess. "I'm sorry if what I did—"

"No." She set down her bun, shook her head, glanced hurriedly over her shoulder at her minders. "No, it was our own recklessness. With Brother Lu in your hospital, we thought we were so clever, tricking everyone. We did not want to be denied the excitement of the masquerade, not when we thought our freedom was so close." She gave a hard little laugh. "It was all foolishness. Perhaps some part of us knew we would never get away, and we wanted . . ." There was a pause, then for the first time Zhafi lifted her head and looked at me directly. Tear tracks marked the cosmetics on her face. "I loved Tuhash, but he did not always make wise decisions. How he behaved after we parted was his decision, not yours and not mine. It was not your fault, Kalina. You protected us. You protected me, when you barely knew me, more than once. Why did you do that?"

The sudden question, and its intensity, surprised me. It was my turn to search for words. "I liked you," I said honestly. "I know what it's like to be more than what people think you are, and I understood how frustrated you must have been. I don't think anyone should be punished for that."

This time she touched *my* hand. "You are a kind person, Kalina Oromani. I won't forget. I will tell my father so, if I have any influence left to spend."

And then all of a sudden she was gone in a whirl of Talafan silks and high emotion.

I took another bite of my cake and chewed, both touched and relieved the conversation had gone as it had. Zhafi was an intelligent and passionate woman trapped by circumstance in a position not of her making, and I had contributed to the death of not just her lover but her dream. The anger and bitterness of thwarted hope could very easily have been redirected at me and my family, or even my country. We had been fortunate indeed to escape it.

"Do you want to make a lantern?" I asked Dee with forced cheer. My niece was studying me interestedly, her gaze assessing behind her glasses and her expression suggesting she had understood far more of that conversation than she should have been able to, for someone who did not speak the language. "Or shall we go home?"

But before she could answer, the empty space left by Zhafi was filled with another, and once again as if on cue I heard a soft foreign voice saying, "A bounteous and fortunate season to you, Credola Kalina."

Unlike Zhafi, the Perest-Avani diplomat had made no attempt at subtle integration or disguise. She wore a high-necked dress and jewelry in her country's fashion, in riotous reds and golds and beads glinting in the sun. I returned the greeting warily, watching her closely as we exchanged ribbons. This woman, with her warm, inviting smile, seemed to be everywhere I was, and it would be foolish to put that down to a coincidence. On my far side, I felt Dee's tension.

The translator bowed her head low with her fingertips touching together lightly in the western style. It exposed the back of her head and the intricate patterns shaved into her close-cropped hair, visible below her ribbon crown. "We have not been formally introduced. I am known as Abaezalla Runkojo, and I am here in Silasta by grace of General Iheanako, benevolent high ruler of Perest-Avana." Her Sjon was smooth and barely accented.

"A pleasure to meet you," I said, watching her closely as she straightened. She was much taller than I, and up close her glorious burnished brown skin seemed almost luminous, her eyes black and liquid as ink in candlelight, the bones of her face like a carving from the sculpture garden. A dangerously beautiful woman. "We have passed each other a few times, have we not? I thought you were on the staff of the High Priestess?"

"Yes, but I do not work for the High Priestess," she said, smiling. Her teeth were very white. "I was assigned by General Iheanako to assist the Exalted One with translation as part of the official delegation, but I am not of the Priestess's order, myself."

"I see."

"I am a linguist. I study languages," she explained eagerly. "It is a great privilege to work directly in another country so I may observe their language firsthand. Are you interested in language?"

"A little," I admitted. It was hard not to be moved by her enthusiasm.

"I hear you speak excellent Talafan. Have you ever visited the Imperial City, Credola Kalina?" Her smile was so warm, her voice soft and sweet, and her tone sparkled with the same excitement as her eyes. "I have spent much time there. It is a most magnificent place."

"I have not," I said, slightly taken aback by her open friendliness. Was she trying to determine my relationship to the Talafan party? She must have seen me with Zhafi. What interest did Perest-Avana have in the Sjon-Talafar alliance? If she thought a pretty face would sway me, she'd be disappointed; I would not volunteer anything. Perhaps she could offer *me* some answers instead.

"Do you speak Talafan too?" I asked.

"Oh, yes! It is the most fascinating. It is such a vast country, you know, and there are distinct groups of dialects that—" She broke off suddenly. "I'm sorry, I am told I am boring when I go on about this. I knew you worked for your diplomatic office though, and thought—" But I winced because she had reached a hand, apparently to gesture to my Guild tattoo, and hit instead my bandaged arm, still sensitive from yesterday's cuts.

Her smile dropped away as if I'd struck her. "I'm sorry!" she said immediately. "Oh my goodness. Please, forgive me. I did know you were hurt, I even saw what happened. It was terrifying! What a careless fool you must think me."

"Not at all," I said truthfully; I would not underestimate her, no matter how breathtaking her smile and charming her apparent naivety. "It was hardly the morning I was expecting, either."

"You are so brave," she said, shaking her head. "You are so calm. I would be a mess. I cried when that bird got up again, I was so scared." And indeed, her eyes filled at the mere mention.

A little nonplussed by the compliments, I shrugged, awkward. "I was petrified. It was Hadrea who's the fearless one."

Abaezalla chuckled. "I have heard such stories, I do not believe that for a moment!" She looked away, smoothing down her dress with sudden fussiness. "I confess I very much wanted to meet you, Credola Kalina. Tales of your bravery have made it as far as my country, do you know?"

I smiled. "Exaggerated tales, no doubt."

"Well." Her smile broadened, exposing some crooked teeth; somehow, the small imperfection only made her more dazzling. "Some claim you were gifted with magical gills to swim up the length of the mighty Bright River, but I will have to report back that I have seen no sign of any fish parts."

Her gaze lingered on my neck, the warmth in her voice making her jest clear. "These things always sound more dramatic as stories than the reality," I said, annoyed to feel my cheeks warm. "I ran, rather badly, and stole an animal and a cart, and blundered my way to the army. It was very far from glamorous. I could do without having to do anything like it again."

Her smile vanished. "Of course. And here I have been a fool again, quizzing you about such things. I always talk too much."

But not too thoughtlessly, despite appearances, I thought, because she would hardly be serving a person as important as the High Priestess if she could not be trusted to mind her tongue. I played along, reassuring her I had taken no offense. My mind raced. There could be valuable information to be learned here. "Have you made a lantern yet? Perhaps you'll join me and my niece? It's traditional to make one and then carry it to the closing ceremony tonight."

Without any signal from me, Dija seemed to understand what to do. All wide eyes and enthusiastic manner, she took Abaezalla's hand with open trust and launched into an explanation of the rules of the treasure hunt as we walked to the lantern making. I kept my eyes on the surrounding crowd, watching not just for assassins but also for any other Credolen. I'd had enough of fencing away their queries and parries today, even the friendly ones. "—and then you bring the completed sheet to the judges, and if you have all the symbols right, you get the treasure." She was showing Abaezalla the list of clues and spaces for marking in the answers.

"And what is the treasure?" the translator asked, smiling down at her, apparently charmed by my niece's enthusiasm.

"Oh, you don't find out till you win," Dee said unconcernedly. "There's a big prize for first, but everyone who submits a list before the time runs out gets something."

"Did you not wish to play? You have the list."

"Oh, no. I just took it to read. I don't like running," she said, tucking it away back in her tunic, but although Abaezalla nodded in agreement, I wondered if that was anything more than an excuse. Dija's brothers were too old now and hadn't wanted to be seen to play a children's game, and Davi was too small to be of any use with the clues even if he could have kept up with the race around town. I felt guilty my niece had made no friends since her move here that she could team up with. But it wasn't just the intensive nature of her work keeping her from bonding with her peers; Dee was an unusual child, talkative with adults but awkward and shy with people her own age, and more interested in her own observations about the world than in getting to know other children. "I wanted to make a lantern anyway. It's very pretty, you know, when everyone carries them in the dark, and did you hear, this year there's going to be a light show?"

Abaezalla looked a bit bewildered as we joined the big central table and collected supplies, Dee instructing her cheerfully about folding and the best colors to paint the waxed paper and barely drawing breath, but I was grateful for the source of distraction. I said casually, "I heard relations between Perest-Avana and its neighbors have improved in recent years. That must mean more work for diplomats like yourself?"

"Yes and no," she said. "My specialties are in other countries, so it makes little difference to me. There is less need for translation and interpretation when it comes to our immediate neighbors, you see. And I saw that you met some of the men of my region the other day, so I am sure you see there are disadvantages to a closer working relationship."

I thought of Duke Lago and his sly looks and Prince Hanichii's arrogance, and returned her rueful smile as she continued.

"Besides, I must confess, it is for farther places my heart yearns." She ducked her head as if embarrassed to have admitted it.

"I understand. I hope to be nominated for the Ambassador position in Talafar myself." Doubtless she already knew that, but I wanted her talking about the Empire. She'd been in the Leaning Lady when I'd been turned away; Perest-Avana was using this opportunity to discuss *something* with Talafar. "We haven't sent a female Ambassador to Izruitn before, though, and there are cultural differences of some concern. His Majesty Prince Hiukipi may be . . . unused to dealing with women in government positions."

She made a face, and dropped her tone. "I am only an interpreter, no one of consequence, but he looked at me in such a way . . ." She gave a little shudder, then glanced at me with her lip caught between her teeth as if worried I might have taken offense.

I felt an answering shudder of revulsion. I'd been on the receiving end of one of those looks myself, and I also remembered how Hiukipi had treated the women at the masquerade. But I pushed down my sympathetic urge. We hadn't originally thought Perest-Avana a truly viable threat because of its size and relative powerlessness, but we might have underestimated the extent to which the western nations were capable of working together. Or could an ambitious general be looking to make a deal with, say, a reckless heir who longed for expansion of his father's great empire? Abaezalla had admitted to spending considerable time in Izruitn, so she could have established many significant contacts. Additionally, it occurred to me, stealing sidelong glances through my lashes, that sending someone who looked like her to a man with an apparent weakness for women would certainly be one way of broaching the subject. Perhaps such a deal was already in motion?

On the other hand, perhaps I was simply projecting my suspicions on an innocent woman. Certainly it was hard to detect any guile in her manner, and while I remained on alert it was difficult not to enjoy her company. Dija, too, seemed genuinely to be enjoying the conversation. Abaezalla had a shy charm difficult to resist; she was a warm and interested conversationalist, and never showed any sign of deception as we chatted and made lanterns together. It was hard not to succumb to the pleasant natural energy of the final festival day. The weather was perfect, with a scrubbed blue sky clear of clouds and the winds too light to dislodge anyone's crown. We'd given out a good half of our ribbons and our crowns were now a riot of colors and textures. Surely it wasn't such a crime to just enjoy myself for an hour or two.

Everyone else seemed to be in good spirits as well. If Tain had invested too much of himself into making this karodee a success, the results showed. The atmosphere was more subdued than a few days ago, but still merry; sore heads and unsettled stomachs had settled, and there was an air of pleasant anticipation for the end tonight. We saw only one small scuffle, which broke out between a young person carrying offerings for the Darfri shrine and a shrill older man with a cane and a supercilious attitude, the former claiming the latter had deliberately tripped her. Though both parties ended up being hit with the cane a few times, the argument never got much further than raised voices, because a pair of Order Guards broke it up before it could.

"Mind yourself, uncle," one Guard said firmly. Her companion was a big enough fellow to physically pick up the old man under the armpits and set him back several paces as if he were an inconveniently placed ornament on a table.

"Be careful with that cane, eh?" she warned him.

"Wouldn't want to see any more accidents," the big Guard rumbled, and the man scurried back from him.

"What color should I make my bird, Dee?" I asked her, holding up my attempt.

"Oh! Is that a bird, Auntie?" She took off her spectacles and rubbed them on the side of her tunic. "I thought you were drawing some kind of root vegetable."

I laughed. "Cheeky little—" I stopped. "Dee?"

Her whole body had stiffened. The glasses she'd taken off to clean dropped to the table, splattering into one of the little tubs of paint.

"What is it?"

She took a sucking, shaky breath. Her eyes were wide and fixed. I started to pivot toward the direction she was staring in, but her hand shot out, fast as a strike, to catch my wrist. She shook her head, still silent, still terrified, and gave a tiny jerk of the head. For a moment she looked so much like Etan that a wave of confused grief overpowered my alarm. Then, because it was what we were trained for, what Etan had taught me, I controlled myself, forced my body to relax, daubed some paint on my blob of a bird, and shifted position so Dee could shrink back behind my frame. Only then did I glance over where she was looking. The old man had moved on and the smaller of the two Order Guards was helping the Darfri youth pick up their charms while the big man stood by, arms folded, scanning the crowd with a practiced, methodical eye. The crowd moved around them, adults and children alike, but nobody I recognized. And nothing to suggest the cause of her fearful, shocked reaction.

"There, I think I'm done, what do you think?" I held my painted paper aloft, giving me another excuse to look around at the meandering people in the market. Abaezalla's pretty nose wrinkled with the effort of thinking of a compliment about my poor artwork, and while she nobly pretended to admire it, Dija leaned in to breathe in my ear.

"The Guard. Auntie." I could barely hear her. "That big one. He was the one in the mask, the one who—the one who took Uncle Jov."

My own breath turned a bit shaky. I turned to her and helped her clean her paint-splattered spectacles. "Are you sure you want to use the blue there?" I asked, pointing at her painstakingly neat pattern of flowers and leaves. I thought I recognized a plant from our own little poison garden, though I couldn't remember what it was called.

Even scared, she was smart and attentive. "I'm sure," she said firmly, her voice barely shaking this time.

"It's a funny place to put it, is all. It's a leaf. You wouldn't expect to see a blue leaf, would you?"

"Yes," she said quietly. "You wouldn't expect it. People might mistake it for a flower, but it's definitely a leaf."

"All right." I gave Abaezalla a tolerant shrug, as if I were indulging my niece, and she smiled back, apparently unaware of the undercurrents. I chanced another glance at the Order Guards. My eyes drifted to the big one's hands. He'd strangled Tuhash with those hands. The dead man's face flashed before my eyes and I felt a wave of nausea so intense it almost buckled my knees. "Oh, Dee, you've got paint into the metalwork," I exclaimed. "If this dries we'll have such a time getting it out." I turned my most charming smile on Abaezalla. "Your company has been a delight, but these spectacles were terribly expensive and they're very delicate. We'll have to go and clean them back at the apartments, we have the materials there. Perhaps we will see you later? Look out for blue leaves and vegetable birds, won't you?"

And I spun Dee away and into the crowd, leaving Abaezalla standing with a paintbrush in one hand, the ribbons in her hair blowing back from her face in the spring breeze.

Our own guard, Lara, looked at me quizzically as she followed a few lengths behind us. I shook my head at her, forcing a smile I didn't feel, then turned away from her to speak softly to Dija. "You're absolutely sure? I thought he was wearing a mask."

"He was, once they moved him," she said, "but in the house, when they first jumped on him, they weren't. I got a good look at his face. It's definitely him." Her hand in mine was sweating, trembling.

An Order Guard. Shit, shit. "What about the other one? The woman?"

She shook her head firmly. "That's not the woman he was with that day."

"All right." I tried to calm my breathing. The Guards were moving on, and we trailed at a short distance; fortunately the big one was so tall he was easy to keep track of in the crowd. He had a kind of prowling grace despite his size; the look of a confident man of violence, I thought. So these Hands had infiltrated the Order Guards, or recruited within it. The thought was more than troubling. Order Guards could be armed, they could go anywhere and carry authority with them. We would have looked to them to assist us in protecting Tain, not as a source of potential threat.

"We should go tell Uncle Jovan, shouldn't we?" Dee asked anxiously. She was turned toward me but her gaze seemed fastened to the man's back, as if she couldn't pull it away.

We did need to tell Jov, but I needed to think, first. "We need to know who he is. As much information as we can get." They would be setting up for the closing ceremony in a matter of hours. If there was someone—or more than one someone—on the city's own security staff who could be part of the threat, we needed to know exactly who they were so we could know where they might otherwise be. My hand was half-raised to beckon Lara to us, but then it dropped. If they'd infiltrated the Order Guards, who was to say they couldn't have done the same with private houseguards? I liked Lara, but she'd only been in our employ six months. How well could we really know her, in that time?

"We'll follow them for a bit, get a name if we can."

Dee stopped walking, her grip on my hand loosening. For the first time she took her eyes off the Guard and stared at me instead. "I don't . . . I don't think we should," she said. Her voice sounded very small. I remembered suddenly what had happened last time she'd decided to follow someone. I felt an idiot, and a cruel one, for even suggesting it.

"I'm sorry." I dropped down to bring myself to her eye level. "You're right. I know this is scary. I won't make you come, but I'm going to have to do this. I can't risk him walking away and us not being able to identify him."

"He's so big, and he's on duty right now," she protested. "The Captain will be able to look up who he is."

"There's lots of big men in the Guard," I said. "And you told Chen he was wearing a mask. We're going to have to find some other way of convincingly identifying him, and that means knowing something about him. Look, you go back to the lanterns and stay at the table until I'm back. I'll send Lara with you. You'll be safe there, just don't leave the table."

She hesitated, and I tried not to show her any impatience. The Guards weren't moving fast, I had time, and she needed to make the decision.

"I'll come," she said, and squared her jaw, once again reminding me of my uncle. A surge of pride filled me. She was only thirteen, and she'd seen something terrible, but she was an Oromani, and she already prioritized duty over safety. Or maybe she just didn't want to be left behind.

"We won't be doing anything dangerous, I promise."

"I trust you, Auntie."

Squeezing her hand, I moved us through the crowd. It was easy enough to blend in; I encouraged Dee to comment on things and people we passed, just as if we were out enjoying ourselves as originally planned. The chatter distracted her, but not completely; her hand still sweated in mine despite the mild weather.

We got lucky before we even left the market square; the woman called him by name—Sukseno. An unusual one, enough to identify him, surely. Was it enough? I glanced up at the sun's arc. There weren't many hours until the closing ceremony. The guilt was back, but I needed two people for this play. "Dee, I'm going to ask you to be really brave for a second, all right? Do you think you can do that?"

Dija was too young for tattoos, and I was grateful for it. To the big Guard she was just a kid, indistinguishable from any other. I'd asked her to cause a minor disturbance, something to distract him. Instead she was standing right before him, bold as anything, holding her treasure hunt list and ask-ing earnest questions as she pointed to various city landmarks. I heard him laugh—actually laugh—at something she was saying.

"That was nice work, back there," I said to the female Order Guard, ges-turing roughly behind me, keeping her attention on me and away from her partner. Dee might be anonymous but I wasn't, and she wouldn't remain so for long if he saw us both in the same company. "With the Darfri lass. It could have gotten ugly if you hadn't stepped in."

"That's what we're here for, Credola," the Guard said briskly. "Keeping the peace, like."

"I've heard things have been tense, since the fire." I adopted a vaguely gos-sipy tone, the sort of tone the Reed cousin had used on me earlier. I wanted this conversation short and as forgettable as possible. "This sort of careful management is just what we need. Will you and your partner be working the closing ceremony tonight? We need cool heads, you know."

"Mm." Her interest had quickly dissipated and her gaze was back to roam-ing the crowd, eyes out for trouble. "No, Credola, 'fraid not. Just looking out for you all here this morning. Plenty of good people looking after everyone tonight, don't you worry."

I chanced another glance at Dee. She was still talking to the Guard but we couldn't have much longer. *Shit.* "You know, I think I saw you and your partner doing just as good a job during the masquerade the other night, weren't you?"

"Not me, Credola." Her patience for the conversation was clearly wearing thin.

I interrupted the intake of breath that promised to tell me to have a bounteous and fortunate season, scrupulously polite as it would be, with a hurried,
"Your partner then, I'm sure I saw—"

"Not our usual work, I'm afraid," she said, a note of irritation at last creeping in. "We're jail guards, usually. Looking after folks like this is easy compared to the types we're normally handling, if you get my drift. So you see,
you're mistaken. Look, Credola, I'd best be back to work, eh?" She tipped her
head and escaped me with barely concealed relief, and I coughed loudly to
signal Dee. She joined me moments later, stuffing the list back in her tunic.
Her hand was shaking so hard it took two tries.

"I was scared," she said. "I was so scared he was going to know me somehow."

"You were right to be scared," I said, "but you were absolutely brilliant.
We can go tell Jov now and decide what to do." *At least*, I told myself as we
left the market square and hailed the nearest litter, *at least he's not scheduled
on guard duty for the arena tonight*. Dee was quiet in the litter, and would not
meet my concerned gaze. "He was so *nice*," she whispered at last. "He killed
that man for no good reason at all. He hurts people and he works for those
horrible people, but he was so nice to me just now." A gleaming tear trickled
out from under her glasses and she hastily scrubbed it away with her sleeve.
"He helped me solve a clue."

I swallowed. It felt like a replay of something that had happened before,
us marking out the same familiar steps. Bad, brutal people who wouldn't
hesitate to murder could be gentle to children, could as easily believe
themselves to be decent. "People aren't only one thing," I said, putting a
hand on her shoulder. I kept my voice low; the street was noisy but litter
carriers could be paid to listen, same as anyone. "You'll see that, as you
grow up." *Especially growing up doing what we're doing*, I thought grimly. I
had struggled to reconcile the generous, faultlessly polite Marco with the
traitor who had killed my uncle and the Chancellor, who had taken people
from the streets and cut off their heads all to help fuel both sides of a rebellion that had cost us so much. "Sometimes they're good actors. Sometimes
they just don't see what they do, following orders from evil people, as being
wrong."

*And sometimes, of course, they know it's wrong and they don't care. They do
what they want for their own ends, and be damned anyone who gets in their way.*
The scar on my abdomen seemed to burn, even though I knew the damage

was long healed. It was all in my mind. *The knife going in. The water clos-ing around my face.* The man's big hands flashed in my head again; I imag-ined them closing around Tuhash's pale neck, squeezing, squeezing. Then it turned into Aven's face, and it was her hands around my throat.

And all of a sudden, something made sense to me.

"Honor-down," I said. "Stop. Stop!" My voice rose to a yell, and the litter carriers slowed and lowered us down.

"Credola?" one of them asked, but I barely heard. Dee was staring at me, her mouth in an *o* of surprise. Now it was my hands that were shaking. "Let me out here," I said. "Please take my niece straight to the Oromani apart-ments, as quickly as possible."

"Auntie?"

"Go straight to Jov. You're to stay there, and don't leave the apartments."

"But what do I tell him?"

"Tell him they've infiltrated the Guard and he has to stop Tain going to-night, at all costs. Tell him not to talk to *anyone* but Tain."

Her eyes were very wide. "And where are you going?"

I closed my eyes, but there was no peace there. The same images that had haunted my dreams for two years, the ones that made me sweat and gasp for breath, from which I woke unrested and fearful, were brought into such sudden painful relief I felt I might never breathe easily again. "I'm going to the jail."

"I know it will be reported. I don't care if you report it straight to the Chan-cellor himself," I told the slightly indignant Guard. "I'll be going right to him after this anyway. There's no law preventing me from visiting anyone in this prison, is there?"

"No, Credola, but—"

"Then you can just put anything you like in the report, mark me down in the log. It's not a secret. But I *am* in a hurry, so I need to see her now. And alone."

"Alone?" The man's mouth worked silently for a moment. "Credola, no, that *is* in the prison code. No one sees that prisoner without a Guard. The Guild sets the code and the Council signs off on it, Credola. You can't just—"

"We have a matter of utmost secrecy to discuss. It must be alone."

"The code is for everyone's safety," he protested. "I can't let you go without a Guard."

"She's at the far end of the central corridor, isn't she?"

"Yes, but—"

"If the Guard stands at the corridor entrance, they'll be able to see me in front of her cell, won't they?"

"I suppose, but—"

"You can search me," I said, applying my sweetest smile. "I'm not carrying a weapon."

"Credola, I didn't say . . . I mean to say, that's not necessary, I know who you are." The man rubbed a hand over his shorn head, looking troubled. "It's for your safety more than the prisoner's. The Guard's there to stop any trouble."

"She's safe in the cell," I said. "The Guard will be able to see us and I can call out if I need help. But I need to talk to her, right away. It's a matter of utmost importance." I took a step closer. "I know it's not fair to ask you to bend rules, but I know you wouldn't be sitting here if you were just a windup doll, following the rules without any judgment. You're a thinking man, you're here because you've been trusted with a position that calls for intelligence and common sense."

The faintest hint of a flattered smile teased the edge of his mustache. "I can't fault you there, Credola."

"So what does your judgment say? You know who I am—and I don't mean my family name or any of that rubbish, I mean you know I would do anything to protect this city. I share that with your Guild, don't I?"

"Aye, you do at that," he admitted. He rubbed his head again. "Look, you can have a short conversation but you have to stay back from the cell. A *short* conversation, mind. And you call out if she tries any funny business, eh? She isn't cowed, not one bit, I'll tell you that for nothing."

"I didn't think she would be," I murmured. Who could even imagine that? Aven hadn't been cowed when she'd been caught and surrounded, or when she'd been tried and sentenced. I'd watched, from a distance, when she'd ridden out of the city south to the mines for the first time. I thought seeing her off would make me feel something, some sense of closure. But she'd been as straight-backed and proud as ever, like a political prisoner rather than the heartless butcher I knew her to be.

I approached down the corridor, leaving the Guard at the other end. The cells down this quiet, lonely corridor were reserved for the most dangerous prisoners, of which we had few. It wasn't a long-term solution, but no one wanted to sponsor the absolute worst of society, so the prisoners in her category were moved between supervised jobs and here in the jail in stretches, depending on whether they were willing to continue to contribute or not. Most of the cells I passed were empty, and the occupied few were silent, though eyes watched me curiously as I passed.

The silence was heavy and my footsteps loud as I approached. Plenty of time for the prisoner to know someone was approaching, and perhaps my footfalls sounded sufficiently different to the Guard's, or the timing of the visit did not correspond to regular Guard visits, because when I came into view the former Warrior-Guilder, my attempted murderer, was sitting in the center of her cell, and registered not even the mildest surprise at the sight of me.

"Kalina Oromani," she purred. "Oh, I so hoped it would be you." She uncoiled herself from her position on the floor, rising with more grace than should have been possible considering the circumstances. The cell was clean, but for the lamp marks on the walls; not uncomfortable, but depressing in a way only a locked room under the ground could ever be. *She is not cowed*, the Guard had said, and that was obvious. She looked—had I thought she would look different?—she looked just the same, really, as she had the day she'd driven her knife into my stomach. Her hair was still long, still scraped back from her face in a plait, albeit a bit neater than it had been on the battlefield. She had not lost muscle, though the ugly cluster scar on her hand where Tain had pinned her with a blade was visible. Her face was still strong, beautiful, charismatic, her bearing still that of a person looking upon creatures of some lesser species; a bird to an insect.

For all my supposed bravery, the sight of her robbed me of speech. How could I be afraid of someone locked up, likely forever, who could not harm me?

But I was. Maybe I always would be.

She cracked her neck and took a deep breath, a small smile of satisfaction playing across her face. I thought she would have been surprised to see me. It had been two years, I thought, anger tingeing the edge of my nerves. Why would she have expected this? Suddenly I was certain it was all an act. She had perfected this image of the confident commander, never surprised by anything, to try to keep others off balance. It wouldn't work on me.

"You don't look well, little bird," she said, with mock concern. "Still sickly? What are all those bandages for?"

"I'm fine. Thanks for the concern. How's life as a mine worker?"

She yawned. "Keeps me strong, you know. Wouldn't want to lose my edge." She smiled, a predator's smile, the same one that haunted my dreams. Fortunes, I hated her. I seized on that hatred, riding the wave of it over my fear.

"Hard to keep an edge when you're never going to be allowed to hold a sword again," I said coolly. That one bit in, and she regarded me with a curl of her lip, her own anger showing this time.

"Don't worry about me, little bird. I keep the practice up." She lunged forward suddenly, driving her hand toward me with a knife that wasn't there, and in that moment my brain forgot she wasn't armed, forgot she was safe behind bars. I leapt back instinctively, almost tripping, and heat flooded my face as she laughed in response. I glared back, heart racing, furious. She pretended to clean her fingernails. "Still. Stabbing isn't always as effective as you'd like, is it? I'd definitely slit a throat next time, if I got the chance."

Again, I remembered the feeling of the knife going in, the terrible pain, the wrongness of splitting flesh, but I battled to keep that memory from my face. I was here, I was alive and well, and she was in jail. Two years of nightmares, two years of her as a demon haunting my steps. I'd paid the price and tenfold. She'd taken something from me, and it was high time to take something back.

I tried to force my voice to calm. "It's boring in there, isn't it? Is this the best you can do to break the monotony—weak threats from your cage?"

"Oh, I'm doing more than you'd like," she purred. "I knew you'd come, you know. I thought it might be your dear brother. It'd make a nice change from that pathetic little creature you've got in charge of the Council." She gave a disparaging laugh. "Fortunes, that boy was as eager to please as a starving street animal when I fucked him, and he's no different now."

Her words opened a horrible tear inside my chest.

"Oh. Didn't you know your beloved Chancellor's been coming to see me, then? He can't stay away, whenever I'm here. Wants my advice. Wants my respect."

She is trying to throw you off balance, I told myself. She's saying whatever she wants to get a reaction. I ignored her jibe. "But you said you hoped it'd be me? Why? I thought seeing me might . . ." Now it was my own turn to examine my fingernails. ". . . upset you."

"There's the smugness," she breathed. "There's the attitude. All of you have it, even the ones who pretend they don't. You think you have the world figured out." She laughed suddenly, loudly, crudely. "But now here you are, realizing once again you've screwed it all up, haven't you. And what is this little visit about—begging me for help?"

"We know about your connections to the Hands," I said stonily, ignoring the heat creeping up my neck. "We've already found your pet Order Guard. Was he always one of yours? Can't imagine this"—I gestured vaguely to her and her cell—"winning anyone over."

"*One* of mine?" Her laugh sounded genuinely merry this time, and it turned my stomach to ice. "Honor-down, little bird, you've only found one? How fucking disappointing. You've left this very late to figure out what's going on, haven't you." She leaned forward and dropped her voice to a dramatic whisper. I had to resist the urge to step closer, knowing she would want that. "You're only just now noticing how much is already in motion, aren't you? You thought one grand gesture would be the end of it? Rebellion isn't some single event you can just squash in one hit, you know. It's thousands of little moments, little voices, little actions. A few seats on your bloated Council aren't going to stop them. All those young people, kicking around your city, still dreaming about unseating the fat families, they aren't going to stop just because you've elected some token commoners to help oppress them."

"Oh, I'm sorry, are you pretending you ever cared about the rebellion?" The mere idea of it was laughable. She hadn't wanted to overturn our society because she'd been worried about how the lower classes were treated; she'd been concerned with how *she* was treated, and how much influence *she* had over our society. "You didn't give a damn about the people you tricked into going to war, and they know that now. Do you think anyone's going to bust you out of here? You think your military empire or whatever ridiculous dream you had was going to make the poorest people in the country happy? They're not dreaming of you as their lost leader, I promise." My turn to laugh coldly. "It's been two years. No one's coming for you."

Aven threw aside the splinter she had been using to clean her nails, smiling again. "Of course I don't care. Means to an end, and all that. But you really are being terribly naive, or is it arrogant? So hard to tell with you coddled little egg yolks. If you think some creative accounting and fifty thousand broke peasants funded the last strike against you, you're stupider than even your bland little faces look. I told your brother two years ago I had friends, and you all still sat back and worried about the little peasants and not at all about the players behind them."

"You don't look much like someone with friends," I said. "Sitting here alone in the dark, reduced to trying to taunt people who've long moved on from worrying about you."

"Oh, I don't know," she said, stretching and yawning theatrically. "I'm doing all right in here. I mean, some little pissant threatened to poison me, a long time ago, but he doesn't seem to have had the guts to go through with it."

In his darker moments, Jov certainly had thought about it, he'd told me. While I had been hovering, fighting infections, hanging on to life, he had dreamed of giving her the death she'd given so many he cared about. But over time the heat of his anger and desire for revenge had faded away. Better to leave her here, rotting, he had told me, and I'd agreed. "Maybe he just thinks it's funnier seeing you completely impotent than dead."

She didn't even bother to reply. "You're not here because you think I'm impotent," she said. "You're here because you know I'm *not*, even if you haven't yet grasped the scale of it."

"I'm here to give you a chance," I said, my tone level. "You know you'll never be offered a spot with a rehabilitation sponsor. If you give us information now, help us stop the next attack, I'd personally speak on your behalf to the determination council. You aren't stupid enough to think nothing could be done to improve your lot in here."

"Oh, you'll 'speak on my behalf'? Very generous."

"Credola!" the Guard at the end of the corridor called down. "That's time now."

I ignored him. "I gave the key testimony against you, remember. My word in your favor will go a long way."

"Hmm, a very tempting offer, but I rather think not, little bird. You see, I don't need to make any deals with you fucking Oromani snakes. I already have deals, and friends, and I have no intention of being in this hole forever, believe me."

"Tell me about the Hands," I went on doggedly. "Tell me what you know about the attack at the closing ceremony."

"Has that happened already?" She looked surprised, but delighted. "It *is* hard to keep track of the days down here. Is that what all those bandages are from? Did I miss all the fun?"

My heart pounded in my ears. I didn't know if she was genuine or just playing with me. Could she really have lost track of times and daylight hours so far? Was that why she hadn't been surprised to see me, because she thought something big had already happened? But she was already shaking her head as her eyes traveled all over me. "No, no, I'm just teasing you, Credola. We wouldn't be having such a lovely relaxed conversation if I'd missed it. Come see me tomorrow, why don't you?" She paused, her smile cold. "If you can."

The Guard was striding down the corridor now, his footsteps tap-tapping as he approached. I stepped closer. "Tell me what's going to happen at the ceremony."

"Oh, you'd love to know, wouldn't you? Maybe it'll be a second rebellion, maybe someone will take off your little Chancellor's head for him. It'll be a lovely surprise."

"Credola! Please step back from the bars."

I took one step back. Aven correspondingly lowered her voice so it was difficult to hear. "It's killing you, wondering, isn't it. What *have* my friends been doing? They didn't pack up and go home when the plans didn't go right. Believe me, they will *never* pack up and go home. Not ever. And this city will go down one way or the other, because you're all too sure of yourselves to bother to heed the threat. It's funny, really."

"Who are they?" I asked, aware I was sounding desperate. Fortunes, she was so confident, so completely unfazed by my questions. "Who are these friends?"

"No friends of yours, that's for sure," she replied. She settled herself back down on the floor, serene as a butterfly landing, and rolled her neck in a lazy circle. "I'm glad you came, Kalina Oromani. It's given me so much pleasure to know exactly how little you understand. You did interfere last time, so I did wonder whether you were clever enough to be a problem, but I needn't have bothered. It was just luck—good luck on your part, bad on mine. Still. This gives me a chance to tell you personally that you and your brother are going to lose it all. And I'm going to be watching and enjoying it." Her laughter echoed until, escorted by the Guard, muttering a string of complaints under his breath, we were almost out of the jail.

INCIDENT: Attempted poisoning of Chancellor Hana Iliri

POISON: Manita fungus

INCIDENT NOTES: This proofer detected manita fungus (likely powder form) mixed in with vegetable paste to be served to Chancellor. Proofed in kitchen and detected early. Meal replaced, Oromani family to conduct surveillance of kitchen workers. *Update:* kitchen worker with ties to C. Senydred Brook followed and payment confirmed. (Note: C. Senydred and Chancellor Hana had personal history suggesting this is not a Family-driven attack.) Kitchen worker arrested, C. Senydred sent a bottle of kori dosed with (non-fatal) quantity of Esto's revenge. *Update:* message appears to have been received and no further attacks forthcoming. C. Senydred accepted Guild position in Moncasta (approx. 1 mth post incident).

(from proofing notes of Credo Travi Oromani)

13

Jovan

"I don't know where he is, Credo Jovan, and I'll remind you not to raise your voice in my presence. I may be old, but I'm not deaf." Argo straightened his glasses and glared at me. His gaze didn't even soften for my sister, which was proof enough we'd really annoyed him. "He's got a lot of things on this afternoon. I've not seen him for hours."

"I'm sorry, Argo," Kalina said, leaning across the desk and taking both the old man's hands in hers, swift enough that he didn't have time to pull away. "We didn't mean to be short. But Tain's in danger and we need to talk to him."

"Sorry," I echoed. "We're just worried, Argo."

"All right," he said. He glared at us each one more time for good measure, but he didn't pull his hands out of Kalina's. "If this is about the Chancellor's safety, you could speak to the Captain of the blackstripes. She's still here."

I'd have preferred to bring it direct to Tain, but we didn't have time to be running around town trying to find him. It was barely an hour until the gates would open at the arena and he would have to come back here first; if we already had his Captain briefed and ready to support us, that might make things faster in any case.

The Captain of the blackstripes was a stern, practical woman with short curls more gray than black, a jawline hard enough to crack rocks off, and a gnarled set of scars down one cheek. She had been unfailingly polite in our interactions thus far, but we'd barely begun telling her our concerns when it became clear she was reaching the end of her patience with me.

"Credo Jovan," she said levelly, "I appreciate you're very serious about this threat but I have already reassured you—several times—that I am taking your concerns on board. The Chancellor will be protected at all times. There will be three guards within an arm's stretch no matter where he is, the whole ceremony. I will personally be there with him."

"We have new information," I said without hesitation.

"Since this morning?" She delivered it without audible exasperation but it was implied in the movement of her eyebrows.

"Yes, since this morning," I continued patiently. "We have good reason now to believe the former Warrior-Guilder has been cultivating a criminal network since she was incarcerated. The man I told you about earlier, Suk-seno, he's on prison duty and six months ago he did a stint at the mine at Stunted Rock, which is where—"

"Which is where the Warrior-Guilder was working," she finished for me. Her voice had dropped to a hoarser level. She blinked a few times. "I . . . can see how this is concerning."

"We don't know whether he took the jobs to get close to her, or he got close to her because he was rostered near her, but either way, we have a Guard who's also a Hand and who's probably had more contact with our most dangerous criminal than any other person has since we caught her. There is absolutely no way this is chance." I gestured to Kalina, looking clammy and out of breath beside me. "My sister talked to Aven and she didn't even try to pretend otherwise."

Kalina added, "She intimated she had many Order Guards in her network, not just one. She laughed at me for thinking it was just one."

The blackstripe frowned, looking uncertain for the first time. "Well, that would be a problem, no lie about it. We'll refer this straight to Captain Chen and she can doubtless find out more information about this Sukseno." She nodded, as if convincing herself of something. "Thanks for the information. We won't have any Order Guards near the Chancellor. Blackstripes only."

Kalina cleared her throat and I squeezed my hands into silent fists. "Captain, some of your blackstripes are army, too, aren't they? Or ex-army?"

She puffed up her chest. "You have the finest people at the Chancellor's disposal here in my company," she said, visibly affronted. "No one protects the Chancellor who I haven't personally vetted."

"And none of them have friends in the Order Guards? In the army? We knew we'd never get all the loyalists out of the army ranks." I tried to rein in my frustration. I needed her onside. Many—perhaps most—of Aven's loyal supporters in the army had rather conveniently announced themselves after the siege by storming the Manor and attempting to burn the entire Council to death. Many had been killed, the rest captured, in that process, and one or two isolated incidents—two attempts to break Aven out of custody and a handful to attack Tain or the Council—since then had revealed a few others. But we'd always known there would be people who had not been part of that coup who nevertheless supported Aven and believed in her ideals. We'd not expected to ever identify them, but rather hoped we could regain their loyalty over time through building a better and fairer city, one that didn't present so many reasons to seek revolution. I liked to think it must have worked for some. For others, perhaps, they'd found new ways to give voice to their dissatisfaction with the city. Whether Aven had found them or the other way around, we couldn't risk giving anyone we didn't trust entirely access to the Chancellor. "One of the reasons Aven even *had* loyalists was that she gave them something the city wasn't giving. Power, prestige. Aven and people who supported her wanted respect, or fear, or both. If they couldn't get it legitimately who's to say they wouldn't get it other ways? Like through a criminal gang?"

"The Order Guards, maybe," the Captain acknowledged, frowning. "But there's none in *my* ranks who'd betray their honor. The blackstripes is a company people respect and honor." A touch of pride in her voice. "It's not like the old days. The Chancellor treats us that way, and the city's followed."

"Some of Aven's supporters weren't selfishly motivated, either," Kalina put in quietly. "Some of them legitimately believed in the rebellion. They might not be Hands, but that doesn't mean they're not still working their cause. Aven was right—we didn't fix everything with a few grand gestures, and there's plenty of people who think we haven't done enough."

The Captain narrowed her eyes. "Are you talking about this business with the boat? Because I don't mind telling you, Credola, I worked for the Ashes for a while earlier in my career, and they make enough enemies as it is. I don't think there's any reason to suspect magical sabotage there."

Neither my sister nor I were so convinced there was nothing supernatural tied up in this mess, but I doubted we would convince the Captain. I glanced at Kalina to convey that we should move on and saw a strange expression, almost guilty, certainly furtive, pass over her face. A corresponding twist in my own stomach echoed it without me really understanding why. Did she suspect Hadrea's disaffected Darfri friends might really have caused it? Did *I*?

"Leave aside the Darfri for a moment, then," I said. "I think it's likely someone's been working divisions where they can, but let's say I'm wrong. Concentrate on tonight. I don't know what's planned for the closing ceremony, but we can be certain of a few things." I ticked them off on my hands, trying to stay calm, stationary, rational. "The Hands made an effort to stop me going, and what I'm known for in this city, to friends and foes, is protecting the Chancellor. So we can assume if they didn't want me there, he's in danger. And we know, for sure, some key people involved in organizing today aren't going to be there. And who *is* going to be there? Representatives—including *armed* people—from what, six other countries, any one of which could have been funding Aven two years ago!"

Kalina added, "Aven is involved, and she's got at *least* one Order Guard in her pocket, likely more. She knows what's going to happen today, whether she's the mastermind or just lending help. She was practically expecting me to turn up at the jail. Bring her in. Question her if you don't believe me."

"It's not a question of believing you, Credola," the Captain said. "But forgive me, it's just that the Warrior-Guilder's grudge against you isn't a secret. She'd have loved seeing you worried, and she'd say whatever she could to make it worse. Maybe she's been turning a Guard or two sympathetic, sure. Maybe even some of them are going rogue, turning to crime. This gang is a problem and no mistake. But I don't see as why a criminal gang has any special interest in murdering the Chancellor at all, let alone at a public event where he'll be surrounded by protection."

"If they were just a gang, that might be true, but if they're working for people who hate Sjona? The city's full of strangers right now, and some of them will be right there with the Chancellor tonight."

"You work in diplomacy, Credola," the Captain said to my sister, throwing her hands up. "Does the Guild think any of the visiting officials are our enemies? Far as I know, every country representative we invited here is an ally. Because I was assured when this was planned and we were allowing strangers into the city carrying weapons that these were allied countries that posed no threat. Was that untrue? Should we be stripping them of privileges and kicking them home?"

"Not that we know, of course," she said. "But *someone* supplied Aven with resources to fund her mercenary army. We know that much."

"No one showed up with a fresh army after the siege, but that doesn't mean one or more of these countries wasn't hoping for our downfall," I said. "Whoever our enemy is has been working through intermediaries the whole time, and right now is no different. Quiet assassins and local criminals, and our own bloody ex-army commander. This is their style. We clawed this city back together but the Chancellor is the one holding all the pieces, you must know that, Captain. You spend enough time with him to see how important he is to stability."

"I don't dispute it," she said, still in the same infuriatingly calm manner, though something else bristled in her posture now. "And I'll thank you to remember I'm personally committed to protecting him, on my life and honor."

Now it was my turn to be defensive. "I didn't intimate otherwise, Captain. We came straight to you, didn't we? You're the person I thought we could *most* trust to focus on the Chancellor's safety."

"And I'd give my life before I let anyone near him," she said. She sighed, and scratched her scarred cheek. "But one part of my job is to make sure keeping him safe doesn't get in the way of his governing, either. He's always made that clear. He doesn't want to be some emperor figure like they've got up north, sitting on a throne and hidden away from the people. He'll let us be with him, protecting him, but I'm not in charge of dictating where he can and cannot go."

"I know." I did sympathize. Tain had grown up in a world vastly different to the one we now inhabited—we all had. Being surrounded by visible protection at all times was galling, jarring, inconvenient, and invasive. But we'd all had to make concessions for the dangers our positions carried with them. To accept the power to effect positive change in society meant recognizing he was more than just a man, and his safety meant more than the average person's. "But he won't be doing any governing at all if he's dead."

We were all silent for a moment. "Look," I said, "the safest thing to do would be to fake something going wrong—some damage to the infrastructure at the arena that makes it unsafe, or something—and cancel the ceremony altogether. If we don't know what they've got planned, or how many people they have, or what they're planning to strike at, how do you protect the Chancellor or anyone else?"

But she was already shaking her head again. "I don't have the authority to pull something like that off, Credo. You get the Council to agree, I'll not get in your way. But I gotta tell you, I don't see how you could even find the

Council before the closing ceremony starts, let alone get them to agree on anything. You've given me plenty to be concerned about, and it's possible there could be an attack, but what you've not given me is any proof it's more than a handful of people who hate your family and the Chancellor behind it, and that we aren't a match for them. Hells, even if you're right about everything, and one of these kings or princes or priestesses or what have you is planning an assassination assisted by Darfri and Hands and half the bloody Order Guards, I will *still* back my blackstripes to protect the Chancellor." She leaned across to me, earnest. "You can trust us," the Captain said firmly. "Even if you don't believe my word on it, you can trust them for one simple reason: if you had blackstripes working against the Chancellor who wanted him dead, he'd be dead already, if you don't mind me saying, Credo."

I forced a breath, and another. A fair point, but more importantly, it was obviously going to be her last word. We wouldn't get any further here. "Look," I said. "If I can get Tain and the Council to agree to cancel, will you back me?"

"I'll do what I'm told," she said. "If they want to play it safe and keep him out, or call the whole thing off, I'm happy enough. But I don't like your chances. This festival's been a triumph for them and they're not going to want to end on a sour note."

That, I thought, would have to do. "Thank you," I said, trying not to sound stiff, trying not to sound afraid, but I met Kalina's eye as we left and saw my own fear reflected there. I was afraid, deathly afraid, we were hurtling toward disaster and the two of us were the only ones looking straight ahead.

Tain returned to the Manor with several Guilders and regional representatives in tow, so there was no proper time to talk to him privately; we had to rudely pull him aside to his study, leaving the others waiting, and hurriedly explain what we'd learned.

"You talked to her?" he said, a strange twist to his lips. "You talked to Aven?"

My heart hurt for the pain he was trying to hide. He had never forgiven himself for the Warrior-Guilder. Not just his infatuation, or for being taken in and used by her after her original plan failed. It was more than that. It was facing that he had admired someone, respected her methods and her manner, who had been capable of the kinds of atrocities we had seen. It had shaken his confidence in his judgment in a fundamental way.

Kalina was regarding him not with sympathy or understanding, but with something harder. "Yes, I did," she said. "She didn't so much *admit* to this as brag about it. She's tied up with the Hands, Tain. Whether she's behind them or just helping, it doesn't really matter. But she knows whatever they have planned today, and she's confident enough to not bother pretending otherwise to me. She was . . ." She cleared her throat, looked away a moment, then back. "She was pleased I'd come. Like she'd been waiting for a chance to crow about it." She looked at Tain with that same odd expression again, something almost accusing. Her lips parted, then closed again, and she shook her head just the tiniest fraction. I was missing something here, but I had no idea what it could be, and we had no time for subtlety in any case.

"You see what this means," I said. "She could have a bunch of operatives working the Order Guards, the army, whatever. Your blackstripes. We can't risk you being there."

"Not the blackstripes," Tain said automatically.

Kalina laughed, a breathy, exasperated sound. "Of course she could have someone in the bloody blackstripes, Tain. There's barely a trained fighter in this city who never trained under her or Marco. Didn't we learn from Marco that people who seem otherwise to hold themselves with honor can be murderers and traitors, if you're on the wrong side of their loyalty and honor? Didn't *you* learn, Tain?"

He didn't seem to want to look directly at her, and the sense of missing information was too great to ignore this time. "What's going on?" I directed the question at my sister, and she bit her lip, clenched her hands into fists. "What? Spit it out."

"Aven said you've been visiting her," Kalina said bluntly, and it was like she'd punched him in the stomach; he folded in on himself somehow.

"Tain?" I squeezed my eyes shut, as if I could erase the reaction and the confirmation. "Have you?"

"Once or twice," he admitted, barely audible. "I thought if I could get something from her, it could cancel out what happened. What I did."

"Honor-down, Tain, we told you after it happened. You had a momentary lapse in judgment and it didn't gain her a thing. She never got to use you."

"But she could have. For all this talk about how *important* I am, you know as well as I do she would have used my weakness to her own ends, and if it hadn't been for you two, we'd not be here. She'd have had Lini killed the second she found out she was alive, and no doubt she'd have disposed of you too, Jov. What kind of decisions would I have made without you two advising me? What kind of weakling fool would this city have been saddled with?" There was a wild, feverish look in his eyes now.

I was right, he really hadn't forgiven himself. For all I'd worried about his health over the past few months, I'd assumed it was related still to the poisoning that had damaged his insides. Kalina had been smarter than me, again, as she ever was; she'd tried to talk to me about his mental state and I'd brushed it aside.

"All right, so you thought you could reverse some of the potential harm you could have caused," I said, trying to salvage the conversation with some desperation. "But she didn't tell you anything. Why'd you go back?"

"I knew she thought I was an idiot," he said. "I thought if I played that up, she might underestimate me, give me something we could use."

"That's not it, or you'd have told us," Kalina said. Her anger was a tightly coiled thing, contained in her shoulders and her neck, rarely provoked and never unearned, and Tain was right to flinch away from her. But he was not a liar. Call him anything, but he was not a liar.

"No," he said. "I also thought, or maybe just wanted to believe, it couldn't all have been show. The things I'd admired. She inspired fierce loyalty in her army, and in the Guild. She might have hated the Council, hated the rich families and how they treated her Guild, but she didn't hate our country. And some of that was fair."

"She didn't hate it because she believed in equality," Kalina said, and her voice had an edge sharp enough to scratch glass. "She didn't believe in the rebellion. She used it to gain power, that's all she wanted. There was a lot to dislike about Silasta's classes but she only cared because it meant she wasn't treated by everyone she met the way she was treated in the army."

"But she also fought her whole life for Sjona. She betrayed whoever paid her off, didn't she? They wanted the two armies to tear each other apart, to destroy the country, and she turned on them."

"For her own reasons!" As Tain's voice had gotten louder, hers had quieted. Her lips were barely moving. I had rarely seen her so furious. "She didn't give a flying *shit* about the Darfri oppression except how she could use it as a weapon. When she found out it was real magic she would have been quick enough to either use it for her own purposes or stamp it out. She didn't battle her way out of the lower classes or the estates, she grew up in the bloody Reed apartments, in unimaginable luxury, same as the rest of us here. You're worth fifty of her, you always were, even at your *stupidest*, Tain Iliri, because you didn't look at the reality of Silasta and wonder how you could turn that to your personal advantage, you kicked the rock over and you've been doing your best to stamp out the grubs ever since."

He blinked, looking down, and with a horrible twist in my chest I saw wet tracks on his cheeks. I took a breath and seized one of his hands, squeezed it. "Tain. This isn't the first time in your life you've been an idiot and it's not likely to be the last. But we can go over this later. Right now, we need to know if you could have told her anything in these little chats, anything at all she could have used. Sometimes the assassin seemed to know where we'd be when there was only a very small group of people who knew—"

"No," he said firmly. "No, I swear. I never told her anything. I just . . . sort of pretended to want her advice about things. General things, never specifics." He chanced a look at Kalina's burning glare and hastily added, "And I never took it. I just thought she might let something slip about who her allies were, maybe try to push me into making decisions benefiting one of our neighbors or something. Or I thought if I could appeal to her moral side, or even her self-interest, she might sell them out. She'd been in there for a long time, and I figured she'd think no one was coming for her, no grand rescue. What good did it do her to stay loyal to someone she'd already betrayed once anyway?"

"What good?" Kalina stood up, but her whole body shook, wilted, suddenly drained of energy. "To ruin us, of course. Maybe you're right and she doesn't hate the country, maybe she doesn't feel any real loyalty to whoever paid her—I'd believe that easy enough. But she hates us, she hates me and Jov, and that's been enough to sustain her in prison and in those mines, and all this time she's been picking at anyone she could reach, trying to get her revenge."

"Lini—"

"No." She turned her back on him, her breath short and raspy. "Jov's right. We don't have time for this. You either have to help us convince the Council to cancel the ceremony tonight, or at the very least, you have to stay away. Fake an illness. We'll bloody *give* you one if you need." She shot him an extremely fierce look, but was distracted by a bout of coughing. Worry pierced my shock and anxiety for a moment; she couldn't have a lung attack now, of any time. I hobbled over to her and she shook me off impatiently. "I'm fine."

We both turned back to Tain. He looked drained too, but any sign of tears had gone. He looked very grave. "I'm not canceling the closing. You had to know I was going to say that. Even if there was time, which there isn't, we have all our allies here, we have thousands of guests. And if our enemies have people in the Order Guards and the blackstripes and fortunes know wherever else, we'd only be putting off the problem anyway. They can strike whenever they want. I'm not ruining an event we spent months, and a goodly portion of the treasury, setting up. We're still a small country around bigger military powers. This karodee shows we are strong, we're united, and this city can offer something like nowhere else in the world. We can't just be an indulgent capital that got torn apart in a civil war. We have to be a beacon again, we have to *matter*, or sooner or later we're going to get swallowed up by an empire or something like it." He shook his head. "Aven's manipulative, you know as well as anyone. If she told you something was planned for tonight, if they've been toying with us, leaving us clues, giving signals, how do you know the point isn't to make us cancel the ceremony and ruin the festival? They want me dead; there's a lot of easier ways to do it than something this public. Someone cunning enough to try to discredit you the way they've been doing is playing a long game, Jov." He stood. "People are waiting for us. We can't cancel."

"And you? Will you go?"

"I'll go," he said, and my heart sank at the finality in his voice. Was this, too, some form of punishment he was imposing on himself? "But I'll take my Captain's advice on the best way to thwart any plans someone might have. I'll do everything I'm told. And you're right about the other leaders having armed guards, so I won't watch the ceremony from the viewing box with them. I'll, I don't know, I'll surprise some of the ordinary citizens by turning up in the regular seating or something."

"We could stop you," my sister said coldly. "If we wanted to."

He blinked, and the look of surprise was chased by one of betrayal.

"We wouldn't," I said, and invested it with all my sincerity, because the Chancellor had to be able to trust their proofer. Always, without hesitation. The proofer takes the harm. Never causes it.

There was a knock at Tain's study door. Erel waited there, dressed more finely than I'd ever seen him, his stray puff of hair even tamed for the occasion. "Honored Chancellor, the others are getting anxious," he said, peering curiously at me and Kalina, taking in our flushed faces and the palpable tension in the room. "Can I say you're nearly done here?"

Tain was looking furiously at Kalina, something I couldn't remember him ever doing before. "Yeah," he said, turning his back. "Yeah, we're done."

Much of my life was spent with an elevated pulse, my brain trying to convince me something terrible was going to happen, might already have happened, and it was probably caused by something I did or failed to do. It was almost a relief to feel the usual sickness in my stomach, the tight chest, the physical symptoms of dread, and know they were not the product of my mind but a normal reaction. The dread, this time, was well justified.

We found Hadrea before we reached our apartments, approaching from the quarry pass with her hair blowing wild and her eyes bright. Her presence gave me heart. Here was one person I would not have to convince of the danger; she listened, frowning and attentive, while we outlined what we knew.

"He is not wrong about the blackstripes," she said, brow furrowed. "You cannot keep him safe if his bodyguards are compromised. So we must act as if they can be trusted because there is no hope if they cannot." She scratched a hand through her hair, which was unbound by her usual scarf and had caught in knots and snarls in the wind. Only then did I notice she was not wearing the traditional Darfri garb.

"Where have you been, anyway? Aren't you supposed to be doing something at the ceremony?" I asked, distracted. "With the other Speakers?"

A hardness stiffened her face, just for a moment, but then she affected a relaxed smile and shook her head. "No. I am going to help you stop whatever is planned for tonight." She put a hand on my arm. "Do not worry, Jovan." My sense of relief grew. Despite her somewhat disheveled appearance, and the air of excess energy that rolled off her, Hadrea's confidence and competence was a balm to my rising anxiety. Together, the three of us would figure this out.

But Kalina had a strange tone to her voice when she said, "One possibility is that Aven has managed to rile up some of the Darfri in the city. She might be using them as part of the disruption tonight." Hadrea was shaking her head but Kalina continued flatly, almost as if she were reading from a script from which she couldn't deviate. "You said yourself there are unhappy people, especially unhappy young people, in the city. There are strange things happening to spirits out on the estates. Jovan saw someone who seemed to be using fresken at that party. We can't rule out the possibility that some of them might be part of this."

"Yes, we can," Hadrea said, a flare of anger and defensiveness in the answer, but she did not look directly at either of us. "There are people who are dissatisfied, yes, and who desire more change, and yes those who do not consider An-Ostada an appropriate teacher, but they are not any risk to the Chancellor."

"They burned down a boat," Kalina said, and Hadrea did look at her then; something passed between them, knife-edge sharp. "What if they did that on Aven's orders?"

"It was not that," she said, her mouth hard and barely moving as she answered. A faint color change was swelling up her neck and into her cheeks.

"You can't know that, though," Kalina said, overly reasonably, "unless you know the people who did it. You don't know the people who did it, do you?"

Her hands tightened into fists and my sister looked at Hadrea with the harshest expression I'd ever seen her turn in Hadrea's direction. And I knew, immediately, with a sour, hot taste in the back of my throat, that here was another thing I'd not noticed, another thing Kalina had deduced and I had missed. Or ignored. Because there was some part of me—a small, honest part—that knew I had felt something was off when she was first accused, and in the way she had responded when I brought it up, and chosen not to tug on that string and follow the feeling. I hadn't wanted to because I had known there was a chance I wouldn't like where it led.

"You were with them," I said quietly, and she shrugged and looked away. I grabbed her arm. A strange surge of emotion flared up inside me as if it had been ignited by the touch; I felt anger, confusion, fear, all white-hot. "The group who lit the fire, you were with them. *Why?* What were you thinking?"

"I told you An-Ostada had driven some of our group out of training," she said, pulling her arm free. "I could not find you after the ceremony and I found them, and they were . . . angry." Her tone, surprisingly, was defensive, almost beseeching. "You know what masquerade night is like, Jovan. Everyone was drinking, eating karodee cakes, and then we were just . . . experimenting, I suppose. Seeing what we could do." She hesitated, rubbing her hands together, and my heart thundered in my chest and the white-hot rage slipped out of me like an unplugged basin.

My voice sounded hollow as I said, "What do you mean, experimenting?"

She pressed her lips together, her jaw tight. After a moment she said, "I told you once that sometimes the Speakers used babacash to help communicate with the spirits. It loosens the hold the conscious world has on you, and makes you more amenable to seeing the secondworld."

"I remember." She had dosed herself with the toxic plant to attempt connection with the great water spirit Os-Woorin to seek his help, and then to subdue him; Salvea and I had given the same to the other Speakers at the lake that day. "And you remember it's poisonous, right?"

"Yes. But some of the—" She broke off, then tried again. "It had been suggested in our training group, not by An-Ostada, that there might be other substances that could help us. Not just to access the secondworld and communicate with the spirits and seek their favor, but to share and use the fresken of the land, the way I did that day. The big feats the Speakers among the rebels performed in the siege are very difficult, exhausting, possible only with coordinated effort and intense emotional investment. They speculated babacash, or something like it, might make it easier to access."

Something about the way she said "something like it" made my skin prickle, and Kalina clearly had the same idea. "What kind of substance are you talking about?" she asked.

Hadrea's hands were threaded tight together and she looked away from us. This deceptiveness from her, of all people, someone who was honest to a fault, turned my insides cold. "There are other things available that change how you are thinking and experiencing the world. Other substances. An-Ostada forbids talk of such things, because it does not fit the order she has determined that we should learn." A bitter twist of her lips, not really a smile. There was a long pause. "Void," she said at last. "Speakers can use it. We found it helps you reach the right emotional state, and to make connections with the living things around you. It is like babacash, but not. Babacash weakens your hold on reality so you can better understand the connections between things. This . . ." She took a deep breath in through her nose, like she was breathing in a delicious scent. "This makes *me* the connection. I felt . . . *more*."

Kalina was staring at her, eyes narrowed, staring as if she could decipher Hadrea like a line of badly printed text in a book. "You know the physics said people have already died using this stuff. And you know the Hands are tied up in its distribution, using it to fund their operations. Why would you take it?"

"And the boat?" I covered my face with my hands, dragged them down my cheeks, trying to smear the whole conversation away. "What was that? Some kind of prank? We've been in Council arguing these supposed Darfri attacks aren't real, accusing people of sowing discord! How many of those things were actually true?"

"It was just a boat!" she retorted. Her pupils were huge. I suddenly wondered if she had taken the drug more often than just that one night; the part of my brain trained to make observations, to gauge symptoms and reactions, kicked in, and I started registering all the things I had ignored or explained away before. Her occasional artificial energy. The evasiveness. The intense late-night visits to my room, where I'd thought we were connecting more deeply than ever before. I felt sick.

"The other Darfri are not criminals. They are just tired of being treated as naughty children instead of respected. They are not hurting anyone. It was just a boat, surrounded by water."

"There could have been people aboard," Kalina said slowly. She was regarding Hadrea with a baffled, hurt look, one echoed in my own heart. How could she have done this?

"No one sleeps on a cargo boat, Kalina. And I would have felt them if they were. I could feel *everything* when I was using the drug. I knew it was safe."

"And what about the damage it did?"

"It is an Ash boat," she snapped. "They will cope just fine. The Ash family never stopped growing fat off our labor. One less boat will not hurt them."

"You used fresken, Hadrea," I said. "After everything we've been trying to build, all the work your mother is doing, you're just blowing it all up? No wonder An-Ostada was worried." I looked at her flushed, defiant face, and felt like I was looking at a stranger.

"This would not have happened if *she* would teach me properly! She calls me too ambitious, as if I am engaged in some petty inter-Guild jostle for position. She says I am impatient, as if not just wanting to learn but to hunger for it is not a desirable trait in a Speaker."

Kalina stayed calm, though I knew her well enough to recognize how much strain she was under. "I know the power was denied you, and you feel cheated, having lost that time. But An-Ostada was a Speaker chosen by all the others for her wisdom, and deemed suitable to be your instructor."

I knew at once she'd made a mistake. Hadrea seemed to grow larger in her rage. "Instructor? Pah! She expects to be our master!" Her words tumbled out in a rush. "She was holding me back on purpose. She learned things one way from her grandmother and she thinks that is the only way to have tah. It is not. I am not a child, to just practice rituals by rote. Every generation we have lost knowledge but she punishes me when I recognize new ways we might use power."

"Maybe she's right to, if this is how you want to use yours!" I held back from shouting only because we were still outside, and anyone nearby might hear. "What were you thinking? You know how frightened people are of Darfri magic and how hard we've been working to reassure them that Speakers aren't an army and fresken isn't a weapon. How many times I've quashed rumors about Darfri assuming the accusers were just trying to cause trouble. If it gets out this was real, that undoes everything I've said, whether it's true or not."

"And if I had not retained those relationships you would not have anyone who could speak to them for you now. You would not know this is not where your enemies lie. If I had stopped them burning the boat, do you think I would be invited in with them again? You do not just need the ordinary Darfri to keep this country safe, you need Darfri with power."

"We don't need another civil war." I shook my head, dazed, trying to get a grip on my anger, trying to reason with her. "Hadrea, the city is only still standing because of you. It owes you everything. *We* owe you. And I wouldn't tell you how to practice your religion, you know I've never tried to intrude. But—"

"You are intruding right now!" she retorted. "This has nothing to do with an attack on the Chancellor or on the ceremony tonight. You are wasting time worrying about your bickering Credol colleagues and a few burnt sacks of rice when there are more important things to be concerned with."

"I don't want to be concerned with fresken or the Darfri or spirits or anything else! But you're being reckless, and you're being secretive, and honordown, Hadrea, I love you but I need to be able to trust you too!"

She squared her jaw, and her voice went very cold. "I thought we did trust each other, Jovan."

A nasty laugh came out before I could stop myself. "If you trusted me you'd have talked to me about An-Ostada and what was going on. You'd have wanted my support. You'd have kept me informed about what was going on with the other students and the drugs and everything else, instead of letting me blunder around defending you in Council." I couldn't look at her, couldn't look at Kalina, but the words kept coming all the same. "You always think you know better. No one's ever on your team, are they? Hadrea against the world. I thought—" I stopped, not even wanting to finish in my head, let alone say it out loud.

Kalina, stricken, touched my shoulder. "Jov, we're running out of time."

I shook myself, tried to clear my head. She was right; we had no time for this. Tain was in danger. "Don't go to the ceremony," I said to Hadrea. "Just . . . just stay away, all right?" And I spun and left her standing there, a sour taste rising in my throat. She didn't answer, and the silence of her still-ness closed around me like fog as Kalina and I walked away.

"You're staying here," I told Dija, and then raised my voice over her loud ob-jection to address the rest of the family, all decked out as they were in their last spring finery. "You're *all* staying here. It's not safe."

"What do you mean, it's not safe?"

"Uncle!"

"What exactly is going on?"

They peppered us with questions with varying degrees of fury; the boys howling their displeasure at being confined, and Dija staring at me with such intensity from behind her glasses that had she been able to use magic I might have been seriously concerned.

"Don't let anyone in, all right?" I instructed Sjease and our houseguards, the latter of whom looked more alarmed than the former, and more inclined to argue. "No one goes in, no one goes out."

I hesitated as I looked over at the doorway to my room, through which Kalina could be just seen, packing clothing with our various substances. Since the siege, since proving how stupidly, insultingly foolish I'd been for obsessing over her health, I had resolved never to be the overprotective, over-bearing brother who had not listened to her. But, honor-down, the conflict inside me was intense. I didn't know what exactly we were going to face at the ceremony. For all her determination and skills, she still could not run or fight if she was in danger, and the thought of losing her—again—made me want to throw up. On the other hand, there was no one in the world I trusted more, no one I'd rather have with me in this. Especially when the two other people I thought I could count on had been keeping secrets.

"Let's go," she said, emerging from the room. She wore one of my palumas as her own lacked the pockets that concealed my potions and chemicals. I didn't like using them offensively and liked even less the idea of Kalina being forced to do so when she was less familiar with their individual effects, but if it came to it, she had a better shot defeating an attacker with poison than with a knife. She handed me the small vial of darpar I'd asked for, and I swallowed its contents quickly and with a twist of distaste. I needed the pain relief and the energy for this if I was going to be of any use, but it felt wrong to take it all the same. Hadn't I railed on Tain for the same thing, in similar circumstances? I shook off that thought. For whatever reasons, Tain didn't believe he could abandon this event, and we would do everything we could to protect him, even if it went against my preferences.

Our path to the front door was blocked by a small figure. Dija raised her chin and looked at each of us, resolute. "I could help."

Behind me, Ana made a strangled, furious noise of protest, and I held up a hand to quiet her. "No," I said flatly. Dija was a good apprentice, a hard worker, and she'd already shown herself to be clever and brave and resilient. But I'd put her in harm's way too much already. "The only way you can help right now is to stay here, out of danger. If—" I cleared my throat, looked over the rest of the family, a small clot of staring, fearful faces, and dropped my voice down so only Dija could hear. "If something goes wrong, you're my backup. You understand? You're the only one who's going to be able to step up and look after Tain and Merenda. I can't control what's going to happen tonight, but I can at least make sure I have someone to carry on if the worst happens, all right?"

"But—"

"I'm the teacher. You're the apprentice. You do what *I* say. I told you that when you agreed to come to Silasta, Dija. I say you stay here and you stay safe. You follow me this time and you're out, forever, whatever happens. Do you understand?" I knew it was coming across too harshly, I could see myself, a cold and emotionless thing, in the reflection before me, in the sudden wetness in her eyes, the quiver in her chin. But I didn't have time to coddle her, not now. "Well?"

"Yes, Uncle," she whispered, and fled back into the apartments.

For once, Kalina didn't chide me for it. She squeezed my hand, and without a further word, we left.

We didn't have a clear plan. We couldn't know from where the attack would come—an Order Guard? Some other Hands in the crowd? A foreign official? We had the Captain's concession that every country's delegation was being watched by double the men as previously planned. The blackstripes would protect Tain from a close-range attack, and the Captain had been right in one respect: if the blackstripes had turned, my proximity wouldn't save him. All we could do was split up and search, and keep our eyes open.

"Want to get a good seat," I told the official at the gate, trying to sound excited. They had done a cursory check for weapons, but it had not been thorough enough to find the pouches under my clothes.

"Enjoy the festival," the official said, sounding bored, their attention already on the next person trickling in.

By my reckoning there was little time until people started turning up in earnest. Officials were still undertaking last-minute preparation and maintenance in the center of the arena, one performer practiced swinging one-handed on a bar at the far end, and some of the general public seats were filling with early entries. Several Order Guards walked a slow perimeter of the field, staggered at intervals, surveying both the seating and the grounds.

I kept well clear of them. We had no way of knowing which Order Guards we could trust. Sukseno might not be on official duty tonight, and Chen had been informed about his betrayal, but I didn't believe for a second he was the only one. And Guards in Hands' pay, or under Aven's instructions, meant they knew where our security was focused. Which meant whatever they planned, it wasn't what we were ready to defend.

I started my search in the lavish section equipped for the comfort of the Council and international guests. Not precisely sure what to look for but hoping I'd know it when I saw it, I ran my hands under the bench seating, squashed cushions, checked vantage points across the arena . . . nothing. No hidden weapons or assassins. I squinted, trying to identify the best position from which to attack with a range weapon.

"Hey!" A woman in an official's sash approached from below, gesturing. "You! Yes, you. You can't be up there."

"Sorry," I called, and climbed down into the regular seating, heading for the other side of the arena. The diligence and the speed with which I'd been spotted was something of a relief; it meant Chen must have at least ordered the Guards to watch for people who didn't belong or were acting strangely.

"Stop!" I froze. "What do you think you're playing at, up there, mate?" a Guard asked.

"Just seeing what the best views look like," I replied, keeping my face turned away. My heart beat hard, and one of my hands slipped inside my paluma. "Wasn't going to sit there or anything. Sorry, I'll move on."

"Mmm." The official looked me over, then glanced at the Guard. "What do you think?"

"Been told not to take any chances," the Guard said shortly. "Let's see what the Captain thinks. Come with me, please."

Chen. Relieved, I followed meekly along, and when Chen strode up, eyes widening as she recognized me, I had pulled my hat off and was speaking before she could say anything. "Captain, I need to call in a favor."

She looked at me with a sharp, penetrating stare, one hand resting on her belt. "Your sister's at the gate, talking about an attack. You're here for the same thing, I assume?" She glanced back over her shoulder. "Bring the Credola out, would you?"

Kalina, a flush to her cheeks, was led out. Chen looked over the two of us and took a breath; for a moment it seemed she might call for someone to escort us out, but instead, she dismissed the other Guard and gestured at us to walk with her. There was no time to dance around it. "Chen, tell me what you think. If you wanted to attack Tain or disrupt the ceremony, but you knew everything about our security, where all our guards would be and who they'd be watching, how would you do it?"

"Jovan, I know you mean well, but—"

"How would you do it?"

She sighed again, louder, but then her lips thinned as she considered. "We talked about this. I s'pose I'd want range weapons, assuming I managed to get them into the city somehow, and in the hands of people I knew you weren't watching. I'd wait till the targets were somewhere predictable and stationary—sitting in their seats—and then cause a distraction—a fire, a riot—then shoot them down. You could hide a few different bowmen in the crowd and they could get lost in the commotion and we'd have no way of identifying them on the way out, even with limited exits.

"But Jovan, even if you're right and there are Hands out there, that plan wouldn't work. Everyone's getting searched on the way in, they can't bring bows in. Not even my Order Guards—and we'll talk later about Sukseno, don't worry, I'm not ignoring that. Though I find it hard to believe anyone in my Order Guards—" she began hotly, but I shook my head.

"You know the Guards aren't immune from infiltration. We found one, and there's likely more—either Aven loyalists from the army, or disgruntled

Darfri she's riled up again, or foreign agents—you've had a massive influx of new people since the siege and no way to be certain of every single person who's been hired."

I checked over my shoulder. We were almost in hearing range of the solo athlete swinging between bars, but they were completely focused on their task and no one else was close.

"You're searching people on the way in," Kalina said, "but you've had Order Guards and officials coming and going all day. What if there are weapons in here already, hidden earlier? Bows, for example? What if you fixed some to the bottom of a bench?"

Chen paused in her stride. "My Guards don't carry bows, and nor do anyone else's," she said. "No one can even bring ranged weapons into the city."

I snorted. "And who does the weapons searches and confiscations at the gates of the city? Order Guards. Who can access those stores anytime they want? Order Guards.

"Look. There'll be people pouring in here shortly. If we're wrong and there's nothing here, nothing happens, all we've wasted is a bit of time and effort. I'll look like a fool and I'll never have been so happy to be one."

There was a long silence as the Captain regarded me, her expression inscrutable. Then she nodded. "I haven't forgotten how I got this position," she said at last. "I know you two trusted me at a time when maybe not everyone around you earned that trust. You always asked people with more experience or knowledge when you didn't know something. I respect that about you both." She looked off into the distance for so long I feared she wasn't going to return, but eventually she looked me in the eye. "I don't believe you'd be here to waste my time or anything of the sort." She squinted up at the sky and then blew her whistle twice, hard. The other Guards in the arena responded smoothly, jogging up toward us. Some of the tightness in my chest eased.

"We're going to do a last-minute search of the arena," she told them briskly. "Checking the seats, every row, anything out of the ordinary. A section each. And you three, go do a sweep under the tiers to make sure no one's hidden down there. Take a lantern, it's dark under there." She ignored the quizzical looks from the Guards and barked, "Get on it! Methodical, thorough. Let's get this done before the seats start filling."

We split up and started. Bench after bench, pace by pace, until my back was screaming from the effort and my ankle burned. Nothing. People had started to file in; several performers began their warm-ups. Sweat dripped down the back of my neck and down my forehead into my eyes as I tried to cover more ground. Nothing, nothing, nothing but splinters, and a growing feeling of despair. I was losing confidence. I glanced over at Kalina, one section over. She was moving much slower than me, and bending awkwardly.

More and more people streamed in and our search continued, row by row. Time seemed both to drag and to speed by. The Order Guards were probably furious by now at this seemingly pointless task. Eventually I stood and caught Chen's eye from a distance; she shrugged one shoulder and shook her head. We'd run out of time; she would need to send her Guards back to their assigned duties. Sure enough, she blew her whistle to attract the others. My breath came quicker than ever. Down to me and Kalina now. I bitterly regretted, now, the heated confrontation with Hadrea; for all that I was furious with her for lying to me, for concealing key information, we had needed her here, and if I could find her I would tell her so. We could quarrel about the Darfri later.

I looked over at the private entranceway through which the access to the upper tiers for the important guests was granted. The Doranite party entered in a large bloc through that reserved entrance and filed along to their seats. The King was dressed in leather and fur, his long, thick hair worn in a heavily decorated topknot. He carried a massive scepter with a gleaming opal at the center, so he was easy to identify. His assorted Chieftains accompanied him, all muscular and powerful figures.

I climbed up to the next row and bent again. The arena was filling fast, and people had started sitting in the area I was searching; I didn't attempt to explain myself and endured their stares and affronted noises. A number of officials were down on the grounds now, talking to the gathered athletes and performers in preparation for the final events, and other important guests were coming in, too. The Costkati Grand Emissary and the Tocatican Prince filed in with their respective parties, and a noisy group of Silastians took seats nearest the box. Then there was the Talafan group, proceeding slowly to the far side of the box, their servants hurrying ahead of the Crown Prince, who was bedecked spectacularly with clothes like an armor of wealth gleaming in the afternoon sunshine.

The noise was building; when had it become so loud? A Marutian Duke whose name I couldn't remember and a huge cast of servants and attendants swept in. Their hats were so tall they obscured the people behind them. More

Councilors. Attentive blackstripes were positioned around the foreign parties, ostensibly for their protection but also to monitor them.

I straightened to stretch out my back and neck with a crack. More and
more blackstripes were visible in positions at the ends of rows and moving
around in the enclosed box, so Tain must be on his way. I was nearly at the
top now. Around me, oblivious people swapped bets and bought snacks from
innovative—and likely un-Guilded—vendors, chatting and laughing and
speculating in a hodgepodge of languages. The noise and confusion would
have made me anxious at the best of times.

Panting, Kalina joined me from the next stand. "Have you found anything?" She moved aside to make way for an elaborately dressed juggler who
was readying himself to perform for the amusement of the crowd. I ducked,
only just avoiding a faceful of pink silk hat, and shook my head; Kalina
rubbed her eyes. "What are we supposed to do now, then?"

I hesitated. Our first guess had been wrong; whatever was planned, if
indeed there was anything, we weren't going to find it hidden in the seats. At
least the Guards were on alert, and at least some of them were on our side.
"We keep looking. Stay out of sight if we can."

We fell in behind another set of performers, this one an acrobat on the
shoulders of another, underneath a single dress so they appeared to be a giant
woman. She waved and bowed as she moved along the path at the base of the
seats, throwing sweets to the children in the crowd, and we kept our heads
down and followed in her wake. No one paid us any heed.

We tracked around the arena as quickly as we could without attracting too much attention; most people were in their seats now, and a massive
cheer signaled the entry of the first performance. We kept wending our way
around, past where a huge contingent of Doranite spectators were sitting,
roaring their approval as one of the demonstration athletes from Doran flew
through the obstacles with great skill. The noise as we passed their section
was so deafening we could not even hear the singer who was attempting to
perform in the stairway. Over the course of the Games, Sjon athletes had
excelled in the team sports, the hurdling, hoop and print, and high jump, but
Doran had dominated in anything resembling the everyday activities of their
culture, which was heavily physical: the log toss, all of the climbing events,
wrestling, and of course the obstacle course, which required dexterous and
bold leaping and climbing through an impressive range of structures. The
Doranite Chieftain had been right to question why many of our traditional

games and sports were ill-suited to our own landscape; I could only assume
many traditions had been carried in with the refugees or imported from set-
tlers from elsewhere over the years.

We stopped behind a ropy-armed elderly woman manning a Guild-flagged
small cart selling dried figs stuffed with white cheese and meat-and-bean
balls on sticks. Kalina pretended to muse over which dip she wanted while
I surreptitiously checked the position of the Order Guards and blackstripes;
there were at least twice as many here as in any of the other sections, probably
because it was where many of the most powerful Sjon families had seats. The
next section along contained the viewing box for the Council. I kept my head
averted in case someone who knew us happened to look down.

"I searched up here first," I told Kalina in a low voice. We had covered the
whole perimeter, and nothing.

"So what do you want to do now?"

We looked at each other a long while. "Find Tain and stick by him. I'll do
a loop outside."

I contented myself and calmed some of my rising panic by pacing around
the edges of the arena fencing, squeezing my fingers and toes as I walked.
Nothing suspicious caught my eye as I circled around; there were more street
performers amusing the waiting crowds as they queued to get inside, a few
Darfri preachers calling blessings, various vendors with prominently displayed official Guild markings, and down alleyways more portable stands
with no Guild markings and vendors with darting eyes and charming quick
tongues. Once I thought I saw the girl who had sent me into the Hands' den,
but when I stepped closer it was a little boy. On a few occasions I briefly went
on alert, but the incidents were nothing more than alcohol- and excitement-
fueled scuffles. Pacing suited both my state of anxiety and my task in any
case, so I continued walking around and around, watching and waiting for
something to happen. I heard the bellows of the crowd, the announcements,
gasps and cries of delight at the demonstration events.

Something would happen. Our enemies would not let an opportunity like
this pass, with so many people gathered in one place, not after all their efforts
to ruin our day.

And yet.

I paced and watched and speculated, and paced and watched some more.
All the while, the rock in my stomach grew heavier. The trickle of people
kept up through the afternoon before eventually slowing. As it turned to

dusk, workers lit huge beacon lamps at various points on the arena, visible like giant candles even from outside. Beyond, the streets were all brightly lamplit and almost all shops, bars, and even bathhouses would be open late tonight, hoping to lure in the unprecedented number of patrons, but there remained plenty of dark hiding places.

Kalina came out and joined me. "No sign of anything inside," she said. "I . . ." She looked tentatively at me, as if fearful I might break. "I found Hadrea. She'd been looking for us. I told her to find Tain and stick by him."

"Good." My voice sounded too jolly, too false, but it was the best I could manage. "I'm glad. I feel better him having her nearby." That was true, at least. For all her temper and her recklessness, Hadrea was smart and observant and swift and strong, and she would protect Tain fearlessly.

"I haven't seen anything suspicious so far," Kalina said. "What about out here?"

"Nothing."

Baina and her team arrived, ready for the explosives display. Chen had said if she were planning something, she would use a distraction. Well, the display would be that, and the arena was full, and it was much harder to see now, with the slowly darkening sky and the brightness and shadows cast by the giant lights. So we tracked in after them. They were all searched on the way in, as were we. The officials were still being vigilant, at least.

The team was chattering, sounding more anxious than jubilant. We loitered near enough them to hear some of their nervous whispers, which were hushed quickly under Baina's glare. "Time to move," she said firmly, and she took off in an unexpected direction, looking over her shoulder. I didn't get out of the way in time and she accidentally caught me with her shoulder, knocking me off my feet. "Oh! Credo Jovan." The engineer peered at me suspiciously. "What are you doing here?"

"Nothing." I got to my feet. "Just making sure everything's all right here."

"Well, look, be careful, mind," she said, already starting to move on. "Don't go knocking people over in the dark. This stuff's dangerous, you know that. And it's worth a bloody fortune!"

"Good luck with the display," Kalina said, and Baina acknowledged her with a wave as she moved on.

"We should go back in there," she said, watching the team move on. "It must be during the display they're going to attack."

But I was still shocked into stillness where I'd half gotten to my feet. It felt like there were insects buzzing around my skull, excited and distracting, stopping me from thinking.

"Jov?"

My throat constricted. *That stuff's dangerous.* Someone had said that to me the other day.

"Jov?"

"The committee." The committee had been worried because Chen's report listed a break-in at Baina's workshop. They'd been worried about the chemicals being dumped. "Someone stole materials from Baina days ago."

Kalina and I stared at each other for a treacly moment before my brain snapped back into action.

Baina's materials were capable of significant destruction; I knew better than anyone, having used one of her devices to blow out the priceless and irreplaceable old Council chamber roof two years ago. I swallowed, and looked at the seating. "We need to get under there," I said to my sister. There were entrances to the under-tier section in each of the entryways, but even faster: from this angle, in the thin gaps between spectators' heads and legs, I could see through to the underside beneath the seats at head height. There was no backing to the underside of the benches. Kalina followed my gaze, and did not hesitate.

Kalina slid beneath the first row of seating, disappearing into the darkness below, and I followed clumsily, squeezing myself through the gap as fast as I could.

We dropped down to the underside of the tiers. I shuffled back until we were able to stand, then stretched out my back. The dull ache in my ankle was slowly defeating the effects of the darpar I'd taken, and a sharp pain lingered beneath my shoulder blades from the frantic searching under benches. It was dark and strange under there, most of the lamp and moonlight filtered out by angles and by the legs blocking the gaps between the seating above. "Didn't Chen send people to check down here?" Kalina said.

"Yes, but they were looking for people hiding down here."

"And what exactly are *we* looking for?" Kalina asked in a low voice, as I strode to the nearest support pillar and scanned it.

"Anything that looks like it doesn't belong there," I muttered. "Something strapped on to a pillar or wall, probably." There was no solid continuous wall at the back, only support pillars and the high fencing erected around the arena that acted like an external wall. "If you wanted to cause maximum damage you'd destroy a support pillar." I looked up.

Nothing on this one. I moved on to the next. Outside, the crowd roared and cheered again as a competitor finished their round. I walked around the pillar; nothing.

"Clear here," she said, from yet another. The anxious, sick feeling of having missed something began to grow in my stomach again. Had I been wrong *again*? Was there really no threat? Was all this for nothing?

"And here." I ran to the fence and along it, searching for any sign of something being attached. Anything at all.

"Nothing under here," Kalina said quietly. She had her head craned up, looking at the seats from below. It was a weird sensation being under all of those bodies. I pictured again the devastation if part of the structure exploded. Maybe I really had imagined it all, dreamed up a dramatic attack where there never was one.

There was a sudden crack and we both jumped, but it was only the first of Baina's decorative explosions. Peering through spectators' feet we saw white fire shoot into the air and shatter into tiny sparkling pieces, like someone had pulled stars out of the night sky and scattered them in the air above the water. There were a few nervous shouts and screams but after the third pop the crowd was making only gasps of appreciation.

Grief hollowed out my stomach for a moment, distracting me from the worry. Etan had been at least partially responsible for the chemical work that had underlain Baina's experiments and successes, but no one would remember his name years from now. Of course, that was how he would have wanted it.

"We're in the wrong section," Kalina said suddenly into the strange quiet. She was counting on her fingers, looking up. "Honor-down, Jov. We were so worried about Tain, but what if . . . Jov, listen. All our allies—the Council, the King of Doran, the Talafan, the western delegations . . . they're *all sitting in the same place.*"

Our eyes met.

"Fuck."

As one, we started to run.

"They're the next section across," I panted. "We'll have to risk going through the entries, there's no time to go out into the arena again." There was a small half door at the end of the section, leading into the next entryway. It wasn't locked, thankfully, but as we shoved it open and half-ran, half-crouched through, the Order Guards manning that passage saw us at once.

"Hey," one said; I kept running and kicked in the half-door entry on the opposite side of the passage before anyone could grab me. "Come with us!" I bellowed at the Guard over my shoulder. "We need help!"

Someone made to grab Kalina but I hauled her through the entrance with me. She gasped and staggered to the side as her leg gave out from under her, and a jolt of guilt pierced me.

"I'm fine!" she barked. Outside I heard the Order Guards giving shouted directions: *You, stay here and keep monitoring the entrance! You get backup!* One man ducked into the space, his baton held out, and stepped toward us. A whistle sounded, but it was buried in another round of cheering and applause, and people stamping their feet in enthusiasm on the benches. The sound was deafening from underneath.

"Stop where you are."

I spun back to face the Guard. "We need to search under here," I said. "Make yourself useful. Anything out of the ordinary, look for a—"

I broke off forcibly as Kalina's hand slapped across my mouth. She gestured. In the dappled light, something was moving, the light shifting. Some-*one* was moving. We stood in silence, watching, as a figure slipped through a sudden patch of bright light; a section of fence had been damaged to allow entry.

The Order Guard, who had also frozen, stepped forward and shouted. "You there!"

The figure whirled round. It was a plainly dressed man, carrying something carefully in his hands. He saw us, and instead of running away or toward us, he ran toward the nearest support pillar. Only as flame flared did I realize what he'd been carrying: fabric or cord of some kind dangled from a clumpy shape protruding from the join point of a support beam and a pillar, and now the end of it was alight, burning like a wick. The man pulled a long knife from his belt and spun to face us boldly. "Shit," I muttered, dread sinking in. He looked familiar in the half light; I was suddenly sure I knew him from somewhere. Something about his posture . . . The skinny man with the high voice, the third Hand.

The Order Guard abandoned his attempt to arrest us and with a cry he charged instead at the Hand, but the smaller man was much faster and easily slipped the angle of his shoulders to avoid the baton strike, then struck back. An explosive round of cheering above us saved the Guard; the man's knife went awry when he looked up suddenly, and the blade thrust under the Guard's arm instead of into his stomach. Kalina came from nowhere and kicked the man in the back of the knees. Even with her relatively tentative force he buckled and fell into the Order Guard, dropping the knife; the two of them wrestled furiously to the ground and Kalina recovered the knife. I had edged around the scuffle and made a run for the lit fuse. I tore off my hat and used it like gloves to try to smother the flame, but my attempts were fruitless. "Here!" Kalina cried, and slid the knife to me across the ground. With a few frantic sawing motions and swearing as the flames bit at my wrists, I managed to sever the fabric so the burning end fell harmlessly to the ground.

The Order Guard was on the top of the struggle on the ground and holding his own. The wick design would have given the Hand enough time to get safely clear of the explosion, but I couldn't just leave the device there. I squinted up at it frantically, trying to see how it worked and how it was attached. The explosives might have used the same combination of chemicals my uncle had put together years ago, but how they were combined in the strange parcel and tube I could not have said. There was a slick, smooth covering wrapping it so I couldn't tell what parts held what components or how they were designed to combine. "Get it down," my sister gasped. "Hurry!"

It was at the limit of my reach but I tugged at it as best I could. "It's . . ." I struggled, feeling around the edges of it. "I think it's bolted in."

I felt in my pouch, thinking to perhaps use Malek's acid, but my hands stopped mid-groping—I didn't know exactly what was inside the casing and what might happen if any Malek's acid came in contact with it. "Shit. *Shit!* I can't get it down, Lini. We need help."

The Guard on the floor had the better of his opponent, who was now covering his head, cowering. "Here," Kalina said, quickly untying and slicing off a section of cording on her dress. "We can tie him up."

The man grunted angrily as the Order Guard forced his arms behind his back while Kalina shakily held the knife pointed at him, and grimaced with pain as he tied the knots. But he peered up at me and his teeth gleamed between the bloody rivulets streaming down his face. He was grinning. Then a wheezy little laugh emerged, and still he stared. "You'll never get them all, though," he said.

"Them all what?" the Order Guard demanded. "What in the bloody hell's going on here, anyway?"

But cold fear had blossomed in my chest. Was this the only device? How many more Hands, how many more devices? I couldn't see any others attached to any of the other visible support pillars or beams. "Stay here," I said to the Order Guard, "until you get more help. There could be other devices and I haven't disabled this one. Don't let anyone get near it with anything burning, all right?"

He nodded.

"Kalina, you have to get the guests out," I said. I squeezed her hand. She couldn't run, now; I could see from the tremors in her limbs and the look in her eye that she had tapped out her supplies of energy. "Get out, call for help, get everyone out of this section but especially the foreign delegations, they might target them some other way. Scream the place down if you have to."

I looked grimly back the way we'd come. "I have to check if there are others. Send me help, get people under here, but first priority is to get the spectators out of the stands. You—you just—" My voice choked off, and her eyes filled with tears, but she nodded.

"I will. Go."

I took off at a run, but not through the doorway; if one Hand had come in through the fence, chances were good that was how another might. I squashed through the gap the man had left and then ran the perimeter, heart pounding, head swimming, looking for another broken section. Thank the fortunes for the bright and clear moon; if there had been clouds I'd never have been able to see. Inside the arena I thought the volume of cries and stomping of feet had increased. A few people outside were staring at me and pointing as I sprinted past. "Get the Guards! Get help!" I yelled at them as I ran, but they only stared back mutely.

Then I saw it. Another broken section, just like the first, masked partially by bushes growing close to the fencing. No time to waste; I hurtled past the bushes, heedless of the scratches to my face and neck, and threw myself through the gap and into another half-lit under-tier section. A light bobbed in one direction. I swore and ran toward it.

The man with the torch saw me just in time to stand up, alarmed, but not in enough time to do anything about my furious charge. I smashed into him with my shoulder, sending him flying and me crashing heavily on top of

him. He was bigger and stronger than me, though, and somehow he turned
us over so it was me on my back, winded, one hand pinned under his bulk.
He punched me in the face and I felt the impact as a heavy, sickening crack,
but my pinned hand had just enough wiggle room, and a moment later he
was reeling back, coughing and panicking, as powder exploded into his face.
I buried my own face in the earth, holding my breath, and as he staggered
off me, shrieking, I crawled away, still not daring to breathe. The torch was
abandoned on the ground and I rolled it in the dirt until it was utterly dead,
thanking the fortunes I'd been fast enough.

Then my relief caught in my throat. I had just enough time to register a
flare of light in the distance and then the terrible boom of an explosion.

INCIDENT: Council poisoning

POISON: Clouddust

INCIDENT NOTES: Water for handwashing at Council table contained clouddust serum; six Councilors used the water before symptoms—blistering and painful burns—were detected. Credola Fonda Leka (known for strong hygiene practices) suffered the most severe damage to skin of her palms. Chancellor Keiki unaffected, this proofer suffered only mild and temporary effects. Disgruntled servant arrested and sentenced by determination council. Grudge appears to relate to working conditions and is not more broadly politically driven.

(from proofing notes of Credola Tasuri Oromani)

14

Kalina

The first explosion rocked the entire structure, sending its evil, destructive wave through the connected sections of the arena like a ripple on a pond. I hadn't even seen the blast itself, just heard the terrible crack, a flare of something bright in the corner of my eye, then I was falling into people and down over suddenly unstable benches and footing, unsure which way was up or down and struggling to breathe. Before I could orient myself, a kind of hollow *pop* sounded, along with another flare of light at my peripheral, and then a third. My ears felt like they were being compressed with heavy pillows, thick and impenetrable, but also painful.

Someone shifted their weight and relieved some of the pressure on my chest. I was able to lever myself out of the squash enough to breathe, but everything hurt and the air felt hot and wet in my lungs. I rolled out and away onto a clear section of ground, coughing, half-blinded with the pain and dizzy with the confusing hollow ringing in my head. One of my hands hurt more than the other and I realized that was because I was still holding in a crushing grip the speaking trumpet I had seized from an official. Not that I'd done much good with it.

I blinked, rubbing my gritty eyes, swallowing down the urge to vomit. My vision went black for whole moments at a time as I tried to look around, so I wasn't sure whether I was not fully conscious or there was something wrong with my eyes, too. Turning my head rapidly to try to get a picture of what had happened only made the urge to vomit stronger. I got to my hands and knees, tried not to weep at the pain, and looked slowly around.

The group of Doranites, including the King, were getting to their feet nearby, shaken but apparently uninjured. At least some of our guests had listened to my frantic directions, but no one had made it far before the explosion had gone off. Dread and disorientation slowing my movements, I looked back over in the other direction.

The blast had torn through the next section over; a terrible hole gaped open in the middle of the seating, twisted benches and debris and bodies—and bits of bodies, horrible bits—scattered around it. Fires had caught, smoking and burning, and people in the lowest levels were scrambling to get off in a panicked, messy rabble. People seated higher were less fortunate. Those who could still move were trying to haul themselves down the wobbling remains of the structure. The top half had destabilized and collapsed into the exit passageway. It was strangely quiet, considering I could see people's mouths open, their faces contorted into screams of terror and agony. My ears must not be working properly. Pieces of the arena hung broken like eggshells. Even as I tried to stand, my brain finally catching up and starting to comprehend the awfulness of what I was seeing, additional parts of the section wobbled and buckled.

A Doranite Chieftain, coughing and staggering, spotted me, and in a few powerful strides he had caught me under the arm, stopping me from falling, but his grip was rough. He said something, right up near my face, but I couldn't understand; only faint sounds penetrated my abused ears. I understood the body language well enough, though.

I shook my head, trying to clear my throat. "We found explosives under here." I gestured down. "Where you were sitting, but—" I coughed, tried to stand straight, to look him in the eye. "There must have been more. . . ."

He clearly couldn't understand me either, but released my arm with an abrupt shake and turned back to his companions. Behind him, a hodgepodge of people were getting their footing; royals, Councilors, dignitaries alike, and beginning to grasp what had happened. I followed their frightened and horrified gazes back at the mess one section over. Beyond, through the smoke, even in the dark, I saw another mass of broken seating and fire, and farther still, another. The pops I had heard after the first blast must have been further explosions. A horrible guilt turned my stomach. We'd disabled one device, but it hadn't been enough. They hadn't been just targeting the supposedly important people, but all of us. How many people had been caught up in this? How many people were dead or injured? I couldn't even fathom the scale of it.

And then my slow brain processed it. *Jov*. He hadn't stopped the explosions; could never have stopped three of them. Had he been right there, in the heart of the first blast? I stared at the ruin of the seating, then at the pit beneath it. How far had Jov run, how close had he gotten?

Though I could barely make my left side work, though every step was an effort, I started clambering over the broken seating toward the smoking crater. "Jov!" I screamed. I think I screamed. My throat registered the burr but I still heard only a muted squeal. My eyes burned with desperate, terrible tears and I couldn't summon any volume to my second scream through my clenching throat. Still, I kept trying, pointlessly, hopelessly. *"Jov!"* I coughed, my brain even now still registering the scope of what had happened. Not just Jov, but Tain too, where had Tain been? "Tain!"

"Who is this?" Someone growled in my ear, in Trade. The Doranite again, clambering after me. I glanced back at him, still half-blinded by furious tears.

"I'm Kalina," I began, but he shook his head.

"No, who is *this*?" He spread his arms to indicate the entire disaster, and I understood. Trade had limited tenses. He meant who was responsible for the explosion.

"I don't know."

"You are trying to get us out." His voice was muffled by the noise in my ears, but understandable. They seemed to be clearing, though the ringing continued. "You know something is happening?"

"Yes."

"Who?" He pointed back behind him, to the crowds of guests, gesturing at the groups in turn. "Is this inside Sjona or is it Maru? Tocatica? Talafar?"

I shook my head helplessly. "I don't know," I said again.

Another noise managed to penetrate my thick head then, and both of us swung round at it—a tortured groan, as the metal supports under part of the seating buckled. People dangled from the broken edge, limbs flailing into the open space. The faintest ghost screams penetrated the overwhelming whine in my head. The Doranite Chieftain shouted something, and moments later I was buffeted by a thundering of boots and bodies pounding toward the wreck; the Doranites, in a pack, the King and Chieftains and servants, too. Racing *toward* the danger, I thought, when Jov had sent me here to get them out of it.

Jov. The swell of fear and grief was so strong it was like my chest was threatening to tear into pieces instead. I staggered after the Doranites, who were leaping with impressive athleticism across the bent benches, heading up to the worst of the damage. My pace as I followed was slow and wonky. There were injured people—and worse—everywhere. The Doranites, making far faster progress than I, had formed a human chain to reach one of the people dangling into the opening.

The horrible swelling in my throat and head intensified. Had Jov been down there, in that gaping hole?

Blood and smoke and the smell of blackened flesh filled my senses as I got closer. People had been ripped apart by the force of the explosion. No one close to it could have survived.

"Help," I heard, and then louder: "Help!"

One of the bodies on the broken benches was moving, the head turned toward me and the whites of their eyes bright in their face in the dark. I crouched to tug away the piece of twisted metal pinning their shoulder but gasped and dropped it with a curse. The metal was hot; I didn't realize how hot until too late and the heat spread deep in my fingers and palm. I hastily wrapped my hand in a handful of my clothes and tried again. This time the metal gave and the woman, gasping with pain, pulled free. Her skin was puckered and burnt where the metal had pinned her but she seemed not even to notice.

"My boy!" she whispered hoarsely, and the moment I'd levered the metal off, she rolled out and scrambled across to a smaller figure. I thought my heart might snap, it felt so brittle. But the boy, thank the fortunes, was alive, and crying, and scrambled into his mother's embrace.

I helped whoever I could, though it was often hard to identify the grievously wounded from the dead. Honor-down, it was grim work. There were dead and injured children, honored elders, people I knew from school and work and everyday life in the city. I realized, seeing a significant number of Credol Family tattoos, that this section had been where most of the Councilors' families had been sitting. Where our own family would have been, had we not forced them to stay at the apartments. I could have been stumbling over *their* limbs, closing *their* eyes and avoiding looking at the things sticking into their chests.

Finally I drew near the shaking broken edges around the main blast site, where the Doranites were working as an efficient team, hauling people out. Avoiding the burning sections, and trying not to get in their way, I peered down, silent with dread, my pulse thumping painfully in my ears.

The Doranites were talking rapidly in their own language, gesturing at their next target for rescue, and blackstripes, Order Guards, and other citizens were joining their rescue attempts. Stinging smoke billowed around from the various fires, including from the wreckage under the collapsed section, masking my view of the worst-hit sections so I couldn't tell who might be . . . I didn't want to think about it. I didn't want to try to identify clothing or speculate about who was sitting where. It was all too obvious no one below the seating where the explosion had gone off could have survived.

I would just have to hope with everything in me that Jov had not been below. After everything we had been through, after all the dangers he had prevented and survived, I couldn't lose him now, not like this. I would not. He was not down there, he had been in a different section, and he would be busy, like me, helping the injured. We would find each other later. I assisted another person, their face smoke-blackened and a chunk of debris protruding from one arm, down to safety. I found I couldn't answer their thanks; in fact I couldn't get my breath out at all, it was trapped in my chest.

"Are you all right?" Someone grabbed my arm to steady me.

I started to nod then shook my head instead, and tapped my chest. Even after all these years, after so many attacks, it was so hard to wrestle with my brain, tell myself not to panic, to relax. The woman helped me to a stable section. "Lie down here," she suggested, but I shook my head harder.

"Stay . . . upright," I gasped. *Breathe, breathe, slow, in through the nose, out through the mouth.*

"The smoke will be making it worse," I heard someone say, a male voice.

The woman, who was peering over me anxiously, glanced over her shoulder and said, "What?" and only then did I realize he had spoken in Talafan, not Sjon. Dimly, I recognized Minister Kokush.

"This condition, it can be triggered by smoke," the Minister said earnestly. "You must get into clean air." He looked at the woman and seemed to suddenly understand the problem. He repeated it in slightly hesitant Sjon; she looked back with narrowed eyes.

"Will you be all right if I go help?" I nodded. "You look after her then," she added loudly, pointing an aggressive finger at Kokush, as if volume were the obstacle. He gave her a little bow and nodded.

Kokush switched back to Talafan to speak to me. "Your physics are setting up a treatment area," he said, gesturing down to the arena floor. "We should go there." He put one of my arms across his shoulder and his around my waist, and led me away from the smoking, burning stand. A section of the field had been hastily marked out with broken benches and a makeshift flag of a physic's blue sash. Several physics, sweaty and grim-faced, were treating the worst wounds, and other injured people were waiting in dazed groups to the side. No one paid me any heed as Kokush led me to join them and gently lifted my hands behind my head. "This opens up the chest, yes?" he said, and I nodded. He seemed both genuinely concerned and distracted; he kept looking anxiously back over his shoulder, inflated with questions he could not ask.

Breathe. Breathe. A fraction longer each time, the tiniest easing in my chest. Repeat. I was getting control back. "Good," he said quietly. "That's right."

I couldn't talk yet, but he read my questioning look. "My mother," he said, understanding what I meant. "We always had to look after her. She would do too much in the fields and my brothers and I would need to watch out that she had not worked her lungs to death. When they smoked the fields or if she got too close to the tanning equipment, it always made it worse."

He was looking back at the blast site again. I wondered whether there were any Talafan unaccounted for. I'd not been in the viewing box long enough to take stock but I'd had the impression of only a small Talafan group—I'd seen the Prince but no women, and no Ectar, either. I hoped he had not come at all, that he had not been elsewhere in the arena.

"Go," I wheezed, waving one feeble hand at Kokush. He nodded and turned back, running into the fray.

Concentrate. Relax. No point obsessing over this now. I couldn't help anyone until I could safely breathe again. Maddening, terrifying minutes passed in forced stillness. I managed a longer breath, and another. Patience was a skill learned in a hundred days of enforced bed rest, in canceled invitations and repeated excuses and missed opportunities. I would not forget it now.

"Kalina!"

Someone swooped up from behind and grabbed me in a fierce hug, momentarily constricting my breathing again. Fortunately I was quickly released and Hadrea pivoted me around to face her. Her eyes traveled over me, searching for injuries, even as I did the same to her. She looked unhurt, only slightly rumpled. "Where is Jovan?" she asked breathlessly.

She read my anguish in an instant. A spasm of emotion passed across her face and she said nothing, just stared at me, mouth slightly open.

"He was down . . . down under the tiers," I said. "I don't know whether he . . ." It was too much, my throat closed over. I shook my head and tried again. "I haven't found him yet, but we will." Then my own fear. "Where's Tain? You were together."

"He is here," she said, gesturing to the crowd of injured people lining up for care behind her, and my body sagged in gratitude. "We were lucky. There was an explosion in our section but we were in the bottom rows and did not get the full force. We were just knocked over." She surveyed the mess of the arena, brows drawn tight. "Three blasts," she said.

"We stopped the first one, then Jov ran," I said. I squeezed my eyes shut. Should I have gone with him? Tried to stop him?

Hadrea pointed. "Look how they are spaced." The three successful blasts were separated by one relatively unscathed section, immediately to the left of the first blast site. "Perhaps he stopped that one, too."

"Maybe." I tried not to think about other alternatives. Then my chest constricted again. "Your mother? Davi? Have you seen them?" It had been such a terrible blur as I had stumbled up those cursed stairs, my legs traitor-ously slow, trying to bellow instructions from a stolen speaking trumpet, and I'd not registered who exactly had been in the main box. I couldn't remember seeing Salvea, though I raked my memory for an image of her. *Don't let them have been in the family section. Please don't let them.*

"Not yet." She spoke with forced calm. "They were down there, near the front, last I saw them. I am sure they were out of the worst part of the force, the same as I was." She shifted her weight between her feet and stared back at the burning wreckage of the arena. I read the impatience in her posture and put a hand on her arm.

"Go look for them," I said, and a smile cut across her face, gone in an instant.

"I will find them all safe, and come back," she promised, and leapt away.

My breathing was feeling better and though the burn on my palm throbbed still, it wasn't serious. I had just begun to move closer to the physics to assist when a crack splintered the air, followed by an animalistic groan of metal and wood from the structure. Everyone flinched, and as one we looked up at the tiers, where a new section adjacent to and above the nearest blast site, swarming with people, had started to collapse. People raced past, and I heard snatches of conversation.

". . . Got a bunch of the rescuers . . ."

"—the Doranites! The King's up there! We need something we can use as a ladder, quick!"

A groan escaped me. There were people trapped up there, people who'd been trying to pull others out, and even as I watched, horror-struck at this new disaster, more of the seating crumpled away and fresh screams erupted. People streamed past me, scrambling up to help, but I felt rooted to the ground, unable to do anything but stare.

But over the now-dull ringing in my ears and the shouts and cries of people on the structure rose an unexpected and distracting sound. A dozen people had formed a pack near the base of the seating and were chanting in a rhythmic fashion: the Darfri, led by An-Ostada at the center, proud and tall. A ripple of reaction spread out from them. "About time!" snapped the physic nearest me. "Let's see if the bloody spirits are good for anything but destruction."

I hadn't been there for the big feats of Darfri magic in the siege. Hadn't been capable of fighting on the walls and witnessing the strange winds and the terrifying disembodied hands of dirt and stone. Hadn't seen the great Os-Woorin tearing apart its false idol and wreaking havoc on the city. Jovan had tried to explain to me what had happened, how the spirit had drunk in the emotional energy of the terrified people fighting around the lake. Was I about to see it now? My heart beat hard in anticipation. There was certainly terror aplenty here today. Were we about to see a spirit coming to our aid?

I wasn't the only one watching in anxious anticipation; others also stopped what they were doing and stared, looking frightened but hopeful, everyone's attention split between the Darfri group and the gaping angry hole and dangling edges of the falling arena. I stood ready, waiting for the sensation Jov had described, and to assist the way he had apparently once been able to do for Hadrea. After a few long moments of attempting to open myself up to it, all I felt was my burning lungs, the throbbing of my palm, and a creeping sense of awkwardness. If I should have felt something as the Darfri asked their boon, I didn't. I felt nothing at all. Just the same physical complaints, the same sting of smoke in my eyes and cold in my heart, the same rising tide of dread and desperate anger at what was happening to us.

As I watched, Hadrea emerged from the ruckus and approached at a trot. "Nothing," she said before I could ask. "I cannot get under there. One side has collapsed over the entryway and it is not safe to get in the other side. Beams are buckling and falling. There is a lot of fire down there. I called out for him, but . . ." She shook her head. "Nothing." Her head snapped suddenly over toward An-Ostada and her group. "What are they trying to do?" she muttered.

I covered my mouth with a loose part of my paluma as we moved closer, trying to see clearer without getting in anyone's way. "They're trying to help. The Doranites—the King, the Chieftains—got caught up in that last collapse." I had left Jov in order to get the Doranites to safety, and now it might have been for nothing. Guilt and rage battled inside me. The sheer unfairness of it made me want to scream. "I guess An-Ostada and her group are asking the spirits to do something? Can you . . . I don't know, help them?" It had never been clear to me how Darfri magic worked, but if a spirit could come hurtling out of the water to destroy the city when angry, could an appeased one not help us now? Or could Hadrea, hero of the battle, not do something similar and bend it to her will?

Certainly whatever An-Ostada's group was attempting wasn't working. We stopped just behind them, and even as they chanted and moved in unison, An-Ostada's hands rising and falling with her pleas, new flames inexplicably burst from the seating, as though it had been doused with oil and lit. Hadrea flinched, frowned, and looked between the flames and the group with narrowed eyes. "What?" she muttered. More shouting and screaming followed and another crash of broken wood and metal. The chanting of An-Ostada and her Speakers grew louder in response, a desperate edge to their voices now.

"Do something," I begged her, and Hadrea closed her eyes and raised her hands. Her mouth moved silently, but her chest rose and fell in time to the rhythm of the Darfri group's chants. A moment later, An-Ostada visibly stiffened and twisted back. She saw us immediately and in the mixed light I couldn't read her expression—anger? Gratitude? Relief? She turned back to face the seating without speaking.

I watched, anxious. Surely, surely their magic could help somehow. As if willed into existence a faint breeze rose and the flames seemed momentarily to dampen; my heart lifted. But it went no further. The chain of people trying to reach the Doranites, half of whom seemed to be dangling on the partially collapsed section, were still being defeated by the unreliable, dangerous footing in the crumpling sections, and the new fires blazing beyond expected levels.

Hadrea let out her breath in a tumbled rush. "It is not working."

"Why not?" My hands balled into frustrated fists. "It worked during the siege, why not now?"

She didn't open her eyes, but the little jerk of her chin in my direction was chastening. "It is not that easy. Speaking is not Summoning, and both rely on the attention of the spirits." Her voice softened slightly as she explained. "The spirits are old and powerful but they are part of the character of the land. A lake is deep and cool and quiet, difficult to stir. So too is the Os-Woorin. It is not—it is not like calling out and being answered, like a person."

A section of seating shuddered and tilted farther, bending into the hole with creaks and groans, increasing the angle at which the people scrambled to find purchase. Sweat poured down An-Ostada's broad back as she chanted. With visible effort, sweat also beading down her face—or perhaps that was just the heat billowing off the flames?—Hadrea made a firm, two-handed gesture, as if pushing something away. She opened her eyes. An-Ostada grunted and shook like we had pulled a foundation brick out of her very structure, but she continued the group's work.

"I am going to try something else," Hadrea said. She slipped something out of her sleeve, and if I could have felt worse, I did; it was a small, pale yellow tablet, and I knew what it was.

"What are you doing?"

She ignored me.

"Hadrea," I began, but a booming voice cut me off.

"Everyone off!" One of the blackstripes had got hold of a speaking trumpet and she and several other blackstripes and Guards were herding people off the tiers. "Quickly! This whole thing might come down and take everyone with it."

Bitter, I stepped back farther to clear space as many of the remaining rescuers hurried off the at-risk areas. This feeling of utter impotence I'd felt twice before, at the bedside of men I had loved but could not help save. Now I was to stand back and watch any chance of rescue diminish, without contributing in any way?

"Had—"

The sight of Hadrea's face sent an uneasy jolt through me. Her eyes had gone very black. With a beatific smile, she spun a slow circle, looking out around at the panicking crowd. At intervals, she stopped moving and stared, until the subject of the gaze returned it, almost as if she had summoned their attention from a distance. Several people did this until there were six of

them. As if as one, they began to approach the wreck. I didn't recognize any
of them; just ordinary men and women, mostly on the younger side, but they
seemed to know Hadrea, and some kind of silent communication passed between them. Like the people surrounding An-Ostada, they formed a group
behind Hadrea. They seemed dazed, almost as if they were sleepwalking, but
they moved in disquieting, fluid unity.

Then Hadrea froze suddenly, the smile dropping from her face. She opened
her eyes and looked directly at me. "Kalina! He is alive! Jovan is alive. I can
feel him."

"What?" But hope flooded me, instant, premature, foolish. She had just
said she could *feel* him, what did that even mean? I didn't understand, but my
singing heart did not care. "Can you—"

She had turned away again, concentration back on her arcane task.

Movement caught my eye behind her: a woman pushing through the crowd
toward us. Perhaps in her sixties, she was strong and fat, with a strip of white
hair amidst her still-dark curls, and such an aura of self-possession and power
I'd have recognized her as another Speaker even without the traditional
Darfri garb and neck laden with charms. My spirits rose again. Perhaps, with
the power of every Speaker, Hadrea could do this.

The seating dropped another few treads with a sudden, terrifying jolt.
This time the screams from within the hole rang clearer. As I watched, my
heart pounding, a section on the side closest to us jerked suddenly, and another set of benches buckled and collapsed, swallowing at least one rescuer
and the person he'd been reaching for. The entire section shuddered and
slipped, and in that moment I knew the entire thing was going to collapse
in on itself. Involuntarily I covered my face with my hands. But gasps rose
around me like birds taking flight and I dropped them.

The structure had frozen, mid-collapse, wobbling like an artful confec-
tion in Etan's kitchen, and the flames diminished down to nothing as if all
the air had been sucked from them. Hadrea had her hands out, as did the
group behind her. They were helping her or feeding her power, somehow, I
didn't understand how, but I recognized the kind of raw-power feat Hadrea
must have used to save us all two years ago. And where An-Ostada had
failed, Hadrea was succeeding. "Get everyone off! They can't hold it forever!"
I yelled, and someone else took up the cry. Armed with the confidence of
this sudden temporary stability, Guards and blackstripes and ordinary citizens climbed up the structure, and limbs and heads and finally whole people

began to emerge from the edges they'd been clinging to, scrambling up and linking hands with their rescuers. The King of Doran himself emerged with assistance from three Guards hauling the massive man together, then immediately turned around to assist someone else. The broken pieces of the arena shakily, impossibly, rose with a slow scream of metal, tipping up, correcting, until the pieces were almost horizontal.

I glanced at Hadrea, biting my lip. She wore an expression of intense concentration and though her body trembled and sweat beaded over her face and neck, she seemed to be in control. It was only purest luck I was looking exactly in the right direction to catch a movement behind her. The Darfri woman with the white strip in her hair, the one I'd noticed earlier, jerked, a little pulse of energy that would have been lost in a thousand other reactions in the crowd if I hadn't been looking right at her, and her mouth opened and eyes widened, like she was surprised—shocked, even. She shook her head, shock peeled away into anger, and something about the way her hands moved made me certain she was using fresken, just like Hadrea was, only Hadrea's apparent success was *not* what she was working for.

I remembered suddenly how Jov had seen a Darfri Speaker using fresken at the Hands' party, and Hadrea had not believed him. He had described drums, and a painted urn, and there, from a pouch around the woman's waist, peeked such an urn. I didn't know what it meant, but I did not doubt that whoever this woman was, she was not on our side.

I made my way closer to her, my mouth dry. And now I could see the actions corresponding to her movements: there, her arm jerked and one of the giant torches at the edge of the walkway, its base already aflame, creaked and started to fall toward the last of the people trying to help the injured off the wobbling, chaotic seats. Her other hand moved and the flames on the other side rose higher. I heard Hadrea's grunt in response and saw the pillar steady, the flames recede.

Trying to move as quietly and smoothly as possible, I slipped between the gawking onlookers—no one paid me any heed at all, so focused were they on the strange, supernatural effort holding together the massive broken structure—and drew closer and closer to the Darfri woman. Watching her I could see her hands regularly returned to the urn at her waist, as if it was part of her ritual or assisting in some fashion. I'd heard Hadrea scoffing at the need for items to focus power, but whatever it was, it seemed important to this woman.

My hand stole down and grabbed a piece of random debris, a piece of twisted metal about as long as my forearm. Sweat made it slippery in my palm, and my skin still throbbed from the burn. Closer I drew, and closer again. Three treads away. Two treads. Right behind her. I lined up the trajectory—side of the knee—and drew the makeshift baton back.

She spun in an instant, and my arm swung into nothing then stopped, ringing pain and reverberation up my arm as if I'd struck metal with all my strength. She bared her teeth and I sucked in a breath to scream, to warn Hadrea, but the woman closed one hand in a soft, strange motion, like she was squeezing an invisible piece of fruit. The air simply . . . vanished. My mouth stayed open, I tried to let the breath and the scream out, but it was as though my mouth and nose had been blocked off somehow. I started to step forward, clawing with my free hand at my throat and face, trying to understand the source of the suffocating, terrifying force, but to no avail.

The Darfri woman's grimace twisted into a grin, and with one more hand motion I felt something gripping my foot, as if it were being sucked down into the very earth. Dirt and grit and stone and rubble rose over my sandal, ate my foot with ease, and crept up to my ankle like loose metal filings onto a magnet. No amount of frantic pulling could free it. I couldn't breathe, I couldn't move, the edges of my vision were growing dark, and random spots were bursting with sparkling light, like staring at the sun. And no one was looking at me, no one but the woman, who wore the most terrible expression yet, a hungry, ecstatic pleasure as I scraped at my throat, my mouth moving soundlessly, panic infecting every pore of my body.

She turned abruptly, her hands going to the urn at her waist, and her focus visibly shifted to the arena again. I tried to see but the terrible pressure of the solid, unmoving air in my lungs sucked all my attention. I fell awkwardly to my knee on the side that wasn't trapped, the bright spots and black corners of my vision growing closer together until I could see nothing, feel nothing but the absence of air.

You know what this feels like, a tiny voice told me, dispassionate, without judgment. My weak lungs, seizing, fighting me. *Drowning, drowning in the river again, drowning in the air.* Aven's face, smiling, amused, as I tumbled back into the water. *Drowning.* The water closing over my face, a cold cloth on fevered skin. *This is how you die.*

But I did not want to die like this. *I will not.* I knew what it felt like to struggle to release the air from my lungs. I'd lived through it a hundred times.

The lack of air would kill me if I let it. *Relax. Don't panic.* I let my body go limp, dropped my hand from my chest, released the other's grip on the metal bar. It dropped from my hand and I could move that arm again, could move everything but the foot captured by the earth. Lightheaded, but the panic receding, I felt a moment of clarity.

I lunged.

My dive stretched the length of my body and it was enough to clumsily catch the woman's billowing skirt with both hands. She was jerked hard to one side and stumbled toward me, taken by surprise. It was enough. The waist sash opened up and the urn tumbled toward me; with the last of my energy I swatted it with one hand and knocked it to the ground.

The woman hissed, furious and guttural, and I could breathe, honor-down, the air was flooding in and out of me, and my foot was free, and I rolled over, sucking in air in grateful, sweet gasps.

As my vision swam back to normal the Darfri woman's face wobbled into focus above me, twisted in its rage. There was no energy left for one last effort, one last trick. I couldn't even move my head. She needed no fresken to defeat me now. She raised a foot to stomp down on my head, but then suddenly it was *her* who was crumpling, staggering, pushed under the weight of some unseen force. A wind had come from nowhere, a targeted, buffeting, silent wind, like a miniature Maiso directed at her. She was knocked off me, almost falling over onto her back, and I had enough energy to look at the direction it was coming from to see Hadrea, her face calm and her hands outstretched, strolling toward her like some savior hero out of a story. She dropped her hands down abruptly and the wind disappeared into nothing.

"Get away from my friend," she said into the sudden silence around us.

Still panting grateful breaths, I scrambled out of her way as Hadrea walked toward the Darfri woman. The latter stood warily, her uncertainty obvious. Her gaze darted between Hadrea and the urn beside me, and her tongue darted out to moisten her lips as she backed away slowly. The crowd near us scuttled away in turn, their faces stuck in silent terror. Too many people here had seen the battle of Silasta, and knew what Darfri magic was capable of.

"Keep back and no one else need be hurt," the Darfri woman said. She had a deep, lustrous voice, and the imperious tone of someone used to being obeyed. She looked directly at Hadrea. "Come with me. I can show you things these fools never could. I can show you real power."

She was facing the woman who had gone toe-to-toe with the great Os-

Woorin but seemed to expect her to be cautious or willing to engage in a discussion before doing any more. Apparently she didn't know Hadrea.

With an almost casual movement Hadrea brought her hands together, and just as the ground had risen and pinned my foot, so it now rose and grabbed at the Darfri woman, pieces of earth and shrapnel and grass and rock swarming like a thousand small insects up her feet and legs and almost to her waist. The woman snarled, jaw pulsing, sweat pouring off her, and flung out a hand. Hadrea was momentarily buffeted backward by another unseen force. But with an answering movement of her own hand the air before her seemed to shimmer, to thicken into a barrier, a retort. The false wind diverted away from Hadrea and blew into the crowd, knocking the onlookers back farther, and the woman's rage was now edged with confusion, and perhaps a little fear. This was not like the battle of the Bright Lake, where Os-Woorin and Hadrea had struggled for control over the same source, tied intrinsically to that being. Hadrea was wielding power without obvious source or effort. She flicked her fingers and the air fell away into nothing.

"How are you doing that?" the woman demanded, and with another guttural exclamation and an ungraceful sweep of her arms, the pieces of rock and earth and broken arena holding her in place pulled off her body, quivering and shivering, still swarm-like, then raced toward Hadrea in a clattering maelstrom.

"Watch out!" I yelled, pointlessly, but if Hadrea heard me she didn't show it. She drew her hands, palm out, in front of her and then slashed them apart, and all of the pieces flying at her dropped harmlessly to the ground in a pattery rain of shards. Her opponent let out an exhausted, frustrated whimper, and Hadrea strolled closer, unfazed as if she were taking a stroll by the lake. Her face looked wrong, not quite like herself; her eyes were too black, the way she held her jaw and shoulders all off. A sudden deep fear stirred inside me, and it wasn't for myself.

"You're not involving the spirits at all, are you?" The woman stared at Hadrea and gradually her anger and confusion turned, not with fear or anger now, but with fascination. "What are you doing? How are you doing this? No Darfri elder taught you anything like this, they wouldn't know *how*. Only through service to *him* can you learn such things."

Hadrea ignored her. "Are you all right?" she asked me, and I could only nod, unsure what to say.

The woman had not given up. In the moment Hadrea took her eyes off the woman to look at me, she dove—not at me, but at the urn I had left on the ground. The instant her arms wrapped around it a burst of light and heat sprang up between her and Hadrea, a giant flaming fireball of angry red and orange, blue at the core. Hadrea braced herself, hands moving in preparation for defense, but the fireball roared into motion not toward her, but straight toward the crowd of terrified citizens who had circled us.

It all seemed to happen very slowly, even though it could not have been more than a few heartbeats. The flame hurtled toward the crowd, but Hadrea brought down her hands with a scream of effort, and just as the heat blasted out in a nightmarish wall and the flames seemed to catch the people who had barely had time to turn, let alone run, an invisible barrier slammed down between them. For a second I could see it, shimmering in the air like a giant bubble centered around the Darfri woman, framed and defined by the shape of the flames. They collided with the barrier like the flames of an oil lantern licking the glass, then in the space of a breath, having nowhere else to go, they bounced back inward.

The Darfri woman erupted in flame like a wick.

"Stop it!" I yelled at Hadrea over the sound of the woman's agonized screams. "Put it out!"

But Hadrea, showing strain for the first time, turned wildly to me, her whole body shaking. "I cannot! It is her fueling it, not me!" Her eyes were wide and frightened.

Oddly, her fear dissolved mine. I seized my abandoned baton from the ground and, covering my face with my dress with one hand, I raced in close to the shrieking, burning pillar of a woman and swung the baton into her middle, where her melting hands still clutched the painted urn. It shattered under the force of my blow and all at once the flames and the heat were gone, extinguished as if they had never been there.

The woman was upright, a half-melted and blackened candle, for a moment, and then she was gone, collapsing into a pile of meat and bones on the ground.

Hadrea took a step toward me, then her legs buckled under her and she fell in a crumpled heap as well.

It had seemed like a dream, or a nightmare, an otherworldly experience. The whole thing had taken so little time, and most of it without anyone even noticing, and already there were too many other competing catastrophes to dwell on the bizarre and terrifying miniature battle we had just witnessed. In the cold reality of the destruction under the moonlight, it seemed a thing we might have imagined, a horror conjured from too much real trauma.

New patients recovered from the freshly damaged section of the arena were rushed in in varying states of crisis. The physics were sweating, running between patients, calling out instructions to anyone able-bodied enough to assist. I picked my way across the space slowly, the various pains I had been able to ignore for a short time returning like an orchestra building to a cre-scendo. My hand throbbed and stung, and my whole torso felt like it was barely hanging together, like soggy paper on the brink of collapse. Still, my injuries were nothing in comparative terms.

Hadrea and the Darfri who had assisted her had all collapsed and been carried by well-wishers to the treatment area; though I'd been left behind in the rush, it was easy enough to see where they'd gone, as a reverent crowd of apparently awestruck onlookers gathered around where they now lay on a cleared section of ground. I battled my way slowly through until I could see Hadrea, her head propped up on some balled-up fabric and her eyes closed. She looked un-injured but it was unclear whether she was conscious or not. People nearby were staring and whispering; no one seemed game to approach.

"Is she conscious?" I asked the nearest man, who nodded and moved aside to let me closer.

"She held the whole thing," he said reverently, staring at her with a half-fearful, half-admiring expression. "There weren't any spirits this time. It was all just . . . her."

"Hadrea," I said gently, touching her shoulder. "Are you all right?"

Her eyes fluttered open and she gave me a faint smile as she focused on my face. "Kalina." She squeezed my hand. "I am tired."

I looked back at the enormous heap of devastation behind us, at the im-measurably heavy pile of broken wood and metal, flaming and smoking, dust rising around it. I couldn't pretend to understand how she had done what she had done. "It must be tiring being a hero all the time." My attempt at a grin was ruined by the crack in my voice.

Hadrea understood. Her grip on my hand grew both tighter and shakier. She unexpectedly touched me on the cheek with the other hand and said earnestly, "Kalina. Do not worry. He is alive, I am sure of it."

I had been fighting through with stubbornness—Jov must be alive, because

SAM HAWKE

I couldn't contemplate anything else—but now a glimmer of genuine hope lent terrifying, treacherous weight to that feeling. Hadrea looked up at me with an almost surreal calm. I didn't quite know how to make sense of it, but a relaxed warmth emanated from her, the sort of peaceful air I'd always envied in her mother, and had never felt from her. It was almost disconcerting. Hadrea was ordinarily such a contained coil of energy that for a moment she didn't really feel like my friend at all. And yet, her surety was comforting. How could I argue with someone who had just turned earth and fire and air to her will like some creature of legend?

"How—" I cleared my throat, tried again. My voice was so high. "How did you do that? You said the spirits weren't answering, but then you did all *that*."

"She did it by meddling in something outside her full understanding, despite the attempts of her superiors to warn her." A harsh voice interrupted us. An-Ostada, looking weak and drained, propped up by a man on either side, but somehow imperious, surveyed the recovering group with an unsettlingly furious expression on her broad, sweat-streaked face. The whites of her eyes seemed enormous.

Any urge to placate seemed to have been burnt out of me. "Her superiors?" I snapped, stepping between them. "How many people did *you* save today, An-Ostada?" Those close enough to hear us in the crowd made murmurs of agreement. An-Hadrea, the hero who had saved us from the Os-Woorin's wrath, had saved not just the people caught in that final collapse but potentially all of us, at seemingly great personal cost, *again*. They wouldn't take an attack on her lightly.

"We have only just begun to repair the harm done to the secondworld and the spirits over the course of generations," An-Ostada said. "The spirits are not an army in our employ to be used whenever it is convenient and they should not be relied upon as such. Speakers cannot compel—"

"Whatever Hadrea did worked," I said. "That ought to be enough."

"What she *did* was not Speaking. What she did was—"

"Was something you had never even taught us was possible," Hadrea said earnestly. She struggled to sit up; I got beneath her shoulder to help her. "We do not *need* to Speak. We do not need to ask boons! We can use the power directly!"

"Can does not mean should." An-Ostada looked sorrowfully round at the group of Darfri; I realized belatedly these must be the students who had left her teachings. The Darfri with whom Hadrea had experimented with Void and arson. "You are children, stumbling around in the dark. Look at you all! You are drugged!"

Hadrea flinched at the barb. She *had* taken Void before attempting whatever it was she had done, I'd seen it. "Our enemies are not sticking with the old ways!" Hadrea flung back. "Look what they brought against us! Did you even see that woman I stopped? She was using power stored in that vessel, and she was using it to attack us! You never taught us we could store and draw power without Speaking, without the spirits at all!"

"Such things are *forbidden*, An-Hadrea." An-Ostada's voice came out quieter but somehow more menacing than before.

"Well, it has not been forbidden to our enemies, apparently! Where are the spirits when enemies are murdering us in the middle of a celebration in their honor? Nowhere to be found. You are right—the spirits are not our army. Do you not see? We have to learn to look after ourselves. Find new ways."

But An-Ostada shook her head. "I warned the Chancellor and the other Elders at the beginning that your gift was strong but your temperament ill-suited. You reach for power before understanding, and your ambition and greed endangers us all." She sighed. "You will never be a Speaker. I will not teach you again. No one will teach you again."

I watched that hit Hadrea like a strike, and my heart ached for her. But she was every bit as proud as she'd accused An-Ostada of being, and she buried the hurt with a scowl, tossing her head. "How lucky for me you have nothing I need to learn."

The women glared at each other, then An-Ostada turned her head in dismissal, and Hadrea did the same.

"Credola Kalina! Is that a burn?" A woman took my arm and examined my hand, where a red welt ran across my palm. I didn't know her but she had a no-nonsense, motherly sort of tone that expected obedience. "You need to get that cooled and wrapped." I was being tugged away from Hadrea; she turned back from her gaze into the distance and dropped her head back onto the pillow.

"I'll check on you in a bit," I told her, but she didn't respond.

Tain and I spotted each other at about the same time; he was holding a wad of cloth against a cut on his face and talking urgently to one of the physics. My heart skipped in relief at the sight of him, alive and apparently unharmed. Our eyes met and he dropped his hand off the bandage for a moment, said something to the physic in apology, and ran.

We didn't speak at first. Relief pulsed through me, reciprocated in his shaking body as he held me close. "I'm so sorry," he said against my hair, voice hoarse and broken. "Honor-down, Lini, I'm so sorry."

"We didn't predict this," I said. An image of a burning woman, a memory of the breath stolen from my lungs. "Fortunes, no one predicted this." We could worry about self-recrimination later. For now, we had to do what we could for our people. "Tain." I pressed my head against the side of his, unable to look him in the eye. "I don't know where Jov is. We stopped one blast but he ran to see if there were others while I tried to get people evacuating."

He stiffened at my words, held frozen still, saying nothing. Then he pushed me away, eyes wild, a suddenly animated statue. "Which direction was he going? Where did you last see him?"

"We were together under the main guest box," I said. "I came out that entrance there—" I pointed, wincing as I moved my fingers; the burn wasn't bad but it still stung. "—and he ran to check for more devices. I don't know in which direction. Hadrea tried to look but she couldn't find him. But she says she's sure he's all right, she can feel it. I think it's something to do with fresken."

Tain released me entirely, his head moving jerkily between the possible exits. "You can't go looking for him," I warned him. "Tain? You're the Chancellor. We need a leader right now." The words hurt to say, and he looked at me as if I'd slapped him, so I softened my tone to explain. "If he went that way, where the . . . where the first blast went off, he'd have been right in the center of it." Tain made a noise of rejection, a painful, guttural thing, and I took his hand with my uninjured one and plowed on. "But if he went the other way, nothing went off in that direction. He'd be fine. And it's a big crowd, we won't find him in a hurry."

"Chancellor!" Someone hailed Tain down, grasping his arm and babbling. "What is happening? What are you going to do? Who's done this to us?"

Realizing who was in their midst, other injured people came forward, pleading and demanding in equal force. *Help us! Why is this happening again? Please, my daughter!* I watched as he masked the hopeless fear with quiet confidence, the face they needed, and let him be swept away. Other Councilors had found their way here now; I saw Eliska and Moest together and Javesto bending over a bleeding relative, and had to avert my eyes from the sight of Il-Yoro bearing down on one of the physics with a child slung over his shoulder. I thought I might be sick.

"Credola, your burn," the physic reminded me.

"The burn can wait," I told her, but she had already deposited me in a line of people waiting to be seen. There was a chain of supplies coming in now, which included hot and cold water; someone gave me a bucket of cold water and I immersed my hand in it gingerly. I yelped at the shock but quickly the seeping cold had a soothing effect, taking out the worst of the stinging from my skin. I watched the other patients almost unwittingly, identifying friends and colleagues with varying degrees of grief.

Missing limbs, projectile injuries, terrible burns, and scores of eye injuries; the blast had not discriminated, hitting people of all ages. Bleeding, silent children lay alongside their moaning grandmothers. I thought perhaps at last I could understand the nightmares that had plagued my brother since the siege; the images of the horrors he had seen in the aftermath of that battle.

I abandoned the bucket, let them bandage my hand to keep it clean, and asked someone what I could do to help. Numbly, I let myself be directed by a brusque physic into helping make crude bandages for anyone who was bleeding, which seemed to be half or more of the wounded here. "Head wounds first," she told me. "Anything bleeding a lot, or spurting out in bursts, you yell for me straightaway, all right?" She'd turned away before she could hear my assent, and said to one of the other physics, "When will they get here? We should have seen the first of the litters by now."

"They can't get in, I'll bet," her colleague replied grimly. "Everyone's trying to get out, they'll be stuck. The Chancellor's got the army trying to clear the collapsed exit to get them in there, that's the closest one, anyway."

Some people were helping by tearing up donated clothing and pilfered banners and flags. I used the makeshift bandages around bleeding injuries, one after another, and another. Helping was better than nothing, of course, but it was beyond frustrating when all I wanted was to know where Jov was and whether he was all right. I kept scanning the floods of people, hoping I would see his familiar face emerge. Thank the fortunes the rest of our family had stayed home, at least, so Dee wasn't caught up in this mess along with the other unfortunate frightened children being carried on adults' shoulders or searching tearfully for their mothers or Tashen.

Covered bodies had begun to be discreetly laid out in one corner of the area; someone had fashioned a rough tentlike structure to shield them from sight but their terrible still forms screamed out at me all the same. I felt I would never grow desensitized to the string of dreadful injuries; each fresh one seemed to carve out a new bleeding hole inside my middle.

I didn't know how much time passed. I was aware of Tain, every now and again, coming by and conferring with physics or being yelled at by terrified citizens or foreigners or Councilors; once or twice he caught my eye, silently asking the question; always, I shook my head. My hearing slowly returned to normal, but the arena seemed no less noisy; though thousands must have fled, it remained crowded. The hospital area had a never-ending stream of new patients as people worked tirelessly to transport the injured and dead from the seating down to the grounds. The moon, brilliant and clear and bold in the sky tonight, gave decent light, but at some point people had arrived with proper lamps and even braziers to take the chill off where the physics were working.

Eventually, access must have been cleared because litters started arriving and physics were able to transport the most seriously injured to the hospital. That in turn relieved some of the pressure on the first-aid administration here at the arena. It felt like a long time I had been making and applying bandages, comforting crying people of all ages, cleaning wounds, directing people, but I was aware my sense of time might be skewed. Just as I finished tying off a bandage around a thickly bleeding leg wound I glanced up and saw him.

It took a moment to recognize him because his head was down, and a bigger man was slung half across his shoulder as he hauled him along. But something about the way he moved set my heart to racing.

"Jov!" I tried to yell but it came out a whisper. He seemed to hear it anyway, swiveling a weary head around as if looking for me. "Jov!"

I dropped the bandage I was cutting on the table and staggered over, half-blinded by tears of relief. Something extremely hard and tight in my chest I hadn't even known was there released in a rush, and my whole body felt like a viscous liquid, so I was afraid my legs would slowly sink into themselves as I tried to run to my brother.

He was too encumbered by his existing burden to hug me but he squeezed his eyes shut and touched my hand, apparently unable to speak. The relief I felt was tempered by guilt; my family was safe in our apartments or relatively unscathed here. Who else could say the same?

"There were too many," he said dully, struggling with the heavier man. I switched sides and helped prop up his charge and together we brought him in to join the queue to be seen. "I got one but they must have had a separate person lighting each."

"We were never going to have enough time. Not with two of us." If we'd used the Order Guards more effectively, though, thought of explosives sooner . . . Even though I'd only just been shutting down that line of thought when Tain had voiced it, it was hard not to obsess over how we could have prevented this. Ash and smoke still floated in the night air and the smells and sounds of death and destruction were a constant reminder of the scale of this disaster. "We have to stop them, Jov," I said quietly. "Whoever this is. Look what they're willing to do."

Tain spotted us soon after and whooped and shouted his way over several obstacles to crush my brother in his grip. The two men hugged hard and silent for a long moment, then pulled me in, too. "You scared me," Tain said, his voice muffled in my hair and Jov's shoulder. "Honor-down, Jov, you scared the *shit* out of me. Don't do that again, all right?"

"I promise, you're stuck with me," Jov said, half-laughing, and Tain stepped back a pace to regard us both with an intense expression.

"All three of us," he said firmly, and when I grinned he gave my shoulder a rough shake until I stopped.

"I swear," I agreed, and for a moment my eyes burned, forcing me to blink hard and look away until the tears retreated. There was enough to deal with, I thought, without us losing one another, even temporarily.

We broke apart and Tain took a few short breaths, staring down at his feet, as if summoning strength for something. Then he inhaled, straightened, and looked us both in the eye. "About . . . about Aven. I'm sorry I didn't tell you about talking to her. I felt shitty about it and I knew I should have but somehow it just made it harder to admit. And then I thought if I at least had something to justify it, it would be better, so it built up and up, and . . ."

"It's all right," I said automatically, then paused and reassessed. "I mean, no. It's not all right that you kept it from us. We deserved to know. But compared to everything else . . ." I gave a brittle shrug and gestured around. "As long as you don't keep something like this from us again. We have to be able to be honest with each other, even when it's hard."

Was it my imagination, or did he react to that, just the tiniest flinch? Even as he assured us it wouldn't happen again, as sincere as ever, worry and disbelief had taken root inside me. We couldn't afford more secrets.

Tain and Jov joined the crews of people helping pull the injured from the wreckage while I continued to assist the physics. The worst part, even worse than seeing the dead and dying, was seeing the reactions of their loved ones when they found them; my eyes grew swollen with tears for other families, and my sense of having been lucky at others' expense grew. Credola Karista, who had been in the viewing box, found half a dozen of her family members being treated for serious wounds, and wailed over the body of an elderly woman who might have been her mother or aunt, her anguish so terrible it felt like a tangible thing, bleeding into everyone around her. For all that our families were not friendly, and despite everything I knew about her, the only thing I could feel for her now was pity.

"Why is this happening?" a girl of no more than twelve asked me, as I helped a physic hold her still so he could secure the shrapnel puncturing her back and side that he could not safely remove. She had her face turned toward me, and tears dripped down over her nose and the side of her face, making tracks in the sooty residue. "Why is this happening?"

"I don't know," I told her, holding her hand. "Shh, just hold still, sweetie. They're going to take care of you, all right?"

"Why," she whispered, her eyes glazed; I wasn't even sure she could hear me.

The question we all would need answered. Fortunes, who hated us so much that they could do this? The rebellion and subsequent siege had killed many, but this, targeted at peaceful citizens enjoying sports and a celebratory display, just trying to bring in the new season with goodwill and cheer; who could hate us like this? Would any of our neighboring countries really commit such unprovoked violence for the sake of trade routes or resource wealth? We had thought only another country could have had the resourcing to fund Aven, but it was hard to imagine even Hiukipi organizing something like this.

And, I remembered now, squeezing the girl's hand and wiping her hair back from her forehead with my free hand, Hiukipi had been there, in the guest box. If Jov and I hadn't stopped that first explosion, every Talafan in that area would potentially have been killed. My heart beat faster as I thought it through. Who had been there? It suddenly seemed critically important. Hiukipi and Kokush, certainly, from the Talafan camp; not the ladies, and not Ectar, and I'd not seen the latter among the wounded or dead, thankfully. The King of the Doranites, and at least a handful of Chieftains. Some of the westerners, though they had been behind the Talafan and I couldn't remember who I had seen; not the High Priestess, I would have known her by the veil, nor Abaezalla. Some Marutian Dukes? Had there been any country missing, unrepresented? I'd have to ask someone who was there to report back. But who would be evil enough to murder not just all those powerful people but also hundreds of regular spectators?

I had always imagined our ultimate enemy to be a pragmatic, ruthless type, someone seeking further power or wealth. That, after all, was the most common form of evil one saw in everyday life; rich families jostling for position in the Council and in business, ambitious professionals politicking and manipulating to succeed within the Guilds, even business owners taking advantage of their staff to gain greater profits. Treating others as less deserving of rights or privileges than themselves. This I was used to, could extrapolate to governments attempting to grow by force or wealth ever more powerful within the continent. But this was no mere callousness, not just a disregard for the lives of the powerless, but actively targeting them. This was beyond Aven's hatred for our family and Tain's, beyond the passionate anger that had driven Hadrea's Darfri peers to destruction. This was someone who wanted everyone here to *suffer*.

As the thought crossed my mind a sound rent the air, a tortured cry of pain, distant but so intense it cut through over the background of wails and tears and shouts in our little hospital area. Heart hammering again, I struggled to find its source. But not for long.

It was Minister Kokush, and he was howling with a sound that felt like teeth clacking and metal scraping. Like worlds ending. It grabbed something deep inside me. I ran toward him. He was trying to lift a body, or what was left of one, and his face and torso were covered in blood and gore. The composed, controlled man I had met—who had talked me through a breathing attack not long ago—was almost unrecognizable, and not just with grief. When he looked up at me, hysterical and unseeing, shouting prayers and begging his god for help, the dominant emotion radiating from him was bone-melting *fear*.

"Minister Kokush," I cried, racing over. "Minister! What has happened?"

But I'd seen now what he was holding, the ruins of the person he had recovered from one of the stands, and the sight of the long clumps of bloody, fair hair attached to broken skull and red meat where a face should have been turned my own knees to water.

The Princess had snuck out from her cage one last time. And now she was free.

INCIDENT: Attempted poisoning of Chancellor Sara Iliri and Credola Jenia Iliri

POISON: Geraslin

INCIDENT NOTES: Series of novels and short stories by an anonymous writer known only as "Y" (sometimes reported as "J") sent to Chancellor and her sister C. Jenia, both of whom were avid readers. Sisters hosted series of literary parties where guests were encouraged to read and discuss literature. At end of one such event sisters both collapsed and showed difficulties breathing. Based on symptoms I examined the books and discovered liberal use of geraslin ink. Chancellor and C. Jenia made full recoveries. Unclear whether intentional poisoning or not. Librarians have been asked to match style of prose with new editions in library. *Update:* author remains unknown. Status of poisoning remains unclear.

(from proofing notes of Credola Ettenna Oromani)

15

Jovan

Recovering the injured and dead was a grim duty, especially when any shifted beam or cleared rubble could reveal the face of a friend, a peer, a child. The deeper we delved into the piles of debris the less frequently we found the living, but there were moments of hope, too, when a sudden cry or moan revealed life where we had expected death.

Tain, cut and bruised and soot-stained as he was, somehow kept up relentless optimism, though whether it was genuine or simply a stream of encouragement to his fellow workers, it wasn't clear. "There are spaces and pockets all through this," he said, perching briefly to examine a section. He looked thin, and sweat glistened on his forehead. "We could still find people. We're not giving up until we've checked everywhere. Just in case."

Erel, too, worked tirelessly beside us, his small form capable of wiggling into tight places. "I'm going to check down there," he told us, pointing to a gap. It was the first he'd spoken in some time and his voice came out croaking like a rusty gear. I'd never seen him so quiet, but then he was only a child, still, and too young for the horrors we'd all seen tonight.

"Company," I muttered, gesturing over his shoulder. Two men approached: Moest and the head of the diplomatic office, Vesko, a bald man with a cane. Tain wiped his hands on the side of his clothes, watching the group trot up with a degree of impatience.

"Nothing back from the scouts yet, Honored Chancellor," Moest began without preamble, propping one foot on a pile of rubble and handing

Tain a waterskin. "And nothing visible from any of the walls, but it's full dark so I can't guarantee anything. We'll keep a full watch up there all night."

"How far out are we sending the scouts?"

While Moest's attention was on the Chancellor, showing him positions on a map by lamplight, I took the waterskin and had a swig. Nothing but clear, too-warm water, a balm against the ashy bitterness in my mouth. This Warrior-Guilder, at least, did not seem to be trying to murder us, which was a pleasant change.

"All right," Tain said wearily when Moest finished. "The priority is getting everyone we can out of here safely and the injured treated, but as soon as we've handled that, we need to know what's coming next." He recovered the waterskin from me and took a long drink, then wiped his mouth with the back of his hand. Behind him, Erel emerged from the gap with a few extra scratches but no new wounded or dead. "Vesko, I assume you're here to tell me what's happening with our international guests."

"The King of Doran and his Chieftains were unharmed in the blast, Honored Chancellor." He was a tiny man, frail, with thin skin stretched over his bones and expensive-looking spectacles that magnified his eyes like a giant, delicate beetle. "They remain in the arena, continuing to assist in the rescue efforts. His Majesty does not seem predisposed to, er, point fingers, shall we say? But we will need to manage that relationship very carefully. If we show what they perceive to be weakness in our management of this crisis, the Doranites will be well poised to take advantage."

Tain nodded. "And the Talafan?"

Vesko cleared his throat with a little *hem* sound. "Ah. Yes. Yes, Honored Chancellor. The Talafan have left the arena. The Crown Prince was . . ." He stopped, his chin quivering, recovered control, and continued. "I think it is safe to say His Highness was incandescent with rage at the loss of his sister the Princess. I did not understand a great deal of what he said to me, but it seems rather apparent he is blaming us for this terrible, terrible tragedy." We all avoided one another's gaze. I had caught a glimpse of the remains of Princess Zhafi, and it was a sight that might have haunted me for the remainder of my days had I not seen fifty such atrocities in the last hour alone. If Hiukipi, who in Kalina's assessment had cared for his sister only as a useful prop in his empire-expanding machinations, had been incandescent, it was nothing to what the Emperor might be. His favorite daughter, the most publicly beloved member of his family, lost to an attack in our capital? We would be lucky if Talafar didn't march on our borders in retaliation for that alone.

Tain took another drink then passed the skin back to me. I accepted it gratefully; the effects of the darpar were wearing off, leaving me with a deep thirst and increasing shakes. Tain glanced back at the section he'd been searching, starting to look impatient. "All right. What else?"

Vesko consulted a note. "We have confirmed the early reports that the High Priestess of Perest-Avana did not attend the ceremony tonight, and remains safely in her accommodation with a number of her staff," he said. "I have assigned some of my people to definitively confirm none of the Marutian or Tocatican delegation were harmed, but we are still waiting on a response from them. There was that unfortunate piece of shrapnel that injured the Costkati Grand Emissary, but I understand the wound is not serious." He looked up, regarding each of us in turn with those huge eyes; an uncomfortable, assessing, unblinking gaze. "I cannot emphasize enough what a diplomatic disaster this is and will continue to be, Honored Chancellor."

"Oh, give it a whirl," Tain said flatly. "What are we dealing with here?"

"The most honored and important guests were here on our invitation, Honored Chancellor," the man said. "Some of them came *only* because we encouraged it so strongly. They will be returning to their own governments with the news that not only is this city a chaotic and unsafe place to travel to or do business in, it is one fouled by internal and external treachery. This has potentially dire consequences for our relationships going forward."

"Not to put too blunt a point on it," Moest said, scratching his beard with both hands now, as if there were tiny insects infesting it, "but if we're attacked with the full force of anyone's army, can we count on our allies to back us?"

Vesko's old face puckered up in thought. "We have treaties with Doran and Talafar, of course," he said, "the latter the strongest in theory, because it agrees to aid the other in circumstances where a country is invaded. They should be obliged to come to our aid if, say, one of the western nations attempted a takeover. Just as we would be required to assist in equivalent circumstances. But of course, with what has happened now, who is to say what the Emperor might do?

"Doran is a different matter. The King doesn't have a standing army there, and though officially we are allies, that's never stopped his rogue Chieftains making plays for our assets near the border with some regularity, as we all know." He clicked his tongue. "The point is, though the King appears sympathetic at present, he would not attempt to force his Chieftains to ride to our aid if some external enemy attacked."

"So we can't count on either of them," Tain said. "Even assuming they're not openly against us. What about the western countries?"

"We have no formal arrangements other than in relation to trade and respecting borders. There is no formal alliance. Honor-down, Honored Chancellor, the way those nations bicker among themselves I think they would be a more dangerous ally than enemy."

"All right. Moest, what sort of state is our army in? If we had no allies standing with us, what would be our defense capability in the event of a full invasion?"

The Warrior-Guilder gave a hollow laugh. "A full invasion, Honored Chancellor? I suppose that depends which army and how big it is. The Sjon army is well trained and disciplined, and notwithstanding the manner of his demise, there was a very fine warrior in charge of training for many years. I'd back my people in a three-to-one-odds fight, that's for sure." He looked off into the distance as if he could see an approaching army through all the walls and buildings. "As you well know, the city has withstood a siege for a time before, even poorly defended and unprepared as it was last time. We could hole up here for a while. But could we protect the entire country? The border cities, the villages? And can we defend anything when we have enemies walking among us? These are different questions."

"We decided two years ago we wouldn't be a city that happens to be supplied by estates," Tain said. "We're a country. If our defense is just to hole up in the capital and abandon the rest then it's not a defense." He shook his head. "What you're saying is we need our allies more than we've ever done before. And we've just alienated all of them. Shit. Fucking *fucking* mother of a fucking—" He remembered Erel—the lad had been so quiet, sitting shocked and still at our feet to catch his breath, that I'd also forgotten he was there—and mugged an apologetic face. "Sorry, Erel."

Despite everything, the boy's mouth twitched. "I've heard worse, Honored Chancellor."

Tain ruffled his hair. "Your boss is probably a bad influence." But he looked back across the ruined arena and the brief moment of levity passed. "Vesko, you're going to need the most knowledgeable people in your office to help us untangle this. I know we went through this two years ago and it got nowhere, but we've got more information now. We need to know what all our neighbors' military capabilities are and we need an up-to-date read on the relationships among the other countries." He hesitated, then added, "Keep the number of people involved who aren't local experts minimal. I don't want stray Guards or servants within hearing range of these conversations, all right? We don't have the luxury of trusting everyone right now, not after tonight. Whoever's behind this, we've definitely got internal saboteurs as well, there's no doubt about that anymore."

There was a sudden uncomfortable silence. None of us had been close enough to witness what had happened between the Darfri woman and Hadrea a short while ago, but I'd gotten details from Kalina and they frightened me. Treacherous Guards were one thing, and criminal gangs, even, but rogue Darfri turning their magic against their own was something we didn't know how to address.

Moest nodded at me. "Thanks to Credo Jovan here, the Captain of the Order Guards has two of the culprits in custody." It felt like days ago I'd battled with them under the arena, not mere hours. "She'll be interviewing them as a matter of priority as soon as the arena is secured. I'm guessing we'll get some more information then."

"Don't forget Aven," I said, more harshly than I'd intended. "She's up to her neck in this."

He shrugged. "I don't deny it. I just don't know if she's the worker or the boss, if you follow. Don't worry, no one's going to forget her in a hurry."

"What's *your* read?" Tain interjected. "Not officially. I'm not asking for formal advice. Just—what do you think? You've been a soldier a long time. Is this an internal or an external thing?"

Moest let out a long, slow breath, and considered the horizon. "There's angry people within the city right enough," he said eventually. "And after what just happened, looks like there might be at least some Darfri rebels bucking for a second go. I don't pretend to understand that side of things. But." His gaze wandered over the wreckage of the arena. "I've never seen anything like this in all my years. Those bombs weren't magic, they were made by people. And besides, there ain't no rebels I ever talked to who'd sacrifice the common folk for the sake of making a point, and two of those bombs went off in areas packed with cheap seats and regular people. The Hands might have been involved in laying the bombs but they sure as shit wouldn't be doing that for their own purposes, because it's in their interest for this city to stay fat and stable and healthy. Better pickings for them that way. So, yeah. Like we talked about at Council, I think most likely we're looking at someone external to the country who either has a real sincere grudge against us, or wants to weaken us with as much chaos as possible before they make their real move."

"We've done our share of terrible things to our own," Tain said, "but the worst disputes Sjona's ever been involved in with other countries are just border disputes. Who could have a grudge like that?"

Moest shrugged. "You can consult the historians and librarians if you want to find out if we've ever offended anyone over something major, but I think we'd know about it if we did."

"So it's the second option," I said. "Some amoral bastard who doesn't give a shit who dies as long as it's bad for us."

"Just my opinion," Moest said. "So we're back to who might want to take advantage of a weakened Sjona to seize control of our resources and trade routes."

"Which takes us back where we started, then," I replied, frustrated.

"On the light side, internal sabotage aside, it means that unless they've turned enough of our people to murder the whole city, we're still looking at an old-fashioned invasion force at some point."

"That's the light side?" Tain asked wryly.

"I'd take an open battle over this, any day," Moest replied grimly, and we all fell into silent agreement. "Anyway, I've taken enough of your time for now. We can talk this all out in Council, eh? I imagine you'll want a full Council meeting once all the Councilors are accounted for?"

Tain, about to clap his shoulder in thanks and farewell, frowned. "Is anyone not? I thought everyone in the box was all right?"

"Yes, Honored Chancellor, but like yourself, some of the Councilors were not in the viewing box."

"Salvea?" I asked. My mouth dried. Hadrea had been looking for her mother and brother last I saw her, but she had been confident they'd not been in the blast zones.

"She's fine," Moest said, and I sagged in relief. "Unhurt. I saw her and her boy out personally an hour ago. And Budua and Marjeta didn't come tonight and they've checked in to say they're safe, and we've had reports that An-Jara is safe at home as well. But last I heard Credola Varina was missing, and Credola Merenda."

"Varina's dead," I said grimly. "She was with family in the stands, not in the box." I'd seen her body myself. Varina, pride of the Theater Guild, and evidence that even the richest and most selfish of the Credolen could change and grow given the chance, had not survived the initial blast.

Moest bowed his head. "That is . . ." He let out a grunt of expressive pain, and I felt it too, like a little hammer punching at my chest. I'd barely had time to process it when I'd seen it, but she'd taken a bad head wound and extensive burns, and the image was so seared into my mind that I wondered if I would ever be able to look back and remember her, vivid and bright, the way she had been. "That is grievous news."

"Yes," I said, unsure what else to say, and finding it hard in any case to form words past the sudden lump in my throat.

"Merenda didn't come," Tain said absently, his attention suddenly focused on something in the distance. "She should have been at the Manor. Hold up—messenger."

"No," Moest was saying, "we sent someone to the Manor to get a head count. The Heir wasn't there."

"She has to have been," Tain said, as the messenger clambered up toward us. "She isn't in here, she'd have found us by now otherwise. She'd know to check in, so she can't—"

"Honored Chancellor!" the messenger's cry rang high with urgency or panic.

It seemed as if all three of us felt it at the same moment, as Tain's correction faded away. The messenger's face was grim, even for the circumstances, and she sunk her head low, briefly covering her face with her hands before straightening and looking straight at Tain. By the time she spoke, my chest was heavy with dread, and I knew from Tain's sudden stillness and Moest's groan that we all predicted the words before they even came out.

"Honored Chancellor. Devastating news. I am so sorry, but your Heir, the Credola Merenda . . ."

Oh, no.

The messenger gulped. "She's been found, Chancellor. Unfortunately—"

"Where?" His voice was tight and tense, his body rigid. "Take me."

The messenger gestured to the site farthest from us. "It looks like a number of people in the highest seats were thrown from the back by the blast. No one found the bodies at first because they were a . . . they were outside, a distance from the arena."

Moest bowed his head and put his hand on Tain's shoulder. "Honored Chancellor. A terrible blow, I am grieved to hear it."

Tain gave no sign he'd heard. "She wasn't supposed to be here," he blurted. "Why would she come? She wasn't like that. She was smart, she was sensible. Why didn't she listen?"

I couldn't summon the energy to appreciate the irony. "I imagine she took guards, and thought she was safe. Same as you." Merenda *had* been sensible, eminently so; indeed, several on the Council had expressed their doubts as to whether she had sufficient charisma or gravitas to inspire the people as Chancellor (naturally, their knives delivered hidden in bouquets; Karista had frequently commented on her "manner of the people" and ability to relate to the common person, and Sjistevo on her "charming transparency"). Had she simply decided our fears were warrantless? Or thought herself clever enough to avoid attention in the arena? "Maybe she had a good reason. We can't know what she was thinking." Now we never would.

"Honored Chancellor?" the messenger prompted, and he nodded, stiff. "Please lead the way."

Moest patted him on the shoulder one last time and Tain and I followed the messenger in heavy silence, and after a moment's hesitation Erel scrambled along behind us. The sounds in the arena seemed to recede as we walked, so I could hear the crunch of our steps and the rasp of Erel's breath and the pulse of blood in my ears. Yet another blow, when we'd already had so many.

"Who's that? Another messenger?"

As we crossed over to the last of the explosion sites, I squinted. Someone was approaching with haste. The messenger leading us broke into a trot to meet them, and I frowned. The runner was closer now and they weren't wearing a messenger sash, but were clearly headed for us. I reached surreptitiously into my pouches and retrieved a small dart, and took a wary step in front of Tain.

But it was my name I heard in the wind. "Jovan! Credo Jovan!"

I knew the voice, and a moment later as they lifted their chin I recognized their face in the moonlight. "Sjease?" A hot, fearful sensation took root in my chest and began to expand, filling the gaps between my ribs, making it hard to breathe. "Sjease! What's wrong?" I was running, too, leaving Tain and Erel and the messenger behind, because Sjease should have been safely at home, had been told not to leave the apartments for any reason, and yet here they were. I didn't want to know what that meant, and at the same time I needed to know what that meant.

They stumbled, out of breath, panting and disheveled like I'd never seen them. They seized my shoulders, frantic. "Jovan! I've been looking everywhere, I tried to find you, but there's so much . . ." They looked around hopelessly, helplessly, at the chaos surrounding us, their words a mess of panic. "Where's Merenda? Where's the Heir? Jovan, she followed, and I didn't realize until it was too late, and Jovan, is she with you? They wouldn't let me in at first but I checked the hospital and I asked so many people. No one's seen her. Honor-down, is she with you?"

My heart. My heart wasn't beating properly. "Sjease!" It came out a shout. "What are you talking about?" But I knew, I already knew what they were talking about, and some part of me just wanted to keep talking, to delay the moment.

Sjease's eyes were red, their cheeks sticky and glistening, and they were gulping air like a drowning person. "The Heir came by the apartments look-ing for you. She said she needed to tell you something, urgently. She looked in a panic. And I said you were with Tain and she said she'd go straight to you, and Dee wanted to go with her and we wouldn't let her, but she must have slipped out afterwards. I didn't realize. I didn't realize!"

"Dija," I whispered, choking it out, and nothing, *nothing* in my life had ever felt like this, this all-consuming, bowel-liquefying, desperate fear and dread, this pre-knowledge I simultaneously needed and rejected. I took a shaky breath to scream but nothing came out, and when I tried to run I fell over instead, and my legs were clumsy and heavy, but I got to my feet and I ran faster and harder than I'd ever run before. *Dija, please, please, please don't be dead.*

I was vaguely aware of the messenger catching up behind me but I didn't need her guidance to find the spot where they'd recovered Merenda's body. People were gathered in a section of gardens near a large broken and collapsed part of the arena, and the air was tense and grim. I could hear crying. There were physics moving about, calling for litters, and—my heart starting pounding harder—the shapes of bodies on the ground. A vise clamped around my chest so tight I couldn't breathe.

Dija had been with Merenda.

Dija had been with Merenda and Merenda was dead and I couldn't see my niece in the crowd. Dija must have been here and there were bodies on the ground, large and small bodies.

"Credo Jovan!" The messenger touched my arm. "The Heir is over here."
She must have thought my wild dash had been for Merenda's sake, and I felt a
burst of impatience, followed by guilt. I followed her to the bodies. The nearest was in plain clothing, but I recognized one of Merenda's blackstripes. Her
chest was flattened, her skull broken. My head swam and I stumbled back
from her, searched out the next body. A dead man this time, oddly peaceful
but for the loose position of his limbs. My heart felt like it was going to crack
my ribs, it was pounding so hard. It seemed quiet now, even though moments
ago people had been talking, shouting instructions, helping the wounded, but
now everything was uncannily *quiet*. A large black bird had fluttered down
from one of the trees and was edging toward the blackstripe's body. I glared
back at it and scared it away with a quick stomp in its direction.

Oh, fortunes. Like a blow to the stomach, I recognized the next body. Merenda lay on her side, almost like a natural sleeping position, but her head, like
her guard's, was broken. I couldn't get any air in my lungs and for a moment
I was dizzy, disoriented, unable to process the awfulness of it. I tore my eyes
from her body, blinked hard against the burning feeling there, and raked my
gaze over the last of the bodies. My frantic pace of moments ago had crashed
into a fearful, juddery halt. There was a smaller body at the end of the row,
covered by someone's coat, and I needed to look closer but I had never wanted
to do anything less in my life.

But Tain had caught my arm to stop me. "Not Dee," he said, and I blinked
at him blankly. "It's not Dee!" he said, and the relief hit me almost as hard as
the fear had, and my legs melted. I wobbled, almost falling, but he steadied me.
Erel, panting, stood beside him, a weak grin on his face as he pointed. "Look!"

A small figure was sitting on a rock at the far side of the crowd, with an
elderly man leaning over her, arm around her shoulder, trying to get her to
drink something. I knew her at once, and the horrible pressure in my
chest loosened, like a tiny leak sprung in an overfull waterskin. "Dee!" I
called out, louder than I'd intended. Her head snapped up, she wiggled free
without hesitation, and hurtled toward me to fling herself into my arms.

It was the first time she had hugged me, and the feeling of her small arms
around my neck was such an unfamiliar and disorienting and precious thing
that my eyes went hot and prickly with tears. I felt simultaneously fierce and
horribly exposed.

Her eyes were puffy and her cheeks wet, but her expression was one of resolute calm as she pulled back and looked at me. "I'd like to go home please, Uncle," she said, her voice low and serious.

I couldn't even answer. All I could do was breathe, shaking, my heart slamming and my head spinning. Those heart-shredding moments had been like nothing I'd ever felt before, not when I'd found out Etan was poisoned, not when he died in front of me, not even when I'd thought my sister dead as well; this was a new flavor of terror. Humbling was the realization that, for all my fears that I made a bad guardian, that I was too slow to love, too awkward for a child to love back, she had taken my heart after all, even if it had taken a moment of thinking I'd failed her to realize how much that meant.

"You're shaking," Dija said suddenly into the silence. We were walking, hand in hand, away from the arena; I would need to take her to the hospital to be properly checked over but she had no obvious injuries other than scratches and bruises, and more than anything we needed a moment to breathe. I'd left a stricken Tain by his cousin's body, unable to think of the right words of sympathy when I had found my heir safe and he had not.

I forced a shrug. "It's the darpar. Gives you muscle tremors."

She wasn't fooled, but one of the things I liked best about my niece was how she didn't push things that didn't need pushing. "That explains the bad breath," she said instead, and I snorted.

Now the fear had passed, exhaustion took its place, both a reaction to the release of tension and the genuine effects of the darpar wearing off. It was as if there were roots growing into the ground and each step I had to pull my foot up like a stubborn weed. There was so much to be done still, so many more things to help with and to figure out.

"Dija!" A small figure sprinted over from the darkness, half-stumbling, sobbing with relief. "Sjease said . . . thank the fortunes, thank the fortunes!" Ana scooped up her daughter in a crushing hug, almost knocking me over.

"I'm all right, Mama," Dee mumbled into her mother's shoulder. Ana pushed her back, held her by the shoulders, examining her, touching her face, her arm, the back of her head with frantic but gentle fingers, then wrapped her in a hug again. Uncertainty twisted inside me as I edged away to give them room. Holding her hand as we walked from the site now seemed a callous and undemonstrative response, another failure of my guardianship.

Ana wiped her eyes, attempted a tremulous smile, and set Dija down. "Darling, can you go with Sjease for a moment? I want to talk to Jovan."

Dija started to say something but her mother set a firm hand on her cheek. "Just for a moment. I'll be right with you."

Dee nodded, looking uncertain, and rejoined Sjease, who also caught her in a hug and swung her around in a full circle. As their heads bent together to talk, Ana turned on me, raking me with a gaze of furious intensity. "I'm taking her home," she said. She set her jaw, and with the look on her face and the shaved patches in her hair exposing her half-healed scratches from the bird attack, she looked surprisingly fearsome.

I held up my hands in mollification. "Of course. I just need to talk to her about one thing and then you can take her home. She's not injured."

"No, you're not going to be talking about anything. I know what your conversations are like, and tonight of all nights she doesn't need to be talking about national conspiracies and murder plots and fortunes know what else."

"Ana, I understand why you'd say that, but Merenda found something out, something urgent enough to come find us when she was ordered to stay at the Manor. Dee was the last person to speak to her. We need to know what she told her."

"She's been through too much. She's seen too much. You can ask her tomorrow before we leave." I felt a dull thud of comprehension: *I'm taking her home.* Ana gave a hard laugh. "Yes, Jovan, I mean *home,* not your apartments. We're going home to Telasa as soon as we can get out of this fortunes-forsaken city."

"Ana—"

"She's seen enough. She's thirteen years old, by the fortunes, Jovan. Thirteen. I never liked her coming here and learning all your . . . all your potions and things. But this is too much. She was nearly killed tonight!"

"We all could have been killed tonight," I reminded her as gently as I could. "I know our family duty can seem like a burden a lot of the time, but it saved you all, didn't it?"

Ana scoffed, her eyes hard. "Maybe it did. But answer me this: Would my daughter be safer in Telasa with us, or here with you?"

I had known it was coming. It had seemed like a good idea, inviting Ana and the rest down to the capital to see that Dija was content and safe here, getting an impressive education and learning the responsibilities of the family. It just hadn't really worked out that way. Ever since the masquerade day

I'd known Ana would try to take her daughter back north with her. I'd only hoped to delay it a little longer.

"If we don't figure out what's happening and stop it, there'll be no place safe in this whole country," I said honestly. "But I can promise you Dija's safety is as important to me as anything in the world. You have my word."

"More important than the Chancellor?" Her hands balled into fists at my sudden silence. "No, I didn't think so. You talk about family duty, Jovan, but that's not supposed to only turn outward, is it. Honorable families should not treat their members as tools. What about your duty to my daughter? What kind of guardian are you being if you put her safety behind your work?"

I couldn't blame her for her anger, but nor did I fancy being lectured about family duty by a person who had lived a comfortable life away from the treachery and pressure of the capital, who never had to make the hard decisions or the personal sacrifices my position demanded of me, and Kalina, and Dija. The scars dotted around my body, the knowledge that my mistakes could cost the lives of those I loved most, the pressure of trying to do the right thing when the right thing could be a complex and deceptive thing. The hole where Etan had been. All the reminders that there was no place for me to run, no way to turn my back on this place.

I held up my hands. "Look, Ana, I'm just saying, we don't know where's safe yet. Until we know who attacked us, we won't know the safest place to be. If I thought sending you and Dee and the boys back to Telasa right away would ensure your safety, I'd do it in a heartbeat. But whoever did this has motive for doing it. Maybe they *want* people to flee the city. Maybe there's an army coming from any direction and people are going to run straight into it. What if the other cities have been attacked, same as us?" Before she could finish drawing breath I plowed on quickly. "We need this information to keep you safe. Right now, we have a fortified city, we have guards around our house and we're about to have more. This is the safest place we can be, within reason, right now."

"The safest place?" She whirled on the spot, gesturing to the chaos around us. "This city is nothing but death. We'll take our chances in our home, as far away from this as possible. She's my daughter and I'll make the decisions about her safety."

"Dee's in *my* care," I said, battling the terseness that rose at her words. "I'm her guardian, not you. But if she wants to go home with you, I won't stop her or try to persuade her otherwise."

A rustle behind her turned Ana's attention: Dija, tugging Sjease behind her by one hand and pushing her glasses on her nose with the other. She raised her chin. "I've got some important things to tell Uncle Jovan, Mama," she said firmly. "And I'm not going back to Telasa. I live here now, with him."

"It's too dangerous here."

"Our family doesn't run away when the Chancellor is in danger," Dee said. She wasn't speaking loudly, but her voice quivered with emotion. "The Oromanis are the Iliris' first and closest friends. That's always been the way. Ever since our families came here. And when the Chancellor is in trouble, when the *country* is in trouble, we stand up and fight for it. That's what we do. It's what we're for. Otherwise, what's the point?"

"Dija, the—"

"No! We can't have everything we have, and control land and people and be in the Council and live like this, if that's not what our family's for." She had pulled free of Sjease's grip, as though her words needed physicality. "You can't run away when you're needed. I wouldn't do that. I said I'd come here, I said I'd do the job, and I know what that means, and it's important, and you're not taking it away from me. It wouldn't be honorable, it wouldn't be right. You know that. You *know* that."

Ana was, if possible, looking even angrier than before. She turned her gaze very slowly and deliberately away from her daughter and to me. "There is no honor in endangering a child," she said clearly, and it landed as it was meant to, like a hook in my chest. There was an ugly silence. Sjease stared at their feet. I stayed quiet; Ana's fear and anger was completely understandable, but there was nothing to be done to assuage it for now.

"We'll talk about this later," she said abruptly. "Tell him what you need to tell him and then you're going straight to bed."

I nodded. "Thank you."

We stepped a little way away and after a moment's hesitation I took Dee's hand again. She held on to it, hard, and some of the uncertainty inside me faded. *I live here now, with him.* Maybe the two of us did understand each other after all. "Dee, your mother's right about you needing rest, but first I need to ask you about why you left the apartments tonight," I said. "Is that all right?"

"I'm sorry," she muttered. "You said not to leave. I know I scared you and Sjease and everyone."

"I'm just relieved you're all right," I said. "But I know Merenda found something out, something important. Dee, I know this is hard, but I need to know what she told you. Do you know what she wanted to tell us?"

She shook her head, like she was clearing it, and maybe she was. "Merenda—" Her voice squeaked into nothing, and fresh tears wet her cheeks. I gave her time to gather herself and she took some shaky breaths before continuing. "She came to find you. She said it was urgent, that she had to warn you and the Chancellor."

"About what?"

"She said something terrible was going to happen at the arena, and—I suppose it doesn't matter so much now because I guess it already did." She was too young for that much bitterness. I squeezed her hand, and she pressed her glasses back up her nose and stared down at the ground. Her shoulders jerked suddenly and she hunched down, obviously trying to force back sobs. She had bonded well with Merenda in her time here and I knew the Heir had liked having her around, as she missed her own children. To have ended their relationship in these circumstances, for someone her age to have seen it happen . . . The only consolation was that the Heir's death hadn't been as brutal as some of the others. Dee hadn't had to see her charge be torn apart by the blast, rent to pieces like poor Princess Zhafi, or burnt to a husk by magical fire. Or poisoned, dying slowly right in front of her. *Oh, Etan. I'll never stop missing you.* My own eyes felt a bit hot.

"If this is too much . . ." I began, even though my insides squirmed to know what had driven Merenda out tonight. What had she learned?

"No, it can't wait." She sniffed, straightened up, cleared her throat. "She found something. A note, or a message? I don't know how, but she found it and it was telling somebody to stay away from the arena, and that Tain wasn't going to be where he was meant to be."

My mouth had gone dry now. "She found that somewhere at the Manor?"

"She must have done, I think, because she said you'd told her not to leave but she had to warn Tain because whoever was planning the attack knew you'd told him not to be in the Council seats." Dee looked up at me seriously. There were tears caught in her lashes but she was no longer crying. "She said it meant there was someone close to Tain who was informing his enemies."

I resisted the urge to spring up and start pacing, but only with great focus and control. Dee had gone through a lot; I had to keep her calm. "Did she say who she thought it was?"

"She didn't know. But it had to be someone who knew the Chancellor had been warned off tonight. That's only really people close to him, isn't it?"

Shit. A horrible cold feeling spread through my chest. I didn't want to do this again. I didn't want to second-guess everyone around me, to see enemies in the Council, in the Manor, among my peers and friends. We had done that once and it had nearly broken us. "She found a message," I said slowly. "Did you see it? Could you tell me anything about what it said precisely?"

She took a deep, shuddering breath. "I don't need to." She reached into her paluma and retrieved a small paper packet. My mouth fell open.

"Dee, you—"

"I took it off her body," she said, her voice tiny, and rushed. "I'm sorry, I just knew she had it and I was afraid it might get lost at the hospital or someone might take it on purpose. So I . . . when I went to see the body, I didn't tell anyone and I stuffed it down my tunic. I'm sorry," she added again.

"I was going to say you did exactly the right thing." I didn't want to uncover another bloody traitor in our midst, but if there was one to be found, a head start on the bastard was no small matter. "Can I . . . ?"

She handed it over. It was on good paper, but not so good that only the rich could have afforded it, just good enough to hold the ink. The outside of the folds was unlabeled and so too was the note, frustratingly addressed to no one. The writing was in Sjon and the penmanship neat but unremarkable.

> *Chancellor is on alert, will not be stationary. Plan will proceed in full.*
> *Do not be at the ceremony or your safety will not be guaranteed. Advise*
> *you leave the country as soon as possible, and await further instruc-*
> *tions. Service to the Prince is always rewarded.*

I read it three times. Merenda had been right—the informant, whoever it was, had known Tain had changed plans. "Service to the Prince," I said aloud. Which Prince? Hiukipi? One of the Princes of Tocatica? The coldness in my chest intensified. The *Prince's* Hands. The crown graffiti outside the warehouse. Perhaps they weren't local criminals giving themselves airs, but genuine agents of a foreign ruler, infiltrating our streets right under our noses. Our streets, and perhaps the Manor itself. Who had written this note—and just as importantly, to whom was it written?

INCIDENT: Cosmetics poisonings (numerous)

POISON: Sweetface (skineater)

INCIDENT NOTES: Numerous reports surfaced of members of wealthy families (incl. at least two Credol Families; see Cs. Ormac and Aijai Brook, C. Megann Reed) having unexpected and unpleasant side effects from medical treatments; further investigation revealed a spate of skin necrotizing apparently resulting from un-Guilded medical "beauty" treatments to remove unsightly moles, skin tags, etc. Traced to Darfri herbalist in lower Silasta going by name of An-Alixae. *Note:* I strongly suspect further work of woman previously posing as herbalist in Harrow village (see earlier entry, Harrow village poisonings); deploy resources to tracing her as a priority (use K for information gathering?)

(from proofing notes of Credo Etan Oromani)

16

Kalina

"How are you holding up?" Jov, blinking wearily, put a hand on my shoulder. I realized the physic had finished with the patient I'd been assisting with and given her some pain relief, and I was just standing there, holding her slack hand and staring into space. I smiled at my brother to show him it was nothing to be concerned about, and placed the girl's hand gently onto her chest. Two people swooped in to transport her to the hospital, and I let them go before turning back to scrutinize Jovan.

He looked bad. He had no specific injuries I could see, but he was moving so heavily and awkwardly I suspected he had a lot more than he was letting on. "I'm all right, what about you?"

He shrugged, avoided looking at my face.

"Hadrea's sleeping still. You got Dee home safe?"

"Yes. She was asleep between Ana and Etrika when I left." He rubbed his forehead. "Ana was so relieved to have her there, she even forgot to be pissed at me. Honor-down, Lini. We were so lucky not to lose our niece."

The team who had pulled her out had estimated that if she had been standing even a few treads over she would have been thrown off the area with the others and almost certainly killed. We'd been more than lucky not to lose her. Luckier than a lot of families tonight, too. "Stay here with me a while," I urged him. "We still need hands and you could use a break from lifting heavy things. Here, help me cut some bandages." Strangely, Jovan's visible distress helped me relax a little into a routine. I recognized the signs; he was reliving every perceived bad decision, imagining how he could have done things differently, and worse, dealing with the insidious voice inside him whispering that he must not have even *wanted* to save everyone. Those dark thoughts were bad enough for him where the scale of the mistake was small; in a disaster like this, I was surprised he was even capable of standing under the weight of that burden. But this was something I could do, and do better than anyone. I knew how to be his big sister, helping him deal with an episode, distracting his brain from one of its obsessive "what if" spirals by teaching it something else. There was no point rehashing how we could have prevented this disaster. What we needed now were clear heads so we could work out what was coming next.

He visibly calmed as he worked at the repetitive task. "Listen, Lini," he said, his voice low as he bent over the bandages. His manner had become furtive, as if he feared being overheard. "Merenda found something before she— before coming here. She was trying to tell us we had a traitor in the Manor."

I looked at him sharply. "What do you mean? What did she find?"

"She intercepted this letter." He passed me a note and I scanned it quickly. "We don't know who wrote it or where it was going. She might have known more, but . . . well. We can't ask her."

"But this is something," I said. "*Service* to the Prince? Do you think the leader of the Hands is an actual Prince, then?" A shudder ran over me as I thought of the Talafan camp. *Oh, fortunes, poor Zhafi.* "Surely not Hiukipi. He was there in the box, he can't have been behind the bombs."

"I guess not." Jov shrugged. "There's a Tocatican Prince here, too. Is that it? The Doranites have a king but they don't do hereditary titles so there aren't any princes."

"If this 'Prince' has his Hands here working for him then he doesn't have to be here, though, does he," I said. "Why bother to come to a city you're trying to destroy if you can just pay people to take it down from the inside?" I remembered something. "Wait. *Service.* The woman who attacked Hadrea, she said something like that. Not about a prince, but she said . . ." I searched my memory, trying to recall the exact words. "She was demanding to know how Hadrea was using fresken without calling on the spirits. She was really shocked, like she thought it shouldn't be possible for Hadrea to do what she was doing. And she said no Darfri Speakers would have taught Hadrea that and she could only have learned it through service to *him*."

Jov rubbed his forehead, looking suddenly guarded. "Hadrea can do things other Darfri can't. We knew that."

"Well, maybe the other side didn't understand that. Maybe that'll help us. More importantly, could this 'him' be the Prince in the note? It was the same sort of wording, and the way she said it, I thought she was talking about a god or something, but this"—I prodded the note—"is the closest thing we've got to a clue."

"But both people who might be able to tell us about it are dead," he pointed out. "We don't even know how Merenda got the note."

"It's something," I insisted, and he shrugged wearily.

"One more thing to try to understand."

I stayed near him until he was settled into a routine and his twitching was less obvious. When the bandages were done there remained plenty more work; none of the physics would let a person stand idle and get in their way tonight. Everyone here, no matter their birth or occupation, was a physic's assistant, and that was probably for the best. Jov wasn't the only one who needed a distraction tonight. I left him with Varina's younger brother, Credo Arran, a good-natured and popular man, if not the brightest of our peers. Last time I'd seen Arran he'd been dancing, drunk and high on the dosed sugar cakes at the masquerade, handsome and energetic, and it was an ugly shock to see him sweating, clutching at the stump of his right leg, which had been tied off and bandaged by one of the physics, and moaning like some kind of wild animal. Emergency assistants like me and Jov weren't supposed to be giving out pain relief but I caught Jov slipping a small amount of a clear fluid to Arran, and guessed he'd raided his personal supplies to give the poor man a moment of relief.

I found myself handling basic aid for the less-urgent cases, giving simple treatments and then sending them to the main hospital to be seen later. "They've got to do the priority cases first, obviously," I told the latest, a young man with a series of bad grazes down his torso and leg but no serious bleeding. I had cleared the gravel and dirt out as best I could in the light conditions but they would be able to do a better job at the hospital. "But they'll get to everyone, you just need to be patient. Head over to the main hospital and walk gently, all right?"

The man hobbled off. Next in the line was a familiar figure, tall and broad, wincing with her slightly uneven walk. "Captain Chen," I said. "Are you all right?"

"I'm fine," she grunted. "So far as anyone is, at any rate."

I closed my eyes a moment. "Yeah." The immediacy of first aid at least gave my brain something to do other than dwell on all the horrors we'd seen, but they could be conjured up all too easily on command.

"But I understand it could have been a lot worse." She clapped a heavy hand on my shoulder and looked at me directly, her honest face only a handsbreadth from mine. "If you and your brother hadn't done what you did—"

I looked away, uncomfortable. "We didn't do enough, though." Two out of five blasts. If only we'd acted sooner, if only we'd guessed what they would try.

She scoffed. "You did more than anyone else did, and a lot of people round here are only standing because of what you did. Like as, you won't hear as many thanks as you ought, but I'm here to give mine." She sighed, straightened to her full height, and looked around the hospital area. "Did you see what happened with the Darfri?"

I shrugged. "I saw it. Can't say I really understand it though."

"These things aren't for us folks to understand." Chen shook her head. "Magic and spirits and fires coming out of nowhere—that's beyond us, I reckon. Now this mess with explosives, that's something we can deal with. And thanks to you two, we've got two of the bastards who set this up. They're stewing in the jail right now."

"What about Sukseno?"

"We'll find him. He can't go home, can't go to his friends. Once we've got everyone safely out of here, he'll be a priority. And a certain former Warrior-Guilder, too."

Aven's smug smile flashed through my mind. She'd been so fucking confident, like she'd known we'd find out enough to come asking questions, but not enough to stop it happening. "She was taunting me," I said softly. "Which means she'll be expecting us to come running."

Chen opened and closed the fist on her right hand as if testing its strength. "Don't worry, Credola. We won't play her game. She can answer to us when we're ready."

"She's not going to tell us anything," I said, and even though I'd been the one to talk to her before, I knew it to be true. "Why should she? She's held out this long and she's finally seeing her people take control again. What can we hold over her now that she hasn't already lost?" A sudden thought occurred to me. "Get someone watching the jail. Not your people, just in case. Ask the black-stripes. I'd bet my family honor breaking Aven out is part of the plan, whether now or later. Someone's going to try, maybe Sukseno or one of her other plants. You might be able to flush out some Hands by being ready for that."

Someone called out to Chen from a few treads away, and she nodded to me. "You take care, Credola. I reckon we've had enough excitement for the day, eh?"

"I reckon," I agreed, forcing a smile as she set off to the Guard who'd hailed her, rubbing irritably at her thigh above her artificial leg as she walked.

I looked around for Jov, and found him wiping the gravelly wounds of a young woman from the Builders' Guild. I dropped off a bucket of water to the fire for heating and stopped by my brother to pass on what Chen had said. But I'd barely finished relaying the conversation when we were interrupted by a horrible, gargling cry.

Arran thrashed in place, spit flying from his open mouth. "Hey, someone come quick!" Jov cried out, but the man stopped convulsing before a physic could assist, and slumped back to lie still. Too still. "Oh, shit," Jov murmured, and I squeezed his shoulder. The first patient to die right in front of me had been an old man with a terrible stomach wound and burns over half his body; he'd never even managed to see a physic before his body had given up. Arran's deterioration had been unexpected, and Jov had obviously been unprepared.

"We can't always tell how badly they're hurt," I told him gently. He looked so drained, so emotionally bereft. He had seen death, but there was a particular horror to the helplessness of this grim little zone. I squeezed his hand and went back to work.

A woman in country garb with one eye almost certainly lost to shrapnel, and a bleeding ear I didn't like the look of, was next in the line. "You'll need to see the physics," I told her, sizing up the head injuries with a frown. "I'll get you to sit—" But before I could finish, she seized me by the arm, and I gasped in pain at the pressure on the still-healing cuts on my bicep. She wasn't the first person in pain to try to hold on to me, but honor-down, it *hurt*. I tried to pull away, unpeeling her fingers with my other hand, but she only gripped harder, and yanked my head down close to hers, so I could feel and smell her breath on my face as she hissed in a furious whisper, "You have to listen to me! No one is listening!"

"I'm listening," I said, still trying to free myself. I looked around for someone to assist me but no one was looking.

She yanked me again so we stood nose to nose, almost touching. "Then listen! We are cursed, this country. The spirits have not forgiven us." Her good eye flashed around manically, taking in my face, darting to the smoking remains of the seating in the stands beyond, and back again, and with her free hand she clutched at the Darfri charms around her neck, matted with blood.

"It wasn't the spirits who did this," I told her, not sure if that was really a reassurance or only a correction. "This was people. Terrible people." Sudden wariness filled me. We still didn't know anything about the woman who had attacked Hadrea and tried to sabotage the rescue except that she was likely the same woman Jov saw at the Hands' party. She had seemingly been alone, but who knew whether there were other Darfri on their side?

But she shook her head furiously. "We turned our back on them," she insisted. "The warning signs were there! Our spirits are being murdered, and no one is protecting them! I tried to tell them we are under attack, but no one would listen to me. Now look where we are! Look where we are!"

She let go of my arm and pulled back suddenly, just as I reacted and tried to catch her hands. "Wait, who did you try to tell?" I asked, but she was distracted now, searching the crowd for something or someone, her head moving in jerky, confused motion, probably the result of her bad eye. She pressed her hand against her bleeding ear. "Hey! Wait, what did you mean?"

But she only shook her head at me. "I tried to tell them," she said. "We have not protected our land or the secondworld. Now *they* have it. It is too late, much too late!"

Something about her manner, or perhaps what she was saying about not being listened to, struck me inside like a gong, my heart resonating with understanding. We had seen firsthand the frustration, the fear, of trying to explain a terrible approaching danger and either being ignored or having our motives questioned. I would not do the same to anyone. Besides, we needed answers, and perhaps we had been focused in the wrong place, asking the wrong questions. "I'll listen," I told her, trying again to catch hold of her hand. "I promise. I want to hear."

"We are forsaken," she repeated, but her voice was slurred now. Blood leaked between her fingers from her ear. I looked around for a free physic.

"Sit down, all right?" I said. "Don't go anywhere."

"Credola Kalina!" Someone tugged on my shoulder: Karista, disheveled and panting, visibly distressed. "Have you seen any of my family? The explosion, they were sitting . . ."

I pointed her in the direction of several Lekas, thinking guiltily of both Varina and Arran but lacking the immediate strength to deliver that news myself. *Coward*, I told myself, but there was just so much pain, I couldn't dole any more out myself. I turned back to the Darfri woman, but she had disappeared. *Shit.* Unsettled, I searched the area to try to find her and asked everyone I ran into whether they had seen her, but she seemed to have gone from the zone without being treated. I found Jov instead, washing out some equipment, looking shaken, but before I could tell him about the Darfri woman he spoke heavily. "Those little twins both died."

I winced. "I thought their burns weren't too bad." Oh, honor-down, them too? I'd sent Karista into worse news than I'd even known; the twins were her cousin's children, and they'd already lost their mother in the explosion, as well as their aunt Varina.

"It must have been shock," he said. "I thought they were all right, too. And Karista's sister bled out before they could get her to the hospital."

"Shit. *More* Lekas?" The family might be our political adversaries most of the time but there were good people among them, including Varina. For all that Karista had done, no one deserved that kind of loss.

Jov was obviously thinking the same thing. "Honor-down, we're losing so many." He looked around the camp, bewildered. I put a hand on his arm and was trying to think of something comforting to say, when a patient, a girl not even old enough for tattoos, started convulsing violently on the pallet nearby. We had to leap out of the way of several physics racing in to help.

"Listen, Jov, there was this Darfri woman here before," I started, but Jov wasn't paying attention. He was staring at the convulsing girl, his mouth a little open, his brows tight together.

"She was fine," he murmured, barely audible.

But it seemed otherwise; moments later she slumped back on the ground, body slack, and despite the frantic efforts of the physic, she could not be revived. I turned away, feeling sick. She was only about the same age as Dee's brothers.

Jov was still staring as if he couldn't comprehend what he was seeing. "That shouldn't have happened. I helped clean those wounds and none of them were that serious. She only needed to be stitched up."

"She must have had internal injuries," I said, repeating what I'd heard a physic say when something similar had happened earlier.

"No," he said, then repeated it more firmly. "No, that's not right, that's not normal."

"None of this is normal." I gestured around us, slightly irritated. "Look around, Jov. We're in a bloody war zone but we don't know who or where the other side is!"

"No, I mean, convulsions like that, that's not . . ." His expression had taken on a faraway quality, the one he wore when he was accessing an old memory, or thinking through a problem. Then his focus snapped back on me. "All those Lekas. The twins, Arran, Karista's sister . . . how many others from that family have died here tonight?"

"A lot, Jov," I said, fully irritated now. Sometimes the things his brain could get fixated on were unfathomable. "Not just Lekas, all the Families. The first stand was where most of them were sitting. A lot died in the blast and a lot more were injured. Explosions don't discriminate, rich people get hurt, too."

I could tell his mind was elsewhere because he didn't retort, just touched his fingers together deliberately, and said, almost dreamily, "That's not what I mean."

"What *do* you mean? Because like you said, people are dying, and frankly we have better things to do than dwell on what wounds they died of."

"I mean," Jov said, toneless, watching as a stricken Karista crouched, silent, her hands pressed over her mouth, beside the girl's body, "if you wanted to do as much damage as you could, why stop with just the explosions? That Darfri woman was targeting the people trying to help the survivors, right? Well, here we are, a whole bunch of survivors and wounded people, sitting right where they left us."

I closed off the sharp retort I'd been about to make. A cold, damp feeling settled over me, like putting on a soaking-wet dress. My brother was still tapping his fingers together thoughtfully, but he had stopped staring at the dead young woman and instead was turning his gaze methodically over the bustling area, from patient to patient, lingering on the physics and the helpers like us. He started walking, almost in slow motion, his weight shifting very slowly, like a hunter trying not to startle an animal. Sweating now, I stepped up next to him and whispered, "What are we looking for?"

"Someone who doesn't belong," he replied softly. "Someone checking on patients who are already treated. Anyone who looks like they're not doing what they're supposed to be doing." Up close it was clear his calm demeanor was the product of intense effort and control. His fingers were stiff where he tapped their ends together, his breathing too even to be natural, his step too deliberate. Emotions roiled palpably from him, if you knew him well enough to notice. "Be subtle," he whispered, his lips barely moving. "Split up. We can't contain things here."

I knew what he meant. It was relatively well lit here where we were treating patients, under a number of lamps and out in the open with the bright moon above, but if we had to chase someone into the shadowy, treacherous ruins of the arena seating, we'd lose them easily in the wreckage. If there was another attack going on right under our noses, we had to stop it without losing any of the perpetrators. My mouth dry, I set to combing the area.

INCIDENT: Poisoning of Chancellor Jesso Iliri

POISON: Scourge (dilute)

INCIDENT NOTES: Chancellor Jesso consumed dilute scourge solution when attempting after a coughing fit to drink from a water jug in the apartment of his lover An-Melisa esCaruso. An-Melisa claimed to have provided the jug by accident, believing it to be water and not the solution of scourge she had used to clean out her oven. Chancellor attested both parties were mostly asleep (query—narcotics?) and An-Melisa sought immediate medical care. This proofer has reiterated the importance of proper precautions in all situations, and does not intend to pursue further.

(from proofing notes of Credola Stefi Oromani)

17

Jovan

We spread out. I grabbed a stack of bandages and Kalina a bucket and we moved around near the perimeter of the medical zone. I stopped occasionally by a patient and performed some menial, short task, all the while looking for someone, anyone, suspicious.

In the end I saw him not because he looked suspicious. He didn't. He wore a physic's blue sash over a plain paluma, stained with blood and soot like everyone else's here. He was standing, back to me, beside a patient examining a stomach wound, nothing unusual about him. My eyes would have gone straight past if I hadn't seen the woman on the makeshift pallet flinch suddenly, a whole-body spasm, and then the glint of metal in the man's hand. Even then, it almost looked as if he was treating the wound, except that instead of continuing to work, he turned casually and moved on toward another patient, while thick, ugly blood spread in a worsening pool at the woman's waist. "Shit," I said, forgetting to be quiet, forgetting to be subtle. I had an agonizing second of indecision, then raced to the woman's side and shoved a wad of bandages against the fresh bulging split in her skin, a mass of terrible wet red parts trying to escape her abdomen. A flash of nauseating, gut-cramping horror almost knocked me to the ground at the sight and smell of it. I pressed the bandages against the wound, hard, trying to keep my eyes on the man's back as he strolled on, bold and relaxed as anything. I could not lose him. "I need some help here," I called out urgently, and a physic rushed to my side.

"Fuck." She practically shoved me out of the way. "What the . . . ?" She leapt into action and I stepped back, shaken, the woman's blood racing down my wrists from my soaking hands. Honor-down, there was so much of it. I didn't bother trying to clean myself; the man had disappeared. I couldn't see him, I couldn't see Kalina, and I didn't know what to do. I turned back to the physic.

"Someone's killing patients," I blurted out. "There's someone pretending to be a physic. He did this. Be careful."

She didn't even hear me, she was concentrating so hard on trying to bring the torn flesh together again. In despair, I strode over to the next pallet, then the next, trying to find the man again. But all the physics looked alike in the circumstances, or at least equally unalike; few were wearing medical sashes because most had simply been spectators at the closing ceremony, not working, and though I had seen the back of the man, he had been of average height, with average coloring, hair a fraction longer than current fashion.

And just like that, the images locked back into place. I *did* know that figure. That hair needing a trim. I'd seen it multiple times, and honor-down if he wasn't taunting me by showing up here where he must know we would be focused on our dead and dying. It was my assassin, the very man I'd been trying to track and identify for more than a month, and he was strolling around our makeshift hospital and killing without effort or disturbance. But now I knew who I was looking for, the game had changed considerably. I scooped up a discarded piece of broken wood and held it in one hand, loose down by my side, a bucket balanced against my other hip, and began to search.

He was targeting people who'd already been treated, so I ignored the line of people waiting to be seen in ragged groups clumped at the edges, and focused on those who were put in a recovery rest here because they could not be trusted to make their way either home or to the hospital, whichever was needed.

There.

My heart felt like it completely stopped when I saw him. I nearly dropped my splintery wooden weapon. I knew that face, would know it in a second. I just needed him not to see me. I dropped my gaze swiftly and got behind the man's line of sight, then casually, oh so casually, approached.

"What are you doing with that? I need hot water," a physic said, stepping out from nowhere. I tried to sidestep quickly to avoid losing sight of the assassin but the physic stepped to block me and I accidentally dropped the bucket;

it crashed into a commandeered metal food and drinks trolley, now covered in medical tools, bounced off, and then landed on the physic's foot.

Everything happened at once. The loud clatter and the physic's cry of pain alerted everyone; faces twisted or rolled toward me, including the assassin's. He glanced back at the sound, his face familiar but blank, emotionless, and our gazes met. There was a heartbeat's pause, then he tipped something into the patient's mouth and ducked away.

Shit, shit *shit*, exactly what I hadn't wanted to happen. But there was no time for anything else. I seized the nearest person's shoulder and shouted, gesturing at the patient, "He needs a purge, someone's just poisoned him!" Then I leapt after the assassin. He was fast, so fast, and not exhausted from trying to rescue people and clear paths, and he jumped the makeshift cordon easily, already halfway toward the arena seats before I managed to even get out after him. "Help! Stop that man!" I shouted, no longer caring about subtlety at all. He would not get away this time, he would not, could not, get away. "Guards, someone!" I bellowed it loud enough that some of the people milling about between the sprinting assassin and the exit looked up curiously, but none of them moved. Everyone just stared.

He diverted from that cluster of people anyway, and disappeared instead into the darkened wreckage. I followed him, sprinting into a side passage blocked by fallen debris and partially cleared; a few people searched for survivors and bodies in the rubble, their efforts lit by lamps set on the floor at intervals. I'd had my eye off the assassin for a bare moment and yet he seemed already to have been swallowed up by the shadows. No one paid me any attention as I ducked under the collapsed piles of wood and metal, pushing my way in underneath the frame and trying not to disturb any of the balancing debris.

From beneath, the instability of the structure was terrifyingly obvious. The supports that had held up the tiers were completely blown out of the middle, where the explosion had originated, and that center was filled with the wreckage of the collapsed sections above, forming a spreading mound, half of it still alight with sullen fire. The frames at either side were buckled and twisted, unsteady. Though the enormous hole in the roof above let in moonlight, the evil black smoke made it darker than when I had been under the tiers earlier.

A movement up ahead. He had one foot caught up in the rubble and was trying to extract it without making a lot of noise. He glanced over his shoulder at me and tugged harder at his ankle; as I closed the distance he pulled it free and turned to flee. Hard as I could, I hurled the piece of wood at him. It struck him on the shoulder hard enough to spin him around and as he stumbled, trying to maintain his balance on the rubble, I leapt after him, heedless of my unstable footing, fumbling in my paluma to reach something more incapacitating. He would *not* get away this time.

I barreled into the assassin's waist, knocking him down. He fell with a heavy *uh* of pain but still managed to lock his arms around me and twist so I went down with him, and not the way I'd intended. His momentum rolled us down the other side of the mound, and a blow to the back of my ribs knocked the breath out of me. We landed hard, him pressed down on my chest and one of his hard arms across my face, smothering me. I couldn't see, could only feel the horrible compression, as if my cheekbones might crack under the pressure. But I still had a small packet of stingbark in my fist and I used it now, cramming it up blindly into the man's face, smearing its contents around his mouth and nose. For one terrible moment the assassin screamed in pain and instead of letting go of me, he arched his back and all of his weight crushed into my chest. I couldn't breathe, couldn't see, wedged as I was between debris and his body, but then he was rolling off and I could take a wheezy gasp of air and scramble to my feet.

I kicked him hard in the ribs and he fell to his side, still clutching at his face. "I think it's about time we met formally," I said.

It was strange, almost surreal, to have at last in our custody the man who'd haunted me for months. He looked unimpressive close up—though perhaps that was because of his injuries. A faceful of stingbark had left his skin red and angry; he had driven the tiny hair needles farther into the delicate skin of his nostrils and around his eyes by rubbing it. It left him a pathetic sight, trussed up with his ankles and hands tied and face puffy and painful. He had stopped screaming and rubbing the affected patches now, and instead sat still, breathing raggedly, staring at the two of us without speaking.

Kalina stood beside me now, watching him warily. "Is help coming?"

I nodded, still breathing heavily. "Order Guard helped me tie him up, and got us a lamp. He's gone to get assistance. Shouldn't be long."

"You checked him for weapons?"

I gestured to the small pile of knives, the length of rope, and several bottles of suspected poison. "There could be more, but that's what we found." He hadn't exactly cooperated with the search, and even with an Order Guard holding a knife at his throat and having tied him pretty thoroughly while he was incapacitated with the stingbark, I'd been reluctant to stay within his range longer than necessary. I'd cut his sleeves off, both to use as binding and to check for identifying tattoos, and emptied his pockets and shoes, but the Guards would have to fully strip him once they had him secure.

"The famous assassin," she said slowly, looking him over. "Who are you, then?" If she'd expected an answer she'd be disappointed. He'd yet to say a word or respond to a single thing I'd said. He was right in front of me at last, but he might as well have disappeared again for what I'd learned so far. His appearance was unremarkable. His skin was a similar shade of brown to mine, and his face dark with a short, stubbly beard that looked more like the result of a hairy man who had not shaved for a few days than a deliberate choice. His dark hair was long enough to be tied into a small knot at the base of his neck, but springy enough to be battling that fate. Older than me, fit and strong, muscle sinewy and hard on his frame. I could have passed him any day on the street and but for the impressive raised patches around his mouth, nose, and eyes from the stingbark, he would not have caused a second glance. But then, that was the point. How else would he have been able to slip into so many places and events without standing out? The best assassins in history had always been ordinary.

Kalina's eyes drifted to his arms, just as mine had done, searching for answers, but while his arms were heavily tattooed, it was not with Guild or family bands but rather a complex design from shoulder to elbow. He wore no Darfri charms or any other jewelry. In short, nothing about his appearance told me anything of much use.

"What does that say?" Tentatively, she took a step closer, and I put a hand on her shoulder.

"Careful." But he only stared flatly at us.

"Raise your arm," she said to him, and he gave no sign he'd even heard. She glanced back over her shoulder at me. "There are words there. In the tattoo pattern. At least, I think."

"Raise your arm," I repeated, this time pointing the knife a bit more threateningly. But I might as well have said nothing, for all the reaction I got. Kalina moved a fraction closer, tilting her head.

"Never mind. *Obey . . . to . . . ascend?*" she read. "Is that what it says?"

I frowned. "The book says something like that."

"The book?"

The only thing he'd carried besides a small armory, it was a slim volume made of a rough-grained leather and well worn from use. Kalina picked it up, but kept her eyes on the man. He flinched when Kalina took it. *So that's important.* She'd noticed his reaction too, and looked thoughtful as she opened the book. For just a second I thought he was going to leap at her; for the first time since I'd gotten him tied up he gave a sign of real emotion. But he didn't move, just continued to watch us, assessing.

"Anything in there?" I asked Kalina. The weapons hadn't been anything distinctive, but the book, perhaps, if it was important to him, could help us.

"It's printed." Disappointment rang in her voice; like me, she'd probably hoped to find a notebook or diary, something that might lead us further along. "I'm not sure what kind, though. It's weird. The printing's kind of wonky." She traced the title with one finger. "You're right. 'Obedience for ascension,'" she read aloud. "Looks like—"

"Over here," I heard, and turned. Three Order Guards, including the one who'd helped me with him before, were making their way across the rubble. "Everything all right, Credo Jovan? Credola Kalina?"

"He hasn't given us any trouble," I said. I glanced at Kalina. Without saying anything, she slipped the book away into her clothing so when she turned to face the Order Guards with a grateful expression, she seemed never to have been holding anything.

"We'll take him from here," one of the Guards said. "If that's all right with you."

I hesitated a moment. We still didn't know if there were any other traitors among the Order Guards. Part of me didn't want to let the man out of my sight, not even for a second. The Order Guard, perhaps guessing at my reluctance, added, "You can come along with us, Credo, if you prefer? Only I know there's still a lot to do out there to get everyone safely out, and I imagine there'll be an emergency Council meeting called, if there isn't one already."

"No, you take him," I said, forcing a smile. There was still an awful lot to do, and there could still be Hands or other agents of our enemy out there trying to sabotage our efforts. "Just be careful, and don't take any chances with him."

"No, Credo, we won't," he assured me.

We walked together behind them as they led him out, all alert and weapons out, watching for any sign of trouble. As we broke out into the open, despite everything, the terrible aftermath and all of the new things to face, I felt a tiny prick of optimism. One more piece of the puzzle had come into our hands. Now we just had to hope we could assemble it in time.

Several times throughout that hellish night and morning, I rested my eyes for a fraction too long and each time when I jerked awake there was a confused period where the horrors of the night might have just been a dream. Perhaps it was the exhaustion, or wishful thinking, but as the night wore on these moments grew longer and longer and my sense of reality grew indistinct. Sometimes, it felt like no time had passed and we were back under siege, the city panicking and grief fresh in my heart.

It wasn't just my tired brain and body that called to mind the siege, though. Moest had called up the army and set roving patrols around the city and scouts out in every direction. The wall guard was quadrupled and messenger birds sent to the three border cities to call their garrisons and be on full alert. Double the usual blackstripes were accompanying Tain everywhere he went and every Councilor had been allocated additional protection. If we felt once again like a city at war it was because we were, even if we still didn't understand with whom we were at war.

On the other hand, perhaps because of our history, the city fell easily into organizing around the disaster. Come morning the rescue and cleanup crews found renewed energy along with the lightness of the sky, clearing rubble and searching for survivors we might have been unable to get out during the dark. Manor staff and a number of city eatery proprietors had been making hot food for the volunteers, and people unable to shift rubble were helping with less physically onerous tasks such as running food to the various work crews.

Dee and Kalina were unloading trays of buns and meat on skewers onto a hastily assembled bench in the arena. "Have they found anyone yet?" I heard Dija ask. "I was thinking there'd be a chance, wouldn't there, that some people could have been knocked out or something, so they couldn't cry for help, or maybe we couldn't hear them?" Tain and I sat together on overturned buckets beside the table. We had just finished combing a section with a group of volunteers and found nothing but stray body parts, but neither of us felt inclined to share that with my niece. Erel had been beside us all morning and his young face had taken on a terrible haunted look I'd no desire to see on hers. Tain closed his eyes and tipped his head back, breathing heavily, and I used the wet cloth they'd laid out to clean my filthy hands and face, stuck with sweat and dust and ash and fortunes knew what else. Normally it would have bothered me more to be so dirty but I seemed to have exhausted my capacity to feel anything, even the usual obsessions and anxieties. "Or maybe the way the structure fell there'd be parts covered up but with gaps, so the people under weren't crushed." Dija's response to trauma and stress was apparently a very vocal one; I wasn't sure she'd stopped talking for more than a few minutes since I'd woken.

"There's definitely a chance," Kalina told her. "Let's get the crews something to eat though, they must be hungry."

I'd sent her home for a few hours' sleep, and though dark circles still made her eyes look bruised, she no longer seemed at risk of falling over. While people cleaned up and ate, she jerked her head to the side and Tain and I followed to the outskirts of the group, looking around warily to see if we were being observed. Other than Tain's ever-alert blackstripes, who followed at a respectful distance, no one seemed to have the energy to pay us attention. "What's up?"

"I had a look at his book."

No need to wonder whose book she meant. We'd checked it briefly after they'd taken him away, and been unable to make immediate sense of it. Kalina had thought it might be a book of fables or some kind of religious text, and wondered whether it was a Darfri artifact, despite the man not being obviously Darfri. "What did you find?" I didn't bother to point out that she'd been supposed to be resting, not reading.

"More questions than answers." She glanced around, slipped it out of a pocket, and showed us. "I'm not even sure it's quite in Sjon. There are definitely Sjon words, but the lettering is weird, like the printer got a bit scrambled or something, look." She was right; though I could mostly read the words it was like trying to read something written by a child with unpredictable and unreliable spelling, and left-handed by a right-hander. I flicked through the pages, seeing the same issues again and again. Words that didn't make sense among ones that did. Spelling errors, misshapen letters. Awkward, ungrammatical sentence structures.

"If this was a Talafan book I'd say it was a non-standard dialect. Regional variations in language happen, especially in big places like the Empire. But Sjona isn't big enough, and we had centralized education for a hundred years.

These differences are too extreme to have just appeared in the last few decades." She sounded both frustrated and intellectually curious.

"There are plenty of cultural differences between the cities and the countryside," Tain pointed out. "Maybe there's some remote villages with local dialects or something. Or a population near our border that's adopted some of our language."

"Or it could be a code?" I suggested.

"Not a very good one, if so," Kalina muttered. "I can read most of it."

I checked around quickly; still, everyone was too involved in the rescue attempts to pay us any heed. "And what's it about?"

"From what I could make out? It's kind of . . . a book of stories, moral lessons. Rules for behavior. There are all these references to some kind of authority figure, or something." She flicked through a few pages until she found what she was looking for: a word made up of symbols I did not know. "My best guess is what I said yesterday. I think it might be a religious text. Rules from, I don't know, a god? This could be the name of a god."

"Or a Speaker, or spirit?"

She gave me a searching look. "Have you spoken to Hadrea yet?"

I shook my head. She'd been sent for observation to the main hospital and I'd had word she was in an exhausted sleep. "The physics said it'd be best to let her wake up on her own terms."

"Do you think she'll understand this?" Tain asked.

"Honestly? No." Kalina flipped through the book again, this time in obvious exasperation. "This isn't Darfri. It's not like any religion I've ever heard of. If these are real rules for life, they're utter nonsense. What foods you can eat when, and what colors can be worn on what day, and a whole elaborate set of rules about tending to—this thing? This word. Which I think might be some kind of sacred animal, and these are the rituals for breeding and killing it, but there's no picture, so the fortunes know what kind. It makes me think they're an animal bred according to some kind of ritualistic method."

My first impulse was that it sounded crazy, but then, we had been raised to dismiss religion as a childish or old-fashioned concept, our city far too enlightened for such nonsense. That worldview had come crashing down two years ago but I couldn't erase decades of habits in my thinking. I had simply not spent much time learning about the religions of the world or even of my own region, so was poorly placed to try to identify this one by its similarities to any others.

"But none of that makes any sense if it's Sjon, does it? Could it be, I don't know, a book from another language someone's tried to translate to Sjon, badly?"

"Maybe." She folded her hands around the book, biting her lip. "Should we be handing this in to the determination council, or Chen? This is important evidence about who he is and where he's from. If he doesn't talk, it might be our best way of working out who he is."

I hesitated, glancing at Tain. He shrugged. "The more people who look at it, the more likely we can find someone able to read it and tell us what it is. Like you say, Lini, Sjona isn't a huge country. If this is a dialect or regional variation or something, surely there's someone here in the city who'd know it."

But I couldn't help thinking about the information Merenda had died trying to deliver us. Someone in the Manor, someone close enough to Tain to have known his movements that night, was passing instructions or information or both to other enemies. Right now, the only people who knew we had it were the assassin himself and the three of us. If there was any head start to be gained, I was loath to surrender it. "You're the Chancellor, it's your call. But if it were up to me . . . I don't know. I'd say let's hang on to it for just a bit. Just until we can figure something out about it, or until we know who we can actually trust."

Tain looked faintly sick, and I almost regretted mentioning it. Delivering the news to him last night that there was another traitor in the house, one close to him, had been a grim and demoralizing task, not least of which because whoever it was had not just been involved in the explosions but had also been the direct cause of Merenda's death. My friend hadn't taken it well. Worse still, he'd not been able to make any more sense of the note than we had; so much for my hope he might recognize the handwriting. But he wiped a tired hand over his forehead and sighed. "All right. But if we can't figure this out within a day or two, we give it to Budua."

I nodded. A few days' head start, at least. That was something. *Just a few days to unravel a conspiracy years in the making.*

"Auntie Kalina? We're out of this lot," Dee was calling, and Kalina glanced back over her shoulder.

"I'd better go," she said.

Tain nodded. "Us, too. Our group's done eating." He rolled his shoulders and stretched out his arms with another sigh. It wasn't worth telling him he needed to rest, too. While there was still any possibility of getting someone out alive, the Chancellor would be here with the rescuers.

"Talk more later." Kalina squeezed my hand and looked at me shrewdly. "Are you going to see Chen now?"

She knew me too well. Whatever she'd told Dee, the chances of finding people alive were rapidly diminishing, and there were plenty of volunteers. "You go on," I told Tain. "I want to see if she's gotten anything out of the Hands or our mysterious friend."

"Be careful," Kalina said, and I managed a twitch of the mouth that might have passed for a grin.

"Always."

The Guardhouse was adjacent to the Warriors' Guildhall and training grounds. It was quieter than usual, presumably because most of the Guards were out either on patrols or assisting with the cleanup. Chen had clearly not slept. Her face looked creased and her eyes red. She moved more gingerly than usual on her false leg, and snapped at a passing colleague who bumped her.

"Any news on our assassin?" I asked her bluntly, sensing she was in the mood to get right to the point.

Chen sank back into her chair and looked at me with an expression both tired and wary. "Ah, yes, this assassin you identified and caught."

"He's the key," I said, unable to tamp the excitement in my voice. "He's not a Hand. He's something different. You might not get anything out of those other two because they're acting on local orders, but that one's different. I was thinking, if he's a hired assassin we might be able to make a deal, or—"

"I won't be getting anything out of those other two, no," Chen interrupted, without a change in tone. She stacked the notepad she held onto a pile on the desk with excessive force. "Because with everything going on last night, the Guards who brought your man in housed him with the two you caught earlier. The ones who lit the devices. And then my people left them there to return to helping at the arena, because we kept a bare-minimum staff on at the Guardhouse last night, for obvious reasons."

A dark shroud settled over my enthusiasm. "And . . ."

"And when someone checked on them next, your assassin had snapped both their necks."

"He *what*?"

"He murdered them, Credo. Then he made a pretty good attempt on the door. I don't know what in all the hells that creature is, but if we'd given him another hour he'd probably have had it down."

I blinked. "Chen, I—I told the Guards to be careful. He's a killer. He's been poisoning people, trying to set me up. He killed Bradomir—"

"Funny, that I should be the Captain of the Order Guards but only now be learning about a murderer roaming our streets," she said. I'd never seen her face quite so set, and realized I'd started pacing back and forth in front of her desk without even noticing. I had the sudden and frantic sensation of control being dragged from me, like I'd been caught in a strong current in the river.

"That's not quite fair," I mumbled. "I've been telling the blackstripes and the Council and anyone who'd listen that there was an assassin after Tain for months."

"But he doesn't seem to have been after the Chancellor." She shoved a stack of papers at me, and the top one fluttered almost off the desk. I snatched it up and read a list of names. My throat felt dry, so dry I could barely swallow. "That's a lot of Lekas, wouldn't you say? Credola Karista provided me with that list of the family members she lost either at the arena explosion or the hospital area afterward, and she's not been the only one. I've been quite popular this morning. I'd say I've had more high-ranked visitors since the sun came up than I've had all year."

The rising wave lifted my legs from the ground, carried me out of my own control. I couldn't get my footing. It felt like my body was a separate thing, a difficult, prickly thing that gave me nothing but trouble. I let the disconnect happen. Honor-down, I was so tired of being blamed. I was so tired of everything. "I caught him poisoning people and I stopped him."

Chen watched me moving back and forth, back and forth. "People are asking questions," she said quietly. "About how a pampered nobleman with barely more martial training than the local baker was able to capture and incapacitate an assassin. A man who, only an hour later, murdered his two cellmates with his bare hands, apparently for sport."

"Some of our bakers are very capable, you know." It wasn't the time for bad jokes, but I'd felt too much, I'd come out the other side. It was oddly freeing.

"And the man seems to have been incapacitated with stingbark to the face," she continued, "which you might know is a substance that causes extremely painful burning to the skin. We found a small paper packet nearby which contained traces of the stuff." She cleared her throat. "A similar packet of stingbark needles, this one apparently unopened, was found in the room where we recovered the body of a murdered Talafan Imperial soldier a few days ago. You remember that incident, I trust, Credo?"

I closed my eyes, crashing back to my body and all its limitations with an almost physical jolt. All of the fear and the anxiety gripped me again, a vise of panic around me. *Shit.* "I remember."

There was a long and unpleasant pause. "May I speak plainly, Jovan?"

I almost laughed. "I'd really prefer it, actually. I think I've had my fill of the other kind."

"Well, it's like this. I've stuck my neck out for you more than once. And I haven't minded doing it, because honor-down, you've done the same for me before. And I've always thought we had compatible goals. I didn't always know exactly what you were about, but I was always sure we were on the same side."

"We *are* on the same side."

"Even last night," she continued, "I trusted you knew something I didn't and that's why you were so set on searching the stands. Of course you were right. But that's the problem, isn't it? I've overlooked a lot of the times you've been less than open with me because you've tended to be right about these things in the end. But every time you give me an explanation for something, five more questions pop up, and maybe some are raising them for their own purposes, but I'm starting to lose track of your stories."

I caught the rhythm in my head, felt the calming influence of knowing I was stepping evenly. *Left, right, left, right, left, right, left, right, turn left.* "What exactly are you saying, Chen?" *Left, right, left, right, left, right, left, right, turn right.*

"I'm saying I don't think you've been honest with me. And it's about time you were."

It was a relief, in a way. Secrets could take us so far but at some point not sharing information hurt us more than the risk of giving it to the wrong person. We couldn't counter what was happening alone; we'd proved that at the arena. If we'd had more people—but no. I'd promised Kalina I wouldn't go over and over, imagining different outcomes. At least not purposefully.

So I told Chen everything. What our family did, had always done. What I'd done during the siege—really done, not what the plays and rumors made out. And what had really happened at the masquerade. Even the strange things

I couldn't explain: weird parcels in our yard, the feeling of being watched, the Darfri woman at the party, the bird attack. She nodded in places, looked surprised in some, and utterly unsurprised in others as I laid it out dispassionately like a report to Etan. In a way, it was a relief. I had missed having someone to report to. It wasn't exactly cathartic, but the familiarity of the exercise called me back to warmer, safer times, when I was confident that older and smarter and more careful people were in charge.

"Right," she said when I'd finished. "Well."

"Yeah."

"I suppose that clears it all up, eh?" She rubbed at her leg, looked at the ceiling, scratched her chin, looked everywhere but at me.

"Does it?" I asked, a bit hopelessly, and she laughed. After a moment, I joined in. There was no humor in it, just shared exhaustion with the utter mess we were in.

"Can't say I'm surprised about most of it. Half the city must know you're always there protecting the Chancellor, but most of us just figured that was 'cause you were in love with him." She scowled suddenly. "I don't like being lied to, though. I asked you straight up about that party and I don't like how easy you lied to me. Or that niece of yours! You watch what you're teaching her."

"It's not an easy life, and you need certain skills to make it out alive," I said, defensive. I didn't need another person judging my guardianship. I hadn't invented proofing or given our family that task; it had been given to me and part of that responsibility was training someone else. *At least that's what you tell yourself,* the insidious little voice inside me whispered. I shoved it down. It had barely left me since that horrible moment yesterday when Sjease had told me Dee was missing. "She was protecting me. Someone had gone to a lot of effort to get me into a fix rather than just killing me straight out, and we didn't want to play right into their hands."

Chen fixed me with a look. "Well. What's done is done, and I don't pretend you didn't have reasons. Don't either of you do it again, and you'll get no more complaints from me about it. Fair?"

"Fair." I didn't hide my relief.

"So. You've decided to trust me, I'd say I owe you the same. There's a few more things you need to know. For starters, this chap we've got in here." She gestured down to the floor. "He's more than just an assassin. If you're right about all those other incidents, he's been waging something of a war on your family, Credo, and I don't mind saying it's been a subtle one. Here's one problem for you, though. This man doesn't speak Sjon."

I blinked. "What?"

"He doesn't speak it. At least not well, anyway."

I shook my head. "You mean he hasn't spoken to you. I imagine he's loyal to his employer and doesn't want to talk. He didn't speak when we captured him, either, but—"

"No. It's obvious he understands when we speak Trade at him. Obeys basic instructions, even—stand back from there, move the bucket over, that sort of thing. He'll answer, too, if he wants. And we spoke to several of the patients and one physic who remember speaking to him out there. They all said the same thing. Heavy accent, spoke slowly, didn't seem to understand what people said to him if it was more than a very simple question or comment."

"But he *looks*—"

She shrugged. "He does. Can't deny that. But people don't have to be born in a place to look like the people there. Look at me. I've never been to Doran but my grandmother's likely why I got the height and shoulders. People come to Silasta from all over the continent, and plenty of Sjons go elsewhere, too. Maybe this chap had a Sjon mother who left the country. Or Sjon blood got mixed up in his from some man at some point. Or it's just coincidence. It's not like you cross an imaginary line on the ground and people just magically look different."

"His tattoo. The book he had. They're in Sjon, though."

"I can read a bit of Doranite 'cause my grandmother had a lot of old books and songs and poems and such she brought over with her. But I can't speak it. Sometimes people learn the writing without having any way to practice the talking. 'Specially in Sjon, since writing won't help you with the talking at all."

"This is good news," I said slowly. "If he's not from here, he's from somewhere else." Suddenly the idea of the book as some kind of code seemed more likely, and the assassin himself vastly more significant. Our enemy would hardly have employed an assassin who barely spoke the language if they'd been hiring locally. I wished I'd taken the book from Kalina; if the assassin didn't want to cooperate our best clues would likely lie in figuring out what it meant. It matched his tattoo. He hadn't wanted her to have it. It meant something important, I knew it.

But Chen still didn't look convinced. "Maybe, but people who do this kind of work for hire could have come from anywhere and be hired anywhere. He might be skilled at killing, but he hasn't been planning interference with business deals and manipulating promotions in the Guilds. You've still got someone giving him instructions. That note the Heir found tells us there's at least one person relaying instructions."

Someone close to Tain. But who? A blackstripe? One of his or Merenda's staff? A Councilor? Without knowing what had been relayed it was impossible to narrow down the list of people who had access to the information. Certainly anyone close enough could have killed him by now if that had been the plan. I put a hand to my forehead as if I could slow the swirl of thoughts there. We could not descend into paranoia, not now. "What else? You said you'd several things I need to know."

"Ah. Well, the other's good news." She gave me a faint smile. "Thanks to your sister's tip, we've captured the Order Guard who was working for the Hands. Sukseno. Kalina guessed breaking the former Warrior-Guilder out of the jail would be the next step in the plan. I set a trap and we got him just before dawn, with a bag of explosives. He was trying to get her out while we were all still distracted here."

Optimism had started to rise in me again. "What do we know about him?"

"He's from the Leka estates, out near West Dortal," she said, consulting notes on her desk. "The mother's dead, got some cousins out there, but the only one who lives here, far as we could tell, is his sister, who's out in the external village. He's been in the Guild for almost twenty years, worked as a private merchant guard for a bit, then for the Order Guard in Moncasta, and eventually moved here. Served under Aven in the army on call for most of that time, so he's got a history with her."

"But he didn't storm the Manor two years ago," I said slowly. That was how we had isolated Aven's most ardent supporters. "Why not?"

"He was injured in some kind of training accident after the forces went south. Was being treated in Moncasta during the whole siege, so he never got a chance to support her or otherwise."

I nodded. "All right. So he might be a full-blown believer. Let's just hope he knows who the Hands are taking orders from."

Chen stood up with a wince and stamped her artificial leg irritably. "Let's have a chat with both of them, eh, before this place is swarming with Councilors again."

But it was as if she'd summoned them with her words. We'd not made it twenty paces from her office before a small crowd of Councilors bore down on us.

"Captain Chen! I sent a messenger some time ago." Sjistevo gave me a scathing look. "Why are you taking private meetings with Credo Jovan instead of reporting to the full Council?"

Chen was a head taller than the Credo and a good deal more muscular; Sjistevo seemed oblivious to the palpable impatience in her scowling form. Whatever deference she usually showed the Council, last night's disaster had burnt it all out of her. "Your message said you wanted a private word. You didn't mention the Council. And now you're complaining your colleague is doing exactly what you asked to do?"

Momentarily taken aback by her uncharacteristic rudeness, Sjistevo mumbled something incoherent; Chen took the opportunity to peer at his companions. "And Credola Karista. Didn't I bid you a hearty farewell less than an hour ago? What a rare privilege to see you again so soon." She delivered the latter in an artificially polite tone and sketched a dainty little bob that looked absurd on her powerful frame. "Credo Lazar. Stone-Guilder. Why, we're well on the way to the Council meeting you wanted anyway, eh, Credo Sjistevo?" She straightened and looked over the group. "What is everyone doing here? Not that I'm looking to tell you all how to run a city but I think there's enough jobs going round that we don't need half a Council to get a report from the Order Guards." She looked over the back and raised a hand. "And here approaches your stalwart leader, too. Perhaps I could persuade you to relocate this little gathering to your own Council chamber and leave me to handle my job. Got a bit on today, as you might imagine."

Tain was indeed approaching down the corridor, and scurrying beside him, taking two steps for each of his strides, was An-Suja, our Oromani estate representative, followed by Salvea, who looked composed but worried. Tain radiated fury, the kind of crackling chaotic energy he only displayed when he was in a real temper. I found my hands tensing, clenching, and tried to force them to relax. Not now, honor-down, not now of all times.

Karista never took her gaze from me. Her eyes burned wild, and her hand shook as she pointed at me, but her voice was all false calm in the heart of a storm. "And where were you going with my dear colleague?"

"We caught the assassin, Karista," I said, trying to soothe the situation. I wished desperately for Kalina; she knew how to burr the edge off dangerous situations in a way I never could. "The one who killed your uncle, and so many more. We were just going to talk to him, to find out who he's working for."

"And do we think that's wise? In the circumstances?" Sjistevo had regained his poise and was smiling a smooth, false smile at Chen, his manner suddenly extravagantly courteous. "Questions have been asked about Credo Jovan's relationship with this man. Would it not be best to—"

Tain strode into the group, the others parting to make way for him. "What in all the hells is going on here?" he demanded. His body moved like a whip as he scoured the group and his voice dropped to a dangerously low, deceptively even tone. His eyes burned no less fervently than Karista's. Though, I thought with a flicker of worry, it was an artificial brightness of the eyes that told me he had used darpar, same as me, to get through the night. I didn't much like it, but hypocritical complaints could wait for another time. "We have a meeting scheduled for later, once everyone's had a chance to have some rest, and Captain Chen will be attending to report then. Most of us have been up all night. So why was I told people are bearing down on the Guardhouse demanding personal reports from the Captain? Is this the most efficient use of the Captain's and your time, do you think?"

"It seems we came just in time," Karista said, with the air of a person triumphantly revealing a surprise. "Credo Jovan here was just attempting to interview the prisoner. Apparently he is not only a one-man army, but a trained interrogator, too. You speak of efficiency, well! Our colleague renders our Order Guards and determination council redundant, apparently."

Sjistevo smirked, and Lazar shifted uncomfortably behind him, avoiding looking directly at me. I felt my stomach turn. Telling Chen the whole truth had been one thing. Explaining my role to the Council was entirely another.

"Credo Jovan tried to warn us a number of times about the threat from this man." Eliska spoke up for the first time. "Now he's caught him, is it any wonder he wants to know more? I'm here because I'd like to know more too, and I've as much interest as anybody in making sure these efforts aren't given any—" She glanced over at Karista and Sjistevo. "—undue hurdles."

"In the circumstances, I think it is best that impartial officers handle what this man may or may not tell us," Sjistevo said, spreading his hands wide and smiling around as though he'd just proposed a solution so eminently sensible no one could possibly object. "There have been some valid questions asked about the circumstances of his capture—"

"Questions asked by who?" Tain demanded. "Chen said Jovan caught this man. I've got my own questions about why anyone would have any interest in keeping him from helping protect us yet again!"

"Chen wasn't there at the medical area!" Karista rounded on him, her temper as fierce as his. "Did you bother to ask anyone who *was* before you marched in here throwing accusations around?"

"I haven't thrown any accusations anywhere yet, Karista," Tain snapped. "But if you'd like me to start, by all means keep volunteering."

"He showed up at the medical area and suddenly people with injuries that shouldn't have killed them were dying left right and center," Sjistevo interjected. "That is what the witnesses report. He was seen giving unauthorized substances to patients! And the people dying were members of the Leka family, relatives of Credola Karista, someone with whom the Credo has often clashed! A family against whom he has a long-standing grudge, I do not think anyone would deny. My colleague is right to say questions need to be asked, questions that should have been asked a long time ago. Credo Jovan undoubtedly tried to stop these explosions or what have you, but that's not to say he's not capable of taking advantage of the chaos to—"

"Very generous of you to acknowledge your colleague probably didn't try to murder half the city," An-Suja cut in dryly, and Eliska was shaking her head, visibly dismissive. Their disbelief was a balm. Not everyone had been influenced by this campaign against me.

"Are you seriously suggesting Credo Jovan murdered injured patients?" Eliska said. "Do you know how insane that sounds? Credo Jovan. Of all people."

"I would trust Credo Jovan with my life," Salvea said firmly.

"I'd trust him with your life, too," Karista shot back. "Just not *mine*."

That set off a chorus of shouting again. Etan had always said no one ever shouted in the Council, that my family's position and honor would insulate me from blatant insult, how I would need to be able to recognize attacks delivered with honey, barbs hidden within questions, double and triple meanings. It seemed a comical and naive perspective now. There had been a hell of a lot of shouting in the last two years. Right now, I felt too numb to participate in it. I leaned back against the wall and closed my eyes. After everything, this latest indignity barely scratched the surface. For all our scrambling and research and attempts to unwind this conspiracy, we'd failed, and it had cost everyone dearly. They'd earned the right to stand and shout and accuse one another of things.

Tain still looked furious. I knew part of that anger was directed at himself. "We were attacked last night, by the same people who almost destroyed our country two years ago, and we're turning on each other," he said. "Were you not watching what happened out there? Don't you think you're doing exactly what our enemies want you to do?"

Lazar, his face puffy from tears, cleared his throat. "We are allowed to have questions, Honored Chancellor. We might all owe Credo Jovan our lives, more than once over for some of us, but that does not give him perpetual freedom from questioning. This is not the first incident that has raised these questions. There has been a pattern—"

"Enemies of Jovan's don't seem to last very long in this city, is what my dear colleague Lazar is saying," Karista said bluntly. "I'm not saying he had anything to do with those blasts, though we all know he has experience in explosive devices. But what I am saying is anyone who opposes him in person or in business seems to end up ruined or dead. You've been his best friend since you were children, Honored Chancellor, do you really think you're unbiased in this?"

"I think it's time we said what a lot of us have been thinking," Sjistevo added. "Which is that either you're working together knowingly, or you're letting your friend do your dirty work and turning a blind eye."

There was a sudden, deep silence. For all that the Council was rarely the diplomatic dance it had been in Etan and Caslav's day anymore, usually the only Councilors blunt enough to directly impugn the honor of the Chancellor were the estate representatives, who had been elected by their regions specifically to be strong in the face of power. Tain had encouraged that. He had never wanted to be free from criticism. But something about seeing one of the old Families, one of the opponents to change and advocates of the old system, make a statement like that . . . it felt like the end of a social norm that had held up for centuries.

Karista slapped a fist on her open palm. "Don't you think it's just a bit strange that every Oromani in the city stayed home? It's the only family that didn't get half wiped out." She took a shuddering breath. "Do you have any idea how much of my family I've lost? My sister. Countless cousins. My little nieces!" On this last, her voice cracked, and despite everything, I felt sorry for her.

"Karista," I said, and the din died down. Every head swiveled to look at me. I took a breath and let it out. "I'm so sorry about your family. And everyone else. What happened was—" My voice caught, and for a moment shared grief and shock connected us. Honor-down, everyone was so tired, everyone had lost so much. My body was so full up with emotions there wasn't any space left for anger. "There are hundreds of people dead. The Heir is dead. The Empire lost its Princess. We lost friends and relatives and yes, Karista, you're right, I did tell my family not to come because I was afraid something was going to happen, so I was luckier than most. But I'd have had all of you stay home if I could have had the time to convince you to. Please, listen now. I know we're all exhausted and grieving. But this is only the beginning, and we have to be ready for what's coming next."

"Is that a threat? He's threatening us now?"

"Sjistevo," Eliska said, with the air of a person very close to packing in her self-control, "if you don't get your head out of your ass, so help me I'm going to make sure you taste what's up there."

I went on before they could start it up again. "This is a campaign. Like the Chancellor said, it started two years ago with Aven and her rebellion and we only slowed it down then, it never stopped."

"Are you saying this is a second rebellion?"

Murmurings, some scared, some angry, sprang up around the group, and Tain scowled round, silencing them with his glower.

"No one's saying that," I said. "For most people, the rebellion was a protest against genuine grievances. But we know some people involved with it had different motivations. What we're seeing now is those people acting directly. This is what they're capable of. Not just targeting people with the explosions but also trying to finish off the wounded. The assassin has been working our city for months, targeting the Families, trying to turn us on each other. I believe he killed Bradomir, and poisoned at least a dozen other people across the city over the past few months."

"This assassin again," Karista scoffed, "a convenient story."

"You can see him right now, if you want," Chen interjected calmly. She had been leaning against the wall, resting her leg. "He's right here. He isn't saying much, but he's real enough. A dozen people saw him posing as a physic at the medical area, and he was found carrying poisons."

"All right," Sjistevo said. "And we are led to believe only Credo Jovan saw this man, chased him down, and captured him? And he now stands here un- harmed? What extraordinary good luck you must have, my friend."

"I recognized him, yes," I said patiently. "But only because I'd seen him

before. Look. I'm sorry I've kept things from the Council about my suspicions, but you have to understand why. You do remember what happened two
years ago?"

"I do. A supposed traitor revealed himself—to you two only—and then
you defeated and killed him. Another bout of extraordinary luck?"

I closed my eyes again, just for a moment. The urge to pace itched in my
feet, but I battled for self-control. I didn't like remembering that terrifying
fight in the dark, against an opponent we had liked and respected and who
grossly outmatched us. Tain, as if he could read right inside my head to the
moment I was stuck in, broke in to save me from answering. "My uncle was
murdered. So was Jovan's. His sister nearly died, I was poisoned and nearly
died, too. And all of it because people close to us betrayed us. Betrayed the
city."

I straightened up, looked each of them full in the face. "Habits are hard
to break, and secrecy's been my way of protecting us. But you're right. I want
to learn where this man is from and who hired him, and it doesn't need to be
secret from any of you. It's in all of our interests to know."

Lazar let out his breath, visibly relieved. "Well, I think that's adequate for
my part," he began hurriedly. "Perhaps—"

"I appreciate your candor, Credo Jovan," Sjistevo said. He put a hand on
Tain's shoulder and lowered his voice as if confiding to a friend. "But you
must understand how upset many of us are, how much we are grieving. It
would be best, just for propriety's sake, would it not, to have the interrogation of prisoners kept well away from the Council. It would soothe poor dear
Credola Karista's worries, and we have many trained determination council
officers, and Order Guards, and military officers, who can conduct interviews
and investigations. It is, after all, their job. Notwithstanding Credo Jovan's
habits and bouts of luck, there are doubtless other things he could be addressing that are a more effective use of his time?"

I could think of nothing to say to it, and apparently neither could Tain. He
looked at me, and I shrugged. Honor-down, I was so tired. "That's fine with
me," I said. "Chen can report to Council later."

"Jovan," Salvea began as the group dispersed, and I smiled at her but
quickened my pace. I wasn't thinking straight. When Sjistevo's manipula-
tions sounded like sense, perhaps I really did need to get some sleep.

INCIDENT: Spring hospital poisonings (various)

POISON: Atrapis

INCIDENT NOTES: Atrapis supply in hospital mislabeled as common pain numbing agents, resulting in the poisoning of at least eleven patients, including two fatalities. Families concerned would not consent to further evaluation. Physic responsible for mislabeling identified as Credola Sjuli Brook—note and continue to monitor.

(from proofing notes of Credo Etan Oromani)

18

Kalina

The Talafan began packing their return barges by the end of the day. Though it could hardly have been a worse diplomatic outcome for them to leave our city, there was no time left to repair what we could of that relationship.

"Short of actually barring them from leaving with force, there's nothing we *can* do," Budua had told me when I asked. "We don't have the legal authority to require them to stay. And considering what's happened here I don't think we're in a position to ask them any favors, are we?"

I held no official office with respect to Talafar, and though our family's involvement in saving the lives of at least the members of the Council and the visiting delegations in the viewing box meant our reputation was publicly stronger than a week ago, I was still not part of the official response team. But I couldn't let them leave without saying at least one personal goodbye, for all the good it would do.

It took a long period of lurking around near the Leaning Lady before I finally caught Ectar out of the building, directing the loading of his cases onto a cart bound for the docks.

"Ectar," I said from the bushes at the side of the road, and he whirled around, looking frantically about as if expecting an attack. "It's only me."

He relaxed instinctively, but then a tension came over him, and though he did not call a guard, nor did he look directly at me. He gave one last instruction to the servants loading his cases and then stepped off to the side of the road, checking his pockets as if looking for a piece of janjan to chew.

"Kalina," he said, sounding throaty. "You should not be here. If His Highness sees . . ."

"I heard you're leaving."

He nodded stiffly. "At first light. We must return the Princess to her father with much haste."

We had sent a specialist physic who dealt with bodies at the hospital to offer her assistance to the Talafan party with storing and transporting the remains of Zhafi and Tuhash, but she had been turned away without even seeing them, apparently on the word of Brother Lu, who considered our medical practices barbaric and blasphemous. I couldn't think of a polite way to ask how they were storing the bodies. Not that there had been much to recover of the Princess. My throat felt tight. I suddenly realized I had not thought this through. What could I say to Ectar to make any of this better? Coming here had led to the death of two of the Emperor's relatives, and while the death of a distant relative and Imperial soldier had been bad enough, how could we be forgiven for getting his most beloved daughter killed? Nothing I could say to Ectar, nothing Ectar could say to the Emperor even if he were so minded, would change that. I could tell him it was not our doing, that it was a third party, one we should treat as a common enemy. But they were grieving, and coming here had caused that, and nothing I could say about conspiracies would sound like anything but an excuse.

"I do not know what to say to . . ." I searched for honest words. "To convey how sorry I am. It is all so inadequate."

He shrugged, staring down at his feet. "Yes. It is a catastrophe. My grandfather the Emperor is in poor health and I do not know what this news will do to him. And the people! The people will throw themselves into the sea with despair at her loss."

I took a hesitant step forward but a sharp movement of his hand sent me sinking back. "And you, Ectar? Are you all right?"

His breaths were short and pained, as if a great weight lay on his chest. He seemed not to be able to bear to look at me. "I grieve," he said at last. "Not just for my aunt, for even if our lives intersected only rarely, by all accounts she was a fine woman. But for our relationship." With a kind of raw groan of pain, Ectar met my eyes for the first time, his gaze intense and tortured. "I do not know what will happen now, Kalina. Between our countries. I had such hopes, and now I find them dashed." He blinked rapidly, looked away, then squared his shoulders in the silence and forced a stiff smile.

"I will not forget knowing you, Kalina Oromani. I hope one day we will meet again."

And he strode away, with only a slight hitch in his step.

I fought back dismay as I walked away, and the sense I had made things worse, not better. With how we had left things we'd be lucky if Talafar didn't tear up our treaty; we certainly could expect no help when our enemy made their next move. And yet, for all that it seemed selfish, and foolish, to mourn a more personal loss amidst the greater ramifications, it was the future snatched away from me that kept returning to my mind. Travel to another country, a chance to use my skills without nefarious purpose to improve relations with our neighbor. A chance to be out of the perpetual suffocating scrutiny of being an Oromani in Silasta. All gone. A stupid and petty thing to be concerned with in the scheme of things, but knowing that didn't make the disappointment and despair any lighter.

"Shall I get you a litter, Credola?" Lara asked. If she had an opinion about my strange meeting in the bushes, she didn't offer it. "Not sure what's operating at the moment but I'm sure I can find someone to—"

"No, I'd like to walk," I said. I had a mind to go and see if Hadrea had woken yet. The physics had checked her over and found no sign of anything wrong other than that she had not woken; her heart and breathing seemed strong, and her sleep appeared natural and relaxed. The walk would give me time to think. There were things I wanted to discuss with her, but bringing up anything of this kind with Hadrea required some planning and forethought. Fortunes knew enough people last night had seen her and her friends working to save everyone, and fighting against the rogue Speaker, and no one could doubt her allegiance. But the fact remained that Hadrea had been using magic in a way An-Ostada had not taught, and aided by narcotics. Questioning her about it, even with a view to learning something about the rogue, was likely to trigger all of her usual defensiveness, and more.

Lara peppered the journey with a long story about her son's first stay in the hospital with a broken bone, but in her usual way she required no input from me to enjoy the telling of it. I let her chatter on as we walked, my mind elsewhere. Once or twice I thought I glimpsed a pale figure in my periphery, and the first time I thought Ectar had followed me. But when I turned to get a proper look, and to hang back to wait for him to catch up, there was nothing behind me but a river of strangers, going about their business with tense and frightened faces. The second time I worried it might be the woman who had been following us before the arena, but nothing happened and she did not appear again, so perhaps it had been my imagination. I felt too tired in any case to worry about birds and smelly parcels in our garden. Everything dimmed in comparison to what had happened since.

The hospital was still the central hive of activity for the city, with a constant flow of people in and out of the entrance hall. It took me some time to find where Hadrea was because the hospital was stuffed above its usual capacity and, just like during the siege, areas had been urgently repurposed to keep up with the needs of the injured citizens. I kept being confronted with people I knew and embroiled in small, repetitive conversations in equal parts depressing and dull: colleagues from the Guild, peers from my school days, our favorite spice merchant, the costumer who had sold me my masquerade costume, a familiar banking clerk; half the city seemed to be lining up or delivering something or visiting their wounded friends and relatives or volunteering to assist the physics. Credo Pedrag, the former Craft-Guilder who had suffered a devastating head injury during the battle for the lower city in the siege, was there in his wheeled chair, keeping the children of visitors entertained with stories. Abaezalla Runkojo was even there, helping unload the contents of a carton of supplies onto trays and trolleys for the physics. She stopped her task when she saw me, though, and hurried over.

"Credola Kalina!" she cried. "I am so relieved to see you unhurt!"

"Kalina, please," I said absently, scouring the room for signs of where I might find out Hadrea's location. "And likewise, Abaezalla." I barely knew her, but every person unhurt was a blessing.

"You must call me Abae," she said earnestly, surprising me by taking both my hands in hers. They were scholar's hands, smooth and soft. "I am trying to help, but I have no medical skills, and I fear I am no help in shifting heavy blocks, either. This is what they have given me to do." She released me with an embarrassed shrug. "I wish it were more. It is so dreadful, what happened. I feel so . . ." She trailed off, spreading her hands and shaking her head.

"Yes, I know," I said heavily. It was hard to articulate this kind of deep helplessness, so I only wished her well at the task and found my way to a service desk, where the frustrated clerk managing visitors narrowed his eyes when I asked about Hadrea, and I gathered from his quizzing that many members of the public had simply wanted to stare at her. Being stared at in

the street didn't bother Hadrea the way it unsettled me, but waking up to a
bunch of gawping strangers would be unpleasant for anyone.

She wasn't in a proper treatment area but a repurposed room for patients
who needed quiet recovery space without the expectation of further urgent
medical care. I pushed open the door. There was a line of pallets set up, with
a patient in each; about half were asleep. Hadrea lay in the farthest bed, facing the wall.

"Hadrea?" I kept my voice low, conscious of the conspicuous eavesdropping.

She turned at once and sat up, pushing her tangled hair from her face.
"Thank the fortunes. Hello, Kalina." She swung her legs off the bed and gave
me a crooked smile. "I am ready to leave. They would not let me go alone, but
you can escort me."

"Are you all right? How are you feeling?" I passed over her shoes, glancing around for a physic. Beside the bed was a small pile of what looked like
nothing so much as offerings at a Darfri shrine. Gifts, it seemed, from people grateful for her efforts. Whatever An-Ostada thought, Hadrea's actions
had only cemented her heroic persona in many people's minds, I was sure. I
looked over them. Posies, mostly, a few loaves of sweetbread, a jar or two of
dried fruit, and a heavy-looking box with a formal card. "This is from the
King of Doran," I said, picking it up and reading the accompanying note. "A
thank-you for saving his life." She grunted, tying the bindings on her sandals,
apparently unconcerned with royal gifts. I lifted the lid and saw the sparkle of
opals. "Are you sure you're allowed to leave?"

Hadrea waved a careless hand. "They checked me over when I woke and
there is nothing wrong with me. I was just very tired. Someone is supposed to
keep an eye on me in case there's something they missed, but there is too much
to be done right now with people who truly need care." She tossed her head.
"Channeling fresken on such a scale takes physical exertion, but does no harm.
I am fine."

"What do we do about these?" I gestured to the pile.

She shrugged. "I am not sure any of the physics have slept in days. I doubt
they are taking breaks to eat properly." So we dropped the posies of spring flowers and foliage by the sleeping patients in Hadrea's room for something bright
to waken to, and the food gifts with the clerk directing traffic. He marked
Hadrea's exit in a log and his hands shook a little; he darted little sidelong looks
at her as he wrote, and swallowed with apparent difficulty. Opals and shaking
hands; admiration and fear. The twin consequences of what she'd done.

I glanced around as we walked. Lara was trailing us, keeping an eye on other pedestrians, but no one was close enough to hear. Still, my heart beat harder with nerves; usually I would never have dared ask a direct question about fresken. "What *did* you do that was so different? Why did it work when An-Ostada's didn't?"

Hadrea walked on in silence for a short while, looking—to my intense relief—more thoughtful than offended at the question. "It is not easy to describe. The words are not right. It is like trying to say what red sounds like, or how sadness smells. The senses do not line up with our words."

"I think what An-Ostada seemed to be saying was that she was asking the spirits for help, but you were doing something else," I prompted.

"Yes. I suppose. Speaking is the art of communicating with the spirits. You might ask them for wisdom or for aid or a boon, or you might simply offer praise or honor . . ." She trailed off, frowning hard. "Offerings are hard to explain. It is about making yourself emotionally open, so the intensity of the things you feel are shared with the spirits. These connections are what become . . . a fuel, you might say. Like oil in a lantern. The fuel that powers the secondworld.

"So. You must follow the rituals, and the spirit must know your presence or it will not answer. It is like if you hear a name called out in a crowd. If it is not your name, you do not turn. If it is your name, but when you turn you do not recognize the person calling, you might walk on." She bit her lip. "So you build up a relationship with spirits by offering these things, regularly, ritualistically. Because you put yourself, your community, into the spirit, to fuel and nourish it, when you call upon it, the spirit knows you. It might lend you strength to perform certain acts. This is what happened during the battles at the siege. But if you neglect the spirit, and pay no respects to the land, no matter how skilled you are in fresken, your cries will go unanswered."

"So An-Ostada called on the lake spirit and it didn't answer."

"Yes. She tried to call upon the lake spirit and then the spirit of Solemn Peak, and I lent my support to her, but it was not enough. They did not answer. They are deeply dormant, and it may be years until they are responsive the way our stories once described them." She raised her chin. "So I entered the secondworld and used what they were offering myself."

We took a few steps in silence as I digested this. "You did what the spirits normally do. You used their power. Is that what . . ." I tried to remember the other terms I'd heard. "Is that what they call summoning? Sorcery?"

"No!" She turned on me, breathing hard and furious, as if I'd accused her of some disgusting act. "Summoning is forcing a spirit to do your bidding. Using them like a puppet. It is a dark and foul act." Her pace quickened, and I struggled to keep up.

"I'm sorry," I said. "I'm just trying to understand. An-Ostada was so angry. What was it you did that she hates so much?"

For a moment I thought I'd pushed her too far. She strode on, color high, lips pressed together. I pushed on after her, breath starting to hurt in my lungs. It was the sound of my breathing, I suspected, that made her stop, suddenly, and something like shame passed across her face. "I am walking too fast," she said, by way of apology, and I took it as it was meant.

We walked on together in silence for long enough that it was a surprise when she suddenly spoke again. "What I did at the arena is not so different from what I did two years ago. The drug. Void. It also makes it easier to act as a conduit for the power, and it is like . . ." She struggled for words again, moving her hands in frustrated expression. "The mind of a person who has opened themselves to the spirits and the secondworld is different from the mind of someone who has not."

I nodded understanding, though with a little sour turn of the stomach. Jov had experienced that opening, that sharing, but when faced with multiple people using Darfri magic, I had not felt the same pull. It was a strange thing to contemplate in the abstract, and a stupid thing to feel jealous about.

"The more you do it, the easier it is for you to do it again, yes? A leather strap grows easier to tie, over time. Void can accelerate that process. It builds a connection between people, also. Those of us who have experimented together are connected, we can find each other easily, even in a crowd, and they could assist me. There were many people in the crowd that night who have used Void too, I think, and whose energy was . . . there. Waiting and undirected, but connected to the secondworld and ready to be used."

Something about that sounded ominous. "So using Void leaves you more vulnerable to this? Like it leaves a hook or a trail or something to your mind?" Any trace of uncomfortable envy vanished in a puff.

"It is no harm to anyone," Hadrea said, bristling again. "It is no bad thing to be more readily able to make offerings to the spirits. Such is fundamental to our beliefs. An-Ostada does not mind that people offer their strength, she only expects it must first be filtered through a spirit."

We crossed a road, pausing in our talk as others moved within range. Two children chased a rogue ball into the traffic and were hauled back by their swearing, overanxious Tashi. A large black bird stole a berry from a woman's basket of groceries and she batted it away. An Order Guard patrolled the street with a tired prowl. Everyday traffic, but with an edge of fear and tension. Once we were clear again, I dared ask, "And the woman? She had that urn thing?"

Hadrea ran a ragged hand through her hair, looking genuinely discomforted for the first time. "Somehow she had stored power in that vessel. I do not know how. I did not know it was possible to do such a thing."

"She said something about being taught by 'him.' Did you know what she meant? Who is 'he'?"

Hadrea laughed, though it was a hard and bitter sound. "Kalina, I have no clue. I have stumbled through understanding my own heritage my entire life, and when I am finally given a teacher, she despises me. The things I do not know are boundless."

Oh, fortunes. Her hard edges could cut, but the hurt beneath . . . I seized her hand on impulse and squeezed it. She returned the grip, and bumped my shoulder with hers, and the silence between us was something comfortable and familiar now.

Eventually she said, "It is An-Ostada, if anyone, who would know who could teach such a thing. There have never been as many male Speakers as female. If she feels so strongly about fresken being used this way, surely she would know if there is a man who is betraying the traditions so. She was less surprised than me at what that woman did."

I remembered something else I had wanted to ask her about. "There was a Darfri woman who tried to warn me at the hospital. She said something like . . . we didn't protect the secondworld, and she'd tried to warn us the spirits were being murdered."

Hadrea stopped. "Murdered? I do not know how you would murder a spirit. Does she mean the spirits that have died around the estates?"

"No idea," I admitted. "I lost her in the crowd. I'm hoping she'll try to find us again; she seemed to want us to listen, and she was upset. It sounded important."

"I will ask around in the lower city, and the outer village," Hadrea promised me. "If this woman has something to say about Darfri matters she will find one of us, I am sure."

"That would be great." I described her as best I could. I had asked at the hospital about a woman with an eye and ear injury but they weren't keeping much in the way of records and there were a lot of people with those kinds of wounds. I hoped she'd been treated. "Could this—any of this—have something to do with some kind of . . . different religion?" I fished out the assassin's book from inside my pocket. Over the last day I'd gone over it in detail, but learned nothing more; likely we'd need to ask language specialists in my Guild for help very soon. Hadrea looked at it blankly.

"What is this?"

"The assassin had it with him when Jov caught him. It's our best clue about where he came from."

She flipped through the book, looking irritated again. "Reading is still not my skill." Although initially keen, she'd proven an inconsistent and often impatient student, and from the sudden tension in her shoulders I suspected she was defensive about it. Instead of asking her if anything was familiar, I read significant passages out while she listened, her nose wrinkling and her frown intensifying as I did. The sections on punishments for transgressions were particularly absurd.

"Most of this makes no sense at all, it's like it's describing all of these cultural rules, but they're not like any country I know of. But this bit, here, talks about how women are more suited to do *something*—I can't read this word—because of their range of emotions, it says. That almost sounds like it could be related to Darfri practices, doesn't it? What you said about women being Speakers more often, and also about how offerings work?"

Hadrea shrugged. "Perhaps there is a similarity, but if your assassin could do what that false Speaker did, he would not have been skulking about poisoning wounded children. I am sorry, Kalina. I do not know what this means. Most of my life it has been difficult for people on the estates to engage with any of our heritage. I cannot imagine there is anywhere in Sjona where these sorts of rules could be enforced. We were not permitted to have shrines by our most ancient spirits if that interfered with the passage of traffic. Is there really a town where someone could make you wear a mask with no mouth if you are caught eating cooked food on the quarter moon days? This does not sound like any place I know of."

"Nor me," I muttered. It had to be either a religion for some far-off place—making the assassin a devout man, to carry his sacred words with him at all times, but then, why would the book be badly translated into Sjon instead of being written in his native language?—or a fiction, some kind of false book disguising a code. I had tried writing out all of the symbols and letters that were unfamiliar or used incorrectly, in the hope I could see some pattern among them. I could not. Etan had once shown me how special codes could be devised if each party had a "key book," but by itself the book was valueless.

We had promised Tain we would ask for help if we hadn't figured out what it meant quickly. So, I supposed, it was time to ask directly.

I went to the Guardhouse the following day, after a fitful night's sleep, part abandoned in favor of rereading the strange book and speculating about its origins. Chen showed me to the cell, well apart from the other holding rooms at the headquarters. "He's still not saying anything, not in Sjon or Trade. The determination council had people in here all day yesterday, trying to get him to speak, but they've had no luck. Hasn't said a word."

I stopped walking. "Thank you for letting me talk to him. I know it's only supposed to be their agents, but—"

"But you got that book, don't you?" She shrugged. "Jovan told me about it. He said you wanted a bit of time to see if you could figure out what it meant, and he explained why." She hunched her shoulders a little, looking sideways at me. "I agreed no Councilors would be permitted entry, and no one at all without supervision. I *might* have implied I'd only let determination council agents in, but I don't know as I recall asserting that precise thing."

"I'll be quick," I promised. "And I won't say a thing to anyone."

"You're here on official records to see Sukseno, given your connection to the former Warrior-Guilder and the fact that she talked to you before. No one could object to that."

"Thank you, Captain." It was an undeniable comfort to have had Jov confide in Chen. Her solid, dependable presence radiated intelligence without cunning, honesty with discretion, and we had been alone with our theories and obsessions too long. She gave me a parental slap on the shoulders, and it gave me a boost of confidence as we approached the assassin's cell.

He was not only confined by the stone-walled cell itself, but also by a rope which bound both wrists to a metal loop fastened to the far wall. "Had to put that in specially," Chen said quietly, following my gaze through the bars of the door. "Seems barbaric, but given he killed two cellmates with his bare hands, I'm not taking any chances with my guards or with you."

"I appreciate that," I muttered honestly. My heart was already pounding, but I kept my face smooth as I approached the door. I would give him nothing without a price.

"You want to stay out here?"

I looked at the room. I could see in and talk through the door, the top half of which was blocked with heavy metal bars, but the light inside was poor, and shadows concealed the face of the man on the bench at the far side of the room. If I was going to show him anything in the book and gauge a reaction, I was going to have to be closer than this. "How far can he reach with those ropes?"

Chen gestured to a mark on the floor. "Full stretch? The point marked with chalk just there. You'll be fine if you stay on this side." She jerked her head toward Lara. "If you're going in, your houseguard goes in with you, armed. And she's on the alert, yeah?"

Lara spat out the last of the janjan stick she'd been chewing and gave Chen a cheerful grin as she accepted the offered short sword. "Won't take my eyes off him, Captain. On my son's life."

Chen unlocked the door and I entered, trying to project calm confidence. Lara melted in behind me and Chen propped at the doorway, her own weapon by her side.

The assassin had watched me come inside without any change in expression or movement. Now, his chin lifted and I got a full look at him. The reaction to the stinging substance Jov had used had receded, though the skin was still raised and red, if less angry. But for that, nothing about his face was noteworthy or remarkable. He looked like an average Sjon, perhaps forty years old. He had been stripped of his previous clothes and given a plain tunic, so the detailed artwork of the tattoo on his left arm was clearly visible. He had a hard, leanly muscled body like an athlete's or a soldier's, and a number of scars on his forearms and legs that looked like old combat injuries.

"Hello," I said, and his flat gaze traveled slowly over me, taking a long time as it focused on my various bandages, cuts, and bruises. As if he were searching out and noting down specific points of weakness. Self-consciously, I felt the urge to step farther away. Though he was tied securely, the prisoner radiated an air of malice and competence and barely leashed violence that reminded me, an anxious ball growing in the pit of my stomach, of Aven. His gaze traced a line across the floor between us as if measuring, counting, assessing. Did he want me to see him gently flexing his hands, testing the strength of his bonds, the tightness of the rope? I wouldn't show him he was unsettling me. If he was like Aven, he'd enjoy my fear, and I didn't feel like gifting him with anything.

"Do you know who I am?" I said it in Sjon first, then Trade. Nothing. He barely blinked. But as I started to ask another question he spoke suddenly into the silence.

"Oromani," he breathed, and my stomach fluttered uneasily at the malice in his tone.

"Where are you from?" I asked, half to myself.

He smiled a wide, toothy smile. "Where from?" His voice was deep and melodious in accented Trade. "From hell."

More discomforted than I wanted to admit, I glanced back at the doorway at Chen, who had made a small sound of surprise, and in that second he burst into motion like a bird taking sudden flight, flinging himself toward me, teeth bared. I leapt backward in panicked instinct and my back slammed against the far wall. My breath flew out of me and my skull rang with the force of my own collision. But of course he was too firmly secured. His lunge cut short by the cords around his wrists, he was yanked back gracelessly at their taut extent and fell to one knee. Lara, who had drawn her weapon and stepped between me and the assassin in barely a blink, brandished her short sword with a threatening growl, and he melted back to sitting on the bench seat without any apparent emotional response. His face returned to the neutral, bland expression. He had simply tested whether at a moment of distraction his bonds would hold, and now confident in their strength, he returned to captivity without any sign the incident had bothered him at all.

Honor-down, who *was* this creature?

"Do you want to kill me?" I asked him, curiosity overcoming the fear response. Chen had said he had not interacted at all with previous questioners. "You said my name. What's so special about my family?"

Nothing. As if attempting to attack me had been the only purpose of the engagement, he looked at the wall of the cell impassively and ignored me. I asked a series of questions, each time first in Sjon, then as best I could repeat in Trade, although it was too simple a language for nuance, and nothing garnered any interest or response, not when I asked him how he had been treated since his capture, how he knew who I was, why he had been murdering patients at the makeshift hospital, who he worked for, who was the Prince? No doubt these were all questions Chen's people and the determination council officers had tried. But things changed the moment I pulled the book out of my pocket, and held it up. "Is this yours?"

It was as though I'd reached inside him and seized his innards. A jolt of energy wracked his body and widened his eyes and he bared his teeth. Behind me, Chen sucked in her breath and even the implacable Lara gave a grunt of surprise. "Take your hands off," he growled, with a voice so menacing it made the hairs on my arm stand up. *A real religious text, then.* He said something else I didn't understand in a voice tight with rage.

"It is important to you," I said slowly. "I understand. Beliefs are important." I gestured to the words on the cover. "You must obey to ascend, yes? Is that why you're here? Did someone send you to kill all those people? Someone you must obey?"

"You read this?" He seemed shocked into answering.

I frowned, and we stared at each other, momentarily joined in mutual confusion. "Yes," I said. "Look, I can help you. If you say nothing, there's a Council full of powerful people looking to blame you for a much bigger plot. I know you work for someone. You barely even speak our language, so I know what you've been doing isn't your own plan. You're taking orders. Tell me about your employer. Who are they? What do they want?"

He turned away again, apparently losing interest. Frustration made me wave the book again, the only thing that seemed to get a reaction. "Does your god want us dead?" I stepped to the limit of the chalk line, opened the book, searching for the name, and held it up, pointing. "This, this right here. Is this your god?"

He stared transfixed at my finger for a long moment, as if frozen in place. He took two slow steps forward—Lara moved her blade in a quiet warning—and stopped, looking between me and the book. Then he spat at me, and it was so sudden and unexpected I had no time to move out of the way. It hit me on the face and I flinched involuntarily.

I wiped it off with my sleeve. "Doesn't even sting," I said, and enjoyed the flash of annoyance across his face. *Good.* Anger seemed to be the trigger, his temper penetrating his desire to stay silent. "Who sent you? What do you want?"

He twisted his wrists so the ropes looped around them, and leaned toward me, arms taut, ropes digging into the flesh of his forearms. "I want? I want to end you," he whispered. He shook his arms so suddenly and so aggressively that I took an involuntary step back.

"Does this tell you to?" I shook the book at him, and again he bared his teeth. The mere sight of me touching the book seemed to be too much for him to ignore. My mouth a little dry, I tried on a smirk and flipped through a few random pages, searching for a phrase I could replicate in Trade. My heart was beating hard—his eyes were wide and demented, and if he were not restrained I had no doubt he would try to tear me apart. "You are afraid of children?" I asked innocently, gesturing at the passages advocating quashing young curiosity. "This sounds like a cowardly religion. Do you really believe this?"

He was actually shaking. "You are not able to touch this," he spat. "It is not for you. You are a thief, a traitor, you are not clean, you are . . . *chamutah*." I had no idea what language the last word was in but the meaning seemed clear from the delivery. "You cannot touch."

"Of course I can," I said, and smiled to cover my nerves. "I read this whole thing. Where are you *from*? Nowhere civilized, based on the contents of this. Some backwater settlement, hiding away from the rest of us, afraid of knowledge, afraid of women, afraid of children . . ."

"Thief! Filth! *Chamutah i esperol!*" He shook his arms so hard the ring clanged dangerously against the wall, roaring with fury so intense I worried he might actually burst his restraints. I backed away, not bothering to hide my alarm, and almost ran straight into Chen, who was approaching swiftly with a bucket in hand.

"Cool off," she said, and doused him in the face with the bucket of water. The prisoner, temporarily spluttering and drenched, stopped screaming, and Chen led me and Lara out of the room. "I don't think you'll get much more from him in that state," she said dryly.

We walked down the hall and into one of the empty rooms. I realized I was shaking. "Are you all right?" Chen asked.

"Just a bit of a shock. I thought he was going to break that ring for a moment."

"You sure pissed him off. Still, that's more than anyone else has been able to do." The captain looked me over thoughtfully. "Was like he just couldn't help himself."

I looked down at the book clenched in one of my hands, and forced them to loosen. "He called me a thief and a *traitor*. Why?"

"Well, you've got his book," she pointed out reasonably.

"He already knew I had it. He saw me pick it up and he didn't react like this then. But those words, why those specific words? Filth, sure. Whatever part of the anatomy he called me with that other stuff, fine. But a thief and a traitor? A traitor to what?"

She shrugged. "Can't say, Credola. Could be they're just the only insults he knows. But I think it's safe to say this man's no simple hired assassin. He's a believer in something, and if he's working for someone they've got more than financial or political motive in your family. It wasn't just the book. It was your *name*."

For some reason, that did not make me feel better.

"What about the other one, then?" Chen gave me a lopsided grin and loosened her powerful shoulders. "While you're on a roll, eh? Since that's what you're officially here for. If you can get him reacting like our mate in there, that'd save me some trouble."

"Aven's man?" I swallowed. "I guess we might as well." Perhaps it was his connection to Aven, or the graphic aftermath of his work I'd seen on Tuhash, but despite the relative scales of their crimes, I was more apprehensive seeing Sukseno than the assassin.

He was held in an ordinary room, without the additional safeguards that had been needed for the other prisoner. His huge hulking form looked too enormous for the bench, for the room, even. Chen had put a chair in front of the cell and I took it, grateful for the chance to get off my feet. My earlier decision to walk to the hospital seemed a waste of my limited energy now. "Sukseno. We've never met. I'm Kalina Oromani, though I think you already know that." He raised his chin in sullen acknowledgment, which I took as a sign to continue.

"Our city's in shambles, and I'm tired, Sukseno. So I'm going to be as quick as possible. The Hands have been running drugs and extortion in the lower city all year, and no doubt worse. We know that. But what happened at the arena . . . mass murder is a whole new game."

I thought I saw a flicker of something. Shame? Amusement? I pressed on.

"You were caught with a bag of explosives so it's a safe bet the determination council will find enough evidence that you intended to set our most dangerous prisoner free. And I have to tell you, after how many people you Hands murdered last night, how many innocent children, it's going to be hard to get a rehabilitation sponsor. Ever. So the only way forward I see for you, Sukseno, is if you help defend the city now, do everything you can to help us stop what's coming."

He blinked, silent, expressionless. Chen had said he was a hard character, displaying no weakness, and there was little incentive for him to help us, if he was the kind of man who could be part of a plan to murder innocent people on the scale he had. But there was one gentle pressure point I could apply. "You were going to break Aven out," I observed. "Was she expecting you at a particular time? Or is she still going to be sitting there, wondering when you'll come?"

The thought of Aven having come so close to breaking free made my heart race and my skin prickle. What would have happened if Dee hadn't recognized Sukseno at the market? What damage would Aven have done to us, if freed? Prison was supposed to be a time for reflection, for penitence, but in her case that had been a fool's errand. She'd never felt sorry for her crimes, only for how they had crumpled, and apparently she'd wasted no time on anything so wasteful as self-reflection; instead, she had turned her considerable talents in manipulation to finding another way out, another way to get revenge.

Well, she could continue to sit in the dark and wonder what had happened with her grand plans and why no one had come to get her. It was enough to give me a small moment of satisfaction, thinking of her triumph and excitement slowly turning to disappointment and fury.

Sukseno was obviously thinking along the same lines. The big, emotionless face had stiffened, his feet on the ground making a little scraping pattern with the toes, back and forth, back and forth. He was listening now, and, I hoped, imagining Aven waiting fruitlessly for him. And that made me suddenly sure of the right way to approach the man. "Getting Aven out was the plan, but you were on your own. No backup, no one to help with the device, no one to use it while you distracted the on-duty Guards. No orders from the top on this little side project."

There, that was a response. Something passed across his face; it might have been anger. "The orders to blow up the arena didn't come from Aven, did they?" I breathed, feeling the truth of it even as I saw the reaction play out in his expression. "She's not in charge of the Hands, is she? Someone else is running this, and they didn't want to bother about getting Aven out. That's why it was just you."

He turned a baleful glare on me, but it was obvious I'd struck a nerve. This was his point of weakness. Aven might have thought she was running things, but whoever her "friends" were, they hadn't made her escape a priority. Maybe they'd never intended to free her at all. Excitement rose in me. We were on the edge of something here.

"Did they cut her loose?" I asked, watching him carefully. "That's what you're worried about. That they never cared about her at all. She let them down last time, you know, double-crossed them. Tried to play both sides and come out on top. You know what I think? I think they were using her."

His hands had balled into fists. Oh, he was a true believer, all right. She'd done a number on him; this was a loyal, loyal man, and the mere thought of someone betraying his commander was cracking him. Fear and disgust and fury tightened in my stomach, and a surprising flash of pity. Yet again, that utterly unworthy human had effortlessly collected adoration and loyalty from others. What had she ever done to deserve such a thing?

"Sukseno, I think we both know I've got no reason to care about Aven getting her comeuppance, but right now, I don't think she's actually the one trying to destroy us. What can you give us to help us stop the ones who are? You might work for the Hands, but you're loyal to Aven. Give the Wraith up, or better still, tell us who's funding this, and we'll see what we can do for you. Who is the Prince?"

The hands on his lap were so tight now they were almost shaking. "What can you do for her?"

For her. Even now he was thinking of bargaining for Aven's conditions, not his own. It made me sick. "We can make her life a lot more comfortable," I lied immediately. "We can organize work for her that's more rewarding than mine work. Give her privileges, let her write to her family more often."

"Make her the Warrior-Guilder again," he said abruptly. Chen, who had been silently observing in the background, gave an audible snort of disbelief, and he swung his gaze to her, fury flashing across his face. "Make her the Warrior-Guilder and she'll clean up this mess."

I had no immediate response. The utter gall of it was almost breathtaking. "Make her the Warrior-Guilder," I repeated. "The woman who murdered a Chancellor and started a civil war. You want us to not just release her but elevate her to a position of power."

A muscle worked in his jaw; he gave me the mean, narrow stare of a person who believes they are being mocked and is on the brink of snapping. "Yes."

"Sukseno, we aren't gonna do that," Chen said. She returned his glare with a flat stare of her own. "You know we aren't."

He shrugged. "You want me to give them up, you're gonna have to."

Chen started to say something else but I cut her off. "You tell me how to find the Wraith, or better still, the Prince she's taking money and orders from, then we can talk about what we can do for Aven. But if you don't give us something, and now, we won't bring this to the Council and ask them for anything for Aven or for you." I turned back to Chen. "The Hands slit the throat of the last guy to displease them, didn't they?"

She followed my lead without hesitation. "Opened his throat and dumped him in a canal," she said cheerfully.

Sukseno's feet, scratching on the floor, stopped still. I yawned—no need to feign tiredness in my state. I'd had more rest than some these past few days, but much less than my body needed. "Well. By fortunate coincidence, we have a few of the Hands in custody, the ones who planted the explosives. It'd be a shame if we let one of them overhear how you folded under our very terrifying threats." It had been a gamble, trusting he hadn't heard what had happened to those Hands.

"The Hands are the tightest criminal gang the Order Guards have ever seen. You reckon they'll be pleased you're sharing anything with us? We'll transfer you to the jail in a nice obvious carriage, and we'll see who comes out to make a play for you." I smiled. "What do you think? Give us a chance to pull in someone a bit more senior."

I was impressed with Chen's cool; she cracked her knuckles and nodded. "I'll give him a day's head start and make a fuss about taking him back over."

A vein pulsed visibly on his temple as he replied with forced ease. "Do what you want. You've already said I'm certain to be convicted so what does it matter?" He folded his big hands behind his head.

I shrugged in false nonchalance. "Your gang's messing about with bigger stakes than drugs and petty crime. If you're not going to help us get to those responsible for the arena I'm not fussed about what happens to you in the scheme of things. If our best bet is using you as bait to draw someone else out, I don't mind the risk."

He clenched his fists, the jaw muscle working, his calculation evident. *Come on*, I thought. *Save your own neck.* Eventually he spat out, "I've got a sister in a chair out in the village, she can't work, and a little niece who's doing most of the looking after her, all right? I support them, people know my pay goes there. The Wraith's vindictive. She'd as soon slit their throats as go after me." He pointed one shaking finger at me, his face still hard and cold even through the fear. "None of this has shit to do with them. Something happens to them, it's on you."

I frowned as I looked him over. He seemed genuine enough. "Does your sister know what you're involved in?"

"She's got nothing to do with this," he repeated angrily, his color rising, and for the first time he seemed unable to meet my gaze. I surmised his sister didn't know the extra work her brother was doing to help support her.

I shrugged. "I don't like it, but if you don't give us something to help stop another attack, we're not going to have a choice. You helped murder hundreds of people, Sukseno, and you're aligned with people who want to kill more still. Do you think the Council's going to lose sleep over a risk to your family?"

The prisoner ground his feet and stared at his lap, furious and scared, stubborn and indecisive, all at once. He looked, in fact, trapped, and despite myself I felt a glimmer of pity. He hadn't always been a criminal. A disabled sister in the external village and not in the city meant money and work were likely a barrier to finding safe, affordable accommodation in the city itself. Maybe falling in with criminals was an easy path to go down in tough circumstances. His own life apparently meant less to him than the safety of his family; I was uncomfortably quick to relate. I shook my head, trying to will myself out of caring.

"Get my sister out," he said at last. "And I'll give you the Wraith. And tell you what I know about that foreign bitch she's taking orders from. She's what started all this."

"A foreign woman?" I asked, cool, as if my heart hadn't started up a staccato beat of excitement in my chest at his words. "It's the *Prince's* Hands, isn't it?"

He shrugged. "I don't know about any Prince. It's just a name, isn't it. The Wraith runs things here, and the money and the drugs come from the foreign bitch, like I said." He folded his arms stubbornly and looked at the wall. "You get my sister out and we'll talk."

"We'll see what can be done." I left the corridor, holding everything inside me so I didn't break out into a run.

New energy pulsed through me as we closed Chen's office door behind us and I spun to face her. "You have to get his sister to safety," I said. "Right away. He knows what we need and he can tell us. You can see it in him. He cares about Aven, not the Wraith, not whoever this 'foreign bitch' is. He'll talk if we give him the right stimulus." *A woman? A foreign woman. But who, and from where? Is the Prince real, or is that a title she uses? And the* he *the Speaker invoked? Are they all working together, or all the same person, or do we have more than one front to fight this battle on?* The questions whirled in my head and I wished I could somehow be delivered straight to Tain and my brother to tell them everything.

Chen leaned against her desk and took weight off her leg. She scowled down at it, rubbing the join, and I suddenly realized she did not share my excitement.

"What's wrong?" I asked. "This is great news. He'll give up the Wraith and more information about her sponsor. Why do you look like someone's just given you cold tea?"

She gave a heavy sigh and looked at me square. "Just . . . don't get your hopes up just yet, Kalina."

"Did you not hear him?" I gestured back the way we came. "He just gave us confirmation someone outside the country is driving this stuff, and told us he'd give us more information. My hopes *are* up, Chen! Honor-down, why aren't yours?"

Chen held up a conciliatory hand. "Look. I've talked to a lot of people in tough situations, is all. They say stuff. You and your brother are public figures, and what you think about a foreign sponsor for the rebellion and all the rest of it is pretty widely known, you know? And this guy, he's had Aven in his ear, telling him whatever the fuck she's been telling him. I'm just saying, he's promising to give you exactly what he knows you want . . . I'm not so sure it won't all come out his ass, is all."

"He was serious. Chen, he really believes in Aven and he's sitting there stewing, thinking the Hands used and abandoned her. Maybe the Wraith never wanted the competition from someone who's used to being in charge. Maybe this foreign sponsor isn't so keen on the person who screwed up their last attempt to take us down. But either way, he feels alienated and betrayed on her behalf, and that's the perfect time to get him helping us."

"Spite's as good a motivator as any," she agreed, but she still looked grim. "Could be we've had a lucky break here. Could be it's something else."

I wheeled in my dismay at her attitude with deliberation, forcing myself to speak calmly when all I wanted to do was shout. "Are we going to bring his sister in then? It can't hurt, can it? All we're doing is protecting an innocent woman, there's no harm in that. I'm not suggesting we let Aven out."

That garnered a small, tired smile. "Yeah, I thought you wouldn't be real keen on that option."

"Warrior-Guilder Aven, bursting out of jail to save us all from the mess she caused?" I wheezed out a laugh of my own. "Can't say it's the ending I've been dreaming of."

"We can get the sister," she said. "But I'm not ordering it myself. The Council's already asking questions about how the investigation's being handled. We do this with full authority or not at all."

INCIDENT: Poisoning of Chancellor Ardana Iliri

POISON: Lendulus

INCIDENT NOTES: Chancellor Ardana struck by dart while recreationally swimming in river south of Moncasta. Initially mistaken by guards for an insect bite, causing delay in treatment. Suspected Marutian assassin (name unknown) apprehended trying to cross border into Doran. Chancellor undergoing treatment, this proofer [text obscured, page damaged]

(from proofing notes of Credola Ettenna Oromani)

19

Jovan

Tain and I were in his office meeting with Moest, Erel taking swift notes in the corner as usual, when a blackstripe knocked at the door and cleared his throat. "Excuse me, Honored Chancellor? I've been told there's a litter just arrived at the Manor from the Guardhouse, and Captain Chen's here to see you."

"Tell them to send her on in here," Tain replied. He was flicking through the messages Moest had brought: responses by bird from Telasa, Moncasta, and West Dortal, confirming there were no signs of approaching armies from across the borders, no acts of sabotage, no violence on the streets.

"We could still be facing a follow-up attack in a more traditional form," Moest continued. "I would not say it is impossible. The Talafan delegation left at first light today but it will be days before they can clear the north border; likewise with the Doranites. There's a possibility an attack could come after other countries' officials are out of Sjona to minimize the chances our enemy would have to contend with either of their armies if their people were trapped here."

"But?" Tain looked up wearily.

"But we must also consider that our enemies may not have the support of a full army. We could be looking at continued acts of internal sabotage, designed to cause havoc and mass harm. Or some sort of supernatural attack, if the secondary attack at the arena was not an isolated one."

"An-Ostada says she doesn't know who that was," Tain said grimly. "But someone trained her, obviously."

I felt a flicker of unease. Hadrea seemed no worse for wear after her extended recovery sleep, but I worried about this terrible rift between her and her peers and An-Ostada. The Speaker was the only person in the city who could teach Hadrea about her gifts, and we might well need them all working together if we had to defend against further attacks like the one the woman with the urn had tried. She had come to me late at night and in the darkness of the bedchamber, exhausted from the seemingly endless day before, and, overwhelmed by the warmth and strength of her body, I'd been too cowardly to start a conversation about it. I had just been grateful to feel alive and connected to her. Later, later we could talk about how fresken fit into this mess.

Footsteps sounded from the corridor outside, and we all looked up to see Chen being led in, closely followed by my sister. She had meant to try to speak to the assassin this morning; my heart leapt at the brightness in her face. She must have learned something important for them to have come straight up here.

"Captain." Tain got to his feet and clasped Chen's shoulders in greeting. "Not more bad news, I hope." He kissed my sister on her forehead. "You still need rest," he chided her gently.

"Speak for yourself," she retorted, putting a hand on his thin cheek. "We need our Chancellor right now. Can't have you collapsing, can we?"

"Sit, take tea," Tain urged them. In some ways it seemed strange, in the midst of this disaster, to still be sitting and taking tea like civilized people, but we still needed to eat and drink even when the world was falling apart. So we sat, and Chen told us what they had learned from questioning not the assassin, as I had expected, but Sukseno, the treacherous Order Guard. Kalina sat beside her, twitchy and energetic.

"He didn't seem motivated by the threat to his own life," Chen finished. "But only by the risk to his sister's."

"So we should get her to safety, as soon as we can," Kalina said, apparently unable to keep from speaking any longer. "She hasn't done anything wrong, so keeping her safe from any retaliation makes sense in any case."

"We don't know, of course, whether or not this sister is just an innocent party or not," Chen said, with an oppressive frown at Kalina. "We've only his word for it. And as someone who's betrayed his Guild and the Order, can't say as I'm thrilled with his trustworthiness. The sister could be neck high in this for all we know."

"I don't think she is," Kalina insisted. "I believed him when he said she hadn't anything to do with it. And he said he had information, not just about the Hands, but about who they're taking orders from."

I almost spilled my tea, and set it down to avoid the accident. "Who? Did he say who?"

Chen was frowning again, but Kalina nodded. "A woman. A foreign woman he says is controlling it all. He seemed to think the 'Prince' bit is just a name, not a person."

I frowned. That didn't fit with the note Merenda had intercepted, or with what the Darfri woman had said.

Moest was watching with great interest. "This is the Guard who was caught trying to free Credola Aven?"

"Yes." *And the one who strangled a man right in front of me.*

"This is good news, then, isn't it?" Tain asked. He took a sip of tea and looked around at all of us over the rim. "Why do you not look like this is good news? This is the information we've been searching for for two years, isn't it?"

"It's just that I'd be mighty cautious with anyone who's working to Aven's tune," Moest said, shifting uncomfortably on his cushion. "It may look like she's not masterminding this, that she's been left behind, but I won't believe that till I see it for sure. She's no one's fool. Maybe this is the break we need, or maybe it's just another trick. We get the sister out, he gives us some information about some foreign agent of some sort, and then he pushes for what he *really* wants, and what do you know, it's about getting Aven out of jail."

"No one is letting Aven out of jail," Tain said.

"And if more things like the arena happen?" I found myself saying. I could see it rolling out in front of me, horribly real. "The Hands kill more of us? What then? If the price is letting one person out of jail, would the Council really not consider it?"

Kalina swallowed.

"Fine. We'll treat anything he says with caution," Tain said. "Chen, you bring this information to the determination council and see what they think, and if it needs to go to Council, then it goes to Council. Like Lini said, we pick up the sister and get her somewhere safe. If he was lying and she is involved, worst case is we've got a new prisoner. And best case, we get some information we need, and keep an innocent woman safe. I don't see how we do anything else."

"Wasn't suggesting we ignore it," Chen said. She'd refused tea, and stood now with a wince, obviously keen to move. "Just wanted to make sure we

had appropriate expectations, eh? Could be this is what changes everything. Could be it's just another cog in their machine and we're being pulled
through. As long as we've got our eyes open, is all I'm saying."

She excused herself to go straight to the Governance Chambers, where
the determination council was housed, and Moest also stood.

"I'm due back at the Guildhall myself," he said. "I'll report straightaway
when I hear from the scouts. Are you happy for me to reduce the patrols on
the wall for now? Unless it's a flying army, no one's going to be within march-
ing distance for days and I've got more critical preparations to do with my
squads, so I could use the extra people."

"I don't want any surprises," Tain said. "So as long as the towers are staffed
and no one decides we should relax just yet, that's fine."

He gave us all a nod in farewell and strode out as well, leaving the three of
us looking at one another with apprehension and hope, both.

"I believe him," Kalina said. "I know that's not scientific but that's my
read. He's devoted to Aven."

"I trust your read," I told her. "What about the assassin? Did you get anything out of him?"

She glanced over at Erel, who was still taking notes. The boy paused, his
pen hovering, and looked questioningly at Tain, who frowned. "Have you
figured out the book, or do you need help?"

"I need help," she admitted.

"Then it's time to bring in Budua and whoever else she suggests, I'd say."
He glanced back at Erel. "Erel, note down that Credola Kalina found a book
in the rubble and has now confirmed it belongs to the prisoner. We are going
to approach members of the Administrative Guild with specialties in language, customs, and religions of other countries to get their views."

"He feels very strongly about it," she said. "Chen says it's the first thing
he's responded to. He hated me touching it, called me all sorts of names in a
language I don't know, but he said one word twice so I remember: *chamutah*.
But also 'thief' and 'traitor.'"

There was a moment of confused silence. Even Erel stopped scratching notes to look up at Kalina. "'Traitor'?" I asked. "Could you have mis-
heard?"

"I don't think so." Her voice shook with remembered feeling. "It was like
I completely disgusted him. And he knew our name, that's what he first responded to."

I spun my teacup absently, thinking hard. Assassins from unknown places, local gangs working for foreigners, spies reporting "in service to the Prince," Darfri taking lessons from mysterious men . . . I was *sure* this was a single conspiracy against Sjona, but honor-down, there were a lot of moving parts. And something else I hadn't really considered. "When you talk to Budua, can you also get her to talk to one of the historians and see if there are any records of a noteworthy scandal involving our family specifically at any point? Business or personal. And Dee can check our journals." I didn't have much confidence there, though, because I had read the Oromani family journals multiple times, and though they were extensive, they focused on our proof-ing duties and political issues concerning the Chancellor's family, rather than much personal detail about the Oromanis themselves. Could our own family have given offense or committed some sin against a foreign trading partner, long ago, who had nursed a grudge? Thin, perhaps, but perhaps there was more to why we were targeted than isolating Tain.

"I'll do that," she said, nodding.

Tain had to go and meet Eliska about the infrastructure cleanup so I walked out with Erel, who kept glancing at me nervously as if he had some-thing to say as we walked out of Tain's study. "What's up?" I asked him even-tually, tiring of his palpably tense presence just beside me.

"What? Nothing, Credo!" He swallowed. "Uh, by the way, how is Dee?" His tone was no more than politely curious to the casual onlooker, but I saw the way he wrung his ink-blotted fingers together while he waited for my reply, and my mild irritation melted away. I smiled.

"She's going to be all right, Erel," I reassured him. "She saw some things up close that are a bit hard to deal with, but you did, too, and here you are." I didn't ask where Erel had been during the blast, but hoped it was somewhere well away from the worst zones. Certainly he had been in the rubble piles helping get victims out, though, so either way he had seen far too much for a boy his age. In some ways the rescue process had been more traumatic than the initial blast.

"I . . . I didn't know what else to do," he admitted in a mumble, avoiding my gaze. "At least this way I'm busy. And the Chancellor needs me still. He's so tired, and he's not well." Then, as if he'd been caught insulting Tain in some way, he hastened to clarify, "Anyone would be tired! He's working him-self to the bone trying to deal with everything. It's normal to forget things and get a bit mixed up."

"I know." Honor-down, no one knew better than me. I put a hand on the lad's shoulder. "You're a great help to him, Erel. I don't know what he'd do without you." Just as Sjease had taken an enormous burden off me and Kalina, I knew Erel had done the same for Tain. It occurred to me, in a rush of shame, that I had not thought to ask him whether his family was safe, and I hesitated to do so now—what if someone close to him had been killed, and I made things worse?—then decided it was worse to never even bother to ask. "Your family, were they . . . was anyone hurt in the blasts?"

"Oh, no, Credo," he said earnestly. "My Tashi took a job back home in Imudush a few months ago, to be closer to my nieces and nephews. All the family's still up there."

"You must miss them." Inked-in members of families were typically even more fiercely loyal than those born into them, and he was still young to be all on his own.

"I'm all right, Credo," he said, puffing up his chest a little, and I suppressed a smile. To be fifteen, and so concerned to be seen as self-sufficient! "The Chancellor treats me very well. Like a member of his own family."

I patted his shoulder. Tain did think of Erel that way. He liked children and would secretly have liked, I suspected, to have brought in one of his younger relatives to train up as his Heir, but the chaos of the post-siege time had meant his older cousin, stable and sensible, was the appropriate choice. He'd been looking forward to Merenda bringing her children into the city. In the meantime, I think he'd enjoyed having Erel around, and not only because the latter remembered when Tain's appointments were and kept his paperwork in order.

My smile faded and the memory of the Heir's broken body, flung from the height of the arena, soured my stomach. I wondered, as we walked the corridor in silence, whether word had yet reached Merenda's brother and daughters. Tain would have to replace her, if we made it through the season.

Erel's comment about Tain earlier in the day stuck in my mind, and I carved out time to prepare some nutritious food for him in the evening. Dija assisted, her eyes a little red and carrying a brittle silence around her mother that suggested they had been fighting again about her staying here. The Talafan had left the city this morning and hundreds, perhaps thousands, more had done the same over the course of the day, in a great fearful exodus. Ana wanted to leave, but had not given up on bringing her daughter back with her. For now we existed in a kind of tense temporary truce, and I had avoided her as much as possible.

As it had been during the siege, these moments of normalcy, carved out amidst the trauma, were slightly surreal. Cooking for Tain was an ingrained routine that gave my body something to do and a way for me and Dija to talk about familiar things and avoid confronting the terrible pressure of what had happened looming over us. We prepared several packed meals and then made time to play muse over sweet nighttime tea before bed, and for a brief stretch, life almost felt like it made sense again.

Partway through a game in the evening, our houseguards interrupted. "An-Hadrea at the door to see you, Credo," Dom announced.

"Yes, of course," I said. I glanced back down at the muse board. Dija must have been distracted, she'd overextended with that red tile. I moved my blue to threaten it.

Hadrea came inside and shrugged her cloak off. Though we were well into spring, the morning and evening winds were still cold, and I shivered as she brushed my arm with her hand in greeting. Though she had insisted she had taken no harm from the incident at the arena, there had been an over-intensity about her since that I distrusted, a look not dissimilar to the one Tain wore sometimes. It called to mind the sensation of walking on a cliff path in high wind. "Your skin's icy," I said, touching her cheek and making room for her with us at the muse board. "Where've you been?"

"It is colder than it should be, this year, I think. An ill wind for the start of the season." She looked distant, as if her mind were elsewhere, but then shook her head and looked down at the board. "Who is winning?"

"Uncle Jov," Dee piped up. "He always wins. But I'm getting better. Do you want to play next?"

I moved my blue again—what was Dija thinking with that red? Had she forgotten they were vulnerable?—and looked up innocently. "Hadrea doesn't like muse."

Hadrea shrugged. "You city folk. You have worked out how to turn even games into something you can pore over like a book. Games are for outside." She stretched out next to us like an animal relaxing by an oven. "Is Kalina here?"

"She's at the Guildhall still. She's got a fragment of language she's trying to identify and she's been in with the scholars and historians all day."

"I have been down in the Darfri districts," Hadrea said in a more serious tone. "I have found the woman Kalina said you were looking for."

"Where?" I started to stand, pleased, but Hadrea shook her head, glancing warningly at Dija.

"Finish your game first." Her expression turned warm as she smiled at Dija across the board, and ruffled her hair. "How are you feeling, little one?"

"I'm not so little," Dee said, without looking up from the game, but her voice had a smile in it. "I'm all right, I guess."

Hadrea looked her over carefully, and then gave me a questioning flick of her eyebrows. I shrugged. Truth was, Dee was handling the trauma remarkably well, better than me, most likely. She still couldn't talk easily about Merenda, and I'd heard her crying in bed at night, but most of the city probably did that. Hadrea watched the girl thoughtfully. She had been as stern as Ana about my niece's recovery when we'd spoken last night, making me promise to give Dija time to grieve for Merenda and to process the things she had seen before she was embroiled once more in my world. It was on her recommendation that I had suggested muse, even though it seemed wrong to do something recreational in the circumstances. As someone who had lost her Tashi at a similar age, she had better experience on the issue than me.

"Did you talk to her?" I asked, trying to keep my tone light.

"Not myself. A friend in the lower town recognized the description as soon as I said she might have one patched eye."

Dija stared determinedly at the board and moved a yellow piece at the other side of the circle, but I could tell by the too-careful frown between her glasses that she was only pretending not to pay attention to our conversation.

"At least, I think it is your woman. My friend says there is a one-eyed Darfri woman saying a lot of things about the spirits to anyone who will listen. He did not think she was . . ." Hadrea tapped her forehead. "Quite right in the head."

"Kalina said she was a bit incoherent, but given the circumstances . . ."

Dija stacked my flame piece under her blue, and I swiftly captured her red piece with my blue and stacked them. "Don't forget to pay attention," I warned her with a faint smile.

"I won't," she said, and though her face remained grave there was a hint of pleasure in her voice as she circled her yellow piece around the board in the spiral dive, a move I definitely hadn't shown her, and captured my blue, creating a red/blue/yellow tower in a very aggressive position on the board. I gaped at her, and she managed a smile, the first I'd seen on her since before the explosions.

"Where did you learn that?"

"Sjease."

"Obviously not keeping them busy enough if they've got this much time to teach you sneaky muse moves," I muttered.

We finished our game under Hadrea's half-amused, half-bored eye—I still won, but only barely, and that multi-tower did a lot of damage to my strategy. "Bed for you, I think," I said, swirling the last dregs of my tea in the cup. Dija got to her feet obediently. The lack of argument worried me; it was as though what had happened had extinguished some spark within her.

"She just needs time," Hadrea said quietly, watching me watch her go off to bed. "She is not broken. Only weighed down."

And what am I doing to lift the weight? I wondered. Ana would not readily cease her campaign to convince her daughter to leave the city, but if she was more subtle about it, I was too tired and too caught up with everything else to have a stalwart defense. I could not guarantee Dee's safety here, but nor could I guarantee it back in Telasa. And she was a thoughtful and intelligent child who seemed to know her own mind, and whose will should not be ignored. But I thought I understood, now, how none of those logical arguments would mean anything in the face of the deep, biological fear that came from loving a child, and it made me sympathetic to Ana in a helpless sort of way.

"So." I packed up the muse board. "Can we go and talk to this woman, right in the head or not?"

"Yes. And Jovan, I think you were right to ask. There are more rumors out of the Darfri quarters in the lower city. People hearing word from families out on the estates, especially to the north. Dead spirits and other strange things, too." She shivered. "I do not like the sound of this, Jovan. That woman I fought at the arena was not just a Speaker who believed in the rebellion. She was something else."

But what, we had no idea. An-Ostada had reported on the matter to the Council yesterday. But it had been a frustrating experience that had given us no more answers. An-Ostada had not known the dead Speaker and seemed to regard her existence as an exhibit of greatest blasphemy. The presence of someone using Darfri magic against us had not, as I'd hoped, made her more forthcoming with information about fresken and how it could be weaponized, but the opposite; she had channeled her offense and shame into a greater defensiveness on the topic.

"We are most likely looking at a lone, rogue woman with Speaker potential, with a grasping ambition, who has meddled in the secondworld and stumbled upon forbidden magics," she had told the Council, glaring around as if we had insulted her. "It is unfortunate, but these dangerous students do arise from time to time." She had looked pointedly at Salvea and me then. "Had we been permitted to practice our ancestral rites and teachings appropriately over the last few decades, such disasters would never have occurred."

Now, I modulated my tone carefully, hoping to distract Hadrea from a topic that led only to prickly defensiveness at best, and open anger and withdrawal at worst. "You're the one who actually understands this stuff," I said. "We're swinging in the dark here. Do you think there's a connection between what's happening on the estates with the spirits, and that woman at the arena?"

"I do not know," she said, appropriately mollified. She looked thoughtful, and worried. "Perhaps. Or perhaps not. But this woman insists she was turned away from the determination council and the Order Guards and any other official she tried to speak to. Your Captain Chen means well, but she is focused on immediate threats to the city, and I fear she does not see Darfri matters as Silastian matters. That is the problem. Even good people treat us like we are a race apart."

I wanted to shout my frustration. She was right; it was wrong-footed and dangerous to have officials acting as if Darfri matters were some special breed of issue, separate from the country at large. It was bloody hard to do otherwise, though, when Darfri leaders like An-Ostada were forcefully resisting the idea. "I'm sure a lot of important things are being put aside at the moment," I said neutrally. "But I think this might be critical. Can we go talk to her now?"

"Yes. I would have liked to wait for Kalina, but I think we ought to go tonight. The woman is staying at a place in the outer village, and from what I heard, I fear if we do not go, we may lose the chance to talk to her. I do not think she will stay for long."

We left with only one guard, and I borrowed one of the boys' jackets. Hadrea kept the hood of her cloak up. I hadn't been out in the outer village much; it had grown out of necessity for a city stuffed to bursting, but the early settlements of tents and poor sewage had gradually improved, so now the stench of shit didn't rise from waste at the sides of the roads, and said roads were well-packed dirt, swept and maintained, and marked out neatly in rows. There were no maintained streetlights at this stage, so our way was lit mostly by grubby light spilling from residences and the few social buildings. It was quiet, almost eerily so, but then I supposed a large number of residents had probably either packed up and left for one of the other towns, or sought shelter within the walls of Silasta proper. Those who remained were probably afraid, and rightly so.

"There." Hadrea, who had been counting buildings as we walked, nodded to a house that looked, to my mind, far too small to function as an inn. No signage or other advertisement for its services marked the outside to my eyes, but Hadrea pointed out a hanging wreath of dried bluehood and thyme on the door. "That is for accommodation," she said. "The Guild is aware, I am sure, but they have better things to do than to try to stamp out this sort of thing when we are not even within city walls."

"Tamarik, are you hungry?" I asked our guard, who shook his head crisply.

"No, Credo. Want me to stay out here and keep an eye on things?"

"Thank you." I had no idea what this woman might tell us, but the presence of an armed escort never really helped me make a pleasant first impression.

The door was unlocked and we walked immediately into a simple tea-room, with unfinished benches and grubby cushions, but a cheerful warmth from a big oven, the smell of spiced roasted meat, and the low chatter of conversation. Perhaps a dozen patrons were taking tea or eating at the benches: men whose build and clothing suggested physical laborers, a few elderly persons taking careful and sparing bites of meat, one family with thin, wide-eyed children, and a surly-faced woman who glared over the rim of her cup as though searching for a fight to pick. A tired-looking elderly woman no taller than my rib cage, presumably the owner, was moving between the rows and topping up tea with an equally elderly-looking pot.

The woman who had approached Kalina was easy enough to spot. She must have gone to the hospital at some point because the bandage covering one of her eyes and wrapping around her hair looked professionally done, not to mention being the only clean bit of fabric on her. There was a wide gap in every direction around where she sat, tearing flat black strips of bread off the round on a plate in front of her and stuffing them in her mouth hastily, in the manner of a person who expects them to be taken away at any moment. Between mouthfuls she seemed to be muttering something, and as we

cautiously approached, she jerked, looking up at us with alarm. She looked
desperate, frantic, half-starved.

"Can we sit down?" I asked her, keeping my hands open and my arms
gently raised, just as if I approached a startled wild animal. "Would that be
all right?"

She looked at her meal, pulled the plate a little closer to herself, then nodded cautiously.

We sat slowly, and after a moment's further staring, she returned to eating. I couldn't make out the words she mumbled as she stuffed the bread
down. The owner came by, offering us cups of steaming black tea and a jar
of honey, her eyes traveling anxiously over our clothes; though my tattoos
were covered we were all too obviously dressed for a different part of the city.
"Haven't seen you here before, neighbors. Are you . . . working in the area?"

"We are not here to report anyone to the Guild," Hadrea said bluntly, accepting the cup of tea, and the woman visibly relaxed.

She set the teapot down and smiled a charming, broad grin, suddenly af-
fable. "We've all had a rough few years, eh? 'Specially those of us nearer to
the bottom of the heap, if you follow. We all try to get by, best as we can."

"Can you bring our friend here some more food?" I asked, gesturing to the
woman beside me. "She looks hungry."

The owner sighed and dropped her voice low. "You know her?"

"No," I admitted.

"She's been on her own on the roads a bit too long, that one, and then she
was at the arena the other night, when . . . well. Don't mind the things she
says. I've told her to go back to the hospital but she's not thinking straight."

The main door opened and another traveler entered, visibly harassed. His
hair was long and wild and his face a crisscross of lines. An assortment of
Darfri charms hung from his neck and he wore traveling boots that had seen
plenty of wear. The owner excused herself and headed over to greet him, and
I turned to the woman beside me. "I'm Jovan Oromani," I said gently. "I'm on
the Council. Someone told me you were trying to warn us about something."

She closed her one good eye, screwing up her face as if she were trying to
remember something.

"Something about the spirits," I prompted.

She opened her eye and it focused on me with sudden clarity. Without
warning, her hand flew out and seized the front of my clothes in a taut, filthy

grip. "We did not protect them," she said in an urgent whisper. "They are murdered before our eyes and we do nothing."

"What do you mean, murdered?" Hadrea asked. "How do you murder a spirit?"

"I saw it," she insisted, but her words slurred a little and she stopped, shook her head, and looked around the room as if surprised to find herself there. "I tried to tell them, but they did not believe me." Her expression grew fearful and she dropped my clothes abruptly and cowered back over her plate of bread. The owner returned with a plate of meat cut from the big roast and a scoop of salty dark rice, and I pushed it in front of the woman.

"Here, eat," I said, and she didn't wait for further invitation, but snatched a dripping slice from the tray and stuffed it into her mouth whole.

"She looks exhausted," I murmured to Hadrea. "I wonder if she's slept since the blast. Might be she left the hospital too early. Thendra said they didn't have the controls to stop people wandering out if they wanted to."

Hadrea, peering at what looked like dried blood in the woman's ear, frowned. "Perhaps we could take her back, if she will let us. A head injury should not be left unattended."

The traveler who had come in before had taken a seat at the other end of our bench, next to a big man who smelled strongly of oku, and the owner was pouring him a cup of tea and smiling. "What can I get you?" she asked, carefully turning the cup on the spot and then pushing it in front of him.

"Some cursed leadership for the country for a start," he said, unwinding his scarf with unnecessary force. "Maybe another shot at the rebellion."

The owner laughed nervously, her gaze flicking over to where we sat. The man hadn't seen us yet but even if she'd not recognized me, the owner must have guessed at our identities. "Mind that talk, now," she said with forced cheer. "Just tea, or something to eat?"

The man requested food but clearly wasn't done with his grumbling; he muttered and swore as he adjusted himself, and when he tried to take a sip of tea his hands were shaking and he put it down again.

"You been inside the walls again?" his neighbor asked. Evidently he was familiar with the story.

"I went all the way to the Manor this time, for all the good it has done." The man made a derisive snort. "I waited all day for an audience and then was turned away without getting near the determination council."

"Oh, ah, bad times abound, though," the neighbor said. "They'll have a lot on their plate, eh?"

"They are looking up their asses is what they are doing. And we all know the only thing you will find up there is shit." Apparently deciding better of his rant, the fellow blew out his breath and turned his attention to his tea and to the plate of rice that had followed. Our own neighbor was shoveling rice with the fingers of one hand and hoarding meat with the other.

Hadrea had been gently attempting to engage the woman in conversation again, to little avail. "What is your name?" she tried. "I am An-Hadrea esLosi. Who are you?"

The woman squinted at her with the good eye. "Dima," she said slowly. "An-Dima esFasa."

Encouraged by this moment of clarity, I smiled at her. "Fasa, to the north?" A village and lands in the Iliri estate, I was relatively sure. "That is home?"

Dima stared at me, her breath coming in short spurts, like she was panting. It was the effort, I realized, the effort of concentrating on us. Her eye kept drooping and her elbows on the table slipping, and I suspected it was only willpower or pain keeping her from falling asleep there at the bench. No wonder she was agitated and incoherent. "Home. They were there. But they are sleeping deeply, and then, the spirits! Murdered!"

"I do not think a spirit can be murdered," Hadrea said, kindly enough, but she looked thoughtful. "But many spirits sleep very deeply, or slowly die from neglect. What spirits have you lost?"

"Outside our village." Her voice was a harsh whisper. "There was a special place. A sacred place. That was the first. They took it. And I tried to tell, tried to warn, but they did not take me seriously. I ran so far and they were there, and they . . . gone. I felt it, and . . ." She trailed off again, rubbing her forehead. Her hand slipped and her head jerked down suddenly as if the hand had been load bearing.

"We should take her back to the hospital," Hadrea said with more certainty. "I do not think she is safe to leave on her own."

I nodded. "Let her finish her food, then we'll see if we can get her there."

Meanwhile, the man down the bench had started up his complaint again. "It was not just for my own sake that I went," he was muttering. "If the local council could not find her, I expected nothing more from the city one. But this is about more than me, and they are running scared instead of listening."

"Any's the wonder?" the neighbor said, a touch incredulously. He leaned closer, brandishing one hand to punctuate his words. "Did you not hear? On top of the arena massacre, the Heir's dead, and most of the Leka family to boot, I heard. You can't trust Order Guards, you can't trust the army. War's coming, my friend, and they're picking off the rich and powerful first. They're right to be running scared."

The Darfri man pressed his lips together and breathed hard out of his nose. One of his hands fingered the charm around his neck absently. "Perhaps so. But they are looking in the wrong places for their war, and if you try to tell them this, they do not listen. The Compact is meaningless. They have learned nothing from their past."

I hadn't meant to eavesdrop, but what he was saying sounded like an echo of Dima's words.

"Excuse me just a moment," I told Dima, who had moved a jealous hand between her plate and Hadrea and was leaning over the food like a guard. I spun around on my cushion and faced the man.

"Where should the Council be looking?" I asked.

The man snorted and set down his tea as he looked me up and down. "The same place as last time. In its own yard. Why, do you have some secret way of making them listen?"

"I'm on the Council," I said flatly. "I'm Jovan Oromani." While he looked me up and down suspiciously, I shrugged the fabric off my arm so he could see my tattoos. "This is my friend, An-Hadrea esLosi. We're here and we're listening. What were you trying to tell the Council?"

He looked taken aback, but only for a moment; soon his chin returned to its defiant, defensive position. "My auntie," he said. "She disappeared. She went for water one night and never came back."

"I'm sorry to hear that," I said. "The authorities couldn't find out what happened?"

He looked like he was going to spit, but glanced at the owner and thought better of it. His expression was very sour when he answered. "The town administrator set one of her people on it. He couldn't find any sign of a struggle or any body so he decided she must have left on her own."

"And you don't believe that."

The man snorted again. "No one who knew my aunt would believe that. Devoted to the town, she was. The administrator knew that too, but it was more convenient to claim Jesta left of her own volition. Allowed her to paint her as unreliable."

"So you took it further?" There was clearly more to this story than just one missing woman and a grudge with a local administrator; however tragic, it could hardly be blamed on the Council. But I didn't want to anger him or have him close up and stop talking, either. "To your local council?"

"Our village does not have a determination council. I walked to the next town," the man said grimly. "But they would not hear my complaint."

"Where are you from?" I asked. "Somewhere local?"

"No. I am from Lot's Rise."

I frowned. There was something vaguely familiar about the name Lot's Rise. I'd never been there but I thought I must have seen it on a map or written down somewhere recently, because I felt sure it was a town to the north.

"In the Iliri lands," he clarified, confirming my guess.

"And what do you think happened to your aunt? Someone killed her? Took her?"

A long pause. "Something bad. I am not the only one. I heard about others, and I met some of their families in the town. There are people all over Iliri and Oromani lands." He gave a mocking little bow of the head as he looked at my tattoo. "Did you not know that?"

Our own lands. I shook my head slowly. "You're saying there are other missing people like your aunt. From other villages?"

"That is what I have been trying to tell the authorities. A girl from Kakiu. A woman in Salt. There was a family I heard of who lost even a grandmother way up in Rokan, and the authorities there were sure she had wandered off into the hills and been eaten by a taskjer or fallen down an old mine. A grandmother who grew up in those hills!" He shook his head. "But no one in the town would listen, and no one in your fancy capital would even give me a chance to speak. No citizens are being permitted to bring appeals to the Silastian determination council, and when I sought to complain about being denied access to this justice I was told the Council itself would not hear complaints, either." He pushed back from the bench and I had to resist the urge to grab his arm to keep him close as he started to stand. There was still more to this story, and something told me I needed it.

"Please. I'm here and I'm listening. The Council might be focused on other things right now but I'm here in front of you."

Something in him seemed to sag, like invisible strings holding him upright had suddenly loosened. He sat again, and dragged both his hands through his wild hair. He looked exhausted.

"We have wronged the spirits. They are abandoning us."

Dima stopped sucking the last of the meat juice from her sleeve and looked urgently down the table. "A hundred and fifty years the spirit's been at our village," she said. "We've driven away its protections somehow and some wickedness has killed it." It was the most coherent sentence we'd had out of her, and her one visible eye gleamed with tears as she said it, as though it was coming at great personal cost.

"You think the spirits had something to do with your aunt's disappearance?" I asked the man, looking between our two sources.

"She disappeared without anyone seeing a thing amiss," he said, and the set of his jaw suggested he'd had to defend this position more than once.

"Wouldn't be the first person to want a change, eh, though? Would she?" The man beside him, who had been silently consuming an alarming number of fried beetles while we spoke, gave his neighbor a nudge. "'S'a lot of reasons someone might want to disappear."

The traveler glared at him. "Jesta would not willingly walk away from her family. Nor her duty to our spirits. She would never have abandoned us without a conduit to them, not now of all times."

"Her duty—was your aunt a Speaker?" I asked. My mouth had gone dry, though I could not quite say why.

He frowned. "Yes. Her grandmother was a very powerful Speaker and Jesta was the last to be taught the ways in a long time." He looked at my tattoos again, and I felt blood rush to my face and shame press against my ribs. The underdevelopment of Speakers across the country was the fault of families like mine, whether through deliberate malice or unforgivable neglect. I made myself meet his eyes, and he continued, with a touch of pride, "Jesta of Lot's Rise is a name known all round our parts. When the spirit at Tenrowan Creek died, who do you think they called on first? To say she would just abandon us is—"

"Tenrowan Creek," I repeated, and now I remembered the map on which I had seen the name Lot's Rise. Hadrea's notes on the missing spirits. "The spirit at Tenrowan Creek died."

"Or left." He scowled. "It does not matter. The fish died, water ruined. Folks lost livestock and wildlife alike."

"An-Ostada was there, wasn't she?" A faint prickle of excitement gathered static in my chest, the feeling I was on the edge of understanding something; something important.

"That Speaker from the city? For all the good that did. Jesta went in to town to speak to her and all she got was a lecture about failing to educate the population. As if it were Jesta's fault Darfri practices have fallen out of favor! No, that investigation was about as useful as the one into Jesta's disappearance." He frowned at me. "What do you know about it?"

I hesitated only momentarily. If I wanted candor it was only fair to offer it in return. "Spirits are dying or dead in places without explanation. That much we did know. An-Ostada and her apprentices reported the first instance probably five months ago now, but we didn't realize it was a pattern until later. An-Ostada thought it was down to neglect." We should have looked harder, but I'd been focusing on more physical and direct threats, and had been keen not to intrude in Darfri matters against the wishes of the elders.

And yet, failing to take the Darfri and the spirits seriously had almost been our country's downfall. Hubris and greed and shortsightedness had led us to forget or ignore our own heritage, nearly to the ruin of all. I couldn't sit back and let that happen again, couldn't assume these events were unrelated. I met the Darfri man's eyes directly. "Listen. I promise, on my honor, on my family's honor, I won't ignore this. I can't promise we'll find your aunt, but I *can* promise I'm going to look." I fumbled in my paluma for my notebook and pencil. "We're going to take Dima here to get some help at the hospital but before we go, I want you to tell me everything you know."

Chen stood stiffly, hands behind her back. There was an air of awkwardness about her posture and expression, and she didn't seem to want to look at anyone directly. Could be she was regretting her manner with the Councilors two days ago; now she'd had a bit of rest she seemed embarrassed to have been so forthright with them. A shame. They could have used a bit of directness. We all could. It was long past the time where coddling us did anyone any favors.

"All parties are satisfied the assassin caught poisoning patients at the hospital is not local, though so far attempts to determine his homeland have failed," she said, keeping her eyes on the paper in front of her as she reported. "The prisoner Sukseno, formerly of my own Guards, has as part of an agreement to bring his sister into safety from retaliation by his employers agreed to divulge some information about the Hands' network. A small team of my people in conjunction with army officials this morning raided a house in the

Weavers' District on the basis of this information and arrested three members of the criminal gang and seized a quantity of money and the drug Void, which was being stored in a disused tunnel accessible from the basement of the house."

"The tunnels we ordered closed off after the siege?" Lazar asked.

Chen bowed her head in acknowledgment. "It appears the Hands had reopened access for the purposes of their criminal activities," she said. "As you can appreciate, Credo, the task of sealing off the entrances took a long time as part of the infrastructure repairs two years ago, and it is not possible for the Builders' Guild to continuously maintain checks on every access point indefinitely."

"Army officials are now conducting a search of the tunnels, as it is likely other entrances have been used by the network," Moest said. "We're hoping to identify some other buildings they're using." There was a pleased murmuring around the table. "Noting the source of our information was a person who had infiltrated our city Guard, please understand this operation is being conducted as secretly as possible. If the Hands are tipped off about our plan, they will have time to respond. So this doesn't leave this room."

"His information was good then," I said. Honor-down, I was trying, but it was hard not to get my hopes up. "What did he say about the foreign connection? Where did they hire the assassin from?"

Chen looked up properly then, and directly at me. "He says he doesn't know anything about an assassin and he doesn't reckon he's got anything to do with them. He claims the Wraith—that's the name he knows the Hands' leader by, claims not to know her real identity—arranged the arena explosions under orders from the gang's foreign backer, and that the entire criminal network was built around the supply of Void from across the border. It's his view that the real money flows back out of the country."

The room started murmuring again. "To where? To whom?" someone demanded.

"So far, he hasn't said. Might be he's holding out for further bargaining. For now, he's told us the foreign agent who gives the Wraith orders is a woman, and she is—or was, at least during the karodee—here in the city. He claims the Wraith took an urgent meeting with her on the evening of the masquerade."

Excitement tingled in my fingers and I had to consciously work to keep them smooth and relaxed on the table. What Sukseno had told Chen checked out with my experience. They'd realized who I was and then come back with a plan to dump me at that party. I tried to remember exactly what the Wraith had said when she'd come back dragging poor drugged Tuhash with her. *The boss suggested it*. He wasn't lying. She really had gone off to meet "the boss" in the interim.

"And he won't say who this person is? What good is this without a name?" asked Ifico, one of the estate representatives, throwing his hands up in frustration.

Eliska cleared her throat. "The Captain has been so good as to provide my Guild with samples of Void, and I've just this morning set my best scientists to analyzing it as we speak. If we can identify the key ingredients we can perhaps learn where it is made. It might also be worth giving some to the research team at the hospital. They can do some testing on animals to better understand the effects on the body, and that might give us some further information."

"My daughter says this drug, this Void, has a particular effect in relation to Darfri communion with the spirits," Salvea said, looking troubled. "Should that also be investigated by the physics?"

Chen scratched her head, the lines between her brows deepening. "Right. On that note, there was one more bit of information we got out of Sukseno. Apparently in the early days, Void was distributed cheaply in the lower city, and it was only later they started marketing it as an expensive and exclusive drug for the upper classes. Parties like the one our Talafan guest died at are a newer source of revenue for the gang."

I felt a dark amusement at the thought of the kind of rich, spoiled people Sjease had said were the type to populate those parties thinking they were partaking in something unique, something to separate them from the masses, when really they were taking the same shit as the people on the streets in the outer village, just marked up in price. "It's an addictive drug," I said. "The physics told me people get badly hooked then do all sorts of things to afford to keep on it. Makes sense that they start it cheap so everyone gets addicted."

She nodded. "But the interesting part, to my mind, was all the sellers in the early days had orders to give Darfri customers discounts. They targeted Darfri districts and sold near Darfri gathering places. Some of the first businesses they started extorting were in the heaviest Darfri-populated areas."

We all digested that. *Why* had the Hands targeted the Darfri? To engender goodwill in those communities? I felt my insides go cold. *Or to help recruit people, people like that rogue Speaker?* The drug was the key. Its sales drove the Hands' success and had allowed the gang to get a foothold in the city, spreading from the lower city all the way to high-class secret parties in the upper. And it had some connection to Darfri magic. But as far as I knew, the Darfri culture and its understanding and use of the secondworld was something unique to Sjona. How did it fit in with a foreign power looking to destroy us?

"Well, it's obvious what that's about, isn't it?" Credo Sjistevo thumped a hand on the table and looked pointedly around at the Council. "They want to recruit for a second rebellion! Our esteemed Darfri leader, An-Ostada herself, said she had had difficulties with some of her students. I don't think anyone could now deny there has been resistance among some segments of the population, sometimes in the form of violence and sabotage, to the new Compact and Council. Our enemies are seeking to agitate old wounds and use these people to their own ends."

"This is not a rebellion," Tain said. "We don't even know what these people *want*, other than to hurt as many people as possible. What we need to find is the common factor between the rebellion and *these* attacks. We can't defend against random, senseless attacks, so we have to make sense of them. Which is why the work the Administrative Guild is doing is of critical importance. We know there is someone styling themselves as a 'Prince'—"

"Talafar? There are half a dozen Princes to the north," Javesto said, rubbing his chin thoughtfully. "Or Tocatica? I didn't like that Hanichii."

"I thought this Sukseno said it was a woman," An-Suja said.

"It's not a single person, obviously," Javesto shot back. "If they've funded an entire rebellion, and been mass-producing a drug, they've got money, they've got lands, and private ways of growing and manufacturing this sort of thing. I've heard from Talafan business contacts there's a lot of drug use in the streets of the capital there, too. Could be it's the same thing."

"The Prince was nearly killed in the explosions," Tain said, "and his sister the Princess *was*. The assassin is not Talafan. The Empire's our best hope for assistance if we fall under a full attack, so we need to be trying to preserve our relationship with them, not accuse the heir to the Imperial throne of trying to blow up our city."

"What about Perest-Avana? Their High Priestess or what have you is a woman, and she mysteriously didn't turn up to the closing ceremony," Lazar said. "Need I remind you all that Marco, one of our greatest traitors, was

Perest-Avani? What explanation did their delegation give for not attending? Very suspicious if you ask me."

Budua pursed her lips. "The diplomatic office made some . . . subtle inquiries in that regard. Evidently the entire contingent came down with a vomiting illness on the evening of the closing ceremony and decided not to attend at the last minute."

"Can anyone verify that?"

There was a quiet cough from the corner, and everyone turned to look at the boy who sat behind Tain, notebook in one hand, the other raised, quavering, in the air. "Uh, Honored Councilors?"

"Yes, Erel?" Tain smiled encouragingly, pushing himself to the side to give the room full view of his nervous young page. "What is it?"

"It's just . . . if you remember, you had gifts made for each of the delegations? The lanterns?"

Tain looked blank for a moment, then suddenly nodded. "Yes, yes of course. The Guild's idea, wasn't it?" He looked over at Budua. Did I imagine a tiny bit of desperation in that glance? What had Erel said the other day? That it was normal to forget things? I scrutinized my friend's dull skin, bright eyes, and thin cheeks, and wondered suddenly just how much of the slack his page really was picking up.

"Yes, each delegation was gifted with a lantern made by one of the Artists' Guild's best artisans," she said, glancing at Marjeta beside her, "with a message of goodwill for the season. The Chancellor added his own signature and delivered them to the delegations before the ceremony."

"I delivered the lanterns to all of the western delegations," Erel said, his voice squeaking uncertainly. "And, well, if anyone was sick in the Perest-Avani residence, they didn't look it, and they didn't say anything. I talked to that, uh, the very . . ." He paused, looked down at his lap in obvious embarrassment, and tried again. "There was a translator, a lady, there in the room when I delivered it, and she said she would give it to the High Priestess, and that was only a few hours before the ceremony." Significant mumbles followed this pronouncement, but I also saw several people around the room give an understanding smirk and realized the reason for Erel's fumbling—he'd been about to describe the extremely attractive diplomat, Abaezalla somebody, who Kalina had dealt with a few times. To a fifteen-year-old boy, she must look like something straight out of his imagination. But more critically, she was someone Kalina already held suspicions about. She'd shown far too much interest in our family and been around town meeting too many other countries' delegations for a supposed linguist here only for translation for a reclusive religious leader.

"We're getting closer to solving this," I said slowly, but with building excitement. "Everyone, listen. We're nearly there, I can feel it. If we just put our efforts into putting it together, we can do this. We've got all the clues we need to find our enemy." I got to my feet, unable to keep still. "We've got an assassin from somewhere we can't identify, working for the same foreigner who's controlling this gang, and they're using the same sorts of tools they did last time. People sympathetic to Aven. Maybe some disaffected Darfri. Someone based in another country, someone with significant power and influence and money, wants our country destroyed. The first plan was indirect and it didn't work, but they've adapted now. They spent the last two years financing a criminal network based on a drug we've never seen, which has an effect on the very people who saved the city from ruin last time. That's not a coincidence. I'm hearing rumors about missing people on the estates, and we already knew strange things were happening with the spirits. They've sabotaged our relationship with our neighbors. If we find out who they are, and we *can*, we're nearly there, then we can stop whatever's coming."

"A lot of this assumes Sukseno's information is good, Credo," Chen said cautiously. "I did warn you people in his position can sometimes give the information they know you want to hear. Like I told you, the next thing he's asking for is going to be Aven's release."

"Aven's release!" Lazar looked like he was in danger of bursting. His eyes bulged and his round figure quivered with outrage. "I would die first!"

"Forgive me, Credo Jovan," Moest said. He looked genuinely reluctant, shuffling his weight between his feet, speaking slower than usual, as if every word had to be dragged out. "I do not doubt the work you have done, the danger you have placed yourself in in pursuit of this enemy. But I think we do have to consider an alternative explanation."

The room went quiet and everyone took their seats again.

"An alternative explanation?" I asked. "An alternative to what?"

"You and the Chancellor both have suffered a great deal of betrayal in your lives," he said, his tone as gentle as Etan's had ever been. "Seen your world uprooted and your families murdered, and given as much as anyone could ask of you to try to secure the future of our country against long odds. It's understandable that you've been putting your best efforts into making sure you stay ahead of another conspiracy."

"Moest, you don't need to read our eulogies," Tain said impatiently. "If you have an alternative theory about what is going on and what our next steps should be, let's just hear it, all right?"

The Warrior-Guilder set his shoulders and looked around the room. "I think there is a real chance every single thing you've told us is right, but you're searching for a missing part that doesn't exist."

"What do you mean?" I frowned. "What part doesn't exist?"

"What I mean is we've seen enough evidence, much of it uncovered by Credo Jovan personally, to satisfy any determination council about exactly what's been happening in the two years since the siege," Moest said. "You just don't realize you've finished already. You're still looking for a mastermind, but looking at what's in front of me, it's clear you already found her." He spread his hands. "I don't dispute there may well be foreign money or drugs involved. But I've listened to a lot of information in the last few days and if you ask my honest opinion, the simplest and most likely explanation is this is *Aven's* conspiracy, just like it was two years ago. It was Aven then. It was always her. You stopped her before, but like you said, she didn't give up. She just had to make a new plan. She's smart and she's adaptive. It's what made her a good commander, actually." He cleared his throat, as if embarrassed to have complimented his predecessor.

"Of course she's involved," I said, not liking the way many of the Councilors were looking not confused or irritated but thoughtful, nodding at Moest. A few shot glances at me that looked almost sympathetic. "But it wasn't her idea to start a rebellion. We always knew she had backers last time, we just never found them."

"Forgive me," he said again. "But I've spent a not inconsiderable amount of time reviewing the reports you've prepared and presented over the past few years. I take the betrayal of my office very seriously. You spent a lot of money on very clever accountants trying to trace the finances, and you never really got anywhere. The spymaster collected dozens of reports from every spy or informant we have on the continent, and none of them turned up any sign of a foreign government working against our country. I've looked at everything, and the only proof we ever had that Aven was taking instructions from someone else was her word. And we know what that's worth."

Tain had gone silent, looking more drawn than ever. His eyes had taken on a hollow, frightened look. Aven was the monster who haunted him, who reminded him of his mistakes.

"She isn't sorry for what she did," I said. "She didn't repent or show any remorse. If she could take credit for the whole sorry mess why would she lie and pretend she was someone else's pawn?"

"Because she wasn't giving up on her plans, of course," Lazar burst in. Nervous agitation ran his words close together and made his hands fly wildly as he spoke. He'd never forgotten the dishonor of our city's greatest traitor being a member of his own family, and presented with this opportunity to denounce her further, he seemed to be embracing it with enthusiasm. "She pretended she had powerful friends waiting so she'd continue to have value, and you'd continue to be looking outside our borders when we should have had our eyes on the city itself! I should have known. When did she ever make friends with anyone? If she had her way, diplomacy would have consisted of asking people which weapon they'd like to be killed with."

Moest nodded. "She's a convincing liar and there's no shame in being fooled by her. Perhaps we wanted to believe there was some evil foreign plan to take us down because that was better than admitting we'd created the situation ourselves, and built the very weapon that would be used against us."

My head had started to hurt. The things he was saying *seemed* to make sense, but they weren't quite right. But the conversation kept moving and I didn't have time to pinpoint the things wrong with it. "We *did* create the situation ourselves, yes, but that doesn't mean someone wasn't using it to their own advantage."

"I agree! *Aven* was." Moest had most of the room nodding along now. I felt the ground slipping away from me, and I could do nothing about it. "Afterwards, we knew we wouldn't get all her loyalists but we were too slow to make links between the drugs and the Hands and her. We thought we had her safely out of trouble, but mistakes were made. She was allowed contact with Guards, given chances to get her message out to her remaining friends."

Javesto leaned in, shaking his head as if from a daze. "You were the one who tried to warn us, Credo Jovan. To our shame, we as a Council chose not to take those concerns seriously enough. Captain Chen brought report after report seeking further resources to deal with crime and drug use but too many of us had family indulging in some of these . . . less savory activities, and we were embarrassed, or perhaps it wasn't in our interest to try to outlaw what we saw as harmless recreation."

"The drugs and the criminal network were how she built up money and control again, right under our noses," Moest continued. "She only needed a couple of the Guards on her side to have regular contact. Who better to have onside than a Guard, who can go anywhere in the city, however unsavory, and pretend to be investigating?"

"But the Prince, and the Wraith—" I started to say.

"There is no Prince, I'd lay bets. Just an excuse for a memorable name and a symbol they can easily mark round the city. And the Wraith's likely just one more henchman. If we were to unmask her, I'd lay odds on finding a soldier or former soldier in there. Someone with a connection to Aven."

Chen, even Chen, was nodding now. "Sukseno told a convincing story about the Wraith not really being in charge, and he's worked around criminals too long not to know the best lies are the ones that are as true as possible. She *was* taking orders from someone, but maybe someone a bit closer to home, eh? And instead of letting us focus on Aven as we might otherwise naturally have done, given her history, he's sending us hunting down mysterious foreign agents and trying to make deals to get her out."

"The Warrior-Guilder confessed her involvement to your own sister," Lazar exclaimed. "And Credola Kalina's word is surely more than enough evidence for everyone here." Funny, how suddenly Kalina was such a respected voice to people who'd largely ignored her existence or infantilized her for years. "It cannot be disputed that Aven established or at least informed and joined forces with this criminal gang. You've all heard they hired an assassin—and such things do exist, you should remember, my dear Councilors! My own dear great-grandmother herself was murdered by an assassin! The famous Red Piper!"

His grandmother had choked on a fish bone and as far as my family knew had never even met the infamous Red Piper, but again, what would be the point in saying so?

"And this was no mere brute of an assassin, as you yourself reported, Credo Jovan! Committing not just murder but nefarious attempts to influence your reputation, so we've heard!"

I tried to keep myself calm, but the twitching had begun and I had to keep track of the flexing of my muscles, counting in my head, over and over, and it was so hard to do that and also make a coherent argument at the same time.

"Yes, true, but where does he come from? If he's just hired by the Hands, why did he have a book in some kind of other dialect or code?"

"Perhaps the Scribe-Guilder could assist here? I understand that evidence is in her Guild's custody."

Budua shuffled in her seat. She had the air of someone considering hard the effect of her words, perhaps sensing the tide of the room and wishing to ensure her answer didn't make things worse. "There has not been enough time to learn anything of significance," she said. "Certainly the language fragments we cannot identify are from no known variation of Sjon, but they appear consistent with the form of the rest of the words."

"What about the contents?"

"An expert in every country on the continent has been asked to consider the document. None recognize the cultural markers described in it. The religion apparently depicted does not resemble any known religion or culture." She scowled and adjusted her glasses, apparently offended to have been so defeated, even if only temporarily.

"The point is, wherever he comes from, it isn't Sjona," I said. "How are the Hands supposed to have found and hired him? And why? He barely speaks the language at all. Have any of you tried talking to him?"

"We've all heard from the determination council, same as you, Credo Jovan," Lazar said, bristling. "The man doesn't speak. He doesn't respond to anything. No threats or bribes or anything at all. What would you have us do? Torture the man?" He gave a theatrical shudder. "That kind of violence is one of the things Sjona has always stood against."

"I didn't say to torture him," I said, reining in my frustration with some effort. "I said he wasn't Sjon. I don't know what he is, and neither do the top experts in the country. Doesn't that concern you? And what about that Darfri woman—who was no Speaker An-Ostada recognized, by the way, but *someone* taught her—where did she come from? And what did she want?"

"Chaos! Destruction! Who knows with these people!" Javesto said. "You're searching for logic in the actions of illogical people! Aven just wants us to burn, she wants the whole city to suffer for her own sense of ego or revenge or whatever it is. She's not the only one ever born with that character flaw, Jovan. There *are* fundamentally bad people in this world, people not all the rehabilitation sponsors in the wide land could help. Our ancestors knew that and we shouldn't forget it, either. Just because we are more enlightened now doesn't mean every child born thinks the same way."

"The assassin did react to your family name, Jovan," Chen pointed out. "It's pretty clear there's a personal focus on the Oromanis. Who hates your family like Aven, eh? Between your sister and yourself you ruined her last plot and so it's personal."

"He makes some sense," Il-Yoro said, grudgingly. "It does fit. And let us not forget the baseless accusations thrown at An-Hadrea only a week ago. It is entirely possible her reputation was a target of Aven's people as well. Did you not say yourself at the time it was likely designed to cause division, to turn us on each other?"

"Well, now, wait just a moment there." Sjistevo waved an angry finger. "There *were* Darfri sabotages. My boat—"

"Your boat was a petty prank, Sjistevo, not a terrorist act."

"Do you know that for sure? Show me the people responsible if you expect me to believe it. Clearly the Hands and Aven had some Darfri onside. At least one Speaker, you can't deny that. Some of us saw her at the arena, conjuring wind and fire with her bare hands!"

"Hold, hold, Credo Sjistevo," Lazar said urgently. He looked around the room, puffing out his chest and holding his hands spread wide. "No one is saying most Darfri or even a lot of them are involved in this mess. We all saw what An-Hadrea and her people did at the arena, and at the siege. We don't doubt her loyalty."

"Well, *some* of us do not," Salvea said, icy.

"Peace, An-Salvea," Lazar begged. "Emotions are high, but like I said, they only need a few bad fruits, so to speak, a few who would have preferred if the city had fallen two years ago. They've been learning some sorcery or what have you. All I'm saying is that all the ingredients for this terrible disaster at the arena could be found right here in Sjona, and we need to find and stop these internal villains as our priority."

My frustration rose. "That's like trying to stop the knife and not the person wielding it. We've got clues, finally, about who it is, and you want to focus our efforts on the weapon."

"I wouldn't suggest we stop looking into the foreign connections," Moest said, in what he probably imagined to be a reassuring manner, but with an edge of condescension that made my anger flare hotter. "There might well be foreign backers. Just that we make rooting out the local conspirators our priority and not allow ourselves to become distracted by the errands this Sukseno, who we *know* is passionately loyal to my predecessor, has left us."

"What do you mean by distracted, though? Wasn't it just a moment ago we were agreeing the Perest-Avani delegation was suspiciously absent from the arena? And the drugs are likely coming in from out of the country? And the assassin definitely did not come from here?" I bunched my fingers in my hair, feeling the strongest urge to pull on it and scream, like a children's illustration of frustration. What was *happening* here, right under my nose? We were close to answers and now they were talking themselves out of looking for them? "This conspiracy is bigger than bloody Aven!"

"I agree it's likely there's some foreigners mixed up in it," Moest continued calmly. "I don't like the coincidental illness but you've got to admit the Perest-Avani are also an obvious target for misdirection. You said yourself the assassin used poisons to cause illness before; let's not rule out the possibility that he's laid a false trail by dosing their delegation. Indeed perhaps this affectation 'Prince' is deliberately intended to throw suspicion on Talafar or Tocatica, and toward male conspirators? It seems within the realms of my predecessor's sense of humor."

I could do nothing but stare at him. The conversation had veered entirely out of my control. "Are we going to at least investigate it?" I asked, incredulous. "We should be getting more information from Sukseno and any of the Hands we've captured. We should be looking into what's happening on our estates. The missing people. The dead spirits. I spoke to some people last night—"

"Honestly, how many more people does this conspiracy need to have to satisfy your sense of scale, Jovan?" Sjistevo looked like he was refraining from rolling his eyes at me only out of white-knuckled effort.

Javesto put up a restraining hand, glaring at his colleague, then turned a sympathetic expression on me. "It's just that we have people being murdered by the hundreds here in the city. Two of our own are dead. Families of Councilors have been attacked in the most cowardly fashion. And conniving known traitors who might well be trying to distract us from the murderer we already have under our noses. The criminal behind the Hands might style himself a Prince, but that doesn't mean he is one, or that he is even a he. Let's keep looking into things, eh, and maybe An-Ostada can send someone back out to the estates, but the priority should be rounding up the Hands first and foremost. Whoever else might be involved, we know they're out there, we know they have money and maybe some more explosives. Let's get them into custody and shut this thing down, and then we can start repairing our relationships with the neighbors we've gravely offended."

"And what of me?" A cold and quavering voice rang out over the discussion. Karista, who had been tight-lipped and stiff at the far end of the table from me, finally spoke. "It is not *just* Credo Jovan's family who has been targeted. It was *my* family murdered in the hospital in droves. That assassin wasn't indiscriminate. He was finding people with Leka tattoos. You say we're being distracted by Aven and Sukseno, well, I see a room distracted from the actions of certain members of this Council, who deal in secrets and lies and do not honor our laws or our division of responsibilities! Credo Jovan dodges questions whenever they are asked. He tells us of a grand conspiracy against his family but it seems to me it is *other* families who have suffered, often to his gain!"

"Not this again." Eliska rubbed a weary hand over her face. "Honor-down, Karista, haven't we had enough of this?"

"How am I supposed to trust this Council when it is ignoring what has happened to my family! One of the most honored, respected families in this country, blasted to a bare few, and we are still sitting here indulging Jovan's farfetched theories! I'll have had enough when people are held to account for their actions, that's when!"

Sjistevo, clearly sensing an opportunity, laid a hand on his colleague's shoulder. "Credola Karista's losses are indeed substantial," he said. "And it is understandable that she has questions that we—"

"*Stop.*" Tain banged the table, but he didn't look angry. He ran a hand through his hair and looked around the table, making eye contact with everyone individually until they all quieted. "There's no one in this room who hasn't been hurt by this. Whoever they are, local or otherwise, the enemy we're facing is picking us apart, and if we can't trust each other, we're going to *lose*. They know that. They *know* that. We can't fight an enemy if we're turning on each other. We have to decide, here and now, to meet this together. Someone is coming for us and we have to figure out where they're coming from and how to stop them. We have to."

Salvea nodded. "I agree with the Chancellor. We are all in pain, but it will be nothing to what will happen if these enemies are allowed to continue to divide us."

But Karista was looking at me with loathing and suspicion, and as I looked around the table as many faces shared the suspicion as not. With a sinking, hot certainty in my chest, I knew, then and there, that the Council would not be united on this, could not trust each other, not with me there. Our enemy had done too good a job, too subtle a campaign. No matter that they did not believe I was responsible for the main attacks, they didn't, couldn't, trust that I was not working as some kind of secret assassin, prioritizing the interests of my family and Tain's over the safety of the city, using the chaos against my personal enemies. Some of them, doubtless, believed I had murdered a man in some kind of drug-addled sex gone wrong, and then used my power and influence to cover it up. And we *had* lied, we had ignored Council structures and made decisions affecting the city without consulting them. And we would do it again.

I cleared my throat. Tain gave me an indecipherable look, but I did not meet his eyes. *Forgive me,* I thought. "If I might address the Council just one more time," I said quietly, and everyone turned to look at me. A strange feeling gripped me, of being on the brink. A dangerous and heady feeling. This time I jumped. "It's obvious to me that on this point, our enemy has won. I haven't been running around murdering my political adversaries or anyone else, and I've never done anything in this room to protect my personal interests over what I saw as those of the city. Some of you know that's true, but some of you don't and can't believe it. And I understand, I really do. This Council hasn't exactly got a long and glorious history of being honest and selfless, has it?

"But the Chancellor is right. The Council *has* to be able to run on trust or the country won't make it through. We're facing ruthless murderers who are targeting the people in this room and any innocent people who happen to be in their way. They've tried to sabotage our chances with our allies. They've turned us on each other. They want us friendless and gnawing ourselves to pieces while they launch their attacks, and so far it's working." I took a breath, determinedly avoided Tain's eyes, and plunged on. "I won't be part of that. So as of today, I'm stepping down from my seat on this Council."

There were perhaps three heartbeats of empty silence as they digested my words. Tain's eyes, very wide, were fixed on me, unblinking, shocked.

Then it erupted.

"What?"

"What?"

"Credo Jovan! You cannot—"

"Jov, no." I heard the last among the glamour, spoken softly, pitched only for me. I felt dizzy, disoriented, but somehow free, like I was plummeting off a cliff with no ground in sight, just tumbling through the air. *I'm sorry,* I thought, but I couldn't look at his face, I couldn't bear seeing my betrayal play out there. Best not to think about him at all right now, or I might lose my resolve. I closed my eyes a moment, then opened them again. I didn't need to count, and none of my muscles were twitching. I felt empty, calm, almost relaxed.

"Credo Jovan!" An-Suja spoke in a shocked, shaking voice. "You cannot step down in the middle of a threat like this. Your heir is a mere child, and a traumatized one at that, who cannot be left to—"

"I was not proposing Dija or anyone else to take my place," I said, and another ripple passed around the room. Lazar and, to my surprise, Sjistevo, of all people, were both shaking their heads forcefully.

"This Council was founded with six Credol Families," Lazar said, sounding on the verge of panic. His chin wobbled as he looked around at the other Family heads, searching for support. "That must be maintained! There has been much change in recent years but I'm afraid this is one I cannot support. I cannot."

"I agree," Sjistevo said, albeit with a trace of reluctance. "This is not the time for an upheaval."

"Then we are agreed this is foolishness, and Credo Jovan will *not* be stepping down?" Tain had recovered from his stupor enough to speak, but his voice sounded suspiciously shaky.

Sjistevo waved a finger. "Now, now, that's not what I said, Honored Chancellor," he said silkily. "In fact I agree it is best for Credo Jovan to step down, given the . . . sensitivities of the situation. But I do not feel the Oromani family should be unrepresented. The issues are confined to the Credo himself, surely?"

My initial disbelief at hearing his objection faded. *Of course.* His loyalty to the entrenched structures of power and wealth here in the Council overrode even his dislike of my family. "Then I nominate my cousin Etrika as a replacement Oromani representative," I said. "An-Suja, I think you've probably had dealings with her, and many of you will remember her from younger days when she spent more time in the city. She is intelligent and capable and, I think, sufficiently removed from me to satisfy those who are concerned with my personal integrity."

"Etrika has a good head," Budua said. "Clever, measured. I taught her in school, you know." She turned her penetrating stare on me, but added nothing further.

Marjeta, beside her, nodded. She looked more sad than annoyed. "I agree. Etrika Oromani is a wise and honorable woman. I would happily accept her as a temporary stand-in for Credo Jovan."

"Temporary," Eliska repeated, voice tight. I found I couldn't look at her, either. Why were they all taking this as a personal insult? They could see as well as I what was happening here. I glanced over at Sjistevo and Karista; they were whispering together at the other end of the table. Salvea, two seats up, looked deeply grieved, one hand over her mouth, apparently unwilling to speak.

"It is all the same to me," Il-Yoro said flatly. "I do not happen to believe this is necessary, Credo Jovan, but if this will enable . . . certain members . . . of this Council to swallow their petty grievances and concentrate on things that matter to the common people of this country—"

"Like staying alive, for example," Ifico interjected.

"—then I am all for it."

"This requires a vote," Javesto said. He wasn't looking at me, just staring down at the table, one hand smoothing his beard, half-hiding his expression. I couldn't tell whether he was angry or relieved or upset. Likewise with Lazar, who picked at his fingernails and mumbled to himself under his breath, visibly flustered.

"Then vote," I said. "Though you will have to ask Etrika about this and it's always possible she will refuse." The thought of Etrika's face when I told her I'd volunteered her for this mess almost made me smile. *I'm an old woman, Jovan,* I could almost hear her complain, even though she wasn't old by any sensible measure.

In the end, they all voted to accept Etrika in my place, notwithstanding she had never been my formal heir. Different degrees of reluctance marked the votes sourced from doubtless different reasons, but they all got there. It came around to Tain in the end, who had sat, spinning the little water bowl we used to wash hands at the beginning of the meeting, round and round and round, eyes downcast.

"Honored Chancellor?" I asked him, hating how stiff and formal my voice sounded.

"Honored Chancellor?" Moest, on Tain's left, nudged him gently. "The vote?"

It was a mere formality. The Council did not need Tain's vote to accept a nominated successor or heir. But I willed him to be sensible about it all the same.

"I accept the nomination," he said at last, sounding choked. "Though I would like it recorded that I find accusations and rumors about Credo Jovan to be unfounded, malicious, and beneath the integrity and honor to which everyone in this room should aspire." Then, his composure cracking, his gaze accusatory as he glared around the room, he added, "Almost everyone here would be dead if it wasn't for Jovan, and turning on him the second you've got a chance is a fine bloody repayment for everything he's given."

"Honored Chancellor, thank you for your support," I said quietly. "But what anyone believes about me now is irrelevant. This is about having a decision-making body that can function without descending into accusations. With me on it, it can't." My turn to look around the room, to make eye contact with every person there. "With me gone, it had better. Call me melodramatic if you want, but we won't need a Council if we're all dead."

I knew he would need to yell at me for a while, so although I left the meeting before anyone could corner me, I returned to the Manor within the hour to meet Tain in his study, alone. I had made some quick enquiries and the beginnings of a plan in the interim, but he wouldn't listen to those until he'd burnt out on the yelling, so I came bearing good tea.

Tain waited until the servant bringing in the hot water left before exploding at me. "What in the *hells* was that?" he demanded.

"The right way forward, I think," I said wearily, sinking onto a cushion.

"My Heir is dead and you thought the only way forward was to take the only person I trust absolutely off the Council? You thought leaving me without my best adviser, supposedly my best friend, was the right move, just because fucking Karista and Sjistevo are bitching about something?"

I turned the teapot carefully, letting the deliberate motions keep me calm. "This isn't just bitching, Tain, and you know that. Most of Karista's family were just wiped out. Sjistevo's isn't doing much better, and they were struggling to keep the family living on as it was. They've inked in more family members in the last few years than in the whole of their history combined. These aren't petty squabbles and political opposition. These are people afraid they're being picked off to extinction."

"Not by *you*!"

I turned the teapot around one more time and let my breath out slowly through my nose. "Well, quite," I said.

"This isn't funny, Jov!" He kicked a cushion into the bookshelf. "Don't act like I'm being some kind of unreasonable toddler. This was the *Council,* that was your job, you can't just abandon it and let whoever is doing this beat us. You can't."

"I don't think you're being unreasonable," I said. Strangely, no painful swelling of feelings choked me, no constant replay of the decision to second-guess myself sounded from the part of my brain usually so reliable to attack me. I sounded calm because I *was* calm. "You're reacting to a blow like any-one would. I get it. I'm not mad about it."

"Oh, how very fucking noble of you!" He glared down at me, eyes wild with fury. "Afraid I can't say the same. What were you *thinking*? They target your family and set this nonsense up to discredit you and you just let them take your position away?"

"They haven't taken anything away." I prepared two cups. "The Oromanis still have a seat. Etrika is wise, probably substantially more so than me. You won't be alone in there. You have plenty of allies, plenty of reasonable voices. Look." I set the cups down and looked directly at him. "It's like muse."

Tain blinked. "What?"

"When we play, I usually win, right?"

This old argument cut through his anger momentarily and a flicker of competitive good nature passed across his expression, as I'd hoped. "Debat-able, but what's that got to do with this?"

"You make fun of me because I'm too measured." He usually used a ruder term, but the point stood. "You're impulsive. You make dumb mistakes but sometimes you're so unpredictable you just surprise me and pull something off."

"More than sometimes," he grumbled. "The point, though?"

I folded my hands in my lap. They felt oddly relaxed, not clenching, not tapping, no rhythm or numbers scrolling through my head. "I played muse with Dija last night and she did the same thing to me. She let me take her red and I thought she was being careless. But you can't play the spiral dive with the yellow if your red is on the board, which is why you barely ever see the move, because people are always so protective of their red."

"Honor-down, Jov, if you don't blow me away with this analogy soon, the next thing I kick won't be a pillow. What is the *point*."

"The point is," I continued, "if someone is concentrating on attacking a particular piece and suddenly you take that piece out of the equation, you can get yourself an advantage."

"And you've taken yourself off the board."

"The person attacking us knows our relationship. They specifically targeted my family because they know we're an important barrier to you, right?"

"Maybe," he said. "We don't actually know the why of anything, do we?"

"Well, we can speculate. They went to all this trouble, over a period of months, not to try to have you killed, but only to try to make me look bad. So the rest of the Council didn't trust me. They know we're friends, they know what kind of position that puts you in. So, let's make all that time and energy a wasted cause. No one can seriously claim Etrika was involved in any of this, so the Lekas and the Ashes can stop obsessing about attacks from me and start concentrating on the things that actually matter."

"They've latched on to this idea that Aven is the ultimate mastermind." Tain frowned. "They're going to put the best interrogators from the determination council onto her."

A dull chord of anxiety struck in my chest, but I didn't let it deter me. "That's another conversation made worse by me being in it. I can't consider her unemotionally or rationally."

He gave a hollow laugh. "And I can?"

"Maybe I'm wrong and she really has been pulling the strings the whole time. Maybe she's been sitting there laughing herself stupid as I dig around audit reports and try to trace payments and suspect all our allies of working against us. Or maybe she's just a distraction they want us to waste time trying to decipher." I took a deep breath. "Look, what's happened every other time we've been threatened? I've hunkered down, stuck to your side, suspected everyone around us."

"And shouldn't we?" The anger flared again in his dark eyes, glimmering and deep. "Merenda died trying to get us information about another bloody traitor. Isn't suspecting everyone exactly what we *should* be doing?"

"I thought that, too. It was all I could think about at first." But I'd shaken off the instinct to obsess and I did it again now. "But two things strike me about it. One, whoever wrote it might be relaying information but they're not in charge. Two, who's likely to be the traitor who wrote that note? Someone we trust, through conscious choice or necessity. Guards and blackstripes who've been in our households for years, been alone with you or me or Merenda a hundred times. Erel's got your schedule and attends half your meetings—he's a kid, but kids can sell information as easily as adults. Even a Councilor, again." I shook my head. "We can't manage this crisis just between the people

we trust absolutely because a handful of people aren't enough to run a country, so we *have* to share information and delegate tasks. It's the only way we'll
get anything done. And proofing isn't the secret it once was. Realistically, if
any one of them wants you dead, it won't be through poison, and me being
here won't change it one way or the other."

"What do you mean, you being here?" His eyes had gone wide with apprehension.

I took a deep, steadying breath, uncertainty wavering my resolve for the
first time since I'd had the idea. "My instinct is to treat everyone with suspicion, but anyone who paid attention last time knows that. They'll know what
happened with Marco and Aven has made us wary and they'll expect me to
focus on finding a traitor here and protecting you, because that's what I do." I
took another breath, making myself look at him. It wasn't fair to make it easy
on myself. "I think I should leave the city."

Tain stared at me, unspeaking, for a very long moment. Then he calmly
poured the tea for both of us, set down the pot, and looked directly at me. "I
assume that's some kind of stupid joke."

"Famous as I am for stupid jokes in the face of crises," I said dryly, "in this
particular instance, no. It's not a joke." I held up a hand. "Listen. Lini will
still be here, and she'll be trying to work out who the traitor is and what the
assassin's book means. Dee will prepare all your food and you can get it from
our apartments or Sjease or Dee can deliver it. You don't exactly eat much
anyway. And I'm honestly doubtful there's any assassination attempt coming.
They already have us divided and scrambling, they don't need to kill you."

"And you?" He was clearly grappling with his temper, but he held his cup
to his lips in a passable imitation of calm. "What are you going to be doing?"

"I'm going to go to the estates. I think what's happening there is more
important than anyone realized, and I think our enemies don't want or expect
us to pay attention to it."

He forgot to be furious for a moment, set down the cup, and stared at me.
"To the estates? We sent An-Ostada to do that already."

"An-Ostada went out there before we knew there were Darfri mixed up
with the other side."

"*One* Darfri. Dozens of Speakers sided with Hadrea and An-Ostada but
no one with that woman."

"Maybe, but we know nothing about her and where she came from, so we
can't be sure there aren't more like her. Sjistevo's right about that—someone

taught her. And anyway, what did An-Ostada report back last time? That it was Darfri business, we just needed better education, better funding, more official recognition of Darfri practices. That's not an investigation. She was looking for the wrong thing."

"Jov, I know we have our issues with An-Ostada, but even if you're right about this being significant, forgive me, but what good are *you* going to do trying to figure out what's going on with spirits? You're not a Speaker, you're not even Darfri."

I almost laughed. "I'm not going to go alone, of course."

A pause. "Hadrea," he said softly. "But she was *with* An-Ostada, and—"

"And she didn't believe it was being properly handled, even then. Maybe An-Ostada didn't trust her with her thoughts, but either way, Hadrea wasn't satisfied the local people were doing anything that could damage the spirits to that extent. And there's a woman in the hospital right now who's been trying to tell anyone who'll listen that the spirits have been murdered."

He leaned forward, frowning. "Murdered?"

"The woman's got a bad head injury she didn't treat properly," I admitted. "The physics did something to put her to sleep while they try to get some swelling down. It'd be better to properly question her when she's had some treatment and rest, or she'll sound like she's raving. But Hadrea took her seriously and I think we should, too.

"But listen, it's not just the spirits. Like I was trying to say at the meeting, there's other rumors, too. I met a man from your own lands last night. Lot's Rise. His aunt vanished just before the villages noticed the well was drying up and the crops failing. She was a Speaker, Tain. He thinks the spirits took her. He went searching for help and got turned away everywhere, including here in Silasta, but in the process he met others." Now he was listening, not just reacting, I pulled out the map and my notes from the Darfri man. "Look at this. There's a pattern to it. Here are the spots An-Ostada reported dead spirits. And here are the places he'd heard of missing people." I traced the affected spots, concentrated on the north and east of the country, predominantly in Oromani and Iliri lands. Almost every missing person was from a town or village close to or right in a place listed in An-Ostada's reports. "Not every place, but I have a feeling that if I go to these places, I'm going to find more missing people." I frowned. "There's something happening here and I don't think it's natural. People on the estates are scared, they're asking for help and they're not getting it."

Tain stared at the map, rubbing his forehead. "What do you think is happening? You think spirits are taking people, somehow? Is that even how Darfri magic works?"

I shrugged. "I don't know. Hadrea scoffed at the idea but she also agrees we have to look into it." My hands clenched and unclenched in the same half-excited state I'd felt when the man described it to me. "This is something, Tain. I can feel it."

"All right, I accept that. There's a pattern there I can't deny. But Jov, it can't be your immediate priority. There's someone attacking us within the damn city, by all the fortunes!"

"Yes, and whoever they are, they want us concentrating on that, don't they? They want us scrambling and afraid and mistrusting." I tapped the map. "I think they're linked. You heard what Sukseno said. The Hands targeted Darfri on purpose. The drug has an effect on Speakers, and that woman used it against us. It's not a coincidence, Tain. There is a connection here, I can *feel* it."

Tain took a long, slow sip of tea. He might have a short temper but he was always capable of listening, of working things through, and I could see he was giving it proper consideration. And then he turned his sharp gaze on me over the rim of the cup and said, "How does Hadrea know what effects Void has on Darfri Speakers? The physics haven't even tested it on animals yet, let alone people."

"She's used it." I sighed. "It works a bit like feverhead, I think. She used it to help her when she was at the arena. Kalina saw her and she admitted it later."

"That's bloody dangerous."

A prickle of irritation flickered up at the force in his tone. "Yes. You might recall I've been fairly outspoken about the health risks of taking these kinds of narcotics. Even when people have noble intentions."

We glared at each other, and he was the first to look away.

"I know you've been using darpar again," I said. "You think I don't know the signs? Me, of all people?"

He stuck his hands in his armpits, arms crossed across his chest, and continued to look off to the side. I was too tired to have patience with this sulky-child behavior, and he must have realized that because even as I sucked in a breath to admonish him, he turned it into a sheepish smile, albeit one gone in an instant. "Guilty. I did use it. But it was just to get through the last few days. Someone's always asking something, every hour of every day, it seems. I just didn't have the energy to get through on my own."

"Well, we can't expect you to be awake day and night," I said, mollified. "I know you want to do your best, but you'll be no good to us if you collapse. Darpar isn't a substitute for sleep. It's just a temporary mask you can fool yourself with. We've had enough two-day recovery sleeps for my liking, thanks." I didn't ever again want to sit by the bedside of a person I loved, wondering if they would ever wake.

"I'll get some proper natural sleep tonight, I promise," he said. "I don't think I have a choice." He looked so tired, so fragile, that a trickle of doubt found its way into my resolve. His health hadn't been perfect since the poisoning during the siege. Was leaving him now, in the most stressful time since then, really safe? But then, all the proofing in the world couldn't help him from losing weight and energy when he simply wasn't eating or sleeping enough. I would charge Dija and Kalina and even his personal servants and staff if necessary with making sure he rested more.

Tain, too distracted to notice my reaction, was frowning in thought. "How is An-Ostada going to react if we send you out with Hadrea? She thinks Hadrea should be prohibited from using fresken at all, you know. She calls her 'a danger to every human in this city.'"

"And people call *me* melodramatic," I muttered. But discomfort swirled in my belly. With everything that had happened in the interim, I had pushed aside the unpleasant truth about Hadrea's involvement with the rogue Speakers, and had never found the time to explain it to Tain. But now was a time for honesty. "Yeah, I think they've, uh, reached the end of that relationship," I said delicately. "Neither of them has been entirely honest with us about how the training was going." I explained what we'd learned, trying hard to keep the hurt and betrayal I'd felt the day I learned of Hadrea's involvement in the boat incident out of my voice.

But his face reflected that feeling all the same. "Does she have any concept of the amount of work her mother and I and our allies on the Council have done over the past few years to push back against this sort of thing?" he asked dully. "The number of fights I've started, the times I've staked my honor on it?"

"I think she does," I said. "But things got bad with An-Ostada, Tain. I didn't realize how bad. I think we might have made a mistake with her appointment."

"It wasn't our call. She was nominated, we just endorsed it. The Council can't be meddling in matters that only exacerbate tensions we can't afford to exacerbate. It's not our—"

"Yeah, not our business," I replied, weary of hearing it. "I know. I've heard that a million times. And maybe it wasn't, but it's everyone's business if it's put us all at risk. We've left the country vulnerable by leaving Darfri matters outside the Council. She's supposed to be training new Speakers, not alienating them and forcing them into bloody rebel splinter groups, and she's supposed to report to the Council on issues that affect everyone, not hide problems from us."

Tain frowned. "She's not been exactly forthcoming, I agree. But neither has Hadrea, you said so yourself. So shouldn't we confront An-Ostada with this?" He shook the map. "Make her explain it?"

"I don't trust her to handle this," I said flatly. "Hadrea's right. An-Ostada's rules and traditions might well be there for a good reason, but none of that means shit if the other side is using it against us. She *can't* manage this problem. She's so busy trying to make sure she distances herself from people misusing their powers that she's no good to us in protecting against them. That woman came from *somewhere*. I'd stake my honor it's connected to what's been happening on the estates. I want to go there, Tain, and I want to do it quietly, without anyone—and I mean *anyone* except my family, and maybe Chen—knowing where I've gone. Let the city think I'm sulking in my apartments, too ashamed of the dishonor of losing my Council seat. Let everyone in the Manor think you're spectacularly angry at my little stunt. Let the public speculate about feuding Councilors. Hopefully the traitor believes their plan worked."

He ran his hands through his hair and sat there, still, for a long time. "All right," he said softly. "You're not a Councilor and you're traveling on your own lands or mine, you don't need anyone's permission. Just tell me this. What do you think you're going to find?"

I shrugged. "I don't know exactly. But this time I'm not going to sit around and be surprised when we find out too late."

He blew out a long, slow breath, his eyes on the map, his hands, anywhere but me. "And what am I supposed to do without you?" he muttered, so softly I barely heard. My heart hurt, but I stood up to leave, pretending that I hadn't.

INCIDENT: Attempted poisoning of Chancellor Caslav Iliri

POISON: Hazelnode

INCIDENT NOTES: Private party to celebrate birth of C. Nara Ash's twin great-grandchildren. This proofer sampled dish intended for Chancellor, detected hazelnode presence in smoked fishpaste, spilled kavcha on meal, and staged argument with Chancellor to facilitate his exit from party. Observed behavior of other guests and based on this suspect Credo Chys Ash responsible for poisoning. Due to relative ineptitude of attempt and likely non-fatal dose, will recommend C. Chys be made subject to a minor scandal and required to return to estates. Marked for discussion with Chancellor.

(from proofing notes of Credo Etan Oromani)

20

Kalina

Jov and Hadrea left the city as anonymously as we could arrange, with Chen's assistance with the Guards at the gate and a cover story of a wealthy merchant family sending their heirs out of the city to safety. It was not an uncommon story, and Jov was banking on no one expecting him to leave the Chancellor in these circumstances. We'd said our goodbyes in private, just the four of us and Dee, to minimize the chances of anyone recognizing our faces at the harbor.

"We'll come back as soon as we can," he'd reassured me. "You know I wouldn't leave if I didn't think—"

"I know," I'd told him, and I did. Tain had done a poor job of masking his anger and hurt—he'd never been terribly good at hiding his emotions—but I understood why Jov needed to go. From a strategic viewpoint, it made sense. It didn't make it any easier to press him and Hadrea close one last time, though, and have the sour fear in my chest that something could happen and we might never see each other again.

They'll be all right, I told myself, like a mantra. Jov was smart and cautious and Hadrea fearless and tough. *They'll be all right.*

I slept poorly over the next few days and woke unrested, symbols moving through my mind and dreams of blood and water and fear clinging to me like cobwebs I struggled to shake off each morning. Fear and boredom were a bad combination, and with every day that nothing happened, my dread only grew.

Every lead we had seemed to fizzle into nothing. The scientists analyzing the seized drug could say only that its core ingredient was likely organic

material from an unknown plant. None of my Guild colleagues had any revelations about the assassin's origin; in such a short time the Council's interest
in him had clearly waned. He was an enigma, but not one anyone seemed
to have any great urgency in unwrapping, convinced as they were that he
was merely a hireling. Like Sukseno he remained in the Guardhouse, and it
pleased me to know Aven was still sitting isolated in jail, unaware Sukseno
had been arrested and her escape plan was in ruins. But it was only a small
pleasure, because he would give no further information without her release,
and no one on the Council had any appetite for that.

Someone had tipped off the Hands, or else they had reacted with spectacular swiftness to the initial raid; no further Hand premises were discovered through the tunnels, and no more arrests were made, no more drugs or
money recovered. The few Hands who had been caught were visibly terrified
and could not be threatened or cajoled into admitting to so much as a childhood memory of the Wraith or her whisperers. The determination council
could and would convict them, but they wouldn't give their employer up.

The cleanup at the arena and the damage to the surrounding structures
continued, but as days went by with no reports of further attacks or signs of
approaching armies, normal city functions began returning. Shops reopened,
as did the markets and factories, even if many businesses were still directing their efforts toward repairs. Moments of peace, where I could almost
fool myself into forgetting how we teetered on the brink, came unexpectedly: morning tea with Dee, a habitual joke at Tain's expense, resting from
obsessing by reading the book of Talafan poetry that had been delivered to
our apartments a few days prior, with a short handwritten note from Abae. If
she hoped to ingratiate herself with us as a distraction from her delegation's
suspicious "illness" during the closing ceremony, I would not be fooled, but I
enjoyed the poetry without resentment or suspicion.

Dija, to her consternation, was required to return to school, and the apparent return to normal routine sat oddly with me, too. How could we go
to school and work and the markets and the theater like our hearts had not
been brutally torn apart? It was not like it had been during the siege, where
staffing the walls and shoring up defenses had been a citywide preparation.
Ordinary people couldn't be expected to prepare for the kind of attacks we
were facing now. People had to eat, and be clothed, and they still needed tea
and conversation and distractions, perhaps now more than ever.

So while I studied reports and sent enough messages around the town asking for updates—from the scientists, from the physics, from the Guild scholars and librarians—to fund a princely lifestyle for the Guild messengers, much of the city went about its business as usual. Perhaps more somber and fearful than usual, but life went on.

And my unease and fears for my brother and Hadrea, and for all of us, only grew, and my temper frayed further. I forgot to laugh in the right places when Lara told me an amusing story about her son, until she faded off into offended silence, and I snapped at Sjease when I stumbled stepping around them in the kitchen and they caught my arm to help me. They both accepted my gruff apologies; guilt turned my stomach when their wounded looks turned sympathetic.

"I think I'll collect Dija from school," I told them with false brightness, stretching my back out with a shuddering yawn. "I think a bit of fresh air will do me good."

"You've been very cooped up the past few days," Sjease agreed, but their eyes were shrewd and concerned, and I knew they weren't fooled.

"I'm just . . . worried."

Sjease squeezed my shoulder in understanding. "Me, too. It's the uncertainty, isn't it? Not knowing what's going to happen."

I supposed, after all, that was exactly how our enemy wanted us to feel. Dread and complacency, afraid and helpless, and knowing we were not adequately prepared for whatever was coming.

"It feels strange being there," Dee told me, an echo of my own thoughts, looking back over her shoulder at the school as we walked away together a short while later. "Everyone's just trying to act like normal, but it isn't normal."

I felt a rush of affection and connection. "Sometimes it's easier to do that. It's exhausting being afraid all the time. Eventually you get a bit numb to the terrible things that happen, and it gets easier to just try to pretend."

We walked along together, Dee kicking a stone along the street, her head down. We were walking along a main thoroughfare and I steered her farther to the side of the road, conscious of the carts and animals and runners moving at pace toward the center. "Anything wrong, Dee? I mean, anything specially wrong? You're very quiet."

My niece turned her serious round face up at me. "It's just . . ." She stared off down the street, thoughtful. It was a busy afternoon in the lower city, and traffic was moving swiftly past us as we walked. There was a heaviness to the air suggesting impending rain, and a corresponding urgency in the passage of pedestrians and vehicles alike. Two women with baskets on their heads wove past us, one of them cajoling the other to speed up. "—not spending the evening trying to dry this out even if you want to—" I heard as they swept past. In the thick of it I glimpsed a pale northern face, watching us from across the street, and felt a brief spike of fear. But when I looked again it was only a Talafan man I didn't know, in Silastian-style clothes, walking in conversation with a friend.

Dee seemed oblivious to the surroundings, caught up in her own head. I gave her time to think; nothing worse than someone demanding your emotions on their schedule. Eventually she said, "I feel like . . . like the teacher's assigned us a really hard problem, and given us the information we need, but I can't . . . but I'm looking at it, and I don't know where to start. And the afternoon's going on and on and the class is running out of time, and I know I should be able to work it out, but I just can't. So I feel kind of sick and embarrassed and a bit desperate." She took off her glasses and rubbed them on her tunic, adding in a mumble, "I feel like that all the time. A few days ago all this stuff changed, and I want to help and do my part but I don't know what to do."

Oof. I took her hand. "I know exactly what you mean." That day at the Guardhouse, it had felt like a tipping point. Like we finally had the tools to tackle the problem, enough information to solve the mystery. And yet I'd found no revelation in the library, no enlightening conversation with a colleague to connect a mysterious religion with our family or the Darfri or even Aven. Jov had trusted me to think this through, and every day that passed without me doing so I felt more of a desperate failure than ever. *The Hero of Silasta,* I thought bitterly, *well, where are my acts of bravery and brilliant intuition now?*

"Oh, hello," I heard Dee say suddenly, and I glanced up; this time it had been me caught up in my thoughts. We were standing face-to-face with Abae Runkojo, and blood rushed to my face with embarrassing rapidity. She was a suspect, like everyone from her delegation, conveniently absent from the closing ceremony with shaky excuses—hadn't I myself seen her, perfectly healthy, that afternoon at the markets?—whom I should regard with appropriate caution. And yet the first reaction upon seeing her was an involuntary but pleasant tightening in my gut. *It's that smile,* I thought defensively.

She seemed not to notice my awkward reaction, but instead beamed as though greeting her dearest friends. "Hello, Credola Dija, Credola Kalina!"

"Hello," I said, returning her smile, cautious. "I thought your delegation might have left Silasta by now, like most of the other visiting officials?" *Why would you stay in a city that has been attacked so ruthlessly? Why, unless you had some nefarious purpose?*

"Oh, no," she said seriously. "The High Priestess offers her prayers and her good works to the people of Silasta. In this time of tumult and fear, she feels she has been sent by the gods to bring light and faith. She would not abandon the people hurt for the sake of her own safety." She indicated the bag she carried over her shoulder with a small shrug. "I have been purchasing papers and inks and writing utensils so she may spread her word and the word of the heavens to those in need."

"I think those in need might need more than words," I replied, a little more tartly than I'd meant, and unfairly, since last I'd seen her she had been offering far more practical assistance at the hospital. But Abae seemed to take no offense.

"Of course," she said, ducking her head in acknowledgment. "And I know you do not share our religion. But there are many Perest-Avani and other wetlanders here in your city, and few places of worship for them. I believe they may take comfort from the prayers of the High Priestess, if nothing else."

It would be easier to believe her a spy or a ruthless conspirator if her eyes were not so honest, her manner almost childlike in its earnestness. "And you? You are not of the Order, you told me. Do you not want to go home?"

"I am afraid," she admitted, and I noticed Dija was regarding her with a peculiar expression I couldn't quite identify. Abae squeezed her eyes shut, and when she opened them tears gleamed at the edges. "Unless I am instructed otherwise, I must stay and assist. But I confess it, I am afraid. If I were given the chance I would turn tail and run home." She looked around us as if fearing someone might overhear. "I am not brave, like you both."

"I'm not brave," Dija muttered, just as Abae's apparent sincerity prompted me to answer honestly.

"Abae, I promise we're afraid, too. That's the right thing to be when people are trying to tear you down. But we don't have anywhere to run *to*." My mouth twisted, the taste in my mouth a little bitter, a little satisfied. "Besides, I spent a lot of my life only doing what I was expected to do, and now I've

broken the habit it seems a shame to go back, especially for the sake of someone who means me ill."

More than one someone. Did her admiring gaze hide a shrewd interior?
Did she know I suspected her? Or had Moest been right when he said the
Perest-Avani were an easy target for misdirection? Marco had been a traitor
to us, but loyal to *Aven,* not his home country, whose more oppressive lifestyle requirements for military men had ill-suited him. Could a small nation
that didn't even share our borders really be tied up in such a grand and brutal
plan? Honor-down, Abae seemed so genuine. Part of me yearned to accept
her at face value, but I couldn't trust that part, not with everything at risk.

There was a long pause, and when I glanced up at her face it was drawn in
a very serious line. To soften my earlier words, I said, "I finished the poetry
book last night. I think the final one was my favorite."

"'The Long Grass'?" She squeezed her eyes shut in delight. "I love that one."

"I did not know a word at the end." I searched my memory. "When she lay
among the grass. *Manassma,* I think it was?"

Abaezalla tilted her head, considering. "It is a Talafan word for . . . it is
the sensation you feel, when you are very small, a tiny part but an integral
one. When you stare at the sky, and see the stars. She lies very low in the long
grass, so that she can see nothing but long stems in every direction, and she
feels alone, but connected. This is *manassma.*"

I repeated the word, liking its sound in my mouth.

Abae glanced up at the sky. "It looks like it might rain." With a regretful
downturn of her lips she added, "I should return to the High Priestess with
the materials she wanted, before they get wet. It was good to see you both."
She turned her smile first on Dija and then, with a hint of mischief, on me.
"Perhaps you can come and visit me sometime. If you are in need of prayer."

We parted ways and began our passage along the crowded route once
more. "Do you think she's working with them? The enemies?" Dee asked me
suddenly, and it was my turn to quickly look around to make sure we weren't
being overheard. "It's just that she's awfully nice."

"I don't know," I said wearily. She *was* nice. But so too had Marco been. A
memory came back to me all of a sudden. I had sat with Marco in a deserted
building, spying on the street below, and he had shared deep truths about
himself with me. And he had never treated me like an invalid when the rest
of the Council had done so. Honor-down, whoever our enemy was, they had
ruined good people as well as bad ones.

The sky had indeed turned an ominous rich indigo hue near the horizon. "Let's go to the bathhouse," I suggested on a whim. There was one with a children-and-families tub not too far out of the way home, where Etan and my mother used to take us when we were young, before she left the city. "Sometimes a good soak makes it easier to get your thoughts together."

She hesitated, looked down at her feet. A kitsa, a stray by its thin looks and the bald patches in the fur around its scaled spine, was weaving in and out of the pedestrians, and it rubbed against her legs. She scratched it absently with one foot, and said nothing.

"Is something wrong? We don't have to go if you don't want to."

"No, it's just . . ." She swallowed and her voice went higher. "I know the one you mean. Merenda used to take me sometimes."

"Oh, Dee." I squeezed her against me on impulse. "I'm sorry. We don't have to—"

"No, I want to. I like it there. And it's nice to re . . . remember good things." She raised her chin to give me a quavering smile, then she turned to continue walking.

It happened so fast.

Someone going in the other direction jostled us and the kitsa suddenly swerved underfoot, just where Dee tried to step to correct. She tripped over it, stumbled, and fell. Directly out into the street.

My heart in my throat, I flung one arm out and caught the back of her scarf, yanking her back toward me, just as a huge oku, lumbering far too fast for a city street, crashed along past us, the wind of its swift passage whooshing into us in a puff of scattering dust and rock. The driver, standing up at the reins, shouted something frightened and angry, though whether it was directed at us or at his rogue beast, I couldn't have said.

Dee and I looked at each other, wide-eyed. We were both panting, I realized, and closed my mouth, but still the pounding of my pulse thundered in my ears. Dija's open-mouthed breathing alternated with a spluttering cough.

"I'm sorry, Auntie!" She stepped back almost up to the nearest building, her eyes still huge, adjusting the scarf my grip had pulled against her throat hard enough to choke. "I didn't see the kitsa there!"

My eyes tracked the animal; after the oku cart skidded up the road and finally slowed down, a flash of fur and glint of scale showed through the continued traffic as it crossed the road in apparent calm and headed down an alley. I glimpsed, just for a moment, a figure scooping it up like a pet, before disappearing. My blood seemed to slow and chill in my veins and my saliva dried up in my mouth so I thought I might choke. At last, I recognized that pale figure.

"Who was that?" Dee asked, gripping my hand a little tighter. "Auntie?"

I forced a smile and tucked her scarf back around her neck. "No one. Just a trick of the light. Come on, that wind's cold."

The encounter unsettled me enough that I took Dee straight back home instead of stopping at the bathhouse like I'd originally intended. Suddenly the idea of sitting among strangers, vulnerable, was not at all relaxing.

With everything that had happened over the past few days, I had neglected my research into Talafar and its witches. They had seemed tame in comparison to murder and explosions, a milder facet of a more serious campaign against us. Now, I wondered whether it had ever been related to the main attacks, or whether what we were looking at was its own unique thing, a case of one of the simplest motives of all: revenge for a terrible loss.

Because the face I was almost certain I'd seen in the alley earlier was that of Lady Mosecca, Tuhash's mother.

A lighter sleeper perhaps might have woken at the commotion, but I was too heavily gone and our apartments too far. I only knew something had happened when Sjease shook me awake; it was still dark and my eyes felt gummy, my limbs slow. Bad dreams clung to me still.

"Credola, the Chancellor's page is at the door," they whispered. "He has an urgent message from the Chancellor."

Erel was indeed waiting in the entranceway to our apartments, his hair sticking up and rumpled from sleep and his eyes wide. "What is it?" I asked him, hurrying over.

"Chancellor Tain bade me come straight to you to tell you in person," he said, shifting his weight anxiously between his feet. "He's gone straight down there but he wanted you to know immediately."

"Know what? Down where?" *Honor-down, there's been another attack?*

"The Guardhouse, Credola," he gasped. "Someone's set off another explosion and busted half of the Guardhouse up."

Oh, no. Dread deep in my heart, I grabbed my cloak and threw it straight over my sleeping tunic. "I want to go down there."

"Yes, Credola, he thought you might. I've a litter waiting, Credola."

I felt like an invalid, being carried down the hill and across Compact Bridge at speed, but I could be realistic about these things. There was no way I could run down there in the middle of the night.

Devastation, smaller scaled but familiar, greeted us in the form of broken masonry, rubble and dust, and bitterly smoldering fires dotted here and there. Crowds, too, and a lot of noise. The Guardhouse was adjacent to the Warriors' Guildhall and in the same neighborhood as several other key institutions, and enough people had still obviously been up and working in the various locations that the street around the broken building was full of alarmed crowds. A huge chunk of wall was missing on the east side of the building, but the majority of the Guardhouse still stood.

"Was anyone killed? How many were hurt?" I asked anyone who would listen, but no one seemed to know for sure. I thought of Chen, and her gruff, kindly manner, and the leg that she'd lost and how far she'd come, and I was disgusted at myself for how I'd last spoken to her, in frustration and irritation at her lack of accommodation for our theories. What if she were blasted to pieces now, like so many others? Her crime being present late at night in her Guardhouse, utterly dedicated to her role?

But to my immense relief, I soon found her, along with Tain, Eliska, and Moest, engaged in furious and intense conversation at the front of the building. Chen had clearly not been in the Guardhouse; she, like me, wore nightclothes and a coat thrust over the top. Her false leg gleamed in the moonlight. Tain spotted me and threw an arm around my shoulders, drawing me close. I leaned in, blinking back unexpected tears. I hadn't cried for days and the one Order Guard I had a personal relationship with was here in front of me, distraught but uninjured. I didn't understand why now, of all times, I should cry.

"—planted it and got out of the way," an Order Guard was reporting. He was very young, with a freckled face and plaited hair, and his voice shook. "A witness across the street saw the flame that must have been the wick. She started to cross the road to investigate, thinking it was an accidental thing, like, and then it exploded." He threaded his fingers together, released them, threaded them again. Repeated it. "She was knocked over by the force of it but she's all right. The physics have her now, she's only got scratches and bruises."

"She see anything else?" Eliska asked. Her face was very sooty. She was still dressed in a paluma; I guessed she'd been working late as well.

"At least a dozen people, with them masks, you know, the masks with the slits, the whisperer masks the Hands wear. They came rushing into the gap. She got out of the way, so she didn't see what happened next, but by the time anyone come to help it was all over. They were gone."

"Five people died in the blast, best we can tell," Chen said, looking over at me. "Then two Guards were attacked and killed by the Hands who stormed the breach."

"What did they want?" I asked, mouth dry, even though I already knew the answer.

"Sukseno," she said grimly. She rubbed her forehead with one hand, closed her eyes, and let out her breath. "The blast broke open his cell and most of the others, too. They obviously knew the layout of the building perfectly, knew where to let off the device."

"Where is he?" I asked. Tain's body had gone very still and stiff against mine.

Chen jerked her head off to the side and I followed her gaze. Inside the Guardhouse, in a section exposed by the blast but still protected from the weather, corpses lay out on the ground in a cleared space. "They cut his throat. Ear to ear. Left him there in his cell." A crack of thunder sounded, making us all jump, and a moment later a heavy, drenching rain hissed out of the sky and fell around us. She raised a weary arm to shelter her face from the sudden downpour. "The three other Hands we had in custody are gone. Escaped with their comrades."

We'd done that, I thought. We'd threatened him that we'd leak that he was talking to us, and the leak had happened whether we wanted it to or not. Now we'd never get anything out of him, not about Aven, not about the Wraith, not about anything. I wanted to scream, or be sick, or something, *anything*, to expel the feelings inside my chest.

But I didn't do any of those things, just asked in a voice so calm I wasn't sure it was mine, "And the assassin?"

Chen frowned. "He wasn't their concern, apparently. They didn't touch him." She glanced over to the pile of bodies again, and my heart skipped.

"Then what—"

"His room got a lot of . . . collateral damage, I suppose you'd say. Your assassin's alive, but his legs got pinned under about a boat's weight worth of stone. Totally crushed."

The sensation in my chest, the clawing feeling like something alive, something conscious, intensified. "How bad is it?"

"He's with the physics, and he's not conscious last I saw." Someone else pulled on Chen's arm for attention and she gave me one tired glance. "Maybe you can talk to him in the morning, if he lives through the night." She opened her mouth to say something, then closed it again. She looked twenty years older as she stomped off into the rain.

Tain and I looked at each other, the rain streaking down around us. "If he dies too, and we get nothing out of him . . ."

"Then we're back where we started. With no information and no way of getting more." He sounded calm but abruptly he spun and kicked a rock so hard it struck a building that must have been twenty treads away. There was something so wild and brittle in his face at that moment that I shivered. "Every time!" His voice wasn't loud, but it carried the weight of a shout with its intensity. "Every time we get close to answers they're ahead of us."

He stamped off, leaving me scrambling to catch up. I stopped and glanced back. Poor Erel was standing, bewildered, his hair plastered to his face, obviously unsure of what he should be doing. "You should go back to the Manor," I told him, but he set his jaw and folded his arms across his chest with a stubborn pose so reminiscent of Tain that in that moment he could have been his nephew, not just a faithful page, and I almost smiled, despite everything. "You can come back afterwards," I said. "Get one of the house servants to get some blankets, maybe some hot food and drink, and you can bring it back here. I promise we won't be going far, and you know he won't take care of himself if we don't help him." Perhaps in his mother's absence my firm tone was an acceptable substitute, because he ducked his head and agreed in a small voice. *One more traumatized child*, I thought, watching him scamper off. What would become of all these children growing up in such violence and turmoil? What kind of shapes were we forcing them to grow into?

I clambered over slippery stones, trying hard to keep my balance, to follow in the direction Tain had gone. A crew of brave—or foolhardy—people were up on the roof of the Guardhouse now, just visible through the sheets of rain, rolling oilskins over the gaping hole in the building to try to provide some cover from the elements. I spotted Tain standing a little ways off, watching them as he fiddled with a water flask at his side; Jov had made him promise he would take no drink from any other vessel, and would let it leave his body only to be refilled by me or Dija.

"Tain?" He jumped as if I'd struck him, then looked at me with an expression suggesting he was on the brink of a cross exclamation, then thought better of it. "There's not much to be done in this." I gestured up at the sky. "We can't do anything for the dead, and the Hands are long gone. We should get under cover."

He nodded, eyes still on the work on the building, but instead he sat on the stone and dropped his chin onto his hands. After a moment's hesitation, I shrugged and sat down beside him. I was already soaked through anyway. He shuffled to free the bottom of his cloak and held it up by one hand over my head, like a particularly pathetic parasol.

"Thank you, good sir," I muttered, and he let out an involuntary snort of laughter that faded into the rain so quickly I might have imagined it. We sat there in the dark and cold and wet for what felt like an age.

"They killed Sukseno," I said after a while. "But they left the assassin. You know that means we were right. The Hands either don't care about the assassin because they didn't hire him, so didn't care to either rescue or kill him. Or else they wanted to silence him but assumed he was killed in the blast. But by all the fortunes they were afraid of what Sukseno might tell us. They wanted to make sure of him."

He nodded, and some of the anger flared up in his face again. "Our complacency. We're so used to the Hands sneaking around in the background, it never even occurred to us they'd try a direct attack."

"One of Baina's engineers on her team must be a Hand, because they've been entirely too free with these devices to not have a person who's worked with those chemicals before."

"Oh. I forgot to tell you," he said, frowning. "Sorry. Yeah. The determination council thought so too, even before this latest. They've been watching every member of Baina's team, and Baina herself, for several days."

"You're supposed to be reporting back on everything that goes on in Council," I said, cross. "It's hard enough putting this together without you withholding things."

A muscle in his jaw clenched. "I didn't withhold," he grumbled. "I just forgot. There's a lot going on, in case you haven't noticed."

I opened my mouth to snap back, then closed it firmly. This was just tiredness talking, tiredness and bickering. It was always hardest to hide our moods from those closest to us. "Never mind."

He took a drink from the flask, then linked his hands behind his back and stretched, then shook his shoulders loose. "Anyway, I know someone on the Council's going to say this but I don't think we can assume it was just revenge or retaliation, what they did to Sukseno. I think you're right and they knew he was trying to make a deal to talk about who they're really taking orders from." He seemed to have regained some energy. He had another swig from the flask and stood, looking more resolute.

I hated to add to the burden just as he seemed to be getting himself together, but the stone dread in my stomach had turned when he'd said the words "revenge or retaliation." "Something happened with Dee this afternoon," I told him, and relayed what had happened.

"Mosecca? One of the Princess's ladies?" He blinked at me. "But the Talafan are gone."

"It was her. I didn't imagine it," I said quickly. "I've seen her a few times. I only just got a good enough look to recognize her today. I don't know how she managed to stay behind but I'm sure it was her. And it fits, don't you see? Those stupid rumors about Jov, and it's possible that Zhafi told her the full story about what happened at the masquerade, too, which means she could blame me, too, for my part."

"And you really think she's . . . what? Using those dolls to do magic?"

"I don't know! I tried to ask Ectar about witches," I said. "After what happened with the bird. And he was really freaked out by it. He said it was forbidden."

"Honor-down, just what we need." He paced back and forth in the rain in front of me, like he was channeling my absent brother. The exhausted defeat I'd seen a short time ago seemed to have been subsumed by something else, something brighter and harder and more fragile. "Witches trying to murder you as well as everything else. It wasn't your fault! The Hands and their employer or owner or whatever they are, they're the ones who are responsible for Tuhash and Zhafi, not you, not Jov. Certainly not Dee! She's just a kid!"

"Funny things can happen to people when they lose a child," I said quietly. "He was her only son. I don't blame her for hating us. The court women live very different lives to us, Tain, but one thing I know is how important their sons are to them. They carry on the family name and ambitions. And anyway, parenthood is universal. Our city took that from her, and as far as she knows, my family was the most to blame."

"You're going to have double the guards," he said, voice speeding up, his posture straightening. "We'll get an artist to draw up a likeness and post it on every streetlamp if we need to. We'll catch her." He stopped pacing, put his hand on my shoulder, and gave me his best reassuring grin. But his eyes were too bright, his voice too fast, and a suspicion had uncurled inside me. I snatched the flask from him and opened the lid, and he cried out in response, trying to snatch it back. That was all I needed. I was no proofer, to test the bottle, but I could read Tain as easily as my brother could read food and drink, and sour anger and worry froze me on the spot.

"I know what's in here," I told him. "That's darpar, Tain. I'm not Jov, I might not be able to tell you exactly what the symptoms are or what it'll do to you, but I *can* tell you that I know perfectly well how it changes how you act, how you move, so don't think you can fool me."

Tain opened his mouth to argue, closed it, dropped his hands away from the bottle, and sighed. "Lini, of everyone in the world, you're the last I could ever fool. Don't know why I'd ever bother trying." He scrubbed his fingers through his hair and then sat back on the rocks. I joined him, frowning, but he raised a reassuring hand and flashed me a weak but disarming grin. "You're right. It's been a bit of an issue. Turns out this stuff's addictive. I used it during the siege and it was all right—maybe because I didn't take much— but this time it's been a bit trickier. But Jov talked to me about it before he left and I'm following his instructions to come off it gradually. You can't do it all at once. Don't worry, he already got plenty mad at me about it." He gave me another weak smile.

I frowned. "He didn't say anything to me about it."

"I didn't think he'd protect my feelings, to be perfectly honest, but I have to say I'm grateful for the attempt." He seized one of my hands with his; it felt strong but bony, as if even his hands had lost flesh. "Even if it was ultimately a useless game. There's no keeping things from you."

"Just . . . no more, all right? There's enough going on without me having to worry that you're poisoning yourself to keep everyone else happy."

"I'll do everything Jov told me to wean myself off it. I promise. You think I want to hear the lecture he'll give me if it's still on my breath when he gets back?"

Reluctantly, I grinned. "Tain Iliri. Fearless in the face of a desperate, cruel enemy. Scared into good behavior by the promise of a lecture."

"Be fair. Your brother's power to both shame and bore is *very* strong."

I snorted, but my amusement faded quickly. Now that we knew who to look for we could keep Mosecca from getting close to me. But my brother, the man she thought had killed her son, was out on the estates. If she could send animals to do her bidding, perhaps the distance between them was no hindrance.

I remembered the great bird, the talons in my flesh, and how easily it had flown away despite the blow from Hadrea, effortlessly gliding above the land, clearing vast distances so quickly it had taken only moments to lose it from sight. I shivered, and not from the rain and the cold, but from a fear and a dread that had taken visceral root inside me.

Erel returned not long after, bearing warmer clothes for us and promises that the Manor staff would be sending down food and tea for the people who had been working out in the downpour to secure the building and take care of the wounded. Despite there not being much we could contribute, he seemed as reluctant as I to leave Tain here, and Tain would not leave until the essential work was done. At least one advantage of the weather was that it had masked the sound and the subsequent commotion so that we were not having to deal with hundreds of bystanders and frightened Councilors in addition to everything else.

Most of the injured Guards had been taken urgently to the hospital and I expected to find the same of the assassin, but he had only been moved inside the Guardhouse near the bodies of the dead, in a hastily cleared room. A couple of physics were looking over him when we came in, and one of them addressed Tain in a low voice, face downcast. Once I got a proper look, I understood why.

I'd seen compression injuries like that after the first explosion. Some during the siege, as well. People could come back from a grievous injury to one limb, or part of it—Chen had lost everything below her knee and had recovered, and hers was far from the only artificial limb around town—but not something like this.

Everything below his hips was ruined.

"We can't amputate," the physic, a short man I didn't know, with spectacles and a balding pate, told us in a low voice, as if not wanting to upset the patient. He needn't have bothered; the assassin had his eyes closed and his body was motionless but for his shallow breaths. "He's on our best pain-numbing agent, and that's about all we can do in the circumstances. Blood loss . . . organs shutting down in trauma shock . . . I'm sorry, Honored Chancellor, but it's only a question of time before he succumbs to one or the other." He shrugged. No

wonder they hadn't moved him to the hospital. Not only would further moving his wreck of a body likely accelerate his death, nothing was to be gained
by taking him there instead of here to die.

Taking with him any chance I had of learning who he was.

"We can send someone for you if he wakes up," a Guard suggested, but
who knew how long we'd have if he did? Maybe, delirious on pain medica-
tion and with only a short time left to live, he'd be willing to speak.

So we waited. Periodically Tain had short, tense meetings with various officials in the corner, or went off somewhere to inspect something. Erel drifted
off to an exhausted sleep once or twice, his gangly, youthful form on an awkward bed of folded blankets. Physics came in and out to check on the assassin
and the other patient, a Guard, whose injuries they considered too serious
to risk transport. Some of his colleagues and then a tearful elderly couple
came to see and murmur gentle words over him. I couldn't sleep, despite my
bone-deep tiredness; I could only sit, and stare, and worry. Tain was right;
no matter what we did, what we seemed to achieve, they always seemed to be
ahead of the game.

But they had left this man here to die, neither bothering about finishing
him off nor troubling to rescue him. Was he so unimportant to them? Perhaps my certainty that his identity was critical to the mystery was a mistake
after all. Maybe he really was just a hired hand, loyal only to the code of his
profession, such as it was. Maybe I was a fool for sitting here in the cold,
betting on the thinnest chance that he would even wake up again, let alone
speak to me.

"Any change?" I asked the physic, for what felt like the fiftieth time,
when he next came in. He adjusted his glasses and gave me a tolerant sort
of look as he shook his head. Erel, who had looked up blearily, closed his
eyes again.

It was perhaps an hour later, when all my joints pounded with a constant
deep ache and my muscles were cold and stiff, that he woke. I had been staring at him without really seeing much, close to drifting off myself; most of
the activity in the Guardhouse had ceased for the night, though the blast site
would continue to be guarded from the outside by some unfortunate soldiers
who'd drawn that wet and depressing duty from their Guilder. He stirred
suddenly, his mouth working, then took some louder and deeper breaths. By
the time his eyes had flickered open, I was already up and by the bedside.

"Can you hear me?" I asked, in Trade, and his eyes focused on my face in apparent response. "You're hurt. Someone is coming to help." I looked over my shoulder. "Erel! Wake up! Find the physic, he's around somewhere."

The man looked at me a long moment. He began to moan, deep in his throat, and the sound grew louder and louder. His muscles worked and jerked and his eyes moved blearily in and out of focus, and still the moan grew until it was a hoarse scream of pain.

A flurry of activity followed; Erel found the physic and Tain came in too, and Chen. She'd managed to get changed at some point, as she was wearing her uniform now, and looked neat and capable and in charge.

"Stay back from the patient, please," the physic said irritably, as Tain, Chen, and I had been crowded close around the man, whose cries paused only for the space of a gulped breath before starting again. My stomach turned. It was a horrible sound, an apt reflection of the horror of waking up to find the lower half of your body gone. The physic took a bottle from a trolley beside the pallet and muttered a soothing string of words—barely audible—as he administered one spoonful, then another.

"It is more than it is safe to give," the physic said, heaving a sigh. "But he should not spend his last hours in that kind of pain."

After that the patient's cries and moans slowly died back and then stopped. His eyes closed again. While the physic checked on the Guard, we stepped in closer again.

"Can you hear me?" I asked him again, and at first I thought he would not respond, but then his tongue darted out to lick his dry lips, then again, and he turned his head a tiny bit to look at us, his eyes roaming over us all.

"Yes," he said, croaky but clear enough.

"There was another explosion," Tain said slowly. "You've been hurt by falling stones."

The pain relief was obviously starting to work. "How . . . bad?" the assassin asked.

"It's bad," I said, and his gaze met mine. "Help us," I said quietly. "You have nothing to lose now. You're not going to have a career as an assassin after this."

"Not . . . assassin." Perhaps it was only the effect of the pain relief, but his expression twisted up so that he looked almost *hurt*. "I am . . . a soldier."

Tain bristled beside me but I laid a calming hand on his, hushing him. But if I had hoped the man might say more, it was another disappointment; his eyelids dropped closed and he didn't open them again. His panting breaths became smoother and even. Too much pain relief might have made his agony more bearable but it also made it hard for him to stay conscious.

We loomed over him for a while longer but he continued to sleep. The physic shooed us away from the pallet again and, frustrated, aware that might have been the only conversation we would have, I returned to my position by the wall. Erel started to fall asleep again, and when his head had completely fallen on his chest I nudged Tain. "I'll stay here in case he wakes again," I said. "But you take Erel back. There's no point the three of us sitting here all night, and he won't leave if you don't. He's seen enough people die."

Tain looked like he might argue, but then crouched by the boy and gently woke him. Erel, hiding yawns behind his hands, made a weak protest, but looked more relieved than anything, and I shot Tain a grateful look as he walked out. "I'll update you later," I muttered.

But truth be told, I'd lost any real hope in learning anything more from him before the man died. He considered himself a soldier, not an assassin; well, that fit with his attitude. His previous behavior had shown us he was more zealot than mercenary. Maybe that was all we would ever know.

At that moment, as if summoned, his body twitched and I levered myself up, hopes rising again. He twitched again, and again, his eyes rolling about rapidly behind the lids, then let out a burbling burp. I stood beside him, optimistic again, and he opened his eyes. This time it was no gentle flutter- ing, but a sudden shocked opening. The groan intensified and then his chest jerked, tendons stood out on his neck, and foul-smelling sick erupted from his mouth and nose. Some of it splashed on me even though I leapt back in disgust. His body was twitching, his face contorted. He vomited again, with less volume but also less strength, and he was unable to turn his own head, so most of it stayed on his face. I stared, horrified. Where had these new symptoms come from?

And then I knew, with a sickening twist in my stomach, where they'd come from. These were not the symptoms of traumatic pressure injuries: he'd been poisoned. Not by the Hands, who could have slit his throat like Suk- seno's if they'd wanted, but by someone after that, someone who did it while he was under our medical care, just like the assassin had done to the victims at the arena. *And I don't know what to do. Honor-down, if only Jov were here!* I opened my mouth to shout for a physic but the words died in my throat. Caution, after all, had been braided firmly into Oromani souls, and at least a dozen people had been in this room and nearish the patient in the time I'd been here, but the person with the closest contact had been the physic. Still, what else could I do? "This man's been poisoned!" I cried out. "Someone, help!"

The Guard who had been sleepily monitoring the patient—even with his legs crushed, after his initial capture and murder of his cellmates, Chen was taking no chances—leapt to attention, and raced out of the room.

The assassin moaned, slumped and drooling on his pallet, and a terrible certainty took root inside me. It was too late for an antidote, even if we knew what poison had been used. He was dying, and quickly. Despite everything, it didn't feel like justice or vengeance or a deserved end. It just felt like another painful, unnecessary bit of violence. "I didn't do this," I blurted out, staring at him in horror. "You tried to kill everyone I care about, but I didn't do this." I didn't know why it was so important to me that he knew that.

The assassin rolled his head toward me, his eyes struggling to focus. His lips, wet with frothy saliva, twisted up into something close to a smile, as if he had just recalled some pleasant memory. His voice was a soft burr, drawn out, as he struggled to form words. "He was . . . supposed to . . . to come for me. I was . . . I was not meant to die here . . . in this foreign place." The smile turned into a spluttery laugh.

"Who is *he*? Why are we important to you, to him?" I asked. My voice was too high, too frantic, but we were running out of time. "Why is my family important? We're not enemies. I don't even know where you came from!"

His laugh became a wet cough, and I kept talking, aware I was begging, but past caring about the power dynamic. "Your employer isn't coming for you. He's sold you out, had you killed when you didn't serve his purpose anymore! You don't owe him anything."

The physic came skidding into the room and pushed past me roughly. "What happened?" he barked, and I stepped out of his way as he quickly examined the assassin.

"He's been poisoned, I think," I said, and the physic looked sharply back at me, eyes narrowed. I gestured at the man in exasperation. "Honor-down, help him if you can!"

"Get me a purge!" the physic shouted to an assistant who had just peeked his head into the room.

"Tell me who he is," I begged again. "Tell me what is the plan?"

The prisoner shrugged, or at least I thought he tried to; the physic was turning him onto his side, letting the bubbly spit and drool drain out of his mouth. He mumbled something incomprehensible, perhaps in his own language, his eyes half-closing.

"Obedience again?" I could have screamed with frustration. "They left you here and then they tried to murder you, why keep their secrets? Whatever you were planning to do, you failed, it's over!"

The assistant raced back into the room, feet slapping, a tray of bottles and pastes rattling frantically in his hands. The physic snatched something off it and forced it into the man's mouth. "Swallow! You must swallow!" he urged, turning his glare back on me.

"Failed?" The assassin choked and spat the dark substance from his mouth and his head flopped back like a doll's. "My work . . . not the goal. Just . . . one of the means . . . to an end. Your end." He laughed thickly, his voice drawling like a drunk's now. Abruptly, his body started to shake with proper force.

"Get out of here!" the physic snapped at me, thrusting a rough hand between us and forcing me a few paces back. "You're making this worse!"

But the assassin, convulsing properly now, kept spitting words out between his clenching and unclenching jaw. "Death . . . is not good enough for you . . . thieves and heathens. We . . . we take *everything* from you first. All . . . your protections . . . all your friends. You are weak and broken. Soon you will know. We don't forget. We are patient. *We are coming.*"

"Get her the *hell* out of here!"

A tentative hand on my arm; the assistant. "Please, Credola," he urged me, and I let myself be tugged backward, eyes still fixed on the assassin jerking and flailing on the bed while the physic riffled through the tray his assistant had brought, pulling out a glass needle. My heart pounded as forcefully as if someone were pressing up and down on my chest. The assistant released me, also unable to stop staring at the dramatic convulsions on the pallet. The assassin resisted the physic's attempts to hold him still, his eyes wild and his muscles spasming. "Help him," I said to the assistant, and he leapt away from me and back to the patient. But the assassin, perhaps inadvertently, perhaps in one last fragment of control, punched out with one powerful hand and struck the assistant across the cheek and jaw; the man crumpled to the ground and his colleague, the Guard, and I all sprang to assist. The assassin fell off the pallet right beside us and his clawing hand caught my coat in his spasming grip.

Almost involuntarily, it seemed, his muscles tightened and he yanked me in close. "They sent me to my death . . . and they will finish you, too. You think I am your only enemy in this city? You are *surrounded*, you fool." He struggled, his body moving in big jerky efforts. I remembered his terrifying strength and speed lurching at me from the cell, but now the effects of the poison had him, and his fist slackened and dropped away. His head cracked against the floor, and with one last twitch, he lay still.

INCIDENT: Poisoning of Credo Evano Brook. *Update:* and Credola Reka Reed.

POISON: Winterberry/slagol

INCIDENT NOTES: C. Evano's body found bloated and covered in own vomit in public bathhouse. Physical examination showed clear signs of slagol poisoning, including distinctive discoloration of lips. Private examination of stomach contents (Brook family did not consent) suggests poison was dissolved in kavcha (substantial quantities of which had been consumed). Widely speculated suspect is rival rushuk player C. Reka Reed, noting considerable history of disagreement and witnesses seeing C. Reka at bathhouse on previous night. *Update:* C. Reka also found dead by the southernmost canal, also slagol poisoning. Further investigation of rushuk team being pursued by determination council.

(from proofing notes of Credola Jaya Oromani)

21

Jovan

We had left the city onboard a passenger vessel heading north, carrying many frightened people, both citizens and visitors, fleeing Silasta and its uncertain future. I kept my head down and my arms covered, and if anyone recognized us, they didn't say. I was grateful for even the illusion of anonymity. I did not want to spend my time worrying about assassins quietly following us through the farms and villages. Truth be told, I had proven myself an easy target. If our enemy had set another assassin to stalk us, it would only be a matter of time before they succeeded, and there was little I could do about it. Most days it was an exercise in self-control to manage my anxieties about everything that was going wrong as it was.

Hadrea, by contrast, looked more comfortable than I could remember. By the time we exited the boat at a routine stop at the first of the villages on the river and made our way inland, toward the Oromani lands, back was the swagger, the self-possession, that had so impressed me when we first met. So too was her urge to tease me in relentless good humor. By unspoken agreement, we had avoided the topic of our last, terrible fight, though the shape of it was still there, like the hole in a hagstone, passive but ever-present. I did not want to damage the peace between us. She had agreed to come with me without hesitation, without second-guessing or criticizing my reasoning, even in relation to my decision to leave Dija behind.

"She would come in a flash, that one," Hadrea had said, her tone admiring. "She is made of fire and stone, both. But out here, we cannot protect her properly. She is safer in a guarded house and in the presence of the Chancellor."

I could not deny that I felt a failure as a guardian, the farther we got from the city, but in any case what kind of guardian had I really been to her? She'd almost been killed. Safer by far to stay with Kalina and Sjease and Etrika and Tain, all looking out for her, rather than follow me into the unknown.

We headed first for the village of Ista, a farming community on my own estates. It was the last place from which An-Ostada had reported, and one of the closest incidents to the city, though still several days' travel out. It was hard to determine a timeline for the incidents, but having studied the map and discussed it exhaustively with Hadrea as we traveled, it was possible to at least approximate the pattern, and it seemed to both of us that the spirits had begun dying or otherwise going missing far from the main cities, then drawing closer and closer to Silasta, like some kind of ominous wave. Hopefully memories would be fresh.

We traveled by back ways and camped in the countryside rather than using the main roads. It was not just to make us harder to follow but to prevent word spreading of our presence. If I was right and our enemy expected us to be distracted with internal intrigue in the city, I didn't want them knowing that we were investigating in the estates. We'd agreed that if anyone asked, we were fleeing dangerous times in the capital to return home to our family croft in Rokan, to the northeast. Hadrea, at least, had the believable manners and speech patterns of someone who grew up in the country, not the city, though she was also a terrible liar.

When I heard sounds of the creek bushes rustling, like someone might be there taking a piss or having a quick bath, I prodded her and spoke in a low voice. "We might have company. Remember who we are."

She rolled her eyes but her grin took the edge off it. "Simple country folk, yes, very frightened of our ordeal in the city. Maybe if you could stop looking so much like someone who is desperately missing his hot food and books, we might be more convincing?"

I gasped in mock indignation but my heart felt oddly light. We were working together, being honest with each other; I felt closer to her, more connected, than I had since those first heady days after Kalina had come home and the world had felt like it was turning once again along the right path. So I grinned back, shook out my shoulders, and kept walking without haste, waiting for the interruption from the stream.

It didn't come. We continued to walk and though I heard rustling again, and closer, it must have been a bird or an animal, because no person emerged. "We might remain city folk today after all," I said, but even as the words left my mouth I saw Hadrea's eyes go wide and her hand fly to the dagger on her belted skirt.

I spun in time for a glimpse at what had alarmed her, but not in time to get out of the way. The creature, an adult taskjer, hit me in the chest with plate-sized paws and knocked me to the ground. I flung my arms up, bracing them between me and its snapping, grasping jaws. Its brown teeth were cracking in alarming proximity to my face, and the reek of its breath dousing me with foulness and gobs of hot saliva, when Hadrea struck it with her pack to the side of its big face. It was a forceful swing and it knocked the taskjer on its side, but it rolled immediately to its feet and lunged back at us again, this time its attention on the greater threat. It almost had Hadrea's leg when I kicked it in the ribs, and it let out a dull yelp and leapt at me instead.

I pulled back just in time and leapt sideways, so close to the crack of its teeth that I felt the swish of its long whiskers brush my leg, and tripped on an uneven patch of ground. My ankle turned and the weight of my pack unbalanced me; I fell, but the ground wasn't where I thought. I rolled, hitting the ground and going over and over, half-bouncing down the slope to the creek in an ungainly and painful set of blows and tumbles through the long grass until I hit the stream in a spray of icy spring water. For a moment it was over my face, up my nose, shocking me with the sudden change in temperature.

I came up with a gasp, shaking water off my face, to see the beast charging down the last few lengths of the slope to hurtle into the water. My bag saved me; I pivoted my shoulder sharply just as the taskjer tried to take a chunk out of my side, and though I felt a painful gouge and sting in one spot, most of the force of its bite struck my pack instead of me. Before it could recover from the surprise of having a mouthful of cloth instead of blood and flesh, I dropped my weight on top of it and pinned it, biting and thrashing, under the shallow flow of the stream.

"Jovan!" Hadrea was coming down the bank now, the belt dagger glinting in her hand.

"Here," I grunted, but with effort; the creature was squirming, bucking, wriggling under my pack, thrashing to get out of the water, and I couldn't hold it. "Quick!"

Without hesitation she leapt into the stream beside me and plunged the dagger, with the strength of both her muscular arms, into the frothing space where the taskjer was freeing itself from my pin. It stiffened in one big jerk, and a cloud of red puffed out in the water. Panting, I let go and stepped back, dripping. Hadrea stood over the creature, holding the dagger firm until it stopped moving and the body lay still, water flowing gently around it, sending the red cloud downstream.

"Careful," I cautioned as she crouched and scooped up the body with a grunt. It probably weighed about as much as her little brother; knee high but muscular, with long coarse hairs along their back in a dusty silver that helped them blend into the grasslands, taskjers were about the only wild animals in Sjona genuinely dangerous to humans. But they usually gave human settlements a wide berth and we were perhaps an hour at most from Ista.

"Did it bite you?" she asked me as she dropped it onto the shore and surveyed the body, dagger still sticking out between its ribs.

I dropped my sodden pack and pulled up my shirt, for the first time grateful for the country-style clothes I wore. There was a scratch and a shallow puncture in the center of a tender spot where I'd caught the edge of one of its teeth, but it wasn't serious. "Got me a little, but it's all right. You?"

She shook her head, and we both stood there, catching our breath, staring down at it.

"They do not usually attack like that," Hadrea said. She pried off one of her wet boots, then the other, and tipped the water out with a frown of irritation. "We saw them sometimes in Losi when I was growing up, but they are shy of people. They only attack if they have to."

"It was like it was stalking us," I muttered. I put my foot on the side of the creature and pulled the knife free; Hadrea took the hilt and crouched by the stream to clean the blade. "Huh." Something caught the light in the fur. I bent to get a closer look, and found a very thin metal chain wound around the creature's neck. It came loose to my tug, and from the end dangled a very small cloth packet, like the kind sometimes kept in beds with perfumed dried flowers and herbs, or clothes chests to repel insects.

"What is that?" Hadrea, one hand squeezing out the water from her skirt and the other drying the knife against the side of her thigh, stepped closer, wary.

My suspicions were confirmed as I shook out the contents on top of my pack. More dirt and feathers, and this time a whorl of hair in the middle of it, dark and curly. Involuntarily I reached a hand up to my head.

"Is it your hair?" Hadrea, face twisted in disgust, peered at the contents, evidently unwilling to touch them.

"Impossible to say, I guess." But I felt sure it was. "Kalina thought there was some kind of magic from the Talafan people. Witchcraft, she called it. If that's my hair . . . do you think it was able to track us because of that?" It sounded crazy.

"Perhaps. I can say that I do not like it." She backed away. "These are dark magics, Jovan."

The remembered smell of the creature's breath in my face made me shudder. "Yeah." I picked up my pack with a shaking hand, more unsettled than I wanted to admit. "Let's just get moving."

We arrived in Ista later in the day than intended, when the shadows were long and the looks locals shot us mildly suspicious. Hadrea pointed out the tree to which an ancient spirit had once been attached. It was a twisted, heavy-boughed old thing, but its spring leaves had shriveled on the branches and it cut an imposing, ominous silhouette against the violent pinks and oranges of the western sky. The village administrator, a woman with a thicket of gray curls and the remnants of a city accent, greeted us politely at her home but with a wary air. These were my family's lands but I felt like a stranger. "We told the Speaker everything we knew," she said almost immediately, before I had even fully explained our visit, her eyes flicking frequently to Hadrea. "I don't see as there's anything else to be said. We've done everything any of those Darfri folk have told us since that Compact. We stopped farming the east field for a whole year like they said. We let them do their dance, or whatever, out by the rise on the days they said. Put their shrine thing in the center of the village." Another bristling glance at Hadrea. The administrator brushed her hands down her paluma more aggressively than its neatly crisscrossed cording could tolerate, then hastily smoothed out the resultant bunching. "No one's mistreating any Darfri round here."

Hadrea raised a brow. "Yes, I can see how supportive you are of your community."

"That's not why we're here," I said quickly, putting hands between the two of them as the administrator's posture stiffened. "I want to ask you about something else."

"Oh?" She looked both relieved and unsettled.

"Has anyone gone missing from the local area? Anytime recently, around the time you first had the issues with the spirits?"

Whatever she'd been expecting, it hadn't been that. She sat down abruptly as if her legs had lost strength. "Well! I suppose the answer to that is yes, truth be told." She blinked several times. "Where's my manners? Let me pour the tea."

"Thank you." We sat, turned our cups, waited for her to elaborate. Hadrea was like a charged presence beside me, but she kept her mouth shut. The administrator fussed with the tea and her cup and drew out the ritual far longer than necessary. I let her gather her thoughts.

"Well," she said again. "We did have someone vanish around the same time; I know it was then because everyone was distracted by that when your Speakers arrived. Our Pemu from up at the way. She was lost and we never saw her again."

"You did not mention this when we were here," Hadrea said; not quite an accusation, but not far enough off for my liking. I touched her leg under the table and she pressed her lips together again.

"Why would we?" the administrator said, and she sounded genuinely puzzled rather than defensive. "It hadn't anything to do with the tree spirit your Speaker was asking about. It was . . . well." She stared down at her tea. "It was a nasty business, I'll give you the drum."

Hadrea and I exchanged looks. "A nasty business?" I prompted, when the administrator had stared at the swirling steam from her tea long enough for it to thin out into weak wisps.

"Pemu was . . . different. She didn't grow up the way children normally do, in body or mind. Her mother took her down to the hospital in the city when she was little and she wasn't learning like the others, but they said there was nothing to be done for her." The administrator sighed, and something wistful exposed itself in her expression, softening the heavy lines crisscrossing her face. "She was healthy, mind! And the sweetest girl, always a smile for anybody. She had such a smile. . . . But she must have been, oh, close to thirty years, and she had a mind like a child's. Loving, inquisitive, but not mature, I suppose. I grew up in Silasta, you know, I've seen people with the same thing. Nothing wrong with them!" She said the last fiercely, as if we had expressed negative judgment. "She was a good girl. Helped her family. Ran errands here into town, you know. Everyone liked her. Well, why wouldn't you?"

There was a long enough pause that I started to fear she expected an actual answer, but fortunately she continued, her voice a softer, ragged thing now.

"She disappeared one afternoon on the way home. We think the smith was the last one who saw her, she got a few hinges and things there. But she never made it back, and her brother, he came up to the town that evening looking." She shook her head with a heavy sigh. "They found her bag, with the hinges and all, behind the laneway fence on the western side of the village. Just the bag, nothing more. None of us ever saw her again."

"That is very sad," said Hadrea in a much gentler tone than before. "I am sorry."

"What do you think happened?" I asked, and the administrator made an ugly little grunt as she shook her head.

"We couldn't find a thing. Never a body, or any more of her things, or even a sign of a struggle. But then she would have gone with anyone who said a kind word, you understand. Wouldn't have known how to distrust anyone." She pressed her lips hard together, but not before I saw the quiver she tried to suppress. "There's a council up at the town by the river; we asked for help and they sent some fellow." She sniffed. "He kept saying she was simple, that she'd just wandered off and fallen in the stream or something. Never mind there'd have been a body! We're not in the wilderness here, there's no predators as would have taken a grown woman and left no trace. No, this was people, sure as every gray hair on my head."

I gave her a moment to gather herself, then set my cup down. "What do *you* think happened?"

The administrator looked directly at me for the first time. Her eyes were a bright, warm brown, and there was the faintest shimmer of wetness in them as she took a hard breath, in and out. "There were some strange folks in the area. I saw them myself."

My heart rate picked up and I tensed in anticipation. "Strangers? Foreigners?"

"Strangers, yes, but not foreigners." She looked at Hadrea, a kind of blazing defiance in the set of her jaw and her glimmering eyes. "A man and a couple of women, and they were an odd bunch. I certainly didn't like the look of him. They were Darfri folks, though; I know because I saw them myself at the shrine, doing some offering or some such."

I squeezed Hadrea's hand under the table but she only looked attentive, not defensive. "They were in the village the day that Pemu disappeared?" she asked, leaning forward.

"A few days before. Not on the day itself, I suppose, but the day before, and the one before that. I told the man the council sent about them, but he didn't think it was important. He'd never met someone like Pemu. He didn't understand how people can be. No one in this village would have laid a hand on that girl, but . . . I tried to explain. Sweet a girl as ever you could know, but she did have a way of staring, and asking questions, that if you didn't know her, well, some folks take offense. She was different, and there are those who can't tolerate that, can't see a thing they don't understand without feeling angry or wanting to force it to be something they *do* understand." She spread her hands hopelessly. "He didn't know what I meant."

"I know what you mean," Hadrea said quietly. She had grown up in a place not so dissimilar from this, and she had been a Darfri child among people who had hated her for her differences. "Did you see them with Pemu?"

"No," the administrator said wearily. "It was only a feeling. I didn't even speak to the man. Asked around and couldn't find a soul who had. But he'd a coldness about him, and a fervor. Handsome enough, but the type I could see taking offense easily. And I didn't like the way he treated the women with him. Ordered them about, had them bringing him things, though he wasn't any fancy lord or even a proper family. He had tattoos, I saw them when he was down by the stream that first day, washing, but they weren't any family or Guild tattoos, they were just nonsense. And he didn't like people looking at him, I saw that right away."

Nonsense tattoos, like the assassin's? "So no one spoke to the man. What about the women? They must have spoken to someone, even if it was just to buy supplies or rent a room, right?" I tried to keep my tone calm but we were dancing on the edge of answers here, I could feel it.

"They were camping, I think, but the miller up the road there sold one of the women some bread and said she was an odd one. Too quiet, sort of passive. Like an oku that learned to walk and talk, the miller said, if you'll excuse the unkindness. He told me when I asked that he'd asked about why they were here and she said her sister was sick and they were stopping to rest a bit longer. Well, I don't know about that."

"You don't think the sister was sick?"

She huffed a little. "I've seen 'sick' like that before, and it's nothing a few days' rest will cure. She'd been using those funny smokes and powders and things they use in the cities. Up in Telasa, even over the border, I've heard. Horrible stuff."

"Drugs," I supplied, and she nodded angrily.

"City business for people with too much time on their hands. No place for it in a good working community like this. Oh, everyone knows some of the old Speakers and such use those things, but they've no business getting young people involved. I'm always on the watch for it after we've had travelers or peddlers through. Twenty years I've been administrator here and I've never heard so many stories as I have these past few years."

Sensing she was hitting stride on a different rant, I steered her gently back. "So one of the women was using drugs, you think?"

"She had the look anyways. Thin, twitchy, eyes all looking at things that weren't there. Giggling or tearing up just wandering round the street. When the man was doing . . . I don't know, his offering or what have you, at the shrine, she was just standing there, mouth open, like she was catching insects." She leaned forward suddenly. "You asked what I think happened. Well, I'll tell you. It's haunted me since, I don't mind saying. I think some of these drugs make people act like they wouldn't act if they were seeing straight. Do things they wouldn't normally do. I think people like that, 'specially ones with a cruel edge anyway, might hurt a person in that state. I think that man saw Pemu and maybe he thought it was funny or maybe he didn't like the way she looked or talked, and I think he took her on a whim, just led her away from us, back to their camp." She didn't bother to try to stop her lips trembling this time, and her voice went high and soft. "I think they tormented her and killed her, is what I think."

We were all silent a moment as this ugly thought sat between us. But then I shook my head. We were past the point of coincidences. However possible the scenario she painted was—and I'd seen the kind of ugliness she was envisioning—this was not an isolated case. Something was happening out here. Drugs, missing women, dead spirits. I frowned, picturing the village layout in my head. "The western laneway where you found Pemu's bag," I said. "Where was that, relative to the Darfri tree?"

The administrator looked up in surprise. "Oh. Close, I suppose. Fifty treads or so?"

"And was Pemu Darfri?"

"No." She looked between us. "What's all this about? Is there some sort of . . . some sort of nasty magic involved?" If possible, she looked even more horrified at this thought, and something shifted, hardened, as she looked at Hadrea. I almost regretted asking the question. This would do nothing to help the Darfri in this town, who doubtless already had been served a balancing dose of resentment along with the changes she'd listed.

"I don't know," I said truthfully. "But Pemu's not the only one who's disappeared from the estates these past few months. Have you heard anything else? Any other missing persons in other local places?"

She shook her head. "Not as I've heard. The man they sent from the town might be able to tell you. But he wouldn't be equipped to deal with anything . . . supernatural."

The problem was, of course, that neither was I.

INCIDENT: Potbelly Market poisoning (19 victims)

POISON: Moonblossom

INCIDENT NOTES: Nineteen deaths and forty-eight non-fatal cases recorded in the hospital were traced to consumption of a red sugar-gum sweet sold in Potbelly Market during karodee. Sweet sellers arrested but early indications are that underestimated demand during busy time led to hasty preparation of sweets and toxic food dye using red color from moonblossom berries, likely negligent rather than intentional. Craft and Art Guilds both tasked by Council with developing standards for dyes to be used in food and fabric, including in relation to toxic substances. (*Note:* this proofer is satisfied sweet producer's mistake was unintentional but intends further investigation into source of moonblossom paste.)

(from proofing notes of Credola Reen Oromani)

22

Kalina

"I begin," Etrika said, as she settled herself on a cushion and pulled the teapot gratefully toward her, "to understand why your brother wanted to flee the city."

Tain, looking harried, sat beside her.

"Council meeting went well, then?" I asked, bringing them each a cup.

"Never in all my years have I heard so many people think of so many ways to chase themselves around in verbal circles. What's the word I want here, dear?" She took a grateful sip of tea. "Oh yes. 'Dithering,' I think that covers it. Honestly, if it were up to this old lady, we'd throw the lot of them in the lake and have done with it."

Tain gave a faint grin and Dee, who was finishing up making the bread with Sjease in the kitchen, giggled. It was a sound we hadn't heard in days, and it both heartened and saddened me. In some ways this state was worse than when Silasta had been under siege. Then, we had been faced with a visible threat: a giant army, surrounding the city. We had known what they wanted and what they would try to do. How could a whole city prepare for bombs in the night? How could we face an enemy who seemed to have infiltrated every stratum of society? Worse, an enemy using our own people against us, to an end game we didn't understand?

"No word on the missing boat hand," Tain said, after a grateful sip of tea. Two days ago there had been something of a breakthrough when a vessel coming south from Telasa had been caught with a crate onboard concealing some kind of dried plant, but the captain of the vessel insisted he had no knowledge of the crate. One of his long-term crew had disappeared the same day as the seizure and hadn't been seen since. "So I think everyone's convinced she smuggled it aboard."

"Does it mean it came from the Empire?"

"The spymaster's agents in Izruitn reckon there's a lot of street people and war refugees addicted to something that sounds an awful lot like Void, though that's not what they call it. I'd say it's pretty likely it's crossing the border from that direction."

"Are they still sure they have the ringleader in jail, then?"

Etrika didn't buy my falsely casual tone, and gave me a level look over the rim of her teacup. "They *are* getting desperate, dear. The Warrior-Guilder and the Captains are all very focused on their raids and their informants, and all the Families seem rather more concerned that none of their own members be hauled up in front of the determination council." She sighed. "Perhaps some of the Council still believe Aven is the ringleader, but it doesn't seem to matter, one way or the other. Whether she's giving the orders or not, this Wraith character and her people seem perfectly able to carry out their plans without contact with her."

Tain set down his tea, looking guarded. Like me, he could not discuss Aven without dredging up memories he'd rather have forgotten. The guilty, pained expression that passed across his face now told me he was still obsessing over the possibility that he had divulged information to her in their conversations that she had somehow used as part of this plot. "I keep telling them we have to be prepared to face an additional external threat, even if we don't know where it's coming from. Some of the room agrees, but right now the Hands have us all running scared. We might have picked up some of the dealers and the muscle this week but no one's got us any closer to the Wraith. And we know she's capable of mass destruction, so that's got to be the threat we're focused on, I guess."

Even with the memory of the assassin's ominous warning waiting behind my eyelids every night, I could understand that. Whoever the "we" he had told me was coming might be, the Wraith was already here.

"Has Aven said anything else?"

"No, I'm afraid not," Etrika said. "The determination council people came in and gave us an update today. If she is behind all of this, she's certainly not saying so. I believe she made one of the interrogators *cry* yesterday. Now, I'm not an unsympathetic woman, but I think perhaps someone might have chosen the wrong career, hmm?" Etrika reached across and patted my hand with her spotted, wrinkled one. "And what about you, dear? Has there been any word from your brother?"

I pinched my lips closed and shook my head. I had known he would not be able to send a message except in the most urgent and dire circumstances, so the silence should have been a comfort. But it wasn't. I missed his counsel, his presence, his brain, and I worried desperately that Mosecca and her strange magics might have followed him from the city somehow. She'd proven herself capable of using even the most innocuous of creatures to endanger us.

Tain's shoulders drooped. He was doubtless thinking the same thing. The morning after the Guardhouse explosion he had tried to convince me we should send a troop of soldiers after them to protect them, just in case, but the truth was, doing that was more likely to draw attention to them than not. Sjease kept me well informed of gossip among the Families through their various sources, and the rumors about Jovan's whereabouts all assumed he was either hiding in his apartments, avoiding the shame and dishonor, or (the more sinister version, usually quickly halted within range of Sjease) with Tain in the Manor, working the Chancellor's will in secret. For now, unless our enemy was sitting in this room with us, they likely did not know where Jovan was. There was a comfort in that. Mosecca was a threat, and a frightening one at that, but she was one grieving woman, and Jov had Hadrea. I wasn't sure there was a person alive who could better protect him from attacks, supernatural or otherwise.

We finished our tea, and Dee and Sjease stacked the bread rounds and packed some up for Tain to take back with him, and for a while the illusion of an ordinary afternoon held. But eventually, after Etrika had excused herself and Dee had settled in the corner with an international botanical textbook and a sketch of the seized plant that Tain had procured for her, trying to find a match, the same worries returned.

Tain gestured at the book I had open in front of me. "Did you get anything out of that?"

The dead man's book. I was reading it as much out of habit as any expectation that it would magically convey new information, but the depth of feeling the assassin had shown as he died had reminded me of an earlier theory. "I've been wondering if it's a cult." He blinked. "I've read about it happening—people in a remote place who are self-sufficient and isolate themselves from the rest of society. There was a place I read about on the other side of a

Marutian swampland that got found after a long drought, where they'd not seen other people in fifty years, and basically treated the village elders as gods. What if it's something like that?"

"And it's a cult who hate us?"

"Think about it like this. What if a person or a family with money was involved in a big scandal, or a loss of honor, some social embarrassment. Fortunes know there've been enough of them over the years. Whole families have had to leave before, haven't they, when their status becomes untenable, as a last resort?"

Tain's gaze met mine. He knew better than anyone about that particular last resort. I hurried on. "Imagine if a group of them left—not just Silasta but Sjona. They've got money but no status because for a big enough scandal word would spread to all the cities. They're bitter and resentful, thinking that Silastian society ruined their lives. What if they started their own community, cut off contact with the outside world over time? If it was long enough ago they could have grown in numbers over time, and all the time feeding an old grudge." *We don't forget. We are patient. We are coming.*

He leaned over the book, tracing the unfamiliar letters amidst the familiar. "And if that happened a long time ago? Over time, language might change, mightn't it? We need new words for things all the time, and the way people use words doesn't stay static." At my surprised expression, Tain raised an eyebrow. "You told me that last week." He adopted a sanctimonious tone and wagged his finger. "And you say I don't listen! Unfairly maligned, again!"

I grinned. "Sorry. Habit."

"Not just a pretty face, you know," he said. He looked back at the book. "So if that's it, what, they just made it their life's work to get back at the city?"

"It sounds stupid when you say it out loud." I pushed the book away and buried my face in my hands. Honor-down, I was tired again. I'd barely left this chair today, but stress and fear used all kinds of invisible muscles and energy.

"I don't know. Is there a reason for blowing strangers up that *wouldn't* sound stupid?" He looked at me seriously. "There was something I was thinking about today too, actually. Just when we were in the meeting, and Jov was gone, and Karista made another comment about her family's state, and I just . . . I know my family has the Chancellery, and yours is publicly associated with mine *and* you and Jov were the reason the last mess didn't kill us all.

Plus you've basically dedicated the last two years to trying to root them out. But why did they target the Lekas so hard?"

I frowned. "Well, that was part of discrediting us, right? And just rousing up animosity with rival families?"

"Maybe." He scratched his head, looking almost sheepish. "But what if it's more than that? There were people from every family at the hospital that night. It was the Lekas he targeted. No one else was poisoned but them. What if causing discord was only a side benefit? What if actually we were targets for a different reason? What do the Oromani, Iliri, and Leka have in common? Could the three of our families have done something particularly to provoke a reaction?"

He'd surprised me again. I hadn't thought of it in those terms at all.

"Anyway, it was just what you said then that made me think of it." Tain shrugged. "I remember Jov said we were looking for a scandal or something that could have caused some sort of intense grudge. What if it's not just your family or mine, but something that involved our three families more than others? We're not close now, but we have been in the past, plenty of times. In recent years they've been the three most powerful, most honored families. . . ." He trailed off. "It's probably nothing. The whole Council would have been blown up if we hadn't stopped that device."

"We shouldn't ignore any ideas. I'll get someone to expand the search to include things involving the Lekas. Dee's been checking our family records, too, in case there's anything in there."

Tain glanced at the window and frowned. "That reminds me. Any sign of our unwelcome northern visitor? Has she been seen?"

"No." I shot a look at Dee, who was flipping through the textbook still, and a little lurch of fear clenched my throat. I had been too afraid to let her return to school since I'd seen Mosecca, now that I knew the latter was willing to strike even at a child to get revenge on our family. I couldn't put Dee at risk, and I couldn't keep her safe if she was at school during the afternoons as usual. Perhaps I couldn't keep her safe at all.

The houseguards had all been shown a likeness of Mosecca and knew to look out for her. A pale northern noblewoman, on her own in a strange city whose language she did not speak, should easily stand out, but if she had come near me or anyone in my family again, it had been without being spotted. Two nights ago I had returned home from the Manor to find one of our houseguards being chastised by his colleagues for falling asleep at his post, and I had found a footprint in the back garden, but nothing unusual inside. I hadn't slept well that night.

"I don't know what we're supposed to do, short of catching her near us and having her arrested. How do you fight back against witches if you don't understand how they work? Our office doesn't know anything about it other than vague mentions from kids' stories. And the way Ectar was talking, it seemed like the Church over there suppresses even mention of it." The very first instance of unusual behavior I'd seen had not been an attack on my family but two separate attempts on Brother Lu's life or health. Perhaps Mosecca had been trying to reduce the Church's influence on the Emperor through particularly direct means? "Do you think they know they have practitioners in the royal household?"

"What about your friend?" When I stared at him blankly, Tain nudged the other slim volume within my reach. "The one who gave you that poetry you're always reading? Did you try asking her?"

"Abae? She's part of the Perest-Avani delegation," I said, stung. "She's a suspect in all this!"

"But she's not a witch, surely," he pointed out. "You're the one who told me you're sure the Mosecca attacks don't have anything to do with the other ones. What's the harm in seeing if you can get some information about Talafar out of her? If she's working with our enemies she might still be happy to ingratiate herself with you by helping with something that doesn't implicate them. Make her think you suspect the Empire of being behind it all. Worst case is that she doesn't tell you anything, then you're no worse off."

"And the best case?" To my intense irritation, I felt heat in my cheeks, and busied myself turning the book of poetry over and over in my hands.

Tain, to his credit, did not smirk or grin or so much as raise an eyebrow. "Best case, she's innocent of all this and might be able to help." He sighed and cracked his neck. "Fortunes know we need all the friends we can find."

The Perest-Avani delegation had not left the city with the Talafan or Doranites. Apparently the High Priestess led prayers for westerners at dawn and dusk every day at a little church in the lower city near their accommodation. It was there I headed now, Lara and Dom trailing from a short distance behind as I walked along the canal.

The church barely deserved that name; there was nothing to distinguish it from the surrounding buildings but for some western-style bells on strings on either side of the door.

I stopped outside the entrance, hesitant. What was the protocol; did one knock on the door of a church, or simply enter? The sound of music and voices raised in song drifted out, muffled but pleasant, and before I had to contemplate my dilemma much longer, a small woman with short hair and a reddish tint to her skin joined me at the door and, giving me a slightly confused nod in greeting, pushed it open and went inside. I slipped in after her before the door could shut.

The inside of the building was as modest as the outside in structure, but the furnishings were more what I expected from a formal church setting. Darfri religious practices were always outdoors, focused on communion and connection with the land and its natural forces. From the little I knew of western religion, it was far more focused on the mind, and the private contemplation of gods and the nature of humanity, and prayer was undertaken indoors, in what often appeared (from the illustrations in texts, at least) to be lavishly decorated spaces.

Lavish was not quite the word to describe the inside of the church here, but someone had clearly devoted significant effort to creating a worship space. The second story seemed to consist only of a walkway around the perimeter of the room, and the ceiling high above was painted in a single scene of a crowd of worshipers before a deity, nude and sexless, its smile benevolent but its eyes unforgiving. Tapestries and bells hung from every wall and smaller hangings from the underside of the upper balcony level, and every item of furniture had been painted in a coordinated theme. I wondered how much of this had been done since the High Priestess arrived.

The woman who had entered ahead of me joined perhaps a dozen worshipers who were kneeling, heads bowed, as they sang. Before a statue of the same deity as depicted on the ceiling sat the High Priestess herself, cross-legged and motionless behind her long, dark veil. I sidled awkwardly to the edge of the room, looking for Abae. She was not among the worshipers; all had bare heads and none her distinctive shaved patterns, nor her long, graceful neck.

I had just thought to leave and try to return later when a small door to the side of the room opened and a bearded man in a tall hat came out, saw me, and approached. He smiled politely, but uncertainly, as if surprised and a little concerned to have a stranger visit.

"May I assist, Credola?" Ah, perhaps not a stranger, then. He'd recognized me. "I trust there is no . . . er . . . difficulty?"

There had been enough rumor and rhetoric around the city to make certain segments of the population fear persecution, evidently. My face arranged into its most non-threatening expression, I said, struggling to remember the correct form of address, "No, of course not, Superior . . . ?"

"Yes, Credola." He relaxed fractionally. "Yes, Superior Kamok. This is my church. Well, it is ordinarily my church. We are fortunate indeed to have our most Exalted One in our fair city, offering us comfort in our time of great and urgent need." With a little bow of his head he indicated the High Priestess. "Have you come to, er . . ." His hands fluttered nervously, as he searched for a possible reason for my visit.

"I don't mean to be any trouble. I was just hoping to—ah!" Behind him, Abae had emerged from the same doorway. Her smile was day to night compared to his expression. I nodded in her direction. "I was hoping to talk to Abaezalla?"

The Superior's gaze swept over Abae in a manner both hungry and, it seemed, angry. It was not dissimilar to the look Prince Hiukipi had worn after being thwarted in his desires at the masquerade. "Actually, Credola, the lady is quite busy at the moment," he said, making as if to step between us. I bypassed him neatly and let my tone cool considerably as I said, over my shoulder, "A pleasure to meet you," then turned my attention deliberately to the diplomat.

"Could we talk outside?" I asked her, returning her smile, and making it clear I was no longer inviting the Superior's views on the matter.

"Of course," she said. She ducked her head deferentially to the Superior as she passed, but did not wait for his permission or approval.

"It is good to see you again," she said as the church door closed behind us, shutting out most of the sound of the song.

"I hope I was not interrupting anything. I should really have sent a messenger first, I'm sorry."

"You were not interrupting," she said. "The High Priestess was conducting the service, and had no need of me."

There was something in her tone that emboldened me to say, "The Superior seemed to think you had some business?"

She pressed her lips together, her eyes downcast, but there was the faintest trace of stubbornness in her voice. "I do not work for Superior Kamok."

"Is he a good priest?" I prodded.

"I do not know," Abae confessed. "I am no judge. He seems to me to be very like many priests I have known."

"That," I said with a smile, nudging her companionably as we walked, "sounded suspiciously like an insult."

Her face dimpled suddenly with mischief, and she giggled. "I would never insult a priest of the Exalted Order, Kalina. To do so would be to insult the gods themselves. I would simply say that a priest is required to deprive himself of many human wants in the name of the gods. Such a lifestyle is very difficult, and many struggle to reach the peace and enlightenment that comes from truly surrendering those desires."

A long way of describing exactly what I had seen in the way he had looked at her. Covetous, but self-loathing, too. "It must be doubly difficult to maintain such a lifestyle here in Silasta," I said mildly. "Many people struggle to adjust from one culture to another. I imagine it's much harder for a priest who worships in the same way as his homeland, but lives among a majority who live differently."

She nodded. "He finds much about Silasta scandalous. He is like many priests. The things he covets the most, he hates." A shadow passed over her face. She was no stranger to being both wanted and hated, I was suddenly sure. "Superior Kamok considers it inappropriate that I be here, working, when my husband remains in Perest-Avana."

"Your . . . husband?" A sudden unpleasant sourness unfurled in my stomach, quickly chased by embarrassment at my own reaction. A woman of her age, her intelligence, her outrageously perfect looks, in a society that placed political status on romantic pairings? Of course she would not remain unmarried. It was hardly my business.

"Oh, I am sorry. It is a word that means a man that—"

"I know the word," I said quickly. "I was just surprised. You hadn't mentioned him, that was all." That was all.

"My husband is an important man," she said. She smiled, but it was the carefully neutral smile I had seen her use on others, the one that did not show the charm of her crooked teeth. Pretty, and bland, and empty. "It is by his status that I was permitted to this role. But the priest believes a woman should remain by her husband's side at all times." She slowed her pace. It was falling dark now, and I could not read her face so clearly in the shadows at this angle. "It would not do to explain to him that my husband prefers me as far from his side as is possible." Then she stopped altogether, shook her head, and her smile gleamed white in the dimming light. "I talk too much, you see, and here I have been doing so again. You came to see me, was there something you needed?"

"Yes, actually," I said.

Was that a flicker of disappointment in her eyes? "Anything! How may I assist?" I must have imagined it, for she was perfectly gracious in her eagerness now.

"You have studied Talafan culture," I said carefully. "And there is an aspect I am interested in. Something that our diplomatic office could not help me with. I could have asked my tutor, but he left the country a few months ago. And when I asked Lord Ectar when he was here, he had such a peculiar reaction."

"What aspect of the culture do you mean?" We started walking again, but Abae looked genuinely curious, the light of pleasure across her face that of a scholar truly enthusiastic about her subject.

"I had read a story about witches in a children's book, and had not realized it was a forbidden topic."

"Oh!" Abae drew in her breath and lowered her voice, though we were quite alone by the canal. "Yes, a lord would not want to be seen to be talking about such things. Did the rumors not reach you here? That witches have cursed the Emperor and are the source of his ill health?"

"What? No, I didn't know anything of the sort. Ectar looked terrified that I'd even mentioned it."

Abaezalla looked up and down the waterway, then drew me by the elbow to whisper close. "It was the Emperor's chief priest who started it, I think. Father Cam. He had been with the Emperor many years. For some reason he became sure there was a bird following him, watching with human eyes, and he was convinced it was a witch trying to stop his spiritual guidance of the Emperor. Everyone laughed it off at first, I think—there are hundreds of similar birds around the Palace grounds, so how could he even think it was the same one he kept seeing? But he grew more and more insistent, claiming they were trying to murder him, and then . . ."

"Then?"

"He managed to catch the bird he said had been following him, and he cooked it up and ate it in a pie. I think he must have been quite mad by then."

She pressed her lips together as if torn between a laugh and a frown. "He was dead within the week."

Birds as spies and mysterious deaths? The awful fear that had gripped me as I pulled Dee back off the road seized me again. Perhaps that priest had been mad, and perhaps not. "How did he die?"

"It was terrible, they say," Abaezalla whispered. "He could not . . . er . . . expel waste? He grew bloated and nothing the physics gave him could clear his bowels. In the end, when they found his body, they say . . ." She looked desperately reluctant to continue, but as I stared avidly she finished. "They say the waste came out his nose and mouth."

I winced. "That is not a nice way to die." I had a sudden disturbing image of a doll being stuffed fuller and fuller until the stuffing burst from the cracks, and shuddered.

"After that, the Church took up the cry against witches." She hesitated. "We have a similar word in Perest-Avana, to mean . . . uh . . . women who can use blood and other natural things to cast spells on others. I am not sure how things are here, but in my homeland it is a grievous charge to lay against a woman. Sometimes it feels like it is something leveled at a woman who has grown inconvenient to someone." She shook her head, looking troubled. She squeezed my arm suddenly. "So it is best not to ask these questions to Talafan men!"

"No, I can see that. I won't make that mistake again."

"Why do you ask about this?" She sounded curious, not accusatory. "There are many rumors in the city, even for a foreigner like me to hear. Some say there was a magical attack at the arena. Do you suspect witchcraft? I should say that I do not know if such things are real, Kalina, not even in Talafar. Father Cam's story is frightening, but birds are often diseased animals, and he would not be the first person to die from eating something he should not have."

"Quite," I muttered, shooting her a sidelong look. How benign a comment was that, really? Her eyes were wide and innocent. Damnit, I didn't know what to think about her. I hedged, using the shadows to hide *my* face this time. "There have been a lot of strange things happening, and I know there to be things in the world that don't obey our understanding of it. We need to be prepared for anything."

"Well, I can tell you what I know from stories, if you like, though they are that. Stories."

"Anything you know would be helpful," I said. There was a stone bench near the canal just up ahead. We sat together, and Lara and Dom took up positions within a respectful distance, their backs to us, scanning the area with easy confidence. I felt strangely conscious of where my arms and legs were; was I sitting naturally? I felt awkward and off balance, and annoyed at myself for it. What kind of student of Etan's was I, to be so flustered by a charming smile and long lashes?

She bit her lip, thoughtful. "All of the stories are about women. There do not seem to be any men who are witches. There is always a witchmother, who teaches a young girl how to use her powers." She smiled. "I suspect many of these stories are meant to be enjoyed by such young girls, who dream of exciting futures and daring escapes. Witches worship a Moon Goddess, and they call her Mother, and they are strongest when the moon is full and clear."

Involuntarily, I glanced up at the sky. The moon was close to full, probably a few days away at most. But all the attacks so far had occurred in daylight, and Lara and Dom were only a few treads away. There were no animals, not pets nor strays nor wild birds, in sight. I forced myself to relax, to breathe easily, to listen.

"In the stories for older children, and the very oldest stories I have read, the girl must usually use her blood, or flesh, or hair, to perform her spells. Commonly they can talk to animals or force them to do their bidding—I imagine that is where Father Cam's fears came from. Then there are even more outlandish tales, of blood binding and healing and powerful magics of the human body. Bringing people back from the dead with the blood of another's sacrifice, that sort of thing."

"Are the witches ever the villains in the stories?" A defense or attack against these mysterious powers, even if simplified for children's consumption, was better than nothing.

Abae stopped and thought again. "I do not think so," she said at last. "Sometimes they are . . . not the villain, precisely, but sometimes the witchmother is harder or more ruthless than the child. Or the child is not sure that it is worth the pain to go away with her."

"The one I had was sort of . . . ambiguous."

She chuckled. "Yes, that is a good word for it. In Perest-Avana our children's stories are usually in a particular format. There is a rule, and a child follows the rule or does not follow the rule, and is rewarded or punished. They are mostly ways to teach about societies through such a viewpoint. But Talafan stories are quite different. Sometimes I am not sure I have translated properly but then later I find a different version of the same tale with the same strange ending."

"If you throw yourself from the peak and so feed your heart to the hungry mountain, but you have flown away from the evil prince who had captured and imprisoned you, is that a happy ending?" I wondered aloud.

"Some of the stories are very unsettling," she agreed. "The blood magic and sacrifice ones make me the most uncomfortable, because in our culture to speak of bringing a person back from the dead, with another's blood, would be a terrible thing. To interrupt the peace of passing, to swap a life for a life . . . this is the stuff of curses."

Hungry mountains and dark sacrifices, I thought. *Not a tale I'd tell a child to comfort them in bed at night.*

A flicker of movement from the other side of the canal made my heart skip. But no animal or woman emerged, just the flap of bedding hanging off a line from one of the buildings. Still, it was getting dark and we were exposed, here, guards or no guards. I started to stand.

And then I saw her.

She was standing among the billowing flaps of fabric, pale and stony, staring across at us with loathing. I had a clear and unambiguous view of her face. There was something in her hand, and before I could even shout, or point, or do anything at all, she had thrown it. I flinched back instinctively, pulling Abae away with me and almost causing her to trip over the bench, and heard a fat *plop* as something hit the surface of the canal. I opened my mouth to shout, and found it full of water.

Stale, tepid canal water, smelling of industry and algae and piss, filled my mouth, drained down my throat, choked me, attacked me. I dropped to all fours, coughing and retching, but no matter how I tried to cough it out, more water filled the space it left. As though they were very far away, the sounds of Lara's and Dom's shouts ricocheted faintly around my skull, but I could barely understand them, because I was drowning again, drowning in the dry, on the land, coughing up water that forced itself ever deeper, blocking out the air. Someone was striking my back in heavy blows, but my vision was all flare spots and shadows and I couldn't make out anything but the pain and the pressure and I couldn't understand what was happening.

I fell, at some point, from my hands and knees to flat on my face, and registered the additional pain on my cheekbone and jaw and skin, but it was nothing compared to the desperate fire in my lungs. And then a cry, or a grunt, some kind of visceral sound that I felt as much as heard cut through the swirling panic in my ears, and the back-slapping stopped.

Drowning again, and not even in the water. The fucking irony.

A loud splash, I heard that much, but it meant nothing anymore. The blackness took over, a blanket flung over me, sheltering me, and my muscles stopped fighting, and all of a sudden I was plunging in the most comfortable sleep imaginable, every part of my body warm and relaxed and the pain miraculously vanished. Only the tiniest moment of regret chased that release.

And then it was stripped away. Someone or something yanked the blanket off, and I was on the hard ground, my face squashed into the stones by the canal, and my stomach felt like it was about to burst, and everything, *everything* from my nose and eyes and ears and throat burned and strained. I coughed and vomited simultaneously, expelling a horrendous flood of water and vomit. For a moment hatred and anger infused me with a powerful and thorough strength and I wanted more than anything to return to the velvety blackness, the point past the pain.

But air was making it back inside me now—fiery, aggressive air that clawed its way back into my lungs and bled me for each gulp, but air nonetheless, and my vision showed colors and shapes again, and then slowly my brain made sense of it all, and I could let myself be helped up by soft hands and remember myself.

Abae was squatting in front of me, crying noisily, and when I looked at her directly and focused on her eyes, she flung her arms around my shoulders. "My God, my God," she sobbed, pressing her forehead against mine. "You are all right. Thank God."

She was wet, and not just from her tears; her whole bottom half was soaking. "What . . . what happened?" I gasped.

"I saw her!" she cried. "The Talafan woman. She threw something in the water and then you were drowning, there was so much water, you were drowning right here on the land, and it made no sense, no sense at all! Your guards chased her and I . . . I didn't know what to do, no matter how much you coughed up, there was always more." And indeed the ground around us was a sodden mess.

But I had just realized what she was holding in her hand, and I knew without her saying what she had done next. "I didn't know what else to do, so I jumped in the canal and I felt around until I found what she threw, and . . ." She held it out with shaking hands, tears still spilling down her cheeks. "The moment it came out of the water, it was as if a plug had been pulled out in you."

It was a poppet, a small and ugly thing like the one I'd found in the viewing box a few short weeks and what seemed like another lifetime ago. But this one had a fingerswidth of dark curly hair, soaking wet and springing in all directions, crudely sewn into the head part. I wasn't sure I had ever seen an object that repulsed and scared me more. I did not want to look at it, but nor had I any idea what to do, how to treat it, whether it could cause me further harm. So I just numbly took it from Abae and tucked it inside my now vomit-stained clothes.

"I do not understand what these people want," she whispered, and I gave a shaky laugh.

"She wants something I can't give her," I said. I coughed again, spat out another smelly mouthful, and shuddered. "She wants something no one can give her. And I don't think she'll stop till we're dead."

By the time Lara and Dom came back from the alley, swearing, shaken, and furious, we were both a sight, soaked with canal water and bile, Abae close to hysterical with the shock of it all, and a horrible numbness and lethargy weighing me down.

"What in all the hells was that?" Lara demanded, roughly pulling me to my feet and inspecting me like a frightened mother. Dom, his baton in hand, was wide-eyed and speechless, his eyes darting between us and the canal and the alley. "Kalina?"

"I'm all right," I forced myself to say, giving her a mechanical smile. I patted inside my paluma, thinking of the book concealed there, and hoping it had not been damaged. "Just shaken up." I took Abae's hand and helped her to her feet. "Abaezalla saved me. If she hadn't been here, I'd be dead. I'm sorry, everyone. None of you signed up for this."

"Dunno 'bout that," Lara said, her eyes still roaming me as if to find other concealed injuries. "I signed up to protect your person, and seems like it needs protecting more than ever." She nudged Dom and added, "We didn't get her, which means we need to not be out in the open right now. Get it together, mate."

Like a verbal slap, her words seemed to bring him back to himself. He shook his head like an animal shedding itself of water. "Right you are," he muttered. "Let's get to cover."

"Who *was* that woman?" Abae whispered as we hurried away from the canal, a guard in front and behind us, her hand still tight in mine. "Why is she trying to kill you?"

Dom was slapping the baton nervously in one of his palms, his head still swiveling as we moved. I swallowed. "I'll explain more once we're safe, all right?"

"Back to your apartments?" Lara asked, as we ducked down a side street and she walked backward, keeping her eyes out for anyone following us.

I hesitated. Home had always been a comfort, but right now it was a false comfort, an empty trick. Nowhere was safe, not really. When buildings could explode in the night and women could drown you on the shore, there was no real safety to be found, not even surrounded by the trappings of family and childhood. There was no escaping fear. Memories of Aven and the river still had their claws deep inside me.

Abae wore a shocked, blank look, reflecting the same hollow fear, and I knew suddenly that I didn't want to answer any questions about what we had seen, to describe it to anyone, not even to Tain or Sjease or Dee. I would not have to relive anything, just for a while. "Not to my apartments," I said, then cleared my throat to continue without the uncertain crack. "We're filthy and Abae's cold. Where's the nearest bathhouse from here?"

Abae blinked at me. "There is a private bathhouse at our guesthouse," she offered softly. "It is close by. And everyone else will be at the church for some time yet."

"Yes, good." No one to ask us questions there. "Which way?" In our hurry to get clear of the area I'd lost track of exactly where we were. Abae looked around dazedly, obviously suffering the same issue.

"It is on Harrow Street," she said uncertainly, and Dom nodded.

"That's not far," he said. "We'll get you there safe and then I'll get a messenger to send word to the Order Guards?" He paused, looked at me quizzically. Ordinarily, such a thing would require sending word to Jov, to Chen, to Tain, but what was there to report? Everyone was already on the lookout for Mosecca. I was not injured and nothing had changed, except that she had proven she could attack me in any situation.

"No urgency," I said. "We'll get clean and warm and then decide what to do."

Unlike the Talafan contingent, who had used their own staff almost exclusively to run the guesthouse during their stay, the much smaller Perest-Avani delegation were being looked after by the ordinary operators of the house. The owner was an ancient woman in a wheeled chair, her face so wrinkled her eyes were like tiny seeds, her hair shockingly white. She saw the state of us and immediately called for servants to heat the baths without asking any questions, then while we were waiting for them to be readied she arranged tea and cheese stew and fussed over us gently.

"Shall we come in with you?" Dom asked. He hadn't put the baton away, and he looked like he'd very much like to hit something to relieve the confusion and tension.

"No, just stay by the door, maybe?"

"I'll patrol outside," Lara said. "You stay here. No one goes inside that room without your say-so." She shot a firm look at the proprietor, who nodded.

"Of course, my dears. You go on in, and I'll arrange for your clothes to be cleaned and bring you something fresh and dry."

"Thank you." My words sounded wooden and expressionless but the effort of summoning up anything more was too much.

The guesthouse bathing area was small and simple in design but it still had a cleansing area with buckets and brushes and soap, and a proper bath, full depth, with soothing oils in the burners by the walls and herbs and flowers in the water, which must have been from the proprietor's own garden, based on the freshness. It was a relief to shed the soiled clothes—placing my belongings, including the book and the witch's doll, carefully to the side so that they would not be caught up—and scrub ourselves clean, and breathe in the pleasantly scented air instead of sour rot, but I hesitated on the edge of the relaxation pool. Perhaps a bath had been ill-advised. I closed my eyes. I had survived a close drowning once before, and had not let it ruin my enjoyment of the simple pleasure of a bath; this time would be no different. A deep breath fell out of me, almost involuntary, as I stepped in, careful to keep my head well above water, but fortunately immersing myself did not trigger any rush of frightening memory.

A ripple and a soft splosh indicated that Abae had joined me, but my eyes, once closed, had no intention of opening for a while. I rested my head on a perfumed pillow and breathed as slowly as my lungs would let me.

I lay there for an indefinite period, but eventually both the cold and the shaky fear had receded in the face of the deep, relaxing comfort, and I sat up to stop myself falling asleep. Abae was on the other side, her face tear-streaked. "What's wrong?" I asked automatically, and then flushed with embarrassment at the stupidity of the question. But she smiled wanly and shook her head.

"I am all right, Kalina," she said. "It feels so safe and calm here, I was just thinking that perhaps it could be a terrible dream. But I have never dreamed such things." Her eyes looked glassy as she stared at a point somewhere in the distance.

"You saved my life," I said quietly. "There was nothing I could have done. If you hadn't pulled that thing out of the canal, I'd have drowned. Thank you."

There was a long pause, during which she took a number of shaky breaths. Her voice, when it came out, sounded huskier than usual. "You were asking about witches, before. You knew that one was coming for you?"

"I'm sorry. If I'd known I was putting you in danger . . ."

"Me?" She shook her head. "It was you who was at risk. I did nothing but pick up a doll."

"You jumped in the water in the dark," I pointed out, "and managed to find what she threw in. How did you even think of it?"

"I do not know," she said. "I was so frightened."

"Me too," I admitted. I squeezed my eyes shut, battling the memory.

"Why does this woman try to kill you?"

My hands twined together under the water. She could still be working with our enemy. But she had just saved my life; surely she was owed the truth. "Because she thinks that my brother and I are responsible for her son's death. He was with the Imperial soldiers, and he got caught up with the same gang that set off the explosions at the closing ceremony. They killed him and tried to make it look like my brother did." I sighed. "It's a long story."

I was half-afraid Abae would ask for the story, but she didn't. Instead she watched me with those dark, liquid eyes, and cocked her head to one side, as if studying a difficult puzzle, or scrutinizing a piece of artwork. "She blames you for something she believes your brother did?"

"No, but it was partly my fault that her son . . . was where he was that night." I rubbed my forehead. Fortunes, the whole thing was such a mess. "The funny thing is that I don't even blame her for hating us. What you said about witches in stories—it seems like the folklore is all about women finding power to escape the traps they find themselves in." I thought about poor Zhafi and her attempts to carve herself out a real existence, her charities and businesses and dreams of freedom. "Mosecca is a widow and he was her only son, and I'm sure she had many hopes for him. I'm not surprised that losing him drove her to this."

"It has been my impression that many Talafan noblewomen choose to realize their own ambitions through their sons," she agreed, a strange twist to her lips.

"How is it for you, in Perest-Avana?" I couldn't help asking. "You said the Superior didn't approve of you being apart from your husband; is that a common attitude?"

She didn't answer. "I'm sorry," I said quickly. "I'm being nosy."

"No, it is not that." Her crooked smile reassured me. "It is very different for women here in your country. I am permitted my employment, yes, where a Talafan noblewoman would not be. But I was not permitted to choose my husband. I was chosen for him like you might choose an item of clothing, or a piece of jewelry, or a very fine chair. And men feel free to look and touch and 'compliment' me in this fashion. At least when I am traveling with the High Priestess, I am extended the courtesy of the holy women."

I slid over and added some water to the hot rocks to create more steam, and to have something to do with my hands. Abae said something over the hiss that I couldn't understand.

"What was that?"

The look in her eyes had changed; her gaze roamed my face with something faintly jealous, faintly hungry. "Women are not treated so here. I have heard men complain of it, back home. They come to Silasta expecting . . . certain pleasures, and instead find themselves rebuffed."

I thought of Hiukipi, roaming the masquerade and rudely attempting to touch strangers. He had been notable for the extremity of his reaction but he was hardly unusual; it was a common joke in bathhouse talk that men from the north and the west, or at least men of a certain social class, could not find man nor woman willing to be with them. "Yes. No one wants romantic relations with someone who speaks to them as if they were a thing, not a person. Some men are left with only their hands to entertain themselves, because no Sjon will consent to their attentions."

She ducked her head, a tiny smile on her lips. "It is a different world, with different rules."

"It is," I agreed. "But it's not so hard to understand." My face was very hot; perhaps I had made too much steam. "It's the simplest thing, really, if you think about it. If people are attracted to each other, they are free to act on that. If they are not both attracted, then they do not." Was she flushing, too? I could see the tiny, perfect water droplets gathered on her smooth shoulders. Her neck was so graceful.

"What is it like, then? If people do not simply take liberties. What . . . what do you say, to show another that you want, or that you wish for . . ." She lifted her chin and met my gaze. Her eyes were very black and her body very still. The warmth in my face spread down into my stomach, and deeper. The lap of the water against my skin sounded so loud, or was that my heartbeat in my ears?

"Well. You might say something to show that you admire them. That you are attracted. Perhaps, if you're poetically minded, you might say that their smile is like the sun through the clouds. Or that their voice is finer than birdsong." My tone was meant to be light, but it hadn't come out that way. I cleared my throat. "You might compliment their gentle heart, or the way their laughter makes you feel. If you are feeling sentimental." Her lips curved, just a fraction, the suggestion or promise of a smile. Something shifted or loosened inside me, something I hadn't realized was there before, and all of a sudden I did not feel uncomfortable or uncertain. "Or you might say that you have longed to touch the skin of their neck, to see if it feels as smooth as it looks. Or that they make you feel better, and braver, than you are, because their regard elevates you." Very slowly, very deliberately, I moved closer; not so close as to be within her space, but closing the distance between us so that if I had reached out a hand I could have touched her. "And then you would wait, to see whether they felt any of those things also. If not . . ." I shrugged, and made to slide backward through the water.

Her hand snaked out and caught my wrist, stopping my retreat. Then she released it, and wound her fingers in mine, instead. "And if so?"

"Well then." Suddenly it felt difficult to get a full breath. My skin felt so hot. A knot of wanting, deep inside me, tightened, tightened. "Then I would ask if I could please kiss her, and hope that she says—"

"Yes."

"Yes?"

Abae squeezed my hand, and pulled, just the tiniest bit, drawing me in without resistance. "Please," she whispered.

So I did. Gently, tentatively at first—her eyes were still so wide, so dark— just her soft lips on mine, then deeper as she sighed, softening against me. The fingers of her free hand traced down my back in the water, and I touched her face with mine, feeling the soft curve of her cheek. She trembled and I pulled back from the kiss. "And then in case there's some doubt, it's easy to ask: Do you want me to stop?"

"Kalina," she whispered, and then her face broke into the crooked smile with the dimple that I now could admit to myself made me want her with quite mad intensity. "I don't think I will want you to stop, ever."

And this time her fingers on my back were not so tentative, and our bodies pressed together under the water, warm skin on warm skin, and all the panic and fear and guilt and cold were nothing but distant memories of a passing storm. There was only this. There was only her.

Dom looked somewhat puzzled when I told him that I would be staying overnight in the accommodation.

"Credola, won't you want to tell the Chancellor? Report on what happened?"

"I don't want to be out on the streets tonight," I said, trying to look worried. "I'm exhausted. The owner has space for me here and I've got some thinking to do. Can you or Lara head back to the apartments and let my family know I'm safe, just following something up. Just—keep us safe here, for now, all right?"

The proprietor, true to her word, had brought clean, dry clothes and fresh tea to Abae's room, where we had briefly enjoyed the latter and completely ignored the former.

Abae was older than me, but in many ways she seemed younger; there was something pure and full of wonder about the way she looked at me, and her touch had a gentle reverence that invoked a confusing jumble of emotions in me that I wasn't quite ready to unpack.

"I have never been with a woman before," she whispered. Dom waited outside, on my request, and occasionally, and with muffled giggles, I reached a toe out and chinked the cups against each other in what I hoped was a convincing show of an ordinary friendly meeting.

"I assumed not," I told her. We lay sprawled out on the floor, legs tangled together, and her head rested on my chest. Her fingers stroked my scar with soft, tingly brushes.

"It is not allowed. I would be banished if anyone knew that I . . . that I wanted these things."

I kissed the top of her head. Enough westerners had fled to Sjona for failing to meet their country's religious or government decrees about sexuality that it was no surprise to hear, but I couldn't pretend to understand how it would feel to live that way.

She twisted to look up at me, her expression shy. "I was a great disappointment to my husband. I tried to be a dutiful wife, but I could not make myself want him. His skin was rough and hairy, and he would lie on top of me so I could not breathe. I would close my eyes and think about the pretty cook downstairs, who was fat and sweet, with round cheeks and a merry laugh. . . ." She sighed. "Such a celebrated beauty, he would say, yet a corpse in bed. When he took a mistress I pretended to be ashamed but in private I wept for joy."

I ran my hand over her smooth stomach, then up, tracing her ribs, and she half-closed her eyes in pleasure. "You," I told her with a smile, "are no corpse."

And we set about firmly establishing the truth of that statement in as many creative ways as we could divine.

When the light of predawn crept into the room, I woke more rested and comfortable than I had for as long as I could remember. With some reluctance I rose and picked up the spare clothing that the proprietor had left for me.

"Must we get dressed?" Abae asked plaintively, opening one eye reluctantly. "Could we not stay like this forever?"

"Don't you have to go to morning prayers?" I peered outside at the sky.

"I'm afraid I feel very poorly this morning," she said, flopping back onto the pillow, and I laughed.

"I do have things to do, I'm sorry," I said. Dee and Sjease would be worried, regardless of the message Lara had delivered. And in the light of day, the attack last night seemed a thing from a dream, and my actions here reckless and indulgent, the product of relief and trauma rather than sound judgment.

As she tied her shirt over her chest, I retrieved my belongings and tucked them into the various pockets of my borrowed clothes. The horrible poppet I didn't know what to do with, and I stopped to stare at it, feeling the remnants of the comfort and pleasure of the last night leaking out of me. Abae was suddenly at my shoulder, her lips pressed into the side of my neck. "What is that?" she asked.

It took a moment to realize she meant not the doll but the book underneath. I tensed involuntarily and she stepped back. "I am sorry," she said, "I did not mean to pry. If it is personal . . ."

I clutched the book, saying nothing. It felt like there were some kind of storm inside me, with wind and tide pushing and shifting and raging. Did I trust her? I wanted to trust her, honor-down, I did. She'd saved my life. I felt, deep to my core, that she was good, that she would never harm anyone, that I had been right to leave myself vulnerable to her. Didn't Jov and Tain both speak of my judgment? Didn't they both trust my read of people?

Or, a little voice inside me whispered, *do you just want to believe that because you let her in, and you don't want to admit that you succumbed to a flattering manner and a beautiful face? Haven't you always wanted to be admired like she seems to admire you?*

But many people had seen this book. Within my Guild, within the Council, and beyond. We already knew from Merenda's last act that *someone* in the inner circle was informing on us. Chances were good that person had seen this or at least knew what we knew about it. And that was precious little, and only a few of us seemed to regard it as overly significant in any case. What would I really be giving up by showing her?

I took a breath. My judgment was good, and I didn't have to share what I thought about the contents. I could just see what she said. So I unclenched my fingers and turned around, offering it to her. "Here," I said. "It's not personal. We took it off the assassin, the one who murdered the people at the arena after the explosion."

Her eyes widened, but she accepted the book. "What is it?" She read out the title, flipped through a few pages. "Oh! This is not Sjon. Not quite." Her face folded into a frown, but it was one of concentration, not displeasure. In fact her eyes were bright, interested, and she sank cross-legged to the ground, fingers tracing the words. "How fascinating!"

I had forgotten. How had I forgotten? "You're a linguist," I said, feeling stupid.

"Yes indeed," she said. "That is my field of study. Most of my work is in translation, of course, because there is the demand for it. But my true love is not for diplomacy. It is for the languages themselves. How they develop, how they change. There are as many variations of Doranite dialects as there are clans, and Talafar has had a very colonizing history, with so many regional languages that are supplanted by the Imperial requirements, but which survive in all kinds of forms." Her eyes twinkled as she looked up at me. "Language is rebellion, Kalina!"

"Our linguists couldn't tell me where this came from," I said. "I thought if we knew where the assassin was from, that could tell us who hired him. But it's all been dead ends." I wished I had thought to ask her earlier.

"Well, the content is certainly not reflective of Sjona, is it?" Abae wrinkled her nose in a few places as she skimmed. "Some of this sounds like things that the Church might like to do in Talafar, but even it is not so powerful and daring and oppressive, yet." She hummed under her breath as she read. "Do we think it is a translation? But these are not mistakes, they are too consistent." She was clearly talking to herself more than me. Her left hand twitched, suddenly, making a pinching motion, and I almost laughed at the familiar gesture. I must have supplied Etan with a pen in response to that movement a thousand times. I retrieved both pen and a sheet of paper from the small desk by the window and she took them without looking up, and began scribbling symbols. "Sjon is fascinating too, you know. One of the most interesting languages in the world, and one of the most difficult to master because of your disconnect between written and spoken—" She looked up and gave me a sheepish smile. "You know this, of course."

I waved her on, letting her go back to murmuring, scribbling, sometimes exclaiming something. At one point I ducked out and found Dom relieved from his shift by Tamarik, and ordered some more tea and morning refreshments from the proprietor. Abae ate them cheerfully and gracefully one-handed while continuing to work. If this was a book she had seen before, her ability to feign excitement and enthusiasm while purportedly solving its mysteries was a masterpiece of deception.

"I am sure you have already concluded this, but this is an internally consistent language," she said after a long period referring between her notes and the book. "If you gave me enough time, I think I could probably come up with much of the missing material. But I am not sure that would help you with what you need, would it?"

"Probably not, unless there's a helpful description of where the author comes from in there," I said with a sigh. "What I want is to know if there's a link between whatever culture this assassin came from and the people who are attacking us. If you were looking at this, what would be your best guess about where it came from?"

"Linguistically? A related population," she said promptly. "A culture with a shared linguistic root. This is absolutely a language which either developed parallel to Sjon, or predates it."

"And have you ever seen anything like it? You've traveled and you pay attention to language. Is there anywhere you've seen this?"

She sucked in a deep breath, stretched her back, and cracked her knuckles. Then she settled again, lips pursed, thinking. "Not really," she said at last. "Well . . ." She looked conflicted, but at my impatient eagerness, she added almost reluctantly, "Not precisely, but this expression . . . obey to ascend. I have seen something like that before, a long time ago, I think. Do not be excited! It is not such a helpful thing. I only remember because at the time I had not yet been to Sjona and I had not seen a population which uses tattoos in a widespread fashion, the way you do here." She seemed to be getting muddled; I put a hand on hers and she took a slightly quavering breath and returned it, then went on more clearly. "It was in Izruitn, when I was there ten years ago. There was a group of merchants doing business in the trading district, and they were dark, but not western, and they had tattoos on their arms. I admit I was being nosy, and was likely being rude, staring. But their tattoos . . . I am sure that that was the expression." She lifted her arm up and traced a line down the soft underside, from armpit to elbow. "Here."

My breath caught excitedly in my chest. Exactly as it had appeared on the assassin's arm.

"One man caught me staring and I went to apologize for the rudeness because he looked offended. They were such fierce-looking men! And no women among them. But I thought myself clever, and I had been learning Sjon, so I attempted to apologize in Sjon, and they did not understand." She spread her hands. "They were not Sjon, you see, it was my mistake. They did not understand me. And I asked one of the officials where they came from, because I was curious, and he just shrugged and said they were from the far east." She frowned prettily. "So you see, it is not much help to you."

But I was sitting very still, and for a moment it was like I was drowning again, because my head swirled, my vision spotting, and I could not seem to make my leaden lungs take a breath.

"What did you say?" I whispered, barely able to choke the words out. "A related population? A language which developed . . ."

"Parallel to Sjon," she supplied, looking utterly bewildered at my reaction. "Or an earlier iteration of it."

I stumbled to my feet, my body clumsy and slow, struggling to balance.

What do the Iliris, the Lekas, and the Oromanis have in common?

Tain had asked me that and I'd been so caught up trying to think of business deals or Guild politics or poisonings that I'd forgotten the most fundamental connection of all, the thing that our families had in common with one another and not with the other three.

"From the far east . . ." I said it out loud, and felt like I might cry with the sheer stupidity, the sheer stubbornness and illogic and willful ignorance of it all. We'd had it all backward. Two years ago, ignoring our country's history had almost cost us everything, and we hadn't learned from it. We'd just made the same mistake again.

"Honor-down," I whispered. "Oh, no. I know who they are."

INCIDENT: Fatal poisoning of Credo Jaco Ash, heir to Ash Council Seat

POISON: Praconis

INCIDENT NOTES: C. Jaco discovered dead in Ash family apartments, diagnosed with heart failure. Servant witness noted presence of praconis plant in Ash gardens, physic confirmed C. Jaco had been taking mild nightly dose of praconis leaves to assist with difficulties sleeping. Family cook confirmed to this proofer that C. Jaco's sister and heir, C. Bela, next in line for the Ash family Council seat, had requested household meals featuring unusually large quantities of lavabulb and pepper seasoning. Suspect C. Bela of dosing brother's meals with praconis seeds. Desirable to ensure C. Bela not ascend to Ash seat. *Further note:* subsequent use of leverage by Iliri family resulted in C. Bela being returned to family estates and cousin C. Kristen taking Ash seat.

(from proofing notes of Credola Para Oromani)

23

Jovan

We headed into my own family's lands, next, northwest and still using the country roads. There was an unsettled air about our travel. No more attacks on the road, and no mysterious animals appearing to follow us, but the story we'd heard in Ista had troubled us both. The spirit at the tree was gone, as we'd already known, and Hadrea had found no clues at the site to explain it. "It is gone," she'd told me, her hands in the dirt beside the whitened trunk and her face bleak. "It is as we found before. There is no sign of a neglected spirit grown fallow. It is just a dead tree."

Our speculation as we left Ista and headed to the next village was wide ranging. Hadrea had finally abandoned the vestiges of her sensitivity to speaking about fresken, and took no offense at my questions. It was easy to see now, observing her out in the open country, how stifled she had been in Silasta, how poorly her studies and the lifestyle she had been forced into by her actions during the siege and her mother's new Council position had fit her. Little wonder she had been unhappy.

"So this man and the women," I wondered out loud as we sat, jostled together companionably on the back of a wagon on which we'd hitched a ride. "Did they kill it somehow? Are they . . . I don't know, murdering people and somehow murdering spirits at the same time? Is that a thing that's possible?"

"I have never heard of such a rite," she said. "Some kind of sacrifice?" Once, the very question would have angered her. But holding on to the idea of Darfri magic being used solely in traditional and respectful ways was foolish in the face of everything we'd seen and learned, and Hadrea, whatever her faults, was no fool.

"Spirits feed on our energy," she mused. "Could the energy of a murdered person have a different quality, something that could *harm* a spirit?"

"People were murdered at the lake that day, and it didn't seem to hurt Os-Woorin," I pointed out.

"No. But he was very mighty, and being fed energy from thousands of people. If they found a way to connect only one person . . . but *why*? What is the point? If it is to harm us, why choose these remote places? Trees and creeks and little rock formations?"

"Maybe they're just practicing," I said, and the thought filled me with dread. "You know, warming up on smaller things so that they can strike at bigger targets?"

Hadrea looked sick at the thought. "It is pointless destruction. But I suppose everything these people do is about pointless destruction."

"What about something like what you did with Os-Woorin then? You battled it. Could they have used the murders to somehow help power themselves in a fight with these smaller spirits?"

She gave me a look, but her tone was still mild. "No, Jovan. That is not what I mean by 'battle.' I did not harm the Os-Woorin, I only contained and calmed it." She stared thoughtfully off down the road as the wagon bumped and trundled along. "But perhaps you are right about the women. They have found some way to store the energy they take from people, especially people using Void; you saw that at the party. They may be doing something similar out here. Though again, if so, why take only one person?"

"They don't want to attract notice. One person going missing—especially someone like Pemu, whose disappearance might be easier to explain away as an accident—well, we saw what happens. It doesn't get the notice of the bigger towns and it never makes it anywhere near the cities. So they've been quietly lurking around the estates for months, maybe experimenting on people, I don't know, not wanting anyone who's looking for them to come start asking questions."

"Perhaps." She leaned forward and rested her chin on her hands. "I suppose we will learn more at the next village."

Kakiu was next, and then Lot's Rise, and then Salt, and the stories we heard at each were similar in some key respects. Always we found at least a few people who remembered a small group of women led by a handsome, aloof man passing through the area some time near when a person went missing, though no one had accused the party of any wrongdoing and it did not appear to have occurred to them that the two events were connected. Frustratingly, there was no real pattern to the victims, other than that they were women; of the three cases we heard directly and the four more anecdotally there had been a range of ages, professions, and family status. Jesta of Lot's Rise had been the most prominent in terms of community standing, being the only Speaker, but not the only Darfri, but nor was that a pattern because only about half the victims had been from Darfri families. Our early theory that this had been a ploy to somehow capture and murder Speakers fizzled to nothing.

In Salt we had heard a rumor that had sent us farther north, and three days later that was where we were headed. We had been unable to find a ride this time, and were back on foot heading toward a mining town in the far northwest of Oromani lands. The road was quiet, barely trafficked, and we had been free to talk as we walked, though our theories were starting to feel circular. There were never any bodies, and if anyone had witnessed either the victim or the mysterious visitors at the site of the dead spirit, they did not remember, or share it with us if so. Hadrea had felt no differences of significance at any of the locations; each time the spirit was simply gone as if it had never been there. In Kakiu locals had continued to leave offerings at the site, but only, Hadrea said, out of a desire to cling to familiarity. "It is like leaving milk out for an imaginary pet," she'd said bluntly. "Your child might enjoy the game but it does no good and you would be better off using your milk on things that are real."

We walked on the road, after a long and tiring day where the Maiso had blown at cross-purposes until the midafternoon, stifling our conversation and requiring all the energy I might have used for thinking just to keep myself from being blown over by the roaring, powerful wind. Hadrea suddenly stopped, her face hard. I had been walking in something of a stupor, but her sudden tension made my mouth dry and my skin prickle. After days without incident, I'd let myself hope that whoever had sent the taskjer on our trail had had only one creature under their control, and grown complacent. Or could it be that despite our requests to village administrators and witnesses we'd spoken to, rumors about our presence on the estates had spread and our enemy had sent another assassin, or a Hand, or fortunes knew what? So my

own hand sought out my version of weapons: a little poison dart tube, loaded
up with a deadly center.

"What is it?" I whispered.

She stayed silent, but her hands slipped into a deep pocket of her skirt and
she came out holding a sling. With one foot she deftly scooped up a large
pebble and flicked it up high enough to catch with her spare hand. Moments
later she had spun about and released the sling, so fast I barely registered what
she'd done. There was a *thuck* of impact and something fell from the bushes.
She padded over to it, already tugging her dagger from her belt.

A fat black bird lay stunned or dead on the ground by the bushes. She
prodded it tentatively with one foot, then, apparently unwilling to take a
chance, struck down with one swift motion, decapitating it as if she'd been
wielding an ax. The dagger, not really designed for the purpose, got a little
stuck in the bird's neck and as she yanked it free a blot of blood and gore
splashed out. The taste of sharp vomit rose in the back of my throat.

"Honor-down," I said, crouching to wipe my arm on the grass in disgust.
My stomach still roiled. "Was it, you know? One of them?"

Hadrea shrugged. "I am not sure. It seemed to be looking at us." She
hoisted the bird up by its feet and gave me an amused grin. "Besides, I would
like some fresh meat tonight."

Her skill as a hunter was far superior to her skill as a cook, though, so the
task of preparing the bird fell to me. I plucked and cleaned it while she found
us an appropriate hollow to shelter our fire and beds from the imminent return of the evening Maiso. *How*, I wondered, *are you supposed to tell the difference between a bird and a Bird?* Would there be any ill effects from eating the
latter? I overcooked it a bit, just to be sure, deciding it was worth Hadrea's
grumbling about dry meat to give its flesh some extra time over heat.

"You burned it," she muttered when I nudged her out of her trancelike
state a short while later.

"You're welcome." I sat beside her and blew on my own blackened piece.
I'd tried some before waking her and detected no toxins or anything unusual
in the taste.

"I am just saying, Jovan. For a man whose Tashi was a cook, your food
preparation can be . . . what is the city expression for it?"

"Shit?" I supplied, grinning despite myself.

"That is the one!" She winked.

"Yeah. Etan used to say that, too. But I've always preferred bland food to food that kills you, so . . ." I shrugged, and Hadrea laughed, waggling her half-eaten leg at me.

"Your problem, Jovan, is that you do not know how to enjoy a bit of risk. I think I would take a few poisonings rather than never eat lavabulb again."

We ate in companionable silence, and if we had just killed and eaten some kind of magical witch vessel, neither of us seemed to take any harm from it. I unfolded the map and stretched out beside the fire, tracing my finger along to mark out the final destination: Imudush North, a mining settlement in the far northeast corner of the Oromani lands. "Last one."

"First one," she countered. It had not been on the list of places An-Ostada had visited, nor on the list of missing people, but a villager in Salt had had a cousin move down from there who claimed the mountain spirit overlooking the town had vanished more than six months prior. That made it, at least as far as our investigations had revealed, the earliest missing spirit. Though it was hard, after hearing so many similar stories, to expect anything different, it was possible that the first instance would hold a clue that the later ones did not. If this really was practice for something else, perhaps our enemies had made mistakes on their first try that they had not repeated.

"I know that name," I muttered, and Hadrea looked at me strangely.

"It is on your lands. Of course you know the name."

"No, I mean . . . I've heard it, or seen it, or it's got some significance." Frustrated, I thought back, searching for context, but I'd spent so much of my time poring over documents of all kinds, it could have been anything. But then again, perhaps it had come up in some business dealing or in the reparation process. I had a good head for information but even I could get overwhelmed with the quantity that had passed my desk in the last few years.

Hadrea stretched, yawned, and wiggled her blanket beside mine by the fire. "Well. We will leave at first light and be there within a few hours at most. Perhaps something will jog your memory. Perhaps there will be something there that we have not found elsewhere."

Neither of us voiced it, but the shadow of our failure to solve this mystery hung heavy over us, and infected the rest of the night. Our coupling had an intensity and roughness that rose from desperation more than passion, and I lay awake for a long time afterward, feeling her body against my back, holding her forearms around my chest with the strangest sense that if she let go, we would lose each other forever.

"Jovan, you are holding too tight," she mumbled sleepily against my shoulder, and I loosened my arms obediently. I was, after all, just being maudlin.

Imudush North was built around a set of mines in the eastern mountain range; it was as remote a community as any, and my first suspicious thought as we finally crossed into it the following morning was that if ever there was an isolated place where a different language or culture might have developed, it would be somewhere like this. It made me more guarded than ever, scrutinizing the faces of everyone I saw.

But truth be told, it was innocuous enough, and though the people we met had stiff country formality, if they were harboring some secretive cult then their concealment skills were superior. The stares we got were perhaps more surprised, more curious, by comparison to the earlier villages, but that made sense. Imudush North was not on the thoroughfare to anywhere. A single road led in and out of the town, which was bordered by the inhospitable mountains, east of which lay only the Howling Plains; though it might have been possible to cross into the Empire through that range on its northern side, there was little point bothering when one could simply travel back west to Telasa and cross at the border there. So Imudush North had no through traffic and no visitors other than periodic traveling services.

The village administrator, a man called Il-Toro, told us all of this in somewhat bemused fashion. Visitors from Telasa were rare enough, but visitors from the capital, almost unheard of. He was helpful enough, though, and could offer a little detail about the spirit. He was a Darfri man himself, and the disappearance of the spirit of the mountain clearly still grieved him. "Things have been harder since then, Credo," he admitted. "But you would know this from our reduced taxes. Your family has been very sympathetic, I do not mean to imply otherwise, always extending us understanding when the mines are less plentiful than they were, and accidents more common."

"Did you tell anyone about the spirit?"

"Tell anyone? What do you mean, Credo? I am not following." He smiled, but his forehead wrinkled in confusion as he looked between us.

"We have heard of many cases of ancient spirits disappearing, dying," Hadrea said. "But we never heard your town mentioned until very recently."

"Yes," Il-Toro said, unconcerned. "Rumors rarely make it to our little corner of the world, you see. And when we do meet others for trade and services we would not ordinarily discuss sacred matters such as this."

"But you didn't want to ask for help?"

"For help?" He blinked. "Help from whom? The great spirit is gone. It has been gone for months and months. Some of us can feel the difference, even if the signs were not clear in the land." He raised his chin, looking somewhat proud, and Hadrea cocked her head in a speculative expression and I thought I could guess what she was wondering. He was young by comparison to most other administrators we'd talked to; perhaps in his forties. Young enough that he could have been sensitive to fresken, a potential Speaker who'd found himself without anyone to teach him.

"Where is your nearest Speaker, do you know?" Hadrea asked, and Il-Toro frowned properly now.

"We have not had a Speaker here for twenty years," he said stiffly. "And as I said before, people do not tend to visit us."

"Did you notice anything strange around the time that the spirit vanished?" I asked to change the subject. I turned my teacup around carefully. "Any visitors to town, that sort of thing? You'd remember visitors here, wouldn't you."

"We would," he agreed. "So I can be sure that we did not have any."

Hadrea looked up sharply. Though we'd had to sometimes work to help people remember in the previous towns, that had been because visitors were not generally a noteworthy matter, so the timing of their comings and goings was difficult for most to recall. "Are you certain?" she said. "We are investigating this damage to the spirits, and one common factor everywhere this has occurred is particular strangers in town."

"We think they are involved," I added unnecessarily.

"Involved in destroying our spirits?" Disgust flickered across his face. "Who would want to do such a thing?"

"We don't know, exactly." I leaned forward over my tea. "Administrator, this is the earliest example we've found. This may have been the first place they did whatever it is they're doing. Did anything else unusual happen around the same time?" At the last few villages we had made it a policy to not put suggestions in their minds; it was too easy for memories to conflate events, and if we mentioned missing persons before they volunteered it, they might falsely associate an unrelated case to the time period. The desire to be helpful and the fallibility of memory was a dangerous combination when what we wanted—needed—was nothing less than the truth.

In this case, Il-Toro still looked politely confused. "What is it you mean, anything else? There were a variety of incidents with the mine, and the mountain stream thinned to a trickle, and—"

"Not to do with the mine. Anything else you remember happening in the town."

"No, Credo, I do not believe so." He set his teacup down and made to stand. "I can look up the village meeting notes from that time."

"If you wouldn't mind."

He returned shortly with a large tome and flipped through it, muttering. He stopped, scanned a few pages, then spun it around to face us. "There seems to be nothing of particular interest there," he said. "I am afraid we do not have many villagers who can read or write Sjon—though we are now sending the children to the tutor in the town most mornings, and over to the big school in Telasa every week, as per the Compact! I do not mean to complain!—so the notes are a bit crude." As I looked down the page, which was mostly simple Trade, the administrator added hastily, "I can read, and write, of course, but I am not always available for note-taking at the meetings."

I glanced at Hadrea. There was nothing of use here, and while I didn't want to lead the man to a false answer, we couldn't afford to miss anything here. *This can't be a dead end, honor-down, it can't!* She gave a tiny nod. "Has anyone from the village gone missing?" I asked directly.

"Missing?" Il-Toro stared at me, his mouth open a little, blinking rapidly. "What do you mean, missing?"

"We have seen people go missing. Mainly women. Same as the strangers in town, whenever we see a dead spirit we're seeing a missing person along with it. They just disappear doing some routine chore and are never seen again. No bodies are found. They just . . . vanish."

"Well, I am happy to tell you there is nothing like that here." He shook his head. "Fortunes, no."

"Are you sure?" I pressed. "Your spirit incident happened a while back. Six months or so. Maybe you've just forgotten? Or you thought it was an accident?"

"We have had three deaths in the mines since then," he said. "They weigh heavily on me."

"Were they all definitely mining accidents?" I asked. "Maybe a missing body, or . . . ?"

"I buried each of them myself." The stiff tone was back, as if I'd dishonored him.

Hadrea and I looked at each other, puzzled. Why was this case different? How had they done what they'd done to this spirit without the stolen woman? If they didn't *need* to snatch someone in order to do whatever they were doing to the spirits, then why bother?

"Would you like to see where our shrine was?" Il-Toro asked after a long silence, and we agreed, because what else could we do?

"I don't understand," I whispered to Hadrea as the administrator led us out through the far end of the village and up to the mountain itself. A large section, about as big and deep as a bath standing on its side, had been carved out of the pale rock face, leaving a hollow in which the remnants of a former shrine could be seen. Unlike in some of the other towns, where locals had maintained the shrine even after the spirit was gone, here there was no doubt that the town was certain their mountain spirit was gone. No one had left an offering here for a very long time. "Why is this one different?"

Hadrea undertook her usual process of connecting herself to the earth and looking for any sign of the missing spirit or evidence of what had happened to it. She tried it each time even though she had yet to find a single trace. While she did so, I looked around, struggling for further conversation with Il-Toro to fill the silence. To the left of the hollow, off to the west, there was a small path that zigzagged off around the base of the stony rock edge and disappeared; it looked well worn. "What's that?" I asked him, pointing. "Is there more of the village that way?"

"Not anymore," he said. "There used to be houses there but no one has lived in them for twenty years now, because of the gas."

"The gas?" My turn to be confused.

"There are strange gas pockets underground east of the village," he explained. "They can burst up through the earth sometimes; it is very unpredictable and dangerous. We had a geologist from Silasta declare the whole area unstable and unsafe. We do not even let our animals near it."

It suddenly clicked in my head with a flood of understanding. *This* was why the name of the town was familiar. I'd heard about those gas pockets; it was a unique phenomenon, and it being on our lands, our family had investigated it at the time. "They couldn't figure out why it was happening, could they?" I said aloud. "I remember. Vaguely. There was some kind of horrible accident, the first time, wasn't there?" *The Imudush disaster.* That was how I'd heard it described.

Il-Toro nodded, bowing his head. "I fear so, yes. I was not administrator then, of course."

"I was just a kid," I said. "It must have been—"

"Twenty years," he supplied. He looked out to the west, sighing deeply. "It was terrible. Twelve people died when the first pocket went off under a group of houses, some in the explosion and some in the collapse. We hold a memorial every year."

I was about to ask more, but Hadrea made a sudden noise, and we turned to see her blinking her eyes open. Her hands still pressed to the hollow, she shook her head at me. "It is the same," she said. "The spirit is gone."

Il-Toro opened his mouth as if he were about to remind her that he had told her so, but the comment died unspoken at the look on her face, sad and furious. "There is nothing more to be done here," she said flatly.

But I hesitated still. The differences of this site to the others had to be significant. I found my gaze drawn back to the path to the west, and realized that my hands were clenching, one after the other. The anxieties had risen up like a slow tide without me paying mind. Ruthlessly I forced myself to calm, counting *one-two-one-two-one-two* between right and left, dragging the twitches back to a rhythm, matching my breath to eight squeezes. Il-Toro was staring at me, but I didn't care. My subconscious had been working faster than I had. Finally, I was settled enough to squeeze my eyes shut, slow my breath again, and relax my hands.

"Jov?" Hadrea asked. She put a hand on each of my shoulders. "Are you all right?"

"Yes." I took a few tentative steps down the western path, thinking hard, and Il-Toro caught my elbow and pulled me back roughly. "Credo! I must insist that you do not endanger yourself."

I shook him off and Hadrea looked at me quizzically; I summarized what I had learned while she had been in her trance.

"It is not safe!" Il-Toro insisted. "You are the head of the Oromani family, and my guest here! If you are hurt . . ."

"When's the last time there's been a pocket burst? It must have been a long time, because if the phenomenon was still active I'd still be hearing about it, at least occasionally. *Someone* working for my family would have tried to find a way to make money off something like that."

He spluttered, wringing his hands. "Not for some time, I suppose. There was a bad one ten years ago, maybe a little less? But the geologists said they are unpredictable—"

"No strangers came to town," I said, switching my attention to Hadrea. "But they got to that spirit anyway, didn't they? Tiny place like this, with a single route in and out? They'd have been noticed and remarked on if they so much as strolled down the main street. I trust your memory, administrator, and I believe you didn't see them." I gestured to the path. "But our friend here said there's houses back there, or at least the ruins of some. I'm willing to bet there's enough shelter for a few people to hole up for some time and to creep along here to get to the shrine at nighttime when there's no one about. And they trust that your town's got a good enough memory to stay out of there, just in case. You hold an annual memorial and everything, still, twenty years later. They'd be safe out there, wouldn't they."

"Twenty years?" Hadrea said. Her eyes narrowed. "You said that before, also."

He frowned. "What do you mean?

My heart started thundering in my chest and the pressure I had forced under control a short while ago threatened me again, knocking at my attention, grasping for my fingers and toes and thighs. "The Speaker," I said slowly. "You said there hadn't been a Speaker here for twenty years."

"Yes." He folded his arms, like a child who perceives they are in trouble for a wrong they have not committed. "Because our Speaker died in the disaster." At our expressions, he continued in a louder voice. "What has this to do with your questions and your investigation? This was twenty years ago! The spirit only died six months ago."

"Describe her," I said. "In as much detail as you can remember."

He blew out his cheeks, clearly baffled, but his eyes rolled up and to the left as he thought back. "Her name was An-Aralina esImudush. She was born here, and she was apprenticed to the Speaker over in the Sho Valley, I cannot recall her name now, and took over the region from her eventually. I was only young then. At the time An-Aralina died she was forty, forty-five, I suppose. I do not really know for sure."

"What did she look like?"

"She was attractive. Quite big and powerful. The kind of person you always looked at when she came into a room, though I suppose that was her presence more than her looks. Charismatic, you would call her. She had a beautiful voice for storytelling and singing, very deep, and when she spoke, everyone always listened." Il-Toro shifted, uncomfortable. "I do not know what else I can tell you."

"Her hair?" Hadrea pressed urgently. "What was her hair like?"

He shrugged. "Long. She wore it in braids back then, we all did, it was the fashion. Oh! She used to have a few white braids. Because she cracked her head helping little Timeo when he was trapped in the well when I was a boy, and the scar made her hair go white in that spot."

"It's her," Hadrea whispered. "That was the woman at the arena." Our eyes met in shared horror and as one we set off down the path toward the settlement.

"She is dead! Dead for decades!" he called after us in open frustration. "What are you *doing*?"

"I bet there were never any gas pockets here," I said as we moved along the path. "No wonder the geologists were baffled." They'd seen the after-effects and not the phenomenon itself, and of course they had struggled to understand it.

The remains of the settlement were soon visible. A spooky, quiet outline of a miniature dead town with half a dozen buildings in various states of ruin; most were roofless, all damaged. Blackened remnants of fire and several blast sites showed among the overgrown weeds and reclaimed fields. Not just among the houses, though an epicenter of damage was identifiable even twenty years later, but also in various spots in the earth, marked out with decaying fencing. Within a dozen treads of the place it was obvious, though, that it had not been abandoned for twenty years. Despite its overall air of ruin, as soon as we drew closer, signs of habitation were apparent; a vegetable bed was nestled in a sunny spot on the far side, several vines grew on trellises up the side of one of the most intact buildings, and behind a makeshift short wall of reclaimed stones there was sign of a regularly used firepit. A trampled section with short grass surrounding a fence post suggested animals had been tied here.

"They've been living here," I said, and Hadrea nodded. "Not just when they killed off the spirit. This has been empty a few days at most, not months. I think this is where they've been hiding."

"So this An-Aralina faked the gas bursts twenty years ago and ran away?" Hadrea squatted by the firepit, testing for residual warmth. "Why? And who are the others?"

The slap-slap of feet on the path sounded. Il-Toro, apparently unable to resist his curiosity, was approaching along the path, dancing anxiously and looking jerkily about him as if he expected the ground to explode any moment.

"I don't know what happened twenty years ago," I muttered. "She's dead *now*, for real, so maybe there's no way we'll ever know. She started experimenting, maybe, and things went wrong? She got a bunch of people killed by accident and then panicked and fled? Maybe she was even kidnapped and drugged and forced to help someone else. But I'd guess that she's spent that time learning new things to do with fresken, things that weren't allowed when she was a proper Speaker. And whether An-Aralina recruited the others or the other way round, now there's more of them. An-Aralina doesn't match the description of the women who were seen near the missing spirits at any of the other sites." I let out a low exclamation. "You can tell, can't you, when someone has potential? Like Il-Toro, here."

He gave us a startled look, but I ignored him. Hadrea raised an eyebrow. "Yes," she said. "I could feel him instinctively reaching for the spirit at the mountain. And he was so certain that it was gone."

"So what if they're not using the people they take for some horrible sacrifice or rite? What if they're not dead, just 'disappearing' the same as An-Aralina did twenty years ago?"

"It is possible," she agreed slowly. "We know one was a Speaker. There have been some very powerful Speakers who had the condition the administrator described in Ista, the condition Pemu had. They were all women, and some Speakers have very particular views about women being more suited to the work, in general. It is possible they identified someone who appeared to have potential and kidnapped them."

I stared around at the settlement. The place was sinister in its silence, nature slowly reclaiming it but leaving the scars of past trauma there to see. And there was something else, something bothering me. The flicker of a memory, of an idea. There was something else about the story of the Imudush disaster, something missing from the story. Some context I was missing. *When*, specifically, had I learned about the disaster? It felt far fresher than a twenty-year-old story I might have overheard as a child, so I must have read an account more recently than that.

Il-Toro joined us, his mouth hanging open. He still looked jumpy, but his attention was fully captured now by the same things that had caught ours; I saw his eyes take in the signs of habitation. "Someone has been living here?" he muttered. "Impossible! Who would be so foolish? It is clearly marked with warnings."

"Is there anything else you didn't tell me?" I asked him. "Anything else about the story? You didn't find An-Aralina's body, did you? Who else died?"

He flinched, eyes haunted. "I helped clean up out here. It was a terrible, terrible day. Three families who lived here died. The speculation was that they were sharing a meal at the time, because the gas pocket burst around the communal oven, and that is where we found . . . that is where we found all the parts and bodies." That sounded familiar. I was sure I'd read that, perhaps seen an illustration of a group of smiling people of all ages gathered around roasting meat, oblivious to their impending doom. I shivered.

Hadrea, meanwhile, was tracing her hand gently over the mossy stone of a wall, talking softly, so that I had to move close to hear her. "So she left, but then she came back six months ago. Whatever they did here, it worked, and so they moved south. Closer and closer to Silasta, perhaps getting better at whatever it is they are doing. To what end?"

Something Il-Toro had said earlier popped back into my mind. "Did you write the account?" I asked.

He blinked. "What account?"

"I've read an account of what happened here. I'm sure I have. The Imudush disaster, I was too young to remember it properly when it actually happened, so I must have read it in my family records, or the library, or something. But you said barely anyone here could read or write well. Did you write a report for the family, or do you know who did?"

He frowned. "It was not me, no. Your family sent someone all the way from Silasta. A proper scribe from the Administrative Guild, though I would have to look up his name. He came up and recorded it in detail, I remember him interviewing us all. He was a very nice man, very sympathetic. The same fellow came back again years later when there was more activity at the site. He remembered us all. Very thoughtful." He went back to staring at the houses, his gaze distant.

Meanwhile, Hadrea was still walking and talking out loud. "No one outside this region even knew they had destroyed this spirit," she said, glaring at me in frustration as if I were the source of the mystery. "This is not like the arena, causing devastation to make us panicked and afraid. These wounds they tried to *hide*. What are they getting out of it?" She looked back to the mountains, chewing her lip. "What have they . . ." And her face changed, then, with a slow loosening and tightening of muscles, and her eyes grew wide, wider still, and her hand on the stone started to shake. "Oh . . ." she breathed. "Oh, no. Oh, no, they can't have."

A deep chill raced over me at the horror and fear on her face. "What is it? Can't have done what?" When she didn't respond I grabbed her arm, shook her gently. "Hadrea!"

"I . . . I thought that they were using Void to draw people's energy." Her voice was a hoarse whisper. "The way that I did, to defeat An-Aralina. And that they had learned how to store that energy."

"Yes, that's what you said before. That vase, urn thing. The one she had at the party, and then at the arena again. That Lini broke."

"I am sorry, I do not understand," began Il-Toro, but Hadrea ignored him, her anguished expression for me alone.

"Out here in the country," she whispered. "Out here they do not have these parties, these huge public events. The Speaker in the town was using the energy from the crowds because that is available, and easy to access. Out here . . ." She looked back at the mountain, and finally I understood what she meant, and understood, too, the horror of it, even though I was not Darfri myself. "What if they have found a way to drain the spirits themselves? To drain them and store their power in vessels to be carried and used?"

The administrator's mouth had fallen open. "Blasphemy," he choked out, and Hadrea rounded on him.

"The worst kind. I think someone murdered your spirit, administrator, murdered it and took its power. And I think that they are planning to use that power against our country." She rounded on me, her eyes alight. "We have to get back to the city to warn everyone. Right away."

We started running, the administrator scampering after us, calling out confused questions. "What is the fastest way we can get back to the capital from here?" Hadrea demanded as we pounded, panting, back into town. "You need to help us with everything in your power, or something terrible is going to happen."

We scooped up our packs from where we'd left them at the administrator's office while he frantically conferred with a few other citizens, pointing out animals, carts, shouting frightened ideas at one another. Our sense of panic and urgency had infected them all, even if they did not understand why.

But my brain was my brain, and when it had an idea that was picking at it, *chip-chip-chipping* away, not even that level of fear could drown it out entirely. There was still something missing from the story, something that I knew about the event. A scribe from Silasta had written the account, so it had been an outsider, not someone involved, no reason to suspect the account had been manipulated or tampered with, then. But *why* had I read it? I was no scientist, and gas pockets had no particular significance to my studies or interests. But there had been a personal connection, something about it that had been of interest, and not twenty years ago, much more recently.

"Are you sure you don't remember the scribe's name?" I asked Il-Toro, who gaped at me as if he couldn't believe anyone could be so idiotic as to be asking about such matters in the face of an actual disaster. Hadrea, though, was watching me with narrowed eyes and nervous anticipation, recognizing how my brain worked. "Who it was?"

"No," he said, indignant. "I do not remember. Why should I? It was twenty years ago, Credo Jovan."

"Wait." I stopped, thought back. "You said he came back. You said there were more explosions, that the most recent was what, ten years ago, and he came back. What happened then?"

"Well, nothing, Credo," he said. "The land had been dormant for a long time, and I think there was talk that Credo Etan might send some scientists back to see if the land had stabilized. But then there were a few more explosions and it was decided there was no benefit in risking anyone's life for the sake of scientific curiosity."

But I shook my head. "There's something missing from your story. Twenty years ago people died, your Speaker among them, and geologists came and studied things and you closed it off. Then ten years ago it happened again, but no one died that time? Did anything else happen? Anything to do with the spirits, anything unusual at all? Anyone else go missing, anything else happen?"

"No. The scribe came back, made a visit, wrote an update for your uncle, but there was no one hurt. Nothing unusual happened."

"Oh, ah," said the man with the graspad standing beside him. "That's not quite true. That was when they found the boyo, too, remember?"

"They found what?" My heart was in my throat. This meant something, it connected something, I just wasn't sure to what. "The boy?"

"Oh, yes, the boy," a woman in the group said. "That was definitely at the same time, because there was some as wondered if he'd a parent killed in one of the explosions. And it wasn't quite ten years ago because I'd just had my twins then, and I was nursing, and too tired to even think about taking on another child. Eight years, must have been."

Eight years ago. About the same time the research and audits suggested that Aven had begun hiring mercenaries, slowly beginning to fan her rebellion.

The first man took his janjan stick from the corner of his mouth, spat, and looked at me. "Mmm, the boy, the little one. Found him on the road, all alone. No one knew where he came from. Didn't say a word."

"Traumatized, poor little laddie," the woman said, shaking her head. "Terrible thing it was. Couldn't even tell us his name, let alone where his Tashi or his mother or anyone was. They thought he must have at least seen an explosion, and it shocked the life out of him."

"Why didn't you tell me this before?" I demanded of Il-Toro. My muscles were shaking.

The administrator, who had been nodding along, crossed his arms over his chest and raised his chin. "I forgot about the boy. It was ten years ago, I wasn't administrator at the time—"

"Eight," the woman corrected him again, "'less you think I don't know my own children's ages, Toro esImudush."

"—and besides, there was never any proof it had anything to do with the gas. It was only speculation because he would not speak and say where he came from. They found him a week or so later, out on the road south, not anywhere near the blast site. Oh, yes, at first there was some speculation that his guardian had been killed by one of the blasts, but they never found any evidence of that, and there would have been evidence! There was no body, no animals or packs or anything to back it up. I think everyone concluded in the end that he had been lost from somewhere else and wandered over here. It was only coincidence it was a similar time to the blasts."

"Thin enough he was, and hungry, too," the first man said. "Could have been wandering for a while. He couldn't tell us, poor little thing."

"Jovan? Jovan, we are in a hurry."

I became aware that Hadrea was looking at me, and that I was pacing, my legs carrying me back and forth, back and forth, without me even noticing, as my mind made the connections. I was mumbling, swearing, under my breath without being aware of it. "How old was the boy? What happened to him?" I forced myself to ask, but I already knew the answer, because I had finally remembered why I knew the name of the village, why the story of the Imudush disaster had been relevant, with a personal connection.

"Well, we couldn't say for sure, could we, on account of him not talking," the woman said. "But I'd say seven or eight. Only a wee lad. And, why, it was the scribe who found him who took him in in the end." My heart plunged like it had been caught up in an icy waterfall all the way to my feet. "Such a nice fellow. He'd come up to report on the updates on the site and found the little fellow on the way. He felt so sorry for the boy and we still hadn't any idea where he'd come from so when the scribe finished writing up his report, like, he ended up taking the lad home with him. Said he was going to use his connections in the Guild to see if he could trace the mother, but it was obvious he'd taken a real shine to the poor lost thing, and I heard later he'd just inked in the boy to his family instead. I do hope he ended up all right."

A good-news story, a heartwarming tale of perseverance. How a child with such a strange and tragic past had made himself invaluable, first to a family, then to a Guild, then to a Chancellor. "He ended up all right," I muttered. "He ended up all the way to the Manor."

And I wanted to scream and rage and tear a hole in the universe to bring myself home in an instant, because that was still where he was, right now, a constant and trusted presence beside my best friend, all the way back in Silasta.

Incident: Poisoning of Theater-Guilder Macea Peralajo

Poison: Feverhead

Incident notes: Intensely erratic and confused behavior of Theater-Guilder during production of *The Adventures of Sunch the Golden Pen* led to rumors about her suitability for the position. Physics treated Macea after collapse during opening night and suspect significant doses of feverhead; Theater-Guilder had been visiting private gaming room using atmospheric smokes. Order Guards visited gaming room, removed toxic substances, and fined operators. Theater-Guilder stepped down from position and retired to West Dortal with family. *Note:* follow up. Last election was hotly contested and there was significant controversy about listed plays this summer. Not convinced this was accidental.

(from proofing notes of Credola Dia Oromani)

24

Kalina

I burst into the Manor, causing Argo to stand abruptly at his desk and crack his knees. Scowling, he adjusted his spectacles with one hand and rubbed his knee with the other. "Excuse me, Credola Kalina, but this is hardly—"

"We need Tain right away," I said. I'd been too agitated to talk to Abae on the way up here, and she was visibly confused and terrified, but the Council and Tain needed to hear from her and I didn't want to leave her behind anyway.

Just in case, a tiny, hard voice whispered. *Just in case she tells someone else what we know.* I knew now who was coming for us, who'd *always* been coming for us, but they had had help. A foreign woman, supplying drugs and running the Hands on our enemy's behalf. A foreign woman with money and connections and who must be able to speak Sjon and understand our culture. *Not Abae,* I told myself, but nor would I let her out of my sight.

"I'll explain it all to the Council, and you'll understand then," I had told her, and now I told Argo the same thing.

"There is no time for me to go through it with you. Right now, Argo, I literally do not care what he's doing. Honor-down, I don't care if he's in the middle of a shit."

"Credola!" A deeply shocked gasp at my crudity, such a visible display of emotion that I wished Jov were here to see it, given his ongoing battles to generate reactions out of the doorkeep.

"I need to see him *immediately,* Argo. I know who's attacking us."

He blinked, then rang a bell. A servant appeared at his left. "The Chancellor is in the elder room with the Warrior-Guilder. Please ask him to meet Credola Kalina in his study right away."

"Better make it the Council chamber," I said. "And bring Moest. I'll need urgent messengers to every other Councilor to get here right away as well." I paused, considering. "And the captains of the Order Guards and the blackstripes. Oh, and when they get Budua, tell her to bring in Vesko from the diplomatic office, and the best historian she can find."

"Anything else, Credola?" He had never sounded so tart with me before, but I had no time to soften anything.

"I suppose An-Ostada, too. That'll do for now."

I let him take Abae's details down in his tome, firing his disapproving over-the-top-of-the-spectacles look at me, shifting my weight and trying to think through all the implications of what Abae had told me. "The Council chamber, then, Credola," he said, and directed a servant to lead me there.

Tain came hurrying in before I'd even managed to take a seat, and for a moment panic seized my heart at the sight of him. His face was so thin it seemed skeletal, and his skin was entirely the wrong color. But when he gripped my hands with his, his voice was its usual comforting weight. "What's happened?" Behind him, Erel followed, eyes wide, clutching his notebook as usual, and Moest behind him, his face grave.

"I know who they are," I said without preamble. "Tain, I know who's been after us this whole time." I swallowed, and took a breath. "Tain, it's Crede."

"Who?" He blinked at me, gave a kind of half laugh, half snort. "Crede? What do you mean?"

"I mean," I said, trying to keep my voice level but failing. "That it's *Crede* that's been financing and running this whole show. It was always them. The rebellion, Aven, the drugs, the Hands. It's them, it's all them. Led, I would guess, by a Prince, and fueled by religious fanaticism."

A silence followed my pronouncement. "Credola Kalina," the Warrior-Guilder said gently, placatingly, "you are talking about the ancient empire from where our ancestors fled, hundreds of years ago? That Crede?"

"*Some* of our ancestors, yes," I said, meeting Tain's increasingly horrified gaze. "And some of us still bear refugee names. We were looking for some reason why three of the Families were getting struck at more consistently than the others? I think that's why." Oromani. Iliri. Leka. Of the very first founding council of Sjona, the earliest government of the freshly unified country, only three of the Councilors had been Credian refugees.

I slapped the book down on the table in front of them. "I think this is a Credian religious text. It looks like Sjon because the refugees who came here brought their written language. But it's been hundreds of years since then and the languages have moved apart, that's why they don't look exactly the same anymore. And that's why the assassin they sent to do their dirty work here had tattoos and a book that looked like Sjon, but couldn't speak it! Don't you see? It fits! Remember what he called me? Thief, traitor? How can you be a traitor if you've never had some allegiance in common?"

Other Councilors were arriving now, in various states of urgency, muttering among themselves as they tried to follow along with what we were saying. "We all know the story," I said. "A bunch of desperate refugees, scientists and writers and artists and philosophers, suffering under a brutal and tyrannical religious regime in the old Credian Empire, staged a daring escape and fled from their oppressors across the Howling Plains. They found welcome and shelter and shared values with the ancient and nomadic culture already here, and together all our people built a new unified country, free from the oppression the refugees had faced. Sounds familiar? We hear it in schools, don't we? The founding principles of our country were those shared values, and we are all here descended from a mix of bloodlines, whatever our family names are. That was how it was meant to be. No religious regimes dictating how people lived or loved. A culture celebrating learning and arts and personal freedom. Sjona was meant to be a beacon for the rest of the world."

"Except it was not," Il-Yoro pointed out roughly. "As everyone in this room well knows."

"No, it wasn't," I agreed. "But that's our shared story, the one we tell, isn't it? The story of the Credian refugees and the culture that welcomed and incorporated them? That's our vision of Sjona."

There were cautious nods and mutterings of agreement around the room. I took another shaky breath. Since I had put this together I'd had the sensation of being on moving ground, like everything could shift out beneath us again, the way it had when we'd started to uncover the truth of what our Council had done and who we'd hurt before. "But do any of you know any more than that? Like Il-Yoro says, we have our rosy tales of our Bright City and we all know how manipulated they turned out to be. What do we really know about Crede? The refugees didn't just flee an empire for a better life. They fled across the most desperate and dangerous place on the continent, and then they helped create a new society with military defenses wildly out of proportion with the dangers from any of the surrounding civilizations. The early Sjons weren't afraid of the Doranite tribes, or the ever-shifting western clans, or even the growing empire to the north. We'd been living here in relative peace for generations. So the new society didn't decide to fortify Silasta to withstand a siege from any of their neighbors. They built it this way because whatever the circumstances in which the refugees fled Crede, they expected to be followed one day, and their countrymen were sufficiently convinced of that risk to agree to it.

"But what we don't know is *why* they were so frightened. Less than a hundred refugees survived the trip here. Why would a great and powerful empire care about a handful of artists and scientists who weren't valued by their society anyway?"

I turned to Budua and the historian she had brought with her. "Scribe-Guilder, you were a scholar first. Tell me, why aren't there books about Crede in any of our library collections? We know less about this evil empire than the villains in a children's story. Where are the accounts of the daring escape written by the people who lived it? How did they get a few score people across the Howling Plains, when not so much as a kitsa or a bindie can survive out in those conditions? Three of the people who led that party ended up on the very first Council. Where are their stories? Why don't we know who they *were*, except in the vaguest possible terms?"

Budua looked thoughtful, her companion intensely uncomfortable. She shifted in her chair, twisted a bracelet around and around her wrist. She cleared her throat. "Er. Well. It was apparent from what we learned two years ago our ancestors were sometimes . . . er . . . reluctant to set things down in writing. They wanted a fresh start, it was always assumed. They did not devote time or energy to recording much detail about the historical cultures of the past, whether in this land or the one some of them had come from. It is a shortcoming in our early records, true."

"A shortcoming that was almost our downfall before, and which might still be," Tain said. "Credo Jovan's stood before all of us dozens of times over the past two years and told us how all the evidence points to someone incredibly well financed with a deep and personal grudge against this country. If that someone is the Credians, then I think we're missing a critical part of the story, don't you?"

"You think Crede is seeking some kind of revenge?" Moest looked less condescending now. His brows were drawn in and he was staring at me like he was contemplating a particularly difficult puzzle. "I've always understood our ancestors were fleeing oppression and terror. That is the story, like you say. Even if the regime there at the time was angry they fled, that was generations ago. All those people are long dead, and their children, and theirs. What possible interest would remain?"

"That's the piece of the story we're missing, I think," I said heavily. "I don't think any of this makes sense if the refugees just ran. Something else happened. There were broader circumstances, and whatever they were, the people who lived them never wanted to speak about them again, or commit them to our histories." I looked down at the book on the table, remembered the fervor in the assassin's eyes, the intensity of his hatred for me, a stranger. "From what I can understand, this book details a culture and religion built around absolute obedience in exchange for eventual 'ascension,' and if this is how they live in Crede, it's every bit as awful as an evil empire from a story. Fleeing from it makes absolute sense. But what if they did more than flee? What if they did something first?"

The silence grew deeper, more frightening, more complex as shock and confusion turned, like a contagion spreading around the room, to something more like understanding.

"Like what?" Karista had been still and uncharacteristically silent this whole time, blending into the background, but she spoke now, and none of her usual arrogance and Leka confidence were there now. She sounded small, alone, and frightened.

I shook my head. "I don't know. Thief, he called me. Traitor. Whatever they did, it had religious significance, enough to fuel hatred lasting generations. Stole something? Destroyed something? Committed some act of blasphemy so unforgivable that the empire devoted itself to revenge?"

"You said yourself this is an evil empire," Sjistevo said. "Let's not start blaming our founding families for some mysterious atrocities when the other side is patently—"

"It's not about blame," I said. "It's about understanding what our enemies *want*."

"They want our destruction! Not every war needs to be secretly our fault, you know!"

"Honor-down, Sjistevo," Eliska said furiously. "I don't think anyone in the room is looking to sympathize with the people trying to murder us all. But not knowing why the other side is doing what they're doing doesn't help us, it helps them!"

Tain was chewing his lip. "There's more than one piece missing, I reckon," he muttered. "Maybe the refugees did do something terrible in their escape, something that soured the story so they didn't want to tell it. Or maybe it was terrible by Credian religious standards but not by ours, but their escape was so traumatic they couldn't bear to remember it. We all lived through a civil war and more than one terrible disaster. I think we can understand there are some things too painful to want to relive."

Nods around the room at that, and a sudden simmering down of the tension among us. The bonds of shared trauma were strong, after all. "But what I'm wondering," he continued, "is why *now*. If this grudge relates to something done generations ago, why didn't they come for us *then*? What's changed?"

Lazar slapped the table. "Yes, yes, Honored Chancellor, Credola Kalina, this is all very fascinating, but isn't that the key point? Crede couldn't come after the refugees because they fled over the Howling Plains! And, well, that old empire is on the other side of the Howling Plains! No one can cross them. People have tried! So where did they come from?"

"The refugees got here in the first place," I said. "So it's possible, isn't it? And it might have taken a long time, but eventually some Credians have made their way out, too. Maybe it took them this long to find where the refugees went and where their descendants still live. Maybe it just took them this long to find another way to this part of the continent, not across the Howling Plains, but via the north, somehow. Maybe by some incredible sea voyage, I don't know. What we do know for sure is that some of them, with the same tattoos the assassin had, arrived in Izruitn ten years ago."

"And how do we know that?"

Abae cleared her throat politely, but widened her eyes in alarm when everyone swiveled to look at her, some with confusion, others with mild hostility. A short time ago people, including me, were speculating about her country's role in all this, after all. "I met some of them there," she said, her voice small. "They were traders, newly arrived, from the 'far east.' I mistook them for your people but they did not understand me when I spoke to them in your language. Yet they had what seemed to be Sjon words on their arms." She shrugged and spread her hands. "At the time, I thought nothing of it. The world is a vast place."

"The reports all concluded the rebellion plan started about that long ago," said Moest, leaning forward, hand on chin, staring at Abae. "Suppose our Perest-Avani friend here witnessed an early party of Credians who had made it to this part of the continent."

Javesto nodded, catching on. "They could have brought new trade goods, different technologies, and built wealth quickly. What about that gemstone, aragite? All the rage for the last five years but the mine locations are a secret. My contacts say it's controlled by a single company in Izruitn and it's devilishly hard to get a meeting."

I knew that name. "Ectar mentioned aragite, too. He thought the head of the company was Sjon and wanted help getting an introduction. I bet they're not Sjon." I'd missed the clue. And I suddenly felt certain the retired Guild member who'd died had meant to tell me something about that company, too.

"And the Void presumably came from them, too," Eliska said. "But they must be manufacturing it somewhere closer to here. In Izruitn, maybe?"

Chen shot me a sidelong look, somewhere between embarrassment and defensiveness. "The Guard Sukseno told us it was a foreign woman who gave the orders and supplied the drugs and money. We thought he might be covering up for Aven, but the Hands did have him killed. Maybe he was being honest. The Credians would have needed locals for cover to do business from the Empire. This mysterious woman could have been their cover."

"She's here in the city," I said quietly. "Didn't he say that, too?" I didn't look at Abae. *Not her. Someone else.*

"With the Talafan delegation?" Chen gave me a sharp look. "Don't you have a Talafan woman stalking your family, Credola? My Guards have been on the lookout for her for days."

"I—" I frowned. My instinct was to disagree. Mosecca was after me for entirely personal reasons, was she not? And the attacks on the city might have been mixed up with Darfri magic but the witch connection seemed unique to her. But then, could I really say that for certain? "There is, but I don't know . . ." I shook my head. "Maybe. Either way, yes, we still have the Hands to contend with."

"And what do we expect from these Credians, then?" Sjistevo demanded. "Will there be an army coming? Are we prepared to defend ourselves?"

"The Howling Plains cannot be crossed," An-Ostada stated with certainty. "We have been safe here for hundreds of years. If they have found another way to come, they cannot do so without crossing another country."

"Talafar wouldn't let a foreign army use it as a thoroughfare, no matter how pissed they are at us," Tain said. He threw a helpless glance at Vesko. "Right?"

"I do not believe so," Vesko said. "Not unless the empires are working together, Honored Chancellor. One does not simply allow a foreign army to freely enter one's borders."

"Not to mention what kind of state an army would be in if it had to travel that far," Moest pointed out. "The logistics of moving any large numbers of troops is a complex matter. And Crede is not on any map I have ever seen, which means it is distant or inaccessible enough by other routes that transporting an army which is then expected to be able to fight immediately would be completely untenable."

"Which is likely why they've used other kinds of attacks against us," I said. "They have money, and time, and motivation, but they don't have brute force, not directly. So they use explosives and assassinations and drugs and criminal gangs to separate and frighten and damage us."

"And some twisted perversion of Darfri magic, do not forget," Salvea said, with an almost challenging tilt of her chin at An-Ostada, though she did not look at the Speaker directly. "They have a variety of weapons, it seems."

But the Speaker only nodded gravely. "They will be using foul perversions of our sacred arts," she warned them. "We must stand ready to defend this city."

"Well, how do we protect against that?" Lazar roared, with sudden and surprising ferocity. "What are we supposed to *do*?"

An urgent tap at the door, and a Manor servant showed in an army messenger, his face slick with sweat.

"There's smoke! In the distance!" The messenger, slightly out of breath, stepped in and addressed the room at large. "Three massive plumes of it; two to the north, one to the west. It's black. It's like . . . it's like the sky after the arena went up." He looked at Tain, then at Eliska and me, and finally at Karista. "Best early guess is there's been some kind of big explosion at three different locations. Sorry to be bearing the tidings, Honored Credolen, but from the direction of it, it looks like the Oromani, Iliri, and Leka lands. Lieutenant Jay's ordered runners out to look in person and we've sent urgent birds to Telasa and West Dortal to ask for reports from closer. It's likely the birds'll be faster given the distances, but you know it's deceptive out on the plains at times, and with the winds . . ."

People scrambled to their feet.

"They're coming now," I said. My words were quiet but they carried over the hubbub. "There's no more time." I looked at the Warrior-Guilder. "Moest, your people need to be ready for anything. They might not be bringing an army, but they might not need one."

The Warrior-Guilder nodded, his alarm fading in the familiarity and comfort of strategy. "We'll need to evacuate the external village first. Get everyone inside the city. Prepare the walls to full capacity."

"We still have the Hands to contend with!" Javesto said. His face had gone a strange color. "We'll only be shutting ourselves in with them!"

"Maybe with allies inside the city, Crede will be more reluctant to strike?" Even saying it aloud I wasn't convinced. "I don't know what to tell you, Javesto. The assassin told us our city was full of enemies and we were surrounded. He said they were coming. Well. They're here."

Over the course of the next few hours, refugees swarmed into Silasta from the surrounding villages and towns, bearing tales of thunderous cracks and shaking earth. Birds carrying messages from West Dortal and Telasa soon confirmed our fears; the Leka, Oromani, and Iliri estates had all been attacked by something that had torn apart the very earth. Explosions, even more destructive than the ones at the arena, had destroyed whole buildings and presumably killed dozens of people. I tried not to dwell on it, knowing the casualties certainly included family members who had been lucky to survive the seizure of the estates during the rebellion. Had my mother died in her laboratory, working on some new variety of tea, ignoring the world as usual? She had always been happiest there. I pushed the feelings away. There was no time for grief now.

Some of the hysterical people making their way into the city swore the spirits had turned on Sjona and, unsatisfied with our attempts at reparations, were punishing the estates for their sins. A few weeks ago, I might have believed that. After all, the only thing we had seen capable of the kind of destruction the villagers and farmers were reporting was the Os-Woorin. But now we knew there were people who could wreak such damage on their own, without a spirit at all, and for whatever reason, they were in service of the "Prince." These were no acts of angered spirits. They were announcements of intent.

"At some point soon, we will need to consider closing the gates," Moest said to Tain.

"There are still people coming in from all over," Tain said. "We have to keep them open while people are still coming."

Moest nodded patiently. "Yes, Honored Chancellor, but sooner or later we are going to see what caused those explosions, and we need to be able to close everything down as soon as we do."

"If they can blow up estate homes, are a few walls going to keep them out?" It was a rhetorical question and no one bothered answering.

Now Moest looked at me. "Credola, the other matter we spoke about?"

I swallowed, and my throat hurt with the effort of it. She helped us, I thought. She trusts me. But Sukseno had said the Prince's Hands were run by a foreign woman, likely one who spoke Sjon and Talafan, and he hadn't lied about anything else. "Do it," I said, and he nodded.

Tain looked at me quizzically and I shook my head. "Just a precaution." Abae would be safe. She just wouldn't be able to communicate with anyone else. *Just in case.*

He took a drink from the flask and I frowned at him. "Now? Of all times?"

"Now, especially," he said. "I need to have my wits about me. And my strength. We don't know what's coming."

"I'm not sure poison restores your wits. You've been taking that for weeks now. I thought you were tapering off, like you said Jov told you to?"

"I am," he said. "Consider it a taper with a long tail, all right? Lini, we don't have time for this right now."

There was no time to argue further, because distant screams could now be heard, and soldiers on graspads came hurtling back to report that the Prince—and somehow it seemed his identity had spread, because that was how I heard him spoken about, in fearful tones—was coming at last.

"Get everyone inside. Ready on the walls. Get those gates closed!"

It was a nightmare made real, a sight unfathomable. I wanted to squeeze my eyes shut, to will it away, but like everyone else I was instead unable to look away. Barely able to blink.

Under our helpless gaze from the top of the west tower, they came, not quickly, but casually, unhurried, up the main road through the external village as if strolling by the lake on a lazy morning. His crown gleamed in the morning light, his clothes in rich fabrics and glinting with inlaid jewels. Yet he could not be mistaken for anything but the brutal architect of years of our country's trauma; his frame was tall and powerful, a warrior's frame, and he held an enormous blade as if it weighed nothing. And behind him, women, women of all sizes and ages, a dozen, more, walking in concert, fanned out like a formation of birds in flight, and everywhere they touched, they wrought destruction.

The ground rippled and tore under their gestures like a great hoe dragging through the earth, tearing up the dirt and tossing stones aside like the bubbles rolling off a boiling pot. Buildings collapsed as their foundations burbled and in their wake a great dust cloud rose beyond. "I am come!" the man cried, and somehow his voice reached us, though he carried no speaking trumpet. It was as if it was the voice of the very wind, it carried so far and so effortlessly. The village crumpled away from the direction of the women behind him, as easily as paper crushed in a fist.

Then the Prince held up a hand, and the women dropped theirs. The earth quieted and settled, and silence fell. The Prince pulled something from inside his cloak.

A green flag unfurled, was caught up in the crosswinds, and whipped back and forth where he held it aloft. When the wind flapped and stretched it a black sigil was visible. "Peace?" Tain whispered, giving me an incredulous look. "He wants peace? He's just murdered the fortunes know how many people on the estates, and he pretends he wants peace?"

Moest was conferring with his lieutenants. "What do you want to do, Honored Chancellor? Councilors?"

"I seek only to speak," the man called out, his voice still ringing up easily. "I can even speak from outside, for now. You need only listen. I will harm no one while you listen. I am a courteous man."

"What's to speak about?" Moest yelled down, even as the frightened chatter on our side of the wall cooled and quieted. "You're killing our people and cutting up our land. Seems like it's about time to cut you down."

"Tut tut! That is no way to treat a flag of parley! Where is this so-called 'honor' your country loves to brag about so much?"

Tain slammed his hands on the stone and leaned down. "Say your piece then!" he shouted. "We're listening!"

There was a pause—it seemed to me, for dramatic purpose—and then the man's voice came up, even louder, slipping through the stones, ringing ears and vibrating muscles, the boom of a drum and the whisper of a lover all at once.

"I am the Prince."

"What Prince?" someone on the wall shouted back, and a faint ripple of rebellious laughter passed through the crowd.

Peering down at him, though, through the crenels, I fancied I could see his face, and it was smiling. "Why, *your* Prince, of course," he said, and again his voice carried as if he were speaking a few treads away, and the laughter died out like a snuffed candle. "Prince of Crede, God's Empire, second son of the one and true Holy Emperor. Prince of the Sun, Prince of the Words, Prince of Vengeance."

But vengeance for *what*? Listening to him felt like a dangerous enchantment, but I could not deny that part of me craved his words. Oromanis, after all, were bred for intrigue and secrets and solving mysteries, and my curiosity about what had happened so long ago it could cause war generations later was intense. And I was not alone. All along the battlements, we hung, staring, listening, unable to stop.

"My people. Long have you hidden yourselves from God's wrath for your sins. Long years passed, and your crimes became stories, and hopes for our vengeance faded. But I alone did not give up on you! I alone, among all my fair brothers, knew that when strife and famine fell upon our beloved Empire, a new leader could rise and take us to glory!" He raised his arms as if to an adoring crowd of cheers, apparently oblivious to the cold and fearful silence. "And only I was brave enough to pledge our revenge at last. Only I was wise enough to find you. Only I clever enough, strong enough, to destroy you even in the face of your protections.

"But I have found you, as I pledged I would! I, your Prince! So I say this to you now, my children. Open your gates to me, and extend to me the humility and deference of my position, and I shall extend to you my benevolence. You need not die."

Moest looked down the line. "Silastians? Shall we give this so-called Prince a taste of our 'humility and deference'?"

There was a slight pause. Then Tain smiled, a faint, crooked thing. "Yeah, I think we should."

And Moest opened his mouth and roared, and we roared back, from the tower, along the line, into the depths of the city itself. Moest and his lieutenants dropped their arms, calling out the command, and arrows plunged down in a thicket of deadly rain from the walls.

But the women raised their hands in response to the barrage, and the arrows skidded and bounced and deflected, like dancing hail on a rooftop. Only there was no roof; there were only the Speakers, or whatever we were to call them. They were in Darfri garb but they sang no songs, no chants; there was no music in what they did now. They were far below us, and I could not make out any detail, but it seemed to me there was something strange and wrong in their postures. Unlike the commanding Darfri woman who had attacked us in the arena, the women looked almost cowed. Nevertheless, they were single-handedly creating some kind of invisible hardened air barrier, protecting them all from what should have been certain death.

"Hold fire for now!" Moest called, and the Prince swept his hand sideways, and the women behind repeated the gesture; the hundreds of spent arrows tipped off in piles on either side of the party. And then, just as the Warrior-Guilder was readying a new attempt, the Prince began to laugh, and once again the sound seemed to reach inside my very bones.

The Prince spread his hands, gesturing to the arrows scattered harmlessly to either side of him. "Is this your courtesy? I welcome it, for how are children to learn but by failing?" He laughed again as the arrows were nocked and bows drawn along the line. "You are, of course, welcome to try again, if you think your luck or your aim has improved. But I think perhaps it is time for a display of *my* strength." He turned his head and gave some direction to the women behind him, and all of a sudden their group was surrounded by a swirl of wind that lapped around the edges of their formation, picking up dirt and debris and whipping them around as effortlessly as a stray leaf caught in the Maiso.

And then they lurched, as one, in a crude lunge of their bodies, toward us, and the wind hurtled up at the wall. The power of it knocked me sideways into Tain, but we had caught only the edge of it. The main force of the blast crashed into the length of wall to our right, and like a great invisible lasso it tore a dozen archers from their places, whipping them up into the air, spinning and tossing them as helplessly and dreadfully as the dirt and rubble, pulled too fast and too rough to even hear their screams. We staggered back to our feet, shock stealing even the cries from our mouths.

The Prince gave another command and the windstorm spun one final, terrible, circular motion, and then it was gone into nothing, and the archers fell like poppets flung by a child, boneless and broken, thirty treads to the ground below.

"The greatbow!" Moest yelled grimly. "Now!"

We moved out of the way as the greatbow, already loaded and aimed, was released. Its massive bolt, as long as a cart, punched down toward them, but some part of me, of all of us, had already expected what would happen. The great bolt was somehow diverted by the invisible force of thickened air so that instead of striking into the Prince or the women beyond, it slipped to the side and hammered deep into the earth, sending up another huge spray of dirt and debris.

Terror and hopelessness sank into my heart, and I saw it reflected in all the faces around me. Crede did not need an army if it had this kind of power at its disposal. I looked around, down the line. Where was An-Ostada? Were she and her Speakers coming?

Oh, fortunes. Where is Hadrea? My eyes drifted north. Somewhere out there was the only person who'd shown herself capable of matching the kinds of feats these women were performing. Had she and Jov seen the explosions and guessed what was happening? Were they racing back to the city even now? Or had they been caught up in it themselves?

"My children!" the Prince called, and this time he sounded reproachful. "You have shown me your 'strength' and I have shown you mine. I trust this matter is settled, unless you would like a further demonstration?"

This time there were no defiant cries back. The splayed figures of our archers were spread out like scattered crumbs on the ground below. The rest of us were hunkered down, fearful. Some people were pushing off the walls, fleeing into the city, others had turned their backs on the parapet and were crouched in tight balls.

"Good. Now you understand. For God does not forget crimes against Him or His people. He does not forget or forgive, and He has been patient, but He is patient no longer. This city, this country, this haven of sin and debauchery, is a place built by murderers and thieves and blasphemers and those who gave shelter and refuge to them. I am His agent, at long last come to deliver Him the vengeance He has so long been denied.

"But, my people!" His voice abruptly took on a softer, gentler tone. A smooth knife through the ribs, a kiss of sweet poison on the lips. "My people.

I am your Prince, and I am benevolent. I do not hold you all accountable for the crimes of your ancestors. God's vengeance is great, but I do not need or wish to destroy you all. I do not even wish to destroy your city. It is a beautiful feat of design, were it turned to the glory of God, and the pious lives of His subjects. You will be permitted to live as subjects of our great Empire. Observe my mercy! Tremble under my compassion!"

He did something with an arm and the women moved in response. The ground below his feet began to rumble, a deep and foul unnatural grumbling that sent vibrations up through the heavy stone of our walls and into our very bones. "I. Am. Benevolence. But I am also Justice, and my revenge, God's revenge, bears three names.

"Leka. Iliri. Oromani."

Beside me, Tain flinched. I found his hand with mine and we hung on to each other.

"Three names for three traitors. Betrayers." It seemed to me then that he looked directly at me and Tain, that I could feel the cold grip of his gaze hooking into me. *"Poison names."*

Tain's hand in mine faltered; I squeezed harder.

"We know these names, in Crede. We remember them. We have whispered our revenge for generations while you have grown fat and stupid and forgetful. The Empire does not forget. We always remember. And we are here for you at last, those who carry that blood. In your arrogance, in your foolishness, you did not hide yourselves away. You flaunted those names, you gave them to your children, those names of the wicked. Murderers, traitors, bearing those names started a war, a long and silent and deadly war, a war their children must pay for." A hiss now, slicing through the air, a blade of a voice. "Such is justice. Such is right."

The rumbling grew greater, louder, more insistent. The very air around the women seemed to thin and glint and tremble, vibrating in my chest and rattling my teeth.

Then, abruptly, it stopped. It was like being released from a too-tight grip, blood seeming to race around my skin, tingling and urgent, burning in my extremities. I sagged against the stone, and I wasn't the only one. All around me people staggered, slumped, let out soft cries. The Prince smiled, raised his arms. The sun glinted on his luxurious clothes and his beautiful skin and his golden crown. "My children. I give you this chance. One evening, one night, to consider all you have seen, and to come humbly to your rightful place as citizens of the great Empire. It is almost complete. I have taken back what they stole. All you need do to show me your true hearts and begin your penitence is one small thing. You must bring me every person who bears those traitors' names. Bring them to me, every man, woman, and child who has freely worn the name of those most treacherous creatures. They will be your offering to God to begin your path to righteousness.

"You will keep your city! You will keep your lives! You will be given the chance to live a pious and obedient life, and if you obey God's word, perhaps one day you too will ascend with the righteous. Men of Silasta, you have much to gain. And if you choose not to obey? You have much more to lose."

He flicked his hand, and the women raised theirs one final time. A massive ball of flame erupted, swallowing the entire greatbow in blue-and-orange fire. The soldiers operating it were caught in the fireball and their terrible screams pierced the air even as the heat of it blasted us backward, roasting and merciless. Tain sheltered me with his body and I cowered, certain we were about to die, but then abruptly the heat and the flames died into nothing. The remains of the greatbow, smoking and disintegrating, collapsed in a heap between the charred and melted corpses of its operators.

"I will wait for you at dawn," the Prince called. "You will bring me the traitors, or I will bring your doom."

One day and one night. An arbitrary amount of time to plan an impossible defense, and a choice that was no choice at all.

"Will the walls hold?" someone asked Eliska, for perhaps the fifteenth time. She apparently had a wellspring of patience far beyond mine because she answered again with unflappable calm.

"Against ordinary forces? Against catapults and rams and people? Yes." She retied her hair in its customary tail. "Against the very ground falling away beneath them? No, we saw that two years ago. The walls are strong and thick but they are, ultimately, built on the earth." She pressed her palms against her eyes. "Against someone who can command wind and fire and earth at his will? I don't know what could stand against that."

Moest's lieutenants were organizing ordinary folk into makeshift troops, ostensibly to fight the Prince in the event that he broke into the city, but mostly to keep them occupied. Children, the elderly, anyone unwilling or unable to fight, if it came to it, would shelter in the tunnels under the city.

"We need to get the Leka, Oromani, and Iliri households somewhere safe, somewhere hidden," Moest told the Council. "I don't want some scared citizen thinking they'll save us all if they just hand over a few kids."

It was a measly number: my small household and the few remaining of Karista's; Tain had no immediate family here. To some, their lives might seem an acceptable trade to avoid facing the Prince and his terrible magics.

"It only takes one idiot to start a whole collapse. Probably best if none of you are visible today," Moest said, but Tain shook his head.

"People are scared, but I don't think any Silastian fancies the lifestyle the Prince is proposing," Tain said, and one or two people managed a chuckle.

"I do not like living under the effective rule of tyrants, even well-meaning ones," Il-Yoro said. "And I take issue with how the current Council hears certain voices louder than others. If I had my way, every one of you rich bastards would be out of this room and onto the street, and see how you enjoy life at the other end of the town. But I will ride a graspad straight into hell before I live as a slave under that man." He slapped the shoulders of the men and women on either side of him. "We stand together."

"I mean to say . . ." Lazar's chin quivered. "Of course! Never any doubt."

"This is not a perfect country," Salvea agreed in her soft, firm voice. "But it is ours, for all our flaws. It is not part of an empire under a cruel and illogical god."

Javesto thumped his fists on the table. "This is *our* haven of sin and debauchery, and may it prosper!"

A tired, ragged laugh sprang up around the table.

"Then we're in agreement?" Tain said. "We figure out some way to fight this bastard?"

And every voice chimed in, resolute. The load on my chest lightened.

"An-Ostada," Tain continued. "We need you. If we can't shoot him down with arrows and he can set us on fire or blow us off the wall at will, we need some way of protecting ourselves from his magic or distracting him long enough to get our army close. Was he using fresken himself, or is it only the women?"

She pursed her lips and shook her head. "From what I have seen, it is only the women, though under his command or control. But they are too strong. I suspect they are using unnatural means to amplify their power."

"The woman at the arena," I said, remembering, and An-Ostada met my eyes and nodded. "She had that urn. When it smashed, it interfered with what she was doing."

"So if we can get close enough, we might be able to do the same," Moest said. "What would we be looking for?"

An-Ostada frowned. "Be alert for something the women are holding, or wearing, with which they are taking particular care."

"And your Speakers? Can they protect us the way his are protecting him?"

An-Ostada raised her chin. "I will gather every person with talent in the city. And you must . . ." She paused, lips tightening as if in anticipation of particularly foul medicine, then continued. "You must announce that citizens who have used the drug known as Void gather at the lake when I am ready. Their weakness was used against us before. We must turn it against our enemies now. We must wake the great Os-Woorin, and we will need their help to do it."

"If we wait until morning and meet him face-to-face, he'll control the conflict," Chen said. "We need to change the narrative. Do something he won't expect."

There was a noise from the corner. Erel, notebook in hand as always, cleared his throat.

"If I'm not speaking out of turn, Honored Chancellor," the boy said, "I think I have an idea."

Dusk fell swiftly, as if the very day was hurrying us to our uncertain future. I handed Tain a second dagger. Around him, a small band of soldiers and blackstripes tightened boots and adjusted weapons, shifting nervously as we lurked in the shadows. On the walls, Moest noisily directed troops, creating the illusion that we were preparing for a battle in the morning. Hopefully, things would never get that far.

"Wait for the signal," I reminded Tain for the tenth time. "We don't know how fast they'll respond. You've got to make sure they're distracted before you go in."

"I know, Lini." He caught my hand. "We'll be all right."

"Don't rush. He knows he's potentially vulnerable in the open so you can't count on him letting his guard down. We'll keep him as busy as we can here, but—"

"Lini." He put his other hand on top of the ones we had clasped together until I stopped babbling. "We know the plan. We'll be careful."

This sewer line drained under the north wall and came out upriver in the marshes; Erel had remembered we'd used it during the siege to set a trap. The Prince and his Speakers were camped out in the abandoned village, arrogantly waiting for tomorrow morning's decision, and there was no significant cover there. Our attack would be two-pronged; part of the army would march on the camp from the west gate road as Moest attacked with barrages from the walls. While the Prince was distracted, Tain and his team would sneak in and target the women.

It was a fine plan, but for Tain's role in it. He was decent in a fight, but he wasn't a soldier. "If something goes wrong, we're handing the Prince what he wants," I said. "He wants a symbolic sacrifice to his god, and you're walking right up to him."

"Yes," he said, a strange twist on his lips, a sadness and a certainty in his eyes that brooked no argument and broke my heart. "But I'd be the first head on a pike if he takes the city anyway. At least if it ends tonight, more people might live." He let go of my hands. "There's no tomorrow that has me in it. Maybe I can do some good before."

Desperation filled me. "Jov and Hadrea are still out there," I said urgently. "They could make it back in time. Hadrea can take fifty princes and anything those damned women can throw at her."

"Well, let's hope for that," he said. "Honor-down, we can all hope for that. But if you see Jov again and I don't, just tell him . . ." He paused, swallowed, faltering. Then he gave me his best grin, his warmest grin, the one that saw straight through me, and kissed my cheek. "Tell him I died doing what I've always done best. Being an absolute bloody idiot."

"Honored Chancellor?" Erel tapped Tain's shoulder. He had been handing around a flask to the team, but Tain refused it with a shake of his head. "It's almost dark. Time to move."

I couldn't bring myself to stay and watch them descend to the sewers. I had the feeling, hurrying back to our apartments, that it was the last time I would see my friend.

"I'm sorry I was away so long," I told Sjease as I stepped inside. "But you all need to pack up and be ready to move soon. Dee, Ana, the boys, they need to be out of sight. If things . . . if things go bad, they're likely to be targets."

Sjease looked unsettled. "Where have you been? We've been sending messages but not even Etrika would tell us anything. Dee's been frantic."

"The Council's working on a plan. You stay with Dee, all right? No matter what happens, you stay with her." They might not be a trained fighter but I trusted them to put Dee's welfare first.

Dija came flying out of her room, followed by her brothers and Ana, and I enveloped her in a hug.

"They wouldn't let me leave the apartments," she said, scowling at our housekeeper, who only shrugged unapologetically.

"I'm sorry," I said again, looking around at my family. "Things are going to get a bit scary, but we're doing our best to end this before any more people get hurt, all right?"

"Why do they hate our family so much?" Dee asked quietly. "What did our ancestors *do*?"

I could only shake my head. A cold, unpleasant prickle ran over my skin.

Reading my face, Dee pressed, "He said they were murderers. He called our names *poison names*. What did that mean? Did our ancestors poison someone?"

"I don't know, and it doesn't matter," I lied. "We're not our ancestors." We had no way of knowing the context or the justification. But Etan had trained me too well and I couldn't help seeds of speculation germinating in my head. Thieves, he had called us. And then, chillingly: *I have taken back what they stole*. I'd thought it so only a few hours ago: Oromanis were bred for intrigue and secrets and mysteries. He had taken back our land's magic, so I could guess what they had stolen, and who they had poisoned.

But most of all, Oromanis were bred for loyalty. "We've got a plan, all right? We're going to stop him. But for now, I need you all to get food, water flasks, and blankets. We're going to hide you in the jail until this is over. Wear scarves and keep your head down. The fewer people who recognize you, the better. There are still Hands out there and we don't know who we can trust." I thought briefly of Abae, under guard on my order, but pushed down the guilt.

"That's why I needed to talk to you," Dee said urgently. "And to the Chancellor. You were gone all afternoon and I need to show you something."

"You'll have to show me later," I said. *If we get a "later."* "We have to move. The plan's already in action and you can't be caught out in the open."

"What's the plan?" she asked promptly. "Where's the Chancellor?"

I glanced uneasily at Ana and the boys, but Sjease had bustled them into action. "We're not able to hurt the Prince from a distance, and in daylight there's no chance of surprising him." I grabbed a satchel and began loading it up with dried fruit and meat, the day's leftover bread, a jar of vegetable paste, greens hanging from the hook above the bench. Anything they could eat in hiding. "They're going to flank him in the dark. Tain's gone with them."

"Auntie, wait, please. I think I found something out. I don't want it to be true, but I'm afraid it is. Auntie, *where's the Chancellor*?"

She sounded so urgent, and so like Jov, that I stopped packing. "They're in the sewers."

"They?"

If I closed my eyes, I could still feel the pressure of his lips on my cheek. "Tain and a group of soldiers and blackstripes."

"Just soldiers and blackstripes? No one else?" She wore the strangest expression.

"Dee, what *is* it?"

"Who thought of the plan?"

I blinked. "Erel di—" I began, but I hadn't even gotten the words out before she slapped her hands over her mouth. "Dee!"

"We have to go after them, right now," she said in a rush. "Auntie, Erel's the spy."

The bag fell out of my hands, scattering food and cracking one of the jars. Oil seeped over my feet. "What?" Already, I was picturing the boy, always there in the background, watching, listening, taking careful notes. "How do you know?"

She shoved a pair of boots on and dropped her spectacles as she bent over. Her hands shook as she pushed them back on her face. "When Uncle Jov and Hadrea went to the estates I had the idea that if there was someone out there, then someone had to be communicating with them from the city. So I used my savings to bribe every messenger in the Guild to tell me who from the Manor sends messages to our estates or the Chancellor's. And I found someone. A messenger who sends letters from Erel to his 'Tashi' in a place called Imudush North."

I frowned. "So . . . Erel writes to his Tashi. Why wouldn't he? I'm sure he told me his Tashi retired back home up there somewhere." My head felt thick and slow.

"He told me that, too. But his Tashi wasn't *from* the estates. Erel was an orphan, he was found abandoned up there, but the Guild scribe who found and adopted him was *Silastian*. He had no connection to Imudush North. That story didn't make sense, don't you see?"

I shook my head. "Dee, he's just a kid, and he's been with the Guild and with the Chancellor since he was a boy. How could he be a spy? And what could he have to do with Crede?"

"I'm a kid, too," she said grimly. "And I knew how to spy on *him*. But Auntie . . . I don't think Erel's who he says he is. I think . . . I think he might be the Prince's son."

INCIDENT: Poisoning of Credo Tamago Leka

POISON: Eel brain

INCIDENT NOTES: C. Tamago died after a feast celebrating opening night of noted playwright Jos Banjrot's *Ascent of the Sun*, but reclusive habits meant servants did not find his body until the following day. Appears to have choked on vomit. Examination of the menu and remnants in the Leka kitchen suggest an insufficiently baked eel; C. Tamago appears to have chosen his own portion and I am satisfied his death was accidental.

(from proofing notes of Credo Etan Oromani)

25

Jovan

We were racing on borrowed graspads along the road by the river when the explosion sounded, sending a tremor through the ground and causing our mounts to shudder and stumble. I nearly fell, but Hadrea, true to her usual impressive but infuriating competence, caught me by the back of my shirt and steadied me.

We pulled up and stared at the rising cloud of ominous black on the horizon. "Whatever they were preparing for, it is happening now," Hadrea said grimly. "Do we go look, or keep on to the capital?"

I considered the geography with a sinking dread. The explosion had come from my family estates. My heart beat fast, and it hurt to take a breath. "By the time we got there, they'd be long gone." Honor-down, I felt like the coldest bastard to say it. "There'll be people closer than us who can help." *If there's anyone left to help.*

She gave me a sympathetic look. "Keep on then," she said, without judgment.

Silasta was upriver, which meant having to ride until the nearest town to hire a boat and crew. Many of the scant and scared population had already fled to Telasa or Silasta when they'd seen the blast. Rumors abounded; there had been three great blasts, we were told, the other two northwest and southwest. Other estates, I guessed. And then on to the capital?

Birds had passed overhead, north to Telasa. "They'll be sending for the regiments from the border cities," I reasoned. "Our enemy must know we'll do that. They won't wait around to be penned in." I looked hopelessly up the river. It had taken us valuable hours to find a boat and willing crew, and we were more than a day away from Silasta even in favorable conditions. Almost everyone I loved in the world was there, being marched on by monsters carrying the stolen power of our spirits. *"Fuck!"* I kicked the nearest stone as hard as I could, the pain in my toes a momentary blessed distraction. An elderly man gave me a startled and disapproving look.

"We will be too late," Hadrea said quietly.

"Yes," I hissed. "You're probably the only person with a chance of stopping them, and we're too *fucking* far away."

Hadrea looked at the position of the sun, her expression thoughtful rather than upset. "The Maiso will begin soon," she murmured.

"Yes, thanks, that's very informative," I grunted.

"Jovan," she said patiently. "The Maiso is very powerful."

"Yes, I know. One more thing that'll make our journey harder."

But Hadrea had stopped listening. She shook loose her scarf, cracked her neck, and sat down.

"What are you doing?" I demanded.

"Be quiet, Jovan," she said calmly, closing her eyes. "I am about to ask a boon."

Darkness fell as we slipped through the water, our passage too smooth and free for a boat traveling upriver, aided by unnatural forces. There was something utterly eerie about the redirected wind. The Maiso had always seemed to have a personality—a capricious one, at times—so it took no real stretch to attribute it to a mighty spirit. And yet the wind's assistance unsettled me more than its opposition. Life was more comfortable when nature was an indifferent and unrelatable feature of the world, with no fragile and confusing connections to humans. Certainly our crew thought so, judging by the fearful glances they shot Hadrea when they thought she wasn't looking.

I took heart from the silence, and when the white city walls took gradual form in the distance, they stood still and unbroken. The outer village lay in darkness, perhaps evacuated. Hadrea, tired from communion with the Maiso spirit, lay back in the boat while I stared ahead, assessing.

Close to the city, we abandoned the boat, cautious despite the dark. Our thoroughly spooked crew left us by the side of the river and promptly turned downriver without a backward glance.

"Well, the walls are certainly active," I muttered as we approached. "Do you think—"

The night burst into life.

A faint whoosh preceded three heavy collision noises as something crashed into the ground to the west of the river. Bright streaks followed; flaming arrows from the walls, a rain of fire. Their landing triggered several bigger bursts of flame, illuminating a ring of half a dozen shouting people who must have been camped there.

More shouts, and the pounding of approaching troops. A dark mass swarmed toward the camp from the other side; our army, I guessed, coming round from the west gate.

Hadrea tugged at my hand, but I stopped. A flicker of light from the river itself had caught my eye.

"What's that?"

Hadrea gestured to the camp. "We should help! Jovan, what are you doing?"

But I'd seen the glint of light again. "That's the sewer drain." If the city were locked up, shut down against a magical foe, the sewers might be one of the few ways to get past our walls undetected. Either someone was trying to get out of the city, or someone was trying to get in.

Hadrea pried open the grate and we crept into the tunnel. Water sloshed cold and sludgy, halfway up my shins. Someone had blocked the flow from the inside. The light I'd glimpsed reflecting off the water now gave off a steady glow, held by someone just out of sight around the curve of the tunnel.

". . . not you."

I recognized my sister's voice in an instant, and my heart leapt; I almost called out, but Hadrea put a cautious hand on my chest.

"You don't know me." I knew that one too, and it made my blood chill. Erel sounded . . . not confident, precisely, but not frightened, either. "You never did. I've *never* been one of you." The sound of someone spitting. "You're all disgusting. Sinners. Traitors."

"That's what he told you." *Oh, fortunes.* Tain, too. What were the three of them doing down here? I tried to picture the dynamic, the possible layout. "If you wanted to kill me you could have done it a thousand times. Why now?"

"What good would killing you do? Someone else would just take your place. It isn't revenge if the whole city doesn't bow down to—Don't move!" Higher, that time. "Don't think I won't."

"Erel, you don't want to hurt me." Kalina sounded so calm. Calmer than me, for sure. Hadrea and I looked at each other in the dark. "Whatever you were taught as a child, you've lived here half your life and you know we're not thieves or traitors or murderers."

"You're not those things, either," Tain said. "I made you my page because I trusted you. You're a good person, Erel."

"I *am* a good person," he retorted. "I am a good and loyal son. My father the Prince prepared me for this my whole life. Twenty years of planning to destroy you and everything your country stands for." He laughed, a little breathlessly. "Everything you've done in the last two years, he knows, because I've told him. Every letter you penned, every report you signed, every recommendation your Council made, came through my hands. I knew how much your stupid, blasphemous carnival meant to you, that it was the perfect way to humiliate and defeat you. *I* knew where your people would be, and where they wouldn't be. I knew the man most of the city thinks is your lover is your poison taster. Oh, yes, *Credola* Kalina, I know about your family. I'm not stupid. You let your guard down in front of children because you don't take them seriously. You, of all people, when you've been teaching your niece to be just like you!"

"If you hurt a hair on Dee's head, Jovan will find you, and he will tear. You. Apart." Tain's words, through gritted teeth, channeled the sudden burst of rage inside me.

"I wouldn't hurt Dee." A bruised tone to his voice. "She's just a kid. She didn't choose to be raised in this place."

"*You're* just a kid, Erel."

"I've never been just a kid. You were lucky with the siege. My father thought I was too young then. If I'd been in charge instead of that woman—"

Kalina sounded incredulous, but still gentle, still patient, when she replied. "Erel, you were thirteen years old. You wanted to be in charge of a rebellion?" She broke off with a sharp intake of breath, and I clenched my fists, agonizing indecision lancing me. Erel must have a weapon on her, but we couldn't see who was where so we couldn't risk storming around the corner. "What happens now, Erel?" she continued after a moment. "There's two of us and one of you."

"I'm the one with the knife at your throat."

"But what are you going to do with it? I know you don't want to kill me. And if you do, you think you can overpower Tain? A grown man?"

"That weakling?" He snorted. "You don't pay attention to anything, do you? My father's lucky he's made it this far, judging from all those secret visits from the physic. Father wants him alive when he tears his heart out, and it would have been disappointing if he'd dropped dead. I'm going to deliver him and neither of you can stop me."

In the silence that followed, my ears rang with the pressure of suspicions I had spent months pushing away. My heart beat so loud in my ears, I was sure the trio around the bend would hear me. I glanced at Hadrea, who was scrutinizing the tunnel, her slight frown visible in the faint light.

"Your father," Tain said. "That Prince out there? The one who dumped you on a road when you were seven? That 'father'?"

"He did not *dump* me," the boy retorted. "He trusted me with a mission."

"What kind of mission is that to give to a little boy?" Kalina asked quietly. "To ingratiate himself with a family—a family who gave him their name, and a home, and love, and support—and then use them to get close to Tain? And we *also* loved and cared for you. Tain treats you like his own family, Erel. What kind of 'father' asks a boy to betray people who've offered him nothing but kindness?"

"What's the love of sinners worth? Less than nothing." But they had the ring of repeated words, a phrase to remind a little boy not to care for the people who cared for him, and Erel delivered them without conviction. A tiny bead of hope formed inside me. Erel had been indoctrinated, fed a diet of propaganda, and put in a terrible position. But he wasn't at heart an evil person. He had only wanted the approval and affection of his parent. He *did* care about Tain. He could be talked down.

"*He* has to be delivered to my father," Erel said. "But you don't have to die, Kalina. My father the Prince must punish the three Families, but women don't matter to him, because they don't matter to God. Women take all kinds of airs here, but that is not what God says a woman is for."

"What does God say a woman is for, Erel?" Honor-down, she was still so calm. How had I ever doubted her bravery?

Erel, by contrast, grew more agitated with each answer he gave. "God chose women to bear life and magic, but they are just a vessel. God does not mean for women to wield power except in His honor and the service of His chosen leaders."

"That's what the book says," Kalina said. "But you're a spy, Erel, which means you're observant, so you can't be foolish enough to think half the population exist as a vessel for anything. They're people, same as you. Good and bad and screwed up and happy and everything in between."

"That isn't what God teaches." But there had been the tiniest hesitation before his answer. A chink in whatever armor this Prince had built around a small boy to make him believe. "God says women can be cunning but never wise. My father has used cunning and ambitious women to do his bidding against Sjona, so you of all people should know they should not be trusted with power."

There was a sloshing of someone taking a step, and Erel shouted, "Stay back!"

My heart sank. I'd been listening carefully and that last made me certain Tain was closer to us, with Erel and Kalina on the far side, giving us no chance to sneak up behind the boy.

"So is it God or your father who wants us all dead?" Tain asked. His tone was as gentle as Kalina's, inquisitive rather than aggressive.

"Sjona is an affront to God, and my father is the man who will finally take revenge in His name," Erel replied, again with the air of rote learning. "He will be declared the next rightful Emperor."

"Why did it take God hundreds of years to get revenge on our families?" Tain asked. "If he's so powerful. Why *now*?"

"Because you stole our link to Him!" he blurted out, a definite edge of hysteria in his voice now. "Your ancestors! They tricked their way into the Palace of the Emperor and found the Holy Vessels, the source of the Emperor's connection to God. They stole what they could and destroyed the rest, and fled here to this cursed place. And they gave it to others, and used it against Crede, to seal us away from the rest of the world so we could slowly stagnate and perish!"

Hadrea stiffened beside me, but Tain's voice was even. "Erel. Those are words someone else has taught you. A story. You've seen firsthand what can happen if people accept uncritically what a society says about its own history. How can you be sure this isn't just some revenge story passed down over the years? What Holy Vessels? Do you really think a few score refugees carried old artifacts across the Howling Plains?"

The boy spat. "The Holy Vessels, Chancellor. The connection to God. Not artifacts. *People.* Your ancestors found them and they poisoned them all."

A beat of silence followed that bizarre pronouncement, then there was a sudden heavy splash. *A body dropping?* Without hesitation or warning Hadrea sprang into motion; I followed clumsily and was met with a flurry of sloshing water, moving shapes and shadows in the poor and flickering light. I had a moment to identify Kalina on the ground on her side, and the other two wrestling for control of a long knife. Hadrea leapt into the fray, seizing Erel's wrist, and I grabbed the boy from behind, but he fought like a wild animal, clawing and biting, wickedly strong. The lantern shattered, leaving us surrounded by blackness and foul water and flailing bodies. Someone or something struck me in the jaw and I fell back, my head ringing.

A light flared into the gloom. Hadrea held a flame aloft in one bare hand, revealing the muddy figures of Erel and Tain, the former with one arm wrapped tightly around Tain's neck and a glinting blade in the other hand.

"*Don't* use your stolen magics on me," he hissed, "or I'll cut his throat right now." His eyes found me in the dark. "Credo Jovan, too? My father will be pleased with me. He'll take both your hearts and he won't even have to break down your walls." I realized my hands were empty, my knife lost somewhere in the sewage during the scuffle.

"Don't do anything, Hadrea," I said. No matter how fast she was, he could cut Tain's throat faster. My breath screamed in my lungs; I felt paralyzed by indecision. Kalina was slumped at Tain's feet but it was too dark to tell how badly she was hurt. Had Erel cut her throat? Hadrea lowered her flame, and light flickered over my sister. No visible blood, but she wasn't moving. Erel stared at Hadrea, seemingly transfixed, and temporarily paying no attention to me. I crept my hand slowly, gently, toward my concealed pouches. In the dark and wet and muck powders were of no use, but one item in there was capable of covering distance.

Erel's voice, when he spoke, shook, and I was shocked to see tears glinting on his cheeks. "You killed my mother," he whispered, hoarse with loss and fear and hatred, and my breath released with a sudden snick of understanding. He was only a boy, after all, raised as a tool and used as a weapon, promised affection and glory and restoration to his rightful place, and above all, the promise of a mother. Realization dawned on Hadrea's face, too, and pity.

"An-Aralina," she said heavily. "Erel, I had no choice. *She* might not have had a choice, either. Your father—"

But Erel wasn't listening. His face twisted into fury, and pain, and desperation, and I knew it was no good, he was never going to listen or surrender, not to the woman who had incinerated his mother before his eyes.

He was just a child.

What kind of man was I, that I would do this? What kind of man would *not* do this?

I felt cold to the core as I raised the tiny pipe to my mouth, concealed by my fingers. This was, of course, the kind of man I was. You never get used to poisoning a child, not even a child like this one. But I could still do it. *I'm sorry*, I thought, honestly. I aimed the dart, and blew.

I didn't see it land because there was a sudden deep *boom* and force rippled through the tunnel, jolting us all. As Erel fumbled for balance, suddenly Kalina exploded into action, yanking Erel's knife hand down, and Hadrea's light bobbed wildly as she sprang forward into what was, momentarily, another terrifying scuffle in the dark. But then the light brightened and Kalina stood, triumphant, foot on Erel's back, prying the knife from his fingers.

"Got him!" she cried, and she and Tain pulled the boy up to yank his hands behind his back.

It was a long and confused moment before they both realized something was wrong. Horror dawned across their faces as Erel slumped, muscles twitching, eyes rolling, needle dart protruding from his neck. The effect of the laceleaf distillation was immediate. The boy's mouth moved but the poison was constricting his throat and no sound came out.

"Do something, Jov!" Tain yelled. "He's just a kid, do something!"

"I can't," I said woodenly, as my gut seized in regret. If I had held off one more moment until Kalina had acted . . . "There's nothing to be done."

We stood there silently, under the cold and invisible specter of my actions, and I felt old and tired and monstrous.

But a war was going on, and we could ill afford to dwell on my mistakes. "Where's Dee?" I asked.

"With Sjease and the others." Kalina looked dazed, sickened. "They're hiding in the jail." She squeezed my hand. "Jov, you did what you had to to save Tain."

"He was fifteen."

"Fifteen and he did not hesitate to murder," Hadrea observed. "Are your guards dead, Tain?"

Tain blinked. He looked like a man who'd been struck across the face with a pan. But he shook himself, spurred into action by worry, and the three of us followed as he sloshed back up the tunnel. "Just unconscious," he called out, relieved. "He gave them something to drink before we left. Something to warm them up. I didn't take any." He looked up at me as he stood, then quickly looked away again. "Jov trained me a bit too well."

"We cannot leave these people here." Hadrea squatted by one of the black-stripes. "They could drown."

We looked at one another. Tain looked up the tunnel. In the distance, the noises of a fight raged. "The element of surprise is gone, Tain," Kalina said quietly. "If we ever had it. Given who proposed the plan, the Prince probably expected you to turn up."

"Then what do we do?"

"We take your guards out, and then we join the fight," Hadrea said simply.

We dragged the drugged, unconscious men and women out of the sewers, puffing and grunting and avoiding looking at one another. *They don't tell you,* I thought, *in the stories of adventures and dramatic battles and magic, that you'll hurt your back dragging men through water and shit. . . .*

But that mundane frustration was quickly replaced by fear, deep in the bowels, as we helped one another to our feet and then looked around in horrified realization.

The jolt we'd felt must have been the gate or the wall, because the noises of distant battle hadn't been from *outside* the city. The Prince was already here.

The clouds had finally cleared and in the bright hard moonlight the Prince's force came like a tide, crumpling buildings as easily as they had torn up the soil. Stone, garden, people, all were flung aside with equal force, indifferent to weight or composition.

"They have taken the power of many spirits," Hadrea said quietly. "I do not know how we will stand against it."

We fell in with the crowds gathering to watch their approach; a terrible blanket of hopelessness seemed to fall with it. There was no order, no organization, no sign of Moest or any of our other leaders. I remembered, dimly, though it seemed laughable now, that Tain and I were supposed to be among those leaders. But what was the point, in the face of this?

The Prince led the charge, flanked by a formation of women behind him, spread out in wings. I was struck by how different they were from Hadrea or An-Ostada. A ragtag group of all ages, they walked with their heads slumped and their shoulders rolled, feet dragging behind. Even from the other side of the lake I found myself trying to identify them. Surely that small figure must be Pemu, and the older woman behind the Prince must be Jesta. He had not needed long, it seemed, to bend them all to his command. Were they drugged, or had destroying the spirits destroyed their own sense of self?

I looked at Kalina. "What Erel said about our families . . ."

She didn't return my gaze. "He called them Holy Vessels. I thought they were some kind of animal, but . . . now I think they must have been the women who could use fresken."

All the air in my chest seemed to have been pressed out. "And our ancestors poisoned them?"

"Not even the Oromani diaries talk about Crede. Maybe they were so ashamed of what they did that they never could talk about it." She gestured bitterly to the approaching wave. "Their Empire's been breeding hatred for us into its children for generations."

"I offered you a choice!" The Prince's voice boomed, mysteriously magnified to ring out over the lake and the gathered people, army and civilian alike. A beautiful voice, a terrible voice. "I am benevolent, I said. I gave you the chance to keep your city, to serve me as part of God's great empire. All I asked was the delivery of a few pathetic lives, remnants of a past that should shame you. Yet you did not deliver. You breached the parley terms. You are betrayers, still. God is good, but He is proud, too, and when you reject my offer you reject His glory! So I think I must show you, once more, a display of my strength, and you will cower and you will beg for my forgiveness and my mercy before the end!"

"Not today!" an equally booming voice cried, and there on the shores of the lake An-Ostada emerged, flanked by the Speakers and the trainees, all in full Darfri traditional wear, their bodies painted. Smaller figures, children on drums, beat the rhythm while the Speakers behind her started a chant. They all seemed to crackle with power. A ragged cheer started up, a cheer that gained momentum, that grew like a living thing, building, filling my chest and my heart. Despite everything, we would stand together, all of us, in the face of this. I felt the pull of it, the drag of my emotions, my head caught up in a rushing current, but it was a good feeling, an awe-inspiring feeling. We were honoring the Os-Woorin, and the Os-Woorin, as it had once raged against us, would rage now against this Prince.

It started to rise. I felt it, and so did Hadrea beside me; caught up in the ecstasy and the majesty of its familiar form, a form that sang to my very soul,

I barely registered that Kalina and Tain were not running toward the lake with us; why would anyone resist?

Os-Woorin rose from the lake, taking immense, humanlike form, massive and glistening in the moonlight, accepting our offerings and offering its in turn, and I realized I was singing with An-Ostada's song, the spirit's song, singing and crying and pouring everything of myself into that beautiful current. This time the spirit accepted us, would fight for us, I could feel it. Grateful tears wet my cheeks and Hadrea squeezed my hand, her face turned up in joy.

The Prince and his Speakers approached the lake, and like last time, I felt the crackle and clash of two great powers meeting, two great forces battling for dominance. I raised my voice louder in song, clutched at Hadrea's hand. We were connected, we were all connected, and our city and our spirits were one, and we would push back this intruder.

And then, like a shift in sandy ground beneath me, something changed.

I was still pulled, still hooked like a fish on a line, but the current had changed, and now I was swept in the undertow, and I was not singing anymore. The ecstasy, the completeness sharpened, soured, and suddenly it was a drain, not a connection; we were being drained away into something else. Not Os-Woorin.

Into the Prince.

The women behind him sank to their knees, collapsing face-first. I could sense the power that flowed, like the last water in a basin, away from their limp forms and into the Prince's luminous one.

He was the vessel now, and the tiny remaining conscious part of my brain understood what was happening, but I might as well have been a toddler railing against his mother's legs as she stepped through the door.

I can't deal with him anymore, Etan. It's too much. Why does he have to be like this? It's too much! And I was small and abandoned and knew it was because of me that she left. . . .

And she was dead, my mother was dead now, our estate home destroyed, and that grief and the gulf between us roiled and spiked, and then that too was gone, into the night, into the Prince.

It was he who crackled with power now, and he stepped easily toward An-Ostada and the Speakers. Os-Woorin, instead of growing and resisting, was punctured and diminished, sinking and losing form until he was nothing but ripples in the dark surface of the lake.

"Jov!" A tiny cry, as if from far away, but insistent. Voices I knew. Voices I loved. "Jov!"

The Prince advanced further, and that small stubborn fragment in me clung to Tain and Kalina's voices. "Fight," I whispered. "Break loose and fight!"

And I heard an echoed whisper next to me, clinging to me, buoying me. Hadrea's hand tightened around mine. "Fight!"

We found something, some anchor, in our shared presence, and together we *yanked* and all of a sudden we were free, and crumpling to the ground. I blinked, dazed, my gaze finding the line of Speakers. I willed them to resist.

The Prince lifted a hand. Something gathered around it, some crackling, thickening air. He drew it lazily in a horizontal line, and as if he wielded an invisible saw spanning the width of the lake, he casually tore the Speakers in half, one at a time. They fell apart like paper dolls, their insides exposed, their torsos falling off their hips and tumbling into unrecognizable meat on the shore of the lake. Hadrea made a noise like she'd been trodden on; a breathy grunt of agony.

An-Ostada he tore last, and even from this distance, and through the vomit filling my mouth and the blackening edges of my vision, I saw his pleasure in skewering her middle with his weapon of nothing, so that unlike her brethren she knew the ultimate terror and agony of a slow death. She fell too, in the end, and then the thickening air was gone, and there was only the Prince, smiling benignly.

"Bow down before your Emperor, your God," he said, and he laughed, and the laugh was knives in my ears and blood in my mouth.

"Get up, you idiot." Among the swirling disaster of my thoughts his voice penetrated.

"Tain?" I blinked.

Tain and Kalina were hauling us to our feet. All around people lay flopped on the grass, unconscious or worse. The Prince walked across the very surface of the lake as if it were a road designed solely for him. He paid no heed to the bodies strewn around him, but strolled off the lake and past us, east into the upper city, his gaze turned up toward Solemn Peak.

Something moved behind the top line of buildings in the city, some rippling and powerful force bending the bright moonlight, and we could only stand, open-mouthed, as black cracks splintered and shot across the face of the mountain.

The Prince continued up the hill, his attention on the mountain. The power that had infused him seemed to leach away; the ground no longer trembled beneath his steps, buildings did not crumble. Whatever the connection he had forced on us, it was broken. He was a man again.

But. "What's he doing?" I said aloud.

Hadrea stared after him. "I think I know." She looked very grave, and beautiful in the moonlight.

"Can you do something?"

Hadrea looked at me for a moment, oddly wistful, but her eyes burned fever-bright. She kissed me, a chaste kiss on the forehead, like a mother to a child.

"Please remember," she said. "Whatever else. I was always on your team, Jovan."

And she closed her eyes, and sank to the ground, and through some remembered connection, no firmer than the impression of her lips on my forehead, I had the fleeting sensation of her reaching out, away, purposeful and swift.

Now that the Prince had turned his attention from us, people were coming back to themselves groggily. Moest and a group of uniformed soldiers and armed civilians swept over Trickster's Bridge and past us.

"He's just one man!" the Warrior-Guilder shouted. "He doesn't have a dozen eyes anymore. No matter how powerful, we can take him! Join me! Together!"

"Come on," Tain cried, and he pulled me along. "If this is going to be the end of our city we aren't facing it on the ground, bowing down to any Prince."

I pulled my arm loose. "Hadrea," I said. She was vulnerable in this state, and I could not abandon her to it. Tain nodded in understanding, flashed me a grin, and raced after Moest. Kalina took my hand and we watched the charge. For a moment it seemed our forces would catch the Prince, for he had settled in the middle of a street in the same pose as Hadrea, apparently relaxed and oblivious to, or unconcerned with, the approaching Silastians. But as Moest's charge narrowed into the bottleneck of the street, and before the first person could reach the Prince, figures melted out of houses, buildings, shadows, armed figures in masks, protecting the street from the high-ground position. The Prince's Hands. At their rear, standing protectively over the Prince, was the black-clad figure of the Wraith.

Tain, blocked by the thick of bodies, led a splinter group to the side. "This way!" I heard him cry, and half a dozen others broke off to follow him up an alternate route. They re-emerged on a parallel street, and then Tain was climbing the side of the building, clambering up to the roof, and others were following him. *You clever, idiotic bastard*, I thought, torn with admiration and despair at his bravery.

Kalina shook on my arm, pointing. "Look!"

"Honor-down," I whispered.

Now we knew what the Prince had been doing.

A great mountain slide, a huge arrow of crumbling white rock, was dropping like a foamy breaking wave from the slopes of Solemn Peak down toward the city, too slow and deliberate for a natural slide. Kalina buried her face in my shoulder with a cry of disbelief as it plunged into the distant shape of the Manor, and ate it effortlessly.

As it hit the Avenue it split into two parts, sliding down each side of the sweeping loop street on which all the Family apartments lay, and it crashed into those too, an insatiable monster. Kalina stared at the passage of the right-hand fork. "Jov," she croaked, "it's going to hit the jail!"

Dee.

"Hadrea!" I cried, urgent, but she was already rising, and something had changed. I felt no pull of connection, no thickening of the air, none of the sensations I associated with fresken. And yet. She looked at me, her eyes black and old and swirling with something alien. I quavered.

"Do something," I pleaded.

Hadrea pivoted to face the mountain, raising her hands like she was lifting a child, and the rockslides simply . . . stopped.

Instantly, the Prince shot to his feet, and across all the fighting he sought us out with his furious gaze. The Prince crouched, then exploded into the air like a bird taking flight. In one leap, buoyed by the air itself, he cleared the distance between us and landed in front of Hadrea.

The soldiers at the rear pivoted and rushed toward the Prince, but bounced back as if they'd struck an invisible membrane. Kalina tested the barrier with a stick; it pressed into nothing and would go no farther.

The Prince ignored the efforts to reach him. "Who are you?" he said to Hadrea, his voice resonant with power.

Hadrea swept her hand and he was flung to the ground as if weightless.

He bared his teeth and clenched his fists, and the ground beneath him rose like a pillar, lifting him. "I hold the spirit of Solemn Peak inside me," he hissed. "This is the power of a god! Who are you to challenge me?"

Without apparent effort, Hadrea swatted him again, and he tumbled into a heap, rocks and soil from his pillar raining down on him. She drew her hands together and the debris drew in around him, caging him, smothering him. The Prince fought back, clawing the cage apart, gasping for breath. He spat dirt, tensed, and air buffeted around him, creating space in his prison. Hadrea, indifferent, expressionless, moved her hands and the rocks closed in.

"What did you *do*?" he grunted. He flung his hands out suddenly, abandoning the struggle. For a moment I thought he'd given up, but then far up the hill, a rumble sounded as the rockslides released again. This time they plummeted at unnatural speed, the very mountain sagging, burying buildings in its wake.

Hadrea, flustered for the first time, stopped both flows, but it cost her concentration on the Prince. Free of his prison, he hurled himself at her. She captured him again in his rocky cage before his clawing hands reached her, but again he seized on her distraction and the rockslides groaned back into motion.

"Jovan," she said through gritted teeth. The apparent effortlessness of her work had been an illusion; veins and tendons now stood out on her neck and arms. "I cannot hold them both. I must let one go."

I pounded at the barrier surrounding the two of them, but it might as well have been solid glass. We couldn't protect Hadrea from the Prince if she burnt herself out preventing both rockslides. I started to gesture to the left, because the right-hand fork would devour the jail, where my family sheltered. Then my mouth went dry. I couldn't get a breath. I traced the trajectory of the left-hand fork and next set of buildings it would flatten, and saw the figures on the roof realizing the same thing, shouting, trying to scamper down, and I had never known fear like I knew in that moment.

Tain, my best friend, my Chancellor, was in one direction. Dee, my niece, my responsibility, my heart, my child, was in the other.

A horrible noise came out of my mouth, an animal's cry, and I couldn't stop making it. I cried a single instruction to Hadrea, and then, as she gasped in release, the Prince's resistance disintegrated and the barrier protecting him fell away into nothing beneath my beating fists. He had just time to look up to see me launch.

I smashed into him with my shoulder, sending him flying and me crashing heavily on top, the remains of his dirt prison exploding around us. I pummeled into his face, pounding it with every bit of my clumsy pent-up fury and impotence and fear. I pummeled him so hard that the wild blood pounding in my head and the horrible sounds of crunching bones—in his face, in my hands—almost drowned out the crashing of the rockslide above.

INCIDENT: Poisoning of Krisover Sjivano / attempted poisoning of Chancellor Jennyon Iliri

POISON: ~~Unknown~~ *Update:* suspect potentially "Esto's revenge" (see p f41), poison unknown at time of entry and evidence not retained, but likely part of broader campaign

INCIDENT NOTES: Krisover was a blacksmith undertaking several personal projects for Chancellor Jennyon, found dead in home of heart failure (signs of seizure, niece and nephew report victim complained of sore ears before bed). Personalized bottle of Swift Slopes kori discovered in Krisover's home and recognized as a gift to the Chancellor from foreign musician Esto Ramasta. Speculate Krisover may have stolen kori intended to poison Chancellor during recent meeting? Order Guards and spies set to locate Esto.

(from proofing notes of Credola Leife Oromani)

26

Kalina

Was it possible to become desensitized to devastation, even on this scale? My limbs, my neck, my head were heavy and sluggish, like I was walking through a thick liquid, but the only internal feeling I could summon was a dull relief. Hadrea had saved us from the worst of it. The Prince had injured many but killed far fewer than initially feared. We had lost the Manor, and all the Families' homes, and a streak of beautiful historic buildings and streets, but there had been limited fighting and most of the destroyed buildings had already been evacuated.

Small consolation in the wake of what I'd lost.

Tain had been on the roof of a building demolished by the slide and doubtless the rocks had swallowed him, too. Even so, I wandered the edges of the wreck in the dark, searching, because if I stopped looking and sat down, I would have to confront what had happened.

I was truly alone for the first time I could remember in months. A kind of peace came over me as I searched, though I also had the sense of being watched—whether by curious onlookers or even my stalking witch I could not say, and did not much care. It was a full moon. Mosecca could do what she would. If she thought our family had not suffered enough, she had not been paying attention.

In the end, though, it was not Mosecca I saw.

A woman in black, long, matted black hair sweeping behind her, disappeared into a half-collapsed building near where Tain had been swept away. I caught my breath. Many Hands had fled in the confusion of the avalanche.

As we didn't know their identities, undoubtedly they would escape justice, just as many of Aven's supporters had done. Perhaps in another two years we would be battling a resurgence of enemies.

I still had a spear; I had been using it as a walking stick. Honor-down, I was so very tired. But I was drawn inside anyway, as if my legs were independent of me.

This building had been damaged by tumbling rocks but not crushed; the frames at either side were buckled and unsteady, but remained upright. Moonlight streamed in where a rock had punched a hole through the roof.

I heard a crack and whirled around.

I was no athlete, but I could collapse like the best of them, and I let my body drop again now, as I'd done to distract Erel earlier, and the chunk of metal whizzed by where my head had been and sailed harmlessly into the wall.

The Wraith walked toward me, face pursed in disappointment at my last-moment evasion. I rolled and scrambled back over a chunk of debris, panic tightening my lungs. I'd been stupid to follow, and so stupid about who I'd trusted. Because I knew that face and it wasn't the Wraith's.

I yelled for help, as loud as I could, but the ruins seemed to swallow the sound up, and no answering cries followed. She tugged free a length of splintered wood and held it like a sword as she picked her way toward me carefully. "I could have just run," she said, in perfect Sjon. "But you recognized me, didn't you. Never trust diplomats, you know."

I felt my way one foot at a time, stepping backward, keeping my eyes on her. If I could stay out of her range and get back into the open, I could find help. "Or Princesses?" Something wobbled under my foot and I hastily shifted. *Honor-down, Abae, I'm sorry for suspecting you.*

Zhafi laughed. "Fair. You're a fascinating woman, Kalina of Silasta. I think we could have been friends. We're alike, don't you think?"

I hated her for giving voice to it. I'd felt connected to her, admired the life she'd built in difficult circumstances. Perhaps that's why she'd so easily fooled me. "You cut your hair," I observed. The Wraith wig had slipped. "You couldn't resist being part of the big night, is that it? What happened to the real Wraith?"

Zhafi tossed the wig and scratched her cropped locks with an easy smile. "She was happy to let the boss take over for the evening. She owes me her whole livelihood, you know. I told her to call them the Prince's Hands but they're mine, and so is she. I made her rich and powerful. Gave her a vehicle for her . . .

more brutal side. That's what I love about your culture. There are so many *opportunities* for all kinds of women in this city. I've always known this is where I should have been born. A place where I would be appreciated for my skills, not my face. Like you are."

She stepped up onto a small pile of debris under the collapsed roof and balanced without apparent effort. Her confidence stripped me of mine. My lungs were so tight. Blood thudded in my ears and the remembered fear always lurking beneath the surface of my thoughts bubbled over. "If you like it here so much," I retorted, "did you consider *not* blowing half of us up? Do you think this culture you admire so much came from starting wars?"

"What else was I to do? Let my dear brother pack me off to some backwater as the face of the Empire, to rule over a people who secretly hate me?"

So I hadn't really misjudged her motivations, just what she would be willing to do to change her position. She had grown up in the halls of power, knowing herself to be cleverer and more accomplished than the brothers in whose shadows she stood. Of course her goal had never been to run away with some boy and leave all that power behind.

"So you swapped one tyrannical man for another?" I asked. Was that something moving there, in the shadows in the corner? I kept talking, keeping her attention on me. "Did you think the Prince was offering anything but a lifetime of subjugation? I thought you were smarter than that."

The good humor on Zhafi's face slipped. It was with a hard, dangerous look that she approached me, fist opening and closing as if imagining me in her grip. She advanced with a swift lunge, but in her haste, the rubble shifted and her foot plunged to the ankle in a gap between broken beams and debris. I raised my spear, mostly for show, and backed farther over the mound. If I stalled her, someone might hear us and help.

"How did you end up making drugs for the Prince, anyway?"

Zhafi freed her leg but paused and regarded me, head tilted and eyes narrowed, re-evaluating how much I already knew and what I might have told others. Ironically only now, too late, everything had started to make sense. There was a word for that, in muse, when you glimpsed your opponent's strategy and disconnected moves became parts of a larger whole. I'd never been that good at muse.

"You grow the leaves on that land you generously donate to the orphanages, right?" I tried to put gradual space between us. "And they process it for you as cheap labor. Ingenious. And you had all those people in your poorhouses to test it on. But why Crede and the Prince in the first place? His idea of a great empire is ten times as oppressive as the one you wanted to escape."

She feigned a stumble as she straightened, but I'd been waiting for her to try something and ducked in time. Whatever she'd thrown missed my head and thudded into another pile.

"Did the Prince promise he'd let you rule here when he went back home to Crede? Is that it?" I laughed. "He *despised* women. He called you 'cunning and ambitious' and said he was just using you, did you know that?"

If I'd hoped to shock her, I'd failed. "He was a religious fanatic, Kalina, he could barely hide his contempt. But he was going to put his bastard on a throne here, and marry him to me. How long do you think that foolish boy would have run things? Sjona would have been strong in my hands." She sent a sharp, angry look up at the remaining roof above us; it was quivering. This time it was me who used her distraction to throw something at her; she easily dodged. But as she did I saw a flicker of movement behind her, something in the shadows. I'd seen it before but now I understood. Burgeoning hope made me more nervous, my words faster and more desperate.

"That story you told about Lord Tuhash. It was all nonsense, wasn't it? You never cared about him. You passed him over to your Hands to be killed and used against my brother without a second thought." It all seemed so obvious now. "Did you originally intend to murder him and pretend you'd run away together? But then when you used him up for the party stunt you got the idea that if your maid Esma wore your clothes and was badly injured enough in the explosion, everyone would mistake her for you, and not come looking after you?"

"You're clever," Zhafi said, scrutinizing my face like Jov examining a challenging meal. "Not clever enough, but I don't love how close you came to ruining everything. Lucky for me you're just an invalid." Zhafi cleared the gap between us too fast for my tentative spear-up in response, and swung her makeshift sword; it smacked into my thigh and I fell hard on my side into the rubble. Unwilling tears blurred my vision of her standing above me, stick raised.

I slammed my fist down on the plank beside me with all the force I could muster, and the other end flew up like a lever, hitting her knee. She buckled and dropped her weapon in her attempt to regain balance. I grabbed a handful of her clothing and yanked, bringing her down in a tangle with me amidst the wreckage. At first I had the advantage, but Zhafi was stronger. She rolled me onto my back and I clutched her wrists, trying desperately to stop her hands closing around my throat.

"I'm . . . not . . . just . . . an invalid," I forced out. We had been speaking in Talafan but I switched to Sjon, deliberately. "I'm . . . a diplomat, Princess. You know what diplomats are good at? Talking to people." My gaze shifted to a point behind her head. "Persuading people."

Zhafi's eyes widened. She jerked her head around just in time to see the figure who had emerged from the shadows, and the arc of a metal bar, swung with brutal force. Then it crushed into the side of her skull like a mallet into a vegetable, and she crumpled.

Mosecca stood over us, chest heaving.

I sat up, coughing, panting, and got shakily to my feet.

"She killed my boy." Mosecca stared at the broken body with a quiet, shaking rage. "He was besotted from the moment we came to court. Princess this and Princess that. She dragged him into this. You heard her, she never cared about him for a moment. He was just a tool to be used."

I didn't know how to respond. Zhafi's head injury was terrible; I couldn't even look at it. Lacking strength or inclination to talk with her executioner, I staggered out of the building and up a side street, blindly, numbly.

That was when I saw my brother.

He sat slumped on the ground by a broken chunk of boulder, his legs splayed bonelessly like a doll's, back and head hunched.

"Jov!" I stepped toward him. "Are you—" My words dropped away into nothing as he looked up, exposing what he had been hunched over.

A head was in his lap, dark curls spread out as if on a pillow, the face turned away from me. I stopped, unable to move. Just as I'd recognized my brother by the top of his head, so too would I know that head anywhere. But if I took one step closer, if I looked one more time, then I'd know, then I'd be sure, then it would be real.

"Jov," I said again, stupidly.

He looked up at me and it was worse, a thousand times worse. His eyes . . . I'd never seen anything like the look in them.

I wanted to scream but there was nothing left in my chest, no will left in my body. I slumped down beside my brother and rested my head on his shoulder. I closed my eyes, and we sat there together with the night breeze cooling our skin. In the distance the world clattered on without us.

INCIDENT: Poisoning of Credola Freja Iliri, Heir to Chancellor Hana Iliri

POISON: Rucho (death feather)

INCIDENT NOTES: Heir participated anonymously in dance audition at Performers' Guild, but collapsed and died on stage. Needle containing traces of rucho discovered in wings by this proofer. Official report was heart failure by physical exertion but suspect another dancer responsible for assassination. Consider re-emergence of Red Piper??

(from proofing notes of Credo Jaya Oromani)

27

Jovan

There were sounds. Sensations, on my skin. Distant voices. The weight in my lap. I registered them, but they floated away again, unimportant.

My sister was there. I couldn't remember her arrival, but she was there, at my side, just as she always had been. Did she say something?

It didn't matter.

At some point I noticed my eyes were open. That seemed pointless, so I closed them again.

The weight in my lap.

She said something, she was moving, and I wanted to tell her not to, because moving made time go on. If time went on, I would think again, and for now, for once, my head was silent and empty. Was this how it felt to be normal? She should stay. The three of us, we were bound together, it had always been that way. It would always be that way. If she moved, if I moved, then it would be broken, and it would not come back together. No, that was a thought. Thoughts were not good. I let it go. I would hold my head still and let them all go.

At some point I was crying, perhaps. I noticed my body was shaking and breathing was hard, but my face felt dry. It seemed wrong. I wanted to stop, but perhaps that was only something I could do before? Maybe I couldn't do that anymore.

It would really be easier not to breathe.

INCIDENT: Poisoning of Al-Anaka esSilverstream

POISON: Beetle-eye

INCIDENT NOTES: Silverstream village "Speaker" (religious/cultural position in some areas of countryside) found in comatose state, unable to be woken. Drawn to our attention by Oromani stewards due to reports that Al-Anaka had made public drunken threats to bring substantial (but unspecified) complaint to the Council. Described symptoms and witness reports of behavior before death suggest beetle-eye poisoning. Further examination of local administrator and officials necessary.

(from proofing notes of Credo Adrea Oromani)

28

Kalina

We sat there together in the silence. Sometimes Jov cried; ugly great squeaking breaths, his mouth hanging open and his chest heaving, like a fish on the shore. He did not seem aware he was doing it.

Eventually I discovered, as he must have, that it is possible to run out of tears.

The longer we sat there, the further apart we grew. Instead of sharing our grief, Jovan had retreated into some private world, into which I could not follow. I was here with the two people who had always mattered the most to me and it felt like I'd lost them both. My initial shock was transforming into something with raw, bleeding edges that hurt to touch, and a tight, spinning core building inside me.

Looking at Tain's silent, still form, it felt like a hot clamp had seized my spine and shaken it. It hurt, my whole body hurt. I thought I might be sick. I had to stand up, had to look away, but the knowledge was a brand in my brain. The thing growing inside me was filling all the spaces, pressing on my skin, until I could have burst.

It was anger.

This wasn't fair. Not fair, not right, that everything we'd done, all we'd lost, fought for until we bled, could end in this.

My whole body shook. I opened my mouth to scream and nothing came out but a tiny, low howl. Again and again, until I was bent over double, leaning on my own legs, my voice reduced to a guttural choke but my fury unabated. I spun on the spot, looking for something, anything, I could smash, destroy, shred. I wanted to *hurt* something.

I saw her.

The sky had clouded over again, obscuring the moon, but by dim starlight Mosecca was visible, dragging something out of the edge of the wrecked building. A leg. Mosecca was pulling the Princess's body from the building. Needing an outlet for the thing inside me before it ate me alive, I stalked over.

Mosecca dropped Zhafi's leg and stepped back warily, but rage made me swift, and I grabbed her arm so tight she cried out. I didn't care, I only wanted someone else to hurt.

"What are you doing?" She tried to shake off my grip.

"What are *you* doing?" My voice was a weird, hoarse whisper, because if I let it go, if I let it go louder, it would be a scream.

"I'm making *sure*," she hissed.

I let go of her arm. Some of the anger was fizzling out. Mosecca had lost everything, too. The rage was already in her, she was no good target for mine. But I hauled it back, clawed it back, wrapped it tight around me, because if the anger wasn't there, if it wasn't holding me upright, then what was left of me?

The two of us stood over Zhafi's body, united in hatred. "I'm making sure," Mosecca said again, and this time she sounded lost and desperate.

I squatted beside the body and groped through sticky blood and dirt on the side of her neck. Her face was a crumpled paper sculpture, of course she was dead, but I felt for a pulse anyway, to make sure. For Mosecca. For me.

Blood oozed slowly over my fingers on the neck. Mosecca sat beside me, quiet. "I can't feel anything," I said, and withdrew my fingers, then froze. Blood was still oozing. Still flowing. I pressed harder against the slippery slick skin and this time I felt it: the faintest, weakest beat.

"Not dead," I whispered, and anger surged again. Her brain was exposed, a gray and white and red wreck, yet she clung to a life she had used with such reckless disregard for others. The ultimate selfishness.

Mosecca looked at me directly for the first time. "I tried to kill you, and your family." She said it matter-of-factly, without emotion. "I am sorry. Now you give me justice for my boy. I owe you a life debt."

I started to shrug—what good did that do me, now? But Abae's voice sounded in my head. *Blood magic and sacrifices, and lives given for lives.* After everything we'd seen tonight, all the magic and strangeness and horror hidden beneath the surface of this world, why should this one thing be out of reach? "My friend," I blurted out. "Can you do something for him? You are a witch, yes?"

She followed my gesture to Jov and Tain. "He is dead?" An edge of sympathy in her voice. But the sidelong look she cast Tain's body was thoughtful. Her eyes darted to my bloody fingers, to the body on the ground, then back.

"You *can* do something," I said slowly. My sluggish body thudded back to life. "This! Do this, and your life debt or whatever, you've paid it! Please!"

She shook her head. "It is likely too late."

But an unrealistic, stupid hope had flared in me. "It is *not too late*. It is not too late until we've tried. You take this evil excuse for a person and you do whatever it is you need to make this right, make it *her* who's dead, not him. You do it. You *do it*!"

My own rage was reflected back at me in her bared teeth and eyes burning with ferocity. But then I understood. It was a smile.

"Something good to come of her blood," she whispered. "I will try." She laughed, a breathy little giggle. "I will try."

We seized hold of Zhafi's legs and dragged her unceremoniously to where my brother sat, Tain still across his lap. Mosecca sucked her breath. "His chest," she said, unnecessarily.

"Yes." I didn't look at it.

"You get me anything I need," she warned.

"Yes."

Jov was still lost in whatever mental world he had created to escape this and barely reacted as Mosecca barked orders—*those sticks, there! A stone, not that one—yes*—and I sprang to them, taking advantage of the wide range of materials between the wreck of the building and what had once been a garden. Mosecca sang under her breath as she worked, swiftly binding two parcels from a piece of her clothing and shaping them into rough poppets, stuffed with some things she had carried and some she demanded I find. When filled to her satisfaction, she dragged the poppets through the bloody mess of Zhafi's face, and then more carefully in some of Tain's blood. His face, by contrast, looked peaceful. Beautiful.

Mosecca placed the rough poppets on both Tain and Zhafi, over their hearts. "Hold her still," she muttered, and I held Zhafi's limp body close. Without further ceremony, Mosecca slashed a metal shard across the Princess's neck, so deep and swift that her head lolled back at the split and my grip wavered as I fought the urge to be sick.

Blood slurped out of the wound and thickened, darkened, the flow moving in a slow, unnatural pattern. Mosecca chanted softly, though I could not understand the blurred sequences of words or discern a tune, and all the while the blood gleamed oily black, forming thick trails like fat slugs. Zhafi's body jolted, spasming, and my heart beat a tinny, nervous rhythm that pulsed through the strangest places—my lip, my temple, my fingers.

But nothing was happening. Tain lay motionless while Zhafi's blood flow grew weaker. "It's not enough," Mosecca said. "Her life force is weak and he is too far gone."

"You make it enough," I bit back. "Take mine, too." I held out my wrist, and she stared at me, then back up at the moon, then took it without comment. The swift, long cut she dragged down my forearm burned. But as my hand moved above one of the poppets she shoved it out of the way, grabbed my wrist again, sniffed my blood.

"No," she said. "No, this one is wrong. I feel it." She rubbed the blood between two fingers. "There must be a . . . congruence. You do not have it. What about him?" she asked, gesturing roughly to Jovan.

My brother had been sitting there, oblivious. He winced when I shook him and looked at me without recognition. I did not hesitate, all the same. "He'd give anything," I said, and tears burned in my eyes.

When Mosecca cut him he pulled his arm weakly away, but my reassuring whispers seemed to calm him back to his catatonic state, and he let us pull open the wound.

"Not that one," Mosecca said sharply, directing the dripping blood only into one of the poppets. "Now. Hold your brother still. This will hurt."

He did snap out of it, then, his eyes flying open and focusing with sudden clarity as the cut down his arm spread and grew into a black tree of strange gleaming threads.

"Jov, hush." I squeezed him tight. "You've got to stay still, all right?"

He began to struggle, and the blood flowed faster, greedily, the black gleaming and reflecting light as it grew stronger and fatter. His body jerked and spasmed, like Zhafi's, and finally, through the haze of madness that had been over me, I realized the danger I had put him in. "Jov, I'm sorry, please."

Mosecca's song was quiet but urgent, and Zhafi's flow had trickled off to nothing. She was dead, properly dead now. But apparently Mosecca was not satisfied, because she took the shard in both hands and drove it with full strength into the Princess's chest. Jov cried out as though it had been his heart, his chest, and then jerked once and fell still. Then he blinked a few times, and seemed to come back to himself. "Did it . . ." he croaked. "Did something happen?"

There was a long quiet. I counted hoarse breaths, and my hopes died away to nothing.

"I'm sorry," Mosecca said.

I stood, my legs shaky, and hauled my brother to his feet. "You tried. Forget the debt, it's paid." I couldn't look at his body and I couldn't bear to be near her. It was time to go.

We went via the physics' area, and found Thendra. "I have seen your family," she said immediately, to my great relief. "Eliska, Dija, Al-Sjease, and the others. They are all fine. They will be waiting for news of you." Her eyes raked over us, cataloging our conditions, heavy with unspoken questions.

"The Chancellor is dead," I said bluntly. "His body is up there. I couldn't bring it down on my own and Jov is . . ." I shrugged. "Someone else will need to do it."

Thendra bowed her head. "I thought he must be," she said. "I saw him leading the second charge before the landslide." She took my hand in hers; I almost pulled away, so unexpected was the gesture. She had treated me for years and never offered physical comfort. "Credola. Credo. This is a terrible tragedy, yes, but you should know . . . you should know the Chancellor was already dying." Her voice was so gentle it was unrecognizable. "He was in terrible pain. He could not keep food down at all, in the end."

Jov stared at her. "He was having trouble with food since the poisoning, but—"

"It was more than trouble, Credo. His insides never recovered. He made me swear to keep his privacy but every day he was coughing blood, vomiting blood, excreting blood. He used certain substances to maintain his energy and attention but they were temporary fixes, and he had accepted that. Grievous as this news is, in a way, it is a blessing. He would have suffered more, before the end."

It felt as if someone heavy had sat on my chest. Some part of me had known something had been terribly wrong with him, but I hadn't pushed him on it, hadn't pushed him about the eating, or the lie about the darpar, perhaps because I hadn't wanted to know the answer.

Jov stared at me, his face twisted bitterly. One more failure in his eyes, that his friend had not told him the truth. A lifetime of defining himself by reference to his role and family honor was not easily thrown away. As if he'd read my mind, he muttered, "I once told Hadrea I was afraid to find out what

I was when you took away the parts of me that counted. I guess this is it." He gave an ugly little chuckle. "Even I'm disappointed in the results."

The words struck somewhere deep and vulnerable inside me, surprising me with their sting. "All the parts of you that counted?" He stared moodily at the ground, and my temper rose in place of the hurt, ferocious and swift. "You had another role before you were a proofer, before you were a friend. You were my brother first, Jovan Oromani, and I *know* what you did tonight, I know the choice you made, so don't you dare tell me you didn't choose to be a Tashi, too."

I ignored his flinch. "Guess what? You don't get to give up. I just lost my best friend too and I'm not losing anyone else, you hear me?" My voice quavered. The anger was draining at the sight of his stricken, heartbroken face; I tried to grasp it, needing the energy it gave me. "We've defeated this Prince, but he was alone this time. There's a whole Empire on the other side of the Howling Plains. We have to gather our friends around us, Jov, and make it up with all our neighbors, because if you think we've lost everything already, I've got news for you, baby brother; we still have plenty more to lose."

I started to cry, and the deep bone-weariness was seeping in once again. "Don't make me handle this on my own, Jov," I said, and suddenly his arms were around me.

"Are you kidding me?" he mumbled. "You're already the bloody Hero of Silasta. You can't take all the credit again."

Half-laughing, half-crying, I buried my face in his shoulder.

We found Hadrea comforting the kidnapped estate women; they were confused, exhausted, and frightened, but apparently uninjured. So too was Hadrea, who pressed her forehead gratefully against each of ours in turn. "You're all right," Jov whispered, clutching her arms with shaky intensity, his eyes wet. "You said . . . I was afraid you were . . ."

"I am all right," she confirmed. "It did not harm me." There was something raw and frightening about the light in her eyes, something unsettling. I dropped my gaze quickly. Whatever she had done, she had saved the city again from catastrophe.

Our losses, while small, were devastating: almost all the Darfri students in the city had died in one heartbeat. Miraculously, An-Ostada was still alive; surrounded by physics, she drew tiny, shallow breaths, her eyes two slits, moving, tracking our approach. Slimy gore, foul-smelling, slipped and slid out of her rent torso as two frantic physics tried to hold her together. She would not last long, but she had breath to whisper.

"You watch that girl," she said hoarsely. She raised her voice to a croak so Hadrea, who stood nearby with another of the rescued women, could hear. "I know where you took the power from, An-Hadrea. You did not find a *new* anything. You are a fool. Wiser, more trustworthy people have known for centuries. How do you think it got there in the first place? What did you think it was *for*?"

Hadrea's jaw was set, but she said nothing, and a tremor passed over her. Almost involuntarily, she turned her gaze slowly up the hill, past Solemn Peak and the mountain ranges stretching beyond under clearing skies and a full, bright moon. Past those mountains lay the Howling Plains, across which the refugees had fled, and into which no one had dared venture for centuries.

I had never really questioned *why*.

"You will be all of our deaths, in the end," An-Ostada whispered. Blood bubbled at the corners of her lips.

"You are agitating her," a physic chided us, and we stepped away, disquieted.

"An-Hadrea," Thendra called, striding over. "I left you on a bed, did I not? You wish to collapse on your feet? Go, now." To my surprise, Hadrea bobbed her head, chastened.

"We'll talk later. Get some rest," Jov said. "Lini, we should find Dee and the others. We have to tell them what—"

He broke off at Thendra's exclamation. "Oh! But you said . . . ?"

My brother's cry was guttural, and he staggered, legs buckling. I was two steps toward him, thinking him injured or ill, when I saw the cause. And then it was me staggering.

Tain walked toward us, walking, breathing, living. He looked dazed, exhausted, thin, confused, but he was there, alive in the suddenly bright light of the moon.

Jov stood frozen. I walked toward our friend, steps jerky, disbelieving. Relief, joy, fear, doubt, all swirled within me. Jov raised a shaking hand to his chest, across his heart, like a Talafan standing to their national song.

"Please excuse me, Thendra," Tain said. His voice shook and he took tentative steps as if unsure his legs would hold his weight. "I'm afraid I don't feel . . . quite my best."

As his body melted and tumbled down, Jov and I were there, under each shoulder, to catch him. "We've got you," I said.

"Always," Jov added.

For just a moment, under my brother's palm and across his heart, I glimpsed something, a raised shape, outlined under the cloth. But I blinked, the moon passed under a cloud, and in the dim starlight, it vanished.

The three of us sat together, shoulder to shoulder on the grass as dawn rose over our partially ruined city. There was no rush to go home, not least of which because none of us had one anymore.

"I don't think the Families can recover from this," I said. I glanced back up the distant hill, which the avalanche had left bare of its landmark buildings: the Manor, all the Family apartments on the avenue, the bank.

Tain shrugged. "I don't think so, either." The hint of a smile played around his lips. "But maybe that's a good thing. If the last few years have taught us anything, it's that concentrating power and wealth on a couple of bloodlines brought nothing but trouble."

"You're still the Chancellor," Jov pointed out.

"I think the title passes on when you die," he retorted, and I flinched. We hadn't spoken of what Mosecca had done, and I wasn't sure we were ready to. Maybe we'd never be ready. Certainly she seemed not to want to discuss it with us, because no one had seen sign of her since.

"How are you feeling?" I asked tentatively.

"Fine. Good." He paused. "Uh, better than good, actually. Everything feels . . . like I used to." He shot me an anxious, darting glance, as if expecting admonishment. As if there would be any point demanding answers for his concealment. All three of us knew why he'd done it. We'd always been like this, protecting and hurting one another as we wound tighter together, and perhaps we always would be. I didn't know whether to be worried or comforted by that.

Tain continued, sounding thoughtful. "So. If we can pull ourselves out of this, I think we're going to have to think differently about the system."

Jov gave him a strange look. "You're talking like a revolutionary."

Tain grinned, his sparkling eyes gleaming, unclouded by pain for the first time in two years. "You know what? Maybe I am."

A smile tugged rebelliously at my own lips. "So what are we going to do?"

"Well, for starters, we're going to make it up with our neighbors. I don't think we've seen the last of Crede. Maybe it'll take another few decades, maybe another hundred years, but they'll be back. Guess we'll need some good diplomacy, eh?" He flung an arm around each of us. "We'll handle it by working together, won't we?"

I looked at him, still unsure what feeling it generated when I did. *He was dead. He was dead, and gone.* But he was also real, and his warm body pressed up against mine. My second brother. "Of course we will. We're family, right?"

Jovan laughed, a little shakily. His hand strayed back to his heart, rubbing his chest as if something there bothered him. "Family," he agreed.

"Will you go straight north?" I asked Etrika a short time later, as we walked toward the temporary accommodation shelter. Dee walked hand in hand with Jov a few paces ahead, Sjease and her brothers on her other side. Tain was talking animatedly, and Dee was giggling. The incongruous sound was both shockingly wrong, and a pleasure to hear.

Etrika frowned. "My home's in Telasa," she said. "I'm too old and too tired for this nonsense. But I daresay a few more visits will be in order." She gave me the ghost of a smile.

Ana, a few steps behind, was watching Jov and Dee, the latter matching her steps to the former, and she wore a strange expression. As Etrika quickened her pace, I fell back beside her daughter.

"My uncle has never been the most attentive Tashi to the youngsters," she said, as if the target of her conversation was the gravel crunching beneath her feet. There was a long pause. "I don't think Dija will miss his guidance too much. Now that she has . . . well. Now that she has a Tashi who cares for her properly." She pressed her lips together and shot me a fierce look, daring me to challenge her. Instead, I took her free hand, touched. What it must have cost her to come to that decision, in light of everything.

"She's got a lot of family who love her and want the best for her," I said, and she blinked rapidly, flustered, but returned the squeeze of her hand. Then she cleared her throat and dropped it, striding up ahead to catch the others. Someone was pointing Jov to our overnight shelter and I watched them go in, my family, homeless, proud and determined, and felt a surge of love, but also a kind of loneliness.

I stood there, hesitant but unsure why, for a moment. Then I saw the figure up ahead, and my chest tightened. Abae, tall, graceful, still as a flag without a breeze. I approached her slowly, unable to label the feelings flooding me. Gratitude, that she was unharmed. Fear, that she would hate me for failing to trust her when it counted.

"Hello, Kalina," she said uncertainly.

"Hello." She was lovelier than ever. I wanted both to send her away and to kiss her, intensely, and instead I did nothing but stand beside her and turn my face away from the wind. The silence stretched out between us. She scuffed one foot on the ground.

"You have had so much taken from you." She made a little gesture, as if to take my hand, but stopped. The wind felt cold off the mountains. I thought of An-Ostada's ominous warning, and resolutely turned my head so I could see no part of the ranges. Crede was a problem for tomorrow. "Perhaps now is only a time for grieving, and for being with family?"

Abae caught my cheek with long, gentle fingers, and pushed the coils of hair out of my face. I flinched. She dropped her hand and I immediately regretted it, wished to snatch up the hand again and hold it close.

She looked at me closely—could she read the conflicted feelings in my face?—and her liquid dark eyes held mine. "You know, I understand now. No one ever asked me what I wanted until you." She smiled, her eyes distant, and took a steadying breath. "I will respect what you feel, and what you want. If you want to be alone, after all of this . . ."

She bowed her beautiful face over her knuckles, and turned to walk away. A suffocating pain twisted in my chest, as if someone were wringing out my rib cage like wet clothing.

"Wait!" I called out.

Abae turned back.

"The Council will want to build relationships with our more neglected neighbors," I said.

She cocked her head to one side, regarding me curiously. "Yes?" she said. She looked like a skittish animal about to bolt.

"Yes. So. We will need a Perest-Avani diplomat. One who speaks Sjon."

The smile she gave me was as warm as a summer dawn. "I might know someone."

I turned back to my temporary home, a kernel of optimism stirring inside me. I opened the door. "Come inside. That breeze is chilly." The icy wind off Solemn Peak whipped my hair on my face again as we went inside together, and I shivered. But Abae's hand was soft and warm in mine as I closed the door behind us.

Acknowledgments

As always, a team of people contributed to bringing this book together. On the professional side, a big thank-you to Tor Books and the team who worked on the U.S. edition, including:

Diana Gill	Acquiring Editor
Steven Bucsok	Production Manager
Laura Etzkorn	Publicist
Renata Sweeney	Marketing
Irene Gallo	Art Director
Peter Lutjen	Art Director
Greg Ruth	Cover Art
Jamie Stafford-Hill	Cover/Jacket Design
Jennifer Gunnels	In-House Editor
Molly Majumder	Editorial Assistant
Kristin Temple	Editorial Assistant
Megan Kiddoo	Production Editor
Christina MacDonald	Copy Editor
Greg Collins	Designer
Lani Meyer	Proofreader
Laura Dragonette	Proofreader

And for the UK/ANZ edition:

Simon Taylor	Editor
Richard Shailer	Cover Design
Phil Evans	Production
Lilly Cox	Marketing

| Izzie Ghaffari-Parker | Publicity |
| Josh Benn | Managing Editorial |

And the wonderful Sales Team: Deirdre, Emily, Gareth, Gary, Hannah, Natalie, and Tom. And a big shout-out to Lucy Ballantyne and Bec Cowie and the great folks at Penguin Random House Australia who brought my book to my hometown.

And, of course, my agent Julie Crisp. Thanks for calmly dealing with my all-caps WhatsApp messages and always being in my corner.

On the personal side, first and foremost, thanks always to my boys: K, Dean, and Liam, who enable the madness of this second career with good humor and patience, supportive cups of tea and surprise chocolate deliveries, and tolerance of my strange behaviors. (*Mummy, I heard you go for a walk in the middle of the night!* Yes, buddy, yes you did. Mummy had to solve a plot hole in her pajamas at one in the morning. Thank you for understanding.) Oh, and the occasional brutal ransom of an innocent and extremely cute pair of shoes.* You three always have my whole heart, and none of this would work without you.

Thanks to my brilliant and generous sister Meg, always my first reader and cheerleader, for listening to me talk through endless plot problems and helping me solve them, for proofreading and poison-inventing, and literally setting alarms in the middle of the night to wake up and check on me when I was pulling an all-nighter. Thanks also to my other wonderful sister Net, who also proofread and formatted this giant sucker under ridiculously tight turnaround times. Special thanks to Mum, Dad, and Stephie for last minute typo checks! And thank you as always to the rest of my incredibly supportive extended family—I love you all and so appreciate your consistent interest and encouragement. Likewise to my friends, many of whom suffered through buying—and even reading!—a fantasy book for the first time just to support me. You guys rock.

If I had one bit of advice to give emerging writers it would be this: find yourself some pals in the industry and appreciate the hell out of them. I feel very fortunate to have, largely accidentally, landed in some wonderful

---

* No shoes were harmed in the making of this book. At least, not physically harmed. The emotional scars will be there forever.

groups of friends and colleagues over the course of the last few years who have made the world of publishing so much more fun. Huge thanks to my glorious friends who beta read one or more versions of this behemoth for me and lent their genius (geniuses? geni?) to make me better—Devin Madson, Kai Doore, Shannon Chakraborty, E. J. Beaton, RJ Theodore, and Russell Kirkpatrick—and an entire ticker parade–level thank-you to Anna Stephens for real-time beta reading and sanity checks, and keeping me motivated through many weeks of very late nights. I really could not have done this without you, you spectacular Goblin, you. And another special shout-out to AJ Spedding who did late-night moral support and productivity sprints with me on the previous manuscript. Also my IRL writing and cocktails buddies Leife and Freya, and my writing S(l)ack and Discord friends, who are an endless source of support, distraction, motivation, and silliness, mixed with brilliant insightful discussions (even if a remarkable number of them somehow end up being about the Untamed). I have murdered as many of you as possible in this book, as a sign of my love.

And I'd be remiss to leave off the community of readers, booksellers, librarians, bloggers, BookTubers, and podcasters who enjoyed the first book and talked about it—special thanks to the Fantasy Inn crew, to my Aussie booksellers who supported the hell out of me for *City* (especially Claire, Jeremy, Paige, and Stefen). I appreciate every one of you, and the pleasure I get from hearing that someone connected with the characters or the story never gets old. Thank you for being patient and hanging in there with me for the sequel. You make it worth it.

About the Author

A lawyer by training and a black belt in ju-jitsu, **Sam Hawke** lives in Canberra. Her first novel, *City of Lies*, received international acclaim and won the Ditmar Award for Best Novel, jointly won the Aurealis Award for Best Fantasy Novel and the Norma K Hemming Award, as well as earning Sam a nomination for the Astounding Award for Best New Writer for the 2020 Hugos. *Hollow Empire* continues her Poison War series.

To find out more, visit samhawkewrites.com